I0761239

JOHNNY NOVA

About the Author

Dolores Ashcroft-Nowicki is one of the most respected and experienced esoteric practitioners currently at work in the British Isles. She was born and currently lives in Channel Island of Jersey off the coast of France. She was trained in the Fraternity of the Inner Light and worked as a Cosmic Mediator with Walter Ernest, the Grand Maistre of British Occultism. Dolores is a third degree adept and Qabbalist.

She not only teaches the Craft but also is the current director of the Servants of the Light, a Hermetic order descended from Dion Fortune's Society of the Inner Light. She travels extensively, teaching a wide range of occult subjects to pupils in both the UK and United States.

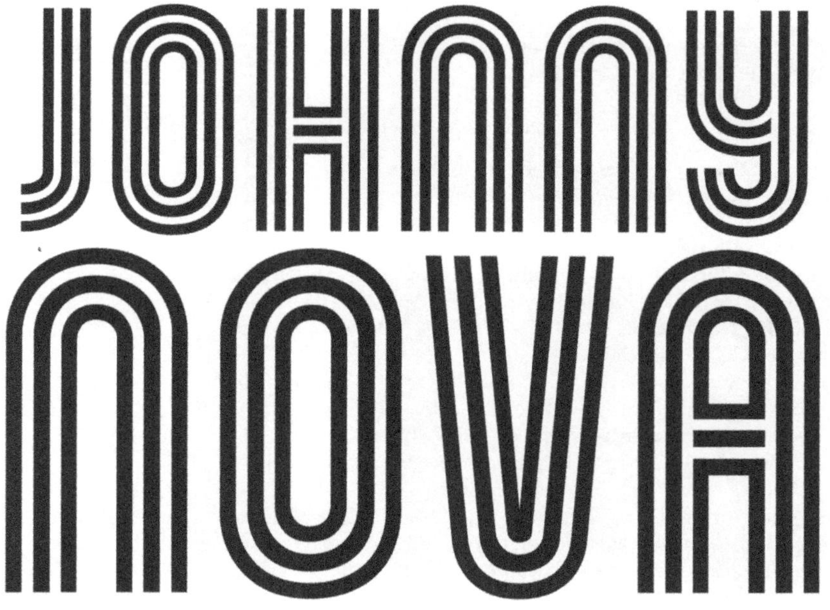

Johnny Nova

A NOVEL OF THE AGE OF AQUARIUS

DOLORES ASHCROFT-NOWICKI

WOODBURY, MINNESOTA

First Edition
First Printing, 2026

Book design by Samantha Peterson
Cover design by Kevin R. Brown

Library of Congress Cataloging-in-Publication Data
Names: Ashcroft-Nowicki, Dolores author
Title: Johnny Nova : a novel on the age of Aquarius / by Dolores Ashcroft-Nowicki.
Description: First edition. | Woodbury, MN : Llewellyn Worldwide, 2026.
Identifiers: LCCN 2025041073 (print) | LCCN 2025041074 (ebook) | ISBN 9780738781747 paperback | ISBN 9780738782034 ebook
Subjects: LCGFT: Novels
Classification: LCC PR6101.S528 J64 2026 (print) | LCC PR6101.S528 (ebook) | DDC 823/.92—dc23/eng/20250923
LC record available at https://lccn.loc.gov/2025041073
LC ebook record available at https://lccn.loc.gov/2025041074

Llewellyn Publications
A Division of Llewellyn Worldwide Ltd.
2143 Wooddale Drive
Woodbury, MN 55125-2989
www.llewellyn.com

Printed in the United States of America

GPSR Representation:
UPI-2M PLUS d.o.o., Medulićeva 20, 10000 Zagreb, Croatia,
matt.parsons@upi2mbooks.hr

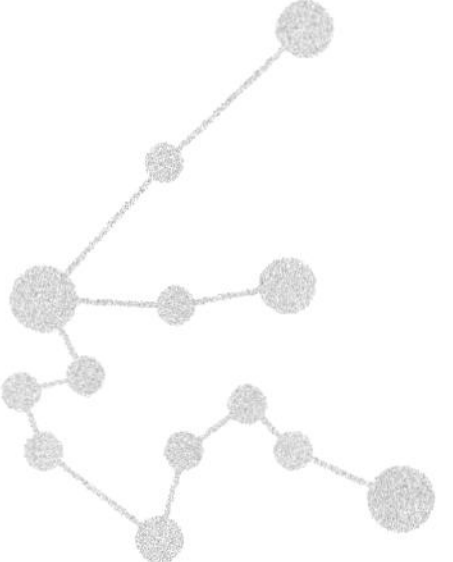

This book is dedicated to
the First Nations peoples of
the USA and the Wanderers
of Europe, the Romani.

CHARACTER LIST

Biff: Bass guitarist for White Heat

Brigadier Sir William Rothely-Smythe: A Watcher and Margaret's partner

Chambha: Member of the Abbey of the Dawn and Nyang Darsip's right-hand man

Colin "Bucky" Buckman: White Heat's road manager

Desiderio "Desi" Agostini: A daemon and Tango's manager

Eamon Merrow: Johnny's father and member of the Abbey of the Aeon

Emir Haroun ibn Sayed al Kerim-Azur: A helper of the abbeys who is often accompanied by his two sons, Hashim and Amal

Florencia "Florrie" Burke: Johnny's aunt

Francis "Frank" Saunders: Plays synthesizer and guitar for White Heat and writes most of the band's music

Johnny Burke, also known as Johnny Nova: Lead singer of the band White Heat and the Forerunner of the Age of Aquarius

Lea Merrow: Tze-Ring's wife

Liam Donahue: Lead guitarist for White Heat

Lyle Barclay: Drummer for White Heat

Mara: Johnny's partner and member of the Abbey of the Aeon

Margaret McDonald: A Watcher, William's partner, and one of Bucky's mentors

Nathan "Wolf" Blackwolf: A shapeshifter who travels amongst the abbeys

Nicholas De'ath: An Undying One and member of the Lords of Darkness

Nyang Darsip, often referred to as Rinpoche: Abbot of the Abbey of the Dawn and Tze-Ring's grandfather

Pacia Adabyo: The Teacher of the Age of Aquarius

Talfryn "Tango" Alvarez Garrett: Guitarist and singer for White Heat and the Betrayer of the Age of Aquarius

Tze-Ring Merrow: Member of the Abbey of the Dawn and Johnny's half-brother

Virginia "Ginny" Donahue: Lyle's partner and White Heat's gofer

THE SEVEN ABBEYS OF LIGHT

An incomplete list of the members of the Abbeys of the Sevenfold Powers.

ABBEY OF THE AEON

In the Pyrenees between France and Spain

Abbot Gregor Theodorakis
Amalia (telepathy)
Dagmar (plant master)
Desmond (mind healer)
Eamon
Eugénie (telepathy)
Genevieve
Juan (kinetic powers)
Leon (far memory)
Mara (healing)
Matthew (illusion)
Maurice (illusion)
Pawel (telepathy and kinetic powers)
René (telepathy)
Venda (telekinesis)
Vivianne (illusion)
Wolf (shape-shifting)

ABBEY OF THE DAWN

On the border of northern India and Tibet

Abbot Nyang Darsip
Abbess Hannah
Adelie
Angeli
Chambha

Devin
Lea (eidetic memory)
Miro
Murad (telepathy)
Nakima
Per
Shuna (weather magic)
Tze-Ring (telekinesis)
Wang Ta (master illusionist and empath)

Abbey of the Snows

Rishiri Island, off the coast of Hokkaido, Japan

Abbess Iwara Sakura
Aoki
Hiro
Yoshi

Abbey of the Throne

Near the Port of Aden

Abbot Khalid ibn Suleiman
Abbess Natasha Darsip
Feisal
Lyrata
Mari-Teresa
Okifi
Yano

Abbey of the Waters

In the Aleutian Islands of Alaska

Abbot Kanien
Chenoa
Siska (teleportation)
Zane

ABBEY OF THE WINDS

In Chile, near the Tierra del Fuego

Abbot Jorje Ortega de Najera
Carl (elemental powers)
Claudio
Colby (illusion)
Dylan (animal communication)
Elissa (sight)
Emilio
Eugénie (healing)
Inez (cleansing)
Maria Teresa
Roger
Simone
Tanaka (telepathy)
Ulrika

THE LOST ABBEY

Unknown

AUTHOR'S NOTE

The term *Age of Aquarius*, as used throughout, can apply to a wide period of time, anywhere between the 1990s and the present. It did not begin in the '60s as many believe, but it is still considered a period of new enlightenment such as that worked towards by Johnny Nova and the inspired visionaries who prepared the way to his ascension.

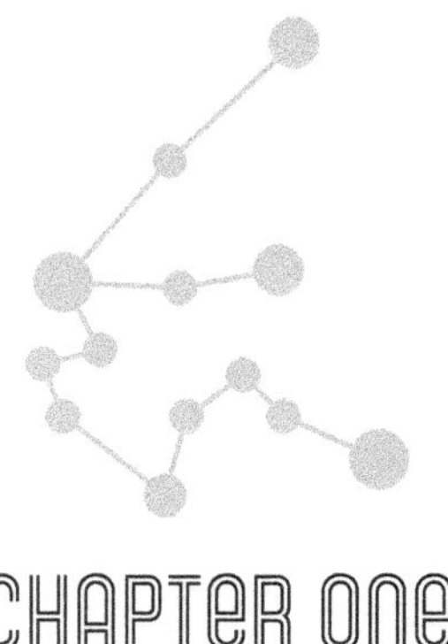

CHAPTER ONE

6 October, 11:00 p.m.
Wembley Stadium, London

The girl gasped for breath as the crowd surged forward. Clutching the edge of the barrier, she drew in a lungful of air, then let it out in a wailing scream that was echoed from thousands of throats. Eyes closed, she swayed from side to side, totally entranced. Along with the others, she chanted her adolescent mantra in a beat as wild and primitive as that of the amplified guitars that howled under the hot stage lights.

John-ny, John-ny, Johnny Nova, John-ny, John-ny, Johnny Nova. It went on and on until all other thoughts ceased to run through the caverns of her noise-deadened brain. Under the emotional pressure, her bladder gave way, and a stream of hot urine trickled down her legs unheeded. All she was aware of was the brightly lit stage and the presence of Johnny Nova as he bounced and capered to the music of his backing group, White Heat, and urged the crowd to even greater roars of adulation.

In the darkened wings of the stage, Colin Buckman—known to everyone in the business as Bucky—rubbed his fleshy hands together with glee. An Australian by birth, he had been the road manager for Johnny and the group for the last three years. During that time, he had pulled them from their squalid beginnings and one-night gigs in working men's clubs to this, the Wembley Stadium. Tonight was the triumphal end to a five-month world tour with capacity crowds all the way.

Along the way, Bucky had grown used to high-quality single malt whisky, Havana cigars, and the trappings of the good life. He had every intention of continuing to gratify his present lifestyle with White Heat and Johnny Nova. Part of the group's success was due to Bucky; his ticket to a wealthy old age was a genius for getting them headlines in the gutter press: Drunken parties with page-three models. Front-page pictures of members of the group in various stages of undress in and around the swimming pools of the rich and infamous had littered their way to the top of the charts. A few cases of dangerous driving and several fines for possession of marijuana (among other things), along with the usual drunken brawls, had boosted their way to fame. Then, last year, a front-page paternity suit (ultimately thrown out of court) against Liam, the lead guitar, had resulted in the names of White Heat and Johnny Nova becoming household names on four continents.

The result had brought condemnation from the tight-corset brigade and mindless adulation from the young and impressionable. It had also brought bookings from every corner of the world and swelled the bank accounts of the group and Bucky alike. Certainly the boys had proved to be highly talented once they learned to work together. Not an easy task, and it had taken most of their first year as a group, innumerable rows, several fights, and all of Bucky's legendary patience. Now, as he watched them on the final night of their third and biggest world tour, he felt they'd all earned a rest.

Well, maybe not too long. He pondered the thought. Hell, he didn't want them totally forgotten. Perhaps the odd concert here and there, or better yet, an album of their greatest hits. Then there were personal appearances and that sort of thing. Jesus, they were on good form tonight. Bucky watched with pride as the audience was skilfully caught up in the magic of the group's frenetic performance. He edged closer to the stage, ignoring the stage manager's pointed look at his massive cigar, and picked out each familiar face in turn.

Liam Donahue. Now he was a real troublemaker, that one, with the morals of a tomcat. A red-headed Irishman from Cork, he had a capacity for booze, women, and drugs that scared the hell out of Bucky at times. He'd cost them a bomb in fines for brawling and fighting, to say nothing of replaced camera equipment. As for girls, it was Bucky's contention that if it had a bum and tits, Liam would screw it regardless of its age, type, colour, or condition.

Bucky squinted round a tower spot at Biff on bass guitar, grinning like a fool with his dyed blonde hair sticking up like a bleedin' bog brush, and shook his head. Biff was Liam's drinking buddy, and his capacity for alcohol was truly incredible. Not that he got off lightly. Bucky had lost count of the times he'd nursed Biff through a particularly vicious hangover. The stupid sod idolized Liam and wanted nothing more out of life than to be like him. He talked a lot about women but seldom made it with any of them. It was Bucky's private opinion that Biff was gay but too bloody thick to know it. Lately he'd taken to smoking grass, and it was only a matter of time before Liam got him on to something stronger.

The snarl of the synthesizer drew Bucky's attention next. Frank Saunders, the oldest at twenty-eight, was one of the best musicians on the musical scene, and after twenty years in the business, Bucky knew a good 'un when he heard one. Frank wrote most of the group's music and could take a lot of credit for their success. Shame he was such an ugly sod.

Leaning forward a little more, he could just make out Tango as he swung in behind Johnny to back him for the chorus. If there was one member of the group the portly little manager could be said to dislike, it was the half Welsh, half Spanish rhythm guitar player. In Bucky's private opinion, he was a good-looking bastard, but with a vicious streak. You could always tell Tango's women; they wore bruises instead of jewellery, and once or twice Bucky had caught sight of a bandage. He thought it more than likely that Tango carried a knife, but short of searching him (unthinkable given the lad's temper), he couldn't prove a thing. For all his faults—and they were legion—Colin Buckman had his own standards, and he never left a girl alone with Tango for long if it could be helped. A nasty bit of work, but a damn good guitar player with a great tenor voice and a body to match.

A flourishing riff of drums shifted his attention to Lyle. Jamaican born and London bred, a superb drummer, and a real gent. No violence for Lyle. Give him good food and a good bed and Lyle was a pussycat. Having Ginny, his tow-headed Cockney girlfriend, on the group's payroll as a general "gofer" made it even easier. Lyle didn't drink, smoke, screw around, or take drugs. He went to church on Sunday whenever possible and loved his Ginny with a total adoration, equalled only by his love for drums in any kind, shape, or form.

Bucky shifted his cigar from one side to the other and pondered the subject of drugs. Grass he didn't lose much sleep over—it didn't do much damage that he could see—but coke, speed, and acid were something else; he didn't even like to think about the other stuff. Drugs could ruin this lot if he didn't watch it. Bucky sighed and eased the ache in his short, fat legs. Christ, he'd be glad to get away for a bit, preferably where there was no bleedin' music.

A sudden roar from the fans caught his attention. On stage, Johnny was announcing the last number of the evening. Ah, thought Bucky affectionately, Johnny was the cream on top of the coffee, a marvellous voice and perfect pitch. Johnny Nova couldn't sing a wrong note if he tried. With justifiable pride, the road manager watched his lead singer work the crowd like a good 'un.

His thick, jet-black hair hung like a shining mane to his shoulders; the olive, almost golden, skin that was part of his Romani heritage; and the brilliant emerald eyes no one ever forgot once they had met him. Johnny, with his lyric tenor that could, according to Liam, part the thighs of an Irish nun with longing. Johnny, with his ability to screw all night, rehearse all day, and drink even Biff, who was part fish, under the table—and often did. Johnny Nova had the face of a fallen angel and was the apple of Bucky's eye. He was White Heat, and Bucky, with an eye on his old age, prayed nightly for his continuing welfare.

The group slid with practised ease into the intro of their greatest hit, "Mountains of Gold." It had been number one, both as a single and on an album, in the world charts for an unprecedented twenty-five weeks when it was first out, and it had never been out of the top twenty since. It had sent the group's ratings through the roof. After a year of hard graft and one-night gigs, they had made it big with that song. There had been other hits, but it was "Mountains of Gold" that had started the avalanche of fame and fortune and had become a standard. Bucky listened as the music wove its spell.

Frank had written the music, but Johnny had insisted on writing the lyrics himself, saying he'd heard them in a dream, a statement that had caused a lot of ribald comments from the group. It had worked, though; Christ, had it worked. Bucky grinned as he listened to Frank coax a mesmerising cascade of sound from his instrument. In the wings, a silently appreciative bunch of stagehands gathered to listen to the familiar words.

I looked for love through the cities of despair
I looked for love, but never found it there
Sometimes I thought I had seen her face
In a downtown bar or a dining place
But when I walked in, she was never there
Just some other girl with dyed blonde hair
I looked at faces till my heart cried, "Enough
You can't go on, you are not that tough"

So I went my way from town to town
Just a desperate man with his shoes worn down
I followed the call and the beckoning hand
To a far-off place in an unknown land
I sat beneath an ancient tree
And my heart said, "Be still and listen to me
I am your love. I have always been here
Rest awhile; there is no more fear"

So the years went by and I grew old
And I found my love 'neath
The Mountains of Gold

Not for the first time, Colin wondered where the hell Johnny had really gotten those words. Ever since writing them a little over two years ago now, he had become increasingly difficult to deal with. His drinking was a byword amongst the groupies; he either fucked like a madman or slept alone for weeks. On top of that, and thanks to Liam, he smoked pot and used coke like it was going out of fashion. *Driven* was the word for Johnny Nova these days, though who, or what, was in the driving seat, God alone knew.

On the brightly lit stage, the three guitarists moved slickly into the choreographed steps of their backing moves. In front of them, Johnny swayed and dipped, eyes closed, letting the words and music flow through him as they always did. The enraptured audience stood silent, caught up in the power of the words and of the man singing them. A shiver went down Bucky's spine. There was something about this song, about the way Johnny sang it, or maybe about the way the song used Johnny, that made his flesh creep. It was the only time the young singer was relaxed and looked like the Johnny Burke he'd been when Bucky had found him, singing for a meal and five pounds cash, up in Leeds.

The number came to an end with an ear-shattering explosion of sound and a high falsetto note from Johnny. For a moment, there was silence, then a demonic ululation erupted from the assembled fans as they realised the concert was over and they were going to lose their idols. As expected, the demand for encores and repeated choruses came fast and furious and went on until, fearing the collapse of the group from sheer fatigue, the front man came on and calmed them down.

Then Johnny, with his usual flair for dealing gently with hysterical girls, consoled and flattered them. He kissed the hands of those in the front row and accepted gifts of flowers, cigarettes, bottles of aftershave, and other, more intimate gifts that were offered. He, along with the others, began to autograph programmes, hankies, bras, panties, and other items of apparel that were handed over the footlights. They answered questions and fended off invitations that were often blatantly sexual.

Halfway through the bedlam, with the bouncers trying to prevent eager fans from climbing over the footlights to get to their idols, Johnny heard his name called in an all-too-familiar voice. He broke out in a cold sweat as he paused in the act of signing a programme and slowly looked up.

In the middle of the jostling crowd, completely at ease, stood a man in the saffron robe of a Buddhist monk. He smiled at the stupefied singer and mouthed his name silently, and again Johnny heard the voice in his head.

"Johnny Burke, soon we will come for you. Be prepared."

A hand tugged at his jacket sleeve impatiently. Johnny looked down into the petulant face of a teenager with short blonde hair, braces on her teeth, and several pimples a day short of bursting.

"Please, Johnny," she whined. "I want it to say 'With all my love, to my dearest Sharon.' Willya do that for me, Johnny? Willya, Johnny, willya?"

He suddenly remembered where he was and what he was supposed to be doing and smiled brilliantly at the dazzled fan whose programme he was holding.

"No sweat, darlin'. 'With all my love, to my dearest Sharon.' There you go."

She looked up at him with total adoration and he smiled again, remembering his own adolescence and its pain. He bent and kissed her cheek. "Take care, Sharon."

He handed the programme over and looked up again, but the man was no longer there. But Johnny knew he'd be back, as surely as he knew the sun would rise tomorrow. He had seen and heard him before, too many times for comfort. Suddenly, he'd had enough; the crowd was too much, and he needed space. He stood up, ignoring the screams of teenage disappointment and tearful goodbyes, and strode from the stage, followed more slowly by the rest of the group. The sudden dimness of the stage after the brilliant footlights made him stumble, and Johnny clung to the coolness of an iron stanchion holding the backdrop together. Frank caught him and held his arm in a steadying, comforting grip.

"You OK, mate?"

"Yeah, just tired, that's all. The noise, lights, and the crowds...It's just getting to me. I swear, if another bra gets shoved in my face to autograph, I'll puke."

The rest of the group passed laughing and joking, relaxing at the thought of a month's vacation time before them. For the moment, the euphoria of the concert still had them by the throat, though it would not last long. Tomorrow they would be wrung out with the aftereffects and as limp as rags. They made their way to the dressing rooms, collecting Bucky as they went, and followed more slowly by Frank and Johnny. The singer stopped suddenly, his hand on the guitarist's arm.

"Frank, I've been hearing the voices again. In fact, I did more than hear them. I saw him, that monk I told you about in Sydney. He was here. Large as bleeding life in the middle of all that mob and no one, not one of them, even blinked an eye. I mean, hell, a Buddhist monk in the middle of a full house at Wembley Stadium, and nobody gave a shit! Come on, man."

He looked pale and distraught and, for a brief moment, close to tears. Back in Sydney, in a rare moment of confidence, Johnny had confided in the older man about the strange events that were invading his life. In a tight, desperate voice cracking with strain, he had spoken of the fear that he was going mad. He was haunted, he said, by voices sounding in his head, calling him by name at all times of the day and night. But lately he'd begun to see things. At first the strangely dressed figures simply moved in and out of his dreams, but then they began to invade his waking life, and all without a warning of any kind.

All this he told to Frank in a night-long session with the best part of a bottle of Scotch inside him, in spite of which he remained stone-cold sober. It had started, Johnny told him, hunched over his drink, just over a year ago while the tour was still in the planning stage. Then the dream voices increased in strength and occurrence. With this came fleeting impressions of some sort of abbey or monastery with priests, "like those Hare Krishna types." Then one figure began to infiltrate his everyday life, appearing in apartments, hotel rooms, and, once, in the bedroom where Johnny was snorting a line of coke. Petrified with fear, he'd spilled the powder on the floor, leaving him with only half the usual amount flooding his system.

In many ways, Frank stood in for the elder brother that had been lacking in Johnny's life. For his part, he was genuinely fond of the young singer and had spent hours teaching him enough music to get by on both the guitar and the keyboard. He was also, apart from Bucky, the only member of the group that knew Johnny provided for the keep and education of a dozen or more children scattered throughout the Third World. A lonely man despite the closeness of the group, Frank had always felt slightly isolated from the others. With his gaunt, angular features, he was not sought after by the groupies and hangers-on, not that he minded; his sex drive was not very high, and Frank preferred writing music to wrestling between the sheets. It was this inner quietness that had drawn the younger man to him, and Johnny decided to confide his problems and fears.

Johnny's sharing of his fears had troubled Frank, for without the younger man's charismatic personality, it was hard to see White Heat surviving. If it went down the drain, his private and long-cherished dream of owning his own recording studio went with it. Studying Johnny now, in the dim light of the theatre corridor, Frank wondered if he was cracking up under the pressure of booze, sex, and drugs. In the state he was in now, he was a fair cop for suicide or death in some shape or form. Nothing lasted forever, but Frank sure as hell wanted White Heat to last a bit longer than this, and without Johnny's incredible voice and blatant sexuality on stage, the group would not last long. He shrugged fatalistically and followed the sound of champagne corks and raised voices to the crowded dressing room.

Bucky, as usual, was holding court with reporters, photographers, and an assortment of groupies and columnists. "There'll be food, booze, and all the little extras you can handle," he told them. A young groupie followed, giggling inanely. She draped her nubile young body over the back of Tango's chair. The reporters smirked and wrote busily, the women among them scowling at the little manager's unconcerned sexism.

"Er, Mr. Buckman, do you plan another world tour like this last one, and if so, when is it likely to come off?" asked a nasal voice.

"Well, the boys need a break. After all these months, they have to have one or they'll go flat."

"They are actually taking a holiday, then? I can quote you on that?"

"When are they going, Buckman, and where? Will it be altogether as a group, or are they going singly?"

"Are they going somewhere exotic?"

"What about Johnny Nova? Is there any truth in the rumours that he's cracking up with all the booze and drugs he's been taking on board lately?"

In quick defence of his own, Bucky spun round, his fleshy body shaking with the sudden movement. His normally pink face was florid with rage that anyone dared to bad-mouth his protégé. "Who said that? I keep tellin' you, there's nothing in those stories, nothing at all. Just bloody gossip, that's all. Christ, can't you buggers let them alone for a bit and get off their backs? Mine too, for chrissakes."

Bucky chomped down hard on his cigar, then remembered that this was, after all, the press. He smiled, albeit a little grimly, and coughed discreetly. "Tell you what. It's a bit crowded in here. Why don't you all go off to the lads' apartment and wait for us to get there? Gotta get them out of here without injury first, and that'll take some doing with all those girls by the stage door. Back there you'll find plenty of food, booze, and company." He winked. "Especially the last lot."

He waved a porcine hand adorned with several gold rings towards the door. Tempted by the promise of free food and the added spice of unlimited photo opportunities and titbits of gossip from the group themselves, the reporters drifted out. There was always the possibility of a drunken brawl or a fight between two of the groupies or even, the God of reporters willing, a photo of one of the lads doing something indiscreet in a bedroom. In high good humour, they headed for the stage door and the limos laid on by the astute Bucky, ready to descend on the group's luxury apartment in the newly developed docklands, overlooking the river.

Left to themselves at last, Bucky shooed out the lingering girls hoping for an invitation to the party. The boys began to shower and change. Comments on the evening, the capacity audience, and the tour as a whole went back and forth as their charged egos calmed down. With the prospect of a normal life for a few weeks, they were feeling great. In high good humour, Bucky filled the rooms with cigar smoke and talked nonstop about the next tour, the big charity concert a minor royal was organising, and the recording contracts in the offing to anyone who would listen. If anyone other than Frank noticed that Johnny was quieter than usual, they said nothing.

The last to shower, Johnny stood under the cascade of hot water trying to relax muscles that had accumulated five months of tension. After tonight, he promised himself he'd book himself into the Betty Ford clinic in the US. He needed to get rid of the shit he'd been taking into his body for the last year and a half.

Johnny may not have had the advantage of a public school education, but he was not stupid. He knew only too well where the booze and the drugs were leading. Come to that, he was pretty sure he had collected something nasty from his last sexual encounter over four weeks ago. The symptoms were distressing and obvious. The trouble was, he'd had no time to see a doctor what with the travelling, the rehearsals, and the concerts night after night. One thing he was sure of, he had to get himself together, and fast. Tomorrow, he promised himself. First thing tomorrow morning for sure. But first, there was this bloody party to get done with.

He shut off the spray and turned. Opening the glass door of the stall, Johnny reached for a towel and froze, his heart racing. On the opposite wall was a full-length mirror. He could see himself reflected in it. A young man a little over medium height, slim but wiry in build, with raven-black hair and brilliant green eyes now wide with fright—no, make that terror. Downright gut-wrenching terror.

Also reflected in the mirror was the monk he had seen in the stadium earlier, only now he seemed taller and larger, and behind him, Johnny could see a room sparsely furnished and filled with the flickering light of many candles and the smoke of incense. Dammit, he could smell the stuff. He stepped out of the shower, almost slipping on the wet surface, and told himself there was nothing there, just a plain mirrored wall. But he still saw the strange room and the smiling monk, who raised a hand and made a beckoning gesture that had him backing up against the shower stall.

"Johnny? Johnny, are you going to be in there all bloody night? Come on out, we gotta go! Get your ass into gear right now, sport."

Bucky's voice and the sound of a fist pounding on the door made Johnny start and glance away, then back to the mirror, a mirror that now simply reflected the shower and his own rigid body clutching a towel.

"Johnny? Johnny, you OK? Quit buggering about in there. Whatcha doin', wanking off or what?"

With an effort, Johnny got to the door and opened it. Immediately, Bucky thrust in a whisky-flushed face and blew cigar smoke in his eyes.

"For chrissakes, Johnny, you ain't even dressed yet."

The singer stammered a placatory reply, then closed the door and dried himself off quickly with one eye on the mirror. In ten minutes he was dressed and followed the others out of their dressing rooms. He was still shaking from his experience, and watched anxiously by Frank. Johnny turned to close the door and saw, sitting in the chair vacated by Bucky, the figure of the monk, smiling and solid. His heart went into his throat, beating there until he thought it would burst. He was going mad. He had to get out of here.

Johnny slammed the door and ran after the others, who were already pushing their way through the crowds outside the stage door. His headlong rush took him through the wall of surprised fans before they realised who it was. By that time he was in the car, huddled into the corner and steadfastly ignoring the pleading faces and puckered lips pressed in adoration against the windows.

"Bloody kids," snorted Bucky. "The car's only just been washed and now it's gunked up with their bleedin' lipstick." He turned to Johnny. "What's up with you, sport? You look as if you've seen a ghost."

Bucky roared with laughter and settled back to tell his latest joke, filling the inside of the limo with smoke and the smell of whisky. Johnny Nova, once Johnny Burke, leaned back against the soft leather, closed his eyes, and prayed. God, how long was it since he had said a prayer? Best forget it, it had been too long. He needed help, that was certain; first the voices in his head, and now the apparitions. Maybe he was going mad, *jawing devio*, as his Romani grandfather would have said. Or maybe DTs; his uncle Luke had died in an alcoholic ward raving about the girl in a white dress waiting by his bed to take him away. If not alcohol or drugs, then maybe a side effect of the dose of STD he knew he had. He had read somewhere that syphilis drove you mad at the end.

Another thought occurred to him. Could it be that the Sight, the supreme gift of Romani blood, had been passed to him after all? His mother and her family on both sides had been pure Romani stock, and the first seven years of Johnny's life had been spent travelling the length and breadth of the country in a brightly painted vardo. His father he had never known, nor would any of his family talk about him. All he knew was that he had been a *gadjo*, a non-Romani, and that he, like the girl he had gotten pregnant, had been gifted with the Sight.

Johnny had once asked his mother what it was like to have the gift. She had told him in her soft, lilting voice, "Ah, Johnny, *miro chal*,[1] never doubt that there is more than the eye can see or the head can understand. Only the heart knows the truth. All of us are born with a destiny we cannot avoid, some greater than others."

Her Sight had warned her of the cancer that killed her, and she had prepared him, with gentle words, for her death when he was sixteen. He had longed for the Gift after she had gone, hoping to see her much-loved face again. But there had never been any sign that he had inherited it—at least, until now. She had been a good and loving mother and had sacrificed her travelling life to give him a chance to go to school. No, only people like his mother had the Sight. People like him died young, riddled with dope.

God, he needed a drink. A drink and a snort of coke. The sooner they got to the apartment, the better. Johnny felt for the flat shape of the leather case in his pocket. It contained a silver tube and a supply of high-quality cocaine, enough to last through to Monday. Maybe a weekend of oblivion was the answer.

By the time they got to the apartment, the party was in full swing. Bucky, surrounded by a posse of reporters and photographers, was setting up photo calls and press conferences, the ever-present cigar and single malt by his side. As usual, Frank was at the piano, content to make music until the small hours even after five months of doing just that. Liam had grabbed a couple of girls and a bottle and disappeared into one of the bedrooms; it was safe to assume that he would not reappear much before noon tomorrow. Biff settled down to some serious drinking with a couple of reporters who were under the false impression they could get him drunk enough to spill some gossip.

Ginny was waiting for Lyle with a shy smile. His face split into a huge grin, and they drifted off to sit in a corner and make plans for their holiday. Watching them, Johnny would have made a bet that the plans included a quiet wedding, if Bucky didn't get into the act and turn it into a three-ring circus.

1. "my boy"

Johnny headed for the bathroom and made up a fix, choosing to inject rather than sniff the coke. With a practised touch, he drew the ligature tight round his arm. It was beginning to be hard to find a decent vein, another reason to kick the habit. At moments like this, he despised himself and the weakness that held him in its grip.

He sat back on the closed toilet seat with his head against the wall, letting the drug rush through his system. Tomorrow, first thing, to a doctor to get some shots for this dose of clap. Then he'd make some discreet inquiries about a clinic where he could dry out and kick the drugs. But for the moment, tomorrow seemed a long way away. First, there was tonight to get through.

After a few minutes, life started to look a little better. Johnny got up and went in search of a drink. He collected a bottle and a glass from the lavishly stocked bar and sat down with a couple of eager-to-please girls to get well and truly legless. Across the room, Tango watched him with a cynical smile that didn't quite reach his eyes, then turned back to the girl at his side. It was 1:05 a.m. Outside, an early autumn mist built up, blurring the outline of the buildings across the river. With the mist came a strange atmosphere of expectation; almost a joyfulness, as if something long planned was about to happen.

At 2:15, Johnny was two-thirds through the bottle and stone-cold sober. The euphoria of his recent fix had disappeared. The girls, finding his company less than amusing, had drifted off to join Biff and the reporters. Now Johnny stood alone on the balcony, looking out over the Thames, nursing his fifth double Scotch and wondering why it was so difficult to get drunk. He needed to deaden the voices that, for the last thirty minutes, had been singing through his head. At times they were quite clear, and though the language was strange, he could almost understand it. Then they would die down just below the level of hearing.

As if that was not enough, Johnny had found himself in the grip of a sudden and unaccountable rage that had caused words between himself and some of the more brash reporters. Bucky had calmed them all down, blaming it on the strain of the tour and long hours of travelling. But Johnny felt tired and sick. The room was stifling, the air rancid with smoke, the smell of alcohol, and stale perfume. One of the girls had been sick in the kitchen, adding to the overall effluvium of degeneration.

Johnny looked round wildly. The walls were closing in on him, and the people laughing and drinking in the brightly lit room had become total strangers with no meaning in his life. He felt totally withdrawn, as if he no longer had any connection with the group, or Bucky, or the life he had been leading until now. He felt he no longer belonged here, that there was somewhere else, another place with different people, a place that was waiting for him. His Mountains of Gold. He felt weightless and without purpose, yet he knew that somewhere, somehow, there was something he had to do.

With a sudden resolve, Johnny threw the contents of his glass over the balcony and went in. He stood looking round at the crowded room. It was filled with gossip hunters, groupies, disillusioned columnists, and hangers-on. He stared at them as if it was all new and strange to him. Johnny looked across at the piano and met Frank's startled and inquiring glance and smiled, a brilliant smile of such sweetness that Frank remembered it all his life. Then he shook his head almost sadly and made for the door.

Halfway there, Bucky caught his arm, alarmed by the bemused expression on his young face. "Where the hell do you think you're going, sport? Every bloody reporter in London is here, drooling for anything you want to give 'em."

Johnny shook off his beefy hand. "I wouldn't give any of them shit. I'm going for a walk to clear my head. I need to get out of here, go somewhere, anywhere." His voice grew pleading. "I have to go, Bucky. I have to get out of here." He started for the door with Bucky hanging on to his leather jacket.

"For chrissakes, Johnny, this mob is waiting to give you the kind of publicity other groups would give their dicks and both balls for, and you want to go walkabout. You're fucking crazy, you know that!"

But he was talking to air. Johnny had already gone, shaking off the grasping fingers and slamming the door behind him. He stood for a minute in the empty corridor, listening to the screams and shouts in the room behind him, to the too-loud music and Bucky's voice trying to make itself heard over the din. Slowly, Johnny walked across the hall and pushed the button for the lift and waited, leaning his head against the welcome coolness of the wall. Oh God, he was tired, tired and sick and lonely. He felt as if he had no real place in this world and no one to anchor him in it. As if the world itself had shrugged him off.

The lift arrived, empty, thank God; he'd had enough of people in the last five months. Enough of the countries, the cities, the airports, the stages, and the hordes of screaming people. Towards the end of the tour, everything had begun to run together, blurring into a dimly remembered dream, or was it a nightmare? He tried to recall the places they had played. Boston, New York, Chicago, Atlanta, St. Louis, and New Orleans. Dallas, Denver, Mexico City and San Diego, Las Vegas, LA, San Francisco, Seattle and Vancouver, Tokyo, Hong Kong, Singapore, Sydney, Melbourne, Perth, Bangkok, and Seoul, and others he no longer remembered. They were just names. He remembered nothing about them except their terrible sameness. The mind-numbing sameness of airports, hotel rooms, receptions, stages, and girls, especially the girls.

The lift opened with a soft hiss, and Johnny walked aimlessly through the deserted lobby, past the dozing night porter. He paused in the doorway, declining the offer of the security guard to get him a taxi.

Outside, it was raining with the soft, persistent drizzle peculiar to London in the autumn. The kind that soaked right through your clothes and into the bone. The street looked wet and shiny, as if it had been freshly painted, and so deserted you could easily imagine there was no one left in the whole city.

Slowly, Johnny descended the steps into the silent street, and the night closed round him. It was 2:31 a.m. on October the seventh. It was also the last anyone saw of Johnny Nova for five years.

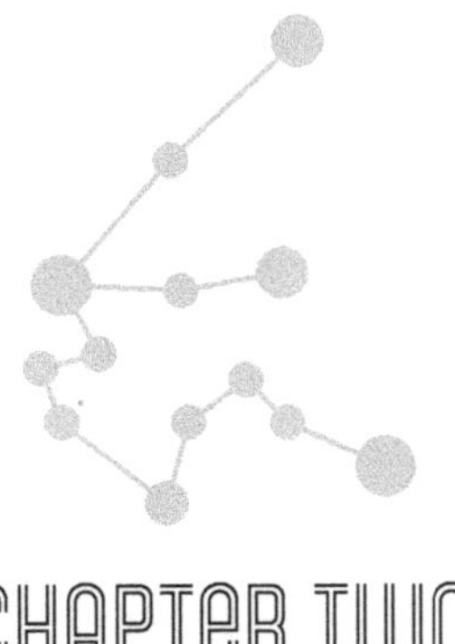

CHAPTER TWO

7 October, 4:05 a.m.
Tunnel Wharf, London

Except for the gleam of two large candles set incongruously into empty jam jars, the inside of the motor yacht was dark. The wake of a passing barge lifted it against its mooring ropes, and the slight bump caused two of the three occupants of the small cabin to stir. The older man spoke in a soft voice, and his younger companion slipped away silently to return a few moments later with a bowl of fragrant green tea.

The old man folded his slender, fine-boned fingers round the fragile porcelain and sipped appreciatively at the hot liquid. Then, setting the bowl aside, he leaned over to look at the third man, lying full-length on the bunk bed. He was tall, well-built, with a sensitive face, the latter made more so by his shaven head. Like his superior, he was dressed in a saffron-coloured robe and was covered with a light woollen blanket against the autumn chill. To all intents and purposes, he was asleep.

"Chambha." The old man spoke quietly, but with authority. "Where is he now?"

"He walks towards the river, Rinpoche. It is a deserted area with many empty houses. The road is narrow and ill lit. I sense much evil in the atmosphere nearby. There is a man and a woman; she has taken money in return for the sharing of her sexual energy. Also, I can see in the shadows ahead two men—no, more like boys, but still dangerous. There is also a young woman. Her aura shows a badly debased pattern, and there are signs of disease that will prove fatal within a short time. They lie in wait for our guest where the road joins a dark alley. One at least has a knife. They are waiting for him to pass, and their thoughts project a great deal of anger, violence, and an intention to commit robbery. There is no one near to see what may happen. He will be injured, perhaps badly, if they are allowed to attack him. There is not much time. We must leave here before dawn if we are to meet with the others at the appointed hour." The speaker did not open his eyes or even stir, yet he spoke with conviction. The abbot sighed and shook his head, then, after some thought, beckoned to the young man in the dark-coloured tracksuit beside him. He spoke quietly in his ear for a moment, then the other man bowed and left the cabin.

Up on the deck, the man vaulted lithely over the rail and onto the sloping dock. With a quick look round to make sure he was unobserved, he took two short steps and leapt. His leap took him a good ten feet to the top of the wharf, where he landed in a crouch. Another look round, then he composed himself, standing quietly and beginning to breathe in a new and deeper pattern. Suddenly he set off, moving with a strange leaping walk that carried him some eight or ten feet with each step. Twice he paused and slid into the shadows, the first time as a young couple passed with arms entwined, and later for a slowly pacing policeman, his tired mind firmly fixed on hot coffee and breakfast. Then he set off again with an unerring sense of direction.

A few streets ahead, in a darkened alley, two youths watched and waited for their victim. They could hear his footsteps on the worn cobblestones separating the derelict houses. Beside them crouched their runner, a skinny teenager with close-cropped hair, a permanently runny nose, and skin marked with small red sores. It was she who had spotted Johnny as he walked the empty streets of London's dockland. One look was enough to see this one was worth rolling. The expensive leather jacket and snakeskin boots, underlined by the flash of a gold watch and an equally expensive gold chain about his neck, said it all. With wolfish anticipation, they had followed him for half an hour, darting in and out of shadowed doorways. Finally, when he turned into the maze of alleys leading to the river, they had raced ahead to find a place for what they had in mind.

With his back pressed hard against the crumbling wall of a long-closed shop, the front man waited for the right moment. He was eighteen in years, three times that in his experience of the streets. Beside him the second youth breathed unevenly, as if he had been running hard, the palms of his hands sweaty with the strain of waiting. He changed a vicious-looking knife from one hand to another, wiping each in turn down the leg of his filthy jeans. Suddenly, they tensed as the oncoming footsteps stopped, and in the cool, rain-washed air, they heard the rasp of a match as Johnny lit a cigarette. After a few moments, the footsteps began again. He was almost upon them.

There was no sound as Tze-Ring approached the trio from behind. For a moment, he regarded them with a sad expression in his dark eyes. He disliked using his skills in this way, but the safety of the man approaching was paramount. So, regretfully, he went into action. The girl knew nothing as selected nerve points were gripped firmly but gently, and with a tiny whimper, she slid into oblivion. Small as it was, the sound drew the attention of her friends. They turned, knives flashing.

With an almost languid grace, the two men were dealt with in the space of seconds. The young lama struck with precise, snakelike swiftness and in total silence. With far less grace, the men slumped to the filthy pavement, unconscious even before they hit its greasy surface. The knives were disposed of down the grating of a nearby drain, and all three were placed in the shelter of a doorway out of the rain. Their intended victim passed by unknowingly, looking neither left nor right, and continued towards the river and his destiny.

Behind Johnny, his unseen guardian bent over his sleeping victims and placed a hand over the heart centre of each of the men in turn, murmuring a Tibetan prayer of blessing. It was little enough, but its power might turn them towards a different path, away from the violence that now possessed them. When he turned to the girl, however, his face changed. His eyes took on a soft, unfocussed stare as he studied her auric pattern.

The disease that ran through her veins was already well advanced; there was nothing he could do to turn it from its course. She was just fifteen and would never see her sixteenth birthday. He delved delicately into her mind and was sickened at the brutal treatment that had turned her from a happy child into a dying, disease-ridden petty thief. He saw the potential that had been there if things had been different. Now it was too late. Unable to help her further, he planted his name into her unconscious mind and instructed her to call him when the time of her death drew near. Then he, or one like him, would be there to help her cross the bridge between life and death and to pass her to those who would care for and soothe the abused young soul. He intoned the same blessing over her, then quietly returned the way he had come, and in the same strange manner.

"The danger has passed. Tze-Ring has dealt with it and now returns," announced the watcher from his position on the bunk. "Our guest nears the river, but his auric pattern is confused. There is much fear and mental pain in him. I think it will take a long time to clear his heart centre, and even longer to train him."

Even in his state of deep trance, the man's voice held a note of disquiet.

"Then we must make use of the time we have been allowed," was the abbot's response. "This young man is of the utmost importance to the world. Without him, the pattern laid down by the Lords of Light will not hold true. If all is now clear and in order for his arrival, you may return."

The abbot leaned forward and tapped lightly on the forehead of the entranced watcher, then sat back to observe the return of his astral body. In less than a minute, a faintly glowing figure passed through the walls of the yacht, pausing briefly before the abbot to bow respectfully. Then it dissolved into a fine mist that extended a stringlike filament and attached itself to the solar plexus of the watcher. Under the keen eye of the abbot, the mist was gathered up and drawn into the body, which jerked a little as the last piece was assimilated. The eyes opened and a deep breath swelled the chest. After a few minutes, Chambha sat up, pushing aside the blanket.

He stretched and swung his legs to the floor, pausing for a moment to test his strength, then stood up and bowed to the abbot.

"Allowing for his slowness of pace, he will be at the meeting point within fifteen minutes. I have set the details of his path into his subconscious, and he will follow them exactly. With your permission, Holy One, I will go to prepare for our meeting."

The old man looked up at his larger companion with affection and nodded.

"The first and hardest part of his training will fall upon you and Tze-Ring. You do understand the importance of the time he will spend with you? You need to approach this task with love and tolerance, though it will be hard on all of you, not least upon the young man himself."

"I fully understand the task laid upon us, and I know Tze-Ring is also deeply committed to its success." Chambha bowed again, then continued, "It is an honour to be chosen. However, having watched this young man for the last twelve months, I find myself doubting the wisdom of the masters in choosing such a...damaged vessel."

A dry chuckle from the abbot whispered round the small cabin. "I learned long ago that the most unlikely lamps may hold the purest light. Do not question too much, Chambha. Consider it a test of your undoubted abilities." He chuckled again. "Tze-Ring is back."

A movement on deck caused the yacht to sway and dip for a moment, followed by the sound of footsteps. The door opened to admit the third member of the group. He bowed and stood waiting for further instructions. Despite his recent exertions, his breathing was unhurried, his manner totally relaxed. The abbot sat lost in thought for a few minutes, then spoke.

"It is of the greatest importance that you both understand the significance of the work ahead of us. When our immediate task has been completed and we, and our guest, are on our way back to the abbey, I will explain more of the reasons for all this—" He waved a frail hand in an all-encompassing gesture. "I believe the expression is 'cloak and dagger' behaviour. But for the moment, we must prepare to welcome our young friend. Chambha, you know what you have to do. Go now."

The monk bowed, adjusted his robe more securely, and left the cabin.

"Tze-Ring, call the others and make certain all is ready. Nothing must go wrong. There is too much at stake for us to fail because of a small oversight. The Lords of Darkness will be watching for the smallest chance. Please hurry."

Tze-Ring inclined his head and went into the forward cabin where, with the help of a radio telephone, he set about contacting the rest of his group. He used a language that had been forgotten for over two thousand years, a language used only by a few erudite scholars and those who lived and worked in the Abbey of the Dawn and its sister abbeys strung across the world. For them, it was only one of many half-forgotten tongues that might be heard in their corridors and gardens. A female voice from the telephone answered in the same language, and after a short exchange Tze-Ring signed off. He picked up a woollen shawl from the bunk and went in search of the abbot.

The old man was on deck, oblivious to the chill predawn wind that fluttered his robe. He neither moved nor spoke as the younger man joined him and placed the shawl about his thin shoulders. He remained wrapped in his own inner thoughts. He was aware that he, like Chambha and Tze-Ring and Johnny himself, was simply one part of the great cosmic plan that was being enacted through them. He glanced up at the rapidly lightening sky. The stars were already fading. Somewhere in that immensity of space, there were beings of great power. Throughout the ages, humanity had known of their existence and had called them by many names: the Archons, the Watchers, the Holy Creatures, Angels, Gods, the Elohim. Some called them demons and had run from the immense power they exuded. Others chose to face them and, having done so, had come to understand that humanity was cherished by these beings. For, with all its faults, humankind was one of the chosen life-waves, destined for greatness and guided towards its full potential. Understanding this, they had stayed to serve with love, awe, and reverence.

The abbot also knew that once every two and a half thousand years, one such being was elected to become the aeon of a new age. When the correct stellar alignments opened the immense Gate of Ages, "it" descended to indwell a human body, a body created by two dedicated initiates through the power and majesty of the Great Rite of Nuit. Encased in human flesh, the aeon took on the task of guiding the planet into the next phase of its evolution, though always at the cost of personal pain and tragedy.

The abbot's task, and may the Lord Buddha give him the strength to accomplish it, was to train the traditional Forerunner, a human being born of an ancient bloodline who would prepare the way for the Aeon of the Age of Aquarius. At this precise moment, that Forerunner was a drug-ridden alcoholic suffering from gonorrhoea, and his name was Johnny Nova.

7 October, 4:35 a.m.
London

The sound of Johnny's footsteps on the rain-washed street changed as cobbles gave way to tarmac. He stopped, and for the first time since leaving the party, Johnny emerged from his dreamlike state and looked round, dazed and weary. He was in the old dockland area, so he must be fairly near the apartment, but where? Wapping, maybe, or what had once been Limehouse Reach. Wherever it was, it was not an area he recognised. He was cold, wet, and the surroundings were uninviting, yet he moved forward again as if following directions.

Johnny turned into a narrow alley leading to a rarely used mooring and began to walk towards the river. Looking ahead, he saw the tide was almost at the full, and the first weak rays of the October sun had touched its normally muddy waters with a sheen of golden light. The early morning clouds, looking like a range of grey-blue mountains, were highlighted in the same way.

"The Mountains of Gold," he murmured, drinking in the sight.

"Yes, Johnny, your mountains of gold are waiting in a far-off place in an unknown land. You received that message very clearly; we were pleased with you."

The singer's mouth opened in a silent scream of terror as from the doorway of an empty house stepped his nemesis, the priest in the saffron robe. He was taller in reality and looked capable of dealing with Johnny if he had to, but his voice, deep and gentle, belied his obvious strength.

"You need not fear me, Johnny Burke. I am here to help you realise the destiny for which you were born. But to do this, we must take you away from here. The boat is waiting, and we must not miss the tide. Come now, give me your hand."

Johnny teetered at the edge of his sanity. He was badly in need of a fix; he'd had no solid food in fifteen hours and two-thirds of a bottle of Scotch for liquid intake. To this was added the toll of the past five months.

He broke. Sinking to his knees in the slime and excrement, both human and animal, that littered the stinking alley, Johnny screamed with primal fear and frustration and a gut-wrenching certainty that nothing would ever be the same again. "For Christ's sweet fuckin' sake, what do you want?"

The answer came at once. "You, Johnny. You. The power and the love that was born in you, the pain and the rage, the hate and the fear in you. Your ultimate humanity, Johnny, that is what we want and need. It is time to leave. We must hurry; the tide will not wait even for such as you. Come."

The breath left Johnny's body in a long, deep sigh that spoke of abject weariness and, for the moment, acceptance. With his companion's help, he got to his feet. As if in a dream, he moved forward, and together they walked to where the yacht was waiting.

The abbot, with Tze-Ring beside him, was on deck. The sunlight that had caught Johnny's fancy a few moments before now edged both figures with a pale gold fire. The young man hesitated briefly, then at his guide's gentle urging, he stepped aboard the small vessel.

"I am most happy to welcome you, Johnny Burke." The old man's voice was a soft, dry sound in the still air. "May I present Brother Tze-Ring." The young monk, a few years older than Johnny, bowed respectfully. "And Father Chambha, with whom I think you are already acquainted." The old man chuckled at his own joke. "They will be responsible for your well-being and much of your training for the next five years."

Johnny's eyes widened, and his apathy vanished.

"What? Five years?! And what bleedin' training? If you think I'm buggerin' off with you lot for years, you can fuckin' think again." He turned to find the gangplank blocked by the not inconsiderable bulk of Father Chambha. "Outta my way!"

The obstacle to his departure moved not an inch, and the abbot's voice drifted over Johnny's shoulder. "I regret that the matter of your departure is now out of your hands, Johnny Burke. Come, you are tired, cold, and hungry. Some hot tea if you please, Tze-Ring. Down in the cabin, I think, where it is warmer. Chambha, please see to the other arrangements."

The abbot bustled the bewildered man down the steps and into the cabin and motioned him to take a seat opposite his own. For a few minutes, he allowed Johnny time to look round and adjust to the situation. On deck, Chambha loosed the mooring ropes, and the tide pulled them into midstream. The engine hummed to life and, guided by a knowledgeable hand on the wheel, the little yacht began its journey to the open sea.

Down in the cabin, their guest took stock of the situation. "I thought monks—you are monks, aren't you?"

The abbot smiled.

"I thought you went in for the poverty, celibacy, and begging bowl lark. All this," he indicated the quiet elegance of the cabin, "must have cost real bucks. These babies do not come cheap."

The abbot placed his fingertips together and leaned back against the padded cushions. "You are speaking of those who practice a different form of the withdrawn life. The Order to which I and my companions owe allegiance is quite different in its outlook and in the work it carries out in the world—and out of it." The last statement was an afterthought, and Johnny, in his hypersensitive state, did not miss its nuance.

Johnny was about to make a comment when they were interrupted by the entry of Tze-Ring, bearing a tray with two delicate porcelain bowls and a matching teapot. However, the aesthetic effect was spoilt by a plate of jumbo-sized ham sandwiches. The abbot looked at them with a horrified expression and raised questioning eyes to his companion. Tze-Ring smiled rather apologetically and murmured, "From a small motorised shop that serves early morning workers. I thought it might make him feel at home."

The abbot nodded reluctantly. "Tea, Johnny Burke?" asked the old man, pouring the pale, straw-coloured liquid into the bowls.

"Yeah, thanks. Lot of milk and three sugars."

For the second time in as many minutes, the abbot struggled not to allow his feelings to show on his face.

"This is taken just as it is, a rare and delicate leaf grown within the grounds of the abbey of which I am honoured to be one of the leaders. Please try it."

He offered a bowl to Johnny, who took it and sniffed it suspiciously, then took a cautious mouthful. The unaccustomed and slightly astringent taste made him baulk, and he looked round vainly for somewhere to spit it out. Finally and reluctantly, he swallowed.

"Jesus, that's bleedin' terrible. It tastes like hot scent. You got any coffee?"

The abbot, with a fixed, immobile expression, summoned Tze-Ring and relayed his request. The young monk left with a wide grin while the abbot watched with fascinated horror as his guest demolished two of the giant ham sandwiches. Then, clearing his throat, he said, "You will have to get used to the 'hot scent,' I am sorry to say. It is the only kind available to us in the abbey. But then," he went on blandly, "there are a great many things you will have to get used to in the next five years, Johnny Burke."

The coffee arrived, hot, strong, and sweet, and Johnny drank deeply, needing the caffeine jolt it would give him. It was only as he reached the bottom of the mug that he saw the powdery remains of a small pill. White-faced, he looked up at the old man, and his fears, somehow allayed until now by the abbot's friendly manner, returned in full force. He leapt to his feet.

"You rotten bastard, you've mickeyed the coffee! You're a nutter. You're all bleedin' crazy! I'm outta here."

He stumbled up the stairs onto the deck and, with a sense of shock, realised they were moving. At that very moment, they were passing the block of luxury flats that held his mates, Bucky, and everything he knew and had worked so hard for over the last four years. For the first time, Johnny realised these people were not joking; they really were taking him away. He lurched forward, the drug already taking effect. He grasped the rail with frantic but now nerveless hands and flung back his head.

"Bucky!" he screamed. "Bucky, for God's sake, help me! They're taking me away, Bucky. Oh God. God, help me...He...lp."

Johnny slumped to the deck, unconscious. Gently, Chambha lifted him into his arms and carried him below. The abbot, who had followed him, remained on deck, looking back at the sun shining on the windows of the nearest penthouse. A man came out and stood on the balcony, looking out over the river towards the vessel. The abbot watched him without a word.

"Tze-Ring," he said quietly. "Please see to it that a supply of coffee and a tea suitable for Johnny Burke's taste are delivered to the abbey. We must not take everything away from him." Then he went below.

7 October, 5:15 a.m.
The penthouse, London

Colin Buckman was dreaming, and he was not happy. He was standing on a bridge spanning a fast-flowing river. A few yards in front of him was Johnny and beside him, a small man dressed like something out of *Lost Horizon*. Bucky was trying to reach Johnny, but there was an invisible barrier between them. Each time he tried, the little monk smiled and shook his head.

Johnny looked scared to death, and he was trying reach Bucky, but with the same result. From a bank of mist behind him came two men dressed in saffron robes. They took hold of Johnny and began to pull him towards the mist. Even in his dream Bucky knew that if they succeeded, Johnny would be lost. Then the group and the life they knew would fall apart. He screamed with rage and frustration, beating with his hands against the unseen barrier.

"Johnny! Johnny, fight them! Fight, you bastard. Don't let them take you, for chrissakes. Get away, Johnny! Oh God, Johnny, I can't reach you."

It was no use. They were slowly but surely drawing him away. With a sudden realization, the dreamer knew that the group, the money, the good life, and all that went with it didn't matter half as much as Johnny. It was a mind-blowing revelation. He, Colin Buckman, the hard-headed businessman who could squeeze the last possible pound out of a reluctant impresario—Buckman, the beer-swilling, cigar-smoking, foul-mouthed Colin Buckman—loved Johnny Nova like a son, and he was losing that son.

Bucky's rage against those he saw as abductors boiled over. He screamed and bellowed and tried to ram the barrier but was thrown back. He could see Johnny's pleading eyes and outstretched hands. Though he couldn't hear it, he knew Johnny was shouting for help, and he knew himself to be helpless. Like all human beings at a crisis point, Bucky reverted to things known and taught in childhood. Things long buried under the glitter and glamour of his life in show business now surfaced. He slumped to his knees, and even in his dream, he knew he was crying.

"Johnny! Johnny, don't go. Please don't go. Let him go, you fuckin' bastards. He's mine, do you hear me? Mine! You'll hurt him. He's sick. He's gotta be looked after. Oh God, please let him go. I'll look after him, I promise. I'll see he gets well, that he gets to a quack right away. I'll give up the booze myself, cigars too, but please, make them let him go. Gentle Jesus meek and mild, oh God, Johnny. Johnny, my boy."

He was gone. The mist had swallowed him and the two men. Only the slight figure of the saffron-robed monk was left. The man walked through the invisible barrier as if it did not exist and stood before Colin Buckman. His voice was gentle.

"Mr. Buckman, I understand your feelings for this young man, but believe me, if he stays with you, he will be dead within a year and his powers will have been wasted. We have great need of him and the power he carries, but we will look after him. Yes, we will hurt him, both physically and mentally; curing someone in his state will always hurt. Training one of his kind to face and control their inner powers will also hurt. But he will become stronger for the pain of learning, and I give you my word that you will see Johnny again. You are a good man, Mr. Buckman. Deep down, you are a good and caring man. Do not keep that part of yourself buried. May He upon whom you called be with you."

Then the man was gone, the bridge was empty, and the barrier was back.

"Johnny! Johnny, come back! Get the hell outta there."

Bucky sat up in bed, sweating like a pig with tears running down his face. His sleeping partner was shaking him, yelling at him to wake up.

"Jesus, Bucky, you'll wake the whole bloody place up! Wake up, you stupid sod. You're dreaming. You've had a nightmare."

Bucky stared at her, still not fully awake but shaking like a leaf.

The woman climbed out of the sweat-soaked bed and ambled, mother-naked, into the bathroom, returning with a glass of water and a sleeping pill. Bucky drank the water but refused the pill; sleep was something he didn't need at the moment. He got up, pulled on a towelling robe, and opened the glass doors to the balcony. It was just after dawn. The stars had gone and the air was clean and fresh. He stood, silent, filled with vague fears and a deep sense of foreboding left over from his dream.

Urged by a sudden premonition, Bucky went back into the bedroom and headed for the lounge of the big penthouse suite. The debris of last night's party covered the room. The stale smell of tobacco and drink pervaded the air, and Bucky cursed as he picked his way over discarded bottles and glasses. He kicked a pair of pantyhose out of his way and headed for the closed door of Johnny's room. His thoughts ran ahead of him. *He'll be there. Shit, what am I worryin' about? The guy just went for a walk to clear his head. It was a dream, just a stupid fuckin' dream. He'll be there, probably with a bird, and he won't thank me for burstin' in either.*

Bucky reached the door and hesitated, then cautiously turned the handle and opened the door. Unlike the others, Johnny was neat in his habits. His early life spent in the cramped confines of a vardo had instilled tidiness in him. While the rooms used by the others looked like a ransacked Oxfam depot, Johnny's was always neat, as it was now. Neat and tidy and with a perfectly made bed that showed no sign of being slept in.

Bucky's nightmare rushed back with full force. He lurched onto the balcony again, his mind whirling and a sick feeling in the pit of his stomach. He grasped the iron railing until the cold metal bit into his hands and stared out over the early morning river. The tide was running full and fast. As he looked, a motor yacht passed, cutting cleanly through the muddy water of the ancient river and heading towards the open sea. A small elderly man in some sort of yellow dressing gown stood on its deck, looking back at him.

"Johnny, where are you?" whispered Colin Buckman. But there was no answer, and he didn't really expect one.

YEAR ONE

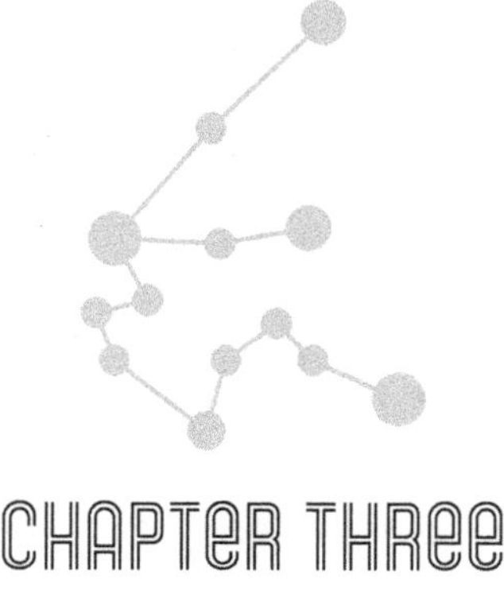

CHAPTER THREE

8 October, 12:00 p.m.
Dockland Police Station, London

Station Sergeant Collins was trying to be patient with the irate man in the psychedelic waistcoat. He'd been there for three hours now and was still insisting that his client had been abducted. Trying not to wince as the eye-twisting waistcoat stopped in front of him, Collins made another attempt to reason with the man.

"Mr. Buckman, on your own admission, this young man…" He glanced down at the note pad in front of him. "Mr. John Burke, known as Johnny Nova, has been missing for roughly thirty-one hours. I'm afraid that is not long enough to warrant a full-scale search for him. He is a grown man known to drink heavily, so maybe he's just gone off on a binge somewhere. I advise you to wait another twenty-four hours, and if he hasn't turned up by then, we can start taking this thing seriously.

"Yes," he raised a placating hand as Bucky began to pound the table again. "I realise that Mr. Nova is a well-known figure, but famous people have been known to disappear for publicity stunts before now. Quite frankly,

Mr. Buckman, I don't want my lads with egg on their faces because some young rock star wants a spot on the front page."

Bucky opened his mouth to start another tirade about slander and police incompetence when Frank Saunders intervened. Uncurling from a chair in a corner of the interview room, he ambled over to the two men glaring at each other over a table littered with plastic cups and the charred corpses of Bucky's cigars.

"You know, Bucky, he thought he was being followed. All through the tour he was convinced he was seeing someone, the same person, wherever he went. He told me about it when we hit Sydney. He was scared stiff; that was why he drank so much."

The two men turned on him as one.

"Why the fuck didn't he tell me? Why didn't you tell me about it?"

"This could put an entirely different light on the matter. You should have given me this information before, Mr. Saunders. Now what exactly did Mr. Burke, er, Nova, tell you about this person?"

Frank shrugged. "Not a lot. He just said that he kept seeing this weird monk type following him about. Johnny said he called him by name and told him he was coming to fetch him. He was real scared about it."

The sergeant looked at Frank as if he'd found him crawling on a leaf. "A monk? What kind of monk?"

"A sort of, uh…Tibetan, you know, robes and prayer-wheel type." Frank shifted his feet uneasily, aware of how stupid it all sounded.

The sergeant closed his eyes and prayed for patience and a modicum of sanity. Taking a deep breath, he opened them again, and with a supreme effort spoke with a fair semblance of his normal self.

"Did you personally see or hear this…this monk?"

"No, I just listened when Johnny wanted to talk. He thought he was going mad."

He's not the only one, thought the sergeant silently. *This whole bloody bunch is round the twist.* He tried again.

"Let me get this quite clear, Mr. Saunders. Mr. Nova, who is given to drinking heavily, told you he was being followed by a Tibetan monk that you yourself never saw or heard?"

Frank swallowed hard and nodded reluctantly. "Yeah. I mean, no, I didn't see or hear him. I only know what Johnny told me."

He looked towards Bucky for help and saw him holding on to the table, white and shaking. His face was the colour of putty, his whole body trembling. Alarmed, Frank grabbed him by the arm.

"Hey, Buck, what's the matter? You look like shit. Christ, sarge, get some water or somethin'. I think he's gonna pass out."

The sergeant took one look at the ashen-faced man and sprang into action. Missing rock stars—especially one given to seeing non-existent Tibetan monks—and a possible heart attack in one day was more than he cared to have around. Sergeant Collins sent for the station doctor and, helped by Frank, got the barely conscious Buckman to an empty cell and laid him down. Methodically, he loosened the man's tie, shirt collar, and belt, carefully turned him onto his side to ease any congestion, and covered him with a blanket.

"Watch him," he ordered Frank tersely and went to hurry the doctor.

Frank didn't feel too good himself. He knelt beside Bucky and patted his hand. "You'll be OK, Buck. They're goin' to get a doc over right away."

Bucky reached out a hand and grabbed him, startling Frank with the fierce strength of the grip. "I don't want no bloody doctor," he wheezed. "I want outta here. I need to think. Frank, listen to me. I dreamt it just like Johnny said. I honest to God dreamt it. The night Johnny walked out, he looked real wild. I tried to stop him, you saw me, but he went anyway. Later on, I had this dream about him." He paused, panting a little, then went on, "I dreamed I was standing on a bridge, and he was there with this small guy dressed in some kinda robe and a sort of shawl round his shoulders. Old, he was—Jesus, the guy must have been touching a hundred, all sorta wizened. I couldn't reach Johnny because of some sort of barrier. Couldn't see anything, it was just there. Then two other guys in the same sort of clobber came out of the fog on the other side of the bridge and took Johnny away. He was screaming at me not to let them take him, but I couldn't get to him. Then the old guy walks right through the bleedin' barrier and talks to me, says he's taking Johnny away because they need him for something big." Bucky closed his eyes and relived the dream.

"It was a dream, Frank, a stupid dream. But then you said, you said…" He swallowed hard, and to Frank's amazement, his eyes were wet. "You said he'd seen them, those monks or whatever they were, that he thought they were following him. Frank, I know I'm right—he's been swiped, and not for a bloody ransom either. One of those bleedin' groups like the Moonies, more like."

The sergeant returned with a young doctor behind him. With swift efficiency, he examined the older man thoroughly. He reassured them it was not the onset of a heart attack but a panic attack, a symptom of severe stress brought on by anxiety. He warned Bucky, however, that a heart attack was on the cards if he didn't lose weight and give up smoking. He slid a needle full of sedative into a vein and wrote out a prescription for a mild tranquilliser, giving it with precise instructions to Frank, then left with a brief nod to the sergeant.

Within twenty minutes, the sedative had calmed Bucky's heart rate down and the colour had returned to his face. After another half hour, much to the relief of the sergeant, he decided to leave.

The sergeant promised to keep in touch if anybody should turn up drunk or, he thought privately, simply dead. He and Frank got the subdued Buckman out of the station and into the custom-built Mercedes taking up most of the parking space in front of the small police station. Normally, Bucky allowed no one to touch his beloved Merc, but he was in no condition to drive, so it was Frank who drove back to the apartment where the others were waiting.

On the way Bucky pressed his companion into giving him details about Johnny's experiences. Frank told him all he knew, but it didn't satisfy Bucky, and he kept worrying at the whole thing like a dog with a bone.

"How come Johnny saw them and you didn't?" he asked for the third time.

"Because they wanted him to see them. I told you before." Frank wrenched the car round a tight corner with a disregard for the paintwork that made Bucky blanch.

"Damn it, Colin." Frank seldom used his real name, and it was a measure of his distress that he used it now. "You've seen them yourself, even if it was only in a dream, so they must've wanted you to see them as well.

I tell you this gets crazier by the minute and—shit, get outta the way you stupid berk—I think it'll get worse."

He turned into the car park of the luxury apartments and eased the car into a private berth marked "C. Buckman, Esquire." Frank turned in his seat to look at the man behind him.

"Buck, in your dream, these monks…They told you they needed Johnny because of his power, didn't they? And something about a destiny? What do you think they meant? I mean, people like us, we don't have destinies. We have careers for a while until we drop out of fashion, then we fall on our arses. Destinies are for people who change the world, not rock groups. I know you and the others think I'm dumb because I don't drink and screw around, but I read a lot. I remember seeing something a year or so back about people who've disappeared over the last forty or fifty years. The writer had studied a lot of cases like Johnny's. Mostly, they never come back, but if they do, they seem…Well, changed somehow."

"How changed?" asked Bucky, leaning forward, a cigar glowing redly in the dimness of the car's interior.

"One guy became a doctor, you know, the alternative stuff. People claimed he cured all sorts of things, even cancer. Another went into politics and changed his country from a dump into a law-abiding, self-sufficient island. Then there was this woman, a teacher. When she came back, she invented a whole new system of teaching kids who were blind to read and learn like the others. There's only one thing though…" His voice trailed away.

"Yes?" came Bucky's voice, although he already knew the answer.

"Most of 'em died eventually, one way or another. Nothing proven of course, but the circumstances were what they call suspicious."

Frank reached out and took the cigar from Bucky's mouth and threw it out of the car window. "The doc said no smoking, remember? And if you're dead, you can't find Johnny, so from now on—" He jerked his head at the smouldering stub. "You can forget those, right!"

For a moment Colin Buckman was about to tell Frank to go to hell. Then he remembered Johnny's face in his dream, how he had held out his arms and begged Bucky to save him. It was something he would never forget.

"Yeah, well…Guess you're right," he said and clambered unsteadily out of the car.

In silence they took the escalator to the front lobby, where they collected the papers and the mail. As they waited for the penthouse elevator, Bucky made a decision and returned to the front desk. He thrust a couple of objects into the porter's hands.

"Here," he said, "I don't need these anymore," and followed a grinning Frank into the lift. The porter was left staring at a solid silver lighter and cigar case half-filled with fine hand-rolled Havana cigars.

8 October, 1:00 p.m.
On board the yacht *Melixanthe*

Tze-Ring glanced up from the book he was reading as Johnny groaned and shifted in the bunk. He was sleeping heavily and obviously dreaming. The young man rose and went over to him, smoothing back the sweat-soaked hair. Turning to the table, he wrung out a cloth in a basin of cold water and wiped the singer's face with a hand as gentle as a woman's. Johnny's head tossed from side to side, and broken words in the Romani tongue he had used as a child came tumbling from his lips.

"*Hom te jov, hom te jov, baulolengro…Miro mam…Tatto si can…Mande kinyo, nastis jalno durroder. Pawni-kekkeno pawni dov odoi.* Please, I must go. Bucky. Mama, it's so hot…*Tatto Mama, tatto. Miri deary Dovvel…*Oh God, my dear God."[2]

The words ran on and on, changing from Romani to English and back again. It was obvious he was getting no rest even with the sedative he'd been given. Tze-Ring hesitated a moment, then sat on the bunk and took Johnny's hand. He probed lightly into his dreams, just enough to ease them into a warm, restful darkness, replacing the churning images with one of Johnny's mother bending over him. He smiled in his sleep and relaxed.

"*Mama, miri mama, so must I ker?…Coin minro Dado?*"[3]

2. "Going home, going home, to big home…My mam…Got to go…My father, darkness, hot water. Hot as kettle, too hot. Please, I must go. Bucky. Mama, it's so hot…Hot, Mama, hot. Dear mother…Oh God, my dear God."
3. "Mama, my mama, what must I do?…Who is my father?"

Linked to him mind with mind as he was, Tze-Ring understood what Johnny was asking. He withdrew from the young man's mind, leaving him to sleep quietly and peacefully.

Tze-Ring stood beside the bunk for a long time, wondering what Johnny would say when he found out his father was not only alive but a high-ranking initiate in one of the Abbeys of Light that spanned the world. What would he think when he found out that his much-loved mother had been brought, with her consent, to that same abbey twenty-three years ago so that the ancient bloodline of the Forerunners could be united with that of a Romani girl whose ancestors had once ruled Egypt?

8 October, 2:30 p.m.
The penthouse, London

For the first six floors, there was silence in the lift. Then Frank asked the question Bucky was dreading.

"What are you goin' to tell the others, Bucky? I mean, they're not goin' to buy this being kidnapped by bleedin' monks, are they?"

Bucky turned and looked at him. "Tell me something, Frank. Do you believe it? Honestly, do you really believe it?"

Frank inspected the scruffy toes of his beat-up trainers for a few seconds, then met Bucky's eyes. He was beginning to realise what losing Johnny meant to the man.

"Yes," he said quietly, "I do believe it. I don't know why I do, but I do. But I still don't think you can tell the others that. At least, not right away."

Frank stepped forward as the lift stopped and the doors opened, then hesitated and looked back. "For what it's worth, I always felt that Johnny was something more than just Johnny, if you know what I mean. That monk was right when he said he had power. He's always had it. You could see it when he was on stage. Wherever it is they've taken him, maybe he'll learn to use it for real."

The door to the apartment burst open and Lyle stood there with Liam looking over his shoulder. The expression of hope on their faces died as the two men pushed past them without a word. Bucky headed for the bar and poured himself a large whisky, looked at it for a moment, then poured half back into the bottle. Frank stood around looking uncomfortable.

"Well," demanded Liam, "what did they say? Is there any news at all? Has anyone seen or heard from him?"

Neither Frank nor Bucky spoke.

"For the love of God, will yez talk to us? Don't just stand there like a dog turd on the pavement! Sure he has to be somewhere. The hospitals, the morgues, or what about Florrie? Would he have gone back there, do you think?"

Bucky tossed back his drink and stood looking into the bottom of the glass as if it might turn into a crystal ball and provide some kind of information. Then he said, "No, Liam, there's no record of him bein' admitted to any London hospital. He hasn't been nicked for anything, and he's not with Florrie 'cos I already phoned. The police won't regard him as a missing person for another twenty-four hours. After that, they'll start..." He swallowed. "They'll start making inquiries and draggin' the river. You know...things like that." His voice trailed away.

The silence that followed was filled with Ginny's sobs and Lyle's voice trying to comfort her. Finally Biff, who had been restringing his guitar, drew a testing flurry of notes from his instrument. Then, laying it aside, he looked up and said casually, "Maybe 'e went off with that weirdo in the orange-coloured robe."

For all his bulk, Bucky could move fast when he wanted to do so. "And just what," he asked, with Biff hanging by his shirt collar from the manager's beefy hands, "just what the fuckin' shit do you know about the weirdo in an orange robe?"

Biff flapped his hands about and tried to speak, but Bucky's hands were slowly choking the life out of him.

"Tell me!" he roared. "What do you know? Tell me, damn it! Tell me!" With each repetition, he shook his victim like a terrier with a rat.

Biff tried desperately to wrench free, but he was fighting a losing battle, both with Bucky and his consciousness. Belatedly, the others sprang into action, Liam and Lyle using brute force to break the manager's grip. Frank helped the terrified Biff to the couch, where he cowered in the corner, staring at his attacker with his eyes starting out of his head.

"Fer the love of God, Buck, lay off the poor sod. You bloody near did for 'im. What are ye tryin' to do, wipe out the whole bleedin' group?" Liam stood with his hands on Bucky's shoulders, holding him steady. "Cool it, man. Do you know somethin' we don't?"

Frank answered for the distraught Bucky. "Leave him be, Liam. He had some kind of attack at the police station. They had to call a doctor to give 'im a shot of something. Johnny told me ages ago that he was being followed by a kind of monk, and Buck dreamed about him being kidnapped by monks the night he disappeared. He's taken a real shock over the last twenty-four. You know he wouldn't really hurt Biff."

"You could 'ave bloody well fooled me," wheezed the shock-headed musician from the couch. "I thought I'd 'ad me friggin' chips."

Bucky lurched over to one of the leather armchairs and sat down heavily. He lowered his face into his hands, still shaking with the aftermath of his rage. He was devastated by his lack of control. In all the time they had been together, he had never done anything like this. He felt in his pocket for his cigars and groaned as he remembered giving them to the porter.

"I suppose all this drama means that at least some of us have seen the ecclesiastical gentleman in question and there is a distinct possibility that Johnny is with him, either willingly or unwillingly."

Tango pushed himself away from the wall he'd been using as a support and sauntered into the middle of the room, hands tucked into the back pockets of his designer jeans. He continued in his carefully cultivated, grammar-school accent that still carried a hint of his native Wales.

"Might I ask if you have told any of this to the police?"

A deep silence descended on the little group. They all looked at Tango, who shrugged and smiled widely, his expensively capped teeth making him look almost feral.

"Oh yes, I saw him as well. I simply took him to be an ordinary fan. Though when he turned up at LA, Tokyo, and Sydney, it seemed a little, well, unusual. After all, monks are supposed to be poor and holy and chaste, aren't they?" His voice took on a sly, mocking note. "But I understand that some of these odd cults have equally odd habits. I thought maybe Johnny knew him well enough to provide him with the money, a sort of…very close friend, if you know what I mean." He laughed again, but there was no amusement there, just a new and rather frightening coldness. This was a Tango none of them knew or liked.

Lyle stepped up to him, easily matching Tango's six feet of height. Quiet-spoken Lyle, who in four years had never raised his voice to any of them. He still spoke softly, but with an edge to his voice that caught their attention and a dignity that held a stinging rebuke for his sneering opponent.

"Watch your mouth, Tango. A holy man is entitled to respect from people like us, no matter what religion he calls his own. Only a fool laughs at a true believer. As for Johnny, he was no saint, but deep inside he was real good, and he cared about people. You never cared about nobody ever. Don't let me hear you runnin' him down again, man."

He turned to Bucky and hunkered down beside him. "I didn't see that guy, Bucko, but Ginny did, and she told me about it. I didn't say nothin' to nobody because…Well, because…" He looked to Ginny for support.

"Because 'e wasn't real, Bucky." Ginny came forward slowly. Her face was white, making the garish makeup she affected stand out like a mask. "I was frightened at first, 'cos I knew 'e weren't really there. I've always been able to see things, ever since I were little. Mum used to beat me something awful if I told anyone, so I got outta the habit of tellin'. I didn't know it was gonna be important, see. I told Lyle, 'cos I knew 'e wouldn't laugh at me. That monk, he was sorta like a reflection of someone who was a real person. He wasn't dead or nothing, it was just that the real part of 'im was somewhere else." She burst into tears. "If only I'd said, Johnny might be here now." She broke down again.

Bucky got to his feet wearily. "You didn't know, Ginny. None of us knew. I never saw the blighter, only in a dream the night Johnny disappeared." He turned to Biff and ruffled his hair. "Sorry, mate. I'm feeling crook after that attack down at the station. I got carried away. I'm just so bloody scared at what might have happened to him."

He walked to the window and looked out at the river for a long time, trying to gather his thoughts. Finally Bucky seemed to make a decision and turned to the others.

"We'll pool all the information we have and see where it gets us, but—" He held up his hand and raised his voice to get their attention. "Whatever happens, I do not want this to get into the papers. Do I make myself absolutely clear? There's always the chance that we may be barking up the wrong tree and Johnny will walk in tonight or tomorrow, and we don't want to rock the boat."

A chorus of muted voices answered him, but in the anxiety of the moment, no one realised that Tango said nothing, had not promised along with the others. He simply smiled and listened.

8 October, 3:00 p.m.
The English Channel

Johnny retched into the toilet bowl for the umpteenth time, but there was no longer anything to bring up. Ever since waking up some hours ago, he'd been glued to the little toilet. At first he had asked for his jacket and his supply of coke, but Chambha had politely refused to give it to him. He kept on refusing, and all Johnny's curses, threats, pleas, and whining had not moved him. His self-appointed torturer simply told him the sooner he got the drug out of his system, the sooner he would be fit enough to make the long journey to the Abbey of the Dawn.

Since then, the stomach cramps had gotten steadily worse. He could keep nothing down, not even boiled water with a little sugar, and his gut was on fire with pain. He shivered uncontrollably as he lay curled up on the floor of the minute bathroom. At this moment, he had forgotten Bucky, the group, his captors, and the torment of the last few months; only the pain was real and immediate. A soft footstep sounded behind him and Chambha stood in the doorway, his dark eyes compassionate as he looked down at his charge.

"Come, Johnny Burke. You will feel better lying down, I think." He lifted the young man to his feet and helped him down the companionway to the forward cabin. There he sat him on the bunk and proceeded to strip him as if he were a small and very sick child. His face remained calm and gentle with not the slightest revulsion of feeling, even when removing the pus-stained briefs to reveal the swollen and infected genitals. He steadied Johnny as a new wave of pain swamped the young man, then gently urged him between the cool sheets and encouraged him to sip small amounts of cracked ice.

"Please," whispered the agonised voice from the pillow. "Just a little. You can't ask me to do this cold…Just a little…That's all I need. Then I could hold out a bit longer…Please, it's in my jacket."

Chambha placed a gentle hand on his shoulder. "What was in your jacket is no longer there, Johnny Burke. It was disposed of hours ago. It will take your body some time to throw off the poison it has accumulated within itself. Until then, you have only your own inner strength to draw upon, and that is greater than you think." He wiped the sweat from Johnny's face with a damp cloth. "Try to sleep, my son. It will be better if you can sleep even a little. I will remain with you."

Johnny felt too weak to fight him and closed his eyes. Tears of weakness and self-pity ran down the sides of his face, and he turned into the pillow to hide them. Then another spasm of pain gripped him and he sobbed aloud, begging and pleading for something, anything, to take the pain away. He writhed on the narrow bed, flinging off the covers and drawing his legs up in an effort to ease the cramps in his belly. A rancid-smelling sweat covered his whole body and slowly soaked its way through to the bottom sheet.

After a thousand years of time, the pain eased, and he relaxed, gasping. Chambha again wiped his face and gave him a tiny spoonful of ice. Johnny lay with his eyes closed, revelling in the cessation of agony, his whole attention focussed on his body and its demand for the drug to which it had become addicted. Then, just as he allowed himself to hope for peace, came the beginnings of another cramp. He threw himself from side to side, screaming hysterically as it gathered strength. He prayed for the pain to go away, but instead it fastened its steel claws into his belly and began to rip him apart.

Johnny flung the sheet aside and tried to scramble off the bed, thoughts of flinging himself into the river at the back of his mind. Chambha gently restrained him. Now the pain gathered strength and dug deeper. Once more Johnny screamed and thrashed about, deliberately banging his head on the wall in an attempt to ease his torment with another and different kind of pain, but it was unrelenting and came upon him in rhythmic waves of agony that threatened to engulf his very sanity. Finally his strength and even his dignity as a man gave way as first his bladder, then his bowels relaxed, covering the lower half of his body with a stinking slimy fluid and staining the white sheets a dirty yellow. He was beyond caring what happened to him or what he looked like. Beyond shame and embarrassment. Johnny Nova, the millionaire rock star, the darling of the fans, lay moaning and shivering, covered in his own excrement and urine.

"Mama, Mama. It hurts, Mama. *Oh Dovvel, miro Dovvel,*[4] it hurts... Please help me...Mama."

Chambha called Tze-Ring to help him, and together they cleansed and bathed the pain-racked body of the young man. Chambha lifted him in his arms so the sheets could be replaced by cool, clean linen, then gently laid him down again. It was a scene that was to be repeated many times as the little yacht sailed on towards its appointed meeting.

The hours ran together. Johnny no longer knew if it was day or night or how long he had been on board. His only criterion of time was the all-too-brief period between bouts of pain and sickness. At short intervals, he would sleep. Then the pain would begin again, and he would battle against it until, too worn out to scream, he would lose consciousness again. But Johnny was never left alone with the pain. There was always someone there, someone to wipe his face, give him water, clean up his vomit and his filth, and change the sheets. Someone who held his hands and encouraged him to bear the torment. Those hands were bandaged now, to prevent him tearing at the skin of his stomach in a fever-induced attempt to stop the pain.

The yacht ploughed on in the heavy seas of the English Channel. The weather was closing in and there was still some way to go. Tze-Ring, now wearing waterproofs and looking like any normal yachtsman, guided her through the intricate sea lanes and on towards the Channel Islands. From time to time, he went below for a few minutes to help Chambha or to see to the comfort of the abbot, who was not a good sailor and who had withdrawn into meditation as a way of keeping his mind off the continually tossing vessel. It was now thirty-six hours since Johnny had come aboard, and ahead in the mist and rain, a Greek cargo vessel stood by off the French coast to pick them up.

4. "Oh God, my God"

At last came a time when Johnny opened his eyes and looked up at the old man bending over him.

"Come, Johnny Burke. Drink this. It will help for a little while."

A cup of bitter-tasting liquid was urged down his throat. Johnny gagged. Then, worn out by pain and far beyond any kind of resistance, he swallowed obediently, and within a few minutes was soundly and deeply asleep.

"Is it necessary for him to endure this, Holy One?" asked Tze-Ring. "It is a simple matter to keep him asleep until the drug has worked its way out of his system. Or, if permitted, I can teach him to control the pain in an hour or so."

The abbot turned to the younger man and smiled.

"It must be this way, Tze-Ring. Unless he has known pain, unless he has fully experienced it for himself, how can he understand what others go through? If he cannot understand, then he cannot help them. It is written that 'in understanding one may find great wisdom,' but first comes the experience that enables one to understand." He stood up and drew his shawl closer about his thin shoulders and stared out of the windows.

"You say we will meet with the cargo boat in two or three hours?"

"Yes, Rinpoche. Alexandros Spiridion and his eldest son are on board, and they will take over this yacht and sail her into a French harbour as if they had been on a fishing trip. His son-in-law, who is a qualified doctor, is also on board, which makes our task a lot easier. The captain, Takis Michalitis, was trained in the Abbey of the Winds for several years. He is a competent initiate of the second level.

"It will take us about four days to reach Crete; maybe a day more or less, according to the weather. Johnny can rest at the house of the Spiridion family. The first stage of withdrawal will be almost over by then, although he will have a long way to go before being free of the addiction. I will stay with him while your Holiness and Father Chambha visit the Abbey of the Aeon. From there, you will return by the usual route to the Abbey of the Dawn. Two days later, Johnny and I will sail for Suez. I estimate it will take six days to get through the canal and on to Muscat. Sister Shuna and Brothers Wang Ta and Murad will meet us there. We fly out the following morning."

For a while, the old abbot and his young companion watched the sleeping man, each busy with his own thoughts. After a few minutes, Tze-Ring turned to his superior, his manner unusually hesitant. Without looking at him, the abbot spoke quietly. "Yes, my son, speak and have no fear."

"Holy One, as you know, my main talent is that of telekinesis, but I have some ability in the art of precognition. It is the way of these things that one can rarely see ahead for oneself, yet I sense my part in the training of the Forerunner will demand more of me than was first thought. Forgive me if I seem presumptuous. I do not seek a greater part to play, just to say that whatever is asked of me, I will give without reservation." Tze-Ring's voice fell into silence.

The abbot turned to him. "You are among those blessed by love and touched by the greatness of the moment, Tze-Ring." The abbot's voice quavered slightly. "As you say, the Forerunner will have great need of you at a point in the future, and I know you will be there. A great and wonderful blessing will be yours at that moment." He sighed and turned away, seeking to change the subject.

"It will be some time before we are back in the mountains. I find this part of the world tiring and long to be where I can contemplate the Land of Snows again. I will rest until it is time to board the *Aghios Loukas*. Wake me then."

Tze-Ring bowed and went up on deck to watch for the signal that would guide them to their rendezvous. Below, the abbot sat in silence, thinking about the events yet to come. Chambha moved quietly about the cabin, packing suitcases. Johnny slept on, for the moment blessedly oblivious to both pain and fear.

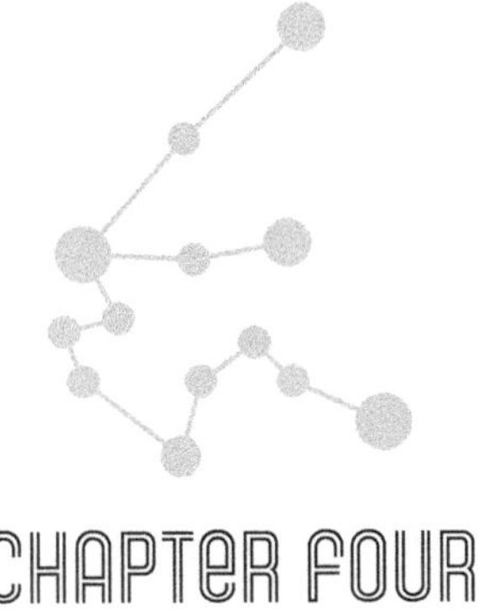

CHAPTER FOUR

9 October, 12:30 a.m.
The penthouse, London

The table was littered with the remains of a Chinese takeaway and several empty pizza boxes. Adding to the air of weariness and gloom was a wastepaper basket full of discarded Coke, lager, and beer cans. They were on the hard stuff now. Bucky sat slumped at the top of the big table, shirt open and sleeves rolled up. His eyes were red-rimmed with tiredness, and he clutched an untouched whisky between his hands. What his thoughts were, the others could only guess.

Through the open windows, the lights of London below looked like a distant fairground. The noise of the late-night traffic was just a muffled roar. Frank stood looking out of one of the windows, hands thrust into his pockets. He, too, looked drawn and haggard. He sighed and turned back to the room, smiling to see Ginny asleep with her head on Lyle's lap, the dark skin of his hand a contrast to her cropped blonde hair.

"She'd be a lot more comfortable in bed," Frank pointed out.

"Yeah, I know. So would I." Lyle lifted the girl's slight weight into his muscular arms and heaved himself off the leather sofa.

"I'll tuck 'er in, then come back. Hush now, honey girl." This to Ginny as she stirred in his arms. "Lyle's right here, so don' you fret yourself." He carried her into the bedroom and closed the door.

"Ginny's sure taken it 'ard, though I don't see it could've changed anythin' even if she 'ad told us sooner." Biff leaned across the table and took the joint from Liam's mouth and drew on it, closing his eyes as the smoke filled his lungs. He leaned back in his chair, propping his stockinged feet on the table.

"For chrissakes, Biff, take your bleedin' feet off the table. Put some shoes on while you're about it. It's bad enough in here with all this booze and stale food without having to put up with your feet as well." Bucky pushed aside his untasted drink and cleared his throat. "Frank, open another window and then get Lyle back in here. Let's go over this once more, see if we've left anything out."

A chorus of weary voices protested, but the fat man was adamant. Frank knocked on Lyle's door and a few minutes later, the drummer joined them round a table cleared of its debris. Bucky scrubbed a hand over his tired face and looked round at them. They'd been at it since midday. Frank and Biff were the worst off, Frank because he had been involved since daybreak and Biff still bruised from Bucky's attack. Liam was slightly the worse for a joint or two but reasonably with it. Lyle had been coping with Ginny's grief as well as his own fears for Johnny's safety. Only Tango looked fresh, even relaxed.

Bucky cleared his throat. "The top line is, Johnny's disappeared. God knows where. He'd been going at the booze like a good 'un since halfway through the tour. We know he was upset about seeing this monk or whatever at least since Sydney and possibly a fair time before that." He paused to collect his thoughts. "We know that was probably why he was hitting the bottle. Out of the six of us, Johnny, Biff, and Tango have actually seen this guy. Four if you count Ginny. Five if you count my dreamin' about him." There was another, longer pause. "Everyone's given the same description that Johnny gave Frank and all agree on times and places, so it's a fair certainty we are talking about the same bloke. It is also safe to say this monk 'as whipped 'im away somewhere. The questions are, one, why? Two, where is he now? And three, what do we do about it?" He looked round at them for an answer. When none came, Bucky sighed and slumped in his chair.

Frank drew a deep breath and spoke. “In your dream, the little guy told you that Johnny has something they needed, something very important?”

“Yeah, like ten million smackers in ransom.” This from Liam as he pulled the ring on another lager.

Frank turned to him. “No, I don’t think…” He stopped and closed his eyes for a moment, then opened them again and resumed, “I know it isn’t the money. I can’t see them like Ginny and Biff and Tango, but I can feel them. I tell you it’s Johnny they want, not money. Besides, it goes against everything a religious order is about, to kidnap someone for money, doesn’t it?”

“Five hundred years ago, religious orders burnt men, women, and children to death because they thought differently to the church. Near enough to five million people died over the course of a couple of centuries. Don’t think they couldn’t take kidnapping in their stride.” A new voice cut into their midst, making them all swing round to the door.

A small, plump woman stood in the doorway, a handsome leather suitcase by her side. Her once-dark hair had been touched up with henna, giving her a slightly piebald look and underlining her lavish use of cosmetics. Johnny’s aunt, Florrie, had been a beauty in her youth, and she had buried three husbands before finally leaving the excitement of the circus life she had married into as a girl. Now in her fifties, the beauty had faded somewhat. But the large, luminous eyes and a warm, generous mouth served as a reminder of the young girl who had once been a graceful bareback rider with a sideline in telling fortunes. Bucky’s face lit up.

“Florrie! You’re a sight for sore eyes!” He heaved himself to his feet and went to greet her, taking her hands in his and kissing her on both cheeks. “What the hell are you doin’ here at this hour? Come and take the weight off your bunions and grab a coldie.”

“Thanks, but I’ll have a gin if it’s all the same to you. I came down from Oxford on the late train and got a taxi at the station.” Florrie handed her coat to Lyle and settled into an armchair, hefting a large handbag onto the glass-topped table in front of her. “I gather there’s been no more news?” She looked round at the circle of faces. “Well, I’m not surprised. I’ve been waiting for somethin’ like this to happen for a long time. It’s not all as cut ’n dried as you might think. I've been lookin' through some papers my sister left, and I thought I'd better come along and fill you in on a couple of things about my nephew. I've a fair idea who took 'im, and I may even have a clue as to why."

Florrie took a hefty swallow of the gin Liam had produced and made sure she had the full attention of everyone in the room.

9 October, 12:30 a.m.
The cargo ship *Aghios Loukas*,
off the French Coast

Johnny opened his eyes and stiffened against the claws of remembered pain, but for the moment there was only a soreness that ran the length of his entire body. He tried moving but desisted when a sudden nausea rose in his throat. For a moment he held it at bay, then, regardless of anything but a need to be sick, he twisted over in the bunk. Even as Johnny started to heave, a basin was under his chin, and a gentle voice called him by name.

For a few minutes he was too occupied to bother about anything else, but when the spasms ended, he slumped back on the pillows and looked up. Then he remembered it all. The voices in his head, the visions that had haunted him, the long walk through the night of rain, the motor yacht, the abbot, Chambha and Tze-Ring. It was the latter who now sat on the bunk and wiped his face with a cool, wet towel and offered a glass of water to wash away the taste of bile. Johnny rinsed his mouth then lay back, closing his eyes and hoping his visitor would go away, but when he opened them again, the young man was still there, smiling. Johnny studied him for a few minutes, then looked round the cabin. Finally he spoke.

"This is a different ship, right?"

The other man nodded.

"When did we change over?"

"About three hours ago. We are now on a Greek cargo vessel bound for Crete. We will stay there for a few days, then go on."

"How much further on?"

The young man regarded him intently. At some point he had exchanged his tracksuit for a full-length robe of dull red, over which he wore a toga-like shawl of the same colour. His shaven head gave his young face a strangely ancient look.

"First to Muscat. Eventually, much further than that, Johnny. The location where most of your training will take place is called the Abbey of the Dawn. It is situated high in the Karakoram Range on the border of northern India and Tibet."

Johnny felt too weak and too sore to make a scene for the moment, and he needed to sleep again.

"The pain's stopped. Did you give me a shot?"

"No," Tze-Ring shook his head regretfully. "The pain will soon return, Johnny. We gave you a sedative to transfer you as quickly and easily as possible." He hesitated, and Johnny saw signs of an inner battle taking place. "I will stay with you when the pain begins again. It may be that I can help you, if only a little. Sleep while you can, Johnny Burke." He smiled and stood up. "I need to speak with the abbot." And he was gone.

Crete, is it? thought Johnny rebelliously. *Well, there may be a way of jumping ship there and getting lost among the tourists, but one thing's for sure: I won't be climbing no bloody Karakorams.*

He turned into the pillow and closed his eyes, intending to sleep, but a few minutes later a familiar cramping pain began low in his belly. He tensed, hoping it was just a passing thing, but it grew with a steady intensity that soon had him writhing on the bunk. Once, twice, three times he gritted his teeth and rode the spasm through. The fourth time, he flung back his head and howled like an animal as the pain locked in and tore him apart. Before it was over, Tze-Ring was there, reaching for his hand as he thrashed about, cursing the pain, the ship, drugs, the abbot, and everything within reach.

Slowly, the pain died away, but Johnny knew it would be back. He opened his eyes and saw Tze-Ring. "You said...Y-you said you could help me. Can you give me something?"

"No, Johnny, I cannot give you anything in the sense that you mean. But I can help if you will cooperate and follow my instructions. Will you do that?"

"Yes, yes! Yes, anything, just help me. Oh God, it's coming again. It's coming. Help me! Please, I'll do anything. Just make it stop, please."

The monk drew a chair to the side of the bed and waited until the pain had subsided a little. Then he began to talk.

"Listen to me, Johnny. This will take a little while, and I have to instruct you in those moments between the pains. Listen to my voice and try to do exactly as I tell you. Listen hard, little brother. The pain is worse because your attention is drawn to that area of your body. You must place the centre of your consciousness in another area and block off the pain. Do you understand?"

Johnny shook his head. "For Christ's sake, give me something, don't just talk to me about some crazy form of meditation." The pain swept over him again, and he arched his body against its onslaught. Over and above it, he could hear the calm voice of his companion giving him precise instructions.

"Johnny, listen to my voice. Concentrate on the point between your eyes. Feel my finger pressing down on that point. Concentrate on it. *Feel* it. Think about nothing but that pressure. That is where *you* are, Johnny Burke, where the real you is to be found. Not in your belly or your bowels. Not in your genitals. That is where the pain is, not where *you* are. Focus, Johnny. Focus *now*."

Johnny tried, but the pain was too great, and the ability to concentrate slipped away from him again and again. But in between the bouts of pain, in the all-too-brief moments of respite, came the calm, gentle voice of Tze-Ring each time the pain renewed its attack.

"Focus, Johnny, here. Here the pressure is. Feel it, Johnny, feel it now. Put yourself there. Put your consciousness in that spot, just between the eyes. Try it again. Don't let the pain win. You can do it. You *can* do it."

So it went on, and time slipped by. The ship surged steadily forward, rounding the point into the Bay of Biscay and setting course for the Straits, battling against the weather and the high seas. In the small cabin, a different kind of battle continued.

"Again, Johnny. Try again."

"I can't, I can't! Just give me something. Anything. I'll buy it. I'll give you a thousand pounds. Two thousand! Oh God, it's coming again. Help me, please."

"Focus, Johnny. Breathe with the pain. Flow with it. Let it lift you up to where you want to be, where you need to be. Breathe. Breathe. Lift your thoughts and your mind. Bring them up to where you can feel my finger pressing, just there Johnny. Just there, between your eyes. Do it. Do it *now*."

Johnny struggled to obey, to lift himself up to where he wanted to be, but the pain dragged him down again. Then, suddenly, it happened—he was there, he reached it. An anger rose in him, a roiling anger that he had allowed this to happen, that he had so casually taken the drugs that now threatened to unman him. Along with the anger, the focal point snapped into being, and he found himself able to use its power to concentrate. He breathed deeply, flowing with the pain instead of resisting it, and felt it lessen and fall away. Tze-Ring's voice was like a rope ladder, and he began to climb up to where the pain could no longer touch him. With no kind of warning, there was a loud, metallic clang inside his head. He was floating free, above a body that lay quietly on a bunk beneath him. He could see the startled look on the face of Tze-Ring as he looked up, clearly able to see him. Then, a quiet chuckle.

"Very good, Johnny. Though a projection of the astral body was not exactly what I had in mind, it will do for now. Set your will towards a point in time eight hours from now. See that time on a clock face in your mind's eye. That is when you will next become fully conscious, no matter what your physical body is feeling. You have done well."

"Yes, he has done very well, but you, Tze-Ring, have not. You have disobeyed my orders, and for that you must answer."

The abbot stood in the doorway, his face cold and aloof. The last thing Johnny remembered was Tze-Ring falling to his knees before the irate figure of the abbot and bowing his head to the ground.

9 October, 1:00 a.m.
The penthouse, London

"I was thirteen years older than Lily. That was Johnny's ma," said Florrie, looking round at the fascinated faces hanging on her words. "My dad married twice. 'e took on Lily's ma as a second wife. In those days, it was a normal thing under Romani law. She was a tiny thing from a family who travelled a different track to ours. Her first husband, Jake, and my dad were brothers, but Jake died a couple of months after they wed. Broke 'is neck in a horse race, the stupid sod. She'd not kindled as yet, so my dad took her as a second wife to raise a child for 'is brother.

"There was only the one, Lily, and she almost died having her. She had a separate vardo with Lily, and my dad shared his time between us. My ma looked after 'er at the birth, and I did hear, listening to tales round the fire, how her family was from Spain originally, and before that, centuries back, from North Africa. Egypt, my ma said. Here, give us a top up Liam. There's a good lad."

Florrie opened her capacious handbag and took out a packet of thin cheroots. She lit one up, the lamplight catching the gleam of gold on both wrists and in her ears as she moved. When her cheroot was smouldering to her satisfaction, she took a mouthful of gin and settled back into her story.

"I remember Lily's ma—her name was Belle, Isabelle really, but we called 'er Belle—as being a really good *dukker-mengra*, you know, fortune teller. I've seen a queue outside her vardo right down the road. As soon as we parked in one of our reg'lar rests, the word would go out and the *gadjos* would come to stand in line for a reading. She was always dead right, and Lily, well she took after her ma, only she never needed to look at a palm. She'd just look into your eyes and tell you true.

"Lily told me I'd never kindle a child and that three men would warm my pillow, and she was right on that. Johnny's the nearest thing to a son I've had, and he's looked after me well these last years." Florrie paused for a moment, thinking back over the years. A little tearfully, she took a gulp of gin and returned to her tale.

"Well now, when Lily was thirteen, 'er ma came to my dad and called 'im to the fire. Under Romani law, that means something serious is afoot. They talked for a long time, first together and then with the rest of the family. I'd never seen my dad so shook up. He got drunk and stayed that way for three days. A while later, a woman we'd never seen before came to the resting place in a big fancy car and took Lily away. The thing was that for all 'er fine clothes and big car, she *rokkered*[5] Romani as good as any of us.

5. Spoke, understood

"Lily was gone all summer, and when she did come back, she'd changed. She didn't laugh as much or play with the others, just sat by herself smiling and singing. Then I got married to a circus man within a month of meeting him and left the family. I only saw them once or twice a year after that, at birthdays and the like. I got word when Lily's ma died but couldn't get back in time."

"What happened to Lily then?" asked Biff, rolling himself a joint.

Florrie, halfway through her gin, looked round hopefully. Taking the hint, Lyle topped up her glass with a wide smile and an admonishing shake of the head. "She was waiting on 'er seventeenth birthday, and I'd just buried my William and had come back home for a bit to get over things. We'd moved up north for one of the big horse fairs, and it was late in the evening. We were just sitting and smoking, you know, relaxing a bit. Suddenly, Lily looks up, and right out of the blue, she says, 'It's time, Dad. He's come for me.'

"She stood up and looked across the fire. A man stood there, looking at 'er as if she's the only thing in the world to see. Not tall, but with a fine pair of shoulders on 'im, hair as black as Lily's, and 'is eyes, ah, they was what you remembered most. Green as a forest pool and bright as a new day, they were. But there was something else, a kinda power round 'im that touched everyone near. 'e looked at Dad and asked permission to come to the fire, just as if he were Romani himself. 'e sat down and drank tea and ate with us, and Lily just looked at 'im and smiled.

"After a while, us women were sent into one of the vardos to wait while the men talked, though we did some talking of our own, I can tell you. Then Dad came and spoke to Lily. He asked 'er if she knew what was needed of her and if she was willing, and she said yes both times. He took 'er by the hand, us following, and led her outside to the stranger. He cut their wrists and joined their hands as if it were a proper Romani wedding. Then the man picked Lily up in his arms, stepped over the fire, and just walked away.

"I remember running after her, calling to her. I mean, she didn't have no coat, no clothes, no money, nothing. The man just smiled at me and said she would have all she needed. Then they left in a car. I could see Lily looking back at me through the car window, waving. It was two years before she came back, and when she did, she brought 'er son Johnny with her."

9 October, 1:30 a.m.
On board the *Aghios Loukas*

"You deliberately disobeyed my orders, Tze-Ring. Twice I told you that this man must go through his pain and explained why that must be. Why, then, have you gone against my wishes in this matter and begun his training already?" The abbot might have been small in stature, but when angered he was a formidable opponent.

The young man hesitated, then raised his head and looked his superior in the eyes without flinching. "Because he was in pain, and that pain became mine, Holy One."

"I see. Did you then teach him to release himself from that pain for his sake or for yours? Are you such a weakling that you cannot bear pain, Tze-Ring?"

The young monk closed his eyes, then opened them and turned to look at Johnny, lying peacefully asleep. He looked back into the eyes of the abbot.

"No, I only knew that I could no longer allow him to be in such agony when it was within my power to help him. It went against the very blood in my veins. After all, Johnny Burke is my half-brother, as you well know, Grandfather."

The abbot went very still, and for a moment there was utter silence in the cabin. Finally the old man stirred, brushing a hand across his eyes as if suddenly weary. He turned, looking for the nearest seat. Tze-Ring remained kneeling, head no longer bowed but held with dignity. It was the first time in his twenty-six years of life that he had dared to defy his much-loved but autocratic grandsire.

Settling himself carefully into a chair, Nyang Darsip, the elected head of the Abbey of the Dawn, sighed deeply and motioned the young man to sit at his side. For a while, he studied the impassive face that held traces of his own finely drawn bone structure and smiled. The atmosphere in the cabin warmed slightly.

"So, you have found the depths within you to stand against me at last. As I might have guessed, it is not for your own sake but for one who, if only temporarily, is weaker than yourself. You are like your grandmother in that respect, Tze-Ring, as you are like her in your features." The old man paused, recalling the face of the girl he had wooed and won in the foothills of the Caucasus Mountains. Then he turned his thoughts towards seeking a solution for their present problem.

"It appears your half-brother is a quick learner, and his powers lie close to the surface. This makes it even more important that he is trained slowly and carefully. Do you understand, *malchik*?"

The sudden and unexpected use of the nickname given to him by his Russian grandmother brought a smile of memory to the young man's lips.

"Yes, Holy One, I understand, and I will try to teach him restraint in such matters. He seems to be sleeping deeply now. It is certain that he will not awaken for at least eight hours." Tze-Ring paused, then added sheepishly, "As he was instructed to do."

"This was a fortuitous flowering of his powers. It may not occur again as quickly or as conveniently. Encourage him to use it only when the pain gets too bad for him to bear. There are also other areas of his health that need attention."

The abbot rose to his feet, accepting the offer of a steadying arm as the ship bucked under their feet in the teeth of a fierce sou'wester.

"Tomorrow Dr. Leonides will examine him before embarking upon the cure for his, ah…other ailments." He headed for the door, then stopped and spoke again without turning round.

"Tze-Ring, I admire your courage in defying my instructions regarding our guest, and I understand your motives for doing so. However, discipline is still discipline. You will hand over the care of Johnny Burke to Chambha until such time as we reach the island of Crete. During that time, you will remain in your cabin, alone. You will meditate on the need for patience and obedience and on the task that lies before your half-brother. You will make no attempt to see or speak to him again until then. Do you understand?"

"Yes, Holy One, I understand. I will ask Chambha to come at once."

"No. He is sleeping. You may safely leave your charge until Chambha awakens in a few hours' time, then I will send him to take up his duties. Johnny Burke will be safe until then."

There was a moment's pause. Then the abbot spoke again, but this time there was a touch of pride in his voice. "You taught him well, *malchik*, very well indeed."

The door closed quietly behind him.

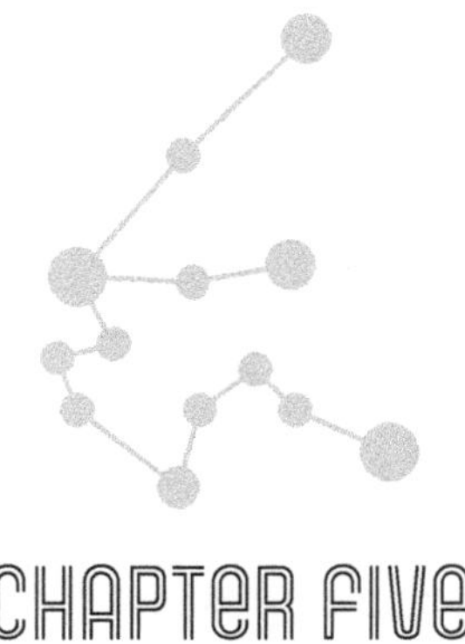

CHAPTER FIVE

9 October, 9:00 p.m.
The penthouse, London

“Florrie, that was a great meal, better than any fancy restaurant I can name.” Bucky’s vote of thanks was echoed by the others as they left the dining table comfortably full. “Florrie and I will clear up,” he went on. “You lot clear off and relax and don’t get into trouble; that’s the last thing I need right now.”

“Ginny and I are goin’ to the youth club, Buck. I promised the rev I’d look in when we got back from the tour.” Lyle took his commitment to the Tanners Wharf Youth Club seriously.

“Yeah, and you can tell ’im the table tennis equipment he needed is on its way, compliments of me an’ Johnny.”

Lyle’s wide grin lit up the room, “Hey, Bucko, that’s great! You’re a king, man.” He slapped five on the manager’s sausage-like fingers and steered the still-pensive Ginny through the door.

“Yeah, well.” Slightly embarrassed, Bucky turned to the others. “And where are you two planning to start a riot?”

Biff shuffled his feet guiltily and looked over his shoulder at Liam.

"Well, personally, I've had enough gloom and doom to last me a while. Biff and I are going uptown to sample a little of Mama Mary's red-hot hospitality," announced Liam with a theatrical leer.

Bucky rolled his eyes at Florrie, who hooted with knowing laughter and disappeared into the kitchen with a loaded tray.

"For chrissakes, be careful. Don't get arrested or photographed, and don't get a dose of clap. That's all I ask," moaned their manager.

Liam opened his eyes wide in pretend amazement. "What's this? Colin Buckman, manager of that world-famous and incredibly handsome group White Heat, afraid of publicity in any shape, form, or content?"

Bucky aimed a ham-sized fist at his head with a wry grin, but Liam ducked and, still laughing, ushered a blushing Biff out of the door. Shaking his head at Frank, who was picking out a sad little tune on the piano, Bucky picked up a sheaf of papers from his desk and followed Florrie into the kitchen.

"That nap this afternoon was the longest I've slept since Johnny went missing," he told her, refusing an offer to finish the apple pie.

Bucky sorted through the papers. "John Eamon Patrick Burke," he read out, "born fifteenth of November, 1970, Lahore, India. Mother: Lily Isabelle Mercedes Burke, spinster. Father: Eamon Zachary Merrow, bachelor. So, they weren't actually married, Lily and—" He glanced down at the paper. "Eamon Merrow. But what the hell were they doing in Lahore? The lads all see to their own passports, so I never knew where Johnny was born. All he ever said was that he was brought up in the Romani way, travelling around until he was seven or eight. Then they settled down so he could go to school."

"That's right," Florrie flicked the ash off her cheroot and began to stack things in the dishwasher. "My ma had gone as well by then, so Lily, Dad, and Johnny stopped travelling, though it was a wrench for the old man. But he was fair crippled with arthritis by then and couldn't take the cold and wet no more." She flipped the switch on the washer and leaned back against the sink, pointing at the papers Bucky was holding.

"Somewhere in there you'll find a letter from a bank in Switzerland telling Lily that fifty thousand pounds had been put into a London bank in her name and she was to buy a house with it. She found one across the river in Rotherhithe, big enough to take in a couple of lodgers as well. Dad couldn't work anymore, so it all fell on Lily. He died two years after that. He missed the travelling, you see, the old vardo and the horses. 'e never settled to *gadjo* life, really."

They moved back into the lounge with their coffee, still talking.

"But if they—whoever 'they' were—could give her fifty grand, why didn't they stake her after that?" asked Bucky curiously.

"If you read through the letters, you'll see that in '79, Lily was warned that someone was after Johnny and she was to sell the house and disappear. She disappeared so bloody well even I didn't know where she was, not until Johnny was going on sixteen. Then, out of the blue, she wrote me a letter saying that she was dying, and would I look after 'im until he could look after himself." Florrie settled herself with a sigh into a leather armchair and looked unhappily at the empty bottle of gin on the coffee table.

"He'd got a bit wild-like 'cos Lily was too ill to do much with him, but whatever else, that boy adored his ma. The night she died, I thought he was going to top himself. I couldn't get him away from 'er. When the undertakers came, 'e took off and didn't come back until the day of the funeral, and then he cried for days."

Frank left the piano to perch on the arm of Florrie's chair, pushing his glasses further onto his nose. "Did she ever say who was after Johnny?"

"Not really. All she said was that one day he would be a very important man, and he had to be protected." Florrie paused and stared up at the ceiling as if trying to recall some half-forgotten titbit. "Then she said something else. Funny, I'd almost forgotten it."

Frank and Bucky leaned forward expectantly.

"She said when the time was right, his own would coming looking for 'im. I reckon this is the time, and they've not only come lookin', they've bloody well nicked 'im."

"What about his real father?" asked Bucky. "I know Johnny never knew anything about him, but what about you? I mean, have you ever heard anything from him since he took Lily away?"

Florrie dropped her bombshell with unerring accuracy and the kind of timing to be expected from someone who had spent her youth jumping from the back of one galloping horse to another.

"Yes," she said casually, "as a matter of fact, I have!"

A stunned silence pervaded the room. Florrie had their undivided attention.

Florrie settled back in her chair. "It was the same woman, all right. I recognised 'er as soon as I opened the door. Older, of course, but I knew 'er. '*Cushti divvus*, Florencia Burke, *sar shin*?'[6] she says to me, bold as you please, as if it were yesterday we'd last met. Well, I wasn't goin' to close the door in 'er face after bein' greeted in me own tongue like that, so I asked her in."

Florrie looked at her rapt audience of three and lowered her voice.

"She had a ruby on 'er hand as big as my thumbnail, and her clothes was good too, not flashy, but good cloth and made special, I could tell. Yet she sat there in my kitchen, drinking tea out of a mug and diggin' into my chocolate cake like she was starved, and lickin' 'er fingers too. We talked about the travelling days and my bein' a '*pivley rawnie*'—a widow woman—three times over, and how there was only a few now to remember the Romani ways.

"'It's time for Johnny to go back to his father,' she says all sudden like. 'He needs to be trained for the work he's got to do. You mustn't worry if he goes missin,' she says. 'He'll be all right.' Then she asked me if he gave me any money, and I told 'er my cheque comes every month reg'lar as clockwork, 'cos Johnny got the bank to see to that. She said that was good, as 'they' didn't want me to go without. Then she gave me an envelope and something wrapped in red silk and says it's from Johnny's father and to read it straight away."

There was a hush in the lounge. From the river came the mournful hoot of a passing boat, heightening the tension in the room. Florrie sat back and lit a cheroot, taking her time over it, prolonging the moment with the touch of a master storyteller. Bucky cleared his throat nervously, then asked the question that hung in the air along with the smoke.

"Er, have you, ah, got the letter with you now, Florrie?"

"Yes, I have," said Florrie. Then, to Frank sitting beside her, "Here, get me handbag for me, will you, love? It'll save me legs.

6. "Good day, Florencia Burke, how are you?"

Eagerly, Frank brought the capacious handbag, and Florrie rummaged through the dumping ground within its maw. "I know I put it in here," she muttered. She loaded the coffee table with half-eaten tubes of mints, old shopping lists and assorted lipsticks, cheque stubs, biros, and out-of-date diaries, along with other unidentifiable objects.

"Ah, I knew it was in there somewhere!" She handed Bucky a large crumpled envelope with an unwrapped piece of toffee sticking to it and scooped the rest back into the bag.

"Jesus, Florrie," complained Bucky, breaking the toffee's death grip on the paper. "Why don't you just carry a bleedin' suitcase? You've got more junk in there than a New York bag lady."

"You never know what you might need in an emergency, and I like to be prepared," she sniffed. "Go on, read it. You and Frank are the two closest friends Johnny has, so you have a right to know what's in it."

Bucky rummaged in his inside pocket for the glasses few people outside the group knew he needed and opened the envelope. The paper was of top quality, the writing firm and strong, and a whiff of elusive scent came from it, reminding Frank of something. It brought to mind stained-glass windows and the sound of a well-tuned organ, time spent learning the intricacies of descant and counterpoint, and the soaring feeling that Christmas Mass had always induced in him.

Bucky cleared his throat and began to read.

The Abbey of the Dawn
1 September

Dear Florencia,

It has been over twenty years since we met, but I think you will remember me as the stranger who took away your sister. You will also have guessed that I am Johnny's father. During the intervening years, you must have wondered why Lily and the baby returned alone and why I never made contact with your family. I assure you that this secrecy was to protect Lily and our son. I did contact Lily, but not in the usual meaning of the word.

I owe it to you to explain what is involved. These are things you must know, for in the near future, Johnny will begin the long and arduous training for his future work. That training will begin in the Abbey of the Dawn under the guidance of its abbot. I write now because I must leave the abbey before he arrives; it is important that we do not meet yet.

We have always known of Johnny's whereabouts, his career, and its success. Strangely enough, it has been a good way of hiding him. It is often the way that those who seek something will miss it placed in full view.

Johnny's ancestry is unique, and his conception had been arranged many years before it happened. That makes it sound cold and heartless, but I can assure you it was not so. I loved Lily deeply, and I love the son she bore me. In a few years I will make myself known to him, but not until his training is well established. You may wonder what that will entail.

Very soon, humanity will be at the most important crossroads in its evolution. Every two thousand years approximately, the earth enters a new zodiacal age. The century leading up to such an event is always one of turbulence, bloodshed, and anarchy, yet also of great advances in science, literature, medicine, and new ways of thinking. The Age of Aquarius is almost here, and it will be the make-or-break point. This time, humanity could destroy itself and the planet. But we have an army that stands ready to do battle for us. This army is composed of what esotericists term the Lords of Flame, Form, and Mind, great, immortal, and non-physical beings.

During the last ten thousand years, a new group of beings have gradually emerged from our species. The Lords of Humanity have joined their strength to that of the others. From these Lords of Light, as the new age approaches, comes a voluntary sacrifice who descends to take the physical body specially prepared for it. This being becomes the Christos of the new age who will lead humanity on to the next step in its evolution. Please do not dismiss my words as foolishness—I am serious. Strung across the world, there are several Abbeys of

Light whose work it is to seek out and train those who have special powers of mind, body, or spirit, sometimes all three.

But before the Teacher of the Age can take up the task assigned to It, there must be one to "proclaim the coming" and to prepare the way—and the people—for the message. One who can train those who will work with the aeon. From time immemorial, a single bloodline has taken on this task. For centuries it lies dormant, each generation training the next in the ancient ways. When the time is right, a mating takes place between the line of the Forerunner and one of the bloodlines of destiny. From this mating the Forerunner is born. Johnny is destined to be the Forerunner for the Christos of Aquarius. I am of the line of those named the Openers of the Way. Lily was descended from an ancient royal house of Egypt. Among her ancestors was the priest magician Khaemweset, son of Ramesses the Great and grandson of Seti the warrior pharaoh. Her family have kept the line intact for over 4,000 years.

As there are Lords of Light, so there are also Lords of Darkness. You, as a woman of pure Romani blood, know this is so. The Dark Ones knew of Johnny's birth and have sought him for twenty-three years. Now the sign of his ancestry has become visible in his aura, and it is only a matter of time before they find him. He will be safe in the abbey, but outside its protection he is vulnerable. That is why he must disappear. He will be looked after; I give you my word on that. For your loving care of my son, I thank and bless you, and I ask you to accept the gift enclosed.

Yours in the Eternal Light,
Father Eamon Merrow

Bucky finished reading and put the letter down. Then Florrie took an object wrapped in red silk from her pocket and held it out to him. He looked at it and then at her, a question in his eyes. She nodded, and he took it from her. A whistle of admiration escaped him as he unwrapped an antique carving of Kwan Yin, the Chinese goddess of mercy. It was six inches high and carved from flawless jade. Silence descended on the little group, each busy with their own thoughts—so busy no one noticed the figure that stood back from the open door, where he had been listening in the shadows of the balcony.

For a long time, Tango stood staring unseeingly into the dark water below. It was happening again. He was being passed over, thrown aside as if he were nothing, as if his gifts and talents had been found wanting. He could hear in his head the voice of his chapel-bred grandmother berating his mother who, drunk as usual, was nursing a black eye from her latest pimp: *How can a child born of sin and lust be anything but evil? He must be made to acknowledge the Lord, beaten until he does, until he bleeds if need be. The body must be mortified to save the soul. If I can't save the mother, I'll save the child.*

Tango remembered those beatings and the endless raving about the love of God for those sinners who crawled on their bellies to Him for forgiveness. He carried the scars on his body and in his mind and would carry them to the grave. He had never given in, had never begged God to forgive him, and never would.

God! He hated God, hated Him for his fear, pain, and rejection in childhood. Hated Him for the feelings of inadequacy that drove him to excel in all he did. He needed to beat others before they beat him. He'd almost managed it with the group until Colin Buckman found Johnny Burke. He renamed him Johnny Nova and made him the lead singer. Johnny Nova! It was his name the fans yelled, his face that dominated the publicity shots and photo sessions. Tango's hands clenched at his sides as he raised an anguished face to the night sky.

Damn him to hell, why didn't he just die and stay dead? Why was he so important that everyone worried about him? He drank, shot dope, screwed the groupies, and punched photographers like the others, didn't he? Now he was doing it again, and Tango knew he would return with a mind-searing certainty. He would come back and reclaim the limelight, playing the part of a bloody John the Baptist. Why was he acclaimed, looked up to, loved?

"You can stop him."

The voice was a deep, rich baritone with authority and power behind it. Tango recognised it at once. It was the voice that had come to him the night his grandmother had suffered her fatal heart attack. This was the voice that had suggested he flush her heart tablets down the kitchen sink and delay sending for the ambulance until it was too late to save her. He'd sat in the dingy armchair and waited until the sounds, the whimpers, and the groans from the front bedroom had stopped.

After his grandmother's death, Tango sold everything he could lay his hands on, and at fifteen he was on the road, alone and free. The voice led him to a holiday camp and a job as a pool cleaner. Here, his rapidly developing body and dark good looks had opened up a world of hungry women and rich pickings and had earned him his nickname.

The voice had given good advice in the past ten years, always in time of need. Now it spoke again, telling him what he needed to hear. "You can stop Johnny Nova and revenge yourself on God at the same time. I will send someone to train you. Place yourself in his hands, and you will have all you have ever desired."

Tango caught his breath. All he had ever wanted could be his, but he'd learned early that nothing came free. There would always be a catch. Would he pay the price? Yes! Because the prize was the heart's desire of six-year-old Talfryn Alvarez Garrett—born the illegitimate son of a Swansea bar maid turned prostitute and the dissolute captain of a Spanish trawler—starved, beaten, and deprived of understanding, love, and recognition.

"What is your price?" he asked the shadows that had thickened round him on the balcony.

The shadow moved to confront him. It swirled and changed until a face hung before him. It was a face of male beauty and of power, holding the promise of dominion over others. The mouth was full, sensuous, smiling. The eyes held a proud and bitter glory that spoke of pain and a loss beyond a human being's capacity to understand. This face had once worn a diadem of light and walked with the source of that light, but now, no more.

"Service. Obedience. Homage."

In the hidden spaces that lie between dimensions, a specific point of time stretched, looped, warped, and split into a crossroads of infinite possibilities. The Lords of Light and their Dark counterparts waited for the outcome as a human being considered the odds presented to him.

Then Tango, having weighed those odds, made a decision.

10 October, 11:00 p.m.
On board the *Aghios Loukas*

Tze-Ring awoke with a sickening jolt, his body beaded with sweat, his mind reaching out to that of the abbot. "Holy One? Are you there? Is everything well with you?" He was already up, reaching for his clothes, breathing more easily, as he felt the answer gently brush his mind.

"I am well, Tze-Ring, but there has been a worrying development. Please come at once to my cabin, and bring the captain with you."

As soon as he stepped onto the deck, Tze-Ring felt the sense of unease surrounding the ship. The wind had risen to gale force, and black clouds scudded across the sky. Lightning flashed intermittently, holding the promise of a storm. The ship seemed to be held within a shell of silence with no link to the outside world. He recognised the work of the Dark Ones and hurried to the abbot's cabin, meeting the captain along the way. The abbot opened the door at the first knock.

"Come in, please, and sit down. Captain Michalitis, I am sorry to have to ask you for help, but I have no other choice. It is important that Father Chambha stays with our guest, whose welfare is of the highest priority. I personally will seek out this focus of power and neutralise it. This means I will leave the protection of the ship in the hands of Tze-Ring and yourself, Captain."

"I am ready and willing to help in any way that I can, though I may not be able to do as much as I would like, Holiness."

"Tze-Ring will show you what to do, Captain. Follow his instructions. At the moment, the focal point is weak, new to this work, and unsure of what it can do or how far its powers extend, but we need to discover who it is, and quickly."

He explained what he wanted them to do and how to make certain of success. The captain waited until Tze-Ring motioned him to follow, and the two men left the cabin.

Left alone, the abbot took a small case from a cupboard and opened it. From its contents, he took a tin containing a handful of earth from the burial site of a Buddhist saint and another filled with the dried leaves of a shrub that grew only in a forgotten area of land far from human habitation. He mixed the two together, then added a handful of ground animal bones from a leather bag. Next, the abbot chose four small candles compounded of a mixture of human and animal fat and wax and a silver gong with its striker. He looked round the cabin and, seeing a small mirror, took it down and placed it with the rest. Clearing a space in the centre of the cabin floor, he sprinkled the mixture of earth, leaves, and powder in a circle, leaving enough room for a person to sit inside. This done, he placed a candle at each quarter and lit them, blessing and intoning a short prayer over each one. The abbot put the gong within reach and propped up the mirror with a book in the centre. His preparations done, he bolted the cabin door and took his place within the magical yantra of protection.

For a while he sat, calming the inner workings of his body. Then he prepared to enter the Levels of Silence. Turning his head slightly, he stared at the light switch. For a moment, nothing happened. Then the switch eased itself down, and with a click, the cabin was plunged into darkness, but not for long. A deep golden glow began to emanate from the area of the abbot's solar plexus. It grew in intensity until an onlooker could have discerned the outline of internal organs. Then a burst of incandescent power leapt from the body and enclosed it in an aura of golden light.

Slowly, the abbot withdrew from the small world of the locked cabin and began to descend through the Silences. The first level cut out external noise; the sound and vibration of the ship's engines faded out. The second level closed off the internal world; the faint sound of the breath, the flow of blood through the veins, the throb of the heart—all were gone. The third level brought complete isolation from both the physical world and the immediate astral. Then, on reaching the fourth level, the sphere of his higher consciousness unfolded its wings and rose up through the centre of the many-petalled lotus.

Emerging into the realm of the subtle levels, the abbot's higher self hovered above the ship. He could see the waves of dark power that beat against it. At the prow and the stern, the astral forms of Tze-Ring and Captain Michalitis stood, buffeted by the raging fury of the Dark. They were struggling to protect the vessel with a shield of astral fire. The abbot checked to see if Johnny and Chambha were safe and was startled to see the young singer's astral form emerge on the scene with that of Chambha's trying to restrain it. It hung in space, looking out beyond the dark sea. The heart centre showed fear and confusion, but above the head shone the form of a white dove, the ancient symbol of the Forerunner. The light grew in intensity, and the dark power shrank back and tried to hide from the radiance.

The dove grew in size and power as it became a direct focal point for the Lords of Light and for the power that has always been wielded by those designated to open the way for the Saviours. The wings changed shape and curved into a half moon. The beak lengthened and sharpened to a point. Suddenly, the dove was a sword of light and flame that cut through the blackness and struck at the very heart of the attacking force.

A roar of thunder and a bolt of lightning split apart the core of the Dark power and broke it into a thousand smaller shadows that sought frantically to escape from the radiance of the Light. Again and again the sword struck, and the Darkness tried to evade its power. The attack on the ship and Johnny's sleeping body was forgotten. This freed Tze-Ring, Michalitis, and Chambha from the need to protect. Led by the abbot, they joined the battle, and the storm on the physical level was duplicated by an even greater storm on the astral.

The Darkness regrouped and tried to attack from a different quarter, but the four spiritual warriors of the abbey stood firm round the central figure of the Forerunner. Above and about the embattled defenders, the sword of the dove ripped at the foulness that tried to engulf them. At last, a vaguely human shape emerged from the heart of the Darkness, and immediately the sword struck at its heart centre. The abbot caught the sound of an anguished mental scream, and suddenly the Dark had gone and the ship was sailing on a quiet, moonlit sea.

They rested, weary and triumphant. The sword resumed the shape of the dove and returned to its place in Johnny's aura, and Chambha led the unresisting astral back to rest. He looked over his shoulder at the abbot.

"I was wrong, Holy One. He may have no conscious knowledge of his power yet, but this is no 'damaged vessel,' as once I called it. When he comes into that power, he will be truly worthy to hold the title of the Forerunner."

Pausing only to make sure that all were safe, the abbot followed the trail of the Darkness to its source and found himself in a London penthouse ablaze with lights. He traced the fading remnants of the power to a corner bedroom and found a young man sitting on the edge of the bed, bathed in the icy sweat of abject fear. He held his head in hands that shook uncontrollably. His aura showed a blaze of dull red with areas of black and grey. Above the head, no symbol of light, but a ragged space where something had been ripped out.

The atmosphere of the room was heavy and dark, but as the abbot's mental form turned to leave, he caught sight of something dark and foul flickering in the corner. Then it was gone. He probed the area, but there was nothing there. Thoughtfully, he regarded the shaking figure of Tango on the bed, then compassionately blanked out Tango's memories of what had seemingly been a nightmare.

The abbot checked on the penthouse's occupants. Frank and Florrie slept peacefully. Lyle and Ginny were making love, and the abbot smiled observing the soft, pulsing colours of the entwined auras. He blessed them and passed on. Liam and Biff were sharing a pile of sandwiches washed down with beer and discussing the merits of Mama Mary's young ladies. Colin Buckman tossed uneasily, half in and half out of sleep. The abbot paused beside him, and the worried mind slid into sleep. Almost immediately, the form of the higher self emerged and faced the visitor. Far beyond the ordinary astral form, it understood on a level the physical would take years to attain.

"You're the one who took Johnny." It was a statement, not a question.

"Yes. He is unharmed and begins to show his potential power. Take care, Colin Buckman—there is danger in your midst. Trust your feelings and let them lead you. Florencia Burke will help you, and Virginia, although young, has a pure seer-ship. The dangers have arisen earlier than I foresaw. We will protect the Forerunner, but you must hold his enemy in check as long as you can. I will see that your own training is begun as soon as possible."

"It's Tango. It has to be him. But why?"

"There is a reason to it all, and he who you call Tango has a part to play—and not an easy one. He is one of the three who are needed to open the new age."

The abbot watched the glowing form settle back into the physical body that turned on its side and slept. Then he sped back to the ship. He followed the silver sound of the gong as it sounded rhythmically on the Inner Levels. The notes guided him like a beacon, and the slumped figure in the circle of flame jerked once, twice, then opened its eyes and drew a deep breath into its lungs.

Immediately, the abbot focussed on the central point of the attack and projected the memory of what he had seen into the mirror before him. It clouded over as if filled with smoke, then cleared to show the sweat-streaked face of a young man with glazed, unseeing eyes. Over his shoulder, another face could be seen dimly: a beautiful, smiling face, but totally evil. The abbot passed his hand over the glass and spoke a short, sharp invocation and the picture froze, sealed into the mirror by his will. Then he rose stiffly to his feet as Tze-Ring's fist pounded on the door.

"Holiness? Grandfather? Are you all right? Open the door, please. It is I, Tze-Ring. Open the door."

The abbot's physical body slumped, but he took a deep breath and extended his will. The light switch obediently clicked, flooding the room with light. The bolt on the door slid aside under the kinetic will of Tze-Ring as he barrelled through the door like a shaven-headed avenging angel.

"Grandfather." His welcome strength enfolded the old man, lifting him and placing him on the bunk. A soft blanket was gently wrapped round the frail figure, and warm fingers tested along the meridians for the vital signs of recovery. Satisfied the abbot was in no immediate danger, Tze-Ring doused the candles and dealt with the debris of the protection ring. An urgent mental request to Chambha for hot tea went winging through the ship.

"Tze-Ring." The old man's whisper brought him to the abbot's side. "Show Chambha the mirror. The image held in its depths is of the new source of Dark power. He is one of Johnny's former associates. Also...one of the three needed to open the age. Chambha will know him. This man has offered himself to our opponents. Do not tell your brother of this; he has enough to contend with without having to face betrayal as well."

The door opened, and Chambha entered with a bowl of fragrant tea. With gentle hands, he raised the abbot and held the bowl to his lips. A few sips were enough to restore enough strength to hold the bowl for himself. The abbot assured his companions he was recovering from the battle and its drain on his powers.

Tze-Ring passed the mirror with its image to Chambha, who looked at it intently.

"It is the man they call Tango, one of the group," he said. "He has much pain and desolation in his life record. He is not evil of himself, but evil finds in him a fertile soil in which to grow. This was the source?"

"Yes," sighed the abbot. "I do not want Johnny Burke to know of this yet. But this man must be held at bay until we can get him to the abbey. Call Wang Ta. As a master illusionist, he must cover our tracks until the Forerunner crosses the boundary. Tell him to seek help from the Abbey of the Aeon. Brother Wolf springs to mind; his shape-shifting abilities can be of help in our predicament. See to this at once, please. And Chambha, is Captain Michalitis all right? And how is our young friend?"

"The captain has returned to the bridge, and Johnny Burke still sleeps, Rinpoche. Little brother here has proven himself an excellent teacher." Chambha smiled broadly at Tze-Ring's embarrassment and disappeared.

"I can sleep now, *malchik*," murmured the abbot, his eyes closing. "Wake me if I am needed."

The tea bowl fell from his fingers, and Tze-Ring drew the covers closely about him, reflecting that at ninety-three, his grandfather had the staying power of a man half his age. Then he switched off the light and left the cabin. He caught up with Chambha, and they walked to Johnny's cabin.

"I may not see him, Chambha; the abbot has laid it upon me as a discipline. But is he all right? I have never seen anything like the power that came from him during the battle. How can he be unaware of such a gift?"

"His conscious self is sleeping, little brother. To know the existence of such power within oneself before one is prepared for it could turn the mind to madness. He will remember at the right time. I will tell him you asked about him when he wakes. Now I must see to my messages."

Tze-Ring checked the rest of the ship on both the physical and astral levels. Only then did he seek his own bed to dream of his wife, Lea, and the dark eyes and wide smile of his baby son back at the Abbey of the Dawn.

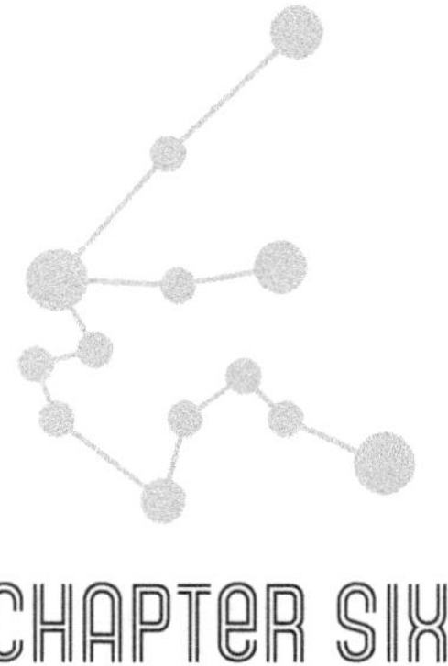

CHAPTER SIX

20 October, 2:00 p.m.
The penthouse, London

Tango drained the last of the lager. He shook the tin hopefully, then aimed the empty container at the bin in the corner, where it joined the others. He was bored, angry, and alone. The penthouse echoed with his frustration. Rising to his feet, he wandered over to the windows and looked at the river. It looked the same as it had twenty minutes ago.

Everyone was out: Bucky, Florrie, and Frank were with solicitors and bank managers; Biff and Liam were on a kid's TV show; and Lyle and Ginny were helping to paint that damned clubhouse. As usual, he'd not been asked to join any of them. He thumped his fist against the window frame. As if he cared.

The comfortable surroundings, deep armchairs, king-sized television, the state-of-the-art music system, his expensive clothes, and the gold watch on his wrist meant little to Tango. Not long ago, he'd owned nothing but what was on his back at the time and a change of underwear. Moodily, Tango flung himself into a chair and closed his eyes as the past flooded back.

"Down on your knees, boyo. And thank God you have a roof over your head and food in your belly, isn't it? Slaved for you both, I have, and not a thank you coming to me from that tainted bitch of a mother of yours. If you have time to read a book, you have time to sweep the yard, and empty the outhouse bucket while you are at it."

His grandmother's shrill voice was as clear in Tango's head as if it were yesterday. Hating the feelings of helplessness that it brought back, he changed the scene to the day of her death in the squalid terraced house that had been his home.

"Me pills, Talfryn boy. Bring me the pills. The pains are on me badly."

Later, "Me pills, boyo, now, or by the good Lord God, I'll take the skin off your back when I'm on me feet."

Later still it was, "Talfryn, *bach*, there's a good lad. Bring me the little bottle from the mantelpiece and you can have some money from me purse. *Duw*, don't let me die. *Bach*, you're Nana's little lad and a good boy. The pills, Tally, the pills! May God strike you down, y'bastard brat. Ah, *Duw*, t'is killing me…*Duw*, *Duw*, Lord God, have mercy. I've been good to the boy, brought him up to fear You. Aah!"

Then a silence that went on and on and on.

"It was, as the saying goes, a good day to die. At least, it was good for you, Talfryn Garrett."

Tango shot to his feet, his heart racing. "Who the hell are you? How did you get in? What do you want?"

The cadaverously thin man with unhealthy white skin and burning black eyes bowed with old-fashioned courtesy. His smile was something no smile should ever be.

"As rude and impatient as usual, I see. We have to do something about that. I am De'ath, Nicholas De'ath, and I walked through the hall, though no one could swear they saw me. Locks and doors present no difficulty to my kind. As for your last question, I come to bring you your heart's desire. I am to be your teacher, Mr. Garrett. My masters, it seems, have need of your talents, such as they are. It would not be wrong to say you are the answer to their hopes."

Tango sat down weakly. The presence of this man—if man he was—was overwhelming, At the same time, it induced a sickness of the soul that Tango had never felt before. He could feel the heat and energy of his body leaving him, drawn off by this stranger. He tried to regain control of the situation. He lit a cigarette with a slightly shaky hand and blew the smoke in the general direction of his visitor.

"My heart's desire, is it? And what would you know of that?"

This time the smile was infinitely worse.

"I know you are so eaten up with envy that your heart, mind, and soul are pockmarked with it. That you cannot forget for one instant the lack of respect you suffer from those around you. I know your greatest rival commands that respect and love from them even though he is thousands of miles away. You know, deep down, that if it were you that had gone missing, the concern, the agitation, the worry would have been far less intense. But I can change all that. I can make your name greater than Johnny Nova's ever was. I can bring the world to your feet. But only if you are willing to pay the price my masters are asking."

"My soul? My signature in blood on a piece of vellum? A little old-fashioned, wouldn't you say?" Tango's mouth twisted wryly.

"They are not interested in your soul, Mr. Garrett—it is of no use to them. They play for much higher stakes. They want rulership over the coming age. To achieve this, they must make sure the birth of the new aeon goes unnoticed. If you play your part well, you could become as I am, an Undying One, an immortal with powers you can only dream about."

He came closer and bent over Tango, his breath a fetid wind that made Tango want to retch.

"Think of it: money, possessions, women, power, adulation, the ability to crush those who annoy you. To be the envy of all the little people who know they can never amount to anything. Doesn't that sound like your heart's desire, Mr. Garrett?"

Tango drew a deep breath. To have the world at his feet. To hear the shouts of the fans and know they were for him alone. To be free of the group, Colin Buckman, and above all, free of Johnny. He looked at the impassive face opposite him and his blood stirred restlessly. He knew this man was totally evil, knew it and was still fascinated.

"Just how does all this come about?" he asked softly. "How soon would we start on this training you spoke about? Are we talking years, months, or what?"

"It all depends on how easy you are to train, how amenable you are to discipline. To begin, you need to get out of this place, away from the influences that fill it." De'ath rose, walked over to Tango, took the cigarette from his mouth, and stubbed it out. "You will also stop smoking and drinking. From this moment, you belong to my masters and, in a lesser way, to me. Pack a bag—we're leaving. The rest of your stuff can be sent on. I have booked a suite at a hotel in the suburbs. It will be our base until I find a suitable house somewhere private and quiet. Leave a note for your friends; we wouldn't want them to worry about your disappearance, would we?"

"Right now? This minute? You're nuts! There are things I have to do. I'm still under contract to Buckman; I can't walk out like that. We have a concert and recordings to do and—"

He stopped abruptly. De'ath had come close to him, his face thrust so close Tango could smell the foulness in his body and retched. Long bony fingers closed round his throat, cutting off his air.

De'ath's voice was soft, sibilant, and full of menace. "I don't think you fully understood what I said. You are now under my orders, Mr. Garrett. You will do as I say or you will regret it very, very much." With each word, he closed his fingers more tightly round the singer's throat.

As his consciousness receded, Tango began to realise the future would hold pain as well as pleasure. Then darkness closed over him, and he sank into it.

De'ath let him lie there on the floor. He busied himself in Tango's room for a time and returned with a couple of suitcases that he set by the door. Then he sat down and waited for his companion to regain consciousness.

The distant hum of traffic was the first thing of which Tango became aware. This was followed by the pain of a badly bruised throat and a splitting headache. Slowly and carefully, he got to his feet. With a sudden spurt of energy, he rushed De'ath, intending to beat the hell out of him. He never reached him; De'ath was not there.

"Still in need of a lesson, Mr. Garrett?" came the mocking voice behind him. "Here it is."

The fight was short and vicious. De'ath had never believed in fair play. His strength was unbelievable for one so slight of build, and it left Tango bruised, bleeding, and totally demoralised. He crouched on hands and knees and looked up at his tormentor, who smiled. Tango shivered at the implications of that smile. Wearily, he got to his feet and went over to the desk. The note was short and to the point.

I have decided to clear out and get my own place. Will be in touch by phone regarding the concert and recordings. I'll let you know where to send the rest of my things when I see you next. Tango.

"I will wait downstairs in the lobby, Mr. Garrett." De'ath walked to the door, stopped, and looked back. "Ten minutes, Mr. Garrett. Ten minutes, or you will have another demonstration of my abilities. If you think I have dealt harshly with your body, you would be appalled at what I could do to your mind. Ten minutes." He left.

Mutely, Tango listened to the lift descend. He looked round the penthouse, remembering the excitement they had all felt when they signed the lease. There had been some good times here. Well, all that was over now. He knew deep down that he had made his choice, and there was no way back from it. Tango picked up his cases, closed the door, and walked to the lift without looking back. He thought he heard his grandmother laughing.

♬ ♩ ♫ ♪ ♬ ♩ ♫

"I don't know, Mr. Buckman. He never left any address or number. Just handed over the keys and said he was moving out. He looked as if he'd been in one helluva fight. And there was this other guy. Jeez, he gave me the creeps just looking at him! Tall and thin, he was, and kinda pasty-coloured skin. And his eyes…I tell you, Mr. Buckman, I don't never want to see eyes like that again. So help me God."

"OK, Harry. Thanks for letting us know." Bucky ushered Florrie to the lift, followed by a worried-looking Frank.

"Hell, Bucky, if he doesn't show for that concert and the recordings, we can say goodbye to everything."

"He'll show. He knows he's still tied by a watertight contract. Don't worry, Frank, he'll be there. But I'd like to know who this new player in the game is and what he's doing with Tango. I have a nasty feeling about this."

Florrie was silent. She was picking up the trail of fear mixed with excitement that Tango had left, and it was making her flesh creep. Her unease grew stronger as they entered the penthouse and intensified when she found small traces of blood on the carpet. This, however, she kept to herself. The others had enough on their plate.

Dinner was a subdued affair despite Florrie's offering of their favourite T-bone steaks and homemade chips with apple pie to follow. Strangely enough, it was Lyle who pointed out that with Tango gone from the apartment, life would be a lot less fraught with antagonism. Biff and Liam lightened the atmosphere with a description of their TV appearance and the delight of the kids in the studio. Bucky suggested asking some of their show business acquaintances to put in an appearance at Lyle's youth club. Florrie left them planning a full-scale programme to be televised from the clubhouse and went to bed early. First, however, she took a quiet peek round Tango's old room.

Apart from the usual clutter, she found a surprising collection of books. Mixed in with the run-of-the-mill novels and thrillers, she found several dealing with occult theory and training. A complete set of Aleister Crowley's works along with others less well-known; some dealt with the darker side of Tibetan magic. If Tango was into that, he was in deep, thought Florrie. Digging into her pocket, she brought out several cloves of garlic and, after squashing them, she used the juice to mark a five-pointed star on each of the four walls and the door panel. That should take care of anything trying to gain a foothold in the apartment through Tango's things, at least for a day or two.

Florrie closed the door quietly and went to bed.

23 October, 1:00 p.m.
Press conference at the Savoy Hotel, London

The press were like rabid wolves, avid for any information they could get. Bucky felt as if he had gone ten rounds with a seasoned heavyweight. After two hours, they were still asking questions, most of which he had already answered.

"Mr. Buckman, would you say that Johnny's drinking problem had something to do with his disappearance? Did he have any driving accidents prior to this?"

"No. If you're asking if he's gone and busted up his face, or been paralysed, or become a bleedin' amnesiac, the answer is no, definitely not."

"Frank Saunders, it has been said that you were among the last to see him and that you were, apart from Mr. Buckman, his closest friend. How did he appear to you just before he left the party? Was he upset or drunk or suicidal, perhaps?"

"N-no, certainly not. He just smiled at me across the room and then he left. He wasn't mad or drunk or any of those things. He just smiled and left the room, and we haven't seen him since."

"Mr. Buckman, is the group going to continue?"

"Mr. Buckman, will there be a new lead singer, or will you become just an instrumental group? Tango Garrett has indicated he is willing to take Johnny's place."

"Have there been any reports of UFO activity in the area?"

"It has been suggested by Mr. Garrett in his statement to the press yesterday that Johnny Nova has gotten religious and become a recluse in some kind of new age cult. Is there any truth to this statement?"

"Tango Garrett is talking through his a—Um, Mr. Garrett must have been mistaken. We do not know where Johnny is at this moment. He's been suffering from exhaustion and has simply gone away; it can happen to people who are always in the public eye. The group *will* continue, and we will be giving more news as to who will take Johnny's place as lead singer on a temporary basis…"

There was a rustle of movement as Tango entered and stood looking across the room at Bucky. By his side was a tall, thin, almost emaciated man dressed entirely in black. An aura of menace hung about the two of them, and those reporters standing near drew back. Looking directly into Tango's eyes, Bucky resumed speaking.

"...in a few days as soon as we come to a firm decision. Now, ladies and gentlemen, if you will excuse us, I think that is all we have to say at the moment. Goodbye, and thank you for coming to this press call."

As the group filed out, last-minute questions were flung at them en masse and individually. Mobile phones were thrust into their faces with demands for an exclusive statement. Camera flashes exploded round them and, at last, Liam lost his notoriously short temper and swung at a reporter. The resulting mayhem cost them another thirty minutes before they were finally free of the milling mass of newshounds. None of them so much as looked at Tango, something not lost on the reporters.

In private, Bucky turned on Tango with a vengeance. "You stupid sod. If you hadn't opened your fat mouth, none of this would have been necessary. You gave your word not to say anything."

"I didn't give my word, but you were so busy worrying about dear Johnny, you didn't notice. Anyway, he's gone, G-O-N-E, and he won't be back. His type always top themselves when the going gets hard. He was never that good, anyway; his voice didn't have as big a range as mine. I can sing better than him anytime. He should have gone ages ago, but you lot sucked up to him." Tango's sneering tone and vicious expression silenced the group like cold water. Lyle was the first to recover.

"You really hate him, don't you, Tango? I didn't want to believe it until this moment, but you do. Probably always have."

"What's to hate? He was a fucking jerk, he had his time, and now he's gone. And if you don't want to break up the group, you're left with me. It's my turn to shine, Lyle baby, and if you don't like it, you can sod off and see how far you get, only don't forget the contract. You opt out, you pay out. By the way, Colin, since Johnny's not around, can we take it that his share gets banged out between the rest of us? Better still, it should come to me, as I'll be lead singer *and* playing instrumental."

There was an icy silence, and Colin turned a face white with barely controlled rage to the grinning Tango. "No, Mr. Garrett, until such time as I know once and for all that Johnny won't be back, his share will, as always, be banked to his account. Frank, I'll need a second signature for the accountant to do that. Will you oblige?"

"Sure will, Bucko. Be glad to."

Bucky turned to the rest of the group and, in a dangerously quiet voice, asked if anyone else objected to Johnny's share continuing as usual. They shook their heads and glared at Tango, who shrugged and poured himself a soft drink from the bar. Turning to the others, he indicated his silent companion with a wave of his hand.

"By the way, may I introduce Mr. De'ath? I have signed him on as my personal PR man. In the future, he will see to all my publicity, press conferences, and such. I suggest we get together soon and rehearse some of the main numbers. I need to alter some of the phrasing and keys to suit my voice. Oh, and I now have a PO box number for any mail and an ex-directory number, which I will give only to Colin here. As the star of the group, I feel the need for more privacy, if you know what I mean."

He laughed and finished his drink, then walked to the door accompanied by De'ath, who had not said a word. At the door, Tango paused and turned to Bucky with a sly look. "By the way, I'm going solo when the contract runs out," and he left.

In the room behind him, the silence was palpable.

"Maybe," said Biff hopefully, "he was joking. Perhaps he doesn't like showing his feelings."

"Shut up, Biff," said Liam savagely. "He's a bastard out for himself, always was. If it wasn't that he's the only singer we've got, and not bad at that, I'd ram his dental caps so far down his throat he'd be able to chew on his own balls. And who the hell was that ghoul with him? God, he gave me the creeps."

Bucky was sitting with his head in his hands. "God, I don't want the group to break up," he moaned. "We're right at the bleedin' top."

Frank pushed his way forward and squatted down beside him. "Bucko, the group is still together 'cept for Johnny, and we can use this as publicity not just for the group, but for Johnny as well. I truly believe that Johnny will come back. Hand on heart, I do. We can push those discs that have his voice on them, selling them as real hot items, you know the sort of thing: the last song recorded by Johnny Nova. The tapes made on that last night we were all together, they're worth a fortune, and it will keep Johnny's name and face before the public. He'll know, wherever he is, that we haven't forgotten him. And as a big, beautiful bonus, it will annoy the shit out of Tango."

A smile spread over Bucky's face. "Yeah, we don't have any bookings for a while, and we already told the press we were taking a break. We'll keep to that for a coupla months, get Christmas over, and who knows, by the time New Year comes, maybe…Well, he might…" His voice trailed away.

Into the silence came a thread of music. Frank had found a piano and was quietly playing the verse to "Mountains of Gold." He sang it softly to himself, knowing they were all listening and hearing Johnny's silver tenor rather than his own reedy tones.

A young man went walkin' in the wind and the rain
He was lookin' for somethin' that had no name
Spendin' his time just growing old and
Lookin', always lookin', for the Mountains of Gold

He came to a place hidden deep in a dream
Where the silence held a music and the air smelt clean
There he found a man, serene and old
And high up above him stood the Mountains of Gold

He laid a gentle hand on the young man's head
He looked into his eyes, and this is what he said
"Wanderin' child, your dreams hold the key
Listen, and I'll tell you how it happened to me"

The words and music died away and Frank said softly, "Tango won't get that one. I'd leave the group myself if he did. That's Johnny's song, and only his." He swung round on the stool and fixed them with a steely look. "We've all gotta promise that. Tango does *not* get to sing 'Mountains of Gold.' Are we agreed?"

There was a chorus of agreement and Frank drew a shaky breath, then smiled. "Let's have lunch, and then I'm going to get some brochures and decide where I'm gonna spend Christmas. You lot comin', or are you staying the night?"

Frank added, "Johnny, wherever you are, I hope you're well," and he raised his glass in salute. "Cheers!"

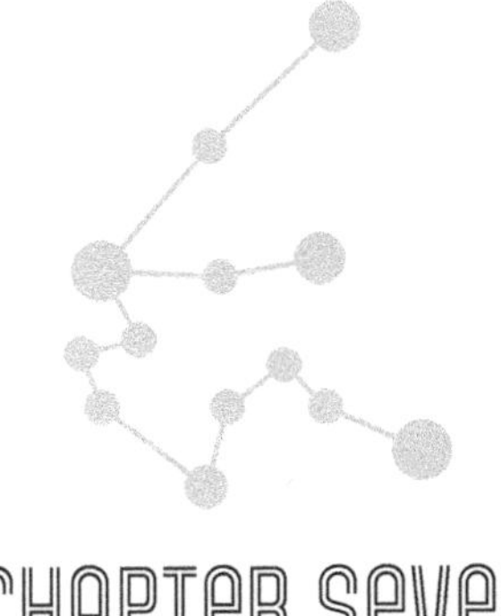

CHAPTER SEVEN

24 October, 2:00 p.m.
On board the *Ortega Star* in the Red Sea

Johnny leaned heavily on Tze-Ring's shoulder and puffed. "That makes three times round this tub, Ring. For Pete's sake, gimme me a break, willya?"

"You are out of condition, Johnny. You need strength for the journey ahead." The young lama was not even breathing hard. Johnny rolled his eyes, limped to a deck chair, and took off his shoes to examine his feet for blisters. Tze-Ring sat beside him and continued his admonition. "You must eat more. You are far too thin. You have hardly eaten these last few days."

Johnny snorted. "There hasn't been anything worth eating! Brown rice, vegetables, milk, fruit, and the odd slice of chicken. I loathe yoghurt, I quit drinking milk when I left primary school, and I won't eat brown rice. I want meat and potatoes, peas, bread and butter, strawberry cheesecake, and a pint of British bitter."

His companion sighed. "What we have offered you is good, nourishing food, Johnny. Besides, the kind of food you want is difficult to get in this area. However," he leaned forward in conspiratorial fashion and whispered, "I managed to obtain a dozen fresh eggs—well, almost fresh—and a small tin of ham. I thought a ham and tomato omelette might tempt you tonight."

"Do I get chips with it?" grinned Johnny, and he laughed as his companion's face dropped. "Never mind, Ring. It's the thought that counts, and an omelette sounds great. And to be on the safe side, I'll make it myself and we'll share."

Tze-Ring hesitated and then admitted shyly, "I would like that, but please do not tell my grandfather. Now I will get us something cool to drink." He turned to leave, then turned back, smiling. "Please do not try to jump ship, Johnny Burke. There are sharks in these waters, and unlike myself, they are not vegetarian."

He disappeared, and Johnny lay back in the chair and propped his feet up on a coil of rope. He closed his eyes and let his mind drift back over the last few days. He was beginning to feel stronger and healthier than he had in years, but Ring was right, he could do with more weight. In the last few days the withdrawal symptoms had begun to loosen their grip on him. He still got one or two bouts during each twenty-four-hour period, mostly during the night, when his body cramped up, but he could cope—just.

Johnny cast his mind back to the night when Tze-Ring had taught him how to beat the pain. He recalled the blaze of exaltation he had felt when he leapt free of his body for the first time and the letdown when it proved so difficult to do it again. He soon found he could only achieve that state when the pain became totally unbearable; the actual pain itself appeared to be the launch pad from which he could soar into a different world. With Ring's encouragement, he'd been able to ride all but the worst of it, and by the time they had reached Crete, he was able to cope with the withdrawal symptoms as they lessened day by day, but he never managed to fly free with such power as that first time. He grinned at the memory of the morning after: The abbot had given him a speculative look and cryptically referred to his abilities on the astral.

The abbot and Chambha had left Crete two days after they arrived to visit another abbey. Johnny and Tze-Ring had stayed in a large and luxurious villa overlooking the harbour. Johnny's plans to escape had been frustrated by guards who looked like nightclub bouncers scattered all round the place. No opportunity had presented itself, and frankly, he had felt too ill to try.

With the treatment Johnny had received on board the *Aghios Loukas*, his other health problems had also started to clear up. He no longer felt ashamed to strip when Ring was around or when his underwear was collected for washing. The cravings for alcohol and tobacco were taking longer to master than he had expected, but he was winning the battle. Even stranger was the fact that, at times, he found himself almost accepting his captivity. There were whole days when he hardly remembered a time when he had not been with Ring. He slept, when the pain allowed, deeply and dreamlessly and woke relaxed and rested. But during this part of the journey, when there was little to do but exercise, sleep, and rest, he had time to think, to remember, and to puzzle over certain things. Today he intended to get some answers. They were, all things considered, long overdue.

Tze-Ring returned with a large jug of fruit juice and two glasses. Johnny accepted a glass and sat sipping the cool liquid for a few minutes and watching the opposite bank glide by. Then, having sorted things out in his mind, he set the drink down on the tray, turned to his companion, and fired his opening shot.

"I'm still determined to get away from you lot, you know. I don't know how, but you can be sure I'll try. You haven't won yet."

Tze-Ring looked down at his glass, then up at Johnny. "You would do well to forget it. The abbey is a place from which it will be extremely difficult to escape. It could cost your life, and that would be a tragedy for you, us, and the world."

Johnny sat up straight and glared at him. "There you go again with all that guff about me being special. I'm a singer, not some bloody male version of Mother Teresa."

He slumped back, frowning, thinking of his former life and his friends. God, what he'd give to see Bucky and Frank, and Lyle with his big, wide grin...Biff and Liam too. Jesus, even that pain in the ass, Tango, would be good to have around! What were they doing without him? Did they know where he was? What had they told the press, and when would he be able to return to them? The questions whirled round in his brain, and his scowl grew blacker.

"You are remembering your friends, Johnny, yes?"

Johnny bit a fingernail, shortening it even further, and spat it out. "Yeah, they must be outta their minds worrying about me, an' we gotta big charity concert to do next month." He looked up. "Please, Ring. The abbot's not here. You could let me send a cable to let them know I'm OK. They must think I've run out on them or topped myself."

"I cannot do that, Johnny. No one must know where you are, even those you love. I keep telling you your life is in danger, but you choose not to believe this."

"Too damn right!"

Silently, they watched the sun move towards its setting in a riot of rose-coloured clouds that painted the cliffs on either side with fire. There seemed to be nothing else in the world but the ship and the cliffs that had seen so much pageantry and pomp pass beneath them. Time had no meaning; there was just an eternal "now" wrapped in a cloak of ancient silence. In that silence, Tze-Ring spoke.

"The sunsets are quite different in the mountains, but just as beautiful. In a few weeks we will be there, Johnny. Then you will understand so much more. Once your training takes shape, you will not grieve for your former life. You will learn to travel to each of the Abbeys of Light in turn, preparing for..." He stopped and looked at Johnny uneasily, then went on, "...for your mission."

The sun had almost dropped below the horizon, and the sudden twilight of the tropics raced towards them. The two young men, with just three years between them, looked at each other, sizing up their likenesses and their differences. Johnny felt a sudden glow of warmth for his companion. He felt as if he had known Tze-Ring since childhood, as if he were more than a friendly jailer. Johnny considered the feeling, trying it out for size, then abruptly decided to put it to the test. Leaning forward, he poured another glass of juice.

"What about these abbeys, Ring? What are they, where are they, and what do they do that is so important you had to kidnap a sick rock singer to help you?"

Tze-Ring heard his own heartbeat in the ensuing silence, which stretched like a cat before a log fire. A lot could turn on his answer. Finally he spoke.

"There are six great Abbeys of Light, Johnny, and they lie scattered across the world. There was a seventh, but its location was lost to us over a century ago. Between them, the abbeys are storehouses of the earth's ancient and magical knowledge, including the books and papers supposedly destroyed when the libraries of Heliopolis, Alexandria, and Carthage were sacked and burned. They, the abbeys, are hidden in very inaccessible places to preserve their peace and to guard the treasures of the world.

"Our records tell us that the first abbey—though it was not called such—was a temple dedicated to the Goddess Neith in the Nile delta, in the time before the first dynasty of Egypt. Its High Priest, Knebt-Tua, was the youngest son of the Bee King, as the ruler of Lower Egypt was styled at that time. He was given a vision of the future, of a time when the ancient knowledge had been lost, destroyed by impious hands and the lust for power.

"He was given instructions to combat the darkness and preserve that knowledge. In dreams, he was directed to an almost-inaccessible area of swampland, and there he built a temple, helped by his students. There was only one way into and out of the swamp, so they became isolated, and only the most determined disciples made it to the temple to be trained. He took only the best and trained them hard in the ways of the priesthood. Then, at the end of his life, he offered his failing strength to the Lords of Light for their purpose. One of the Great Ones of the Light manifested through him and laid down the principles that became the basis of the abbeys' rule as we know it today.

"This last effort caused Knebt-Tua's death, but he had accomplished his task. Those he had trained divided into three groups. One stayed in the original temple to train those who might come. The others left to establish their own temples. One was built on a mountain named for the moon god, Sin; later it was called Sinai. The others sailed to Hellas, or Greece, and took over a site sacred since Neolithic times. It was overgrown and deserted but for a profusion of snakes. As Delphi, the Temple of Apollo, it became a place of pilgrimage throughout the Mediterranean world.

"So it went on. From age to age, they taught and trained the best of the many that came to them. The locations moved from time to time, but the teaching went on. Always mindful of that first vision of Knebt-Tua, copies of everything were sent back to their brethren in the other hidden temples so nothing would be lost if disaster struck.

"Alexandria fell, like Heliopolis and Carthage before it, but the teachings were safe. Over a period of time, there came to be seven such places of teaching and worship, though never of one form of worship alone. All faiths and forms of religion were welcomed; it was the heart of the belief that mattered, not its form or its dogma. In addition to books and knowledge, each temple—later, abbey—was and is the guardian of a…" Tze-Ring paused and chose his words with care. "A certain type of relic, some of which date back before the Age of Pisces.

"One abbey contained a very important relic for the present age. But it disappeared and we lost all contact with it. We are still trying to find a clue that will lead us to it. It was briefly rediscovered in the late nineteenth century by a young explorer called Nicholas Roerich." He glanced at Johnny. "You may have heard of him, but he hid the maps giving its location, and they have never been found.

"During the Dark Ages, these hidden areas were the only places to keep the flame of ancient knowledge alive, though they had to survive many attacks and infiltrations by those hostile to their work. At the present moment there are, as I have told you, six, though not all are working at full strength. The Abbey of the Waters is based in the Aleutian Islands off the coast of Alaska, while the Abbey of the Winds is on one of the islands along the coast of Chile, close to Tierra del Fuego. Then there is the present motherhouse, the Abbey of the Aeon, high in the Pyrenees between Spain and France.

"The Abbey of the Dawn is situated on one of the lesser ranges of the Tibetan plateau, at a point where several countries come together. It was originally a lamasery. It still is; we share it with our Buddhist brethren. It is not the original building, of course. It is the tenth to stand on that spot. Alexander reached it during his foray into India and stayed to learn many things. When he moved on, he left some of his own priests there and took some of the lamas with him. We have many artefacts and books copied from the scrolls he left. You will see them yourself when we get there.

"On this ship, we are within a few hundred miles of the Abbey of the Throne. It is hidden in an ancient, ruined city not far from the Port of

Aden. Lastly, there is the Abbey of the Snows, the most isolated of all in our present era, situated on Rishiri Island, Hokkaido. It is also the newest of the abbeys and, together with the Abbey of the Waters and the Abbey of the Throne, does not have a full complement of personnel. It is hard to find people with the right talents who will give up a normal life and live in such isolation."

Tze-Ring paused, and Johnny, who had been listening, jumped in with a question.

"OK, so you have places full of old papers, books, and artefacts, and judging by the help you are able to call up, you're not short of cash. What I want to know is, what do you do? I mean, *why* do you hide yourselves away? Is it some crazy new religion? A kooky occult group that believes it can save the world?"

"After more than four thousand years, we can hardly be called new. But yes, religion comes into it. Not just one religion, as we come from all denominations, faiths, and creeds. Occult? Well, it depends upon what you would term 'occult.' Your own Romani blood will tell you that there are things science finds difficult to explain and even more difficult to accept. We, on the other hand, not only accept them, we actively seek them out and train them. You will find all races represented in the abbeys, but only one aim: to keep the ancient knowledge intact, and to train the individual talents of the men and women who come to us to the highest degree of perfection."

"You've said that before, and I still don't understand. What do you mean by talents?"

Tze-Ring took a deep breath, looked at Johnny, then silently indicated the almost-empty jug of fruit juice. For a moment, nothing happened. Then the jug lifted smoothly from the tray, poured the remaining liquid into Johnny's glass, and returned to its former place.

The glass dropped from Johnny's nerveless hand and shattered on the deck, the juice staining his white deck shoes. There was a pause, then the scattered fragments of glass clustered together busily and lifted themselves en masse to drop in a compact heap on the tray.

"Talent as in telekinesis, Johnny Burke," said Tze-Ring.

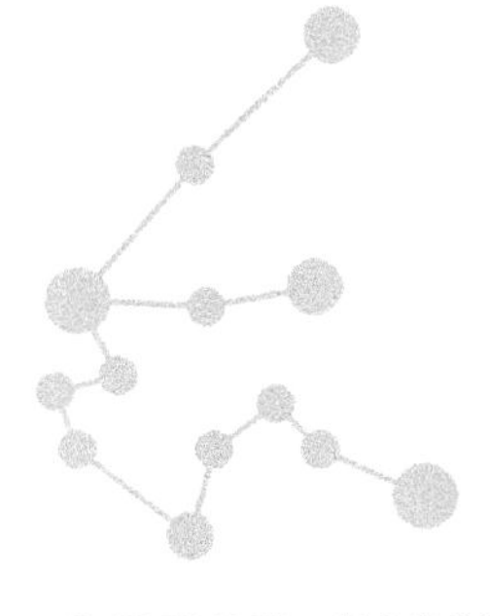

Chapter Eight

25 October, 1:00 p.m.
The coffee shop in the British Museum, London

"Mr. Buckman," said the gentleman from the London Buddhist Society. "I assure you there is nothing in our records whatsoever concerning this Abbey of the Dawn. Unless you can give me more detailed information, I cannot help you. 'Somewhere in northern India, a place with a lot of high mountains, and an abbot who is small, old, and frail' is hardly a viable set of directions. India is full of mountains, especially in the north, and most abbots are old and frail. I rather think someone is pulling your leg about all this. Perhaps you might try some of the English lamaseries. There are quite a few, you know."

"Yeah, I've already tried a few of them. They didn't know either. Well, I tried. Anyway, thanks for meeting me and talking like this."

Bucky chewed on an unlit cigar for a few moments, then stood up, extending his hand to the other man. They shook hands and the man left, leaving Colin Buckman to return to the books he had left in the Reading Room of the British Museum. For the last ten days, he had picked his way through everything he could find on Tibet, India, lamas, Buddhism, and anything that looked likely. There were more books in the apartment, filling a newly bought bookcase in his bedroom and spilling over onto every available space.

At least it was quiet at the moment. Biff and Liam had left for Florida, Lyle and Ginny were in Greece, and Christ alone knew where Tango had gone. And Bucky didn't care, just so long as he kept out of his way. Frank was in India; he had some crazy idea that he might find Johnny among the millions of people already there. For the moment, the furore Johnny's disappearance had stirred up was forgotten for a newer piece of excitement, but Bucky knew it would surface again soon.

Entering the domed and hallowed haven of the Reading Room, Bucky collected a pile of books being kept at the desk and carried them to a vacant seat. He looked round, savouring the silence and the atmosphere and letting the ambience of a hundred years of scholarship and learning soak into his soul. He loved it here. From the first day, it had somehow got under his skin and gentled him. His love of history had been nurtured during his schooldays by a sharp-tongued but observant teacher. Forgotten in the years between, it surfaced stronger than ever, and he indulged it to the hilt.

Bucky sighed and turned his attention to the books in front of him. He was about to pick up the first one when his eye was caught by a book left by the occupant of the next seat. The title was enough to intrigue him: *With Mystics and Magicians in Tibet*, its author Alexandra David-Neel. He picked it up and looked at the contents page, then dipped his way through it, reading a few pages then moving on and becoming more and more enthralled.

He set the other books aside and concentrated on the slim volume in his hand. Oblivious to all else, he read through the afternoon until the library closed, by which time he was more than halfway through. He handed in his pile of reading matter and asked if the book was still in print. On being assured it was available from a bookshop nearby, Bucky left with a thoughtful expression. He did not notice the tall, distinguished gentleman who followed him out and across the courtyard.

♫ ♩ ♫ ♪ ♫ ♪ ♫

"We are about to close, sir. Could you not come in tomorrow?" The elderly lady with a soft Scottish accent looked at him earnestly over her gold-rimmed spectacles.

"It's very important that I get hold of this book as soon as possible, miss. I'd be much obliged if you'd let me buy it tonight." Bucky shamelessly turned on the charm, and the woman's eyes slid into a slightly unfocussed stare and narrowed slightly. Then she nodded and opened the bookshop door.

"Well now, if it is so important, then you shall have it. It's right here on the shelf. And if you have the exact money, sir, it would be very helpful." She took a small paperback off the shelf. "I'm thinking this will be the one you mean, sir?"

"Yeah, that's it." Bucky glanced at the price and thrust a ten pound note into the woman's hand. "I don't have the right money, but put the change in the charity box. Thanks, miss, you're a darlin'. Er, I mean, you're very kind." He thrust the book into his pocket and hurried into the street.

The tall gentleman who had entered the shop after him and the elderly shop assistant watched Bucky hail a passing taxi and clamber into it. As it passed the shop, Bucky was already leafing eagerly through the book. Brigadier Sir William Rothely-Smythe tapped his cane against a hand-stitched and impeccably polished brogue and remarked to his companion, "I think the abbot is right, Margaret. He has a long way to go, but the abilities are close to the surface. A little muddied by his present lifestyle, but the aura beneath shows a good, clear blue and gold. He will undoubtedly make a good Watcher later on."

"Aye, but the poor man is surely bending under a weight of worry. I'm thinking I'll start a novena for him this very night."

The brigadier looked down from his considerable height at his fellow Watcher and chuckled. "Ever the mother hen, eh Margaret? And a heart as golden as your aura. Goodnight, dear lady."

With old-fashioned courtesy, he doffed his hat, kissed her cheek, and strode off into the dark and crowded street.

♬ ♩ ♫ ♪ ♬ ♪ ♫

Much later that evening, Bucky finally closed the book and turned out the light. He lay there quietly, thinking and turning things over in his mind for a while. Then, feeling rather foolish, he sent a tentative thought out into the darkness.

Er, sir? Reverend...Uh, Father? What the hell do you call a Buddhist abbot, for Christ's sake? Can you hear me? It's me, Colin Buckman. Is Johnny with you? Is he all right? I mean, he was pretty screwed up when he left here. I've been reading these books, see, but I can't find anything about your lot. I remember dreaming a few weeks ago that you were here talking to me. The books say you can go places when you're asleep, and I want to know if I can go see Johnny.

Bucky stopped and listened, but there was nothing. He tried again.

Look, I know you need him for something big, but I need him too. Not just for the group, but because he's like family, see? I want to know if he's OK, right?

Again he listened but heard only the muted klaxon of a passing tug. Bucky waited a few more minutes, then laughed at himself for even hoping for an answer. He pummelled his pillow into shape and turned on his side with a deep sigh and closed his eyes.

Bucky drifted in and out of sleep for a while. Then a light appeared behind his closed eyelids. It grew larger and more solid and finally formed into a human and vaguely familiar shape.

"You have surprised me, Mr. Buckman, with your determination and your ability to persevere in your aims. Johnny is well, and at this moment, he is on his way to the Abbey of the Dawn. He has a long way to go—his training has not even begun—but he shows great promise. My advice to you is to continue your reading along the line you have chosen. But for your own sake rather than Johnny's, I must ask you not to call me this way again, or at least not until you are given permission to do so. All my attention must be given to the task ahead, and any distraction, however small, will lessen that concentration. I give you my word that you will see Johnny in the future. Meanwhile, you will also receive help as and when you have need of it. Will you promise not to call me again in this manner, Mr. Buckman?"

Bucky came awake with a sickening jolt in the pit of his stomach. He knew the face and the voice; it had been imprinted on his memory since that first dream. Standing at the foot of his bed, outlined with a soft golden light, was a small, frail figure wrapped in a large woollen shawl. This was real—he was not imagining it. Bucky lay sweating with fear and fighting to keep control until he managed to speak.

"Yeah, Father, so long as I know he's OK. I promise."

"Thank you. I will see to it that you are helped to extend your knowledge. You already have a book to which your attention was directed. Others will follow. You also have a part to play in this drama, Colin Buckman, but not yet. First, you must lay the cornerstones of wisdom; they are discretion, discrimination, dedication, and faith. Also, please remember: That which is built upon falsehood and envy will eventually cause its own destruction. Think on this when events threaten to overwhelm you in the future."

The image faded, leaving a faint scent of incense behind it, and Bucky lay back against the pillows and waited for his heart to stop pounding. It had really happened. He'd done it, just as the books said. He clambered out of bed and went to the bookcase and eagerly rummaged through it, seeking a specific book. On finding it, he returned to bed and leafed through its pages until he came to a chapter marked "Astral Communication" and settled down to read it for the umpteenth time.

> *Still the mind and relax completely. Fix your inner sight on the face of the person with whom you wish to communicate. When the face is as clear as you can get it, visualise over the person's head a light bulb shining with a blue light. Flash the bulb off and on with a steady rhythm until the figure becomes aware of you. Project your message as clearly as you can, and as far as possible in picture form. Keep relaxed, and signal the end of your message with the same flashing on and off of the light.*

Bucky put down the book and lay with a grin on his face. He'd truly done it! Then he grew thoughtful, as if turning over an idea in his mind.

Finally he relaxed again and carefully and precisely built up a picture of Florrie.

Ten minutes later, the phone by his bed rang. Bucky picked it up and said quietly, "That you, Florrie?"

"Wot the bleedin' hell do you think you're playing at, Colin Buckman? All this readin' has gone to your head! Playin' about with this stuff is not on, 'specially when you barge into me sleep demanding I ring you up. Your psychic talents may be opening up, but don't forget your manners. I could've been doing somethin' private."

"God, Florrie, I'm sorry! I was trying something out, honest to God. I didn't mean to wake you. I'll call tomorrow and tell you about it, OK?"

Florrie's reply was blunt, precise, and to the point. Bucky grinned, repeated his goodnight, and put down the phone. He lay for a while mulling over his conversation with the abbot and wondering whether or not to ring Frank in Mumbai, then decided against it until tomorrow. Johnny was OK, that was the main thing, and he would see him again. He could wait.

Bucky turned over and wriggled around until he was comfortable. The soft *put-put-put* of a passing barge became a soothing lullaby, and his eyes grew heavy, his breathing deepened, and night wrapped him with sleep.

A mist drifted in through the half-open window and hung for a moment in the air. Then it thickened and grew, extended and swirled and reformed into a female shape. Margaret McDonald was still woman enough on the astral to take a decade or two off her physical age, but the dancing hazel eyes were the same.

"Well now, Mr. Buckman, let us see how well you cope with your first lesson. Not that you'll remember much about it—that will come later. Out you come, my fine laddie."

Colin Buckman emerged from his sleeping body like a chick from an egg, making hard work of the whole thing. Margaret encouraged him with gentle words and the occasional sharp comment until he stood swaying like a pendulum in a clock, as pink and naked as the day he was born. With a mind for his later embarrassment, Margaret clothed him with a plain brown robe and settled him down on the side of the bed.

"Well now, open your eyes, laddie! Have a look round you and tell me what you see."

Slowly, Bucky opened his eyes and stared at her, taking in the fact that a strangely familiar woman was in his bedroom. Normally he did not mind a woman in his room. However, he could quite clearly see his wardrobe through this one, and that he minded a great deal. He leapt to his feet and found himself flat against the ceiling, floundering like a beached whale. His companion *tsk-tsk*ed impatiently and berated him in her soft Scottish voice.

"Colin Buckman, come down off the ceiling this minute. Never make a sudden move when you are out of the body or for sure you will end up on the other side of wherever you happen to be." She reached for him mentally and guided him down, turning him round so he could see his sleeping form splayed out across the bed and snoring loudly.

"That's a terrible loud snore on you, laddie. Let's go somewhere quieter. Are you there, William? I need a little help."

"At your service, dear lady," said the brigadier, striding briskly through the adjoining wall. "Right sir, follow me. Margaret will hold your hand until you get the hang of things. Don't worry if you find yourself swinging from side to side; that's usual on the first couple of tries. Let's see…Somewhere you are going to recognise and feel at ease with, I think."

His mentors marched Bucky at a brisk pace straight into his bedroom wall. Before he had time to howl a protest, they were through and standing on a headland overlooking a sandy bay. Breakers swept in from a blue sea with surfers riding them like chariots. He had no difficulty in recognising Byron Bay in New South Wales, no more than forty miles from where he had grown up. The sun was shining, and a few people lay scattered about in the early summer warmth.

Bucky looked round. He knew this place, had swum here during his teens, and had lost his fifteen-year-old virginity to Bruce Duffy's sister down among those trees bordering the beach. This was for real. Then he recalled something that had been said and turned to his companions, fixing Margaret with a belligerent frown. "What do you mean I won't remember it in the morning?"

The couple looked at each other and laughed. Then the brigadier laid a hand on Bucky's shoulder and said gently, "Sit down, Colin. There'll be a time when you will remember, but for now it is better this way so it won't interfere with your other life. My name is William. This is Margaret, and we work for the abbeys. The abbot has asked us to look after you and give you some basic training. I left that book for you to find, and Margaret here took over a friend's shift at the bookshop. There are many like us all over the world and in every walk of life. We look for the odd, the unusual, and the out-of-step people that could be of use to the abbeys. You might like to think of us as psychic talent scouts. We are called the Watchers."

26 October, 1:00 a.m.
In a hotel suite outside London

"No, not like that. Relax into your breathing and hold the image steady in your mind. Now push your consciousness through the top of the head as if it was a spray of water. That's right. Now let the spray fall to the floor and allow it to assume your usual form."

Tango's astral wavered and rocked backwards and forwards as he tried to stabilise himself. De'ath's black, pupilless eyes fixed on him intensely. The physical body lay inert on the bed, limp and pale. As the semi-transparent double grew more solid, Tango's voice emerged exultantly from its lips.

"I did it, I did it! It's fantastic! Christ, it actually works!"

"I'll thank you *not* to use that name in my presence. It ruins my mood and plays hell with my concentration." De'ath rose from the chair in which he had been sprawled with a face like thunder. "Now give me a moment and I will join you. Then we can go hunting."

Within seconds, De'ath's astral had separated from the body and stood facing Tango.

"Let's go. You need energy and so do I, and I know where to find it." He rose up through the ceiling, followed by Tango.

From high above the hotel, De'ath surveyed the city below.

"Some advice, my friend. Never take energy from the old, the sick, or the weak. You need young, fresh power to add strength to your own. That way, you will keep your youth and add to your strength."

Tango shuddered. "You mean take blood, like a vampire?" he whispered.

"Nothing so crass or outré as that, my friend. I speak of ingesting pure energy, life energy, drawn from source, as it were. Young, innocent women offer the sweetest and ripest kind and are bursting with life. Young men of the same age have a rawness that is offset by the virility of the energy they secrete." He looked at the sickened Tango and grinned wolfishly. "You'll get used to it, even come to crave it after a while."

De'ath swooped suddenly, dragging his reluctant companion with him. To Tango it was all a blur of speed, colour, and sound that momentarily drove him into unconsciousness. Opening his astral eyes, Tango found himself in a small bedroom with walls covered with posters. Most of them displayed football players, martial arts experts, and track and field personalities. A young man in his teens with a towel draped round his waist was lying on the bed engrossed in a dog-eared porn magazine. De'ath and Tango watched as he turned the pages, lost in the erotic images. After a few minutes, the man threw the magazine aside and rose from the bed. He unpinned three of the biggest posters and turned them round to reveal hard-core porn centrefolds pasted to the back of them. These he re-pinned to the wall and then took off the towel and lay down on the bed again.

Fixing his eyes on the nearest pin-up, he began to fondle his half-erect penis. De'ath licked his lips and drew nearer to the bed. The boy's hips began to buck and he grabbed the pillow and buried his face in it, mumbling love words to his paper goddess. As his hand moved faster, De'ath's astral floated above him, waiting for the peak moment. Tango saw a brilliant thread of energy beginning to form over and around the boy's genitals. It wound upwards in a spiral of pulsing energy that grew brighter and brighter. It drew him closer until, despite his disgust, Tango found himself craving a taste of the energy being generated. He took his place beside De'ath and waited for his share of the outcome.

A final groan buried deep in the pillow heralded the climax and the semen jetted upwards. Simultaneously, the spiralling energy was released and avidly ingested by the waiting astrals. It roared through Tango's system like a shot of pure heroin, the ecstasy flinging him back into the physical on the rebound. His body lay limp, drenched in sweat and flooded with adrenalin, relishing the last few moments of sensation. Then the realisation of what Tango had just done dawned on him, and self-loathing overcame him. He made it to the bathroom just in time.

It was some time before De'ath returned to his body, and Tango watched, sickened, as time after time, the limp figure on the bed moaned and writhed as sexual energy was gleefully ingested by De'ath. Finally it was quiet, and his cold, dark eyes opened.

"Aaaaaahhh!" He stretched luxuriously, then relaxed, laughing. "You left too soon, my friend. My, what stamina these young boys have! I feel twenty-five again." His eyes glinted. "Not bad when you are well over two thousand years old."

Tango's jaw dropped. "Two thousand years? You're joking—or insane."

De'ath came to his feet in one lithe movement and strode across the room. With effortless strength, he gripped Tango by his throat and lifted him arm's-length above his head.

"I never joke, Mr. Garrett. Nor am I insane, though I may very well drive you insane just for the pleasure of seeing you lose your mind piece by tiny piece. However, I was sent to train you, and train you I will. My masters think you are worth their time and my expertise, so I must oblige them. Yes, my cocky Welsh friend, I am two thousand years old and more, and if you play your cards right, you could be as I am. Though, personally, I doubt you have what it will take." He let Tango drop to the floor. "Now, let's begin at the beginning, shall we?"

26 October, 3:00 a.m.
On board the *Ortega Star* in the Red Sea

Tze-Ring was walking the grounds of the Abbey of the Dawn with his beloved Lea. They paused at the balcony overlooking the breath-taking sweep of the mountain range and let its beauty sink into their hearts. An almost-full moon coloured the peaks with a silver radiance, giving them a translucent appearance. An observer would have noticed that Tze-Ring's form seemed less solid than that of his wife's, more tenuous and bordering on the transparent. No words disturbed the utter silence; nevertheless, Lea was speaking with her husband as she wrapped her thick cape round herself more closely.

"I have missed your physical presence, my love, but these times on the Inner Levels have helped me bear my loneliness. In a few weeks we will be together again, and you will see how fast our son has grown."

"The time has been long for me also, Lea, but filled with much that is new. Johnny is different to what I imagined. He is like two men, one filled with anger and fear, the other beginning to see the inner truth of things. It is like watching a closed lotus bud unfold petal by petal. There is much that is good in him, but it is overlaid by his former way of life. You will like him; he has an inner gentleness that comes from his mother. He loved her dearly and called for her continuously when he was in pain. The serenity of this place will heal the hurts in his life. I have spoken with my father and told him about Johnny, and I reassured him that he carried the spark of greatness. I wish he could be here when Johnny arrives, but Grandfather will not allow it."

They stood looking out over the mountains for a while, savouring their closeness, then turned to face each other. The faint light outlining Tze-Ring's form flickered and brightened, then extended, wrapping itself round the woman's body. Her head went back; her breath caught; her hands reached instinctively for her lover but passed through him. Slowly but surely, Lea matched Tze-Ring's auric power with her own until they were melded together in an embrace far more subtle than any physical act. Colours flashed and shifted through the spectrum in a fountain of emotion as the entwined auras pulsed with increasing power. Lea's hands were clasped at her breast, her eyes tightly closed, her breathing rapid.

"*Mon cher, l'homme de mon coeur, je t'aime. Je t'aime.* Aaah…" Her long, audible sigh was echoed by its mental equivalent from Tze-Ring. Lea sank down on to the stone steps and leaned back against them to raise laughing eyes to her love.

"Ring! Hey, Ring—wake up!"

"That was unexpected but welcome, my dear love. I think—" Lea broke off, her attitude changing in an instant to one of alertness. Tze-Ring's form shimmered and almost disappeared, then suddenly snapped back. His dark eyes were stormy and full of anger.

"Ring, wake up, you bald-headed son of a bitch! Wake up! I want some answers."

"I must go, Lea. My physical body is being awakened very forcibly. It's Johnny; I must go. I love—"

Tze-Ring's form faded completely. Lea waited for a few more minutes, but when he did not reappear, she rose and made her way thoughtfully back to her own quarters.

♬ ♩ ♫ ♪ ♬ ♪ ♫

After several hours of hard thinking and mood swings that ranged from an abject fear of the unknown to a towering rage at being hoodwinked by illusionist tricks, Johnny was mad. He was also drunk, having found the cook's hoarded bottle of rum in the galley. He had kicked open the door to Tze-Ring's cabin and was now shaking him awake.

"Shit, man, you sleep deeper than a bat in a cave. C'mon, wake up, damn you!"

Johnny's tirade slowed down as Tze-Ring opened his eyes and sat up. He held his head in his hands, desperately trying to gather his faculties into some semblance of cohesion. The erotic interlude with Lea and the rough awakening had strained even his highly trained physical and mental abilities to their limits. Johnny stood swaying beside the bunk, his red-rimmed eyes glaring at him.

"Now you and I are goin' t'sit down and have this out. I'm not goin' nowhere until I have some fuckin' answers to all this shit. I don't want no stupid tricks, no hypnit…hypnut…No buggerin' about with my mind. Jus' straight answers, or I'll beat 'em outta you, see." He thrust a belligerent face into Tze-Ring's and waved a clenched fist under his nose.

Still disorientated by his fast return to consciousness, the young man reacted in a totally uncharacteristic fashion. Tze-Ring came up from the bunk like a tiger, grabbing Johnny's T-shirt in his fist. His habitual calm and forbearance went to the wind. He swung a left into the bleary-eyed face in front of him, relishing the dull thud as knuckles made contact with flesh and bone.

Johnny reeled back against the wall, the pain in his jaw jolting him into full awareness. With a roar, he launched himself at the other man, swinging wildly with both fists. Tze-Ring dodged and landed another blow under his eye, then felt Johnny's fist sink into his gut in retaliation. In minutes they were rolling through the open door and onto the deserted deck. Punching and kicking, they struggled to their feet, one too drunk and the other too mentally shaken to do more than just stand and slug it out.

The fight gradually shifted to the open arena of the forecastle where, as luck would have it, one of the crew on painting detail had left brushes and several tins of white paint. Johnny seized one of the tins and, beside himself with rage, hurled it at Tze-Ring, who didn't even bother to duck but simply batted the missile away with a blast of kinetic energy.

The tin hit the deck and split, dumping its contents everywhere. Johnny, lunging forward to follow his abortive attempt to stun his opponent, slipped and brought Tze-Ring down with him. Oblivious to all else, the two of them rolled around on the deck, each trying to get the upper hand. Tze-Ring won and, straddling the younger man, gripped him firmly by the throat and raised his fist, ready to deliver a knockout blow.

Johnny looked up at him, and his eyes bulged. A second later, he was choking with laughter—as much as the death grip on his throat would allow—and flapping his hands weakly on the deck.

"Ring, ol' buddy, you should see…Ha ha ha, you should see…Ha ha… Hell, man, you're mother-naked an' covered with paint from neck to prick! Ha ha ha." His voice tailed off into another bout of laughter that made him clutch his bruised ribs in protest.

Still poised to strike, Tze-Ring looked down at himself. The paint had done a good job, and not only on him—Johnny was covered with it as well. His T-shirt hung in shreds, and his shorts were unrecognisable. His black hair was matted and, like his half-brother, every bit of bare skin was covered in white paint. Tze-Ring, who slept nude, was by far the worst. Sheepishly, he lowered his fist and raised himself off Johnny, who curled up and laughed himself silly. After a few minutes Tze-Ring joined him, and the two men gave themselves up to laughter.

Slowly their hilarity subsided until they were sitting side by side on the deck, quiet and subdued. Johnny touched his right eye, now discoloured and swelling. A dark bruise ran along his jaw.

"Man, you pack a mean left, Ring. What the hell were we fighting about anyway?"

Under a covering of paint, Tze-Ring blushed. "I was awakened too quickly, Johnny. You did not know, but I was on the astral and…uh, very involved on the higher levels. Your shouting and shaking me caused me to snap back into the physical body too quickly. I reacted from frustration and disorientation. You see, I was with Lea, my wife."

"You're married?"

"Yes. Is that so surprising, Johnny?"

"It's just that I thought, well...I thought that monks were, you know, celibate."

Tze-Ring threw back his head and laughed. "But Johnny, I am not a monk, not in the sense that you mean. I have certainly gone through the training of a monk—or rather, that of a lama—but those I serve do not ask for celibacy unless that is something the individual wishes to offer. Most of us choose to marry, and when we mate, we mate both for love and, when it is needed, with others of our kind in the hope that the children will inherit our special talents."

Johnny stared at him, aghast. "That's immoral."

"No, Johnny. It is done with love. Nothing is ever forced upon us; we always have a choice. I have a son by Lea. His name is Taras. He is now three years old and already he can bring his toys to his hand. And sometimes, when he is being more naughty than usual, he hides them in places where they should not be. His kinetic powers will far outrival mine by the time he is grown. But I also have a daughter; her mother is from the Abbey of the Waters. She is Inuit. Siska is a lovely, gentle girl, and she and I made Tilkit, our daughter, with love between us, and with the knowledge and consent of Lea.

"Siska's talent is a rare one; we have found only one other like her, and in that other one, the talent is not as strong. She cannot move objects as I can, but she can move herself from one location to another. Not far, it is true, but over a distance of roughly one and a half kilometres. Tilkit is just six months old, and it is too early yet to know if she has inherited her mother's talent, but there is a strong chance she will because my kinetic talent may boost it.

"Lea, my wife, has an eidetic memory. She is a language expert and speaks fourteen major languages and ten dialects. Taras already speaks and understands three languages. When he is grown, they will be multiplied by four or five."

"You mean you're all freaks of some kind?"

Tze Ring's head snapped up. He spoke sharply and with some heat. "No, Johnny, we are not freaks, simply ordinary people with extraordinary abilities. Left to themselves, such people would not survive the trauma of living in a world that does not understand them and actively fears and hates them. I will tell you about some of them, but first, let's shower off this paint. In the morning, we must face the captain's displeasure and clean up this mess."

Thirty minutes later, smelling strongly of paint remover and shampoo, the two men sat down to coffee, Johnny boasting a rapidly closing eye and an assortment of colourful bruises and Tze-Ring nursing tender ribs, a cut lip, and bruised knuckles. Johnny raised his coffee in salute.

"Here's to your left hook, Ring. God help anyone who tries to stop us when we stand together."

His companion smiled ruefully. "That time may come quicker than you think, Johnny Burke."

"Now," said Johnny, "you were going to tell me about some of the people in the abbey."

"Abbeys," corrected Tze-Ring. "Remember, there are six of them, which means there are about…" He made a rapid calculation in his head. "One hundred and twenty-one people altogether. The ideal number for each abbey is twenty-six, though many are understaffed. The ideal complement breaks down into twelve men and twelve women, plus an abbot and an abbess. Of the twelve—again, ideally—there will be six Fathers and six Brothers, six Mothers and six Sisters."

"What's with the fathers, mothers, sisters, and brothers act?" asked Johnny, his mouth full of cheese sandwich.

"They are titles of degree. Father is a title given to an initiate of high degree; so is Mother. Brother or Sister simply means that the person is still training, although they may have already undergone several degrees of initiation." Tze-Ring warmed to his theme. "Then, of course, there are the Watchers. They are located all over the world. Their task is to—"

"Whoa there, Ring, let me catch up on all this. You mean there's more of these fre—Er…super talented people stashed all over?"

"The Watchers are those whose talents, while more pronounced than usual, are not trainable to the degree we need. Or they may be good, but they do not wish to live in or be part of an abbey. They may have a business to run or a family that knows nothing of this part of their lives. Some are teachers in schools; some are professors and doctors in universities.

We have medical doctors, lawyers, and priests of all denominations. Some rank high in the parliaments of their countries. But we also have nurses, policemen, milkmen, shop assistants, housewives, bank clerks, and sea captains.

"Other helpers are people and corporations that have in the past needed our special skills and called on us. In acknowledgement of their debt, they provide what we need when we need it: boats, planes, helicopters, trained personnel, and of course, money, et cetera."

"Jesus." Johnny put down his sandwich and tried to grasp the enormity of what he had heard. "You're a bloody worldwide organisation!"

"Indeed, and our work is of the greatest importance."

Johnny thought this over and came up with the obvious question. "Ring, just what is it these abbeys *do*?"

"We guard the Light, Johnny. We stand against the Darkness that waits patiently for any opportunity—both spiritual and economical—to overwhelm this planet and those who live on it. We are the guardians of ancient knowledge that scholars think was destroyed long ago but that, in fact, rests in our abbeys. Alexandria may have been burned to the ground, but not one page of its library was lost. Long before that, everything had been copied and sent out to the other abbeys. Alexandria was the first and only abbey to have made itself public. That, of course, was the reason for its destruction; the newly established Christian church felt vulnerable and needed to make itself the only way to the Light. But it isn't, Johnny. There are many ways, and just as many ways to the Dark."

Tze-Ring rose and began to pace the cabin. "You think of talented people as freaks, but they are simply people, Johnny. At this moment, the abbot and Chambha are visiting the motherhouse, the Abbey of the Aeon, high in the Pyrenees. One of our most talented people is also there. He is a Navajo man that everyone calls Wolf. His talent nearly caused his death when he was a child because he is what fantasy novels term a shapeshifter. We do not understand how he does it—neither does he—but he can and does change into a wolf and back again.

"He was born and grew up in Page, Arizona, in a Navajo community. At the age of six he caught a fever, and during a delirium attack while his temperature was running high, he shifted in front of his mother's eyes. She had been brought up in a strict Catholic school and was terrified. She ran screaming to the local priest, but he did not believe her. She was also a recovering alcoholic, and he thought she was back on the drink. The local shaman told her that her son was 'one of the Old Ones,' a being of two worlds and ancient bloodlines. But she was convinced he was a devil, so she tried to burn her little son to death by setting fire to his bed."

Tze-Ring paused and looked across at Johnny's horrified face.

"His older brother saved him and took him to the hospital in Flagstaff. There was a nurse there, a Hawaiian girl whose grandfather was a Kahuna, a special kind of healer. He was also a member of one of the abbeys. She understood the problem and called the old man long-distance. Within hours, Wolf was in a private nursing home in Wyoming. A wealthy rancher who was also a Watcher flew him there in his own plane, then flew the Kahuna in to heal Wolf's body and his mind. When the boy had recovered from his burns, his mother refused to have him back, so the Watcher and his wife adopted him.

"He grew up with them in Wyoming, slowly coming to terms with his talent and the rejection from his mother. Wolf studied the history and heritage of his race and trained with Native shamans of great power until he was fully grown. Then he was admitted to the Abbey of the Aeon, and under Abbot Gregor, he has continued to train and utilise his unique talent.

"Then there is Inez. She is Colombian. She was found wounded and starving, wandering the streets during an armed uprising. Men from both sides had raped her. She was just thirteen. A news reporter found her cowering in a doorway and took her to a convent and gave the nuns money to look after her. By the most amazing coincidence, Inez was noticed by a Watcher in Bogota, and from there was sent to the Abbey of the Winds. Her power is new to us. She is a cleanser, a barometer of evil; she can tell you where it is and what type. Sometimes she can banish it simply by absorption.

"Elissa was born in the *barrio*, the shanty town behind Sao Paulo in Brazil. She was thrown onto a rubbish tip when she was just a few hours old. Why? Because her eyes are facetted like those of a bee. Her sight is quite different than ours; she can see colours above and below our limited scale. We think she is beautiful. The world did not and would have killed her.

"Barnaby is deaf and does not speak. He was not born like that; his father beat him so often it damaged his ears and he became deaf. Barnaby was born in a poor area of Jamaica, an almost fully developed psychic and a materialising medium. His father made money off of his talent. When Barnaby was too tired to work, or if he refused, he was beaten. Barnaby is now a trained Watcher.

"There are others, Johnny, over a hundred of them. Not all of them are at the abbeys because of persecution; some found their way there by themselves, some were born in the abbeys, and others are the children of Watchers. One little boy was discovered by a vagrant who is also a Watcher. This boy can communicate with animals. He is very intelligent, and he kept his secret from both parents and siblings. A convenient scholarship to a particular school was arranged. It also provides special holidays, which are spent at one or other of the abbeys. He is now thirteen and continues to surprise us with his talent.

"Juan is a friend of mine. The youngest son of an old and wealthy Spanish family, he was a famous racing driver until he crashed during a race and almost burned to death. His buried talents of precognition and conscious projection were forced to the surface by pain and trauma.

"Danny's talent is a rare one. He can find buried artefacts and gold and silver simply by walking over the ground. He is just fourteen.

"These people cannot exist outside of the abbeys, Johnny. The world is not a safe place for them. If we did not find them, train them, and give them safety and hope, they would be persecuted, perhaps murdered or driven to suicide, or taken over by the Dark. Then their talents would be used against and not for humanity."

There was still one important question Johnny had to ask. "What about me, Ring? I don't have any talents, so why take me?"

Tze-Ring sat down on the bunk, his hands hanging between his knees, his head drooped with utter weariness. Then he looked up and across at Johnny.

"You are important not for what you have, though that is or will be considerable, but because of who you are. Your future will mark a turning point for this world and all life on it. For that future, I will give my life if need be, and so, my friend, will every person in every abbey. There are some rare and wonderful people who are the treasures of the earth, whose names ring down the corridors of history—" He broke off, wondering how much to say without permission.

The moment stretched into infinity, where time and space had ceased to be. Wordlessly, Tze-Ring sought permission for what he was about to say, and in the Abbey of the Aeon, thousands of miles away, the abbot smiled and whispered, "Tell him, Tze-Ring."

The young lama's words dropped into the quietness.

"You, Johnny, are one of those treasures. Your conception was ordained by the Lords of Light and accomplished by the Rite of Nuit. You are of the bloodline of John the Baptist and Khaemweset, the magician son of Ramesses the Great. You are the Forerunner to the Aeon of the Age of Aquarius." He paused, then went on. "Do you understand, Johnny? You are of the chosen. It is you who will prepare the way for the new Christos."

In the silence, there was just a ship, a small cabin, and two people. In the uttermost depths of the cosmos, the Lords of Light waited impassively for their protégé's reaction.

Johnny rose to his feet. Deep within him, something was waking up, something he had never known was there until now. It felt as if, inside him, an eye had opened after a long sleep. It was more than he, so new to these revelations, could cope with.

Johnny opened the cabin door, and the first rays of the sun hit him full in the face. He laughed and turned his head. "Hey, Ring, the sun's up. It's a brand new day, man."

But Tze-Ring was sleeping and made no answer.

27 October, 5:20 p.m.
Delhi

"Yeah, you too, Bucky. It's hot and sticky, and I feel as if I've taken a bath in molasses. The food doesn't taste the same as the Tandoori House back home either. You were right, I was foolish to think I could find Johnny here. Hell, there must be four times the population of London crammed into this burgh... Yeah, I know, bloody incredible. Reminds me of our early days with the group, sleeping in the waiting room on Lime Street station.

"I'll hang round a few days, then head for the mountains. I've a yen to see the Himalayas close up…Yeah, a place called Srinagar, a kind of jumping-off point for the big peaks. I'll be back about end of November. See you then. So long."

Frank wandered onto the balcony and looked out over the gardens at the setting sun. He was bone-weary and frustrated. He had been totally naive and stupid to hope that somewhere in this teeming country, he would find Johnny.

He wandered back to fling himself on the bed. Maybe a nap before dinner would help. Gradually, the outside world fell away. The noise of traffic faded until silence claimed its territory. The lilac shadows of sunset turned to a deeper mauve and then to purple, but Frank slept on. He dreamed he was standing in a busy marketplace, though he knew he was still in India. He marvelled at the way so many people crammed themselves into one small area. Then, over the noise of the milling crowd, he heard, crystal clear and resonant, Johnny singing as only Johnny could.

"Wanderin' child, you need wander no more
Love is the key that opens the door
Let your soul fly free, for the story is told
Go seek your place on the Mountains of Gold"

The young man stood tall, and he raised up his eyes
He spread out his wings and he took to the skies
He rose like an eagle through the wind and the cold
To meet with his soul on the Mountains of Gold

A glow spread through Frank's dream body. He was here! Against all odds, he had found him. Johnny was here! He woke with a start and rolled off the bed and onto his feet, still hearing the song. Still clinging to the hope that it was Johnny.

But the room was empty and dark with evening shadows. The reality was too much to bear after the dream and the hope. For a moment Frank stood with tears running down his face. Then he went to the wardrobe, took out his suitcase, and began to pack.

No more waiting. Tomorrow he would head for the mountains.

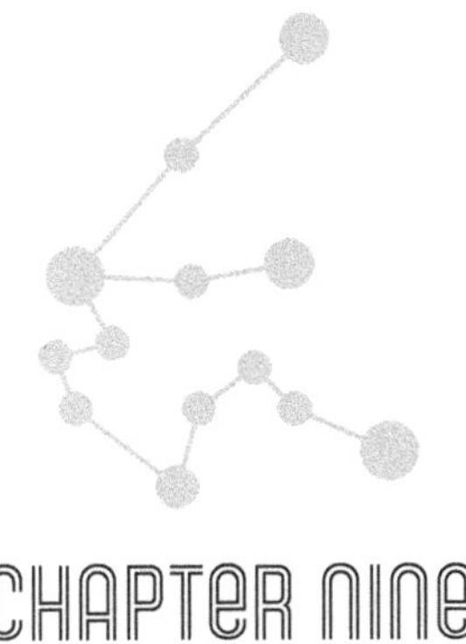

CHAPTER NINE

27 October, 6:00 p.m.
On board the *Ortega Star*, near Aden

Johnny and Tze-Ring sprawled in the shade of the awning and looked out over the harbour of Aden. They had spent the entire day scraping white paint off the deck and were now too tired to do more than just lie around. Both were feeling subdued from the telling-off they had taken from the understandably irate captain. Johnny had tried to take the whole of the blame, saying that he had started the fight, but both had been held responsible and put to work. There had been no time or leisure in which to follow up their last topic of conversation until now.

Johnny had harboured a hope of jumping ship here, but on going through the clothes he had been wearing when kidnapped in London, he had found no money, no credit cards, not even his diary. At a pinch he could have gotten over that hurdle with a phone call to Bucky. But with no passport, things would be more than a little difficult. Which reminded him…He turned to his semi-comatose companion.

"Hey, Ring ol' buddy, what did you guys do about a passport? I mean, how did you get me this far without one?"

Tze-Ring waved a hand that still smelt of paint remover.

"You are travelling on an Irish passport, Johnny. Arranged weeks beforehand, as were all the visas that were needed. Did you think we would leave such things to chance?"

For a while there was silence under the awning, with only the sound of iced fruit juice being poured down thirsty throats to be heard. Then Johnny spoke again.

"Where do we go from here?"

"Muscat."

"Where the hell is that?"

"Two days from here, maybe three. We lost a day in the Red Sea when the ship before us ran aground. We will be late for our rendezvous, but I sent word ahead. My colleagues from the abbey will meet us in Muscat. From there, we fly to Karachi and on to Nepal."

"Nepal! Hell, you're taking me halfway round the world. I can't believe I'm taking this so calmly. Do you really think you can take an unwilling prisoner across India without someone noticing?" He jumped up and began to pace up and down. "I could get away at the airport, the hotel, a taxi—anywhere. And I will. Make no mistake, Ring, I will try."

"I would be disappointed if you did not, Johnny, but you will fail. We fly into a private airfield in Karachi in the early morning when there are few people about. From there we drive over the border to the palace of His Highness the Rajah of Bhimpur. We will be his guests for a few days." He yawned and turned onto his stomach, resting his head on his arms. Then a thought struck Tze-Ring, and he raised his head. "On the way to Kathmandu, we have to get you into shape to climb the mountains. That's why we are taking it slowly: so you can get used to the altitude."

Johnny paused in his pacing and looked down at his companion with horror. "Mountains? Did you say *mountains*? You're gonna take me up a mountain?!"

"Several of them."

"You—you can't. I won't. I couldn't. Ring, I have a thing about heights. I can't even climb a ladder. It makes me dizzy to look down the gangplank over there. I can't go up a bloody mountain!" Johnny's voice rose, bordering on hysteria.

Tze-Ring sat up and spoke sharply. "Stop it, Johnny. You can do whatever you have to do. When the time comes, I will be there to help you; there is no point in dwelling on it until you are there." He rose to his feet and put a hand on the other man's trembling shoulder. "The effort needed to climb the mountains will flush the last of the poisons from your body, Johnny. You need to be fit for your new life. By the time you reach the abbey, you will be in better condition than you have ever been in your life. Now go and sleep for a few hours. When we leave Aden in the evening, I will show you some exercises that will stretch your muscles and make them ready for the climb ahead of us."

Tze-Ring walked with Johnny to his cabin, and as they passed the gangplank, Johnny tensed, ready to leap down and away, but his companion's hand was firm on his arm and the moment was lost. Once in the cabin, he lay down at Tze-Ring's bidding, but he was still tense. Hesitantly, the young lama sat on the bed and smoothed back the dark hair with a gentle hand.

"If you will let me, Johnny, I can send you into a restful sleep. It is quite easy."

There was a silence as Johnny looked at the serene face above him. "I'm scared, Ring. This time on the boat, it's been like a dream, not real somehow, but now it's time to wake up. I don't want to play your games anymore. I want my own life back."

"It is too late, Johnny. None of us can go back to what was before this time, but I will be with you every step of the way."

He laid two fingers between Johnny's dark brows and pressed lightly. A low humming noise came from his throat and emerged from between his lips in a long, hissing syllable.

Johnny's lids fluttered down over his green eyes, but before he plunged into a dreamless sleep, he reached out a hand and grasped that of his companion.

"You're a friend, Ring. You feel like a brother somehow. I should hate you for all this, but I can't, and I don't know why. It's like I've known you all my life."

Tze-Ring opened his heart centre and let its power wrap round him.

"I know, Johnny. I understand. Now sleep, little brother. Sleep and grow strong."

Obediently, Johnny closed his eyes and slept. His brother sat beside him for a long time, watching him. Then, finally, Tze-Ring rose and went to his own cabin.

30 October, 10:30 a.m.
The harbour of Muscat

The harbour of Muscat looked like the maritime equivalent of a London rush hour at Christmas time. Craft of every type, size, and description seemed hell-bent on getting either into the harbour or out of it, most of the time with complete disregard for the rules of the sea. Johnny was fuming. He had been locked in his cabin for the last few hours as the *Ortega Star* jockeyed first for entry, then for her berth, and he was ripe for a showdown with his jailer. He flung himself down on the bunk, wincing as he did so. In the last couple of days, Tze-Ring had put him through a series of muscle-toning exercises designed to stretch and make limber arms and legs made soft by easy living. He could not deny that he felt better and stronger, but he also felt more confident that he could make a break for his freedom—that was, until he found his door locked.

The sound of the key being turned brought Johnny to his feet.

"Ring, you son of a bitch! At last! What the hell goes with you, man..." His voice tailed off into silence as the opening door revealed not Tze-Ring, but a girl. About 5'5", slim but not skinny, just rounded and feminine.

She held out a small, capable-looking hand and said, in faintly accented English, "Hello, Johnny Burke. I am Sister Shuna from the Abbey of the Dawn. I am pleased to meet with you."

Her voice was a husky contralto that matched the dark mahogany-red of her hair and the gold-flecked hazel of her eyes. For a moment Johnny was dumbstruck. Then, remembering his manners, he smiled. When Johnny Burke smiled, Lyle had once remarked, the angels stopped singing for a moment. It began slowly: First with the eyes wrinkling at the corners, lighting up with warmth and laughter; then it sort of spread downwards, lifting the edges of his mouth, broadening the lips, and finally taking over the whole face.

Shuna watched with fascination, having heard about the famous Johnny Nova charm. It was, she admitted to herself, pretty lethal, but she was not there to fall over some swivel-hipped rock star, just to get him to the abbey safely. She offered a small, tight-lipped smile and picked up the canvas bag from the floor.

"If you will follow me, we have a car waiting." She turned and led the way along the deck towards the gangplank.

Johnny lengthened his stride to catch up. "Excuse me, but where's Ring? I haven't seen him for hours, and I don't think I should go without seeing him."

"Brother Tze-Ring was needed urgently in northern Pakistan. He has already gone, but he left you a note. I do not have it with me, but I will give it to you once we are in the air."

"In the air? We're going by air? What about customs? And I haven't said goodbye to the captain. Ring didn't say—"

The girl swung round on him and spoke sharply, her eyes locked on his.

"Mr. Burke, you will make things easier for all of us if you will stop chattering and follow orders, as I am trying to do now. This was not a pleasure cruise; the captain is not expecting a handshake and a gratuity from the famous Johnny Nova. He has done what was expected of him and is now unloading his cargo. You, on the other hand, are expected on the far side of this harbour, where a sea plane has been waiting for twenty-four hours. There will be no customs clearance; officially, you were never on board. Only Tze-Ring was required to go through customs. Now, if you will follow me."

Hurt and bewildered by the girl's attitude after the relaxed manner and friendliness of his former companion, Johnny stopped dead in his tracks. His first reaction was anger against an unjust belligerence. The second, a determination to escape the minute an opportunity presented itself. Seething, he followed the girl to the gangplank. He was so angry he was halfway down the walkway before he realised it, and he had to close his eyes against the vertigo that threatened to disgrace him in front of his surly companion.

At the foot of the gangplank stood two men. The younger was of medium height, slim build, and wearing a necktie of an awesomely hideous design. His face split in an enormous grin at the sight of Johnny, and he introduced himself as Wang Ta, shaking him by the hand and excitedly assuring him he was a long-time fan of White Heat, and of Johnny in particular. A derisory snort from above his right shoulder made Johnny exert more than his usual charm. Wang Ta introduced the older man as Brother Murad, and the singer felt his scalp crawl as he looked up at this newest acquaintance from the abbey.

Murad was big. At 6'5" and three hundred pounds—not an ounce of which was fat—he was impressive to say the least. Getting away from him was going to take fancy footwork and a lot of courage. Murad smiled. To be exact, he bared his teeth. Jesus, the man was the size of a bear with a disposition to match; you could get hugged to death by those biceps.

"Actually," said Murad in a bass voice with a cut-glass Oxford accent, "my wife said the same thing to me a few days ago. I was too enthusiastic in saying goodbye. Being this size can be a terrible bore at times, though it has its uses on occasion."

Johnny closed his eyes and sagged against the door of the waiting car. A telepath! Then he opened them again and looked at Murad.

"You're one of them, aren't you?" he accused. "One of those 'wild talents' Ring was on about. God almighty, I'm surrounded by them."

"Just get in the car, Mr. Burke. We are already behind our schedule." Shuna's military background, courtesy of the Israeli army, was showing through. She got into the driving seat.

Johnny tried again to get through her reserve as he climbed into the back of the car followed by Murad's impressive bulk. "What's your speciality, Shuna?" he asked, settling back against the leather seat. "Ring said that—"

"Brother Tze-Ring has already said far too much in my opinion, Mr. Burke, and perhaps you would be good enough to remain silent while I get us out of this chaos." She slammed the car into gear and moved it out into the seething mass of humans, animals, and cars that crammed the wharf.

Johnny subsided, crushed by her antagonism, but Wang Ta, his natural courtesy irritated by the woman's rudeness, pointed out various things of interest as they threaded their way through the melee at a snail's pace.

Johnny answered in monosyllables, unreasonably angry at Tze-Ring for leaving him with this weird trio and too demoralized to even think about escaping.

Murad grinned across at him and nodded. "Good," he said.

Jesus Christ, thought Johnny, *not even my thoughts are my own with this lot.* He sat back, closed his eyes, and began to mentally recite all he could remember of a racy poem that should give Man Mountain something to think about. As the verses ran through his head on automatic, he wondered where Ring was and what he was doing. Unconsciously, he held the young lama's face in his mind and heard the sound of his voice in his inner ear. He could almost smell the odour of incense and herbs that hung about Tze-Ring when he wore his robe.

Abruptly, Johnny was no longer in the car but with Tze-Ring in a private jet. Two seats faced each other across a folding table covered with maps; two astonished faces looked at each other. Then Tze-Ring threw back his head and laughed.

"Oh Johnny, Johnny, you never cease to amaze me! I think that by now you must have met with Shuna. I can imagine what you must think of her." He wiped his eyes on the back of his hand and regarded Johnny's astral self with great amusement. "This will make them all sit up and take notice."

Johnny tried to speak, but the words came out silently. "Ring…how the hell…did I get here…? Where am I…what…?"

The plane and Tze-Ring faded out, came back, then faded out again. He just managed to catch the answer as it trailed behind him. "Do not worry, Johnny. You did well to find me. The bond is very strong now. I will see you soon."

Johnny's body jerked convulsively, and he came to to find three pairs of eyes regarding him with varying degrees of astonishment and concern. Shuna was the first to recover.

"We have arrived. Please do not try any tricks while we transfer to the seaplane. Murad, see that he makes no attempt to escape. Ta, come with me." She climbed out of the car and went to bargain with a water taxi to take them out to the plane, riding at anchor beyond the harbour entrance.

Murad leant back and looked at Johnny with respect. "That was some trick you pulled. Two-level thinking needs a great deal of concentration.

I got so wrapped up in your distraction ploy, I didn't realise you were projecting until it was too late. You and Tze-Ring must have a very strong bond if you were able to find him two hours' flight away, and in this country, where the astral is thick with thoughtforms. My congratulations."

"Thanks," said Johnny, wondering what he was talking about but determined not to let on. "Ring taught me to get out when I was ill back on the boat."

Murad looked at him thoughtfully but said nothing more. A few minutes later, Wang Ta returned, and they walked to a flight of stone steps leading down to the dirtiest stretch of water Johnny had ever seen. A small and very unstable-looking boat bobbed alongside the step. Its owner looked even more unsavoury than either his boat or the water. *It is now or never*, Johnny thought.

He spun on his heel, pushed Wang Ta into Murad, sending both off balance, and ran for his life. Ignoring the shouts behind him, he dodged in and out of the crowds, changing direction every few minutes. He heard the sounds of pursuit behind him and ran until his lungs were bursting. Men, women, donkeys, and bicycles laden with boxes and sacks scrambled to get out of his way as he plunged into a maze of dockyard buildings. Ahead, he saw the dark opening of a warehouse and made for it. It was dim and cool and smelled rank, but there were places in which to hide, and that made the smell worth it.

Just inside the door, Johnny leaned against the peeling paintwork and risked a look behind him. It was clear—for the moment at least.

He sank down on a pile of sacking and tried to catch his breath. Slowly, his heart rate decreased and his lungs ceased to burn, but there was no time to rest. He waited for a few minutes, then looked round for a better hiding place. He got to his feet and made his way farther into the dimness. A pile of broken packing cases had been stacked haphazardly in one corner. It leaned perilously to one side, looking in imminent danger of collapse, but for the moment Johnny could think only of hiding.

He inched his way into the least-revolting case. It smelt to high heaven and was furnished with a less-than-tasteful array of cigarette butts, to say nothing of the stains of chewing tobacco on the floor outside. The Hilton it was not, but it gave him breathing space to work out a plan. But first, he must blank out all thoughts as far as possible so that Murad could not trace him. He settled back and closed his eyes and tried to think of the blank screen of a TV.

The heat and the stench began to close in on Johnny. Thoughts of a cool beer, a lukewarm shower, and the feel of a guitar in his hands kept coming to mind. Frantically, he began to recite multiplication tables, nursery songs—anything to keep his thoughts from broadcasting his whereabouts. Then he realised anything would be likely to do just that. Johnny wracked his brains for bits of conversation he had had with Tze-Ring, trying to remember anything that might give him a chance to outwit his pursuers. Finally he dozed off.

♬ ♩ ♫ ♪ ♬ ♩ ♫

Johnny woke with a start and looked at his watch. A full hour had passed. Silently, he crept from his hiding place and made his way to the door. It was past noon, and everyone would be heading for shade and a nap. It was the best time to get away. After all, what was that phrase? *Only mad dogs and Englishmen go out in the midday sun.* Well, this Englishman was plenty mad.

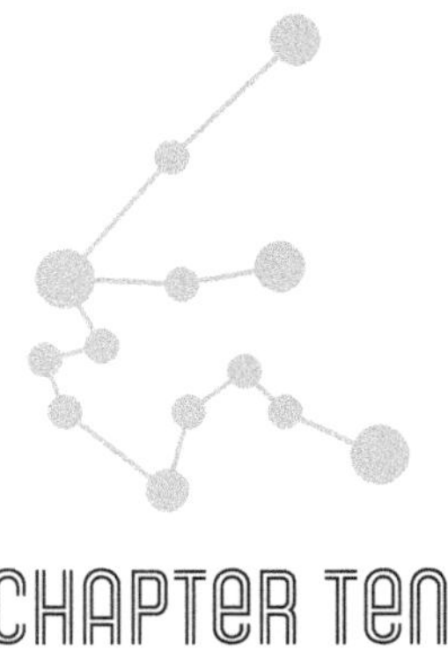

CHAPTER TEN

31 October, 10:30 p.m.
Muscat

Shuna was beside herself with rage. Thirty-six hours and Johnny Burke was still loose in Muscat. All Murad's powers had not been able to pick him up. The abbot had left the Abbey of the Aeon and was en route for his own place. Since his route was, to say the least, unusual, and since Murad's powers did not extend below the earth, he was effectively out of touch. Tze-Ring's plane had hit bad weather and made a forced landing near Rawalpindi. During the landing he had been knocked unconscious and was now recovering from a head wound and concussion. Murad refused to worry Tze-Ring until he was over it, saying that it would cause too much stress on him to search for Johnny using the strong emotional bond between them.

Shuna paced back and forth, promising herself that she would tear the hell out of Johnny Burke when she found him. Shaking with anger, she stepped onto the balcony of her hotel room and looked up at the clear night sky. Her talent reached out and began to pull and weave at the weather patterns. From nowhere, dark clouds suddenly appeared, racing across the sea and massing overhead. Thunder rumbled, and a jagged fork of lightning split the air with the sound of ripping silk. Within minutes, Muscat became the pivotal centre of a violent electrical storm that raged for the best part of three hours.

Some miles away in the car, Wang Ta shivered nervously. "Shuna sounds plenty mad. I hate it when she does this. It makes it hard to think straight."

Murad grunted. To an onlooker, he seemed to be asleep. In actual fact, he was scanning the immediate area round them for any trace of Johnny Burke's thought patterns. But there were none.

Johnny himself was some six miles away, huddled in a filthy alley, gnawing on a piece of bread he had stolen from a stall earlier in the day. He was not proud of it, but he was hungry. Of all the stupid places to make a break, Muscat was the prize. There was no embassy, no consul, and so far he had been unable to make any kind of contact with a European. He'd tried, but being accosted by a wild-eyed individual babbling about kidnappers and claiming to be a famous rock star was not the best way to win friends and influence people. He had spent the night under a wooden bench in the railway station surrounded by decaying vegetables, puddles of urine, and other less-savoury things he would rather not know about.

"Oh God, Ring, where the hell are you? Please get me out of here."

He had over-estimated his own fitness. His empty stomach and the dirty, uncooked food he had managed to find or steal had given him a bellyache. Johnny had literally begged for water from a vendor earlier in the day; it had tasted all right, but he was not sure of its purity. What if his withdrawal pains returned? God, he didn't think he could take that again. Where the hell was Ring? If he had been there, this would not have happened. It was that bloody woman. She'd gotten on his nerves.

"Ring, please, if you can hear me, come and find me."

Within seconds, there was an answer singing in his head, along with feelings of dizziness and pain.

"Johnny, I am here. Hold on to the pattern of my name. Pull me towards you, Johnny. I am trying to find you."

Johnny lurched to his feet, hope flaring in his heart. "Ring! Christ, Ring, where are you? I'm here. It's an alley downtown somewhere. I don't know the street. Oh God, Ring, I'm so tired."

"I do not need the name, Johnny. Just keep talking and try to focus your thoughts. Think of a lighthouse. Make it taller than the buildings round you. Make its light the focal point of your thoughts and keep repeating my name. Good. Stronger, stronger, yes. Yes, I see it! Murad, in the old town there is a neon sign advertising Coca-Cola, and next to it a cinema. Wait, there is a street name. Ham…Hamrudhin, I think. It is difficult to hold it when my head hurts."

"Ring? Ring, are you there? What's wrong with you? My head is hurting, I feel dizzy an' sick. Ring, it's you, isn't it? I'm picking up the way you're feeling. You're hurt! I'm comin'. Hang on, fella."

Johnny staggered from the alleyway into the main street and reeled towards the general area of the harbour. The late-night crowd drew away from the strange, filthy figure. Dark eyes watched speculatively from shadowy doorways. He leaned against a shop window to catch his breath and was chased away by its irate owner.

Weaving his way through the crowds, Johnny came to a wooden bench alongside a bus stop and sat down to collect his thoughts. Murad—he must get hold of Murad. Head in hand, he built up a picture of the dark brown face and silently called his name.

Almost instantly, Murad's voice sounded in his head. "I have you, Johnny. Show me where you are. Look round and feed me what you can see."

"Er, a main street not far from the harbour. There's a sort of market nearby with food stalls, clothes, pots and pans, things like that. There's a small park area behind me with a fountain in it. A bus stop and a bench. Did you hear Ring? I think he's hurt. I could feel his head hurting. God almighty, I'm beginning to act and sound like one of you lot."

"Tze-Ring's plane had to make a forced landing, and he was knocked unconscious. He's all right—just a touch of concussion and several stitches in that hard head of his. The Dark Ones seeking your whereabouts thought you were with him and engineered the crash. Johnny, you must help me to find you."

"Uh, there's a sort of mosque over on the right. Big place. There's a board with some writing, but I can't read it; it's in Arabic."

"Visualise the writing in your head, Johnny. Damn this storm, it's shortening my range. Shuna, for the love of Allah, stop messing around! Ah, got it. Ta, turn right at the lights and take the first left; I'll guide you from there."

The voice in Johnny's head fell silent and he shivered, still partly linked to Tze-Ring. Bile and sickness rose in his throat, and he lurched to his feet and threw up in the gutter. By the time the car screeched to a halt in front of him, Johnny was swaying from side to side and almost out. Murad slid out, picked him up bodily, and bundled him into the back seat, instructing the empathic Wang Ta to stabilise him. Then, taking the wheel, Murad sent the machine speeding through the night towards the hotel where Shuna waited, weak with relief that her charge had been found. Facing the abbot was not going to be pleasant.

Twenty minutes later, they parked the car in the underground lot of the hotel. Heaving the almost-unconscious Johnny out of the back seat, Murad carried him into the lift and up to the fifth floor. Wang Ta went ahead to open the door. It was flung open as they approached, and a furious Shuna opened her mouth to scream abuse, then shut it when she realised the object of her scorn was in no fit state to listen.

With a mixture of gentle bullying and sheer strength, Murad got Johnny undressed, showered, and into bed, then left it to Wang Ta to feed him hot, sweet tea and soothing vibrations. Johnny fell asleep before finishing the first and during the second.

Shuna stood at the side of the bed, looking at the exhausted figure. The eyes, dulled by his condition, opened, and a whisper hung on the still air.

"Sorry, Shuna. That was a dumb thing to do."

Shuna gnawed her bottom lip, watching him for a few minutes, then returned to the lounge. The others were waiting. Murad glared at her.

"I blame you for this, Shuna. If you hadn't been so determined to make a point about hating rock stars, he wouldn't have tried it. We'd never have found him if Tze-Ring hadn't regained consciousness when he did. Without their mental bond, it would have been hopeless. He is not the weak lout you took him to be. He has an amazing mind. Mostly subconscious as yet, but its power is there, ready to be tapped. If ever he—"

Murad sat up as a bubble of displaced air popped loudly and the small, frail figure of the abbot, edged with light, stood before them. He was, to say the least, irate. His astral form literally quivered with tightly controlled anger.

"Sister Shuna, Brother Murad, Brother Wang Ta, I believe I am owed an explanation."

An hour later, a subdued trio watched room service wheel in their delayed meal. As the door closed behind the waiter, Wang Ta voiced the thought uppermost in all their minds.

"I would not like to go through that again," he said. "I do not think I have ever seen the abbot so angry. I fully understand that we learn by experience, but as far as I am concerned, that experience was a one-off." Wang Ta shuddered. For an empath, close contact with any strong emotion was uncomfortable unless trained to use a shield, and the abbot's icily controlled anger had dispensed with his in the first few moments.

Murad heaved his bulk out of the armchair and went to check on Johnny, then returned to his chair and reached for a plate. "That makes two of us, my friend. Or can I make that three?" He cocked an eyebrow at the silent Shuna.

She nodded, still in shock after enduring forty-five minutes of the abbot's condemnation of her dereliction of duty.

"I admit I was taken in by his reputation. I thought he was all mouth. But when he projected like that, and the power he built up when he thought Tze-Ring was badly hurt...God, the entire city could have run for a week on that charge. Me and my big mouth."

Wang Ta was already tucking into the food. "I suggest you use that mouth for eating and get this food down, you. We must be on our way earlier than we had planned. Now things have changed. I must file a new flight plan first thing in the morning."

They ate in silence, then divided up the remaining hours with one keeping watch and two sleeping. Tomorrow would be a long day.

3 November, 8:00 a.m.
The Khamal Hotel, Tibet

Frank Saunders rolled out of bed, yawned widely, and glanced down at his watch. *Holy shit! Eight o'clock already.* He wandered over to the window and out onto the small and rickety veranda. He yawned again as he took in the scene round him, then forgot to close his mouth. Last night when he had arrived, it had been too dark to see anything other than the dim lights on either side of the hotel door. Bone-weary and sticky with sweat and dust, he had eaten, showered, and was in bed and asleep within thirty minutes. Now he was awake and he could see the mountains.

In the morning light, they were breath-taking. The colours ran from palest blue through to deepest purple. It was not just one range, but many that seemed to go on and on to the ends of the earth. In the clear air they looked near enough to touch from the veranda, sharp enough to cut the hand that touched them. Icily remote and so arrogant in their beauty, they defied comparison with lesser peaks.

He'd been right not to stay in Srinagar, thought Frank—too much like civilisation everywhere else. The hotels were full of Americans, Germans, Australians, and the odd Englishman looking for adventure with all mod cons. So he'd moved on to one of the little hill towns. The so called "bus" to the area had been little more than a truck with wooden seats, shared with humans and livestock alike. But this…Frank let his eyes, mind, and soul feast on the sight before him. This was worth every ache and pain collected along the way, and that included the splinters!

He showered, dressed, and went in search of food. Three cups of coffee and an unidentifiable omelette later, he ambled into the one and only street. It was market day, judging from the crowds. Small wooden stalls had been set up and a variety of offerings laid out for sale: brassware and embroidered waistcoats, leather slippers and belts with huge buckles inset with turquoise. Frank bought several to take home. The lads would like them, and they would look great on stage.

A herd of sheep and goats milled past Frank on their way to be sold, and he stopped for tea at a tiny, one-roomed cafe filled with herdsmen and chattering women eating momo, a steamed, meat-filled dumpling that smelt terrible but tasted delicious. Around midday, just as Frank was thinking of returning to the hotel, a procession of monks entered the town and settled themselves in the local square. They unfurled prayer flags and richly hued banners and, with the aid of the householders, hung them from the balconies and roofs of the houses and shops. This done, they arranged themselves into an orchestra of sorts and began to chant to an accompaniment of drums of all shapes and sizes, cymbals, and the huge *radung*, ten-foot-long horns that took Frank's breath away when he heard them sound.

A hand on his shoulder made him turn. It was Dawa, the manager of the hotel.

"You are lucky, Mr. Frank. This is a special day. Very lucky indeed. Today we will see *thangkas*." He gestured towards the huge banners with a reverent hand. "*Thangkas* bring good luck and prosperity to those who see them. Come, sit closer." He herded Frank to the front of the crowd and sat him on a wooden seat hired from a shopkeeper and produced two cups of liquid, one of which he urged on his guest. "It's good. We call it *chang*. It's made from barley, like your English beer."

No, thought Frank, endeavouring to breathe through a throat that had suddenly turned to fire, *not quite like beer*. He wiped streaming eyes and smiled at the beaming Dawa. "Yeah, it's good." Frank smiled weakly.

Squatting comfortably beside him, Dawa began to explain the ceremony now in full fling. "These small drums are called *daru*. They are beaten to send away evil spirits. We also use cymbals. Evil spirits do not like loud noises. Ah, look, Mr. Frank. Here come the dancers!"

Down the small street came a group of fantastic forms dressed in elaborate red and yellow costumes with collars of beaten silver decorated with semiprecious stones. They wore masks painted to look like demons and carried *dorje* ("thunderbolt," translated Dawa) as weapons. Slowly they danced, miming out their intent to enslave the monks and those they protected. Then from the opposite end of the street came the good spirits, equally intent on defeating their opponents. The two groups came together, clashing their cymbals and thunderbolts and leaping high into the air. Over it all was the incessant drumming and the chanting of the monks. Frank was entranced; the noise did not affect someone who had spent most of his adult life around amplifiers and rock bands. He clapped and swayed and shouted encouragement like everyone else during the performance.

Then suddenly, it all stopped. The drums, the bells and cymbals, the chanting and the dancing—it just ended. Everyone began to walk away. The monks gathered up their instruments and the offerings given to them throughout the day. Frank, taken by surprise, stood up and looked round him. And in that instant, he saw Johnny.

He was just across the street, standing in the middle of a small group of people. They surrounded him as if acting as protectors: a short, slim man, and beside him a dark-haired woman talking to Johnny; behind them stood a very tall man, broad of shoulder and looking like an all-American quarterback. Next to him was another man, slim with a shaven head and wearing the saffron robe of a Buddhist monk. In the fraction of time before Frank yelled "Johnny! Johnny!" the monk and the tall man raised their heads and looked in his direction. Johnny looked up as well. For a split second, everything stopped. Then Frank began to run across the square.

At that moment the monks, now finished with their performance, formed into a procession and began to move. This meant Frank had to dart in and out of their ranks to get across. He could see Johnny being hustled away down a side alley and frantically pushed and shoved against bodies in an effort to get closer. Frank could hear Johnny's voice calling to him. Then he was on the other side and the alley was empty.

"Frank! It was Frank, my buddy from the group. Shit, Ring, you gotta let me speak to him, just for a moment. Please, Ring, just one moment. Frank! Hey, Frank! Tell them—tell them I'm OK! Frank—"

♬ ♩ ♫ ♪ ♬ ♪ ♫

Frank searched every alley in town. He looked, called, asked, offered money, and threatened. Finally he admitted defeat and returned to the hotel. Dawa protested that he had seen nothing but had returned to the hotel to arrange the evening meal. Frank said nothing. He went to his room and sat facing the window and the mountains. His system had undergone a severe shock. Against all odds, his dream had come true. He had found Johnny, only to lose him again. Unseeingly, Frank stared through the open window at the sun setting over the distant mountains, turning them to gold.

"They look like the mountains in Johnny's song, do they not, Mr. Saunders? His words and your music, they blend well together."

The voice was cultured, the English precise. Frank turned slowly. The young monk was standing in the doorway, his hand on the doorknob.

"May I come in?"

Frank nodded and went to stand on the veranda, his hopelessness making him indifferent to this stranger who had spirited his friend away.

"I know how you must feel. Coming all this way on just a 'hunch' is proof of your affection for Johnny. If that had not been so, you would never have found him. There is between all of you a bond that we in the abbey have greatly underestimated."

"Why have you come here?" asked Frank dully. "And why didn't you let us speak to each other? You could have done that at least."

Tze-Ring moved closer and laid a gentle hand on Frank's shoulder. Its warmth flowed down and filled the emptiness inside.

The musician turned and looked at him. In this place, with the mountains so close and the whole atmosphere feeling as if it was out of step with time itself, Frank felt a faint stirring of foreboding.

"Things will never be the same, will they?" he said, knowing it to be true. "Even if he came back now, things would never be the same."

"No, they can never be the same, but because they will never be the same, a new stage in the evolution of humanity will happen. It is the reason for which Johnny was born, Mr. Saunders. The reason I was born three years ahead of him to wait and to be by his side. He is my half-brother. We share the same father, though he does not know this yet. You will see him again when the time is right. You will play together again, but not in the same way or for the same reasons."

Frank turned and looked fully at his visitor for the first time. Close up, he could see the resemblance to Johnny. It was there in the bone structure and the wide set of the eyes, not green like Johnny's but dark as bitter chocolate. Though this man was taller, the build was the same, and odd quirks in the way of standing and smiling linked them together.

After a few minutes of silence, Frank spoke quietly.

"How can I tell Colin and the others that I found him and lost him again?"

"You need tell only Mr. Buckman. He will understand." Tze-Ring's voice turned urgent. "Mr. Saunders—Frank—I have instructions for you from the abbot. It is imperative that you keep the man you know as Tango in the group, no matter what happens. He is the focal point of the Dark seeking to destroy Johnny. If we know where he is at all times, it is easier to foil their plans. Do you understand me?"

A clarity filled Frank's mind, a sense of being part of a greater whole. With it came a feeling of joy and a bitter knowledge. "Johnny is in danger, isn't he?"

"The Forerunner is always in danger, Frank Saunders."

Frank looked out at the deepening shadows and was silent for a time. Then he said, "I think I'll go home tomorrow."

There was no answer, but he knew he was already alone.

CHAPTER ELEVEN

8 November, 11:00 a.m.
Somewhere in the Karakoram range

Johnny shut his eyes tightly, clamped his hands to the rock on his left, and hung on for dear life. His stomach told him there was nothing below him for several thousand feet. His mind told him he was on a reasonably wide (all of three feet) ledge and firmly roped to a solidly built Sherpa in front and Man Mountain Murad behind. None of this helped. Johnny was frozen with fear and could move neither backwards nor forwards. No amount of coaxing or bullying had any effect.

Murad sighed and sat down with his feet dangling over the edge of the chasm. This was the third time since sunrise, and Allah alone knew how many times since they had left the main track and begun the long, slow climb to the pass. He looked at the heights above them and calculated that the unscheduled stop had cost them the time needed to make the pass today.

A shout from the forward line of porters heralded the arrival of Tze-Ring, the only one Johnny would trust. *Thanks be to Allah*, thought Murad, *that Shuna went ahead with Wang Ta, taking the usual route. She would have blown her top with these constant halts.* Then they would have had blizzards to contend with as well as Johnny's vertigo.

Tze-Ring came down the icy slope like a lithe snow leopard. Hearing his voice, Johnny made the mistake of opening his eyes just in time to see Tze-Ring step fearlessly right to the very edge of the path as he passed the Sherpa in front of him. With a moan of terror, Johnny closed his eyes again and buried his head against the wall of snow.

"Johnny, calm down. You must try and make the effort to conquer your fear. You will not fall, I promise you."

Murad cast unbelieving eyes in the general direction of heaven and crossed the fingers of both hands inside his mittens. It was his personal belief that Tze-Ring's genetic makeup carried a large proportion of mountain goat. It made even him feel queasy to see the young lama take these icy paths at something close to a run.

The mountain goat in question was untying Johnny's rope from the Sherpa's waist and re-tying it round his own. Then Tze-Ring motioned for Murad to pass his rope to the Sherpa and go ahead and tie on to the leading group. Johnny was now securely tied between the man he trusted most and a solidly built Sherpa who could easily hold his weight should he slip. With his eyes still closed, Johnny began to inch his way forward, following the sound of the calm and encouraging voice ahead of him.

"Johnny, open your eyes. Don't look down, just look at the wall beside you and keep close to it. Follow it as it bends around to the left. That is good. Now, there is a slightly tricky bit here."

Johnny's eyes flew open, and he stared with horror at the broken rock and gaping hole in the path before him. The little colour left in his face faded away, and he looked ready to faint.

"If you faint on me now, Johnny Burke, I swear I will drop you off the edge myself. Get a grip on yourself or I will black your eye as I did on the *Ortega Star*."

The words stung. Johnny's head came up. His green eyes glinted angrily.

"You can bloody well try, mister, but don't forget who won that round."

"We both did, just now," came the answer.

Johnny looked down and found himself on the other side of the broken path. He looked at his companion, who grinned widely and turned to continue the climb. The path now broadened out to a point where it looked passably safe, although the drop on the far side was still a nightmare as far as Johnny was concerned.

The twelve figures climbed steadily upwards, following an ancient path. Since they had started a few days ago, the gradual increase in altitude had played havoc with Johnny's system. Bouts of nausea combined with dizziness and an accelerated heartbeat had slowed them down. Although there was no actual climbing as such, the slow upward haul took a toll on a physique that had not long ago shaken off drug and alcohol addiction. They had come across several small villages and rested there, but it was too late in the year to wait for long, and Tze-Ring urged them on.

They had used four-wheel drive for the first hundred miles, but their route led deep into uncharted peaks and valleys, and the only way in was by tough little mountain ponies and yaks. Then, finally, by foot. Each day took them deeper into the high Karakoram peaks and further from all that Johnny knew. This was a place where the mountains were higher than the clouds, where the sunshine was made twice as bright by the whiteness of the snow.

Johnny's manner had been subdued since his abortive escape. It had resulted in an acerbic telephone call from the abbot and a promise that if he tried again, he would be punished. As they approached the high passes and had to negotiate the narrow ledges that passed for paths spiralling round the closely packed peaks, Johnny began to react. His attacks of vertigo and panic made them all doubt the wisdom of the decision to bring him over the mountains. It had toughened him in one way but had taken its toll in others.

By the fourth day they were climbing well out of the usual routes and into virtually forgotten land. They were on the borders now, but no one could have said if they were in Pakistan, India, China, or Tibet. It was simply a wilderness of snow and ice. At night they camped beneath overhangs of rock, a cave if they were lucky, or else simply against the wall of ice that towered over them, making Johnny feel more like an ant than a man. In the few moments when Johnny forgot his fear and looked round him, he felt the vastness of the ranges and their mystique. He discovered they had voices, high, windy voices that called, sang, and howled without stopping, hour after hour, day after muscle-cracking day. Terrified beyond measure, Johnny fought his inner battles. Both Tze-Ring and Murad knew it but could not help. Victory, if it came, had to come from within.

Then they came to the bridge. If the narrow paths had been bad, this was worse. Made from waist-thick rope, four strands (two top and two bottom) launched themselves across empty space. The lower strands supported pierced and weathered boards, each tied firmly to its rope support on either side. The top strands had been covered over the years with brightly coloured prayer flags until it was hard to see the actual rope. Thousands of feet below, a river roared and plunged its way between sheer walls, fighting its imprisonment by the might of the mountains. But here, close to the peak, the bridge swayed and tossed in the freezing gales that cut through the gorge on their eternal journey to somewhere else.

The leading Sherpas, used to such hazards, crossed easily with their packs perched precariously on their broad backs. They leaned and balanced and swayed with the gusts, and it seemed to Johnny that they were dancing with the wind itself. Then it was his turn.

Johnny thought about just sitting down and refusing to move, but that would make him out to be a coward, and worse, it would let Ring down. Putting the first foot on the bridge had been fairly easy; taking the other foot off terra firma and putting it alongside its twin was quite another thing. As there were two others ahead of him, the entire bridge was dipping and swaying with their weight as well as with the wind. The drill was to cross no more than three at a time, and it was his turn.

Johnny clutched the ropes as if clutching to life itself and inched out over the empty void below him. The bridge pitched and tossed as the wind howled with fury and tore at his fur-lined chuba and ski mask. Never in his life had he felt so alone and vulnerable as he did on that swaying bridge over a drop of sixteen thousand feet.

A third of the way across, Johnny's nerve crumbled and he tried to turn, but someone was behind him—he had to go on. It was an insanely inappropriate thought that saved his sanity. That morning he had asked Tze-Ring the date, and in the middle of his battle on the bridge, Johnny remembered the answer. It was the eighth of November, exactly one week from his twenty-fourth birthday, and he was on a rope bridge thousands of feet in the air somewhere in Tibet. It was all too much. Then his feet slipped from under him.

Johnny's gut-wrenching scream of fear bounced off the mountains round them and ricocheted from peak to peak, intensifying both sound and fear a thousandfold. Its vibration dislodged a mass of snow that roared down the slopes to leap out into space and tumble endlessly, down and down, until it melted in the speed and friction of its fall and rained on the river below.

Those waiting behind Johnny flung themselves flat and hung on to whatever they could grab to keep themselves from being taken over the edge with the avalanche. Johnny hung by his hands to the top rope, his feet flailing in the thin air. He could feel his grip going. The wet surface of his sheepskin mittens could not hold more than a few moments. *He was going to die.*

Then a large brown hand gripped Johnny's wrist and held him fast. In the intensity of fear, Johnny's mind tuned in to the highly trained talents of the abbey. There were no sounds and no voices, just lightning-swift impressions that snapped back and forth over his head.

Tze-Ring: "Murad, for the love of all that you hold dear, hang on to him."

Murad: "I have him, but I cannot lift him alone—the angle is wrong, I have no room to manoeuvre. You will have to use your talent to help me lift him."

Tze-Ring: "I will take as much of his weight as I can from this side of the bridge. On my word...One, two, three, *now*."

Tze-Ring was on his hands and knees at the very edge of the chasm. Murad, also on his knees, had Johnny's wrist in a one-handed death grip with his free hand bare to the cold, gripping the top rope.

Even as Tze-Ring spoke, Johnny's hands finally slipped from the rope, and only Murad's strength lay between him and the end of all their hopes. Johnny could no longer think or feel. He had passed beyond the boundaries of fear; he simply waited for the outcome of the battle for his life. Mentally, he reached out, and in doing so touched a watching Presence and sensed that It, too, was waiting.

Johnny looked up into Murad's fear-filled face and felt a great love for this man he hardly knew. Incredibly, he smiled and touched him mentally, taking it for granted that he would receive the message. *Whatever happens, Murad, thank you.*

Then Johnny felt a pressure build up beneath his booted feet. It reached up and encompassed his knees and thighs, and slowly he began to rise, pushed upwards by Tze-Ring's kinetic talent. The young lama had never lifted a dead weight before, especially one so precious. But his brother's life depended on getting him to a point of balance where Murad's physical strength could take over.

Minute by agonising minute, Tze-Ring inched the weight up until, with a shout of triumph, Murad grabbed Johnny's coat with his other hand and heaved him onto the bridge. For several minutes, the two men simply crouched with their arms round each other. Then Murad lifted his head, his eyes wide.

"Tze-Ring!" he shouted to Johnny above the wind. "I can't sense him."

Murad handed Johnny over to one of the Sherpas and literally ran across the bridge to where his friend lay unconscious, the snow beneath his head stained bright with the blood that flowed from his nose. Johnny was only a few seconds behind, having crossed the bridge without a second thought.

With Murad carrying Tze-Ring's unconscious form, they made their way further from the bridge and sheltered beneath an overhanging rock. The Sherpas built walls of tightly packed snow round them, and within the small three-man tents, they made camp for the night.

It was midnight before Tze-Ring came around, weak but fully conscious. His first words were typical: "Next time, we will teleport you across." Then he turned his face into Murad's shoulder and slept.

Johnny stayed awake far into the night, listening to the wind that had so nearly snatched him to his death. He searched deep inside himself, looking for the taste and smell of the fear that had beset him at that moment, but it had gone. He had faced death and won, faced fear and sent it scuttling back into the darkness. Now he had to learn to face himself.

Johnny snuggled down into his sleeping bag, one arm thrown protectively over his brother, and slept.

13 November, 4:00 a.m.
Deep in the Karakoram range

"Johnny, Johnny, come quickly. As quickly as you can, or you will miss it!"

Lungs bursting, Johnny hauled himself up to where Tze-Ring stood waiting for him, his dark eyes crinkling with amusement at his surliness.

"Hurry! I want you to see it while the sun is at the right angle."

"See what?" wheezed Johnny, sagging limply against the snow wall. Tze-Ring simply gestured with a gloved hand, and Johnny looked down and outwards.

Far below lay a wide valley with fields laid out in neat shapes that scored the brown wintery earth. A broad, swift-flowing river cut through the fields and tumbled over rocks and boulders as if hurrying to warmer climes. Along its banks, herds of animals—rough-haired goats, sheep, and the inevitable yaks—were taking their first drink of the day before making their way to the sparse pastures sprinkled with overnight snow.

Beyond the fields, Johnny could see a village of stone houses mostly roofed with snow-covered turf and wearing the inevitable brightly coloured prayer flags like hair ribbons. At first it looked like any of the hill villages Johnny had seen since they had entered the high country, but a second look told him this one was different. At the western end of the valley, where the ground rose sharply and steeply to become one with the mountain range, sat a many-times-larger-than-life-sized figure of the Buddha. Skilfully cast in bronze it sat, serene and beautiful, gazing down the valley towards the rising sun. Even allowing for the distance, Johnny estimated it must be at least sixty feet high. But it was not just the figure that demanded his attention and made his breath catch in his throat.

Some five hundred feet above the valley floor, built on a natural plateau, stood the Abbey of the Dawn. The dark shadows cast by the overhanging rock and the early morning mists rolling away down the valley gave the building the appearance of hanging in mid-air. It rose, tier upon tier, nestling back against the protective breast of the mountains. It looked as if it had been waiting for him since the beginning of time.

But it was the colour that created the real magic. Like some cosmic alchemist, the winter sun cast a golden haze over the lowest part of the valley. Slowly but surely, it crept up over the fields, the dusting of snow crystals catching the light and reflecting it back to the mountains. It touched the feet and then the folded hands of the Buddha, turning the bronze flesh into a flame that could be seen for miles. The light climbed the white stone walls of the houses and lingered to join the wind as it danced with the prayer flags. As Johnny stared, the full impact of the sun's light hit the sheltered plateau face on, illuminating the abbey and making it burn with solar fire. Wherever they touched, the rays enhanced the awesome beauty of both the abbey and its surroundings. It gilded the walls and underlined the mysterious shadows cast by the dark red of the wooden roofs. A moment more and the colour spilt over the snow-draped mountains, turning the valley as far as the eye could see into a cascade of molten gold.

"You see, Johnny, here are your Mountains of Gold." Tze-Ring stood by his side, sharing the experience. "As often as I see it, it never fails to lift my soul. Its true glory is best seen like this, at dawn, though sunset has its own kind of beauty. Then the shadows seem to race through the valley like a great dragon eating up the light to store as flame for the next sunrise.

"It will take us the rest of the day to descend this mountain, and we will camp tonight at the entrance to the valley, but soon you will enter the Abbey of the Dawn."

Tze-Ring turned away, but Johnny remained standing and looking. Then he too turned away and followed the Sherpas along the narrow ledge that led gradually down towards the valley floor. Johnny plodded along after his guides with only part of his mind on what he was doing; his thoughts were full of what he had seen and its implications. It was only later, when they halted for a while to eat and rest, that it occurred to Johnny he had walked along the very edge of a precipice that fell sheer for thousands of feet without a qualm. He grinned into his bowl of tsampa. Tze-Ring was right—you could get used to anything.

But beautiful as it was, Johnny didn't intend to get used to living in the Abbey of the Dawn. At the first opportunity, he planned to escape. And this time he would make it.

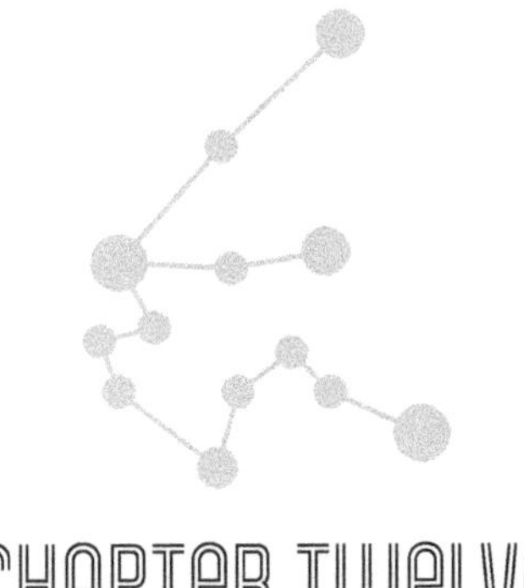

CHAPTER TWELVE

13 November, 7:30 p.m.
The penthouse, London

"Whaddya think, Florrie?"

Colin Buckman performed an exaggerated catwalk twirl with one hand on his hip. Florrie swallowed the last of her gin and eyed him up and down. In the past six weeks he had lost twelve pounds in weight, cut his alcohol intake to less than half, and almost lost his craving for tobacco. In his new tuxedo, he looked almost handsome.

"Quite the nob, Bucky, and not before it's time neither."

Bucky came round the sofa and pulled the giggling Florrie to her feet. He planted a kiss on her slightly over-rouged cheek. "That's my girl. Now, let's paint the town. We deserve something to take our minds off things."

They fell silent, both remembering it was the disappearance of Johnny that had brought them closer together.

Florrie picked a non-existent piece of fluff off Bucky's lapel and smoothed his sleeve. "I know, *miro chal*, but we must believe what we've been told. We'll see 'im again. After all, Frank said he looked well when he saw 'im."

"Yeah, well, let's go then." Bucky held out Florrie's wrap and escorted her to the door. He went on, "I've booked a table at Quintana's after the show; I thought you'd like that. Then we'll come back for a nightcap." He looked round at the empty flat as he closed the door and sighed.

As the lift descended, Florrie tried to lift her companion's spirits. "Lyle rang me the other day to tell me about the weddin', said the invite was on its way. I gather 'er mum and dad refused to come, so you're going to give the bride away. I'm looking forward to a knees-up at this weddin', so I'll be stayin' over."

"You know there's a place for you anytime, Florrie love. Johnny's room is yours as long as you want it."

"Yes, well, I may, and then again I may not," said Florrie mysteriously. "By the way, what's this I hear about Tango cutting a solo record? I thought you had 'is contract sewn up nice an' tight."

"Nothin's settled yet," said Bucky, hurrying her through the lobby to the waiting limo. "He says he's had an offer from the US to record the title song for a new Bond film. He's been blowing his mouth off to the press as usual. Did you know he's moved out of the penthouse? Bought a place in the country, out in the boonies. Never took him for a country boy. He's up to something, Florrie—I can feel it. When Frank phoned from Delhi on his way home, he said that abbey bloke had warned us not to let Tango out of our sight. They reckon he's mixed up with some lot over on the dark side. Frank's back tomorrow...We'll know more then, I hope."

The car slid through the brightly lit streets towards the West End and the glittering night that awaited them, but Bucky was thoughtful and withdrawn. Florrie put a gentle hand on his arm and queried his mood.

"What's wrong, Colin m'dear? It's not just Johnny, it's somethin' else. I can feel it. Do you want to talk about it?"

"Ah, Florrie, it's no good trying to hide things from you. Yeah, things are happening to me inside, Flo, things I don't understand. It's like I'm finding a part of me that's been lost since I was a tike. I dream a lot, usually about the same things. There's a woman; I'd say in her early seventies and Scottish by her voice. Sometimes a man. Tall, with a pommy accent. Y'know, Guards stuff. But I can't remember the dream in the morning. I know it's important, and it links in with what's happened to Johnny."

Florrie noted the shadows beneath his eyes and the slightly haunted look about him. This was a man undergoing some kind of inner battle. She had never been blessed with the full Gift of the Romani, but she knew enough to know that Colin had changed a great deal over the last month; what she knew of Johnny's mentors told her that they were at the root of it.

Then the limo drew up outside the Palladium and the trivia of the outside world thrust itself upon them.

♬ ♩ ♫ ♪ ♬ ♪ ♫

By the interval, Bucky was fit to be tied. The show was gaudy, badly written, had little in the way of talent, and he hated the music. Only the fact that it was Florrie's long-promised night out kept him from sitting it out in the bar. At curtain fall, he heaved a sigh of relief and said to her, "You don't really want to go backstage in that crush, do you Florrie?"

She chuckled and patted his cheek and suggested they have dinner, then go back to the penthouse for coffee. Evading the throng hurrying to congratulate or commiserate with the cast, they made for the lobby. The limo picked them up with little trouble, and within thirty minutes they were seated at their table.

Bucky perused the menu and, after consulting with Florrie, ordered their meal, then sat back to watch her enjoy herself. He pointed out the celebrities as they entered and laughed at her enthusiasm for star spotting. He was used to the glitz, but her glee at mixing with film and television idols rubbed off on him. Some stopped at their table to speak with Bucky, and Florrie found her status as Johnny's aunt was up there with the rest of them.

As their first course was being served, Colin heard a voice he knew coming from behind him. Florrie saw the blood drain from his face, paused her acerbic comments on the almost-non-existent dress of an up-and-coming starlet, and looked to see what had alarmed him.

An elderly couple were waiting to be shown to a table. The woman was small and slight, her dress of dark green velvet highlighting her fresh complexion. Her companion was tall and upright as only a trained soldier can be, immaculate in his evening wear and with an air of authority that stood out in the crowded room. The authority, however, did not bring him a table in the restaurant. The maitre d' was desolate but adamant.

"Are you certain you booked the table for tonight, William? Could it not have been tomorrow, do you think?"

The soft Scottish accent was one Colin Buckman knew well, just as he knew the clipped tones that answered her.

"Damn it, Margaret. I told Masters to book for the tenth. I can't look over the blasted man's shoulder all the time."

As the couple turned to leave, Colin rose to his feet.

"Uh, please excuse me, but I think we've met someplace before. If you'd care to join us as my guests, it would be real...I mean, we'd be honoured."

The couple paused and looked at him. Then the woman smiled and inclined her head.

"Why, William, it's Mr. Buckman! What a pleasant surprise to see you. Are you enjoying all those books you've been buying?" She held out her hand encased in a white kid glove, and as Bucky touched it, everything he had experienced with the two Watchers flooded back. His smile matched hers for brilliance.

"Ah yes, Mr. Buckman. From Australia, I believe." The brigadier shook hands, bowing slightly. "What a charming gesture to invite us to join you. It's a sort of anniversary for us, and I'm afraid my man got the dates mixed. Damned annoying!"

Beside himself with glee, Bucky tipped the waiter to add two chairs to their table and introduced them to a flustered Florrie. Dinner was ordered, and the evening got underway.

Despite their differences in background, the four got on well. Florrie, with her sharp sense of humour, regaled them with stories from her circus days, their guests listening enraptured. In turn the brigadier offered tales of jungle warfare and espionage while Bucky and Margaret talked books. They ate their way steadily through several courses, with their guests insisting on providing the wine to accompany each one. Finally, well-fed and mellow, coffee at the penthouse was agreed upon, and they all drove back in the limo, laughing and chatting like old friends.

Once there, Margaret went into raptures over the view and the brigadier over Bucky's collection of single malts, but when Florrie had served the coffee and liqueurs, she stopped all conversation dead with her next statement.

"If I'm not mistaken," she remarked, sitting back with her coffee, "you'll be something to do with the people who've got my Johnny, and possibly them as is responsible for Colin being so jumpy of late."

In the ensuing silence, Florrie sipped her coffee, then went on. "You needn't looked so shocked. I'm Romani and I can tell an outsider a mile off. I've seen it coming over Colin for some weeks now, but you two, you're old hands. I think it's time we all came clean."

The Watchers looked at each other and then at Florrie and Bucky. The brigadier cleared his throat. "I'd say it looks like we have two of them instead of just the one, Margaret. What do you think?"

"Och, I think it's always much nicer to work with a partner anyway. Now that the earth-level meeting has happened, it will be much easier if Colin has someone with whom he can talk and share things." Margaret leaned forward and patted Florrie's arm. "Suppose you and I meet up tomorrow and have a wee talk, just the two of us, without the menfolk cluttering up the place. Tea at the Savoy, I think. Public enough for safety but discreet enough to talk. Would 3:30 suit you, Florence?"

"I'll be there on the dot. I've decided to stay on in London for a few days to do a bit of shopping and suchlike. Perhaps…" Her voice tailed off. A subtle and terrifying change had come over the room. It infiltrated the atmosphere of friendship and trust that had been building up, turning it into a miasma of desolation and emptiness.

As if on a pre-arranged signal, all four became alert and defensive. Every sense was quickened and ready. The room lost its heat, the lighting became flat and dull, and a feeling of bleak loneliness surrounded them. Tendrils of coldness stole into their veins and numbed their thoughts, and it crossed Bucky's mind that this was what it must be like to be a zombie. Then a passing barge hooted loudly and broke their paralysis.

Instinctively, all four rose to their feet, facing to the quarters, and for a moment everything was still. Then the brigadier lifted something from round his neck. Colour flashed as he held out a chain, from which hung a golden Eye of Horus centred with a star sapphire. His voice, used to commanding men in battle, rolled sonorously across the room. The ancient words gathered strength and something even more powerful: the very essence of Light itself, a vibration that held an echo of the First Word of Creation.

"I am a child of Light, and I cannot be overcome by the Darkness. My sword is a trained will and my shield is a pure heart. Mighty is the power of that which brought the universe into being and holds the power of Light in Its hand. The Eye of the One, who is the rightful Lord of both the Light and the Dark, is upon this place, and It will suffer no evil to maintain itself within these walls. By the power of this talisman, and by the power I command as a High Priest of the Sun, by the authority of the One, blessed be His name, given into my hands in another time and in another place, I command thee to go hence and leave this place, lest the mighty warriors of Michael are summoned against you."

There was a loud crack. The lights flickered madly, and a choking mist began to fill the room. Margaret drew close to her magical partner, standing slightly behind him with one hand resting lightly upon his shoulder, adding her lunar power to that of his solar strength. Florrie reached out for Bucky's hand and he clutched at it tightly, holding his breath. He pushed her behind him and sought deep within himself for courage to face the unknown attacker. The books had given no information on this kind of thing.

A dull orange globe emanated from the focal point, a reading lamp on the desk. Swirling and pulsing and filled with a feeling of hatred, it advanced toward the brigadier as if defying his invocation. The older man stood fast, the talisman held in his outstretched hand. His voice, when it came again, was strangely gentle.

"Return to your Dark master, my son, and do not enter this place again. It is now forbidden to you. The One true Master of Light be with you in your prison of desolation. You must fight to gain your freedom from that which consumes you or remain a slave to the Lords of Darkness forever."

The globe expanded, contracted, and expanded again. For a second, a familiar face was clear within its depths. Then it fled back to the lamp, which exploded, sending glass shards into the wall and leaving the metal stand bent and twisted.

The dead weight of silence filled the room. The four people standing close together could feel the gradual return of normality. The warmth and soft golden light from the remaining lamps seeped slowly into room and bodies alike. The air freshened, and the outside noises of the city became noticeable again. Within a few minutes, all was as it had been before.

The brigadier sighed, sat down heavily in his chair, and with slightly unsteady hands replaced his talisman. His face was drawn and haggard, as if the power he had called upon had used up his own physical vitality. Margaret knelt beside him, her face lined with worry.

Bucky went to stand alone by the window, his body shaking with reaction. The face in the globe had been Tango, he was certain. The lamp was one Tango had brought with him when they had moved in. Even knowing what he knew about Tango, Bucky could hardly believe what he had seen.

It was Florrie, for the second time that night, who steadied them all. She thrust a glass of brandy into Bucky's hand, then went to stand behind the brigadier, placing one hand over his heart and the other on top of his head. A faint humming sound came from between her lips, soft and drowsy like a cloud of honeybees. Margaret, watching her, caught a glimpse of light beneath Florrie's hands, so swift she might have imagined it, and so bright that for one instant she saw the finger bones through the skin and flesh. Then the colour was back in William Rothely-Smythe's face, and he was breathing easily and naturally.

Later, in the kitchen making a fresh pot of coffee, Margaret asked quietly, "Florrie, the healing you did for William was of a high level. The only other person I have known who worked with sound healing like that is Johnny's father. Did you ever meet him?"

Florrie was quick to notice the change from "Florence" to "Florrie" and smiled broadly. "I met 'im only for a short while, but 'e passed his gift of healing to Johnny's mother so she could help the boy if it was needed. When she was dying, she passed it to me for the same reason. I haven't used it since. He was so bad after 'er death. I didn't think just now. It welled up in me, and I knew I could help."

Margaret was silent for a minute. Then she said, "I know this place, a sort of school in the Pyrenees, right away from the usual holiday venues. You would love it, and they could teach you a lot about healing there."

Florrie leaned against the dishwasher and roared with laughter. "Margaret McDonald," she said, wiping her eyes, "I'll bet a bottle of Bombay gin to a new hat, that 'place' in the Pyrenees is run by your lot. You, my girl, couldn't tell a fib if you was paid for it."

The two women laughed together and went in to join their menfolk.

♫ ♩ ♫ ♪ ♫ ♩ ♫

Long after their guests had left, Florrie and Colin sat close together on the sofa, talking over the evening's events. Bucky, elated at having met his mentors at last and shaken by the psychic attack, was spinning. Florrie fed him hot sweet tea, made soothing noises, and let him talk until he was spent, then shooed him off to bed. For a while afterwards, she sat alone, looking down on the brightly lit city, reliving memories, and thinking things over. Finally she came to a decision.

Bucky was dreaming and enjoying it. A warm, soft body was snuggling into him, and an extremely knowing hand was sending his blood pressure up through the ceiling. On the border between sleeping and waking, he turned over and, with a sigh, nestled into an opulent pair of breasts.

Bucky contemplated this miracle in silence for a moment. These dreams were getting very real indeed, he remarked to himself.

"Give over, Bucky. I'm no dream, my lad, and just to show you..."

Bucky yelped and came fully awake on the instant. Sitting up, he fumbled for the bedside light and looked down at his night visitor, unable to believe his eyes.

"Florrie?" he queried, his voice rising to a squeak.

"I've always said that worries shared are worries 'alved," said Florrie, pulling him down under the covers. "Of course, there's sharing and there's *sharing*. And you know what they say about older women!"

"Ooooh, aah...Uuuh, god...Florrie!"

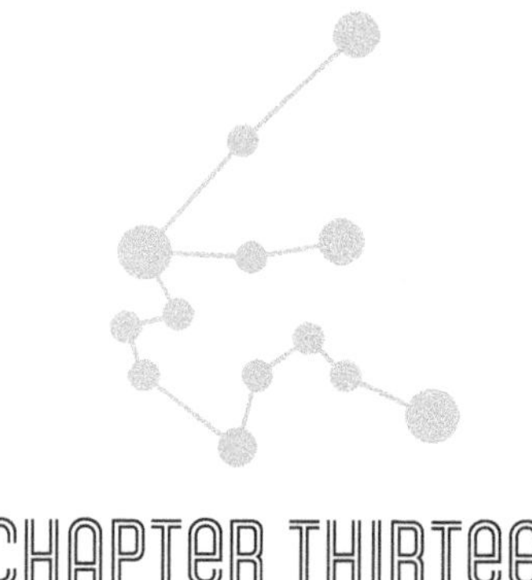

CHAPTER THIRTEEN

14 November, 1:00 a.m.
A small manor in West Wales

In a strangely furnished cellar sixty miles away, Tango bent over, fighting the pain that wracked his body. What the hell had he done wrong this time? Bucky should have been alone. It should have been easy to force him into a heavy sleep and find out what he knew about Johnny's whereabouts. Damn and blast him to hell and back.

The pain eased off and Tango relaxed, the sweat rolling down his chest and back. Everything he did wrong caused him pain; everything he did right brought him unbelievable pleasure; both drove him on to perfect the talent that had been born and then twisted within him.

Painfully he got to his feet, wrapped his silk robe round himself, and staggered to the door. He locked it carefully behind him and began to climb the wooden stairs to the front room. There Tango poured himself a stiff drink and lay back in the armchair. As the tension eased, he went over the night's procedure step by step. Where was the flaw? Who had been there with Bucky? He knew Florrie was there; he thought she'd returned home, but obviously not. He hunched over his glass. The question was, who were the other two? The power that had lashed out at him was beyond anything Bucky was capable of for all his reading and studying.

After a while Tango got up and went over to an ornately carved box standing on the sideboard and opened it. Wrapped in black velvet lay an eight-inch sphere of flawless crystal. He brought it back to the chair, turning out the main lights on the way, and spread the velvet on the small table beside him. He balanced the crystal on its ebony plinth and leaned over to look into its endless depths. Within, things swirled and coiled, things not human but with an intelligence that glittered in the crystalline pupils of their eyes.

First he needed information about the two people that had been with Bucky and Florrie. Tango's concentrated will summoned a face into the crystal, a small, sly, cunning little face with overly sharp teeth. A curt command sent it scurrying away, and for a few minutes the crystal roiled with smoke and then cleared. Tango leaned forward.

A tall, military-looking man entered a comfortably furnished room decorated with prints of early military uniforms and photographs of various campaigns. Behind him came a smaller man, a servant of some kind, with whom he seemed to be in deep conversation. The second man then left the room, turning out the main lights and leaving only the soft amber glow of a table lamp. The tall man walked over to a silver and crystal tantalus standing on the sideboard and poured a drink, then sat down with it, resting his head on the back of the chair.

The brigadier looked tired and older than his years, but he had a task to perform. He thought for a moment or two, then set his drink aside untouched. Settling back against the chair, he relaxed and began to regulate his breathing in an ancient and complicated pattern.

Tango watched in the crystal as a multicoloured flow of energy began to build up round the brigadier. As the flow increased, it enclosed the whole body in an oval of pulsing light. Simultaneously a power sigil became visible above the head. Tango caught his breath as it appeared. Two golden wings enclosed a shimmering silver chalice upon which was engraved the Chi Rho. Out of the chalice itself rose a multipetalled lotus.

The old man was more than he seemed. The sigil proclaimed him an initiate of high degree linked to the Abbeys of Light. Tango swore viciously and dismissed the image before his enemy could become aware of him. He paced back and forth for a while. Then his mind turned to the other person. Yes, what about the unknown woman? He summoned the imp of the crystal for the second time and concentrated.

Again the crystal clouded, swirled, then cleared to show Margaret McDonald kneeling at a small prie-dieu in her bedroom. True to her promise, she was making her nightly novena for Colin Buckman. Wrapped in her prayers and totally oblivious to the astral intrusion, Margaret slid the next bead of her rosary through her fingers and began to whisper. "Hail Mary, full of grace, the Lord is with thee. Blessed art thou among women and blessed is—"

With a rush of rage, Tango saw something shining over her head. Again a pair of golden wings, but this time surrounding a triple flame. The wings were open and fluttered gently over the kneeling initiate.

Still new to his powers, Tango's fury overcame caution and he took advantage of the moment. Using the image as a target, he threw his hate, fear, and anger at Margaret, smiling as it became an astral arrow sinking deep into her back. She half rose, a cry of pain choked off in her throat as a massive heart attack gripped her system.

The winged flame turned to face the attacker. Too late, Tango saw that it was far from being an initiatory sigil. It was an angelic guardian, and it was looking for the source of the attack. He had only seconds to deflect its power.

Tango flung the crystal across the room with every ounce of strength he possessed. It struck the wall and shattered into a thousand fragments, breaking the focus and leaving the guardian unable to identify him.

"That was a mistake. A very stupid and costly mistake," said a voice behind him.

Ice crawled down Tango's back as he rose to face his uninvited guest. De'ath was back, and he was not pleased.

"Never underestimate an enemy," the smooth voice continued, and Tango screamed as a wave of pain engulfed his body. "Especially an enemy who is highly trained and highly placed." The second wave of pain sent the younger man to his knees, sobbing. "The Watchers may not be in the abbeys, but they are part of the abbeys and as powerful as any inmate."

Now beyond screaming, Tango's body convulsed as the third lash of pain struck him. He rolled over and vomited onto the carpet. His tormentor watched dispassionately.

"In striking at a Watcher, particularly one at prayer, you have openly declared war. From now on they will be on their guard, and worse, they will actively seek us out. We need to begin building our defences much earlier than I'd planned, and all because you wanted to show off your piddling little powers. This, my friend, is real power."

An invisible force lifted Tango from the floor and flung him across the room. He tried to scramble up, but it knocked him down again and again. After the third effort, he simply lay there, and the smell of his fear-loosened bowels began to reek.

De'ath stood over him. "Get up, you pathetic object. Go and shower and then clean up this disgusting mess. One more unauthorised action like tonight's fiasco and I will not be so forgiving. Do you understand me?"

On his hands and knees, Tango nodded, looking up at his tormentor. It belatedly occurred to him that it was like being back with his grandmother all those years ago.

De'ath laughed maliciously. "But of course, your memories of that time have given me a great deal of information on how to control you, Mr. Garrett. Now get out!"

14 November, 1:30 a.m.
Wimbledon

Margaret stirred and pulled herself up on her hands and knees. Slowly and carefully she crawled to the bed and tried to lift the bedside phone, but the attack had left her too weak, and she collapsed again.

There was a flare of light above her head. Three times the guardian lit up the room, then hung over the woman and pulsed gently.

Two miles away, a black Porsche raced through the night towards a small house on Wimbledon Common. The grim-faced driver had the copper-toned skin of a Navajo man and the face of an avenging angel. Nathan Blackwolf was the name on his birth certificate. The Abbey of the Aeon called him Wolf. But no matter how well they knew him, they walked softly round him.

On the car phone he first called the brigadier, then an ambulance, and finally the Abbey of the Aeon, giving them the news that a Watcher was down and seriously injured. Wolf had been playing a waiting game ever since the abbot had requested his presence as an extra guardian to keep a watch on Tango. He had kept an astral watch for the last week and had found little difficulty in keeping track of Tango's comings and goings.

Tonight a sudden strengthening of the power round the house had alerted Wolf, and he raised the alarm. It was picked up and relayed to Abbot Gregor at the Abbey of the Aeon. Then a weak, almost inaudible, call for help from Margaret McDonald had come through, followed by a stronger call from Margaret's angelic guardian. Caught off guard by the unexpected attack, Wolf cursed as he guided the powerful motor towards the faint mental call still ringing on the astral. Coming up was the turning he needed, and he mentally called ahead to tell her help was on its way, but there was no answer.

The wheels spun on the gravel as he swung into Margaret's driveway, the engine hardly dying before he was leaping up the steps. With no key and no time to pick it, he placed his hand over the lock and concentrated. The tumblers clicked, moved, and the door swung open. "Miss McDonald? Mother Margaret?" he called.

A weak mental reply sent him up the stairs to the front bedroom. She was on the floor beside the bed, her cotton nightdress soaked with sweat. Gently Wolf turned her over and her eyelids fluttered open, her usual smile a pale shadow of its usual brightness.

"Wolf, dear, how nice to see you. Sorry I was so careless. I didn't expect…"

"Gently, Mother Margaret. An ambulance is on its way, and I've called the brigadier. He will meet you at the hospital." Wolf lifted her onto the bed and covered her with a blanket, then moved about the room gathering a few things into a small case to go with her. That done, he returned to sit beside her, holding her hand and pouring his young strength into her until help arrived. Shortly after, the ambulance turned into the driveway, and within fifteen minutes Margaret was on her way to safety. He could not go with her; there was work to do.

Wolf returned to the car for a map of the area, then made several more phone calls. Satisfied with the information he now had, he settled down on the sofa and composed himself for sleep. It was 4:15 a.m., and he would need all his strength for the coming night.

14 November, 6:30 a.m.
St. Asaph's Private Nursing Home, London

"William, I'll take over now. You go and get somethin' to drink. Florrie's rustled up coffee and sandwiches. Then you can stretch out on the couch in the waiting room. I'll call you as soon as anything happens. Cross my heart, pal." Bucky's hand gripped the older man's shoulder. "You have to get some rest or you'll be asleep when she wakes up. Trust me, I've said I'll wake you if there's any change, and I will."

Eyes bleary with sleeplessness, the brigadier looked up and managed a faint smile, then sighed and rose stiffly to his feet. "Thank you, Colin. I'll just have something to drink and perhaps a turn or two in the corridor to get my blood flowing again. Then I'll be back," he said, moving to the door.

Bucky nodded, knowing full well that Florrie would make him rest, or else; at his age, the brigadier couldn't take much more of this stress. Then he settled down to watch over his charge. The dim light in the intensive care unit was just enough to outline Margaret's face, emphasising its pallor. Her silver hair, loosened from its usual tidy chignon, lay spread over the pillow. The only noise was from the respirator as it breathed for her, taking the strain from her faltering heart.

They had been devastated when an early morning call from the brigadier gave the news. Their time together had been so short, and yet it seemed they had always known each other. At 5:30 a.m. they were at the hospital, but this was the first time they'd succeeded in getting William away from her bedside.

♫ ♩ ♫ ♪ ♫ ♪ ♫

"Get this coffee down, you," ordered Florrie, wasting no time on the niceties. "You're no good to 'er if you get sick yourself." She looked anxiously at the old man, shoulders drooping and head bowed, and tried to think of a way to take his mind off the still figure in the next room. "How long've you known Margaret, William dear?" she asked.

"Since World War Two. Her husband was in my regiment, a major. We all grew up together. He was badly wounded in the Desert Campaign and lost the use of his legs. Then the plane that flew him back had to make a forced landing. The crash did more damage, and he was paralysed from the neck down. Margaret went to pieces over it. She'd left the abbey to marry him, though he knew nothing about all this. But she loved him so much it didn't matter. I loved her too, always have done, but she chose Hugh." He paused, then went on, memories allowing him the luxury of sharing old pain.

"After the war I decided not to return to the abbey but to become a Watcher instead. I did a lot of travelling about, collecting talented children and adults. There were so many displaced people after the war, and conflict on that scale seems to bring talents to the fore. Some were so traumatised we couldn't help them; others just gave up and died. Margaret helped when she could, but looking after Hugh was a full-time job. I made the time to go and sit with Hugh at least once a week, more when I could. It gave Margaret a respite. He knew I loved her. We were friends, and I made no secret of it. One day he made an excuse to send her into town and asked me to 'babysit.' We talked for hours.

"You see, Margaret's faith has always been a mainstay for her, and Hugh's...incapacity...made it impossible for him—for them—to have any kind of intimacy. He asked her for a divorce, but she wouldn't hear of it. She said she had married him for better or worse, and that was how it would stay. But they had always wanted children, and it was the one thing that devastated her.

"That day we talked it over, Hugh and I, and he asked me, begged me, to become Margaret's lover, to bring the glow back to her face and perhaps to give her a child. In the midst of his own pain and broken dreams, Hugh thought only of Margaret and of the man who loved her and thought the fulfilment of that love was impossible.

"When she returned, I tried to tell Margaret, but she was furious and hurt that we had talked it over without her. Of course, she was right. She threw me out of the house, and it was three years before I saw them again.

Hugh was still alive despite the doctor's prognosis, but Margaret was as thin as a rake and very depressed. Hugh made a last effort and called in a friend of his, a priest from County Clare where he'd been born, and told him the story.

"You know, Florrie, there are some priests who are truly called to minister; that man was one of them. He listened, made no judgement, but went off and prayed most of the following night. Then he came back and talked to Margaret. She never told anyone what they spoke about, but a week later she rang the bell of my apartment in Kensington. I opened the door, and she walked into my arms and wept. The first night we ever spent together, we simply slept in each other's arms. After that she came to me when she could, always with a message of love and friendship from Hugh on her lips. We never abused his trust; he always knew when and where. We kept nothing from him.

"Margaret was thirty-five when she became pregnant. We could hardly believe it. Hugh insisted, and rightly, that they move from St. Albans so that Margaret would not have to deal with any gossip. Abbey connections got him into a select nursing home for the last three months, and Margaret stayed with another Watcher in the West Country. On Christmas Eve 1955, Margaret gave birth to our son, and two months later they moved into the house in Wimbledon. Neighbours assumed that young Noel was adopted and that I was a relative."

"Oh, William, did the boy ever get to know?" asked Florrie, almost in tears.

"Yes, Hugh told him. Noel was twelve, and Hugh was dying. He came out of the room ramrod straight and stood in front of me. Told me he knew I was his real father, but for him Hugh would always be Dad. I told him that was as it should be. If things had been different, Hugh would most certainly have been his real father. He was quiet, then said he thought he was luckier than most, as he now had two dads. Hugh died that night in Margaret's arms.

"I've often asked Margaret to marry me, but she never would, said she owed her husband that much. Noel's an orthopaedic surgeon in New York now, married with three youngsters of his own. No talents among them, but that's how it goes." He covered his face with a gnarled hand. "Oh God, I don't want to lose her, Florrie."

"Well, who says you will? We don't know what's going to happen until it does. Lie down on the couch for a while. Bucky and me'll look after things." Florrie tucked him up and watched until he slept, then went to see Margaret.

The doctor was there, talking with Bucky. He drew Florrie aside and told her there was still no change, but at least no deterioration. They sat side by side until morning brightened the room, and Florrie told him the story as the brigadier had told it to her.

A nurse popped in to tell them that Margaret's son had phoned and was on his way from New York. He expected to be there in the late afternoon. After a brief examination, the nurse was able to tell them the vital signs had stabilised, and there was reason to hope.

An hour later Margaret opened her eyes and smiled at William sitting beside her, squeezed his hand, and asked for a drink of water. Choked with tears he was not too proud to show, the brigadier knelt at her bedside and offered thanks for her return to life.

Their son was due to arrive in the afternoon and the doctors were making hopeful noises, so Bucky and Florrie left and went back to the apartment to catch up on much-needed sleep.

14 November, 6:00 p.m.
Wimbledon

Wolf finished off his sandwich and drained the last of the coffee, then washed up and put away his used dishes. The news from the hospital was very encouraging, but he still had a score to settle. He went outside and looked at the sky, sniffed the wind, and allowed his carefully honed senses to inform him. It would rain soon, and heavily. Wolf went over to the car and checked it out. Nothing must go wrong. Then he returned to the house and secured it; it would be some time before Margaret would return.

By 7:00 p.m. the promised rain had started, and the wind coming in from the east blew it across the open spaces of the common. Wolf zipped his leather jacket, drew on his gloves, and settled into the low seat of the

Porsche. The map he had been studying for the last few hours was clear in his head; he wouldn't need it again.

The traffic was light as he drove through the town area and out on to the main road. The rain had set in for the night, and as he came onto the A3, it hit the windscreen with the intensity of a whiplash, forcing him to slow down. Wolf's dark eyes narrowed and took on a strange yellowish gleam that called to mind the name his grandfather had given him at his birth. Wolf was on the hunt.

At 8:15 p.m. the wind and rain were joined by lightning and the intermittent growl of thunder. Wolf drew into a lay-by and waited for a lull in the storm. Just before 9:00 he was on his way again, and shortly after he came off the A3 and turned west. The weather was much worse, still raining hard, and the wind came in gusts that threatened to blow the sleek black car off the road, but the hands that held the wheel were like tungsten steel.

Some twenty minutes later, Wolf was going south again, as fast as he dared to drive in the worsening conditions. He began to count the exits. Three…Four…Five…Six…He came off the motorway and switched on the powerful extra lights. Within minutes Wolf was on a minor road that twisted and turned, making him slow down even more. Small villages came and went in his headlights, their houses huddled together as if for company. What few lights he saw shone dimly behind closely drawn curtains.

By 10:15 p.m. the storm was moving away as Wolf drove slowly and quietly through a small hamlet and eased the car into the yard of a conveniently derelict farm. He sat listening for a few minutes, then switched off the engine. The wind had died down, but the rain persisted. For a few minutes more he waited quietly, "casting" ahead of him in the darkness of the countryside. A lot of time had been lost with this damned storm; his prey might have flown the coop. He could sense nothing at this distance. He had to get closer.

Wolf slid out of his leather jacket and the turtleneck sweater beneath it. There was the swish of leather and the rasp of a zip. He opened the car door and sat sideways to pull off his leather boots, then stood and peeled jeans and briefs down in one movement. Naked to the rain, he shivered, then locked the car and placed the key on a chain round his neck. In the darkness his copper-coloured skin made him hard to see, but what came next was an even better advantage.

Wolf looked round carefully, then crouched down on all fours. He shook himself like a large dog once, twice, three times. Then the human body seemed to fold in upon itself and disappear. For a moment nothing moved, but there were noises in the dark: liquid, grating, cracking noises. Then a stifled groan of something close to pain and from the ground rose a different shape, lean and rangy and four-footed. Its muzzle lifted, sniffing the sharp early winter air. Then, with a menacing whine deep in its throat, it loped off into the darkness. It was 10:35 p.m., and Wolf had gone hunting.

CHAPTER FOURTEEN

14 November, 6:45 p.m.
The Karakoram range north of the Xiancheng Glacier

They always stopped before sunset to prepare for the night, but today there was no sign of stopping. As the sun edged towards the rim of the mountains, Johnny pulled on the rope that linked him to Tze-Ring and called out.

"Hey Ring, when are we going to stop for the night? Another few minutes and we won't be able to see the edge of the path."

"It's all right, Johnny, we do not need the path anymore. Do you see that cairn of rocks ahead of us? It was set in the shelter of an outcrop to protect it from the wind, so it is rarely hidden by snow. It acts as a signpost. The outcrop is the mouth of a cave going back into the mountain. It becomes a tunnel descending right to the valley. It is just one of several special entrances to the valley and used only by those connected with the abbey."

Johnny snorted. “You must have been reading *Lost Horizon*. It’s all so bloody new age. I suppose the valley is unreachable from the outside, has perpetual summer, and everyone lives to be two hundred.”

“James Hilton based his book on legends going back thousands of years. He put what he read and had been told into a highly readable piece of fiction. Our valley *can* be reached from the outside. Not easily, but it can be done. While we don’t have summer all year round, the mountains shield us enough to allow the growing of crops. Because of our way of life and the techniques of breathing and exercise that we utilise, we do have a somewhat extended life, though we are subject to accident and illness just as you are. How old do you think the abbot is, Johnny?”

“I dunno. Pretty ancient, I expect. About eighty, I’d say, give or take a year.”

“Nyang Darsip is in his ninety-fifth year and has had two wives. The first was a Chinese girl from a noble family; she was seventeen and he was twenty-eight. They had three daughters, but only one survived. The twins died at birth, and their mother followed them into the Light.

“He lived alone for many years and was nearly fifty when he met and fell in love with a Russian girl. She was from the Caucasus mountains and much younger than he, but she returned his love and made him very happy. They had a daughter, Natasha. She is my mother.” Tze-Ring paused and then went on, “My father is also an initiate of an abbey. The oldest member of any abbey is around one hundred and thirty years.”

“You mean the old man is your grandfather?”

“I’m afraid so, Johnny Burke. Does this make a difference to our friendship?”

Johnny stopped and turned, looking directly into Tze-Ring’s dark eyes, then put his hands on the other man’s shoulders and gripped hard.

“No, Ring, nothing could do that. There’s nothing that anyone could do that would break us up. Remember that, no matter what happens in the future. Promise me you’ll remember that.”

“I will remember. I am glad our paths have met, Johnny, and I promise you that I will always be there for you to share any burden. Now, here is the cave.”

Beside the cairn of stones was a narrow entrance hardly visible in the failing light. The Sherpas were already squeezing themselves and their packs between the rocky walls. It seemed to go right through the mountain, for Johnny could see the dim light of the fading day ahead, but as he pushed his way through, he saw off to his left a tunnel, and just inside it a flaring torch.

The tunnel led downwards, and at intervals, torches set into iron sconces gave just enough light to see the way. Rough steps had been cut in the rock, but these were made treacherous by nodules of ice underfoot. A heavy chain bolted to the wall gave a degree of safety. The Sherpas laughed and joked with each other as they descended, each step taking them closer to home.

A thunder of sound came from below, making it difficult to hear and speak. Then, after descending a couple of hundred feet, the steps gave way to a large and surprisingly dry cave. And, to Johnny's unbelieving eyes, electric light.

Tze-Ring laughed at his amazement. "Did you think the valley was so isolated that we have no electricity? Let me show you. It is not done by magic, I assure you." He led the way into another well-lit tunnel that led away to one side where the noise was deafening, and Johnny could see why. A torrent of water issued from a fissure on the far side and flung itself down into the darkness. Johnny compared the noise to Niagara Falls and guessed the water was used to feed the large generator he saw set into a corner of the cave. It was this that provided the electricity.

Trying to make himself heard over the roar of the water, Johnny yelled in Tze-Ring's ear, "How the hell did you bring all the gear to build this thing up those mountains?"

"We brought it by road to within a hundred miles of here and then by one of the underground roads. You will see those later. Now, let's eat before we go on."

Murad and three of the Sherpas were pressing on to prepare the way. The tall man smiled at Johnny and warned him not to think of escaping tonight; a blizzard had hit the peaks soon after they had entered the cave, and Johnny would probably walk straight off the edge if he tried. Murad laughed at his own joke and sent the echoes rebounding off the wall, then disappeared after the others.

The Sherpas prepared a simple meal of bread and goat's milk cheese and a hot drink. Now out of the biting wind, they all felt much warmer. After the meal and a short rest, they started again and began the long climb down to the valley floor. Johnny's ears began to pop as they descended, reminding him of how high they had been up on the mountain pass.

They descended for two or three hours, with frequent stops to ease aching muscles. Sometimes there were steps, but for the most part it was simply a slippery rock path. The sound of the rushing torrent lessened as they descended and finally died away altogether. Tze-Ring explained that the tunnel was taking them in a different direction. By now everyone was exhausted after a longer day than usual, and Johnny was beginning to stagger. He was about to ask for a rest when the tunnel came to an abrupt end. Before them was a wooden door that opened to reveal a rough platform with an iron railing round it. Johnny's eyes bulged. A lift in the middle of a Tibetan mountain!

"A simple hydraulic convenience," explained Tze-Ring. "With all that water providing electricity, why not use it? It is not elegant, but it will take us the rest of the way down. Before we had this to help us, it was a dangerous climb down the last thousand feet or so." Tze-Ring, three of the Sherpas, and most of the packs went down first, and Johnny watched them disappear into the darkness with mixed feelings. It was nearly an hour before the lift came back and the rest of them piled onto it. The last man turned off the tunnel lights and hit the switch.

The descent was slow by normal standards, but a lot quicker than it would have been on foot. It was accompanied by creaks and groans and an odd moaning noise made by the wind forcing its way through the crevices and fissures in the tunnels with which the mountain seemed to be riddled. It would have been bad enough with a light to see by, but in the Stygian darkness, it was just short of terrifying. The platform slowed to a halt after some thirty minutes, and the glimmer of a fire greeted them. The sight of the tents, set up and waiting, reminded Johnny how tired he was.

The smell of real coffee hit him, and his face lit up as the hot metal cup was thrust into his hands and Murad's beaming smile welcomed him into the valley. He could see nothing, but he knew that somewhere out there was the end of his journey. He savoured his coffee—his first since leaving the plains—then rolled into his sleeping bag and fell into an exhausted sleep. Beside him, Murad was holding a mental conversation with the abbot.

"Rinpoche, we are camped at the entrance to the valley, and all is well so far. Our guest is extremely tired. The journey has been difficult for him. I must admit it has not been easy for any of us; his fear of heights made the journey here quite hazardous."

"You are to be congratulated, Brother Murad, for your fortitude. Tze-Ring has told me of the occurrence on the bridge. I must admit that Johnny Burke's ability to cope with all the changes he has been forced to undergo is proving quite remarkable. Sister Shuna and Brother Wang Ta arrived three days ago. Both have requested personal silent time to get over their...er...dealings with our guest."

"He can be difficult, Rinpoche, but there is a purity within him that bodes well for the future."

"Considering his ancestry on both sides, that is to be expected. Sleep well, Brother Murad. I shall see you tomorrow."

"May Allah overlook your rest, Holy One."

Johnny stirred. "Murad, you think too loud. For heaven's sake, stop chattering."

Taken aback, Murad raised himself on his elbow and looked down at his tent companion. He was about to ask how Johnny had heard him telepathing the abbot, then noticed he was fast asleep. Murad grinned and lay down again. This lad was going to be amazing when fully trained.

♬ ♩ ♫ ♪ ♬ ♪ ♫

A silence settled over the valley, but in the abbey, one light still burned. The abbot was thinking. At his age he needed little sleep, and three or four hours was more than enough to recharge his energies. He had spent some time with Father Chambha, linked by the man's remarkable powers to both London and the Abbey of the Aeon. From London the news was good and bad. Margaret McDonald would recover, though she would never have her former strength, but Brother Wolf had gone hunting her attacker, and that worried him. Nothing had been heard from Wolf since his last message to the Aeon, and they could ill afford to lose someone as valuable as Wolf, headstrong though he was.

The abbot sank deep into silence, pulling it round himself like a cloak. After a short rest, he rose and left the room. The corridor ran parallel with the top balcony, its windows looking out over the valley below. The whiteness of the snow-covered peaks glimmered in the darkness. The abbot reached the outer door and stepped out into the bitter cold, automatically adjusting his breathing pattern and raising his body heat. He crossed the open space without stumbling. Then he climbed the steps to the wide doors of the Hall of a Thousand Candles and, without hesitation, pushed them open. For a few seconds the whole of the forecourt glowed as light poured out from the holy place. Then it was gone and the bronze doors were closed again.

The Hall of a Thousand Candles looked as if it were made of fire. True to its name, one thousand candles lit the vast interior. The sudden gust of wind from the briefly opened door made their flames dance and flicker and project patterns onto the ceiling high above. The atmosphere was warm and inviting, made more so by the statue that dominated the hall. Dolma, the White Tara: the Tibetan version of Kwan Yin, Goddess of Mercy, the Eastern counterpart of Mary and the patroness of the abbey. She sat cross-legged, her many arms reaching out to those who came to Her. On each palm there was an eye centred by a gemstone, symbolising Her concern for Her children. The serene face looked down, the eyes lowered beneath heavy lids. Between the finely arched brows, a third eye kept watch, its pupil an egg-sized diamond.

Slowly the abbot walked the length of the hall, mounted the three steps of the dais, and bowed before the statue. He sprinkled incense over the charcoal in the brazier resting before the goddess, then turned and sat on a cushion, folding himself easily into his accustomed lotus position. In a semicircle before the dais stood twelve candlesticks—as always when no ceremony was in progress—each five foot in height and carrying in its holder a candle some four inches across and twelve high. The flames held steady, and the abbot concentrated on the pool of light they cast upon the polished floor. After a few minutes he began to chant in a thin, rather shaky tenor.

"*Om tare tuttare ture soha. Om tare tuttare ture soha.*" The words ran into one another as the chant continued until it became one long sound that rose and fell. Time passed on velvet paws, though whether it was one hour or several was impossible to tell. Then the chant ceased and the waiting began.

The silence grew deeper until it seemed to have actual weight. The candle flames lit the far corners of the ceiling, illuminating the *dakinis* painted there. The silence grew until it formed a ring of its own substance round the hall. The flames changed shape and became geometric forms pulsing with colours far beyond the human eye's ability to see. But the abbot had risen far above the physical. His breathing had slowed to the bare minimum, and his skin took on the colour of old wax.

An air of anticipation and joyfulness filled the hall. Forms flickered in and around the spaces between the candles, with snatches of sounds like liquid silver flowing down the side of a crystal mountain: sharp, clear, and unworldly. Colour, sound, silence, and pressure came together, and where the candles had been, there now stood twelve forms that seemed to be made of fire. Only vaguely human in shape, gloriously bright and beautiful beyond belief, the Lords of Flame, the Elohim, had answered the abbot's call.

"My heart is glad to greet you," whispered the abbot as the beings gathered about him. As one, they reached out and wrapped the small figure with filaments of their own substance. The saffron-robed figure quivered, then levitated smoothly to a height of some four feet above the cushion.

"You are precious in our sight, Nyang Darsip. This phase of the work draws to a close and another begins. We are well pleased with what you have accomplished."

Though just one voice was heard by the abbot, its substance came from them all.

"There are difficulties ahead, but we do not doubt the ability of those who serve the Light to overcome them. The Forerunner is almost here and will soon begin his training. Now we can give you more information. This coming divine incarnation will be the last undertaken by one of the Elohim, and there will, of necessity, be new aspects to the way in which it will be presented. We consider humanity will, after this age, be sufficiently advanced to provide its own saviour with no further input from our kind."

A shockwave ran through the frail body of the abbot.

The voice continued. "As always, the Forerunner will be human. But, inevitably, the incarnate memory will make its presence known at some point in time. Watch for signs that this is approaching. We will help in this matter, but it is well that you understand the situation. The present Forerunner has a human body and mind, but within that mind lies full cosmic consciousness. Its awakening will cause a tremendous physical shock to the human being; it will need your strength and that of your associates to mitigate this effect. However, until that time, the training is paramount."

"Your words lift my heart, children of Light. Be assured that my strength, my very life, is at your disposal. All will be done according to your wishes," said the abbot.

"We now address ourselves to the continuation of the physical line. Have you thought more concerning our suggestion on this matter?"

The abbot paused, then spoke. "The girl is young and still bears the mental scars of her early years, but there is no doubt that as a descendant of the Romanov line, she is a suitable choice. The Forerunner is one easily roused to the idea of protection; this can be fostered until it becomes a true emotion and not one imposed upon him. I am confident all will proceed as you wish.

"However, I am concerned with the continuing lack of success in tracing the whereabouts of the Lost Abbey. Even our strongest seers are unable to seek it out. The way is clouded by a power that is neither of the Light nor the Dark, nor can we find any clue to the place of the maps hidden by the Venetian. This is beyond our comprehension and experience. The crown must be examined, perhaps repaired, and the abbey itself must be cleansed physically and spiritually. We are running out of time."

The voice asked, "May we have permission to indwell your physical brain for a time in order to ascertain at the deepest level what you have understood so far?"

The abbot replied, "My overself at all levels is at the disposal of the Light."

A single beam of light emerged from the centre of each being to coalesce in a sphere of brilliant, constantly moving particles. It centred itself over the abbot's head and made contact with it. The abbot threw his arms wide at the shock of entry as the sphere sank into his brain. The frail body began to pulsate and glow until the bone structure could be seen clearly through the skin and flesh. Then the glow died and the sphere left its momentary housing to return and be absorbed by the Elohim. The abbot's semi-conscious body descended gently until it touched the cushion once again, where it relaxed and slumped over on the cushions.

The voice said, "We regret the necessity of using your vehicle in this way, but we will make sure that it is revived to its former state. We have the information we require. The power guarding the secret of the Lost Abbey is an elemental power. It will need much work to persuade it to open to us. Our blessing lies upon you, child of Light. And now, rest."

The beings came together in an explosion of light and energy that made the hall incandescent with power. Then they were gone.

The candles burned low as the abbot passed from trance into a deep, healing sleep. At dawn when the *chelas*[7] came to prepare the hall for morning worship, it was filled with perfume emanating from a single rose lying in the abbot's lap.

Chambha was summoned to assist. Reverently, he lifted the small figure into his loving arms and prepared to take his teacher back to his quarters. A thin whisper halted Chambha and he listened intently, then spoke quietly to one of the chelas. The boy reverently took the rose in his hands and placed it at the feet of the Tara. Only then did the abbot allow himself to be taken away.

Later in the day, the radung horns of the abbey sounded across the valley, waking the echoes and sending them tumbling from mountaintop to mountaintop until the whole valley was alive with sound. The people lined their simple street to welcome the porters home. Shouts of wives and children greeting husbands and fathers came from every side. Laughter and jokes made Tze-Ring smile but flowed over Johnny's head as first one then

7. Students at the abbey

another porter dropped away, their loads left by the front door to be carried up to the abbey later.

Murad, Tze-Ring, and Johnny stopped for a short rest and to drink some tea at the house of the head Sherpa, then set off on the final leg of their journey. As they climbed steadily, Johnny became silent and withdrawn. After so many weeks of travelling, so much physical pain and mental anguish endured, it was hard to believe the feeling growing inside him: a feeling of coming home. He could almost remember the way, almost remember the view as it unfolded below him. Johnny knew he had been born in India, but as he had left at six months old, he held no memories of its landscape. But here, in a land of snow and ice, high mountains and glacier-carved valleys, he knew he belonged.

Johnny stopped to look across the valley far below him. The air was crystal clear, making the mountains on the far side seem right on top of him. In the stillness he could hear the voices of children playing and of women calling them in to eat. Something deep inside him was waking up, and he knew without the slightest doubt that once it awoke fully, his life would never again be his own.

A flash of light at the corner of his eye made him turn. From the topmost peak above came a fall of particles of light. They looked like a flock of tiny birds whirling in a dazzling display of flight. All at once Johnny was covered with them, and what he had thought was a trick of the light was a reality.

Johnny raised a hand to brush the flock away and a point of light zoomed in on him, becoming a tiny face with enormous eyes and hair that looked like ice filaments streaming behind it. He fell back in alarm, his arm still raised, but was caught and held.

"Don't hurt them—they are just curious about you. They can sense that you belong here and are welcoming you in their own way." Tze-Ring held out Johnny's gloved hand, and a ring of the strange little creatures settled on it and whirled in a circle.

"Let your eyes go out of focus," advised Murad from behind him. "That's the best way to see them."

Johnny stared at the lights hovering above his glove and felt his eyes begin to cross. As they did, the figures suddenly became clear. For a brief moment he saw, as if under a microscope, tiny forms that were elongated, sexless, opaque, and totally unhuman, though they had arms and legs. As suddenly as they had appeared, they were gone.

"What the hell are those things?" asked Johnny, sweating slightly.

"Sylphs," smiled Tze-Ring. "Come on, we have another two hundred feet to go yet. You can play with them another day."

The abbey was close now, and Johnny could see the layout. It was composed of many small buildings built next to or on top of each other and other older buildings. The walls were creamy white with curved, sloping roofs painted dark red. Terraces and balconies alternated with solid walls, and small windows looked over the valley in three directions. Trees peeped over the edges of walls, and roofed walkways reminded him of cloisters in old cathedrals back home. The place seemed to be full of red- and yellow-robed figures, some in strangely shaped hats that clung to the top of their shaven heads.

Set back against the mountain itself was a larger building taller than the others; it seemed to be the focus around which all the others huddled together. Further up the mountain, Johnny could see openings in the side of the mountain, and before some of them he could just make out tiny figures.

"They are natural caves," explained Murad. "Some of the lamas and monks prefer solitude or are undergoing a voluntary penance. Some go there to think and meditate upon the mysteries of the universe round us and to write down their thoughts."

"But some of them look as if they are…uh, naked. Well, almost."

"They are. The cold does not bother them. They know how to keep themselves warm without clothing." Murad grinned at his companion. "You must try it sometime."

Johnny snorted. "Not bloody likely!" Another thought struck him. "Murad, I thought from what Ring was saying that the abbey was made up of all kinds of people, but it looks like there are only Tibetans here. How come?"

"The Abbey of the Dawn is only part of what you see. The rest is still a lamasery that we share with our Buddhist brethren. Alexander and his armies came as far as this point on his march into the East; notice that the strange shape of the monks' headwear closely resembles the ancient Greek helmet with its horsehair plume. Alexander stayed many months, learning from the priests of that time. When he left, some of his people stayed behind while some of the monks from the lamasery went with him. They became the Watchers of their time, sending back to this place those with talent and the will to learn. Over the centuries it became part lamasery and part abbey. We are lucky it is fully staffed. Some of the others are far below their capacity, but the right talents are hard to find. Here are the gates."

A turn in the narrow path brought them face to face with the entrance to the abbey. Two great pillars of natural rock, with a third forming the lintel, supported the wooden gates themselves. The stone had been roughly carved into fantastic faces that conveyed the power of the Four Winds. Native sculptors had compromised with regard to representation; the air-filled cheeks and pursed lips might have been seen on a Greek temple, but the fantastic headdresses were purely Tibetan. Both doors were painted red and ornamented with a frieze of symbols surrounding the central figure of a woman with three pairs of arms. Her face was gentle and welcoming, but two of her hands held weapons in a state of readiness.

Tze-Ring took up a horn that hung on one of the stone pillars and, taking a deep breath, he blew through it. The sound was incredibly deep and mellow, and it woke the ever-present echoes and sent them scurrying from valley to peak in wave upon wave of sound. The doors swung back, and the bright faces of two young chelas peered round at them. The greetings were warm, voluble, and to Johnny incomprehensible. Just inside the gates was a wooden wall, again painted red and covered with symbols.

Murad explained, "The belief is that demons can only move in a straight line—they cannot turn or swerve as we do—so a wall keeps evil forces at bay…at least for a time."

Chattering like magpies, the chelas led them along a winding path with wide steps that lifted them another thirty feet or so. On the left were long, low buildings with narrow verandas. On the right a balcony led round a natural curve in the rock, through an archway, and onto a large and impressive forecourt half the size of a professional football pitch. Around the edges were stone seats and carved statues, adding beauty and grace to a breath-taking view. Steps on one side led to another walkway, but before them arose a structure as big as a Western church. Steps led up to an ornate wood and bronze door, on either side of which stood the life-sized figure of an elemental guardian. The roof was covered with birds. Johnny pointed them out to Tze-Ring.

"This is the Hall of a Thousand Candles. The heat rising from them keeps the roof warm and free from ice. The birds rest there through the night. When the weather is very bad, we put bales of straw on the roof and tie them to the posts; then they burrow in to keep warm. Come, the abbot is waiting."

They crossed the cloisters that led along the edge of the plateau and entered the main building. Out of the wind it was warmer, and a series of oil lamps lit their way up a flight of stairs. At the top, Tze-Ring paused and turned to Johnny. "I know you are tired and need to rest, but the abbot has asked to see you at once. He will not keep you long. Then I will return and take you to your quarters." He opened the door and gently pushed Johnny inside.

It was dark inside, and for a moment Johnny could see nothing in the dim light of a single large candle. As his eyes adjusted, he saw the small figure of the abbot wrapped in a woollen shawl sitting on a pile of cushions. He seemed to be outlined with light coming from a window behind him, but as he drew near, Johnny saw there was no window—the light was coming from the abbot himself.

"Ah, Johnny Burke. You have arrived at last, I see. Welcome to the Abbey of the Dawn."

CHAPTER FIFTEEN

14 November, 11:10 p.m.
Penwyllt, West Wales

The manor house was small and had a dark, brooding atmosphere that had put off would-be buyers. Film units had used it in the past for horror classics, but few visitors bothered to stop at the gates for photographs now. The long, tree-lined avenue framed the house in a way that reminded one of looking down the wrong end of a telescope. After the death of its last occupant—an event hastened by his own hand—it had remained empty for ten years. The name on the present three-year lease was that of Talfryn Alvarez Garrett.

The gardens had been left to grow wild, and the new lessee liked it that way. So did Wolf. He slid through the tangled undergrowth like a shimmer of grey moonlight and stretched out beneath the cover of a two-hundred-year-old yew tree. From here, he could see the whole frontage and any comings or goings that occurred.

He stared intently at the house. In the light of a half-moon, it looked like a black and white film clip, eerie and desolate. To the keen senses of the hidden shifter, it gave other information. It was a place where the Dark lay hidden and evil waited to be set free on an unsuspecting world.

The night was into the small hours before the silent guardian saw any sign of movement. The light over the door went on and a tall, thin man in a black leather overcoat emerged. He turned in the doorway to speak to someone, his tone of voice betraying anger and cold disdain. Wolf edged nearer. The person inside the house came forward, and the light fell full on his face. Wolf's eyes gleamed as he matched the face with a picture he had been shown a few days ago. It was Tango Garrett.

As the visitor walked towards the sleek black car parked at the side of the door, his scent reached Wolf's sensitive nose. Evil had a smell that was impossible to disguise. In the nostrils of the shapeshifter, that smell evoked rotting flesh and carrion under a hot sun. The wet black nose wrinkled, the lips lifted and rolled back over sharp white teeth, and a low, rumbling growl escaped from the throat. Soft though it was, the sound carried. The man swung round, the unhealthy whiteness of his thin face clearly visible to the wolf.

"What is it? What did you hear?" asked Tango, coming further on to the gravelled drive.

"Shhh, there's someone or something out there. I heard it. I can smell it. It's one of them."

Wolf retreated back as far as he could, but the man in black had hearing as sharp as his own. The man reached into his coat and brought out a snub-nosed revolver that gleamed a wicked blue-black in the light of the open door. He moved with a light, almost gliding, step towards the trees that edged the drive. Tango, unsure of what was happening, followed him.

"Get me a torch. Quickly."

Tango disappeared for a moment, then returned with a powerful torch that sent a wide beam of light towards the trees. Stealthily, Wolf inched backwards until he was free of the branches, then padded into an overgrown shrubbery, keeping the undergrowth between his pursuer and himself.

The man's deep-set, soulless eyes searched this way and that for whatever had alerted him and found the flattened grass where Wolf had lain. "Something was here. I knew it. I could feel it. It has to be someone from the abbeys. I told you that little trick of yours would have them down our necks, but I didn't think it would be as soon as this."

The man began a systematic search of the trees and shrubs. Wolf kept backtracking, unable to use his super-senses to distract the man. That would work with Tango, but not with this soulless thing. Trying to keep out of the torchlight and not make a noise and keeping his thought patterns under tight control combined with two days and nights of minimal sleep made Wolf careless. He backed right out of the trees and onto the driveway just as Tango turned and saw him.

"There it is on the drive! Bloody hell, it's a dog. A grey dog. The biggest bastard I've ever seen! A rottweiler or a mastiff. Quick, don't let it get away! There, there on the drive, man! To the right."

The beam swung round and Wolf decided he might as well live up to his name. He came racing down the drive and leapt right into Tango's face, his teeth reaching for the throat. Tango screamed and fell to the ground trying to fight off the powerful body, the raking hind claws, and the slavering teeth that nipped and tore. Wolf kept seeing a frail old lady caught unawares, kneeling in communion with her God, saw her face and lips blue and cyanosed, and ripped a jagged eight-inch tear across his adversary's chest that reached to the bone.

De'ath sprang from the overgrown shrubbery, his coat flapping like the wings of a crow. He crouched, both hands holding the gun steady, and fired. Wolf felt the bullet go in deep. It was time to leave.

Using his powerful back legs, Wolf thrust upwards, throwing himself back and somersaulting in mid-air. Then, as his paws touched the ground, he was off down the drive, racing for what he knew would be his life. A second bullet hit the gravel a few inches behind him, and he swerved. Another creased his side, drawing blood. His heart was pounding. His tongue hung from his mouth. The pain was beginning to build up, making it hard to hold on to the shape, but without it, he had no hope at all.

The gates at the end of the drive were in sight. Wolf dodged desperately from side to side. The fourth bullet went wide, and the fifth spurted dust beside his front paws. He could hear the pursuit getting nearer, could feel his strength running from him.

Four feet from the gates, Wolf gathered himself together and leapt, flinging every ounce of strength left into a last bid for freedom and life. He sailed over the gates as the sixth and last bullet ricocheted off the metal and pierced his flank. Then he was on the other side and lost in the darkness.

De'ath thudded to a halt and swore extensively in a language that, in another time, had been his mother tongue. It was useless trying to find the creature in the thick woods out there, and no doubt his superiors had already been alerted. There would be another time for the final reckoning. He turned, pocketing the gun, and went back up the drive to where Tango lay covered in blood and sobbing from a mixture of pain, fear, and hysteria.

A cursory examination showed extensive lacerations to his chest and stomach, plus a rip along the base of his throat. He'd lost a lot of blood and would need a fair amount of stitching. With little grace and no gentleness, De'ath hauled the wounded man to his feet and dragged him into the house and up to his bedroom. He stood looking down at him for a few moments, planning the best way to deal with the situation, then went to the phone and dialled a Reading number.

After some time, the phone on the other end was lifted and a querulous voice answered. De'ath ordered the voice to get out to the manor as soon as possible, giving details of the emergency and what would be needed. The voice at the other end was peeved at the prospect of driving so far at such an early hour and tried to argue. De'ath was not sympathetic. In a voice like oiled silk, he offered a few inducements.

"Dr. Morrissey, I suggest you cast your mind back to June of last year and a day that could have ended your career, cost you your family, and maybe even your life. I was instrumental in saving all of those things. You would have gone down for twenty years at least considering how much money you made selling illegal drugs from your practice. Be here within an hour, or I might let Scotland Yard have some papers still in my possession. By the way, how is that attractive young daughter of yours? Let me see, she must be nearly fifteen now. Such a worrying age for parents. All the drug peddling on the increase, and as for rape and assault—you must take great care of her...What? Yes, one hour will do nicely. Thank you, Dr. Morrissey."

De'ath replaced the receiver with a mirthless grin on his face, then returned to Tango. He washed most of the blood off and staunched the gashes as much as he could but refused to give him the brandy he asked for. "You'll need a local, probably several, and a tetanus shot. At least you don't have to worry about rabies."

Tango froze. "Rabies? Jesus, the shots for that are bloody murder. My God, do you think that hound could have been rabid?"

"That hound, my impetuous friend, was a wolf. Or rather, it was a shapeshifter, and such creatures are not rabid. And I would rather you didn't use the term 'my God.' It seems a little out of place, don't you think?"

"A shapeshifter? You've got to be joking. No, you're not, are you? You mean there are such things—I mean, people—who change into…things like that?"

"You sound surprised, Mr. Garrett, yet you accept your own psychic gifts and those of others. Why is shape-shifting so mind boggling? It simply requires a certain type of physical and genetic makeup and training. Like this, see…"

De'ath's features blurred and his body fell in on itself. A stomach-churning crack sounded through the room, and from the tangled heap of clothing scuttled a black rat the size of a terrier. It ran across the room, leapt onto the bed beside the fear-frozen man, and sat there regarding him with glittering red eyes. It bared a set of gleaming teeth in a ghastly parody of a human smile and began to clean its whiskers with handlike paws.

As if from a long way off, De'ath's voice sounded in Tango's head. "It's quite easy once you know how."

But Tango had fainted.

♬ ♩ ♫ ♪ ♬ ♪ ♫

Wolf dragged himself the last few yards to the gate of the deserted property where he had hidden the car. The loss of blood was telling on him now. The first bullet had lodged in his shoulder, and a long, bleeding crease down his back showed the path of another. The third had passed through the flesh of his right thigh.

The whine of an electric motor made Wolf use the last of his strength to roll into the deep ditch at the side of the road. A milk float rounded the bend and crawled up the hill to the village, its driver casting an incurious glance at the open gate and the Porsche. *High-living coke snorters from London, probably.* Well, it was no skin off his nose; live and let live. The driver whistled cheerfully as the cart took him into the village.

Wolf lay in the ditch, his mind dull and unresponsive. In a few minutes he would be unconscious; then the cold and loss of blood would finish him. He lit the symbol of a beacon in his mind, but it was weak and very faint. His last thought was of Mother Margaret. Was she was still alive, or would she be waiting to help him cross over?

"No, lad, she's just waiting to give you a piece of her mind about haring off across the country on your own, hellbent on revenge."

"Strewth, I've seen a few things in ditches in my time, but never a naked Navajo riddled with bullets."

Wolf's eyes flickered open, and he looked up into the bright blue eyes of Colin Buckman and the darker, sharper ones of the brigadier. He licked dry lips and whispered, "But then you were never in Vietnam, Mr. Buckman. The ditches there were full of my people," and he let the warm darkness wash over him again.

"Get him into your car, Colin. It's bigger and more comfortable than his own. I'll drive the Porsche, but first I'll ring Florrie so she can tell Margaret he's all right, or will be when we get him to a doctor."

Together they lifted Wolf out of the ditch, then Bucky hoisted him over his shoulder and got him back to the Mercedes. Some rough and ready first aid was applied in the backseat while Wolf was still unconscious. He came round again briefly as the brigadier took the keys of the Porsche from round his neck, then slipped into the pain-free darkness again.

"Where to now?" asked Bucky, easing himself behind the wheel.

A black car shot round the bend of the road and up the hill, going towards the village and the manor. The brigadier looked after it thoughtfully, then turned to Bucky.

"For a start, out of here as fast as we can. We are too near the scene of last night's debacle for my liking. If I am not mistaken, the driver who nearly ran into us just now is one Dr. James Morrissey. He, like your friend

Tango, has gone over to the Darkness. Let's head back to London on the A31; it's quieter than the motorway, and I don't want to risk being stopped by traffic police. We'll branch off at Farnham on the A287. I'll lead, but if we get separated, look for a sign that says Tanesford. It's a village with a pub called the Ducking Stool. Park there and wait for me."

Then the brigadier shook his head at Wolf. "Gregor will give him hell when he gets back to the abbey, but Wolf adores Margaret. She kept him on the right side of sanity when his adopted mother died, and he was just trying to avenge her.

"Don't go too fast, Colin. We don't need a speed ticket at this stage of the game."

They set out, the Porsche leading, and began to make their way towards London.

15 November, 9:30 a.m.
The Ducking Stool, Tanesford

The brigadier drew into the rear car park of the Ducking Stool and, having looked round carefully, disappeared into the pub through a side door. A few minutes later, Bucky parked the Mercedes beside the Porsche and waited. A large, broad-shouldered man came out, followed by the brigadier. Within minutes, the unconscious Wolf had been taken into the house and up to one of the bedrooms, where a statuesque black woman with a soft voice and gentle hands waited with hot water, towels, and a doctor's medical bag.

She went to work quickly and efficiently, dealing with the shoulder wound first. The bullet was in deep, and it took all her skill to extract it without causing more damage. Then she attended to the other wounds and administered an antibiotic. An hour and a half after being brought in, Wolf had been made comfortable and was sleeping normally. His nurse went downstairs and joined the others in the bar.

Harry Scrimshaw, the landlord, was a bluff, hearty man in his mid-fifties with a Yorkshireman's deep-set blue eyes and genial manner. He looked up as the woman entered. Turning to Colin, Harry smiled broadly.

"Mr. Buckman, I'd like you to meet my wife, Anna. She was a theatre nurse in Angola for some years, so she's used to dealing with bullet wounds. She kept digging them out of me for years."

Bucky put down his glass of bitter, took the strong, capable hand held out to him, and shook it warmly. "I'm honoured to meet you, Anna. We sure needed your help."

"Happy to help the abbeys anytime. Nice to see you, William. We heard about Margaret being attacked; the grapevine is humming with it. How is she now?"

"Waiting to give Wolf hell the moment she sees him. Otherwise, weak as a kitten. Colin's lady, Florrie, is with her now. It was Margaret who picked up Wolf's track. She just opened her eyes and said to me, 'Billy, Wolf is in trouble. He's gone after the boy who attacked me.' She gave us the details, picking him up as clear as daylight. Then she went out again. Whenever she calls me Billy, I know it's serious, so I grabbed Colin and we high-tailed it down here."

"Wolf will be all right now, but he should have some blood put back into his system as soon as possible. I sent out a call for someone of his blood group as soon as we got your message; he should be arriving soon. Meantime, I'll see about some food for you menfolk." Anna Scrimshaw disappeared in the direction of the kitchen and Bucky turned to the others.

"I swear, I've never seen anything as organised as you lot. It's like an active system inside the country that no one knows about. How long has this been going on, Bill?"

"Not as long as the abbeys themselves. For the last fifty years at this level, but long before that, we had people all over the world. Our ways of communication don't use computers or fax machines, though we do make use of them, naturally. You'll get used to it soon enough, you and Florrie. The old abbot was most impressed with your little sortie into the astral."

An ear-splitting howl interrupted him, announcing the arrival of a Harley Davidson FLH Electro-Glide in the car park. A few seconds later a beefy, leather-clad biker sporting a pickelhaube and a chest-length beard put his head round the door.

"I 'eard one of our lot was in need of some of my personal brand of tomato sauce, mate," said the biker.

"Upstairs, Barney," came Anna's voice. "Get your shirt off and lie down on the bed next to Wolf's. I'll be there directly."

"Promises, promises," said the biker with a grin and disappeared.

Anna entered the bar with plates of bacon, eggs, freshly picked mushrooms, and fried bread. "Coffee's on the hob," she told them and followed the biker.

"Colin, your mouth is open," chuckled the brigadier. "And to answer your unspoken question, yes, Barney is a Watcher. He has an unusual talent; you should ask him to demonstrate sometime. He can grow a plant from seed in ten minutes flat. I've seen him grow a five-foot sapling from a three-inch seedling in an hour."

William indicated two massive climbing plants on either side of the bar's front door. "See those plants? They're African creepers, only grown here in hot houses. Barney brought them from Africa as a present for Anna after she'd nursed him following a bad knife battle. Normally they wouldn't stand a chance in England, but Barney got them to grow and thrive. I swear they're part human now. I've seen them move and bend when either Anna or Barney talks to them or waters them. They're carnivorous, and Anna feeds 'em chicken heads from a nearby farm. Barney is good with people as well; he can mobilise a biker gang with a variety of physical attributes in an amazingly short time. Using them and their bikes in relay, we can get things and even people from John o' Groats to Land's End in a few hours, day or night, and with complete security. So, you see, we are a resourceful lot."

"I'm glad to hear it," said Bucky, downing his beer, "because the other side has just arrived!"

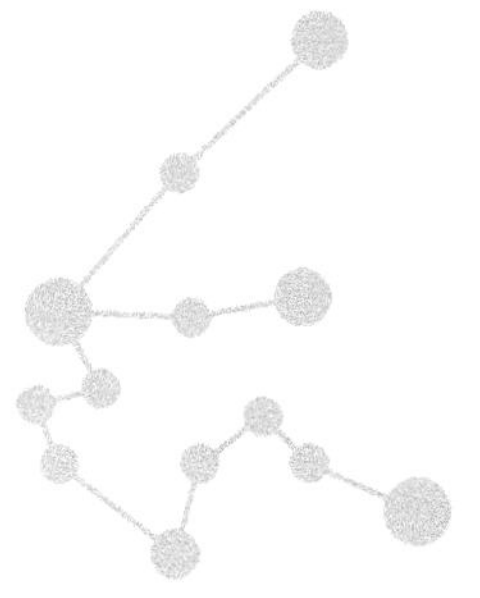

CHAPTER SIXTEEN

15 November, 11:30 a.m.
The Ducking Stool, Tanesford

Harry Scrimshaw straightened up from his position at the bar and went to the window, the other two close behind him. A minivan was disgorging a gang of hoodlums into the car park, all decked out in dirty jeans, variously emblazoned jackets, and Doc Martens boots. Most sported tattoos on arms, shoulders, and even their shaven heads and carried weapons of one sort or another. Plainly, all were hell-bent on trouble. They milled round, screaming and shouting and generally getting up steam.

"I'm glad we parked the Porsche and the Mercedes round the back and out of sight," observed the brigadier. "I rather think that lot means trouble, though I thought there would be more than that."

Harry snorted. "There's enough. Those bastards are animals. They don't need to be big, just close enough to slash your face, throat, or balls. Well, they're going to get more than they bargained for. William, you and Bucky get upstairs and look after Wolf. Anna and me'll deal with this lot."

"And miss a fight? Come off it, Harry," said Bucky. "William should go upstairs, I agree. I don't want to have to tell Margaret he's down as well.

But me, I can swing a bottle as well as the next man. If you've never been in a fight in an Aussie pub at closing time on Melbourne Cup day, you don't know what a fight is."

The men were looking through the windows, making obscene gestures and daubing the glass with spray paint. One opened his fly and urinated on the "open" sign by the door. The three men inside just waited. Then, at Harry's urging, the brigadier reluctantly went upstairs, leaving him and Bucky to wait for the inevitable.

There was an explosion of sound as the door was kicked back on its hinges. The intruders ambled in, laughing and joking, kicking over chairs, stubbing out cigarettes on the parquet floor, and sweeping glass ashtrays off the tables. One, the leader, swaggered up to the bar. He was a slim, ferret-featured young man with a livid scar curving from his right ear to the point of his chin. He rammed a razor-sharp knifepoint into the lovingly polished bar top and hooked a booted heel onto the brass footrest.

"Landlord." The voice was startling, high pitched, almost childlike, as its owner attempted a bad imitation of a posh accent. "Landlord, me and my friends 'ere desire to quench our furst. Set 'em up if you please. Free double whiskies all round I fink, and take one for yourself." He giggled inanely at his feeble joke and looked round for support and approval from his friends.

Harry strolled round the end of the bar and pulled the drying cloth from its position over his shoulder, carefully winding it round his hand.

"Certainly, sir. Or is it madam? Would sir, or madam, care for a cherry in it, or has sir, or madam, lost his cherry already?"

The atmosphere, already charged, suddenly became deadly. The laughter stopped, booted feet shifted uneasily, knives and chains were grasped more firmly, and all eyes turned to the leader.

A dull, red flush crept up the ferret man's face. His mouth worked silently, and a dribble of froth emerged and ran down his chin. "Fuckin' bastard!" he screamed. His hand jerked the knife from the bar as he lunged for Harry's face.

Despite the danger of the situation, Bucky's sense of humour got the better of him, and he laughed. As he laughed, he moved to a point before the door, effectively blocking any getaway and removing a large eighteenth-century, hand-carved cudgel from the wall as he did so. He was getting used to the ways of the abbey and its people, and Bucky would have bet half his considerable offshore bank account that Harry Scrimshaw was a damn sight more than he seemed to be.

His laugh distracted some of the mob from Harry and they turned towards him, knives out, bodies crouched low as they tried to outmanoeuvre him. Bucky hadn't been in a fight for years, and though he was out of condition, he'd lived and worked in places where dirty fighting was an art form. He swung the three-foot cudgel in a wide arc and heard it connect satisfyingly with a leg bone, then dropped to one knee, immediately pulling the shaft back. It broke the kneecap of the man coming up behind him.

At the bar, Ferret Face was having a hard time breathing due to the fact that Harry had a hand round his throat. To be accurate, Harry had a paw garnished with three-inch claws round his throat. Harry had also grown a faceful of hair and slavering canines to match the claws. His shirt had split and hung in tatters from a well-muscled, fur-covered torso. He flexed those muscles and drew the man's throat slowly, almost tenderly, within reach of his teeth.

"Harry, don't you dare eat that man before he's properly cooked," came a sharp command.

An immediate hush fell on the crowded bar. Anna was in the doorway. Her superb breasts were bare, and below her waist gleamed the sheen of silvery scales. Her body swayed up and down and from side to side as she glided into the room, balanced delicately on her massive serpentine coils. A slender forked tongue flicked lazily from between her lips. Razor-sharp fingernails glinted as she reached for the nearest hoodlum. Bucky and his erstwhile playmates watched in horrified fascination as the woman's jaw unhinged and her mouth gaped, opening wider and wider as the head of her hypnotised prey was pulled closer to her curving fangs.

Someone screamed a long, high-pitched scream that spoke of a mind past breaking point. Then the bar was full of thudding feet and jostling, sweating bodies wearing jeans that were suspiciously wet and reeking. Within the space of two minutes, the bar was empty except for the weakly screaming form still clutched in Harry's paws and the unconscious one on the floor in front of Anna. The werewolf leapt lightly over the bar and onto the floor, still carrying its prey. Harry scooped up the second body and loped to the door, then dragged the unhinged ferret man and his companion into the car park. He dumped them outside the locked doors of the van as its terrified passengers fought to keep away from the windows. Then their tormentor stood shaking his massive fists and roaring as the minivan jerked to life and sped onto the road. Harry grinned wolfishly and returned to the pub.

"Somehow I don't think we'll be on their visiting list again," he said, beginning to change back to the benign, middle-aged landlord of the Ducking Stool. "It takes a while to get rid of all this hair," he offered apologetically, "but give me another thirty minutes and I'll look a little less like Lon Chaney Junior."

Bucky was about to brush aside Harry's apology when a choking gurgle over his head made them look up. Up near the ceiling, the African creepers had wound several tendrils round the throat of a forgotten hoodlum and were swinging him to and fro as if he were a doll. His face was becoming a fair match for his blue sweatshirt.

"Cecily, Gertrude," said Anna sternly, "put him down. He's bad for your digestion. I'll give you both an extra chicken head tonight."

There was a thud as the youth's body hit the floor.

A chuckle came from the door at the bottom of the stairs. Barney, still feeling the effects of parting with a pint of blood, was leaning against the wall. "That was some show, mateys. I reckon Colin here got two of them besides the one you scared to death, Anna, and Harry's little friend will sleep with the light on for many a night to come."

Barney crossed over to the plants, stroked their wrist-thick stems, and crooned over them. "You did well, girls. I'm real proud of you." Then he picked up the barely breathing ruffian and casually flung him through the door. "He'll find his way back to London eventually. By the way, I traced the contact back as far as I could. They were certainly hired by someone from the dark side, but whoever it is, he's playing clever. I couldn't see the face, but I'd bet a full tank of gas I know the smell of 'im. I'll figure it out and let you know. Now, for God's sake, gimme me a drink. I need to make up the blood that's haring round Wolf's veins instead of mine. Then we'll clear up."

Some time later, the brigadier and the now-normal Anna emerged from the kitchen with sandwiches, coffee, and a warm, mellow brandy. Harry, wearing fresh clothes but still a little hairy round the ears and arms, lifted the temporary blocking illusion that had prevented unwanted customers from entering the pub during the fracas, and the victors sat down to relax.

Gradually, the bar filled with the usual crowd drinking beer and dry white wine. Bucky kept looking round the room as if to convince himself that things were back to normal. He had hardly said a word since the battle. The brigadier patted his shoulder and smiled.

"I know it's hard to take in, Colin. Within the last two days you have seen and done more strange things than in your whole life. Believe me, it's not always like this. Such times are normal close to the end of an age. Especially an age when the Forerunner walks the earth. The Lords of Darkness will try anything to kill him before he begins his mission. To protect him, we will use all our powers—and our lives, if necessary. You are part of that ring of protection, meaning you are also a part of the Abbeys of Light."

"How can I be?" said Bucky shakily. "I have no talents. I'm not a werewolf like Harry or a shapeshifter like Wolf. I don't have the knowledge you and Margaret have, I can't talk to plants like Barney, and I don't even know what Anna is!"

"I'm a lamia, Colin. Look it up in your books when you get home," Anna said. "But it's not just wild talents we need. You may have something deep inside you that you don't know about yet. I can't switch my talent on and off at will; I have to get plenty mad before it triggers on. Harry manifested his talent during the last Angolan war when he was captured and tortured; the pain and fear he endured forced it to the surface. His captors actually helped him to escape after that! If you are here with us, it is because you're meant to be here. There is a purpose to everything. It's all part of the great plan.

"Wolf is conscious again, but I'll keep him here for a day or so. And I phoned the hospital; Margaret's out of danger now, though still weak. I think you'd better start back for London soon."

Bucky looked round at the people that he had known for so short a time. They were his friends and would lay their lives on the line for him, and he would do the same for them. Anna had hit the nail on the head: He—and Florrie as well, for that matter—was now part of something greater than he had ever dreamed. White Heat, the world of rock and pop, even Johnny, seemed far away. Bucky had changed, changed for good, and he could never go back. For a moment he felt very lonely, but not for long.

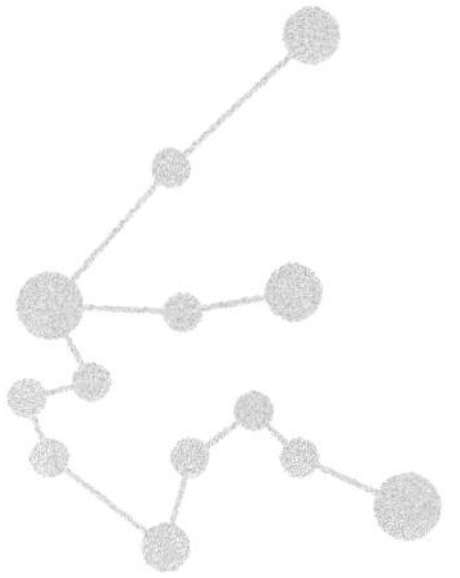

CHAPTER SEVENTEEN

30 November, 2:00 p.m.
Topnote Studios, Kingston upon Thames

"No, no, no!" Frank shouted, signalling to the recording crew that he'd halted the take. "Tango, you can't muck about with the phrasing like that. You'll have to take a breath after the next bar to compensate and that'll throw the following bar out of whack. Sing it as it's written."

"Why should I? It suits my voice better this way, and you can rewrite the music to fit in." Tango's voice was sulky. It was the third time they had blown the recording, and Frank was outraged.

"Rewrite it?" Frank screamed. "Do you have any idea how much time that takes? It's not a matter of adding a few bloody notes, you stupid sod. The whole thing is balanced round the main theme and a particular rhythm. You'll sing it as it's written or you won't bloody sing it at all."

"Then I don't sing it at all," snarled Tango. He flung down his guitar and ripped off the headphones. "You can all go to hell. You're still hankering after your precious Johnny. Well, he's not coming back. You're stuck with me, so get it into your heads and let's get this track down."

Frank opened his mouth to scream at him again, then shut it. He remembered a small room in the foothills of the Himalayas and heard the voice of the young man standing with him: "It is imperative that you keep the man you know as Tango in the group, no matter what happens."

He realised the others were looking at him and wondering what he was going to do. Frank took a deep breath and hid a grin inside himself. If Tango wanted the song rewritten, he'd get it rewritten. But it wouldn't be as easy to sing—he'd make sure of that.

"OK Tango, you win. I'll juggle it around, but it'll take time and I can't do it in a few minutes. Let's do 'Moonshine Boy' and leave this one until tomorrow. I'll figure out a new rhythm for it. That suit you?"

"Yeah, that suits me. You're getting to be real sensible, you know that, Frank?" Tango scooped up the headphones and fitted them on. "Just remember who's the lead singer now and you'll do fine."

Frank gritted his teeth and began to play the intro to the next track of the new album. In the sound box, Bucky silently applauded Frank's forbearance. During the last few weeks, he'd put up with a great deal of arrogance from the triumphant Tango.

Bucky had been busy as well. A vaguely worded statement to the press had revealed that Johnny Nova had been the victim of a breakdown due to overwork and stress; he was officially "resting." Tango had reappeared in their lives to cut the new album, for which (thank God) Johnny had already made several tracks.

Using his finely tuned ability for observing and assessing character, Bucky looked at each member in turn and marvelled at the change in them in so short a time. Tango, no longer in Johnny's shadow, was the most obvious one. Had things been different and had Johnny never joined the group, there was no doubt in the manager's mind that the Welshman would have made it to the top. Probably as a solo artist, which was where he was heading now, so he said. Tango certainly displayed a more positive approach to the work now that he held top place. To his credit, Bucky had to admit that he was good. Different than Johnny, but still good.

Lyle and Ginny were getting married in four weeks' time in the little church they attended every Sunday. The boys and girls from the church youth club were preparing a surprise for them. Trained by Frank, they'd be the choir for the wedding and would sing a choral version of "Mountains of Gold." This had turned out to be so good that Bucky was now negotiating a deal to record and release it as a single. The proceeds would fund the youth club's planned extension. The vicar was ecstatic.

Liam and Biff had drawn closer together and further away from Tango. Bucky sighed and wondered how much longer he could keep the group together.

Leaving the control room, Bucky made his way to reception. He'd felt Florrie's presence as soon as she came through the door. Both knew where the other one was at all times. Such small talents he had ceased to find amazing.

Florrie was leaving next week for the Abbey of the Aeon. She was taking Margaret, now out of hospital, to recuperate and while there would learn to use her own healing powers more efficiently. He would miss her. He'd not realised how deeply she had become a part of his life until now. What if she liked being in the abbey and didn't come back? Bucky stopped walking, his gut twisting at the thought of no Florrie in his life. No laughter, no cosy chats in the evening, no deeply satisfying sex, no companionship, no...Florrie!

Bucky began walking again. This was something he would not let happen. He pushed open the soundproofed door to the foyer.

"'Ello love," said Florrie affectionately. "How are they doin'?"

"Not good. It's taking longer than it did with Johnny. Tango throws a tantrum every time we think we have it right, so it means another try. At this rate it'll take twice as long to get the album cut. Florrie, are you sure you have to be away for six weeks?"

"Now we've been over this a dozen times, Colin. You know why I'm going, and we agreed on the time I'd be away. Margaret can't go by 'erself, the brigadier is tied up with things here, and the abbey can't spare anyone. Besides, I need to get a grip on this healing thing." She paused, looked at his woebegone expression, and smiled. "Oh, love, the time'll go quickly, you'll see. You have a lot to do, what with all that reading and studying. Plus you've got that big charity event next month, and now this album." She took his face, no longer so chubby, in her hands and kissed him gently. "I'll miss you too, *miro chal*."

"Will you marry me, Florrie?"

Florrie's handbag hit the floor along with her jaw. She stared at her companion, lost for words. Bucky took her silence for hesitation and hurried to fill the gap.

"I know I'm not much to look at, but I love you, Florrie. God knows I didn't look to love anybody. I've always thought the business would be the only love I'd ever have. But over these past weeks, well, it's been so good. I've never felt so close to a woman before. I would have gone to pieces without you, girl, and still would if I lost you. Florrie, please say something—anything—preferably yes, but a maybe would help me over the next six weeks. Whaddya say, huh?"

To his consternation—and that of the receptionist, who had been shamelessly listening in—Florrie burst into tears. Bucky staggered as she flung her arms round him and wept happily down the back of his neck.

"Yes, Colin, yes! Yes! *Meery Dovvel*,[8] I love you so much, but I thought… I didn't think you…I mean, I'm not so young or even pretty anymore, and I know you get a lot of young women round you—all them gropies."

"Groupies, Florrie, not gropies. I dunno, though, it sure describes 'em well. Here, dry your eyes, girl. I'm not so young either, and I'm sure as hell not pretty, but I know I want to be with you all the time from now on. I'll look after you and I'll love you and be with you for the rest of our lives, and that's a promise."

A loud sob followed by a ferocious nose-blowing made them both jump. The receptionist, the doorman, the security man, and assorted onlookers had gathered and were listening avidly to the conversation. Florrie laughed and dried her eyes and turned to the embarrassed Bucky.

"I've got witnesses now, my lad. You asked me to marry you and I accept, here and now, in front of all these people. You're hooked, Colin Buckman, and you can't get out of it."

Bucky, red-faced but happy, grabbed Florrie and kissed her thoroughly. "Let's go buy a ring, girl. Then I'll believe it's really happened."

"What about the session?" asked the delighted Florrie.

8. "Good God"

"Sod the session. Let them sort themselves out for once. Come on, let's get back to London and buy that ring. What would you like, sweetheart? Rubies, emeralds, them blue ones? Or would you prefer a diamond?" They departed amid good wishes, much back-slapping from the crowd, and more sobs from the receptionist.

Wrapped up in their newfound happiness, they didn't notice the tall, thin, black-clad man who stood aside to let them pass. He looked after them, his eyes narrowed and thoughtful, then entered the building and approached the desk. The girl looked up inquiringly.

"Mr. De'ath to see Mr. Garrett, if you please." He smiled as he spoke, but the air chilled. For a moment the girl wanted to call the security guard but dismissed the thought. A customer was a customer, and he might be important. But she was glad there were other people in reception—he gave her the creeps.

De'ath probed the atmosphere round him. Traces of the happy emotions of the past few minutes were still there. He grimaced. Happiness offended him. He preferred gloom, despair, and fear. It made him feel strong and powerful. Most of all, he enjoyed bending potentially powerful people to his will, like Tango. Things were coming along nicely there.

Tango reminded De'ath of someone else, someone way back in the past whose life he had left in ruins. In the recesses of his mind, De'ath remembered the sobbing of a young girl. *Bakr, please don't go. Please stay with me. Those people will hurt you, change you, I know it. Bakr, please.* The sobbing died away, slipping back into those parts of his mind and memory that he kept locked away. What De'ath had once been—who he had been—was no longer relevant. He had power now, wealth, and a life that would be as long as he wanted it to be. He had known poverty and the lash too, but no more. The Lords of Darkness had been good to him, and as long as he found and trained talents for them to use, he was safe.

"I *said* let's go. Shit, man, what's wrong with you? You sick?" Tango stood beside him, shaking his shoulder.

De'ath turned on him like a feral animal. "Don't touch me. Don't ever touch me, do you hear?"

"OK, OK. Now can we go? I'm starving and I have to be at the photographer's by five. C'mon, let's get the hell out of here."

The others watched the two of them leave the building. Lyle drew a deep breath. "That guy gives me the creeps. He smells like his name. Ugh."

"He sure in hell has Tango in his pocket, though." Liam was not given to deep thinking, but his Irish ancestry had bequeathed him a modicum of feyness, and it was telling him not to cross Mr. De'ath.

"Where did Bucky and Florrie go, June?"

"Oh, Frank, it was so romantic. He proposed right here, right in front of my desk. She said yes and they've gone off to buy a ring. It was just like the movies and right here before my eyes. It was lovely." The receptionist dissolved into happy tears again.

The four men stood as if pole-axed. Then Frank regained his power of speech. "Bucky? Colin Buckman proposed…to Florrie? Holy shit!" They looked at each other, then let out a combined whoop that had the security guard looking out of his office.

"Florrie's cooking for keeps!" exulted Liam. "Homemade steak and kidney pie, dumplings, apple and ginger cobbler, and chocolate pudding. God be praised, I can throw away the magnesia tablets."

"No more sneaking off to Mama Mary's and rolling home at three in the morning for you," warned a grinning Lyle.

"I'll have socks without holes, and that'll be great, but she'll make me tidy my room," mourned Biff. "I'll never be able to find things. Still, it means I won't have my underwear dyed red from being washed with your sweaters, Ly."

Laughing and joking, they left the building and piled into Liam's Range Rover. Only Frank was quiet. He was thinking of Johnny and how happy he would have been to hear the news.

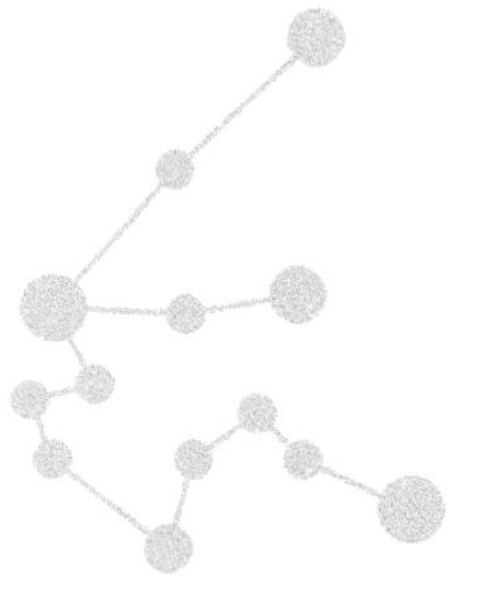

CHAPTER EIGHTEEN

20 December, 6:00 p.m.
The abbot's study, Abbey of the Dawn

"You have disappointed me greatly, Johnny Burke. I knew you to be headstrong; I did not think you were a fool. How far do you think you would have travelled before succumbing to cold, hunger, and hyperthermia, quickly followed by death?"

"I knew this place was just a hundred miles or so from a road. I figured I could make it that far." Johnny stood erect and defiant before the abbot. "I had food and a tent and maps from the library. I knew I couldn't make it back the way we came, so I tried for the road. I followed the Sherpas at a distance for the first three days. It was no picnic, but if it hadn't been for the avalanche, I stood a good chance of making it."

"What you did not know, young fool, was that the Sherpas were never going anywhere near the road. Within hours they would have disappeared from sight and you would never have found them! They intended to take another route, about which you know nothing, and which you would never have found. Fool! Fool! To put at risk all we have accomplished so far..."

Johnny had never seen the abbot so angry. Normally the abbot controlled his emotions with an iron hand, but today he let his anger show in no uncertain manner. Johnny wished fervently he could be dismissed and go. He was cold, hungry, tired, and thoroughly dejected by the failure of his second attempt to escape. Beside him Tze-Ring stood quiet and withdrawn, his face unreadable. As usual, Chambha stood silently, waiting and watching.

God, Johnny felt so sick of all this humbleness and boot licking. He'd been in the abbey over a month now, and apart from being taught how to meditate (which he did with bad grace and little enthusiasm), he had done nothing but help out in the kitchen, sweep up, and take food and water up to the hermits in their spartan caves. Johnny had spent his spare time in the library poring over maps of the area and stealing and secreting the things he deemed needful for his escape. Every day was the same as the one before. Jesus, he didn't even know what day it was. Christmas could have come and gone for all he knew!

Tears stung behind his eyes. Christmas. Florrie's roast turkey with roast potatoes and Yorkshire pudding, and gravy, parsnips, and sprouts. Rum pudding and hot custard, mince pies and Christmas cake. Christmas was special to him, always had been. With Johnny gone, who would remember that Florrie liked Chanel no. 5 perfume and that Bucky counted on Havana cigars, single malt, and new waistcoats, the louder the better? He missed London, Trafalgar Square, and feeding the pigeons. He missed the smell of chestnuts roasting on the braziers outside the British Museum and the cheery banter of the street vendors. The Christmas lights, the crowds, the blast of hot air as you entered a store from the cold street, the familiar black cabs and their voluble drivers, the decorated trees in the windows of houses, and the feeling of that special day coming nearer and nearer...This year Christmas would pass Johnny by and he'd never know. It might even have gone and would never be back, just lost forever.

Johnny became aware that Tze-Ring was speaking to the abbot. He spoke in Sanskrit, a language everyone in the abbey seemed to speak except him. Johnny listened without understanding as Tze-Ring entered into a spirited conversation with the both the abbot and Chambha. They obviously did not like what they were hearing, but the lama was insistent.

Finally the abbot seemed to agree with Tze-Ring. Chambha made a gesture of despair and turned to the window. The abbot turned to Johnny.

"I have to tell you, Johnny Burke, that much against my better judgement, I will give you another chance. I had thought to incarcerate you for the rest of the winter, but my grandson seems to think there is another way." The abbot paused and then went on, his voice deliberate and intent. "If you try to escape again, Mr. Burke, I will punish you so severely you will remember it for the rest of your life. Make no mistake, I can and will do it. Now take him away. It will cost me many hours of meditation to regain my inner peace."

Tze-Ring hustled Johnny out of the panelled room and down the stairs to the outside. Without speaking, they crossed the courtyard and finally arrived in Tze-Ring's own quarters. Lea was waiting for them. She spoke anxiously to her husband in her native French and listened to his reply. Anger flared in her eyes, and she swung round on Johnny as if to strike him, but her husband caught her arm and spoke again, gently. She pulled away and left the room.

"I have asked her to bring some food for us. She is a little upset, but she will get over it. Sit down, Johnny, please."

"Why is she angry? I guess the abbot has a right to be mad, but why Lea?"

"Johnny, you must give up these attempts to escape. You will never make it, believe me." Tze-Ring's tone of voice was evasive. He looked steadily into the flame of the candle in the middle of the table. "You need a lot of expertise to get over these mountains. Even I would not try it alone, and I know the tracks well. Lea is angry because I promised my grandfather that I will persuade you to give up the whole idea of escape. Please do not make me ashamed before him."

Before Johnny could answer, the door burst open and a small whirlwind dressed in a quilted coat with yak-skin boots and mittens threw himself into Tze-Ring's arms.

"Papa, Papa! I went over the snow on my new skis a long, long way, Papa. Right down to the big gate."

"So far, small one! That is a great improvement. Tomorrow I shall put on my skis and go with you. Shall we ask Brother Johnny to come with us?"

The child turned and looked at Johnny, one finger in his mouth, then said, "Brother Johnny's head says he does not know how to ski, Papa. But we can teach him, yes?"

Tze-Ring laughed ruefully. "You must forgive him, Johnny. Taras does not understand yet that one must not go into the mind of another without permission. Ah, here is dinner. Lea, that looks delicious."

Silently Lea placed bowls of hot chicken with vegetables and rice broth in front of the men, with a smaller one for the child between them. Warm bread straight from the oven added to the taste. Johnny tucked into it. He had not eaten a full meal for a week. Food had been scanty and always cold during his abortive escape. Between mouthfuls, he questioned Tze-Ring.

"I thought you didn't eat meat, Ring. How come you're scoffing this down?"

"Lea is not a vegetarian, so I modify my diet to link with hers. I eat a little meat with her sometimes, and she joins me in my more spartan food. In the abbeys we try to give and take, Johnny."

"Papa, why is Brother Johnny thinking of trees with lights on them?"

Startled, Johnny raised his head, then laughed. "I was wondering if I had missed Christmas, Taras. Those trees in my head, they are Christmas trees. We decorate them at this time of year with lights and things that glitter and sparkle. We put presents under them for our friends and people we love. Sometimes we stand round them and sing special songs called carols." He paused, then quietly asked, "Have I missed Christmas, Ring?"

"No, you have not missed Christmas, Johnny. It is only the twentieth of December today. I will obtain a calendar for you in the New Year if that would please you."

"Yeah, I'd like that. Thanks, Ring."

In silence they finished the broth, and Johnny played for a while with Taras, showing him how to make a glider out of a piece of paper. Finally, as Lea took the boy off to bed, Johnny rose and yawned. "I'd better get going as well. At least I'll sleep warm tonight. Lea, the broth was great! Just what I needed. But I'll get back to my room and sleep now. Guess I'm more tired than I thought. Ring, I'm sorry I let you in for it with the old man. G'night and thanks a lot."

"I will walk back with you, Johnny."

The two men walked back to the main building under a moon that poured molten silver light over the mountains high above. The intense cold was dry and caught at their lungs in the thin air. They descended the steps and crossed the cloisters that led along the edge of the plateau, then entered the main building.

Tze-Ring said, "You need time to get used to the altitude, Johnny. That is why we have not demanded too much of you yet. Soon you must begin your real training."

As they went down the steps that led to Johnny's room, Tze-Ring paused and grasped his shoulder.

"Johnny, I have some news for you about your friends."

His companion swung round, immediately alert, fearful.

"Are they all right, Ring? Has anyone been hurt? It's not Bucky, is it?"

"No, no. Please do not worry; the news is good. The man you call Lyle, he and Virginia are getting married in two days' time. Also, Colin Buckman and your aunt Florencia, they too will be married in the New Year. Your aunt at this moment is in the Abbey of the Aeon learning to refine her healing talents."

"Wait, Ring, hold on. I can't take it all in. Just back up. Lyle and Ginny… Well, we always knew they would marry. I'm real happy for them. But Bucky and Florrie getting married?"

"Yes, soon. I believe they plan it for the first week of the coming year. Much has happened since you left, Johnny. Your aunt has developed a unique type of healing skill, and Mr. Buckman has been undergoing training as a Watcher. The abbot is proud of his rapid advance. He always had psychic talents but used them unconsciously in his role as a manager. His grief at your disappearance forced it to the surface."

Tze-Ring paused before Johnny's door. "Come, let us talk in your room. It will be warmer."

Once inside with the fire built up, Tze-Ring told Johnny what had been happening since he left. The news had been filtering through for several weeks. The young singer leapt to his feet and walked up and down agitatedly, asking questions and seeking reassurances. Finally, worried he would not be able to relax enough to sleep, Tze-Ring persuaded Johnny to lie down and gently induced a light trance, then left him curled up under the covers to drift into a natural sleep.

As Tze-Ring walked back to his own quarters, he reflected that maybe it had not been a good idea to tell Johnny so much. But it was done now. He sighed and wondered what the future held for them all.

"You look worried, *mon cher*." Lea had come to meet him. "I should not have allowed myself to become angry or for Johnny to see it. I did not realise the truth of the matter. He does not know what you have done, what you have offered in exchange for his good behaviour. Is it not so, my husband?"

"No, Lea, he must not know. The burden would be too much. I will rely on our bonding to persuade him to remain of his own free will." He turned Lea in his arms. "Have I told you today how much I love you, my wife, or are you tired of hearing me say it?"

The woman's laugh belled out in the still, crisp air. "Perhaps instead of words, a little action would not come amiss, *mon amour*."

He bent to lift her into his arms and carried her to their quarters and into the warmth of the bedroom. Her thick fur wrap fell away as he laid her down on the bed and the firelight gleamed on her naked body. She smiled lazily and held out her arms.

"Come to me, my love. Quickly! I am cold and need your warmth inside me."

It took only moments for Tze-Ring to shed his heavy outdoor boots, the thick, quilted outer robe, and the silk one beneath that covered only a linen loin cloth. Already hard and ready for their joining, he covered her slim body with his larger one. Soft curves and hard angles fitted one into the other. He nuzzled her breasts, still firm after childbirth, and kissed his way down to the junction of her thighs. He cupped her mound, threading his fingers through the soft curls to find her wet and ready for him. The fire died down, but the heat between them increased. Their bodies entwined and locked together. Tendrils of thought went between them, carrying delicate, intimate messages as fragile as the wings of a moth.

"Tze, oh love…Yes, like that…just like that. Aah, yes, there. Ooh."

"So soft, Lea, like satin. Hot, wet satin. No, don't move, not yet. Let me have a moment more of you, aah…Yes…Now, my dove."

Lea arched under him and called out her love in breathless words in a dozen different tongues. He caught them from her lips with his own and fed his soul with their passion. She locked long, slender legs about his waist and wrapped her arms round him tightly. His movements became stronger, quicker, and more forceful, his breathing harsher. She answered with her own deep sighs and gasps, drawing him deeper into her liquid depths until there was no beginning and no end, just a wave of sensation that tumbled them over and over into climax, then exhaustion and sleep.

As he drifted into the warm darkness, Tze-Ring caught a faint mental call, a pain-wracked whisper of sound. But before he could respond, sleep had claimed him.

21 December, 3:00 a.m.
A row of derelict houses in East London

A narrow sliver of moonlight fingered its way through a tiny crack in the boards that had been nailed over the broken window. Slowly it crept across the dirt-encrusted floor, lighting up scraps of carpet and broken lino—all that had been left in the derelict house.

Something shifted restlessly in a far corner. A faint moan of pain was followed by the sound of sobbing. It continued for a few minutes, then died away as exhaustion and sleep overtook the frail figure huddled under a tangle of dirty newspapers. The night padded by on cat paws of silence. The figure stirred again. Hunger and thirst were added to pain and despair, and they combined to bring an unwanted wakefulness.

The moonlight inched its way across the pale face of a young girl, her skin drawn tight over the bone. Blond hair hung in lank, greasy tendrils down her neck, sticking to the open sores there. She hunched over as the stomach cramps began again. Too weak to cry anymore, she lay there hopeless and helpless, waiting for the dawn. In the far corner, a rat watched with bright eyes, sniffing her scent. It, too, was waiting.

A memory stirred behind the girl's closed eyes. A dark alley and a man walking alone in the night. Two men with knives and another man, tall and strong, coming from the darkness behind them. A sharp, clean pain in her heart, and then a slow warmth filled her with something she had not felt since she had been a small child. Someone cared about her, fed her emotionally. She remembered it even now, when the pain was so bad. There were gentle hands in the memory and a voice that spoke in her head, a name: Tiz...No, Tz...She fought to bring the sound into focus. *Say-Ring.* Yes, the sound was right. Another name followed, but she could not find the right sound for it. It didn't seem to matter because the name had a life of its own. It blazed across her brain and spread out, warming her for a brief moment. Then it was gone—no, not gone; it was in her heart, promising help and comfort.

In a corner of the room, a sphere of light appeared and moved to the centre, attracting the girl's attention. It grew larger, extending and becoming an ovoid holding the figure of a man. With a whimper of fear, the girl huddled closer to the corner. The ring of light narrowed and grew faint, changing into a man who stood in the cold, dark room. He bent over her, smiling. Although his lips did not move, she heard the voice of the stranger who had told her his name.

"Do not be afraid, little one. I promised I would help you when the time came. Soon there will be others here. You will not be cold and in pain for much longer. I cannot help as much as I would like; I am far away, and what you see here is only a sort of dream. But I will stay with you until help comes."

Two miles away, over the river, Sir John Bernard-Fox QC came fully awake. The abbey emergency call was still ringing through his head like a clarion. *BROTHER TZE-RING, ABBEY OF THE DAWN. EMERGENCY. HELP NEEDED. TRANSPORT TO AN ABBEY-RUN MEDICAL CENTRE. YOUNG GIRL, 15/16 YEARS, DESTITUTE, HUNGRY, COLD, IN URGENT NEED. CANNOT OFFER PHYSICAL HELP; AM IN A BODY OF LIGHT.*

Sir John glanced at his sleeping wife, leaned over, and gently pressed her temple with two fingers.

"Liz, sleep soundly without waking until I return unless there is danger to you or to the house, in which case you will wake quickly. Do you understand, dear?"

The sleeping woman murmured and snuggled deeper into the warmth of the bed. Satisfied, her husband sent out his ready-to-assist signal. *FOX HERE, READY TO HELP. WHERE ARE YOU LOCATED?* Back came the precise details, by which time Sir John had thrown on a tracksuit and sneakers and was heading down the stairs to the garage.

Miles away in a private nursing home in Harrow on the Hill, the matron and the head of night staff met in the corridor, the matron in her dressing gown.

"Did you get it as well? I estimate they'll be here within an hour. Sir John drives a Jaguar, so he should make good time. I'll get dressed, have a private room made ready, and deal with the admission papers."

"I'll wake Dr. Anderton and brief her on what's happening."

The women disappeared in opposite directions, intent on different tasks.

Back in the derelict squat, the girl was being held in a light trance to ease her pain. Tze-Ring stood beside her, his aura enclosing her with love and warmth. Gently, he probed into her past to a time when she was happy and felt safe. He found the memory of a Christmas party with presents and friends round the girl. He gathered her memories and gave them back to her as a dream. She relaxed, smiling as she relived the party. The young man beside her bowed his head and offered heartfelt prayers that his own children would never know such despair. Then Tze-Ring thought of Johnny and his childlike delight in Christmas and smiled; it might make him feel better if some kind of festivity was arranged for him.

A car drew up outside the rubbish-filled, overgrown front garden. A man got out and looked round, then sent out a call.

"Brother Tze-Ring?"

"I am in the house, Sir John. The girl is entranced to keep her pain at bay. But I can do nothing else for her on the physical level."

Sir John entered the room, paused as he saw the light-rimmed figure of the young lama, and bowed slightly. "Greetings, Brother, in the name of the Light we both serve."

"And mine to you, my brother in Light. Has all been prepared?"

"Yes. Dr. Anderton called me on the car phone. They are waiting for us." Sir John bent and gently lifted the frail body into his arms. "Poor child. There are so many of them like this, alone and destitute. Do you know how long she has until transition?"

"A few days only. I summoned the Priests of Anubis from the other side of life; they will attend her until it is over. She needs warmth, love, and medication against the pain. A hand to hold. The rest will follow. I must go—the pull is strong, and I cannot hold on anymore. My thanks for your swift service."

Sir John carried the girl to his car and laid her in the backseat, covering her with a rug. Then he got into the driving seat and, with a mental goodbye to the fading Body of Light, he drove away.

Tze-Ring's last thought before succumbing to the pull of his physical was that Sir John's legal colleagues who saw him as a hard-hitting barrister would have been amazed to see his gentle handling of the girl. He heard Lea's voice calling. It was time to let go.

"Tze, wake up. Gently now. Come back, *mon amour*. Gently, my heart."

Tze-Ring opened his eyes slowly. His head was cradled on Lea's breasts, and remembering the young girl he had left close to death, he wept against their softness for all those he could not help.

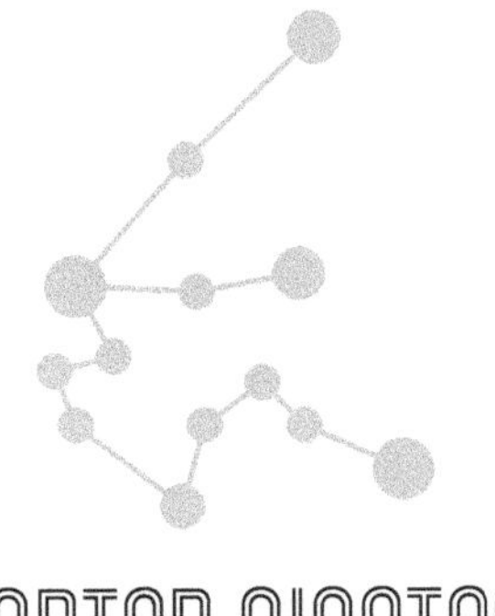

Chapter Nineteen

24 December, 7:30 p.m.
The penthouse, London

The apartment was ablaze with lights, the Christmas tree in the corner almost solid with decorations, and piled beneath it boxes and parcels of every shape and size. Candles gleamed on tables and window ledges, and lamps added their glow to the room, offsetting the chilly darkness outside. Inside it was warm and filled with the scents of Christmas: pine needles, oranges and apples, the clove and cinnamon of mulled ale in the punch bowl, the aroma of brandy, and, more faintly, cigars.

Margaret and Florrie had returned from the abbey to celebrate Christmas Day with their menfolk. Liam had gone home to Eire and taken Biff with him; Lyle and Ginny were on honeymoon in Hawaii; where Tango was, nobody knew or cared. So Bucky, Florrie, and Frank invited Margaret and the brigadier to celebrate with them. Now, after a gargantuan meal, they lay sprawled in chairs and on sofas, replete and sleepy.

Florrie bullied her comatose companions into a sense of interest. "Colin, Colin, wake up! Don't go to sleep. It's time to open the presents. Come on, Frank, you do the handing out, there's a love."

Ever obliging, Frank heaved himself out of the armchair and ambled over to the tree. Running his eye over the gaily packed heap, he chose the first one.

For the next hour they worked their way through the pile of gifts, the carpet becoming a wasteland of Christmas paper, ribbons, and cards. Giggles, laughs, and gasps of delight (mingled with a few of indignation) filled the air.

"Florrie, silk boxer shorts with hearts on? Have a heart, love," Bucky teased.

"I will, Bucko. I'll pick one really special heart, but not until later."

"My word, Colin, where on earth did you get this?" The brigadier held aloft a medal won at Rorke's Drift and smiled happily; it would fit a long-regretted space in his collection. He leaned over to show it to Margaret, who was exclaiming over a delicate, eighteenth-century silver posset cup.

Florrie, eagerly unwrapping a large box in plain red paper, stopped suddenly, her eyes filling with tears. She put a hand up to her mouth, stifling a sob. Bucky rose quickly and went to her.

"What is it, Florrie?"

She offered the box for his inspection: a coffret of Chanel no. 5 perfume, toilet water, soap, talcum powder, and creams, and wrapped round the perfume, a lustrous double string of pearls.

"Oh, Colin, it's from Johnny! My little lad, he remembered. Oh…" She dissolved into happy tears.

Bucky patted her hand and looked helplessly at Margaret, who came to Florrie's side.

"William and I had a call from the abbey. Johnny sent word that he wanted you to have Christmas presents as usual. There are presents for Colin and Frank and the others as well. Johnny wanted you all to know he was thinking of you even though you couldn't be together."

Margaret rose and went to get the other gifts and handed them to Bucky and Frank. They unwrapped them in silence. A lacquered box inlaid with ivory for Bucky, and inside a six-inch crystal ball wrapped in silk. For Frank, a set of antique silver and turquoise buttons, handmade and delicately engraved by Tibetan craftsmen.

"Once his training is underway, in a year or two he will be taken to each abbey in turn. When he goes to the Abbey of the Aeon, it is possible you can meet him there. That's the message from the abbot. He's well and healthier than he's been for a long time—you're not to worry."

Florrie raised her head from Bucky's shoulder and blew her nose. "If we had something for 'im, is it…I mean, would it be possible to get it to 'im so he'd know we hadn't forgotten 'im? He loved Christmas so much. I got 'im something, but I didn't put it under the tree. I thought I'd keep it on the off chance that he…" Her voice trailed off.

Bucky cleared his throat. "Yes, well, I got something myself. Like Florrie, sort of…just in case, you know…"

"Me too," said Frank gruffly, cleaning his glasses with unnecessary vigour. "We all did."

Margaret looked at the brigadier. "I think we could get them to him, though it might take a while being such a long way away," she said. She rose and went over to the punch bowl. "Let's drink a toast. To Johnny, and to his future."

25 December, 5:30 a.m.
The Abbey of the Dawn

"Brother Johnny, Brother Johnny, wake up! Wake up please."

Johnny opened his eyes to find an excited small boy bouncing on his stomach. He groaned, turned over, and came face to face with several other children currently residing in the abbey, their eyes regarding him with varying degrees of excitement.

Taras yanked the thick, feather-stuffed coverlet off him, unconcerned that this left Johnny in the nude, and began dragging his clothes from the chair close by.

"Brother Johnny, get up now. Now! We made you a tree, a real Crystalmus tree."

"Christmas tree," corrected Johnny automatically and grabbed the covers back. "And Taras, you shouldn't barge in here like this. It's…" He peered at his watch, only lately restored to him. "Christ almighty, kid, it's only five-thirty in the morning."

"Happy Crystimiss, Brother Johnny," chorused the watching choir.

"Children, *alors mes enfants*, go now. *Allez vite, vite s'il vous plait*. Go and wait in the schoolroom until Brother Johnny has washed and dressed himself." Tze-Ring shooed the miniature Christmas tree committee out the door and turned back with a broad smile on his face. "They spent the last three days preparing this surprise for you, and their enthusiasm ran away with their manners, I am afraid."

Johnny, now thoroughly awake, headed for the minute bathroom that had been one of the more pleasant surprises about the abbey. "It's the first time I've been up this early on a Christmas morning, I can tell you." He flipped up the lid of the chemical toilet. "Ring, did you manage to get those things for Florrie and Bucky and the others?"

"Yes, Johnny, they have received their gifts from you as I promised. You must thank Father Chambha for this; it was he who mentally relayed the requests to the receiver at the Abbey of the Aeon. I will make tea while you dress, then we will go and see the tree the children have prepared for you. Taras told them about the custom of the Christmas tree in England. We have so many different cultures here that some traditional customs get left out. But the tree caught the imagination of the children so much that Lea suggested they make one for you. The decorations may seem strange to your eyes, but they were made with much love.

"When you have seen the tree, we will have breakfast together. By the way, Shuna and Ta will be there. They have now emerged from their time of silence. I have rarely seen Shuna as rattled as she was after dealing with you," he chuckled at the memory, "and Ta was so traumatised he could not use his powers for weeks. Only Murad was able to cope, just. You made your mark there, Johnny."

Johnny emerged from the shower and began to shave, grabbing the cup of tea his companion held out with his free hand.

"I can get along without Shuna. She's a pain in the ass. Ta's all right, though."

Johnny dressed quickly, shivering; with the fire almost out, the room was overly cool. Ten minutes later the two men headed for the schoolroom run by the abbey for both their own children and those of the locals.

A tumult of noise greeted Johnny's appearance, and dozens of small hands grabbed his padded coat and dragged him to where a rather lopsided and worse-for-wear fir tree stood in the corner. What it lacked in elegance it made up for in ingenuity where decoration was concerned: Brightly coloured berries, scraps of silver paper, ribbons, and jewellery loaned by the women had been used to make the little tree as bright as possible. It was lit with tiny handmade candles and crowned with a star of silver paper. As Johnny stood and looked at it, a lump rose in his throat, and his eyes grew hot with tears he could not shed.

Taras tugged at his hand. "You like it, Brother Johnny? Is it like Cristimiss trees in England?"

"Christmas tree. It's a Christmas Tree." Johnny lifted him up and hugged him. "Yes, Taras, it's just like them. Even better, in fact. Thank you, thank you everyone who had a hand in this present. Thank you very, very much."

A small girl clapped her hands in glee and pointed. "No, Brother Johnny, it's not a present, it is just a tree. The present is here, see, under the tree."

Taken by surprise, Johnny lowered Taras to the floor and looked at the circle of smiling faces. He bent to look under the tree and saw a large parcel wrapped in red cloth. As he drew it out, silence fell round him. He looked up and saw most of the abbey personnel had arrived to watch. Even the abbot was trying to look as if he just happened to be passing by.

Johnny unwrapped the present. *A guitar.* Not the electrically enhanced instrument he used to play in the group, but a superb, handmade Spanish guitar. Johnny had not realised how much he had missed making music, and for a moment he couldn't speak. He ran a hand lightly over the strings to find it had already been tuned, and by an expert.

Lea brought a chair and Johnny sat down. The children drew close round him. He began to play, and as he played, Johnny Nova sang "Mary's Boy Child."

"How appropriate," said the abbot to Chambha, "the Forerunner singing of the new Christ child on Christmas Day. I wonder if that young man realises he is literally prophesying the coming of the new Christos as all Forerunners do. I think, Chambha, that on occasion, the Elohim enjoy a joke at our expense."

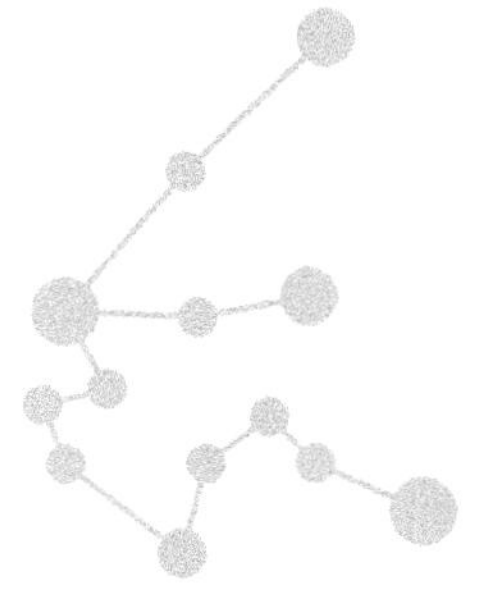

CHAPTER TWENTY

7 February, 8:00 p.m.
The Abbey of the Dawn

They brought Johnny back with his hands tied behind him. *Like a bloody criminal*, he thought bitterly. *They're the ones that should be locked up for kidnapping me in the first place.* "I'll bloody well do it again as well!" he shouted defiantly as they dragged him across the courtyard.

As they neared the abbot's door, it opened and Lea came out, accompanied by a worried-looking Wang Ta. Her face was blotched with tears, and when she saw Johnny, she turned her head away as if she could not bear to see him and wept on Wang Ta's shoulder.

"Lea, what's wrong? Is Taras OK? Is it Ring?" He looked back over his shoulder as the Sherpas pulled him away. "Let go of me! Lea, what is it?"

But she had gone.

In Johnny's quarters, Chambha was waiting for him, his face giving nothing away. "You will remain here until I come to fetch you, Johnny Burke. You would do well to pray and ask forgiveness for the sorrow you have caused." With that he left, locking the door behind him.

Left alone, Johnny went to the window and looked out over the icy landscape he had tried to cross. One part of him was glad to be back in the warmth and safety of the abbey but another longed to fly free and return to what he still thought of as home. God, he was tired, tired and cold and angry and fearful. The abbot had threatened to punish him well and truly the next time he tried to escape; well, the next time was here. He shivered wondering what the punishment would be. He promised himself not to give in no matter what the old sod thought up.

Curled on the padded seat, Johnny looked up and saw a new moon above the peaks. He watched it, imagining it over London, turning the Thames to silver. After a few minutes he bowed his head on his arms and fell into a deep sleep. Hours later Chambha found him and put him to bed, covering him with a fur rug. For a few minutes Chambha watched the exhausted man sleep, then sighed deeply and left him to rest. Tomorrow he would need all his strength to face the punishment decreed by the abbot.

It was stony-faced Chambha that came for Johnny after a tense day of wondering and waiting. He brought a robe of unbleached wool, a pair of soft leather slippers, and a cord of white silk, and he handed them to Johnny with instructions to put them on. Then Chambha crossed to the window, his back to the room, and stood looking at the snow-capped peaks. Johnny hurried to obey, throwing off his thick sweater and woollen pants and tugging the high leather boots from his feet. The silence to which he had been subjected since he had been brought back from his abortive escape had unnerved him, and he sought to alleviate the gloom.

"Chambha, what are they planning to do with me?" he asked, pulling the robe over his head. "I mean, am I going to have bread and water for a month or be put on latrine detail?"

There was no answer.

Johnny tried again, seeking to lighten the atmosphere with an attempt at a bravado he did not feel. "Maybe it'll be solitary confinement up on the mountain with the loin cloth brigade, huh?"

Chambha continued to gaze out of the window silently.

"Well," Johnny tried a weak laugh, "just so long as they don't hang me by my balls out of the window. After all, the abbot keeps telling me how important I am to his plans, so I guess he can't do too much to me, eh?"

Still no answer.

Fear and a growing uncertainty, plus day-long tension, finally snapped Johnny's temper. He grabbed Chambha's arm, turning him to face him. "For Christ's sake, why can't you give me some clue as to what it is they're planning? All this silence and secrecy is screwing me up. You think you're so clever, but I'll tell you this: Whatever it is, I'll take it. And I'll try again and again and again until I do get away. What do you think about that?"

"I think, Johnny Burke, that it is time to go," was the answer.

Chambha crossed to the heavy wooden door and opened it. As Johnny prepared to follow him, he caught a glimpse of himself in the wall mirror. For a moment he stopped, surprised. The robed figure reflected in the glass was a stranger he no longer knew. Then he followed Chambha through the door.

In the corridor Johnny straightened up and put on a show of nonchalance he was far from feeling. He'd show them what he was made of. He'd stick it out to spite the abbot.

The Abbey of the Dawn was empty and quiet. Their sandaled feet rang on the flagstone floors and a chill draught caught the tapestries on the walls, making the figures on them ripple with a sort of half-life. As Johnny followed his silent guide, he saw it was not only corridors and rooms that were empty. The whole place was deserted. No chelas scuttled along the labyrinthine ways of the monastery; no pacing figures deep in meditation were circling the courtyard or sitting, wrapped in thick cloaks, listening to the pleas, prayers, and complaints of the local people; even Mother Anjeli's brood of school children were absent, their voices and laughter gone from the rooms where she and Sister Lea taught them each day. A hushed, anxious atmosphere hung over the entire building. They crossed the courtyard, Johnny shivering in the thin wool of his robe, and climbed the steps up to the Hall of a Thousand Candles.

The spectacle of the candlelit space never failed to catch Johnny's breath, but this time the atmosphere was different. As usual it was ablaze with light, with a thousand flames multiplied and reflected back from the crystal-studded ceiling, and hazy with the smoke rising from the huge, spiral-shaped incense cones. At the far end of the hall the statue of Tara gazed down, calm and benign as usual. But it was the sight of every monk, chela, and servant in the lamasery gathered together and waiting in silent array that stunned Johnny. The candles captured their shadows and threw them against the walls to make a monstrous tapestry of leaping figures that dipped and bowed and flickered as if in some frenzied but silent dance.

On the dais, beneath the looming figure of the Tara, there had been placed two ornately carved chairs side by side. A semicircle of lesser chairs curved away on either side to accommodate the other members of the Abbey of the Dawn. At the foot of the dais were placed two large, round drums, the skins bound with red cords and hung with tiny bells. Crossed on the top of each drum lay a pair of aged human thigh bones. The sweet, heavy smell of incense filled the air, adding to the dreamlike quality of the scene. Then he saw it in the middle of the open central space, and it took the breath from his lungs.

Square in shape, it stood higher than a man, high enough that Johnny could not touch the topmost edge with his fingertips and wide enough for his outstretched arms and legs to hold his body taut. Iron rings were embedded into the seasoned wood at the top and bottom, and from them hung leather straps, supple but strong enough to hold a man's weight. The frame was supported on a base of the same dark wood and showed old scars where something had bitten deep into its surface.

The hair on the back of Johnny's neck rose. His heart began to race. Icy sweat gathered in his armpits and groin and ran in musky rivulets down his back and legs. His hands, clammy with fear, clenched at his side. He did not need to see Murad, stripped to the waist and standing beside the frame, or the coiled whip in his hand to know what lay ahead.

Johnny clenched his teeth to keep them from chattering. From somewhere deep within himself, he found a forgotten morsel of courage that lifted his head high, and with Chambha following him he descended the short flight of steps leading to the tiled floor of the hall. There was no way he was going to let them see the sick dread inside him. He promised himself he would keep silent as long as he could bear the pain, but already in his mind he was anticipating the sting of leather across his back and the bite of the straps cutting into his wrists and ankles.

Chambha escorted him to a seat within a few feet of the whipping frame and remained silent at his side. Deep within the building a gong began to sound, long, shuddering notes that crashed against the ears and vibrated through the hearts and brains of those gathering in the hall. On the fifth stroke the central doors opened, moving silently on their oiled hinges to admit the members of the Abbey of the Dawn, headed by the abbot and the abbess.

They processed into the Hall of a Thousand Candles, their gold and white robes in contrast to the red and saffron clothing of the monks. They moved silently to the measured resonance of the gong. Light from the candles multiplied their shadows until it seemed the hall was filled twice over, once with real men and women and again with wavering, semi-human forms that might have emerged from a nightmare.

The gong fell silent as the leaders of the abbey took their places and the others arranged themselves on either side. From his place Johnny could see Lea, her face drained of colour, flanked by Shuna on one side and Abbess Hannah on the other; both seemed to be supporting her. From the shadows at the back of the hall came two monks from the lamasery, who seated themselves at the foot of the dais with the drums between their knees. Johnny's mouth was like a desert, not even enough moist to swallow. Every muscle was drawn as tight as a finely tuned piano wire as he fought down his fear and dread of what was to come.

There was a long, drawn-out moment of waiting. Then the thin, dry voice of the abbot cut through the silence.

"John Patrick Eamon Burke, you were warned after your first attempt to escape that future tries would result in a severe punishment. You ignored that warning twice. Each time you have been brought back to the abbey to face a period of discipline, but nothing has had the desired effect. You must now face the consequences of your actions."

The abbot raised his hand, the gong sounded once, then the drums began a steady beat. The bronze inner doors opened again to reveal two well-muscled monks. Between them, and clad in a robe identical to Johnny's, stood Tze-Ring. They moved slowly down the hall to just before the wooden frame, where they stopped. The drums fell silent and Chambha stepped forward, his face more impassive than ever.

Still Johnny did not comprehend, until…

With swift, deft movements, Chambha bound the unresisting Tze-Ring to the frame. Each limb was stretched wide and lashed securely until he was spreadeagled across the wood. This done, Chambha took a step back, and with one muscular effort he ripped the robe down the back from neck to hem, leaving Tze-Ring naked but for a loin cloth.

It was the sound of ripping cloth that shocked Johnny out of his stupor and into a stark awareness. The full horror of his "punishment" dawned on him, and he swung round on the abbot in a fury.

"You said I would be the one to be punished, so why is he here? It's my mistake, my punishment. It's nothing to do with him, so let him go *now*!"

"It has everything to do with him, Johnny Burke. After your second attempt to escape, Tze-Ring offered to stand surety for your good behaviour. He was to convince you not to try again, and if he failed, to take your punishment. That was the bargain."

"I didn't know that! If I had, do you think I would have tried to escape again? No way! I was not told of his promise, so it doesn't—it cannot—count!"

The abbot remained impassive and silent, deaf to Johnny's plea.

Johnny ground his teeth in rage. This sanctimonious little creep had watched his own grandson be prepared for the whip, had commanded the presence of Lea at the "punishment" of her husband. He tried again. "You have no right to do this, no right at all. Jesus Christ, man, think! He's your own grandson!"

"Exactly, Johnny Burke. He is my grandson, and..." The abbot paused to allow his words to sink in to the full. "He is also your half-brother, for you share the same father. This is why he was chosen to help with your training and why he volunteered to be your...I believe the term is 'whipping boy.' I am aware of the regard and affection that has grown between you; now it will serve a useful purpose. You will watch every lash descend, hear its impact, and see its effect. You will endure every moment. So will I. So will Sister Lea. Brother, grandfather, and wife, we will share Tze-Ring's pain and your punishment together."

Johnny's eyes were starting from his head. At last he understood so many things that had puzzled him over the last few months, understood the feeling of closeness, companionship, even love he felt for Tze-Ring, who had shared his battle against the drugs and the booze. The man who had washed away vomit and filth from his body, who had held him like a child when pain, despair, and desperation had overwhelmed him. The man who had coaxed, bullied, and almost carried him over a mountain range. The one who had laughed and wept with him, who had listened to him when he spoke of the love he had felt for his mother. The man who had shared his family with him. His brother. Sweet God in heaven, they were going to beat his brother, and all because of him!

"Bastard! Fucking bastard! You dirty, rotten, lying, cheating little shit!" he screamed and launched himself at the abbot. The men who had escorted Tze-Ring leapt to their feet and caught Johnny long before he reached the impassive figure above him. He was lifted and carried, kicking and screaming, back to his place, where they forced him to his knees and held him there, facing the silent figure on the frame. The two brothers looked at each other, Johnny's eyes full of fear, anger, guilt, and self-loathing, Tze-Ring's calm, accepting, and infinitely loving. At a signal from the abbot the drum masters began a steady one, two, three, four beat. Murad loosed the coils of the whip and drew back his arm to its full length.

"Noooo!" screamed Johnny, struggling violently in the hold of his captors. "Nooo, not him! Me, me, meeeee, not him. Bastards! Dirty rotten bastards! Let him go! Oh, Jesus Christ, don't beat him. Please don't. Please, please don't beat him."

The whip sang through the air and landed across the unprotected back of the young man. Tze-Ring arched against its force but made no sound. It was Johnny who screamed, screamed again and again, time after time as the whip rose and fell. It was Johnny who flung himself from side to side, trying in vain to reach his brother, to cover him, to protect him from the next lash and the next and the next. Murad's arm rose and fell rhythmically, and with each new cut across his brother's back, the hall was filled with the sound of Johnny's screams and sobs and his unavailing pleas for them to stop. On and on it went until even Tze-Ring's iron will cracked. A whimper escaped his bitten lips, and he slumped forward.

For Johnny it was the moment of truth. He realized they intended to carry on until he gave his word not to escape again. He flung back his head and howled his rage and grief into the face of the gentle Tara far above him.

"All right, I promise. I promise on Tze-Ring's life. I promise, no more escapes, no more." He turned a ravaged, tear-blotched face to the abbot. "Only please, for the love of God, for the love of Tara, don't beat him anymore."

The drums stopped on the instant, the whip was halted in mid-air, and utter silence descended on the Hall of a Thousand Candles. Only the subdued sound of Lea's sobs were heard. The restraining hold on Johnny's arms fell away and he sank down, his legs unable to hold him. Sobbing, he crawled on his hands and knees towards Tze-Ring, now hanging unconscious, held only by the straps that bound him to the frame.

Alternately praying and cursing, Johnny levered himself up and tried to undo the knots now slippery with blood and sweat. Chambha came to help, cutting the thongs with a small knife, but it was Johnny who caught and gently lowered his brother's limp form to the floor. With strips of the torn robe he tried to staunch the flow of blood, all the while begging Tze-Ring's pardon for the suffering he had endured on his behalf.

"Hang in there, Ring, please, for my sake. Jesus, boy, I didn't know, didn't know they'd do anything like this. Oh God, oh sweet God, what have they done to you? What have *I* done to you? Chambha, help me. There's so much blood, I can't stop it. Forgive me, Ring, please. You gotta forgive me. I'll stay as long as it takes. I'll do everything I'm supposed to do, only you gotta make it, Ring. Please, *miry prala*.[9] Please, brother, make it through."

They came with a soft cotton sheet and Johnny covered the still figure with tender hands. Then he took the limp body in his arms and rocked backwards and forwards, his tears clearing rivulets in the blood where Tze-Ring had bitten through his lips.

How long Johnny stayed like this he never remembered, but finally he felt a touch on his arm and looked up. The hall was empty but for Chambha and two monks with a stretcher. They went to lift Tze-Ring, but Johnny shook his head. This was his father's son; it was his task. He got to

9. "my brother"

his knees and gathered his brother into his arms. Then, with a superhuman effort, he struggled to his feet.

Staggering under the weight, Johnny made it across the hall and through the doors. The others followed silently, waiting until his grief-fired strength gave out. Then Chambha took on the burden. Johnny followed him to the abbey hospital suite. A pale, silent Lea awaited them. There was no reproof, no anger or blame from her, which made Johnny weep all the more. Together they washed away the caked blood and gently smoothed healing salves into the smaller wounds. Mother Adelie stitched the longest and deepest of the cuts and gave Tze-Ring an antibiotic shot, then sent the young man into a deep sleep to recharge his spent energy levels. She gave instructions to call her when he regained consciousness or if he ran a high fever, then left them.

Chambha advised Johnny to return to his own room, promising to call him as soon as Tze-Ring came round, but he refused. Covered with his brother's blood and wrapped in a blanket, Johnny remained by the bed, his hands folded round those of the man who lay so still and quiet. Lea sat silently on the other side of the bed.

Johnny watched the pale face on the pillow with sunken, red-rimmed eyes, watched every shallow breath and every shudder as the abused body slowly relaxed into sleep. Just before dawn Johnny's head slumped onto their linked hands. Worn out with guilt and sorrow, Johnny slept. He never heard the abbot enter, nor did he see him bend over his grandson and smooth the slightly fevered forehead.

Even now the abbot's training prevailed, and he shed no tears but instead opened his heart chakra to the full and bathed the two half-brothers in its healing, loving light. Silently, Chambha came to the side of his beloved superior and waited. The abbot raised his head, his eyes shadowed with a pain he would not allow himself to admit, and smiled gently at Chambha and then at Lea.

"I think that Johnny Burke is finally ready. Tomorrow we may begin the real training of the Forerunner."

YEAR THREE

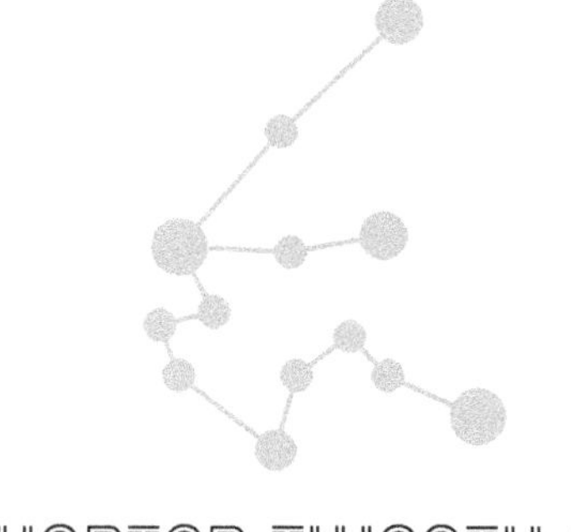

Chapter Twenty-One

28 April, 5:00 a.m.
The Abbey of the Dawn

The room was filled with the translucent light of early dawn. It stole quietly through the fine cracks on the wooden shutters and amused itself making patterns on the polished floor. At one end a platform had been built to hold a low wooden seat, piled with yellow silk cushions for the comfort of its occupant. Watching the abbot as he sat motionless, Johnny reflected that he had never yet seen him take advantage of a chair back. The abbot might well feel the need for a cushion or two between the wood and his bony little butt, but his spine was never anything less than ramrod straight.

Quietly, Johnny eased his own aching thigh muscles. After more than two years in the abbey, he had yet to feel comfortable in a full lotus position. He and the others, having been summoned from their beds before dawn, had now been waiting over an hour. They had not been told why, nor did they expect to. Such occurrences were part of the training, to obey instantly and ask no questions. Johnny was well aware that there were times in occult work when instant obedience could mean the difference between life and death, or worse. Johnny's concentration slipped, and he winced as a stab of cramp flared through his leg. Deliberately, he fixed his mind on the muscle and willed it to relax.

The abbot opened his eyes and gazed at the group of three men and two women sitting in a semicircle before him. All were concentrating on the circles painted on the floor before them, filled with early morning sunshine. His trained sight touched each in turn, pausing on Johnny. Gently, the abbot brought his greater will into synchronisation with that of the younger man, and the stubborn muscle relaxed and adjusted itself to the position required of it. Johnny's thoughts linked gratefully with those of his teacher, for whom over the last two and half years he had developed a respect bordering on love.

"Thank you, Rinpoche. I never could get the hang of this position. My legs don't fold up like yours."

"Perhaps Tze-Ring's stretching exercises would help, my son."

Johnny groaned inwardly and felt the silent shimmer that indicated the abbot had come as close to laughing as he ever did.

"We will commence this morning's exercise by building the Body of Light, and you may begin now." The abbot's voice, soft as it seemed, carried across the room without effort. "Please pay attention to detail, and do not forget the importance of the solidity factor. You have ten minutes in which to accomplish your task."

The class closed their eyes and began. From each solar plexus there emerged a grey mist that centralised itself and began to spiral inside the circle. As it did so, it gathered into itself motes of sunshine from the sun's rays. Concentration was etched deeply into the students' faces as four out of the five struggled to form the shape of a robed and hooded figure from a mixture of astral proto-matter, ectoplasm, and solar particles. In the fifth circle, a shape built quickly and with little effort on the part of its creator. As the other forms grew bigger and more defined, it became obvious the fifth bore no resemblance to them.

Beside Johnny, Sister Devin took a sidelong glance at his circle. Her eyes widened in shock. Then she gave an uncontrollable shriek of mirth. Her ample frame shook with laughter and her half-formed Body of Light imploded with a sharp clap of sound. It was closely followed by more explosions as the others also lost control of their tulpa thought-forms.

Held firmly in Johnny's circle was a circus clown dressed in a garish suit of bright yellow and red. Four large blue buttons adorned the front along with a flashing neon bow tie. Its feet sported outsized patent leather boots with silver buckles. A multicoloured wig topped by a bowler hat sporting a wilted white rose crowned a painted face, smiling on one side and weeping on the other. On its shoulder it carried a walking stick, from which hung a bundle tied in a red-and-white handkerchief. Johnny sat with closed eyes and a faint smile, holding the clown firmly to the physical plane.

For some minutes the room rocked with a mixture of laughter and shocked comments on Johnny's audacity. Then the abbot's voice cut through their mirth with the cutting edge of steel.

"Brother John, you maintain your Body of Light in its present form. The rest of you come to order and rebuild your efforts as before. *Now*."

Silence descended and four minds bent to their task. Johnny began to sweat. Why hadn't the abbot chewed him out or dismissed him from the room? He was up to something, but what? Johnny wrestled with the effort needed to keep his highly detailed astral joke in its present form. Then the abbot spoke again.

"Good. Most satisfactory. You are all to be congratulated on your efforts. Now, if you will allow me a moment of time to prepare my own form, we will proceed to the next part of the exercise."

With practised ease the abbot constructed a Body of Light so solid it could have passed for the abbot himself—and, as Johnny well knew, frequently did. What did he have in mind? Johnny began to regret the burst of boredom and mischief that had tempted him to try his long-suffering teacher yet again. He listened as the abbot's voice issued from his Body of Light.

"We will now proceed to pass through the upper astral level to that of the higher mental level. We will begin now."

Johnny's sweat turned to ice. Take this joker up to the gateway of the angelic levels? The abbot couldn't be serious! He tried to loosen his hold on the form but found his mental power over it had been frozen. A will stronger than his own held both mind and tulpa firmly together and literally hauled both through the astral dimensions and into the rarefied atmosphere of the Briatic level.

A cool voice sounded in his inner ear. "This will be something new for those who dwell at this level. Do you not think so, Johnny Burke?"

"Sir—Rinpoche—Master, please let me reabsorb it. What will they think? I admit I was wrong to do such a thing. Please let me destroy it."

"I think not. It may shed light upon the power of the human mind when spiced with a sense of humour. It will also teach you something new, Johnny Burke."

In the luminous sphere of the higher mental levels, the six forms and their teacher hovered gently, five of them discreetly robed and the sixth, with its trapped portion of Johnny's consciousness, bobbing like a balloon on a stick.

A swarm of scarlet geometric shapes swooped past them with a sound like a chime of bells. They circled once and then drew up in a shimmering phalanx, tinkling insistently. One dropped closer to inspect them. It stopped short on reaching the clown and emitted a discordant chime that intimated disbelief. Linked to the abbot's mind as he was, Johnny understood what the shape was and what it communicated to the old man. As one of the Choir of Michaeline Angelic Warriors that guarded entry to the Briatic level, it had inquired if the form required healing, for it was undoubtedly ailing in some way. If not, why was it here?

Johnny squirmed mentally and tried again to pull away from the iron will of his teacher to no avail. Giving the sign and uttering the multitoned note that was the password for this level, the abbot asked permission to enter the upper level of creation called Briah. The angelic warrior flashed through a complicated rainbow of colours, communicating with others of its kind in the upper level. Johnny sensed that it was with reluctance it allowed the clown to pass.

The abbot offered no answer to the question that had been put to him. Angelics of the lower levels were curious creatures but had no ability to reason beyond the most mundane level. They had been created to act upon certain signals and nothing beyond that.

Six figures, four of them drooping with fatigue and one rapidly deflating clown, were drawn further into the bright realms of Briah. Johnny struggled to maintain full consciousness, remembering a similar physical distress when crossing the mountains two and a half years ago and the feeling of not being able to breathe properly.

A double row of translucent pillars appeared and the abbot led them onwards, between the giant columns. At the furthest point appeared a sunburst of light radiating a power that was too much for some of the figures before it. Two of the figures fell in upon themselves and were caught up by the geometric shapes that had followed at a distance, alert for such a happening. Gently, they were carried away and handed to angelic healers who would see them returned to safety.

The other figures clung to the last of their strength. The sunburst moved nearer and a thread of Light reached out and touched them, feeding them just enough energy to hold their forms together. It caressed the abbot, and Johnny understood from the interchange that it was greeting him with affection as one who was known and loved. Then it turned to him.

In desolation, still encasing Johnny's consciousness, the clown waited for ignominious dismissal. In the infinite radiance at the Level of First Entry, the Light touched it, fed it, loved it, and laughed with it, spoke with it. The silver chiming slowly became words he could understand.

"Thou of grace and Light, I bid thee welcome. Hold no sad thoughts. Hast thou not been taught that the Fool is the highest form of all? It echoes the simplicity of Kether, the first and most blessed manifestation of the One. Full knowingness has yet to touch thy mind, but that time is near. Then many things will become clear to thee. Laughter is a holy thing, and you will have need of it in the days to come."

The wondrous eyes dimly seen in the depths of the gold and scarlet light burned into Johnny's mind and drove his consciousness from him into blessed darkness.

♬ ♩ ♫ ♪ ♬ ♪ ♫

Johnny opened his eyes to find himself looking at the ceiling of his own room. He tried lifting his head and winced as pain struck behind his eyes.

At the sound of his groan, someone moved beside him and placed a cool cloth on his forehead. A familiar chuckle sounded in his ear.

"Ah, Johnny, Johnny. How do you get away with it? Your first summons into the presence of an archangel, and Michael at that, and you make your entrance as a circus clown. Only the Forerunner could get away with that."

"How was I to know what was in the old boy's mind? He's as devious as a cartload of monkeys." Johnny reached out mentally and touched his brother's mind with an affectionate thump. "How's Lea? It's not long to go now."

Tze-Ring smiled broadly. "She complains of the child's excessive movements and longs for the birth to be over. If you feel well enough, shall we walk a while? I have news for you."

Johnny sought his high leather boots and shrugged into the fleece-lined chuba that, even in late April, was needed this high in the mountains. The brothers walked along the balcony in the clear sunshine and looked down over the snow-covered valley and the mountain range beyond. Then Tze-Ring said quietly, "In six weeks' time, you are to leave us and go to the Abbey of the Aeon for further training. There will be letters from Mr. and Mrs. Buckman, Frank Saunders, and your other friends. Also, Lyle's ordination will take place in June, and at the same time his and Virginia's daughter, Mary-Clare, will be christened. Such good news should cure your headache, Johnny."

Johnny stared at him for a moment, trying to take it all in. Then he whooped with joy. Seizing his brother round the waist, he whirled him into a dance of celebration.

"Hey, is this a ritual dance for the coming of spring?" asked Murad, emerging from the library with Chambha. Grinning, Johnny 'pathed him an image of a mating dance he had seen on safari. Murad laughed and changed the face of one girl to that of Johnny, then ducked his retaliation.

"Your telepathy is as good as mine now," Murad told him. "Father Chambha will have no difficulty picking you up from the Aeon." They laughed and joked together in the sunlight for a while longer, then Murad and Tze-Ring left to attend to their various tasks. Chambha placed a hand on Johnny's shoulder and drew him aside.

"Do you have time to spare, Johnny Burke? I have been instructed to show you something. The Holy One thinks you should see this before you leave."

Johnny looked at him, sensing that whatever it was, it could not wait. He placed his hands palm to palm and bowed to his superior. "My time is yours, Father Chambha. Whatever it is, I am happy to be instructed by you."

Chambha chuckled and acknowledged the courtesy. "How different you sound to the Johnny Burke that first arrived here. You have worked hard in these two years, and I sense that soon you will reach a new point in your training. Your auric colours are changing again. But come, we have things to do."

He led Johnny through the courtyard into a little-used passage leading to the mountain. Reaching it, they climbed in silence to save their breath in the thin air. For almost an hour they climbed. Then Chambha paused, watching Johnny as he pulled himself up the slope. He smiled but made no offer of help.

"I can remember a time when you would not have dared to climb this path," Chambha said as the younger man came level with him.

"Yeah, well. Things change, Chambha, things change. Where're we going anyway? As far as I can tell, this path leads up to the glacier, right?"

"True, but we will take another path leading away from the glacier, one you have not seen before." Chambha turned to climb once more, with Johnny following.

Below the ridge Chambha turned off the main path onto a narrow track hidden by two large boulders. He leaned his weight against them, and they swung open to a wider path paved with small stones to give their feet a better grip. The path followed the edge of the mountain for some thirty yards, then turned at a sharp angle into the mountain itself. The opening before them was set into the mountain, and from the valley it was totally invisible. Awestruck, Johnny paused and looked up at the entrance. The pillars and lintel had been carved by skilful hands, but time and the wind had erased all but a faint trace of the graceful Greek sculptures. Under Johnny's feet, the stones were worn smooth by the tread of feet over countless centuries. He shivered as if the wind had laid its icy hand on his heart, then followed his companion into the mountain.

Two winged statues stood inside the portal. Johnny recognised them as Hypnos, the Greek god of sleep and dreams, and facing him, his brother Thanatos, the god of death. On one side of the small entry hall stood an ancient wooden coffer banded with iron. Chambha opened it and took out two thick capes of yak skin lined with sheep fleece. He gave one to Johnny and pulled the other over his shoulders.

"It will be even colder where we are going," he told him. "But it is well lit."

Steps had been cut into the living rock, and the imprint of sandaled feet told a vivid story of devotion where they had worn the stone away. The two men descended into a silence that became more profound as the cold became more intense. Only a faint hum could be heard—a small generator, Chambha told Johnny; it was switched on only when extra light was needed. Wrist-thick candles set in tall iron lanterns offered a flickering light that, with their exhaled breath, combined to produce an eerily glowing mist.

From far below came the sound of voices, and as they rounded a bend in the steps, they came face to face with two young chelas from the abbey. They resembled polar bears in their thick chubas and fur-lined boots and carried armfuls of candles to replace those that had burned out. They bowed respectfully and hurried up into daylight.

"They are the guardians of this place. They work in pairs, keeping the torches renewed and the steps free of ice," Chambha revealed as they reached the end of the steps. "Now we have a long walk, but it is more level."

They set off along a passage connecting the local mountain range with others to the east of them. Natural caves for the most part, but helped by the hand of man where it was needed. They had walked in silence for almost a mile when Chambha halted and waited for Johnny to catch up. Then he pointed. Ahead was an arch of rock lit by a faint blue glow. The arch led into a cave so vast and majestic it took the breath away. As far up as the eye could see, there was a hazy blackness from which hung stalactites, some thicker than three men standing together could encircle with their arms. From the floor rose stalagmites shaped and carved by water seeping through from the glacier above. The walls were pitted with natural alcoves leading away into an echoing emptiness that amplified and threw their hushed voices back to them. Over it all glimmered a pale blue light, coming from small arc lamps set here and there against the walls.

Chambha produced a torch from his chuba and led the way across the rough, rock-strewn floor to a row of alcoves flanked by frozen waterfalls that had ceased to flow long before the building of the pyramids. Johnny followed, looking round in wonder at the massive ice formations. Then Chambha spoke, catching his attention, and held the flame close to one of the niches.

"This is what I have brought you to see, Johnny Burke. It is fitting that you look upon the faces of those who have gone before you. This is where we keep our dead, and where the abbot, your brother, you, and I will stand in our turn."

Through the thin veil of ice, Johnny saw a face as perfectly preserved as if sleep had closed the eyes a moment before. Lost in wonder, Johnny went from one niche to another. A few were young; most were old. A bronze plaque at their feet proclaimed their identity.

"Mother Shahnaz, 1749–1850. Sister Hua'ahali, 1901–1945. Father Chen-Liu, 1780–1871. Father Jarush, 1869–1950, Abbot. Mother Sybilla, Mother Irene, Brother Bruno, Father Mattias…" Johnny crossed to another row and went down it softly, murmuring the names of the dead, his awe making them more of a prayer than mere words. Johnny turned and saw them all around him, serene and patient, as if waiting to speak.

He wandered from one place to another, lost in the wonder of this icebound necropolis. Finally he came to a group set farther back into the shadows and lifted the torch to see the names. His eyes widened and he swung round, calling to Chambha.

"Chambha, c'mere, quick! I don't believe it! Surely it can't be true. Look at these names, the dates." He lifted the flame close and the ice wept tears from water tens of thousands of years old. The first copper plate said simply, "Phidias of Macedon, revered by Alexander."

"Ah, yes," said Chambha quietly. He drew Johnny away from the silent figures towards another row of tombs. Here the dates were much later, coming into modern times. Johnny walked along looking at the names and Chambha, suddenly watchful, walked with him.

Danang Golmud, 1896–1952, Watcher. Frances Marriner, 1903–1944, Watcher. Mother Olga Besmarrianova, Birthdate Unknown–1969, Beloved Wife of Nyang Darsip. Johnny raised questioning eyes to his companion.

"Tze-Ring's grandmother. She was a very beautiful woman; I have seen pictures of her when she was young. But another beautiful woman lies next to her, and this is the real reason why I have brought you here, Johnny."

Johnny looked and was unable to believe what he saw. Encased in the ice, her sweet face captured forever at the moment of death, was Lily Isabelle Mercedes Burke. The plaque gave her name in full and added in elegant script, *Beloved Wife of Father Eamon Merrow & Mother of the Forerunner of Aquarius.*

♬ ♩ ♫ ♪ ♬ ♪ ♫

"How, Chambha, and why?"

They had returned to the entrance and now rested, drinking the hot tea provided by the anxious chelas when an ashen-faced Johnny staggered up the last flight of steps.

"It was fitting that she should rest in the company of those with whom she lived even for so short a time. You were conceived in the Abbey of the Dawn, Johnny, in the Hall of a Thousand Candles with the White Tara guarding the two who fashioned your body. You would have been born here also, but it was thought too dangerous. What was buried in her grave in Rotherhithe was an unfortunate victim of suicide who thereby received a decent burial. The body of your mother was embalmed and brought back to the abbey to rest. Your father came here often. He was totally distraught until the abbot sent him to another abbey to help him come to terms with her death."

"Distraught! He never came to see her—or me. He never cared for us, or he'd have been there when she died." Johnny turned away.

Chambha waited for a while, then spoke.

"He loved you both deeply, but your safety, the safety of the Forerunner, was the most important thing to both of them. That is why your mother retained her maiden name. As for not meeting, Johnny, you should know better than that. They met on a different and higher plane often, and still do. They gave up being together physically so that you would have a normal life before beginning your training. Father Eamon has watched over you from the upper levels since the day you left India for England.

"Come, Johnny, let us return to the abbey, for your father is waiting there to greet his son."

Johnny raised his head and stared at Chambha. "My father, he's in the abbey now?"

"Yes, Tze-Ring is with him. He arrived late last night, and you will travel back with him to the Abbey of the Aeon. He is nervous, Johnny. He knows how much you have blamed him and has borne much sorrow because of it. Draw on your training and on your knowledge of what lies ahead and how important it was to keep your whereabouts secret. He gave up the wife and son he loved so dearly to ensure your safety. You could not know it at the time, but your father was with your mother in her last moments. She stepped from her body into his arms. He was the one who gave her into the hands of those who waited for her. As he now waits for you, Johnny Burke."

For a long time Johnny stood at the very edge of the mountain path, looking down on the abbey where his father waited, going over many things in his mind. Then he turned to Chambha and smiled as only Johnny Nova could smile. "Let's go!"

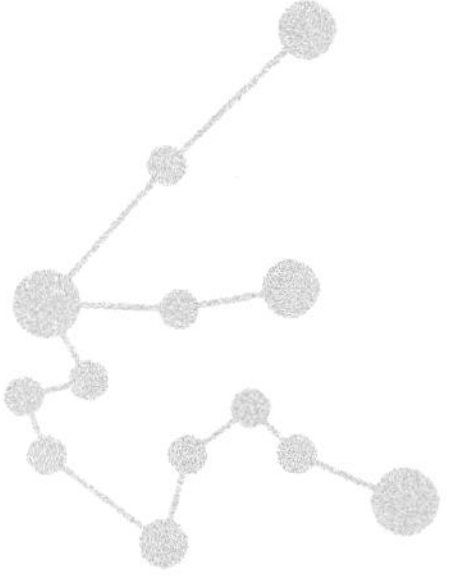

CHAPTER TWENTY-TWO

28 April, 7:00 p.m.
Glastonbury

"And now may I present the star of this performance: Tango Garrett, backed by the one and only White Heat!"

A roar of adulation went up from the packed house as the curtains swept back and the mobile floor moved slowly downstage, carrying the group with Tango centre stage and loving it. As it stopped, Tango leapt down and, with a lavish bow to the audience, went straight into his opening number, his handsome face alight with pleasure at the applause. That it was as much for the group as it was for Tango Garrett made no impression on him. Hips gyrating, head back, his silver costume catching and reflecting a myriad of lights, Tango was lost in the power of fan worship.

Moonshine Boy, she's not for you
She's a gal with silver in her shoe
An' her daddy's gunnin' for you, sure, Moonshine Boy

Oh, I know you love her true
But you must find somebody new
'Cos she's meant for blood that's blue, Moonshine Boy

Man, it was just a stolen kiss
From a teasin' Southern miss
So don't count on married bliss, Moonshine Boy

She didn't mean a word she said
Wouldn't have you in her bed
You were just a passin' fancy, Moonshine Boy

Two and a half years of star billing had made a difference to Tango, and he'd lived his publicity to the full—much to the disapproval of Bucky and the rest of the group. Tonight he was on top of the world, jubilant with the thought that his contract with Bucky had finally run out and he would be free of them all. True, he'd made a name for himself as a solo singer of film title hits, but he craved the freedom to scale what he saw as the *real* heights. By the end of the week he'd have a film contract in his pocket, and to hell with the group and Colin Buckman.

Tango finished the song and collected the applause without a thought for his backing. Then, with a change of mood, he played a lyrical ballad Frank had written for him; Tango was not to know it had been written as a means of getting "Mountains of Gold" away from him.

Had there been any with the Sight in the audience, they would have seen the aura of Dark energy that now almost enclosed Tango as he moved about the stage, seemingly secure in his newfound power. He had worked hard—and suffered, too, at the hands of De'ath and the Darkness—to hone his psychic abilities. Tango didn't know he'd reached the peak and could go no further without committing himself fully to the ultimate sacrilege: the murder of the Forerunner. There remained within a portion of Light that was still untouched by the Dark.

From his box, De'ath savoured the moment. The idea was already planted; the scene was set; the play would open on the world stage. When

Johnny returned and took up his ministry as the Light intended, Tango would see it as a threat to himself and his hard-won popularity. Inevitably, there would be comparisons between them. Already there were disturbing rumours going round concerning the singer's strange nocturnal habits, his phenomenal energy levels, and their source. De'ath smiled. It had not taken long for Tango to get lost on the left-hand path.

From the wings, Bucky watched, as he always did when White Heat was playing. He knew in his heart it was the end of an era. In a few days the group would cease to be, but thanks to Frank, Bucky, and the power of attorney signed over to him by Johnny, the recording studios of Saunders & Buckman and its imprint, NovaTones, would keep them all in work for the foreseeable future.

In June Lyle would be ordained. Bucky smiled, remembering his shock at the announcement that Lyle was entering the ministry. Almost as much of a shock as seeing little punk Ginny in her fairy-tale wedding dress with her hair six inches longer and a butterscotch brown instead of bleached blonde! He'd been as proud of her as if she were his own daughter. The birth ten months later of Mary-Clare had been a real family event, with the whole group pacing the waiting room floor. Even Tango had made a brief appearance. Bucky sighed, then brightened at the thought of seeing Johnny again, and for the hundredth time he wondered if Johnny had changed much. *God knows*, he thought, *the rest of us have.*

In the front stalls, Florrie was thinking the same thing. Now with a better grip on her psychic talents, she saw the darkness that was growing in Tango and shivered. She looked up at the box where De'ath sat in solitary splendour. He caught Florrie's thought, looked down at her, and inclined his head in recognition. She looked away quickly and concentrated on the spectacle before her.

Tears ran down Florrie's cheeks as she realised this was the last of White Heat as live performers. There was the farewell concert next week, and that was it. She'd miss all this, but things had to change in order to get better. She focussed on the stage. When she got back to the apartment, she'd write a letter to Johnny that would be there for him when he got to the Aeon.

28 April, 7:00 p.m.
The Abbey of the Dawn

"He waits for you in your room, Johnny," said Tze-Ring quietly. "It will be difficult for him, knowing you blame him so much. Think before you speak, little brother. Try not to add to his pain."

Tze-Ring drew Johnny to the door and opened it.

Their father stood by the window looking over the valley. He was not a tall man—both Tze-Ring and Johnny were taller—but was broad in the shoulder, and at fifty-five his black hair was only lightly touched with grey. He heard Johnny enter the room, and his whole body tensed. Then he turned slowly to face his two sons.

Johnny Nova looked and saw much of himself in that face; Johnny Burke looked deeper and saw the father he had longed for and never known until now. The Forerunner looked deepest of all and saw the lines that sorrow had drawn on this man's face as well as the desperate loneliness that darkened the brilliant green eyes.

The silence between them stretched and tautened. The harsh words Johnny had prepared for this meeting died on his lips. He walked forward into his father's outstretched arms, and Tze-Ring quietly slipped away.

14 May, 8:00 a.m.
The Abbey of the Dawn

Chambha looked away from the sight of the sun's rays bathing the mountaintops and leaned forward to lift the delicate porcelain teapot. "More tea, Father Eamon? Murad? Johnny?"

All but Johnny offered their cups for refilling. He grimaced and shook his head. Chambha chuckled as he poured the fragrant liquid into the cups. "Brother John has never acquired a taste for our brand of tea," he said and set the teapot down on the carved table.

"Too right," came the answer. "This stuff's not like the brew Aunt Florrie used to make. I'm looking forward to that, and things like croissants running with butter, marmalade, ice cream, jam doughnuts, real beer... God, it'll be like heaven." Johnny moved from the parapet and joined the others as they sat outside enjoying the early morning sun.

"I could do with a cup of that if there's any left." Tze-Ring, looking more than slightly frazzled, joined the little group and sat down.

"Any news yet?" asked his father concernedly.

Tze-Ring drained his cup and set it down. "No, it is too soon. She is only in the first stage of labour. They threw me out because I was distracting her." He stood and stretched, yawning as he did so. "I will go back in an hour or so. Until then, I will see if I can help somewhere. It will help to pass the time."

Tze-Ring headed off across the courtyard, looking back to call out, "I will see you at dinner, Father. By then you should be a grandfather again!"

The men laughed and for a few minutes talked among themselves of the coming birth and Tze-Ring's delight at the addition to his family. Then Father Eamon rose and excused himself, explaining with a smile, "I have a meeting with the abbot." Chambha left to take a class of new novices while Murad returned to his endless searching of the abbey's thousands of books and papers, seeking a clue to the Lost Abbey.

Johnny stood alone, looking out across the mountains. He felt restless, almost apprehensive, as if something important was hurrying towards him. Two and a half years he'd been here. What would the outside world be like now? He'd kept up with world news—they all did—but to really *be* there…to be close to Bucky and Florrie and Frank. He wondered what it would be like to see Lyle in a clerical suit and if Liam and Biff were still drinking buddies. He wondered how they were doing as a group, or what was left of it now that Tango had gone.

He left the balcony and carried the tray of dishes into the kitchen, where he carefully washed and dried them. With nothing to do, he headed for the Hall of a Thousand Candles, "Tara's Hall," as he had mischievously named it on his arrival long ago. He felt the need to offer thanks for his new happiness, not the least of which was his reunion with his father. On his way, Johnny stopped to sweet-talk Abbess Hannah into giving him three of the roses lovingly cultivated in her hothouse in return for tidying up the compost heap later.

The Hall was warm, welcoming, and familiar, with scented candles filling the air with perfume. Johnny laid the roses at the feet of Tara's statue and knelt before Her. He did not pray with words; they were useless for the kind of interchange he had been trained to use between himself and the Inner Level Adepti. Instead, he created images and scenes in his mind and offered them to the Lords of Light, of whom the statue of the Tara was just one of many.

He saw the Tara as a real woman and danced with Her in a field of wild flowers, filling the ecstasy of the dance with his joy and praise. He took Her in his arms and let Her feel the joy in him and offered it to Her. She took it from him with love and sweet acceptance. Releasing the images, Johnny opened his eyes and for a second felt Her presence bending over him, Her eyes bright with tenderness, and gloried in the softness of Her lips on his.

There was a feeling of not being alone in the hall, of something hastening towards Johnny from a long way away. The back of his neck prickled; the shadows deepened and thickened about him. He rose to his feet and slowly, almost fearfully, turned round.

There was nothing there. Just a semicircle of tall candlesticks before the steps, as always when no ritual was in progress.

Obeying an inner summons, Johnny sat down facing them, folding himself a little clumsily into a full lotus. For a long while, nothing happened. The semicircle of flames in front of him burned steadily. Then, without warning, all the other candles in the hall began to go out one by one.

Slowly, Johnny's body heat began to decrease, and a chill enveloped him. At first he counteracted it with a different breathing pattern, then realised that some phenomena was about to happen and it needed his energy to manifest. Johnny broke into a sweat of fear. He had only experienced this approach of power when others were with him: the abbot or Chambha.

Scent filled the hall as if the perfume of the roses he'd offered to the Tara had been increased a thousandfold. Along with the scent, the atmosphere changed. The entire temple was filled with a feeling of joy—no, more than just joy: a Divine joy that became part of the very air he was breathing. The central flame in front of Johnny elongated and widened. He gazed at it, mesmerized, as it imploded with a soft whoosh of displaced air and before him stood a woman, Her body outlined with light.

She was neither old nor young, beautiful nor plain, reflecting whatever She needed to be. Though it seemed She stood before him, Johnny saw Her feet did not quite touch the floor. She held in Her hand the roses he had offered Her. She raised them to smell their perfume and lay the soft petals against Her even-softer cheek. The wisdom that shone from Her eyes spoke of knowledge and understanding beyond time and space.

Johnny's training had not been wasted; he knew with utter certainty that the change the archangel had spoken of was close at hand. He summoned his courage and spoke to the radiant form before him in the way he had been taught. "I greet thee, Eloi, and open my heart to thee."

"It is time for that heart to be opened, the mind and the soul also. Knebt-Tua, Priest of Neith, you have been brought full circle on the Wheel of Life, and what you began you must now prepare to finish. Open yourself to memory and look back into your past." She held out the hand holding the roses and let them fall.

Johnny's consciousness, gripped by Her will, went spinning into a vortex of stars. Snared in a net of time and space, he hung in the void and watched them dance their pattern of creation. Sometimes near, then far away they gyrated, always to a set rhythm. He knew without being told that they were moving back in time, looking for ancient bodies they had once occupied. Aeons slipped past him. Then the dance slowed as the stars moved to their appointed place. He opened his inner eyes and looked round.

He was in a small, bare room furnished with a bed, a chair, and two wooden chests. An old, old man sat in the chair, watching the sunset through the open doorway. He turned his head slowly, and Johnny looked at himself, at his own aged face, across a distance of six thousand years and two ages. Knebt-Tua's wrinkled visage lifted into a brilliant smile of welcome. He gripped the sides of his chair and struggled to lift himself. Johnny went to his side.

"Please, Holy One, do not stand. I will sit."

The priest sat down, bowing his head in respect. "Great One, your presence is an honour you do me. I have been waiting for you."

Johnny was taken aback. "Holy One, I am not a Master; I am just beginning my studies."

Knebt-Tua smiled again. "I know what you think you are, and I know also that you are part of me, as I am a part of you. The essence of our soul is one and the same. You are now what I, Knebt-Tua, will become after many lives of service on the Wheel of Time. You have a message for me from the gods, and I am ready to receive it.

"No, do not touch me yet." He held up his hand. "We can speak together only if we do not touch and so complete the circle."

Johnny stood before him and heard the whispered voice of She who watched over his physical body in Tara's Hall thousands of years in the future. He relaxed, allowing his training to overcome fear. Her voice came from his lips, a soft, husky contralto.

"Knebt-Tua, I am She whom you call Neith, though I am known by many names. You have served me and my kind well for many years. Soon you will call your people together and give them instructions on how to ensure the continuation of what you have built here. It is for you the last night of this incarnation, for what is before you will demand all your remaining life energy. It is time for you and your future persona to meld together so that the first part of his enlightenment may take place in his own future time.

"Know that he is—and you will be, in the far future—the Forerunner to the last Osiris to be drawn from the gods. After that time, the saviours will be all human. The life-wave of the planet in his time has reached a point where they are capable of producing one of their own to carry the burden. It is and always has been the task of the Forerunner to prepare the way. This is your future, but now you must call on the power and wisdom of all the incarnations of this essence, up to and including yourself, and pass the knowledge to the One who will be the companion to the Christos of the Age of Aquarius, an age like no other...One in which the human race will either win or lose everything it has created."

The voice faded into silence, leaving the two men alone. Knebt-Tua sighed deeply, then slowly and painfully got to his feet.

"Come with me, my son, for indeed you are so close a part of myself that I may use that term. We will go to the temple, for such a passing of power must be accomplished in a holy place." The frail old man took his staff in hand and led the way through the door of the small hut.

Outside the sun had almost set. All were preparing for sleep. No one saw as the old priest and the shining figure of what he would one day become passed on to the mud-brick building that served as a temple. It was small, scrupulously clean, and austerely beautiful. Bundles of tall reeds had been bound together and covered with clay to act as pillars holding up the fragile roof of woven grass and papyrus stalks. The floor was of earth, trodden by countless feet over the years into a firm, almost polished, surface. A simple altar and a roughly carved statue of Neith stood at the far end with offerings of fruit and flowers. Hanging on one wall was an oval of highly polished bronze with small oil lamps burning on a ledge before it. Beneath them on a low table stood a basin of clear water, and on either side, bowls of burning incense scented the air.

"It is not as big as temples in the towns further south," said Knebt-Tua softly, "but She was content with what we could achieve by our own hands. It was the teaching of those who came to this place that was important to Her.

"Come, I must not waste one moment of the time left to me. Before another sunset comes, this body will lie before the altar, and I shall have taken my place in the death barge of Upuat."

Knebt-Tua sat Johnny before the bowl of water and stood behind him, complimenting him on the strength and solidity of his Body of Light. As Johnny looked down, he saw that he appeared solid even to his own eyes. He realised he was there in full consciousness and not merely animating a tulpa with a small part of his mind.

He looked as instructed into the bowl of water. The light from the oil lamps danced and flickered on the surface, reminding him of the shadows in Tara's Hall, now so far away in time and distance. For a fraction of time, he was back there, and Knebt-Tua's urgent voice followed him.

"Back, come back! Do not allow yourself to think of anything except what is here in this temple. Be here *now*!"

Johnny clawed his way back into the dark, smoke-filled atmosphere of the ancient temple and looked into the light-filled water. Behind him, Knebt-Tua, supporting himself on his staff, summoned all his reserves of strength and magical power and gazed over his shoulder into the bronze mirror. Focussing on the thread of life within himself, Knebt-Tua followed it back into the darkness that was and is before life. The warm, nurturing darkness of the cosmic womb loomed before him, and he sought out his own life patterns decreed from long before this cosmic day. He selected the threads of life matching his own and gathered them together.

Further and further back he went, gathering the accumulated wisdom of each fraction of existence. Past the earliest lives that might be called civilised to the nomadic wanderers and cave dwellers. He recalled holding the flickering light of a torch so that an aurochs might be drawn on the wall of a damp, dark cave. He danced the dance of the hunter, feeling the newly taken skin of his kill along the length of his spine and the weight of the horns on his head, felt the power and the joy of mating with the Tribal Mother. Deeper still to the time of the Great Cold that brought the Fear of Not Moving to many of the tribe.

Time extended back to the warmth of the salty sea and the mindless drifting with no knowingness of self or the potential before it, beginning with a microscopic cell of life and moving forward into short spells of existence in a myriad of forms until one approximated to a human being. Backwards through times of darkness and non-knowingness that alternated with those when bright forms gathered round him, others like him, feeding them energy and a sense of personal consciousness. A moment of blinding pain when a minute point of Light from the Body of the One was planted deep within the primal pattern that would be his for eternity. The birth moment of the I AM that would become Knebt-Tua/Johnny Burke. Then, finally, Knebt-Tua began the long journey back to his own time, slowly dragging the weight of life memory with him.

Time went by as he drew his burden up to where the recipient, Johnny, waited. He dared not look back, dared not stop to rest lest he lose his grip on the past. He was aware of signposts passing him: A cave. A fire. A dancing man. The feel of a boar's tusk in his groin, ripping its way into his gut. The first taste of cooked meat and the wonder of it. A field of wheat. A pillar of stone. The strange feeling of holding a child and knowing it was a part of himself. The sight of a stormy sea. The feel of ice slowly entombing him. A hot sun and a spear in his hand and the wide maw of the lion that would kill him. The feel of a staff in his hand and the weight of a starched linen crown on his head. Slowly, Knebt-Tua became aware of a light before him, a light that danced and flickered in the depths of a basin of clear water from which the last of the images were fading.

Johnny had caught each vision of the past in the reflections cast by the mirror onto the water, where they floated like so many salmon waiting to be caught. He had fished for each one, captured it along with the wisdom and accumulated knowledge encased within it, and taken it deep into himself. It was all coming together in his mind.

He looked down at the simple bowl, smiling. The Grail of Knowledge. The first of many to be called by that name. As Johnny had been the first Fisher King, now he would also be the last. The one who rose and faced the old priest was not and would never again be Johnny Nova or even Johnny Burke—he had let go of those names forever. He bowed before the old priest, blessed him, and set his name among those of the gods.

Before the simple altar, Knebt-Tua poured water over his hands and feet and held before his eyes the sacred symbols of ancient Sothis, the dog star. He hallowed him with incense and poured fragrant oil over his head, hands, and feet. The night had passed, and soon the sun would rise again. The old priest sent a mental call winging through the pre-dawn mists to summon those who were needed. They came, crowding into the temple, filled with awe and wonder at the godlike figure beside their beloved teacher, one who wore his face as a young man.

In the little temple, Knebt-Tua took the pesh-en-kef knife and made ready the tongue of the initiate. An awestruck acolyte crept close to offer the magical Ur-Hekau. It opened the mouth of the newly Justified One and made him Master of the Words of Power for all eternity. As the ancient symbol touched him, Johnny felt a rush of power. He knew with certainty that this was not all there was. More would come, but for now it was enough.

They listened as the shining stranger spoke of the work that was to be theirs from now on. He spoke of what lay ahead and how the seed they had planted would grow and prevail through the ages. Other voices came from his lips as past personas spoke and taught until it seemed that a multitude of gods stood round them. Finally Johnny blessed them and their work. Then, as the first rays of dawn filtered into the temple, he knelt before the old man and asked for his blessing.

The gnarled hands of Knebt-Tua hesitated for a moment, then settled upon Johnny's head. The past and present met, blended, and became one. The two parts of the single soul came together, and it seemed to those looking on that their teacher became young again and, leaving an outworn body lying before the altar, went forth from them, star crowned, into the light of the early morning sun.

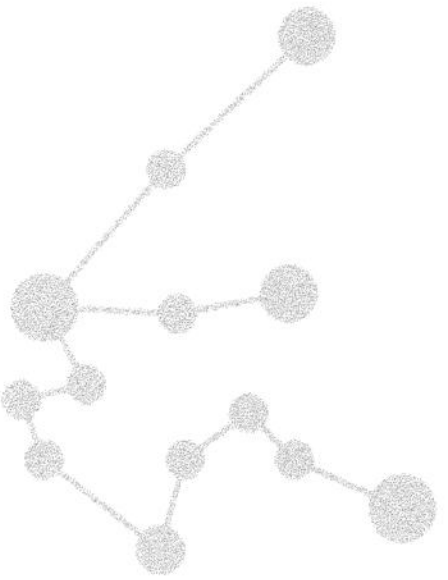

CHAPTER TWENTY-THREE

14 May, 9:30 a.m.
The Abbey of the Dawn

With a start, Johnny woke from his trance and looked up to see the three roses still falling through the air. With a whisper of sound, they landed at his feet. He stared at them, remembering.

Deep within Johnny, the power stirred, filling him as wine fills a cup. The candles burned with a steady flame, and all seemed to be unchanged. But Johnny knew nothing would ever be the same again where he was concerned. The inner change had gone deep, and it was permanent.

The air about him was filled with voices he knew to be the conversations of the abbey. If he focussed intently, he could sense even further. In a sudden blaze of self-knowledge, Johnny knew that should he care to do so, he could touch the mind of anyone within a thousand miles. Confidently, he focussed on the abbot and found him reading in his room. Johnny touched the abbot's mind as gently as a mother would touch a sleeping child and saw him start and look up from his book.

"Rinpoche, it has begun. I am in the Hall of a Thousand Candles and I have need of you. Come, please."

"Johnny Burke? Aaah, so soon? I had not expected this before you left for the Abbey of the Aeon. I will be with you in a few moments. Do not overtax your newfound strength, my son. Wait for me.

"Chambha, summon all available abbey companions to the Hall of a Thousand Candles, if you please."

Then Johnny heard Tze-Ring's voice. "Johnny? Something of great importance has happened to you. I can sense it strongly. I do not want to leave Lea; the second stage is taking longer than we thought. But if you have need of me…?"

"No, Ring, stay with Lea. I'll fill you in from here." Johnny swiftly encapsulated what had happened and transferred it telepathically to his brother, registering Tze-Ring's stunned amazement at the ease with which this was accomplished. "It's OK, Ring, don't think about it right now. Stick with Lea."

The door of the hall opened and the members of the abbey entered in twos and threes, greeting with varying degrees of amazement and satisfaction the star-crowned figure that awaited them, among them his father, looking at Johnny with a loving pride that filled his heart. The tall candles were removed, and the members took their places in a semicircle before the new initiate. Chambha, ever thoughtful, had brought Johnny a robe and slippers and helped him to change from his everyday clothes. Then he stood quietly to one side and waited for the abbot.

When the old man arrived, he came forward and bowed low before the one who had brought him to this focal point in his life. The abbot took Johnny's hands and looked deep into his eyes, and Johnny opened himself to the psychic search willingly. What had once been the priest Knebt-Tua looked back at his mentor and blessed him for his part in keeping alive the work that the humble priest of Neith had begun. Nyang Darsip, abbot of the Abbey of the Dawn, swayed a little from the shock of recognition, then stepped back and, a little shakily, knelt before Johnny and bowed his head.

As one, the rest rose and followed suit. Johnny looked at them lovingly, the people that for over two years had sought to train him in spite of himself. Chambha, now a close and much-loved friend. Nakima, almost as old as the abbot but with a startling sense of humour that endeared him to Johnny. Per, who had patiently taught him, hour upon hour, how to build a Body of Light. Mother Miro, with whom he had battled so fiercely at first; without her skilful training in the art of scrying, he would not have been able to gather up and retain the visions of knowledge he had been given by the persona of Knebt-Tua. Shuna, from whom he had learned control of the elements, and Wang Ta, who had spent endless hours teaching him to reach into the emotional self. Abbess Hannah, who to some extent had filled the gap made by Florrie's absence and had comforted him when life seemed too much to bear. Murad, almost as close as Ring and who once, on a swaying rope bridge, had risked his life for Johnny.

Everyone in the abbey had offered themselves and their talents to train him, and his brother had always been beside him to support, encourage, and listen, as he had promised. For the first time, Johnny really understood why he had been brought here and why his life was so important to them. Now he also understood the true importance of his mission and how dangerous the Dark forces ranged against him could be. He sensed there was more to know, more to be learned from his past, but for now he gave thanks for this beginning.

Then, into the silence of the hall, came Tze-Ring's anguished mental call.

"Johnny! Oh God, Johnny, it's all gone wrong. I am going to lose them both, the baby and Lea. The child lies across the birth canal. Mother Adelie has twice tried to turn it, but it is wedged too tightly. Lea has no more strength, and the child's heartbeat is faltering. Johnny, what can I do? Even with surgery, I will lose one or both. There is no more time."

Tze-Ring's cry cut through every mind in the abbey capable of receiving it. Instantly they were all with him, seeing through his distraught eyes the exhausted, white-faced form of Lea and tracking the faltering heartbeat of the child still enclosed in her pain-wracked body.

Mother Adelie and her team were frantically preparing for surgery when Johnny's voice bade her stop. He stood at the foot of the bed, swaying slightly with the rush of pure energy that had teleported him bodily to the birth chamber, leaving a totally stunned group of adepts gaping at the empty space left in the hall, their ears ringing with the implosion that had accompanied his departure.

"Without surgery she and the child, one or both, will die. I cannot delay, Brother John."

"Peace, Mother Adelie. All will be well. I give you the word of the Forerunner, which may not be broken."

She fell silent and backed away from the bed. Effortlessly, the man who had once been a burnt-out rock star reached into the world of the eternal Christos and demanded the presence of Raphael, the Healing Hand of God. As that Being responded, Johnny aligned himself with Its power, absorbed it totally, and became one with the ultimate power of healing. Lea's pain-drenched consciousness was withdrawn from her body and placed in the care of Mother Sarah the Seer.

Placing his hands gently on Lea's swollen belly, Johnny brought all his newfound power to bear upon the tightly wedged form of the child, simultaneously directing Mother Adelie and Chambha to aid its faltering heartbeat. The Raphaelite power now enclosed within him became a pulsating force of Light. Johnny's hands grew misty and insubstantial. He reached into the torn womb and gently but firmly released the wedged infant, then eased the tiny, slippery form into position, head down towards the tunnel of flesh that led to the light and life. Johnny's voice sounded throughout the Abbey of the Dawn.

"My brother, now I give you back the life you gave to me when we crossed the bridge on the mountains. Now I repay the agony of the whipping you once took for me."

Johnny touched the part of Lea's brain that controlled the contractions and set them in motion again, strongly and rhythmically. Mother Adelie waited close by with a warm towel, clamps, and scissors. Once, twice, three times the unconscious female body convulsed. Then a tiny, wrinkled head filled Johnny's waiting hands. He sent out a silent summons for the aid of Father Nakima, the Inuit shaman and spirit talker.

"Father Nakima, call the child's spirit. It has lost hope and prepares even now to return to the Inner Worlds. Summon it quickly—its body is almost born."

A distant drumming filled the air and a seed-filled gourd added its special sound. Their inner ear heard the uplifted voice of the old man, still strong and vigorous despite his years. Father Nakima chanted:

Spirit, I call thee back from thy journey home.
See, here is thy body waiting for thee.
Come nearer and see the house of life prepared for thee.
A strong body to serve you with many years ahead.
Child of the Light, power-given birthright is yours.
Behold, the Great Ones gather to greet your first day.
Your life has been given back to you to use.
Do not go from us. You are asked to stay and be welcomed.

A shimmering sphere of light appeared by Johnny's shoulder as the rest of the baby's body slid into his hands. The skin's colour was pale blue, for the cord was wound several times about its neck, and Mother Adelie was quick to clamp and sever it. The tiny lungs struggled to inflate. The mouth gaped wide. Johnny looked up at the sphere and grinned.

"Get your ass in there, buster, and be quick about it."

The sphere chimed at him and nose-dived into the soft top of the baby's head. Seconds later came a weak cry that grew steadily stronger, and the abbey drew a collective sigh of relief. But even as Tze-Ring cradled his newborn son in his arms, Johnny began a second fight to save Lea. With the afterbirth came a haemorrhage, and once more Johnny used the healing power he had summoned so peremptorily from the archangelic world. Even so, it took another hour before the lacerated womb had been healed and the mother was out of danger. Only then did Johnny leave her.

He walked out of the room to find Tze-Ring, his father, Murad, and the abbot waiting for him. He saluted them cockily with the old Johnny spirit. "I'd like a double Scotch on the rocks, and hold the water. Do I get a certificate for this, Rinpoche, or just a Boy Scout badge for midwifery?"

Then Johnny's mind went blank. Murad caught him as he fell and lifted him into his arms, weeping unashamedly as he did so.

"It would appear that Brother John has not acquired his power at the cost of his sense of humour. I am glad." The abbot was silent for a few moments.

Then he said wistfully, "I will miss Johnny Burke. It has been an…ah… interesting two and a half years.

"Take him to his quarters, Brother Murad, and stay with him. The reaction to this overuse of his powers so soon after their acquisition will be severe."

The abbot watched Murad carry his precious burden away, then said quietly to the others, "He will be one of the greatest initiates of all."

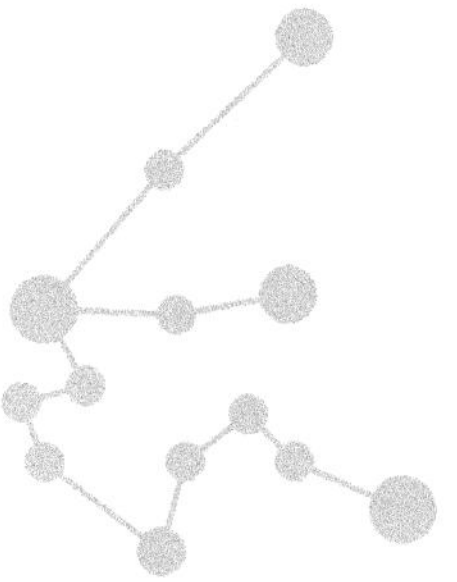

CHAPTER TWENTY-FOUR

19 May, 12:00 a.m.
A small manor in West Wales

The house held an uneasy quietness that was palpable. The absence of sound was deafening. The place had the feel of being somewhere other than "here"—a place to pass time, but not to live in the usual sense of that word.

The wine cellar was the oldest part of the house, but the wine racks had disappeared long ago. The floor had been covered with parquet at the same time and the brick walls painted a cheerful yellow, but that was before the present owner had come. Tango had left the flooring as it was, but the walls and ceiling were now black and draped with heavy velvet curtains in a dull red. In the centre of the floor was a double circle of black, and within the inner circle an inverted pentacle in silver. The space between the two circles was filled with cryptic symbols and names that sent a shiver down the spine just to read them, let alone speak them. Beyond the circle stood an altar of black stone. The only thing on it was a distorted chalice that had once been a thing of beauty and symmetry. Now it was twisted and blackened, and there were stains in the bowl of a darker hue than wine.

At the far end of the temple hung a larger-than-life painting of a young man. The eye was drawn to it immediately on entering the cellar. The figure was seated on a throne draped in scarlet, one leg thrown carelessly over the armrest. Its nudity was blatant and all the more disturbing for its breath-taking but totally evil beauty. The head was thrown back, and dark brown hair curled about the shoulders. The eyes were heavy-lidded and slumberous under arched brows, and the sensual mouth hung open just enough to show the red tip of the tongue beginning to protrude. One hand hung down, a half-empty wine glass dangling from the limp fingers. The other hand openly caressed the erect phallus. Power emanated from the picture and permeated the whole room, creating a feeling of decadence carried so far beyond the norm as to be vileness itself. It was a power that demanded worship, that needed feeding with adulation and human energy. At such times it seemed to come alive, the eyes watching and following what went on, the tongue licking the obscenely full red lips in anticipation. This was one of those times.

Penny Jessup was frightened. The effects of the alcohol had worn off, and she found herself lying stark naked on a cold wooden floor. The room smelt funny, like old Mrs. Harker's place when she held her séance nights, only this was worse. She tried to get up, but her limbs were heavy and unresponsive. Slowly she rolled over and whimpered when her head exploded with pain. Now balanced on her hands and knees, she raised her head and saw the young man she had met in a bar hours ago. His face was familiar, handsome but marred by viciousness and self-indulgence.

He sat in a high-backed chair with ornately carved arms and feet and watched her as she tried to stand and failed. A robe of vivid red silk covered him from neck to ankles, throwing his dark hair and olive skin into greater contrast. A thrill of fear covered the girl's flesh with a fine sheen of sweat and she shrank in on herself, trying to cover her nakedness from the gloating eyes.

Slowly Tango rose to his feet and let the robe slide from his body. Round his waist he wore a leather belt studded with small silver stars. The centre of each star was raised and sharp enough to cause pain and draw blood, but not enough to injure. He walked over to the girl and knelt in front of her, clasping her wrists and drawing her to him.

Penny tried to pull away but was no match for his strength. Tango's lips caressed her mouth gently, first outlining them with his tongue, then slanting across their softness, enticing her to open for him. When she did, he bit down, hard. The girl screamed and Tango raised his head from the kiss, his lips now as red as her lipstick. Blood red.

Tango raised a hand and slapped her back-handed across her face, dazing her with its force. Then, before she could recover, he turned her in his arms and forced her back onto hands and knees. He tightened his grip, and the studs on Tango's belt dug into Penny's skin, drawing more blood. The more she struggled, the deeper the studs ground against her.

Tango reached down and pushed her thighs apart, then positioned himself against her.

There was no gentleness for young Penny, no sweetly arousing caresses to ready her for the invasion of her still-innocent body. The charming stranger with the soft voice and nice manners who had romanced her to the envy of her friends had gone. In his place was a violent adult male who liked to hurt. Too late, she realised her mistake even as she screamed and fought to free herself.

Penny's body tensed for the pain she knew would come, then arched in agony as it did. Tango's teeth bared in a smile of delight as she twisted and turned, trying to escape, each movement impaling her further on his heated shaft. Dazed with pain and fear, her head held back by the man's grip on her hair, her eyes were caught and held by those of the figure in the painting. Now Penny simply shuddered with each thrust as Tango took pleasure both for himself and for his master, who watched the writhing forms avidly.

Slowly, softly, Tango began to chant the praises of his Dark Lord. As he did so, the picture began to emanate a reddish glow, and the figure seemed to take on weight and substance. The picture had changed. The figure no longer reclined. It stood, then gracefully, almost delicately, stepped down from the frame.

Tango withdrew from the girl's body, reluctantly yielding his place to Asmodeus. The Dark Lord paused behind the distraught girl, savouring the moment. The phallus elongated, thickened, then split into multiple tentacles, threadlike, obscene replicas of itself, each terminating in a tiny claw. They reached forward and entered the girl's body, inserting themselves into both vagina and anus, then reaching up and over her back to enter mouth, ears, and nostrils. Penny's screams now reached a new crescendo, taking on a note of madness as her mind gave way and tumbled into the abyss of insanity.

The sight counteracted the drugs in Tango's system. He stood appalled by this hitherto-unknown side of the Darkness, then turned away, unable to watch, sickened and overwhelmed by his own part in this degradation of innocence.

He turned back again almost immediately, some small part of the old, gentler Tango intending to stop it. But what he saw almost unhinged his own mind: a Dark Lord fully manifested in its true form and intent on absorbing the offering made to it.

"*Duw*," he whispered, unthinkingly pronouncing the name of God in a place where God was never meant to be.

A scream of fear, hate, and anguish ripped across the room as the ever-watchful Lords of Light took advantage of the moment. Tango may not have used the name as an invitation for Light to manifest, but it did. The Dark Lord reeled back, seared by its intensity. Like a huge slug, it writhed and flopped painfully along the floor, leaving a trail of putrescent slime in its wake. It reached the frame and disappeared into it.

Tango crawled forward through a pool of blood and urine and pulled the silent figure of Penny out of the circle. Weeping for the first time in two years, he tried vainly to revive her.

"Forgive me, Penny. I didn't know what he—what it—really was. I didn't know. I didn't know. Forgive me, please. Please, Penny."

Tango lifted her limp form and carried her up the stairs and into the living room, where he placed her on the sofa and covered her with a woollen rug. Trembling, he wiped the blood and slime from her face. She was alive, just, but in his heart, Tango knew that her mind had gone from this world. Behind him, De'ath screamed with rage.

"Fool! Fool! You misconceived apology of a man, do you realise what you have done? You actually called on the name of—Ah, I can't even say it.

And at the supreme moment of sacrifice! Do you have any idea how this will affect my standing, to say nothing of yours? Are you so weak you cannot offer one measly sacrifice?" De'ath was beside himself with rage. "And what will you do now? No hospital will take her—she is dying anyway. How will you explain that? I could kill you. *They* could kill you, and may yet do so. May Dagon smite you, Talfryn Garrett. If you were not the only link we have to the Forerunner, I would leave you to their will right now."

De'ath flung himself through the door and into the night.

Wearily, Tango carried the girl upstairs and gently washed her whole body clean of the stinking slime, then dressed her in a pair of his pyjamas. Then he showered and dressed himself. This done, he sat beside Penny and held her hand in his. He knew he could do nothing for her, but equally he couldn't bring himself to leave her. She would become part of the statistics of missing people. Somewhere she had a family who would wait anxiously for her to come home. But she never would.

Just before dawn, Tango came to a decision. He thought about it for a minute or two, then got up to rummage in a drawer. He drew out a battered tin that had once held tea and spilled its contents on the dressing table. He hunted through the odd coins, thimbles, and bits and pieces of his mother's and grandmother's cheap costume jewellery, such as it was. There was something he needed, something he remembered from childhood.

He found it at last, carefully wrapped in a piece of cotton wool: a tiny golden cross on a broken chain. Tango had delivered a lot of papers and run a lot of errands for this. It had been a Christmas present to his mother the year before her death. The last thing—the only thing—of value he had ever given her. He held it in his hand. Tango's eyes blurred with tears he would not allow himself to shed as he told himself he didn't care, that it meant nothing to him. Then he placed the cross carefully between Penny's hands.

As dawn's light began to fill the room, something woke him from a light doze. Standing beside the girl's body was...something bright and warm. As It bent over her, her essence rose to meet It and was enfolded within Its brightness. Then It turned to look at Tango. He flinched away from the eyes that gleamed from the light-filled form. The voice was cold, a coldness that made him sweat, but hidden within the coldness was a tiny promise of hope.

"You have chosen in this life to give yourself to evil. For this, you must eventually pay the cost. But by this one small act of remorse, the door will remain open to you unless your future actions close it forever."

Then It was gone and the room was cold again.

♫ ♩ ♫ ♪ ♫ ♩ ♫

Tango dug a deep grave in the garden and laid Penny to rest. Over the next few days and weeks, he planted flowers there. It was a place where he went to be quiet and to get away from De'ath, who shunned it.

To his companion's disgust, Tango took to alcohol again, defying orders not to do so. He unblocked the cellar windows, opening them to air and light, and burnt the empty picture in its frame. Then he locked the cellar door, nailed it shut, and never spoke again of what he had seen and done that night.

De'ath did not return for weeks. When he did, he was less communicative, less friendly, sullen at times, and concentrated simply on refining Tango's developing psychism. The boy was important to his Dark masters until he had fulfilled his purpose. Then would come the final reckoning, and De'ath was determined to be there when it happened.

Over the next six months, De'ath would drive his charge long and hard, polishing the psychic skills his mixed blood had given him. Work became paramount for Tango, and his career took off with dazzling speed now that he no longer felt hampered by Bucky and the group.

Tango's first solo effort, the title song to a blockbuster movie, reached the top ten long before the film premiere and remained there to win a platinum record. A six-week TV series followed by a US tour made him a rival to the memory of Elvis. Tango had made it to the top, and he intended to stay there despite the dark memories hidden in his mind.

The disappearance of Johnny Nova was yesterday's news, forgotten by the public, though White Heat's records still sold to the fans. The standards and film scores written by Frank kept money coming in at a satisfying rate.

As a group, though smaller, the boys worked contentedly together in the studio, recording and backing big stars. Each, in a way, had achieved tranquillity. It was as if Johnny's newfound inner peace had overflowed onto them. Those who watched them built on the group's inner strength and companionship. In a few years, it would be tested almost beyond endurance.

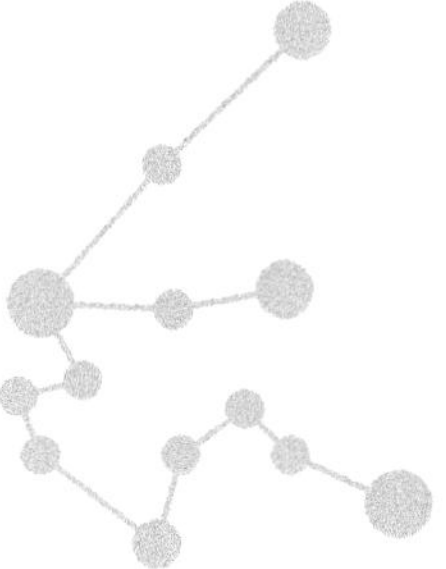

CHAPTER TWENTY-FIVE

11 June, 1:00 a.m.
Somewhere beneath the Karakoram range

The small truck scampered along the endless tunnels, its headlights augmenting the scattered overhead lights. Johnny, huddled into the thickest chuba he possessed, shivered miserably. "When the old man said this was the quickest way, he forgot to add it was also the coldest," he grumbled. "How in the name of God did they find all this?"

His father, equally cocooned against the bone-numbing cold, glanced sideways at him. "There are underground tunnels similar to these under almost every mountain range in the world. They've been known about for thousands of years. Some are natural. Others have been, shall we say, helped along. In the outside world there are scores of legends and stories about them, mostly unbelieved by the majority of people, thank goodness. These are not the oldest. There are some that are prediluvian, way up in the Caucasus, Taurus, and Armenian ranges."

"They may be quick and handy, but couldn't the abbey run to a more comfortable car? Even with the heating full on, I'm freezing my balls off, and I'm wearing most of what I own."

"Have you forgotten all you learned in the abbey, Johnny?"

"I never did get the hang of that personal central heating exercise," mumbled Johnny, huddled under the fleece rug.

"In the Abbey of the Aeon, there is someone who can help you, and I can give you some personal tuition myself. But not now. If we stop for too long, the engine will freeze up. I estimate we have another eight hours or so before we emerge, and another three hours after that to get to the nearest rest house. Try to sleep; it might help."

There was silence in the cab for a while as Eamon concentrated on his driving. Every now and then, as the truck passed over a sensor, extra lights went on, illuminating a curve ahead, then went out behind them. At intervals they passed larger pools of light showing a cache of petrol, tyres, spares, simple food supplies, water, and basic facilities.

They had a thermos of tea and food in the cab, but Eamon was anxious to press on, and he was used to driving long distances. He glanced at his watch. They had been driving for six hours now with one half-hour break. In another hour they would be close to one of the main halts where they could eat and sleep and get warm before tackling the last leg. With luck, they would be in Gilgit in another nine or ten hours. While the tunnels dispensed with the need to cross over the mountains, they were tortuous, cold, and dismal. Eamon blinked tired eyes and began a re-energising breathing pattern, mentally repeating a mantra at the same time.

Beside him, Johnny slept deeply, though he had not expected to, and in his sleep he walked the gardens of the abbey he had just left. By the fountain stood two women, one he recognized with a leap of his heart, and he went towards her, arms outstretched.

"Mama? *Meery Dovvel*, is it really you?"

"Ah Johnny, my Johnny. I am so proud of you, *miro chal*. Such a man you are now."

"I'm dreaming, aren't I? This is just a dream."

"Whatever you think it is, Johnny, it will be. Does it matter? A dream can be as real as you want it to be. I'm glad you have met your father at last; he was so unhappy that he could not be with you sooner. But we had to keep you safe. I want you to know that from now on, I will be with you. You may not see me, but I will be there."

The image began to blur, and Johnny fought to keep it.

"Mama, Mama, don't go! Please don't leave me again!"

There came a light touch on his arm, and Johnny looked down. The second woman stood beside him, her sapphire eyes large and brilliant, her smile warm and a little shy.

"My name is Mara, Johnny. We will meet soon."

"Johnny, wake up! We are at the midway halt, and we can eat and rest here for a few hours."

Johnny opened his eyes and stumbled from the truck in a daze. He looked at his father blankly and then round at the harsh lights and seemingly endless tunnel ahead. Eamon indicated the portacabin against the tunnel wall.

"There's heating, camp beds, and hot food and drink in there. Go in and put the kettle on while I insulate the engine against the cold. Otherwise it will freeze."

Johnny climbed wearily into the comparative comfort of the cabin and busied himself preparing hot soup and mugs of steaming tea. Slowly thawing out, he wrapped his cold fingers round the mug and sipped gratefully.

"I was dreaming of Mama," he said, looking across at his father. "But I lost her again."

"No, son, neither of us have lost her. She is with us. She surrounds us both with her love, as she has always done." There was a ragged edge to Eamon's voice that alerted Johnny. He looked and saw the sheen of tears on his father's face, realizing for the first time how desperately lonely these years had been for him.

Suddenly, he too felt lonely. His confidence drooped and an overwhelming fear swept over him. He felt the loss of the abbey, the abbot, of Ring and Chambha, Murad, and the others. He was "outside" and alone, lost and unprotected, and he panicked.

But as the fear rose in Johnny, those watching from the abbey linked minds and gathered him into their midst. For a long moment he rested in their love and strength and knew his father to be a part of it. Then the Forerunner blessed them for their gift and gently disengaged himself. Consciously, he took his stand alone, as he must do from now on. His father watched him, a quiet pride shining in his eyes.

"Eat," said the Forerunner. "Then rest. Later I will drive."

"You have never driven these roads, Johnny. They can be misleading and treacherous. I will be ready to drive again after an hour or so of rest."

"You have done more than your share, Father. It is time for me to take on at least part of the burden. I have a lot to learn still, but what is within my power, that I will do."

The older man did not argue but finished his soup and tea, then gratefully lay down on the narrow bed and closed his eyes. Johnny, on the other bed, stayed awake; there was something he had to do. He was being called.

Slowly, carefully, Johnny shut down all outside stimuli, withdrawing further and further into himself until all his energies were tightly focussed on building a Body of Light. He rose like a shooting star through the layers of rock that recorded the passages of time and into the world beyond. He knew the restrictions placed upon him in the abbey had been removed. He could go anywhere he wished, and for a moment he was tempted to go and see Bucky and Florrie. But he knew he must be cautious and not draw the attention of the Darkness to himself too early.

Looking at the snow-capped peaks, majestic in their cold beauty, Johnny became aware of many watching eyes. He smiled and turned to greet the devas of the high ranges. Like snow flames, they dipped and swayed in a dance of welcome. Their thoughts sang in his mind in the thin, high winds that were their voices. He listened intently.

"Welcome, Beloved One. Thou who dost open the Gates of the World Mind to the coming of the Chosen One, be welcome. We rejoice in thy presence. Long have we awaited thy coming and thy teaching. Not only for human children is the message that you bear, but for all who have their existence on this earth. Give us your message, Forerunner. Who is it that comes to us from the One?"

For one heart-stopping moment, Johnny saw into the few short years to come. The demands that would be made upon him. The healing, support, comfort, and love he must somehow find within himself, enough and more to give out to all in need. The devas were right: It was not just for the human race that he came, but for all that lived and existed in cohesion with the ultimate Unity. These Shining Ones of the Snows were as eager to hear of the coming as those of his own kind.

Far away, in a place where all dimensions come together in the Great Unified Continuum, the primal spark that had always been Johnny stirred and reached out to its latest and last human form. It had waited for this moment throughout the dance of an entire Great Year. The primal spark touched Johnny's mind and slid into it, bearing as a gift the memories of over thirty thousand years and countless incarnations.

Johnny knew what he had been, what he was, and what he would become. He knew what his task would be and how best to do it. He knew what awaited him, its time and place. He knew who would be there and who had been appointed, and he smiled. He knew also what he would leave behind and how it would grow. He knew a choice would have to be made and that it could go either way, for the Light or for the Dark. He opened his heart centre and spoke to the waiting devic energies gathered about him.

"I am the Opener of the Ways. I am the eagle who has looked upon the sun in its glory, and this is the message I bring to you."

Thunder rolled among the mountains, and in the foothills the villagers scurried into their houses and shut the doors tight. "The gods are talking in the mountains," they told each other.

There were some, however, who smiled and knew that of all the beings on Earth, the devas of the sacred mountains were the first to hear the message of the new aeon.

Johnny touched his father's mind, easing him up through the layers of sleep until his eyes opened. Eamon's abbey-trained senses came online immediately.

"You've been 'out.' For the love of heaven, Johnny, why? You have probably broadcast your whereabouts to the entire Inner Levels."

"No, Father. I was kept safe by the devas. Their auric power acted like a shield. I was quite safe. You see, I heard them calling me, and when they asked, I could not deny them the message."

Eamon caught his breath, searching his son's face for verification.

"The message has started to come through?" he asked. Even now, after all that had happened, he found it hard to believe that it was his son who was the Forerunner of the Christos to come.

"Yes. Not all—there is more to come. It will take time, but a start has been made. We must go. I cleared away in here; we can leave now." Johnny slung his backpack over his shoulder and left the cabin. Eamon followed, buttoning his fleece-lined jacket and pulling on hat and gloves. Johnny, in the driving seat, leaned across and opened the door.

"Spell me in a couple of hours," he said, switching on the ignition.

They travelled in silence, as Johnny was disinclined to talk. He went over the message in his mind. It seemed very simple, yet it had sent the devas into an ecstatic delight. He smiled, remembering the flashing colours that had illuminated the peaks and the sounds made by the winds and the thunder as they had absorbed the words of the One.

Beside him, Eamon was thinking of the moment of Johnny's birth and the brief joy of holding him, watching him sleep and feed and grow. He remembered the pain of parting from the two people he held so dear, the knowledge that his boy would grow up without him. He thought about what he had missed: his first words, his first day at school, learning to ride a bike…So many things had been given up. Eamon's human side rebelled at the cost; his spiritual side gave thanks that he had been strong enough to pay it.

He felt Lily's mind touch his and shared with her their joy in the man beside him. The man who would open the way for the Teacher of the Age of Aquarius. The truck rushed on, cleaving the darkness and carrying its precious cargo towards the outside world. The Forerunner was on the move.

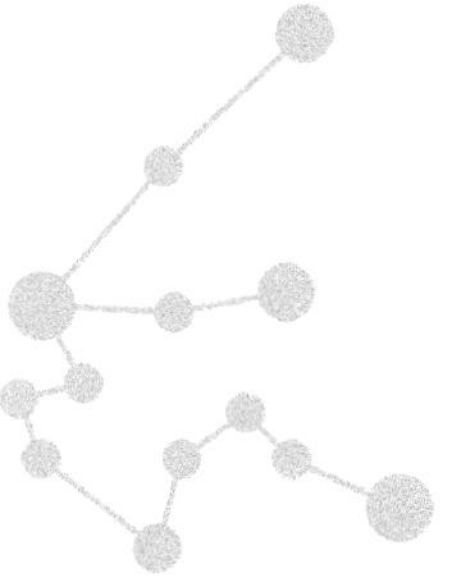

CHAPTER TWENTY-SIX

11 June, 4:00 p.m.
The foothills of the Karakoram range

They came into Gilgit in the late afternoon in a dilapidated Ford driven by Prakesh, the local agent of the abbey. Prakesh had been waiting to greet them as they emerged on foot from a concealed entrance. His wide smile and cheerful local chatter gave Johnny his first contact with the outside world in two years.

Johnny looked about him eagerly as they stopped outside a building declaring itself to be Sanjay's Guest House, adding in small letters, *Very Clean, No Bugs.* Johnny eyed the sign with raised eyebrows but was reassured by his father that the abbey people always used it and that there were, indeed, no bugs.

Inside, it was sparsely furnished but surprisingly comfortable. After a cool shower, both men tucked into a well-cooked and ample meal. As they were finishing their meal, Prakesh brought a message from Lahore to the effect that a private plane would be waiting for them in three days' time to take them on to Karachi.

"I see the abbeys haven't lost their ability to call in favours when needed," said Johnny, pouring his third cup of real tea.

Eamon chuckled. "One of the things people do not understand is that spirituality does not have to mean poverty. The abbeys earn the respect of those who hold wealth and power. We help them in many ways, but we also try to curb their less-desirable traits. We have many Watchers in high office; others in lesser roles are just as important. The power of the abbeys has prevented many small wars, though others we have been unable to prevent. In return, we ask for what we need when we need it and get it."

Later, standing by the window of his room, Johnny thought about the work of the abbeys and their widespread influence and wondered at the part he had been called to play in it all. He recalled his farewell to the Abbey of the Dawn. They had gathered, all of them, and lined the way down to the main gate, chanting an ancient Tibetan blessing. As Johnny passed, each member had bowed low and offered a personal wish for his fortune. At the gate stood those he loved so dearly: Tze-Ring and Lea, with Taras jumping up and down and bursting with pride at being able to offer him the traditional loaf of bread and packet of salt for the journey. Lea held his godson, Patrick, in her arms, her lovely face streaked with tears. Murad, tall and serious for once. Even Shuna and Wang Ta were there. Chambha, serene and patient as always, and close to his beloved teacher.

The abbot, looking frailer, had tried hard to remain impassive, but the tears had escaped as Johnny had knelt before him and kissed the ragged hem of his robe in homage. Then, with a typical grin, he had looked up and said quietly, "Rinpoche, it is really time that you invested in a new robe. Chambha, please see to it. It will be a gift from me."

Chambha had smiled and nodded. The abbot laid his hands on Johnny's head and, in a voice quavering with emotion, had blessed him with all the love held in his heart for this brilliant, wayward, lovable young man, destined to prepare the world for the Coming.

The abbot had stood bareheaded in the cold wind and watched as they descended to the village. Not until they had disappeared from sight had he moved. Then, leaning heavily on the arm of the faithful Chambha, he returned to the abbey.

Now, looking out at the high peaks above him, Johnny wondered if he would ever walk again in the gardens of the Abbey of the Dawn. A touch on his arm made him turn.

"Remember, you can return in the Body of Light at any time. You are not cut off from them forever. They are a living part of you, and you of them. Because of their work, you are now able to complete your task. Do it well for their sake."

The Forerunner nodded, understanding the words and what lay behind them. The inner Johnny wept silently for the peace he had been forced to leave behind. A third part of him realized that all he had been before had gone. It was an entirely new Johnny that stood poised on the edge of the future.

♬ ♩ ♫ ♪ ♬ ♪ ♫

They set off at dawn the following day, with the voluble Prakesh at the wheel. Johnny stood it for a while, then elected to travel in the back of the truck where, he said, he could see the mountains. They came into Srinagar late that night, and all three fell into bed and slept until noon. Prakesh then returned to Gilgit, but Eamon insisted that he and Johnny rest for the remainder of the day.

"You have descended many thousands of feet in a few days. You must get used to living at a lower altitude slowly and carefully," he said, curbing the young man's impatience.

"Where do we go from here?" demanded Johnny, his mouth full of buttered toast.

"To Lahore," was the answer. "A helicopter will arrive tomorrow morning, early, and take us to the airport at Lahore. That is where you were born, Johnny, in the house of a Watcher."

"Tell me about it, Dad."

Eamon stopped, his cup of coffee halfway to his mouth. "It's the first time you have called me that. It sounds so good, Johnny, to be plain Dad for a while rather than Father Eamon."

Johnny smiled. "It feels good to me too, Dad. So tell me what happened when I was born."

His father hesitated for a second, then said, "Why not? You are big enough to handle it."

Eamon was silent for a moment, gathering his memories.

"The abbot was there with Mother Loana from the Abbey of the Throne. She was one of the finest seers the abbeys have ever had. Abbot Gregor from the Aeon was also there. They set up a *kylkor* of protection round the house, which was owned by a doctor who was also a Watcher. Your mother—Lily—was calm, but I was a nervous wreck. Just before midnight, a tremendous storm blew up, but over the house it was almost silent. The moment of your birth was awaited by three of the wisest and most powerful guardians in the world.

"We set up a sacred space with the bed in the centre of a manifestation triangle. In fact, you were conceived within the same kind of triangle in Tara's Hall, as you so aptly named it. Each guardian took one of the points, with the doctor in the centre with Lily and me. As midnight began to strike, the whole room filled with spinning wheels of light, the Aralim, the angelic forces of Binah. It was like being in the middle of a firework display. You were born on the last stroke of midnight, and as you took your first breath a sound came from all around us, like a tremendous harmonic chord. Then both the sound and the lights died away. It was an hour or so later, when you and your mother were back in the bedroom, that the attack came. Lily was sleeping under sedation, and you were in a cot by her bed."

"An attack?" Johnny leaned forward.

"Because we knew you were the Forerunner, we reckoned the other side knew it as well, which was why we took so many precautions. We thought the protections round the house would be enough since the most likely time of attack was at the actual moment of birth." Eamon paused, reliving a moment of terror. "We were betrayed." His voice took on a bitter note. "While the rest of us were downstairs making plans, the doctor had been waiting for his chance. It was Loana who sensed him as he allowed his true aura to manifest. She screamed and ran for the stairs, and we followed. The doctor was bending over your cot with an obsidian sacrificial knife in his hand."

Eamon shuddered and covered his face.

"I'll never forget the look on his face or the feeling of total helplessness as we were caught in the web of Darkness covering the doorway. Lily still slept, thank God, and knew nothing. Then Loana gathered all her strength and tore down the web. It was a time for instinct, not power. She threw herself over you as the knife came down. You know about the power of the willing sacrifice, Johnny? Well, it was that power that saved your life. Loana gathered up the force of the doctor's hate and sent it back through the knife; it hit him with the power he himself had filled it with. His body combusted where he stood. In less than a minute he was just ash on the carpet, though nothing else was touched. Loana died a few hours later, but she had saved you and had no regrets.

"Now you know why Lily and I decided you had to grow up without me beside you. You needed to be well hidden. Lily never again used her divinatory powers; they could have been traced too easily. My presence would have been an even bigger giveaway. But I watched over you both from the higher levels. I saw you grow up, Johnny, though I never held you or spoke to you. Your life was—and is—too precious to risk, but I never ceased to love you. Just as I have never stopped loving your mother."

Johnny was silent for a while. Then, with studied nonchalance, he asked, "What about Ring's mother? Did you love her too?"

Eamon smiled and leaned back in his chair. "Has that been bothering you, Johnny?"

Johnny squirmed. "A little. But it doesn't stop me loving Ring," he added hastily.

"Of course not. Tze-Ring is a special human being, born to be close to you when you need him. The eternal half-brothers manifest in each age. Castor and Pollux, Anubis and Horus, Jesus and John…All of them loving and supportive, though often from different mothers or fathers.

"Yes, I loved and still love Natasha. She is gentle, kind, and beautiful, and her telekinetic powers are very strong. They linked well with my own, plus my ability to apport. We came together to provide the body for a child that we hoped would be better than either of us. We were not disappointed. Tze-Ring is my son as you are my son. I love Natasha, but I was *in* love with your mother. I saw her for the first time when she came to the Aeon. She was young with dark hair and eyes and a laugh like rippling water. I fell in love there and then. Four years later I went to claim my love and brought her to the Abbey of the Dawn."

"Wait, Ring's mother is still alive?" Johnny asked.

"Yes, she is the abbess of the Abbey of the Throne. You will meet her when we visit her abbey. You will visit and stay with all of them eventually."

Johnny sat back in his chair. All this just so he could be born. He pushed back his chair and stood up. "I need to get my head round all this," he told his father and walked out into the small garden.

Eamon watched him go with some apprehension.

"Do not worry, Father Eamon," said the abbot's voice in his head. "Believe me, he is strong enough to cope with this. After two and a half years, I have come to understand him very well."

"My thanks for your reassurance, Rinpoche. You trained him well."

There was a small sigh in his inner ear.

"I miss his laughter, and his…ah…unpredictable ways. You are expected at the Abbey of the Throne. There have been further developments concerning Talfryn Garrett. Abbess Natasha will have the information waiting for you. May Tara keep you both safe."

14 June, 8:30 a.m.
The city of Lahore

Lahore was hot, dusty, and smelly. As the private jet had not yet arrived, Johnny and Eamon drove into the city to buy clothes more suited to the heat.

Johnny looked in the mirror and thought about the suits, shirts, and casuals that must be still hanging in his wardrobes back in London. One thing was certain: They sure in hell wouldn't fit him now. The young man that looked back at him was taller by an inch and a half, broader in the shoulder, and well-muscled. The black hair was shorter, the facial bone structure firmer and more defined. Johnny Nova had been a boy. This was a man.

He turned away.

"How do we pay for all this?" he asked, looking at the assorted bags of clothing. "Wait," Johnny held up a hand. "Don't tell me. This guy is a Watcher, yes?"

The rotund proprietor nodded and smiled. "I am very happy to be serving anyone from these sacred places, sir."

Johnny grinned back at him. "OK. I give up. Thanks! Now let's be on our way."

Cooler now and feeling less out of place, the two men drove back to the airport, where the jet stood ready on the runway. With a minimum of formalities, they went aboard. Johnny looked round appreciatively at the fittings and settled into one of the seats. "It's a long time since I've been in a plane. Mostly I've done my own flying—astrally, that is. This is less tiring, and the view's better." The last statement was aimed at the trim figure of the air hostess. "How long will it take to get to Karachi?"

"I would think we should be there by the afternoon. We'll stay at the Hilton overnight and catch a scheduled flight the following morning to Aden. After that, another helicopter flight to the Abbey of the Throne. Abbot Gregor thought that as we were so close, it would be a good idea for you to spend a few days there. It is a stark place, but it has its own kind of beauty."

They buckled up and in a few minutes were airborne. For some time Johnny looked out of the window at the land below. Then he turned to his father. "Tell me about the Abbey of the Throne, Dad."

Eamon stretched out his legs and gathered his thoughts together.

"Some miles east of Aden is an area called the Hadhramaut. It is mostly desert with a few cities, some very old. Tradition says it was the Kingdom of Sheba. On the coast there is a long inlet, rather like a fjord, leading in from the Gulf of Aden. It narrows as one goes further in and ends in a natural harbour. Atop the cliffs are the ruins of an ancient city well over two thousand years old and built on even earlier ruins. The Abbey of the Throne is hidden in the oldest part. Few know of the ruins. Fewer still go there; the heat is almost impossible to bear, even for those born in the area. The last outsiders to even see it were two naval officers pleasure sailing in the 1800s. They discovered the ruins and actually sent back its location to the Royal Geographical Society. It is marked on maps, but the heat is such that no one bothers about it."

"Why build the abbeys in such places?"

"They need to be hidden from the world at large. All six are hard to get to, often almost impossible unless you know the hidden ways. The Throne is mostly underground, partly for coolness and partly because that is where the treasure they guard is concealed."

"Treasure? There's treasure there?" Johnny's eyes gleamed as he leant forward.

"Each abbey guards a treasure, Johnny. All are priceless, ancient, and full of power. Some are hidden behind walls of stone; others are in plain view but still hidden. Tell me, when you were in the Hall of a Thousand Candles, what lay before the Tara?"

"Just the usual offering. Fruit, flowers, a cup of water."

"Did you ever look at the cup?" asked his father. He smiled as Johnny shook his head. "That simple wooden cup was the treasure of the Abbey of the Dawn. It has had many hiding places, but now it will remain where it is until the coronation of the Aeon of Aquarius. We hid it in full view, Johnny. Where better to hide the Grail than a place where everyone can see it but not recognise it?"

"When I first arrived there, it was one of my chores to clean and refill it every day." Johnny's voice was choked with emotion. "My God, I touched the Grail every day without knowing it."

He looked at his father, bright-eyed. "You say there's a treasure in every abbey?"

Eamon nodded.

"Tell me more," demanded Johnny, impatiently waving away the offer of more tea. "All this is news to me."

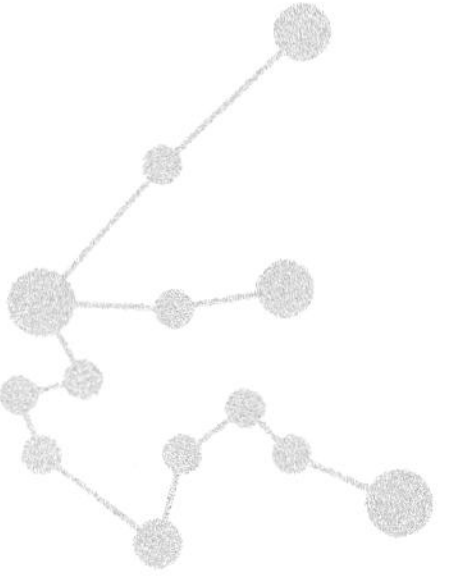

CHAPTER TWENTY-SEVEN

14 June, 11:45 a.m.
St. Giles on the Thames

The little church was full, a measure of the deep affection the local people felt for the young man who now lay face down, arms outstretched before the altar. The ancient ceremony of ordination moved with dignity and power towards its conclusion.

Bucky and Florrie clasped hands tightly and watched with tears in their eyes as Lyle Barclay received his priesthood at the hands of the bishop. Beside them, his mother and grandmother sobbed happily, but Ginny, holding her tiny daughter in her arms, looked with rapt attention at the hovering angelic forms. Margaret, fragile and ailing now, watched her from her wheelchair, the brigadier, as always, close by her side.

"She has such a pure sight, William," she whispered. "I wish we could get her into the Aeon for training."

"We can't kidnap the entire group, Margaret m'dear." The brigadier chuckled. "I find it extraordinary enough that in such a small bunch there are five incredible talents. Of course that includes that Tango feller. Virginia will certainly have her hands full with Lyle taking up a parish and a young baby."

He looked round the church. Liam and Biff sat beside Colin and Florrie, both self-conscious of the three-piece suits Florrie and Margaret had alternately bullied and coaxed them into buying. Liam had been amused and Biff highly embarrassed at the numerous fittings and detailed measurements that ensued.

Frank was in his element conducting his specially written anthem "It Is My Commandment That Ye Love One Another."

All the youngsters from Lyle's centre had turned out to honour their much-loved and respected friend and to sing in the choir, albeit most wore tracksuits and Reeboks under their surplices. It didn't matter; they were there, and that was enough.

An amazing number of theatre people, friends from the old days, and even some fans had packed in. The media, as always, had arrived in force. After all, it was not every day that a member of a respected rock band was ordained as a priest! The rest of the congregation were locals. *A good turn-out*, thought the brigadier happily. Then the hair rose on the back of his neck.

As Lyle went forward to be invested with his clerical garments, there was a stir at the back of the church. Florrie turned and gasped and dug Bucky in the ribs with an elbow.

"Well, I never," she whispered. "Look who just came in."

Tango was dressed to kill. His handmade silk suit was a masterpiece of the tailor's art, his shirt hand-stitched, his tie immaculate, and his shoes custom-made. He stood for a moment in the entrance, and those who knew Tango well were surprised to see a fleeting look of regret on his face. Then he headed for the front pew. Halfway there he stopped dead, and a spasm of pain crossed his face.

Margaret and Ginny both gasped. Ginny clutched her baby to her breast, her face a mask of fear and horror. Margaret whimpered deep in her throat, and William knelt to put an arm about her.

"Don't look. Don't look, my dear," she whispered. "The Darkness, it's all but enclosed him now. The guardians are attacking."

Tango was doubled up in pain, and for a moment the whole ceremony was halted as every eye focussed on his agonised form. For the first time in his life, Liam took charge. Grabbing Biff, he pulled him out of the pew, gestured to the bishop to continue, and the two of them hauled Tango out of the church.

Frank whispered to his front row of voices, and within minutes a beautifully harmonized sevenfold "Amen," sung a cappella, filled the church as the ceremony continued.

Ginny watched the angelic guards erecting an astral barrier at the door and sighed with relief. She caught Margaret's eye and nodded, then turned back to look at her husband. The ceremony went on to its conclusion enclosed within a barrier of angelic light.

♬ ♩ ♫ ♪ ♬ ♪ ♫

Liam watched with distaste as Tango spat out the last of the bile and wiped the back of his hand across his mouth. In the last ten minutes, his erstwhile friend had brought up everything but the soles of his hand-sewn crocodile-skin shoes. Biff, slightly green himself, watched from a distance.

Tango eased himself into a standing position and looked at Liam warily. "Thanks," he said. "I don't know what came over me. Must have been something I ate."

"More like it was somethin' yez did, boyo," opined Liam with rare insight. "What the hell got into yez, man? Surely you must have known you'd not be welcome in there."

"I just wanted to…to…well, to see everyone again, if you must know. God damn it, is that such a hard thing to understand?" Tango dug his hands into his pockets and kicked out at the church railings. "I thought it might be time to meet up again and find out what you've all been doing." His tone took on a casual note. "Heard anything from Johnny lately? How's he doing? Getting over his breakdown?"

Biff's hands clenched at his sides, his face turning red with suppressed anger at the obvious seeking for information. Liam moved to avert a fight, coming to stand between them. Liam shrugged.

"Haven't heard for a while; I've been away in Ireland. Bucky's the one to ask, or Florrie." He was on safe ground there, knowing they were the last two people Tango would ask for anything. He went on smoothly, "They'll be coming out soon. I'd blow if I were you. It would be for the best, don't you think, boyo?"

Tango nodded.

Liam walked him to the silver-grey Aston Martin parked at the curb. "Nice, very nice," he observed. "Yez doin' well, Tango me lad. These babies do not come cheap."

Tango grinned, pleased with his reaction. "Better than when I was with you lot. In more ways than one." This, last, as an afterthought: "You're right, it might be as well if I'm not around when they come out. Tell Lyle I said hi, and give Ginny my love if she'll accept it."

Opening the car door, Tango hesitated and looked back. For a moment, Liam had the feeling he was feeling lost and lonely, then dismissed the thought. Tango cared for nothing but himself and what he could get.

The church door opened and people spilled out onto the pavement. Without a backward glance, Tango let out the clutch and drove off.

Bucky hurried towards Liam and Biff, his face anxious. "What was all that about? Why was he here?"

Liam calmed him down, taking his arm and leading him back to the others. "He said he wanted to touch base, but I'm thinking it was really information about Johnny he was after. What happened in there?"

Bucky shrugged. He didn't want to go into details with Lyle's church friends round. "Let's say the other side has it in hand. Give the brigadier a hand with Margaret, lad."

With good grace, Liam and the ever-present Biff went off to help. They adored Margaret and were always on hand to push her chair or carry her up and down stairs. She greeted them now with a smile.

"Here come my gallant knights of the chair. Biff, my dear, will you give me a hand up? I want to stand for the photographs."

Biff lifted Margaret bodily out of the chair and gently stood her on her feet while the brigadier fussed with her wrap and handbag. Liam folded the chair out of sight, and they lined up for the official photographs.

Determined the incident would not overshadow the event, Bucky marshalled the BBC cameras and the reporters and introduced the bishop to them for an impromptu interview, then had the choir sing the anthem again, unaccompanied, for the cameras. Well pleased with the publicity his little church was getting, the vicar beamed at everyone and completely forgot the interruption.

Nothing was said about the incident until the reception in the new church hall was over and they were on their own. Then Margaret and Ginny described what they had seen.

It had been a year now since the rest of the group had gradually been brought in to the real cause of Johnny's disappearance. Biff and Liam had scoffed at first, but once exposed to Margaret and the brigadier and Bucky's increasing abilities with what he referred to as "his other suit," they found themselves roped in as abbey extras. Margaret was gently encouraging Biff to open up his modest and unrealised talent of empathy. It was slight and unreliable, but it was there. Liam cheerfully acknowledged he had nothing in the way of talent to offer but a good pair of knuckles, but his Irish blood let him go along with it all.

Lyle had been the surprise. Though he knew about and accepted Ginny's gift, his rock-solid Christian beliefs had made it difficult for him to grasp what Johnny's role was to be. The work of the abbeys and their occult talents had given him many a sleepless night. Finally the brigadier had invited Lyle to meet some friends of his over dinner. There Lyle found himself face to face with a high-ranking Jesuit priest, a rabbi, and a seemingly dour Scottish minister. They had argued, discussed, and fought amiably all through dinner, then invited a bemused Lyle to a game of poker, during which they all happily cheated via the medium of their various talents.

Later in the evening, over coffee and brandy, Father Andrew had gently demonstrated his talent of empathy. Having asked for and received permission, he gently aligned his emotional self with that of Lyle and guided him back to a time when Lyle was fourteen. For an electrifying quarter of an hour, Lyle relived his darkest secret: He had been an unseen witness to a rape and murder in his old neighbourhood, and though he knew who the assailant was, he had not come forward for fear of retaliation. The man had killed twice more before being apprehended. His reluctance to identify the killer had weighed heavily on Lyle's mind ever since.

Father Andrew gently lined up the fear, disgust, and confusion of a frightened young boy with his own trained powers. He siphoned the guilt away and absorbed it, transmuting it to Light within his own heart centre. Later he explained to Lyle how he had discovered his talent through the hearing of confessions and had found himself able to truly release troubled souls from their self-imposed purgatories. His ability as a high-level exorcist was often in demand, though not always by his own church.

Lyle wept as the feeling of being cleansed and forgiven flooded through him. The others had been there for him instantly, supporting and holding him steady until he regained control. For a while he was part of a total unity of minds full of love and light. Lyle then understood what the task of the Forerunner would be and was astonished to find he had a part to play in it. He had returned home at peace and determined to be ready for what was to come. Though he had no extra talents, Lyle's profound faith would be one of the mainstays of his ministry.

♬ ♩ ♫ ♪ ♬ ♪ ♫

Tango drove back with a vicious headache and a mixture of despair and frustration eating at him. The sight of the close-knit friendship of the group had awoken a feeling of bitter loneliness in him. He despised the feeling, but deep inside he longed for a return to the old days. He wondered what Johnny was doing and if he had changed.

On a whim, Tango drew in to the parking lot of a suburban hotel and went in and ordered a drink from the bar. He wandered into a small, enclosed garden area and sat away from the other drinkers. Putting down the untouched glass, he leaned back, letting unspoken thoughts reach out.

"Johnny, where are you, and what are you doing? Where did things go wrong? Why am I not as happy as I thought I would be away from the group and you?" Without thinking, Tango reached out, striving for some small thread of the old Johnny he remembered.

With a sense of shock he recalled that not once, in all the time he had known him, had Johnny ever bad-mouthed him, blamed him, or put him down. He had never forgotten Tango's birthday and had always come up with just the right gift to please him. It was Johnny who suggested Tango put a memorial stone on his mother's grave when the money started to roll in. It was Johnny who had gone with him to see it done and had brought flowers to put on the grave. Tango had not been back since, and it was probably overgrown by now, but he remembered how supportive Johnny had been at the time. Perhaps next week he would pay a flying visit to the grave and his old haunts.

Yes, said another and darker side of his mind, *but it was Johnny who took the limelight and the front of the stage, Johnny who had been the idol of the fans*. He, Tango, was the one who had it now, while Johnny was forgotten by all but a few.

Tango relished the glow of self-satisfaction for a few minutes, then downed the warm beer in a few swallows and stood up. He had a rehearsal to go to and a meeting with De'ath in the evening. He badly needed energy, so perhaps they would go hunting tonight.

Tango pushed aside his thoughts of Johnny and strode out to his car. Within minutes he was on his way.

"It would appear," mused a Being of Light, "that there is still a small part of him that resists the Dark. It might well be that we can reach him through this small point of inner Light and alter his pattern of self-destruction."

"True," answered its companion, "but it is deeply buried and will take much effort to bring to the conscious mind."

"There is the spirit of the young girl who died. She has forgiven his part in her death and, through this act of love, has achieved great merit. She would, I am sure, willingly act as an interceptor to the influence of the Darkness."

"Let us speak with her. If there is the slightest chance that Talfryn Garrett can be turned from his present path, it must be taken. It will make no difference, of course, to the outcome—the law is the law. But if it can be done with love and not hate, the tide will turn in our favour."

The two figures came together to form a spiral of light that spun into a star. It hung for a moment in the clear upper air, then imploded and disappeared.

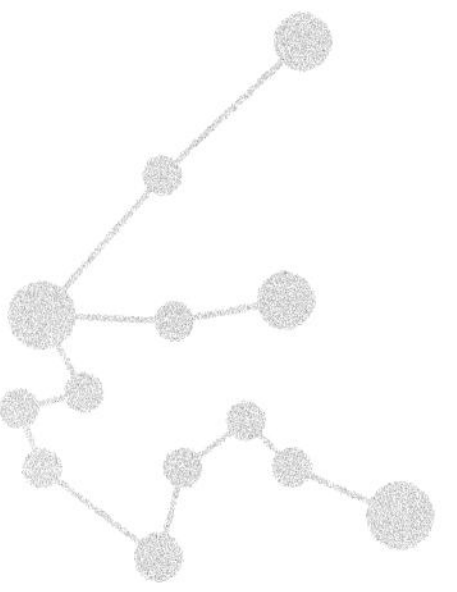

CHAPTER TWENTY-EIGHT

15 June, 2:00 p.m.
Somewhere off the Gulf of Aden

Helicopters, Johnny decided, were the absolute pits. He disliked the sensation of falling forwards as it took off. He disliked even more the feeling of disorientation as it ducked, twisted, sidled, and occasionally flew backwards as Eamon edged his way through the narrow fjord leading to the Abbey of the Throne. It did nothing for Johnny's peace of mind to know it was his own father at the controls. Damn it, what did he know about this man's ability to keep this benighted piece of machinery up in the air?

Johnny grabbed the armrests as they dropped fifty feet in the space of a heartbeat, then closed his eyes as the copter danced horizontally across a massive cliff face. When it shimmied through a gap between two sandstone outcrops like a bee heading for its hive, Johnny decided he'd had enough.

"Holy shit!" he yelled. "Are you trying to prove a point, or is this the usual way in?"

Eamon looked over his shoulder at his white-faced passenger and chuckled when Johnny yelled at him to look where he was going. Minutes later, he landed with pinpoint accuracy on the only flat surface for miles. The fact that the surface was atop a three-hundred-and-fifty-foot pinnacle of rock made Johnny's stomach turn over. He undid his seat belt and slid cautiously out of the machine.

Eamon grabbed their bags and started off to what appeared to be the edge of the minute landing pad. Then he stopped and looked back, jerking his head at the bemused figure behind him.

"C'mon, it's just a few feet and then we're inside the rock." He descended out of sight, leaving Johnny to gather his courage and follow him. A few feet from the helipad, a spiral of steel steps led to a ledge cut into the rock. From there a narrow causeway led to an opening in the cliff face, where a woman in a deep red robe waited.

As he crossed slowly, Johnny found the courage to look over the side of the narrow bridge. Four hundred feet down on one side, the gorge ended in a series of huge, jagged cliffs peppered with small openings that could only be caves. On the other side, the narrow, winding inlet they had just traversed led to the sea and the gulf. He found it hard to believe they had flown through those tortuous gaps without coming to grief. A few more gut-wrenching steps and he stood at the entrance to the Abbey of the Throne.

The woman was a petite figure, with the same elegant bone structure she had bequeathed to her son. Johnny knew her at once. This was Tze-Ring's mother, the abbot's daughter, and the abbess of this abbey.

Eamon drew Johnny to his side.

"Johnny, this is Abbess Natasha, Tze-Ring's mother." He smiled, but his eyes were anxious as he stepped back, leaving them face to face.

"Abbess Natasha, I am honoured to meet you. Tze-Ring and Lea send their love and photographs of Patrick, your new grandson. I greet you, lady, mother of my brother, and so, if it be your wish, my mother also. I thank and bless you and my father for giving me the gift of such a one to stand beside me in the trials to come," said Johnny and lifted her hand to his lips.

"Brother John, I am pleased to welcome you. Tze-Ring speaks of you with such love. Your father may not have told you, but I was with your mother at the Abbey of the Dawn. I helped to prepare her for the Rite of Nuit and your conception. She was much loved by us all."

The tiny abbess tiptoed up to kiss his cheek.

"I greet you, Forerunner of the Aeon of Aquarius. The Abbey of the Throne offers itself to your service. I bore my son to be your brother and companion, as your mother bore you to proclaim the coming of the new Word. I gladly offer myself as a mother to you now, and all that I am to your destiny."

The Forerunner stepped to the edge of the rock and looked out over the desolate beauty of the landscape before him. On the very top of the cliffs, now glowing red in the setting sun, he could see the ruins of a once-thriving city. Old memories stirred and surfaced.

"I remember the old city centuries ago, but the memories are deep and far away."

Johnny turned and smiled at his companions. Knowing what the future held, the brilliance of that smile caught both Eamon and Natasha by the throat.

The abbess pulled herself together.

"Come, Johnny. I may call you that, yes? You have travelled a long way and for many days; now it is time to rest. Your rooms are ready, and there is a meal prepared. Come, come." She bustled both men out of the heat that in a few hours would drop by twenty degrees or more.

♬ ♩ ♫ ♪ ♬ ♪ ♫

Johnny looked round with interest. The corridor before them had been carved out of solid rock and felt oppressive to someone used to the freedom of the high mountains. Other corridors led off at intervals, but they kept to the main one. It widened out into a large, softly lit cavern, in the centre of which was a pool. From the wisps of steam rising from it, Johnny surmised it was a natural hot spring. The coolness of the cave was welcome after the heat outside, and Johnny eyed the pool with longing. The abbess laughed.

"You will find many such springs here, Johnny. We use them to relax and also for healing. Let me show you to your quarters. There you will find all you need, including a hot bath to soak in."

From the central space, more corridors led upward until natural rock gave way to man-made walls. Along these Abbess Natasha led her guests to two small but comfortable rooms with a connecting bathroom. She lingered long enough to say ruefully, "I know you would prefer to eat quietly and then sleep; your journey has been long and arduous. But the others have waited so long to meet you, Johnny. It would be a great kindness if you would share our evening meal."

He turned to her with a gentle smile. "I am anxious to meet them also, Abbess Natasha, and I look forward to dinner both because I am hungry and because this is my first meeting with abbey members other than those of the Dawn. Give us an hour and we will be with you."

The abbess nodded and went to the door, then looked back, smiling.

"I see both your father and Tze-Ring in you, Johnny, but there is also much of Lily's brightness there. She is so proud of you."

"Well," said Eamon as the door closed behind her, "what does your heart tell you about Natasha? Do you understand now when I tell you that I love her, but I was *in* love with your mother?"

Johnny went to his father and hugged him. The Forerunner in him would always be lonely because of what lay ahead, but the human part of him reached out to this man who had sired him with such love and dedication of purpose.

They showered and put on the light woollen robes of wine red laid out for them. Johnny queried their colour, for up until now his robes had been white or saffron. Eamon explained, "Each abbey chooses its own colour. At convocations it is a moving and colourful sight. Come, they are waiting for us."

The dining hall had once been part of the original buildings, and though not large, it was comfortably appointed. As Johnny and his father entered, the abbess came to greet him, bringing with her the abbot, Khalid ibn Suleiman.

The tall, white-bearded abbot looked into the eyes of the young man, and the Forerunner met the searching glance with love, dignity, and respect. Silently, the dignified abbot knelt and pressed his forehead to Johnny's feet.

Johnny hurriedly raised him up. "I do not deserve such a greeting, Holy One—I have not yet come into my full power as the Forerunner. But I thank you for your welcome."

"Then, for the time left to you to be just a man, be welcome and share these few days with us." The abbot's voice, despite his age, was deep and resonant. "Come and meet our small family."

Proudly he introduced each member of the abbey, giving their name and origin as he did so. Johnny could feel the closeness of this small community and the devotion that held them in this remote and inhospitable place. They sat down at one long table, and Abbess Natasha invited Eamon to bless the food.

Eamon thought for a moment, then spoke. "Let the spirit and power of our mother, the earth, be with us as we eat together. Let the power and love of the One Creator be with us as we speak together. Let the spiritual power of each of us be enhanced by our coming together. Selah."

"Selah." The word echoed round the hall.

The designated servers of the day brought in the food, and Johnny was delighted to find meat on the menu. He tucked into the meal with an appreciation that made Brother Yano, the cook, beam with satisfaction. Yano's face split in a broad smile as the guests complimented him on the dinner and began to plan another specialty for the following day as they ate.

The conversation rolled to and fro as the meal progressed, with questions and answers from both sides adding spice to the meal. Later, replete and rested, coffee, fresh dates, and figs were served. Then Sister Lyrata leaned forward, excitement showing on her delicate features.

"We have a surprise for you, Brother John. Being so isolated here, one of our greatest pleasures is listening to music. We have a large and varied collection of recordings and an excellent sound system. When your visit was confirmed, we wanted to offer you something close to your heart as a gift. A few weeks ago, we learned that a newly composed piece was to be premiered at the Royal Albert Hall in London, so we arranged to have the actual performance recorded for you. Also, there is a personal message from the composer that you may find interesting. Brother Feisal, if you please."

The portly figure of Brother Feisal bustled over to a cabinet and opened it to reveal a state-of-the-art music system. For a few moments he busied himself with the equipment, then returned to his seat. Almost as one, the members of the Throne leaned forward, their eyes on Johnny. He poured himself a second cup of coffee and was lifting it to his lips when a familiar voice filled the hall.

"Hi Johnny, this is Frank. I don't know when you'll get this message and the recording, but I want you to know that it was written for you. We miss you and love you. God bless."

"Hi there, Johnno me boy. Liam here. Hope you're keeping off the booze wherever you are. By the way, seeing as how you're not here to wear it, I've taken back that cashmere sweater I gave you when we were in New York. Hope to see you soon, eh!"

"Er—Ah—Umm, Johnny, this is Biff. I wish you were back with us. Things aren't the same without you. I hope you like Frank's music; it's different from his usual stuff."

"Johnny, this is Lyle, in case you've forgotten my voice. I pray for you every night, man, 'cos I know you're doin' somethin' real important. Ginny and I love and miss you. She's right here beside me." A soft cooing noise interrupted him, and his rich laugh filled the hall. "That's Mary-Clare, sending her love in her own way. God bless you, Johnny."

"Johnny, oh Johnny, *miro chal*. I miss you so much. A lot of things have happened since you left, but we're all keepin' together and waitin' to see you when you're ready. Me an' Colin talk about you all the time. The recording studio's doing well, an' we're all excited about Frank's new piece. When you listen to it, think of all of us being there in the audience. Don't forget your old Florrie, love."

"Johnny, it's Bucky. God, I can't wait to see you, son. They say you've changed a lot since...well, since you went away. I suppose we all have in the last few years. Things are different now, but just as exciting in their way. And married life is a blast, I can tell you. Come back soon, son. We need you. God bless." Bucky broke off, close to tears.

"Frank again, Johnny. It's about the music you're going to hear. I took the main theme from 'Mountains of Gold' and used it as a basis for a choral tone poem, the first serious music I've ever written. It's called 'The Golden Mountain,' and it's dedicated to you."

There was a pause. Then the voice of a BBC announcer introduced the first performance of "The Golden Mountain" by Francis Saunders, conducted by the composer. For a few moments they heard only the muted murmur of the audience, then a burst of applause heralded the entrance of the composer as he took his place on the podium. Breathless with excitement, Johnny visualised Frank standing there, his endearingly ugly face taut with concentration. Then came three taps of the baton, and the noise died away.

A single trumpet filled the silence with a long, slow wave of golden notes, underlined by the accompanying deep tone of a Tibetan radung horn. A trio of woodwinds followed in its footsteps, opening up a vision of high, open spaces. The entry of the strings gave voices to the eternal winds, with echoes provided by the violas. Note by note, instrument by instrument, the main theme built up. Suddenly it was there, created by the cellos and a soft, fluid rumble from the percussion. In the mind's eye of the listeners, there gleamed the snow-clad summit of a high mountain caught in the glow of a new day. Female voices eased in slowly and softly, more of a murmur of sound than anything else. Then a deep, low humming from the male voices took up the theme.

With a sure and confident touch, the composer built the visionary landscape, easing it majestically through the day from sunrise to noon and on to sunset. The golden mountain came alive and lived in the hearts and minds of all there. As the piece progressed, it became more and more real until there seemed to be nothing but it and them. Again the soft and wordless chant from the choir underlined the ethereal sunset vision painted by the music. Night fell gently on the mountain and finally, almost reluctantly, the instruments faded away one by one until only the radung horn was left to sound the long, melancholy closing note.

The following silence dragged on and on as the audience struggled to come to terms with the fact that it was over. Then an overwhelming burst of enthusiastic applause filled the hall. Emotion coloured the voice of the announcer as he described the scene of a standing ovation and the calls for the composer to take a bow over and over again. It was, declared a music critic, the birth of a major new talent, one comparable with Benjamin Britten, Ralph Vaughn Williams, Edward Elgar, and William Walton.

The recording cut off, and in the Abbey of the Throne, all eyes turned to Johnny.

He sat with tears streaming down his face, for a long time unable to compose himself. Finally Johnny wiped his eyes, stood, and went to each one in turn to thank and bless them for their wonderful, caring gift. For a while he'd been back with people he loved, in a world he knew, but one of which he would never again be a part. In a voice choked with emotion, he tried to tell those round him what this had meant to him. Abbess Natasha came at last and pressed into his hands a portable CD player, earphones, and a precious copy of the recording.

Eamon took him away then, guiding Johnny's weary footsteps back to his room. He helped Johnny undress and got him into bed, reflecting with a few tears of his own that this would possibly be the one and only time he would "tuck in" his son.

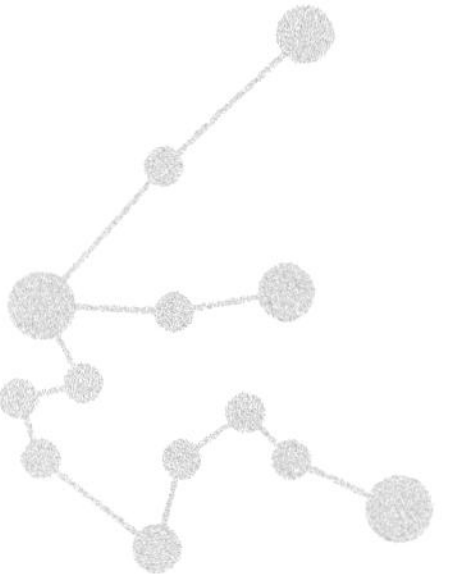

CHAPTER TWENTY-NINE

16 June, 1:00 p.m.
The Abbey of the Throne

The corridor was dim and cool, and the walls had been decorated with murals depicting desert landscapes, caravans, and market scenes. The abbot explained as they walked, Eamon following a few steps behind.

"They are the work of Mother Okifi. She finds it hard to live underground most of the time, so she paints the outside world she remembers as a girl. Our work is demanding and onerous. The concentration needed is intense, so we work in small groups, each group doing a maximum of three hours and then breaking off to do something different. Okifi finds relaxation in her artwork, and it gives pleasure to those of us who see it every day."

"What is the nature of your work, Master Khalid?" asked Johnny, lengthening his stride to keep up with the tall, vigorous figure of the abbot.

The older man chuckled, opened the door they had just reached, and ushered them inside. The underground room was vast, over a hundred feet in length and all of fifty wide. Shelves from the floor to the ceiling over twenty feet above them held row upon row of books, scrolls, parchments, and boxes of vellum. Several large desks occupied what floor space was left between wooden boxes and containers of every kind.

On one side stood a long trestle table carrying modern office equipment ranging from computers to fax machines, radio telephones to scanners, binders to printers. Two large photocopiers were busy in the corner. The atmosphere was more cool than usual, and Johnny shivered.

"It is necessary to keep the books at a low temperature. Almost every one of them is in a very fragile condition," explained Eamon. "They are slowly being copied, some by hand and others typed, so that the originals can be then packed away and kept safe, but the knowledge they contain will be accessible to future generations."

"What books?" asked Johnny, though he already knew what the answer would be.

"Did you really think the teachers of ancient times would risk the destruction of the great libraries without making sure the knowledge they contained was safe?" Abbot Khalid moved to one of the desks where Sister Lyrata and Mother Mari-Teresa were working to translate an early Aramaic script. "Almost without exception, in all the ancient libraries copies were made of important books and scrolls and taken to one or other of the abbeys of the time. With the modern techniques now at our disposal, we thought it time to bring everything together. We re-copy it, translate where the older translations were not correct or inadequate, and store the originals safely. This is our life's work," he added simply.

Overwhelmed, Johnny walked up and down the vast storehouse of knowledge, keenly aware that here, hidden in safety, were books from the most ancient of times, many thought irretrievably lost.

"Will they one day be made available again to the world?" he asked, holding in his hands a treatise on the movement of planets written by a long-dead Chaldean priest.

"If and when the world is ready for what they contain," he was told. "We are the guardians until that time comes. What we have here is far more than even the Vatican library can boast."

"In fact," added Eamon mischievously, "some of this came from the Vatican, either hand-copied, scanned, or photocopied. We have, shall we say, 'friends at court' who have proved very helpful."

"Come, Brother John." The abbot took Johnny's arm. "There is something else that we guard and which you should see." He led the way from the library and out into the corridor. "Father Eamon has told you about the treasures that each abbey contains, has he not?"

"Yes. I must admit to feeling ashamed that I did not recognise the Grail when I held it in my hands almost every day."

"You will hold it again, and at that time you will most assuredly know it for what it is. We need to descend quite deeply now; please take care. There is a rail to hold on to, and I advise making use of it. These steps have been in use since the time of the Queen of Sheba and have worn away almost to nothing in some areas." Khalid spoke casually.

Johnny stopped dead, causing his father to bump into him. "Did you say the Queen of Sheba?"

Unperturbed by his tone of disbelief, the abbot continued to descend the narrow and uneven steps. "Oh yes. It was she who built the city now in ruins above us. Of course, it has been rebuilt many times since then, but it was her son Menelik who brought the treasure to this place on the instructions of his father, King Solomon. It has been here since then, for this is where his coronation was held and where the Teacher of the Age will be crowned."

Again Johnny came to a full stop. "Crowned?"

This time the abbot also stopped and turned round, his bearded face showing his astonishment. "Really, Father Eamon, has the Dawn taught him nothing of this?"

Eamon shrugged. "It was the decision of the abbot of the Dawn that he learned gradually about the…er…finer points of the abbeys' involvement with the work and training of the aeon."

The older man threw up his hands in a show of dismay and then continued downwards. His voice floated back from the near darkness. "When the time comes, Brother John, the Teacher of the Aeon of Aquarius will come here to be invested with the symbols of rank and crowned."

They came to the bottom of the steps and a wide corridor. On either side, niches had been cut into the living rock to hold life-sized statues. Each was veiled, but such was the skill of the sculptor that the form beneath was almost—but not quite—revealed. It was, thought Johnny, just as well, for the forms were in no way human.

At the end of the corridor was a door of dark, heavy wood with massive iron hinges and a lock to match. Hanging beside the door on a simple nail was the key. "If there's a treasure of great value inside, Master Khalid, isn't it silly to have the key in full view?" asked Johnny. "Or," he went on, "is there something I should know about the door, something not immediately obvious?"

His father laughed and turned to the abbot. "He learns fast."

With a smile, Abbot Khalid thrust the key into the lock and turned it. The door swung open on silent, well-oiled hinges. Eamon and the abbot stepped back, drawing Johnny with them. A gust of scorching air that was the salamander guardian blasted out of the darkness beyond the door.

The heat was intense, the feeling of raw power even more so. Khalid stepped into the maelstrom of elemental energy, raised his right hand, and chanted. The fire entity shimmered, dipped in acknowledgement of the blessing, and retreated into its own dimension, leaving the way open. Khalid beckoned his companions forward, and they passed into the temple of the Abbey of the Throne.

The first thing Johnny noticed was the acoustics. Every sound was amplified by the soaring sandstone walls and the great stone arches that rose over fifty feet above them. The floor, also of stone, had been laboriously levelled and made smooth, then covered with thousands upon thousands of mosaic pieces in brilliant colours to display a giant zodiac with each planet in its rightful house. As a labour of love and dedication, it spoke for itself. That the work was still ongoing showed in the areas of bare rock at the far sides.

Almost afraid to breathe, Johnny stood taking it all in. At the far end of the cathedral (as he felt it should be called) stood a triple-tiered dais with three steps leading up to each successive level. The top level was hidden by a curtain of deep purple silk. The lighting, explained the abbot, was twofold. Huge arc lamps hung from red-painted stanchions that crossed the centre space, and smaller lights were hidden in niches carved from the rock itself. These, like most of the electricity in the abbey, ran off the solar panels situated on the plateau above them and from the generator in a cave far below them. The dais, however, was lit by just two twelve-branched candelabra. Carved wooden chairs were set in semicircles, leaving a ceremonial pathway from the door to the dais itself.

To one side stood an organ big enough to grace any church Johnny had ever been in. His stage-trained eye also found discreetly placed amplifiers, and he smiled. In true Abbeys of Light tradition, no expense had been spared. He turned to the abbot.

"It is magnificent, Master Khalid, and worthy of the amount of work that has been devoted to it. But you spoke of a treasure?"

Silently, the abbot led the way to the dais and bent to remove his sandals, intimating to the others to do the same. From a wooden chest he took three plain white cotton robes and cords. Their own robes were discarded and the new ones put on. Then all three washed their hands and feet in a stone basin standing to the side and fed by a continual stream of fresh water. Satisfied, the abbot led them to the dais.

They mounted to the first level and paused, the abbot ringing a silver bell attached to the cord about his waist. A feeling of weight descended upon Johnny as if thousands of years were pressing on his shoulders. All his trained senses came alive, and he found himself mentally linked to his companions and murmuring the same words.

"*Baruch Atah Adonai Eloheinu.* Praised are you, oh God. Bless us, *Adonai Ha-Aretz*, Lord of the Earth, and permit us to approach thee. Thou art the Source of all things; Thou art the One, the most holy, and the most high. We come before Thee with open hearts, trusting in Thy love."

They mounted the second level and the bell rang.

"Thou art *Aloah va Daath*, the chord of harmony manifested in the heart of humanity. We lay our souls before Thee. Behold, we come with pure hands and hearts ready to do Thy bidding. Thou art the One, the compassionate, the beloved, the only Source of life."

They mounted the third level and again the bell was rung.

"God of Abraham, *Eheieh*, the inestimable One, *Hashem*, the first and the last. Permit us to stand upon Thy holy ground. Allow us to come to Thee for Thy blessing. Forbid us not. We bring before Thee Thy chosen one. Lord, bless the chosen and mark him as Thine own."

The bell rang. Silk rippled as the curtains parted, and Johnny raised his eyes.

Power raw and primal slammed through him, forcing him to his knees, filling him with a heady mixture of awe, terror, and a soaring exultation. His companions hid their faces in their hands as the light emerging from the Ark of the Covenant bathed all three in a radiance that burned without heat. Eamon fell and curled into a ball against its intensity. The abbot lost consciousness and tumbled down the steps. But Johnny opened his arms and took the light into himself, unafraid and unharmed.

Torn from his body, Johnny's consciousness was whirled aloft. He saw galaxies born and die. He entered into the heart of stars and spoke with beings whose bodies were those same stars. He beheld the moment of creation and experienced its ending. He looked at the task ahead of him and wept. Then, remembering his debts, he asked for a blessing on those who had shared his life to this point and who had trained and supported him. Johnny saw the Betrayer, knew him, and loved him for what he had once been, and he blessed him also.

The light dimmed, and gentle darkness claimed him.

♬ ♩ ♫ ♪ ♬ ♪ ♫

Eamon was the first to stir. Slowly, he raised his head and looked round him. The curtains were closed again. He winced as he got to his feet; his hands and face were on fire. Eamon looked down and saw blisters and knew it was the same on his face.

The abbot groaned, and Eamon went to help him to his feet. Then, together, they went to Johnny. He lay as if asleep, smiling faintly. His father raised him and supported him against his knee. On Johnny's right temple a red mark caught Eamon's eye: the mark of the chosen, a perfect tau.

20 June, 8:00 a.m.
The Abbey of the Throne

The Abbey of the Throne had gathered to say goodbye. In the past few days Johnny had endeared himself to all of them, and he in turn had come to see them as much-loved friends and companions. When he saw them waiting for him, it brought back bittersweet memories of saying goodbye to the Abbey of the Dawn. This time, he told himself, he would be strong, but it was still a wrench.

Abbess Natasha tiptoed up to put her arms about Johnny's neck. He laughed and lifted her off her feet to hug her. She smoothed down her robe and shook an admonitory finger at him, but her smile was warm and loving. Abbot Khalid said little, but he lightly touched the now-healed mark of the chosen and blessed Johnny. The others crowded round to wave and wish them well as Johnny and Eamon crossed the causeway and climbed the narrow stairs to the helipad.

Eamon lifted the copter off smoothly, and within minutes they had left the Abbey of the Throne behind. Understanding his son's need for silence, Eamon concentrated on flying and, except for the odd glance, kept his gaze fixed ahead. Not until he landed at the Aden airport and turned to gather up the bags behind the seats did he look directly at Johnny.

The Forerunner met his eyes silently, asking for permission. On receiving it, Johnny reached gently into the man's mind and linked it to his own. In the space of a few moments, Johnny poured into his father's memory the whole of his childhood: the talks and the laughter he had shared with his mother, the stories she had told him, and their shared loved for each other. In return, he took from his father the knowledge of his love for Lily and the memories of his short time with her. Then Johnny gently broke contact, climbed out, and walked into the airport, leaving his father stunned at the ease with which it had all been accomplished. The tears on his face were reflections of those on Johnny's.

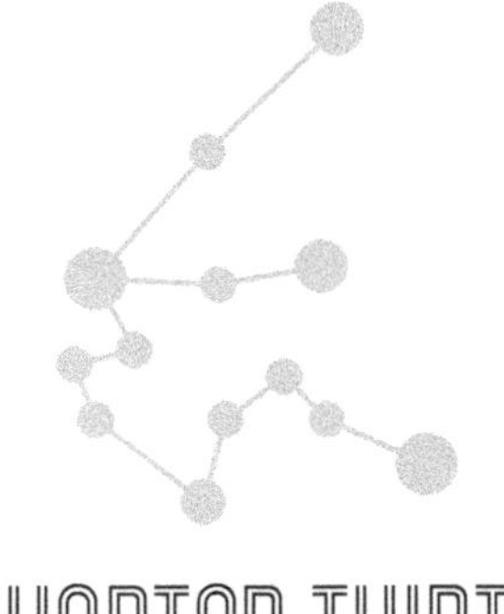

CHAPTER THIRTY

20 June, 12:30 p.m.
The penthouse, London

Bucky was on the balcony looking over the river with a sense of sadness. Ever since Johnny's disappearance, he had stood on this balcony every day and looked at the river. His memories were always the same: In his mind's eye, he saw a small motor yacht moving through the water, taking Johnny away from him. He'd had plenty of time to think about that morning long ago and knew with utter certainty that Johnny had been on board.

Bucky sighed. So much had happened, and so much more was still to happen. His own training had made him privy to exactly what being the Forerunner meant. He was still coming to terms with that.

"Such sad thoughts, *miro chal*," said Florrie's voice behind him. "We still have time with 'im, and it won't all be painful."

Bucky turned, smiling, and put his arm round her. "I know, love. It just sort of gets to me at times. I miss him so much. We all do."

The phone rang, demanding attention. Florrie went inside and lifted the receiver. Bucky turned back to his contemplation of the river, half listening to the conversation. Then a change in Florrie's voice alerted him.

"Well, I'm really not the one to ask, Tango. You'd better speak to Colin; he's the one who makes all the arrangements. Frank's away at the moment, but talk to Colin."

She held out the receiver and silently mouthed, "Tango, for you."

Immediately on his guard, Bucky took the phone from her and prepared to throw up a psychic guard if it was needed.

"Hello, Tango. What can I do for you, if anything?"

"Well, it's the other way round for a change." Tango's voice was light and well controlled, but Bucky discerned a note of anxiety. "I've been asked to do the background vocals for a big new film. The thing is, they want Frank to write the music and the group to do the backing. We've tried to get hold of Frank, but Florrie tells me he's out of town. Can you get in touch with him, and do you think he'd do it? Would the group do it? I realise I'm not high on your list of favourite people, but this is a really big thing. It could even mean an award for both of us, the group and me. What do you say?"

Bucky was stunned but also wary. How he answered could affect many things. On one hand, he wanted nothing to do with Tango or his companion. On the other, it was a priceless opportunity to keep an eye on Tango and suss out his intentions. Then again, it meant Tango might get to know Johnny's current whereabouts, if not through talk, then through other means. He decided to stall.

"On the face of it, it sounds a good deal," he said easily. "Thing is, we haven't a clue where Frank is at the moment. He went off somewhere to work on his new piece. How soon do you need an answer?"

Florrie, listening in, stood open-mouthed.

Bucky listened to Tango's response, then said, "Yeah, well, he said he'd be back by the twenty-second or twenty-third. That's just a coupla days away. How about I talk it over with the others first, and then Frank when he gets back? I'll get back to you by the twenty-fourth at the latest. OK?... Fine... Yeah, you too."

Bucky put the phone down, turned to Florrie, and blew out a lungful of air. "Whew. What a turn up for the books, girl. He has a big deal going down for a film background vocal. The producers want Frank to write it and the group to back it."

"What?" Florrie's voice rose several decibels in outrage. "That two-timing *jukkal* and his *mulengro. Meery Duvvel…*"[10] She went off into an indignant volley of Romani epithets.

"Calm down, Florrie. Let's look at this from another angle. It'll mean we can keep a closer eye on him than we've been able to do lately. We'll have to keep a guard up at all times or he'll suss out Johnny's whereabouts, but I think it's a chance worth taking. I'll ring William and Margaret and ask them. If they think it's a good idea, we'll double-check with the abbey. We've got three or four days grace. Meanwhile, we'd better double the protection round this place. At least I'll feel we're actually doing something."

Bucky dialled the number.

"Rothely-Smythe here."

"William, it's Colin. Something's come up, and we need to talk." He quickly outlined his conversation with Tango and his reasons for not giving Tango a definite refusal. "I'm hoping it will give him the idea we're off guard, so to speak. He might say or do something we can pass on to the abbey."

Bucky stopped to listen to the brigadier voicing his doubts, then continued.

"Yeah, I know, William, but surely we can guard ourselves enough not to give anything away. That bodyguard of his is good, but they are two to our four. Doesn't that count?…Oh, hello, Margaret. What do you think of it?"

Thirty minutes later, Bucky put down the receiver and looked at Florrie.

"Margaret thinks it's tricky. William thinks it's worth a try. I'll call Abbot Gregor."

He dialled the number and Florrie went to make tea. Some time later, Bucky put down the receiver and looked at Florrie.

"We've got the go ahead, girl."

"Well, thank goodness that's settled," said Florrie, finishing off her gin. "For a while I thought we'd never get all the details straight."

10. "That two-timing dog and his scoundrel [De'ath]! Good God…"

The penthouse was unusually full, with Colin, Florrie, Margaret and the brigadier, and all of the group bar Frank. The afternoon had been one of phone calls, faxes, and hurried meetings taking place in three different countries, and they were all exhausted. Bucky rose and went over to a note board. For a moment he studied the notes in his hand, then picked up a marker and turned to the others.

"OK, let's get it down where we can see it as an overall plan. I'll call Tango and tell him we're open to the idea of the whole thing, providing the contract and financial terms are to our liking. It's what Tango will expect from me as a manager and from the group as a whole. During the call, I'll tell him Frank was not keen on the idea and had to be persuaded by the rest of us. I'll make it a condition our involvement includes Frank writing the background score as well as the prime vocal. We'll let Tango think the idea of an Oscar for the best score or song is our prime reason.

"When he gets back, Frank meets with Tango and the producers to look over the script. They'll talk about what they want and what Frank can offer. The usual wrangle will go on and will be settled within a week or so. We'll sign the contract and, as far as they know, everything will be straightforward.

"Frank works on the vocal first, writing it in such a way that it will need an extra instrumentalist. He'll call a couple of preliminary recording sessions to work out phrasing, range, and background tone. After the second or third, he'll throw a wobbly and say the backing needs another 'sound' to add depth of tone.

"Frank will ask for a bass player to give the vocal a richer timbre. That'll please Tango, and it will sound genuine. Liam will say he knows just the person we need, an American finishing a contract over here and looking for another one. We book another session ostensibly to look the guy over and then bring in Brother Colby from the Abbey of the Winds. He damps down his talents at the first meeting and 'broadcasts' an open aura for Tango to look at. If we can get De'ath out of the way for that first meeting, it will be an advantage. Once the contract is signed, Tango can't get out of it.

"Colby's cover is a laidback guy with a pot habit. He'll lay down a psychic cover to stop Tango getting to know Johnny's whereabouts from any of us. He'll also be close enough to Tango when De'ath's not round to get a handle on what stage his training has reached and what his plans might be. Only Colby sends back details to the Aeon. That way, we're not involved and nothing shows up if De'ath tries to pick our brains. On top of this, the Aeon will set up a psychic barrier over this place so we can sleep safely. Everyone clear on all this?"

All voiced their agreement, and Bucky heaved a sigh of relief.

The brigadier smiled. Colin Buckman had changed considerably from the corpulent go-getter of years ago. Slimmer by more than thirty pounds in spite of Florrie's cooking, there was a determination and sense of purpose about him that commanded respect. Not just from his peers in the music business—he'd always had that—but from his newfound circle of friends in the abbeys as well. Though tumultuous times lay ahead, Colin Buckman would keep his head, of that the brigadier was certain.

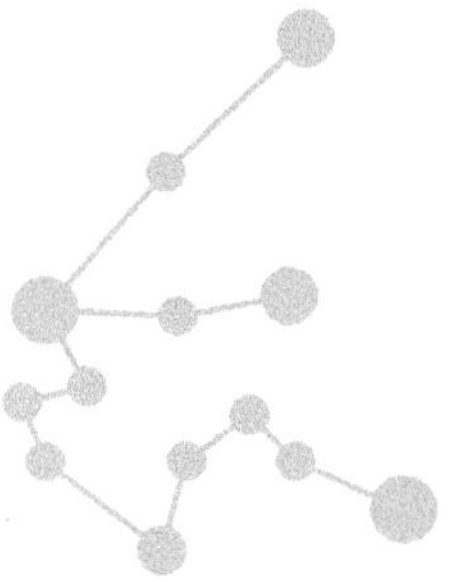

CHAPTER THIRTY-ONE

20 June, 4:30 p.m.
Cairo, Egypt

Eamon and Johnny took a scheduled flight to Cairo. As they circled the airport, Johnny looked down. The part of him that had been Knebt-Tua marvelled at the city below, amazed that the pyramids and the sphinx had survived the centuries, albeit—his memories informed Johnny—the human head had been that of a lion in his time.

As they braved the Cairo traffic in the Rolls that had been sent for them, Eamon bemoaned the fact that they had no time to visit the Valley of the Kings. Johnny laughed. "Dad, there are at least two bodies I've used in the past still undiscovered down there. I don't need to see my tombs again. After all, I designed them and had them built!"

Johnny laughed again at his father's expression as they turned in at a pair of imposing gates. Despite being within the city limits, the palace of Emir Haroun ibn Sayed al Kerim-Azur managed to give the impression of being an oasis. Fountains, pools, palm trees, and colonnades offering shade from the sun abounded, and the efficient but silent servants whisked them and their luggage to a suite of rooms that took Johnny's breath away.

"Wow," he said, trying to take it all in. "This is some pad."

Eamon, remembering the distant gaze and aloof dignity of the Forerunner, marvelled again at the way in which his son handled the two very different sides of his nature.

Having bathed, shaved, and changed, they were escorted through numerous corridors to a dining room to meet their host and his other guests. Instead of the lavish set-up Johnny had envisaged, the room was small, intimate, and comfortable. The emir sat in a wheelchair, a cashmere shawl covering the lack of his lower limbs. Behind him stood his sons, Hashim and Amal.

Eamon bowed. "*As-salamu alaykum.*"[11]

The emir smiled widely. "*Wa 'alaykumu s-salam.*"[12]

He turned to Johnny, his faintly accented English warm as he introduced his sons. Amal extended a hand and said with a grin, "I have all your recordings, and I am hoping you can be persuaded to autograph them for me."

"It will be a pleasure, sir."

"Good! Make that two, as I have my own collection. My brother would not allow me to use his." Hashim elbowed his brother out of the way to offer his hand.

Johnny laughed. "If I had a guitar with me, I'd even give you a personal show."

The brothers looked at each other, and Hashim lowered his voice. "Well, we did ask a few friends round tomorrow, and one of them plays a guitar."

The emir cut in. "My apologies for my sons' enthusiasm, Brother John." He sent a stern look in their direction. "It is hardly fitting to accost a guest with demands the moment he places a foot in my house." He turned to Johnny with a smile. "But I must admit that I will put aside my morning's work and join you."

The meal had been chosen with care, taking into consideration that Johnny's restricted abbey diet now had to get used to a new regime. While they ate, they spoke of mundane matters, then retired to a balcony overlook-

11. "Peace be upon you."
12. "And upon you be peace."

ing a garden of night-scented flowers. There they drank coffee and worked their way through a bowl of *lokum*. Johnny had never tasted it before and went into raptures over it. It was years since he had tasted candy of any kind.

Once the servants had discreetly withdrawn, the emir leaned forward. "There is news from the Aeon," he said quietly. He told them of the plan Bucky and the group had set up to keep track of Tango, and the forthcoming film deal. "It will enable them to keep track of what he does and where he goes. Also..." He paused. "It will enable the Watchers to ascertain just who—or what—is controlling him." He sipped at his coffee. "Abbot Gregor suspects it is an ancient evil, one who keeps itself alive by ingesting human energy. It makes sense, considering the importance of the situation, that the Lords of Darkness would employ an entity capable of delaying—or even of destroying—Brother John's mission. So, my friends, I have taken the liberty of cancelling your flight to France. Instead, Amal will fly you to a private landing strip outside Sète."

Amal leaned forward eagerly. "My brother will drive you. He will take the D612 to the motorway at Beziers and then turn south towards Perpignan and the N116. It is a winding road that leads to the border, but you will turn off at the junction of the N20 and aim for the Tunnel de Puymorens. This runs along the eastern border of Andorra for about two miles. But about a mile inside is the Old Road leading to the Aeon."

Johnny looked at his father. "The Old Road? Like the one we used before?"

"Yes. It is deep underground and, as I remember it, cold, damp, and unpleasant. However, it is safe, and at this stage we cannot be too careful. Thank you, my friend. Your evaluation of the situation could have saved us from a possible kidnap attempt or even an assassination."

The emir bowed slightly. "It is as always an honour to serve the abbeys. Now I suggest you rest, since my sons seem to have arranged your time tomorrow. I will see you then."

The silent servants appeared as if from nowhere and conducted them to their suite.

"I gather," said Johnny, sliding between silk sheets, "that the emir and his sons are part of our lot."

"His planes, ships, houses, and money are there if we have need of them, as are both his sons. Amal can fly, steer, drive, ride, or float anything that moves. He is also a high-level master of ninjutsu. Hashim is a shadow rider, a talent we have only just discovered and, as yet, know little about how it can be used."

"And the emir? Does he also have a talent?"

"Haroun was and is a diviner of precious metals. Twenty years ago he was abducted by the other side to help them uncover a cache of gold, jewels, and art hidden by the German High Command in 1944. He led them in circles for weeks while our side uncovered it and restored as much as we could to its rightful owners, mostly Jews. When they discovered Haroun's deceit, they shot him in both legs and left him to die miles from any help. Too weak from loss of blood to even raise the distress signal, he was found after three days by a Romani woman and her son. She cared for him while the boy went for help. It was too late to save his legs, but her herbal knowledge saved him from fatal blood poisoning. Now he puts his knowledge, his wealth, and his sons at our disposal and helps to train others. His is a rare talent, and because of its link to riches, it requires a pureness of heart and mind to control the vice of greed. Now sleep. You have a 'show' tomorrow."

Johnny turned over, and deep inside he recalled the words and music of "Mountains of Gold." There were many kinds of gold, he thought. There was the kind men would kill for, and there were words, deeds, and acts of courage of a different kind of gold, and far more precious. Johnny reached out and, without thinking, touched the mind of someone he knew who was also thinking of him: Frank.

A chord of music rang through Johnny's head, and he sent out a sleepy thought. "No, Frank, it would sound better in the minor key!"

Then he slept.

21 June, 1:15 p.m.
Somewhere above the Mediterranean Sea

Eamon extended his foot rest and turned his head to look out of the window at the Mediterranean far below them. Across the aisle, Johnny dozed fitfully. In the cockpit Amal, at the controls of the Learjet, talked quietly with his brother.

"I may not have the inner talent some of our kind have, but I can feel waves of power radiating out from him. Yet when we were all singing together, he seemed to be just…well, just Johnny. One day that power will change the world we live in—or at least, the Teacher will change it. I wonder how it will be. We may not live to see its fullness, but he…He will not see it at all. It seems so unfair."

Hashim touched his brother's shoulder. "It is what he was born to do; it is not for us to question. It is the will of Allah. But think of it, Amal: a world where it does not matter by what name you call your God, how you worship, where you worship, or with whom…In such a world, you and I could walk into a synagogue with old Jacob Hertz and not start a riot."

Amal nodded and adjusted his course. "We should be landing about 2:15. The car will be waiting. I'll re-fuel and then head back. I have to get Baba to the French consulate by 10:30 tomorrow. When can we expect you?"

"I'll stay at the Aeon overnight, then drive down to Barcelona and get whatever flight is available. With luck, I should be back for dinner."

"Any delays, just call me and I'll come and get you."

Eamon appeared in the doorway with coffee. "Johnny's still asleep. All this rushing round the globe is getting to him. But a couple of months at the Aeon should get him up to scratch."

Amal laughed. "Get Pawel to work out with him."

Eamon winced. "I want him beefed up a little, not massacred and toothless."

Hashim drained his coffee. "How long will he be with Gregor?"

"I would think about three months, a little more if it's needed. Mara will arrive in a week or so. Then, if things go as planned, we can get him to the Abbey of the Winds. Fancy a trip to Chile, Amal? If I can wrangle it, I'd like to take him via London so he could link up with his old friends."

Hashim shook his head. "I can't see that happening. He would be very exposed there, literally in his enemies' backyard. You'd be better off breaking the journey halfway and taking them to him for a couple of days. Not too long, though—you don't want to upset his training."

Eamon slapped him on the back. "There are times, Hashim, when talking to you is like talking to your father's twin."

Amal grinned delightedly. "You could not have said anything more suitable to him. OK, we are in sight of land now. I'll have you down in under an hour. Hash, call ahead and make sure the car is waiting. I'll contact the landing site."

With abbey-trained efficiency, everyone went about their tasks while Johnny slept on peacefully.

♬ ♩ ♫ ♪ ♬ ♪ ♫

Amal made a feather-light landing at 2:20 p.m. A dusty, bedraggled, well-used, and less-than-elegant four-by-four was already waiting. Passport control and customs made an appearance so brief Johnny hardly had time to open his mouth. The jet was already being refuelled. Since they only had a suitcase apiece (and Hashim an overnight bag), by 2:50 they had said goodbye to Amal and were on their way.

An hour later Johnny plaintively made it known he needed two things: a toilet and food. Hashim grinned and drew in to the next available stop, where, having dealt with the first pressing need, Johnny munched his way through a steak, onions, and his first fries since leaving the Abbey of the Dawn. The others had salad.

"They used to make eggs and fries for me once a month at the Dawn," he told them. "I lived for those special days. Ring's wife, Lea, made them for me. But I really miss meat." A thought struck him. "Are they vegetarian at the Aeon?"

Eamon made soothing noises. "No. Some are, but they do have meat as well, so you'll be OK until you get to Chile. Then it's back to the green stuff, I'm afraid."

Hashim looked at his watch. "We need to get going. I want to be in the abbey before it gets dark."

Once back in the car, Johnny curled up in the back of the car and dozed. The others were silent with their own thoughts. The signs for Perpignan began to show up more frequently, and a few miles further on, Hashim turned off onto the N20 and began the long, slow climb to the mountains.

The traffic increased, and Hashim cursed softly in Arabic as he wound his way through lines of traffic, stopping several times to avoid the odd breakdown.

Johnny woke up and peered through the window. "Where the hell is everyone going?" he asked. "I thought this would be mostly light traffic. Skiers, etcetera."

"There is a festival going on somewhere, I think. Plus Andorra is known for cheap wine, spirits, cigarettes, perfume, and all that. It's always like this on weekends and holidays. We will be at the entrance to the tunnel very soon."

Thanks to a lorry shedding its load and causing a heated argument between its driver and the cars behind it, it was already dark when they arrived at the entrance to the Puymorens Tunnel. Hashim was fit to be tied, and Eamon insisted on taking over the driving so he could rest. Among the cars jostling for entrance, their dingy, run-down, and barely roadworthy conveyance aroused little interest, though Johnny would have bet his next ten years that the engine under the hood was super tuned.

They entered the tunnel and drove in silence for the next mile. Then Hashim turned to Eamon. "The next lay-by," he said quietly.

Eamon nodded and turned to Johnny. "Get your bag ready."

A lay-by came into view, and Eamon turned into it. Hashim got out. Going to a wall phone, he dialled a number and spoke briefly. A door opened and a man in overalls came out.

Hashim gestured to his passengers, and they grabbed their bags and followed Hashim into a workshop. The workman gave them a smile and a salute, got into their vehicle, and drove off.

Eamon opened a large cupboard and, with a heave, slid a portion of the back wall aside, revealing a lift.

Johnny finally found his voice. "When it comes to secrecy, you guys really have it covered."

Eamon nodded. "It is essential. 'Wild talents' have always brought out the worst in those without them. If they knew we walked among them, not one of us would be left alive. Instead of using our skills to build a better world, we would be slaughtered en masse."

The lift came to a halt and the door opened onto the Old Road carved from the mountain untold ages ago. A trolley was waiting, and they piled their bags onto it and crowded into the small seating space. The rough road turned and twisted and gradually descended while Johnny, open-mouthed, took in the prehistoric paintings and carvings that covered the walls.

"This place is priceless. Just think what the archaeologists would give to see this."

"Which is exactly why they won't see it," said Eamon. "Within a year it would be crowded with tourists, and what happened to Les Ezyies would happen here. It would all be destroyed beyond repair…Now we are almost at the end of our journey."

Ahead was a tightly barred gate, and beyond a smooth, modern road where a car waited for them, driven by an excitable and voluble Frenchman who greeted Johnny with a kiss on both cheeks, then thrust several CDs under his nose to be autographed. He talked nonstop in French the entire journey to the abbey until Eamon spoke to him in his own language, explaining that Johnny had travelled from Egypt and was close to being exhausted. More French, this time with apologies, which Johnny gratefully accepted.

They drove in silence for several miles, then turned into a chateau built against the solid mountain wall and guarded by gates that looked capable of deterring a commando unit. The grounds looked extensive and heavily wooded. A signpost welcomed them to the *Société du Mont Dupre*, care home for the elderly and disabled. The whole structure held an air of genteel decay that made Johnny smile and applaud the clever disguise. Waiting on the steps was an imposing figure: Gregor Theodorakis stood a full 6'4" with shoulders like battering rams. A chest-length beard, meticulously neat, was topped by a pair of piercing dark eyes.

Eamon bowed and attempted to greet Abbot Gregor in Greek. A booming laugh emerged from the beard, and Eamon was scooped up in a bear hug that lifted his solid weight a clear two feet off the ground. "Your Greek is as bad as ever. Welcome back, Eamon."

Abbot Gregor turned to Johnny and Hashim. "Salaam, Hashim. My respects to your sainted father. Tell him we would welcome his presence here." He came to Johnny and placed a hand on each shoulder. "A warm welcome to you, Forerunner. We are honoured by your presence. But," his eyes twinkled, "that does not mean your training here will be any easier. Come, you will be tired and hungry. Enter. The Abbey of the Aeon is at your disposal."

The abbot led the way into a large hall, where a member of staff took away their bags. "You will want to shower, eat, and then rest. All has been prepared. Eamon, Hashim, you know your way around. Take Johnny to his room, and I will hurry dinner long." Gregor winked at the bemused man. "I hear you are fond of meat, so how does chicken pie with roast potatoes, parsnips, and green beans sound, with apple pie to follow?"

Johnny swallowed hard. "Bloody marvellous," he said and was nearly floored by a thump on the back.

"Go and wash up. Dinner in thirty minutes."

♬ ♩ ♫ ♪ ♬ ♪ ♫

Eamon sat on the bed and took his shoes off. Unbuttoning his shirt, he looked at Johnny standing by the window. "I hope you don't mind sharing a room, lad. It's just that, well, after being separated for so long and missing so much of your life, I want to be with you as much as possible. There's still so much to know and even more to share with you."

Unspoken words of the fate of the Forerunner shimmered between them.

Johnny turned from the window. "I know what you mean, Dad. I feel the same way. I want as much time as I can get with you as well. You know so much about all this abbey stuff; you know the people, the way they run things, and what makes them so different. I don't even know what makes *me* different, except it appears I was born to carry out a certain task. But right now I want a shower and food and sleep. By the way, can you drop a hint that I really don't want to sing, sign CDs, or talk about White Heat?"

Eamon laughed. "Take a shower. I'll use one in the other room. Then we'll eat."

♬ ♩ ♫ ♪ ♬ ♪ ♫

Two hours later Johnny crawled into bed, replete with real food in his stomach and weary to the bone. He was asleep in seconds. Eamon sat and watched him, longing to hold him but content to just be with him. His son, a son he had been unable to see growing up. He had not seen his first steps or heard his first words, never been able to teach him to ride a bike, never witnessed his first day of school, never watched him open Christmas and birthday presents…He'd sometimes seen Johnny from across a road, in a school playground, or playing football in the street, but he'd never been able to approach him. Eamon had been at Johnny's first gig with White Heat, had bought their CDs and watched them on TV, but he had never been able to turn to someone in the crowd and say, "That's my son."

Eamon sat for a long time and watched Johnny sleep. He prayed for the strength to let him go when the time came.

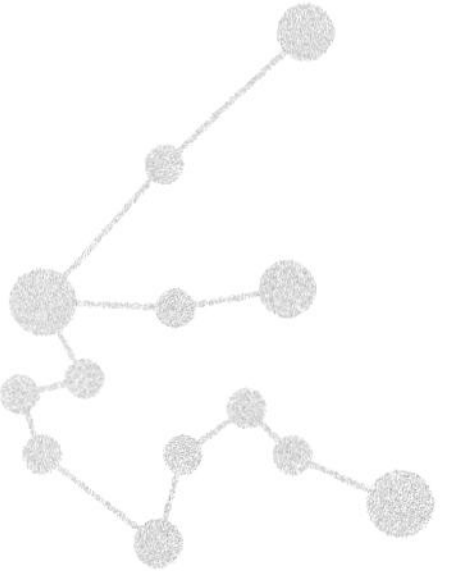

CHAPTER THIRTY-TWO

22 June, 8:00 a.m.
The Abbey of the Aeon

Breakfast was a riot. Johnny, who was used to the quiet serenity of the Abbey of the Dawn and the organised, tightly run Abbey of the Throne, found the Aeon full of laughter and music. There was an almost casual approach to their work that reminded him of how things had been with White Heat.

The first meal of the day was a time when everyone met up. The rest of the day was spent on their individual tasks and training, so they made the most of it. The members of the abbey exchanged and shared ideas, thoughts, jokes, and their unique talents with each other. Abbot Gregor had declared Johnny's first full day would be one of relaxation so they could get to know each other. For the next few months, they would work together, sharing their knowledge and skills and helping him prepare for his own work.

Over mugs of coffee and a plate of scrambled eggs and slices of the first bacon he'd tasted in years, Johnny began to put names and faces together.

Maurice, a Frenchman, apologised profusely for demanding signed CDs and, as an apology, offered to make a strawberry pavlova for dinner. Cooking was his passion, but his real skill lay in his ability to create an illusion so real it could—and did—fool the sharpest eyes and to hold it long enough to be useful. Belgian-born Sister Vivianne had the same skill, but not as strong. Matthew was her tutor, and the two of them constantly tried to outwit each other, often to the dismay of the others.

René, another Frenchman, was a long-range telepath, as was quiet-spoken Pawel from Gdańsk. They were a bonded couple and worked hard to extend their range and accuracy between themselves and other abbeys.

Sister Venda from Zambia was rescued at the age of fourteen from her own mother. The woman had tried to burn Venda to death because of her telekinetic powers. Now seventeen, she was still badly scarred and subject to nightmares. She was hesitant about meeting new people because of her looks but was fascinated by Johnny's former fame as a rock star. A local missionary had hidden Venda in a cave for three weeks before being able to get her to a Methodist Church school in a distant town. They got in touch with Hashim's father, who supported the school, and within a week she was in the Aeon. Here, her talent was being schooled by Juan Artez y Ortiga. An elegant Spaniard from a titled and wealthy family, his face and body, like Venda's, bore the scars of his own brush with fire, and she felt at ease with him. A multiple-car crash had forced his kinetic powers to the surface, and he was capable of moving unusually heavy weights.

Leon was a Basque. His gift of far memory was rare, and he often spent time at the Abbey of the Throne helping them decipher the oldest and most delicate records. Johnny was looking forward to working with him, recalling his time as Knebt-Tua, and hoped to connect with former Forerunners to learn how to prepare the way for the Teacher of the Age of Aquarius.

Wolf's talent was the rarest of all. Gregor estimated that just one in half a million was capable of shape-shifting, mostly as very small forms and for short times. But Wolf's talent was the strongest and most varied of any other yet encountered. Wolf's talent being so rare meant he was often on call and needed to travel at a moment's notice. Soft-spoken and withdrawn, Wolf, like his namesake, was a loner. He moved between abbeys all the time, going wherever he was needed. Abbot Gregor was hoping the kinetics would one day be able to move a human body from place to place; at the moment, they could only move a body several feet, but minus clothing or whatever was needed to carry.

♬ ♩ ♫ ♪ ♬ ♪ ♫

To the outside world, the abbey was a large chateau where wealthy families hid their aging parents from view; the important areas had been carved into the mountain itself. Here their working places and the Hall of Ceremony were located. The abbey grew most of their own food, and everyone shared in the necessary fieldwork aided by a few well-trusted locals. Chickens, cows, and an orchard provided 80 percent of their needs.

The first time Johnny saw his father milking a cow, he doubled up with laughter—until he found himself with his head pressed up against the side of a cow, a bucket and a warm udder in his hands.

"Sing," his father told him. "It makes it easier to milk them. They prefer ballads."

"Mountains of Gold" increased the milk flow by 20 percent. Mother Genevieve, who looked after the cattle, found this hilarious. She also taught Johnny to groom the horses (two of them, Ozzy and Dulce) and the orphaned donkey, Lulu.

All through that first week, between looking after the animals, cleaning out stables, and helping Sister Dagmar with weeding and preparing vegetables for the kitchen, Johnny fell into bed every night and slept like a log. Slowly, Johnny learned of the different skills the abbeys fostered.

Also during the first week, Eamon stayed with him, and they explored their personal relationship. It was a different life from that of the Dawn, but to Johnny's delight, he was able to communicate with Tze-Ring, Chambha, and the abbot several times via the Dawn's newly installed computer. He was also making progress in extending his own telepathic powers, but as yet he could not seem to make the important spiritual connection he would need in the future. Finally he plucked up the courage to ask Gregor if this was all he had to do in this abbey.

Gregor looked up from his desk and took off his glasses. "We wanted you to get used to the abbey and its people. Some you have yet to meet. Desmond comes from a small island off the French coast. There are several of them; Jersey is the largest. He has a talent I've never seen before: He heals minds. He has changed Venda's life since she came to us. At first, she hardly left her room, and when she did, she covered her head and shoulders with a cloth. Juan no longer has nightmares and can stand near an open fire—though not for long.

"We have yet to understand exactly what your own power will be. We know it involves far memory, but according to your brother, Tze-Ring, there are signs of other talents that come and go. Since you arrived, you have been under observation. Mother Amalia and Sister Eugénie have been observing you mentally, physically, and psychically since your arrival. You have puzzled them both, but you obviously feel the need to be more involved.

"Tonight, we will discuss how we can be of help to you in your task. Tomorrow, Sister Mara will arrive. She is in London, where our former abbot, Jerome, has been undergoing treatment. He is close to passing and returns to the Aeon to prepare himself.

"But to answer your question, yes, it is time to assess and measure your talents. According to Abbot Nyang, you seem to be multi-talented, with a unique ability to contact the higher levels. Not entirely unexpected considering the task before you. So, until tomorrow." Abbot Gregor turned and went on with his work.

Johnny, feeling a bit lost, went in search of his father. He found Eamon working with René and Pawel and Sister Eugénie. All four were telepaths, but of different strengths and with additional talents. They were playing bridge, one pair against another, and using their talent to pass information back and forth; René worked with Eugénie and Eamon with Pawel. One in each pair was trying to break into the thought stream of a rival and attempting to send information to their own partner. It was a test of skill, swiftness, and recognition of a totally different mindset.

Holding his own talent in check so as not to confuse the players, Johnny watched until the game was over and its value discussed. Then Sister Eugénie, a rotund Breton with a beaming smile, laid a gentle hand on René's arm. "René, dear, how about some coffee? And, from the aroma coming from the kitchen, there might be an apple pie looking for a home. Join us, Brother John. I'm sure you can spare a few moments before Sister Dagmar comes looking for you. I swear she actually plants weeds for you to find and dig up."

René obligingly went off, but Pawel turned to Johnny and said, "Tomorrow you will meet Father Jerome and Sister Mara. Brother Desmond will be here in the evening, the last of the Aeon's personnel." He paused and ran a critical eye over his companion's body. "I would like to see you in the gym at 6:30 tomorrow morning; you need to toughen up and build some muscle tone." Johnny looked at the Pole's bulging biceps and cringed mentally; suddenly his morning job of weeding the gardens seemed much more appealing.

A plate of apple pie under a layer of fresh cream was thrust into Johnny's hand by Eugénie. "Eat," she said through a mouthful.

Johnny's face lit up, then dropped again when Pawel took it away.

"No," he said firmly. "Cake is not good."

Johnny grabbed it back. "A condemned man has the right to a last meal."

Pawel gave him an evil grin. "You just added fifteen press-ups to the twenty I was going to insist on tomorrow."

♫ ♩ ♫ ♪ ♬ ♪ ♫

The following morning, true to his word, Pawel woke Johnny just before 6:00 a.m. and handed him a set of gym shorts and a vest. "Don't bother to shower," he said. "You can do that after I have finished with you. You will certainly need it then."

Johnny stumbled out of bed and stared at his grinning tormentor. "I need to pee first." He headed for the bathroom, pointedly ignoring the muffled snort of laughter coming from his father's bedcovers.

For the next hour, Johnny prayed earnestly for Sister Dagmar to demand his presence in the garden, to no avail.

When, at long last, Pawel called a halt to the seemingly endless methods of torture he had devised, Johnny felt numb. Though he'd not thought of them for weeks, he longed to be with Frank and Bucky, Liam and Biff and Lyle—even Tango—at the breakfast table, swapping jokes and extolling the attributes of the latest lot of groupies. Sheer pride made him stagger from the gym rather than crawl, as he wanted to do.

Johnny stank to high heaven. The gym kit was sodden with sweat. His hair hung in lank strands, and his mouth felt like something had died in it. Pawel slapped him on the back and said happily, "Same time tomorrow, Johnny. See you at breakfast!" He walked off, whistling.

Holding on to whatever was steady enough to take his weight, Johnny limped, stumbled, and hauled himself to the foot of the stairs. He paused and looked up at them before trying to climb them. Johnny let loose with a string of epithets that would have made a builder proud of him.

"I haven't heard words like that since my father found my mother in bed with the rent collector."

Johnny turned round. In that moment, he understood why Eamon had left his wife and child because he was a danger to them. Why Lyle lit up like Christmas tree whenever Ginny walked into the room. Why Lea glowed when Tze-Ring smiled at her.

She stood there, and the light from the open door curved round her like a shawl. A sapphire could never match the blue of her eyes. No field of wheat would ever be as deep a gold as the braid of hair that fell to her waist. A rose would have given its scent to be as soft as her skin.

A thud was not just the gym shoes falling from Johnny's hand. It was his heart falling at her feet.

A small, delicately boned hand was held out to him. "I am Sister Mara." She smiled at him, and the world and everything in it went away. In that one moment, Johnny lived a lifetime with her: remembered hot summer days spent swimming in the sea, running through piles of autumn leaves, pelting her with snowballs, and kissing her under a branch of mistletoe; the feel of her hand as he slid a golden ring on her finger; the weight of a baby in his arms, the birth cord still attached; the sound of her name on his lips as he drew his last breath and fulfilled his destiny.

She freed her hand from his death grip and said, "I'll see you at dinner," then followed the men carrying Father Jerome's stretcher to his quarters.

Johnny stood at the foot of the stairs, and a wave of energy rose from his Achilles tendon and roared through his body. He sprinted up the stairs and headed for the shower.

Breakfast over, Johnny spent the morning in the garden, planting and weeding. Though he looked for Mara at lunch, she did not appear, and he spent the afternoon with Juan, playing kinetic chess with the board covered and both players sitting with their back to it. Johnny's game was so erratic Juan called a halt and substituted a game of table tennis. To his amazement, Johnny won two of the three bouts. "How did you do that? Have you been practising?"

Johnny laughed. "No, I just put a face on the ball each time I hit it."

Juan threw back his head and roared with delight. "That is something I can use! It combines kinetics with emotions and will double the power. It's brilliant; I must tell the others. Come, Johnny, let's find something long and cool to drink."

Johnny smiled and hid the fact he had imagined the handsome Spaniard's face on the ball, for he was an opponent for a seat next to Mara at dinner. He planned to outsmart him at dinner.

Dinner, as usual, was laid out on the side table, and everyone helped themselves according to their tastes and appetite. Johnny, used to the spartan fare at the Dawn and the boarding school set-up of the Throne, found the long refectory table covered with white linen an amazing contrast. The snowy napkins and crystal wine glasses were Maurice's contribution, and they all appreciated his efforts and complimented his cooking.

Johnny hung round for a while as if trying to make up his mind about what to choose, but he was actually waiting for Mara to appear. Juan appeared with her on his arm, and Johnny went red with anger. He fought to keep his feelings in control and was ready to leave and go without dinner. Then Juan, having seated Mara, came to stand beside Johnny as if choosing his meal. He filled a plate with food he knew Johnny liked, placed it in his hand, and said quietly, "The seat next to her is empty—I'm sitting at the other end. Grab it before Pawel does."

Johnny looked at Juan, then at Mara, and he placed his hand over the Spaniard's heart. A wave of healing power filled the organ, and in the next beat all Juan's past fire trauma was gone. In its place was the ability to govern that element. Everything in the room froze—something new and precious had entered the abbey. Voices stopped. Eyes turned to Johnny as he made his way to the seat beside Mara and sat down. Then everything went back to normal, but what happened in that moment would always be a wonder to those present.

Every evening, Maurice used his talent to create an illusionary centrepiece. Tonight it was a pair of swans, their necks entwined, resting on a nest of flowers. Johnny was enthralled and wanted to know how he created such beauty and kept it in full appearance for so long. Maurice promised to show him how his unusual talent came about and to tell him about his time in the circus as an illusionist. Then everyone tucked in. Flushed with the success of the swans, their creator kept changing the colour until Mother Amalia complained of being dizzy. Johnny watched and drank it all in, something deep within him telling him that such memories would be there to hold on to in the future.

Gregor watched Johnny, quietly listening to his occasional comments, and assessed the way in which he gathered the laughter, voices, images, and atmosphere together as a whole and drew it within himself as a keepsake for the future. Catching Eamon's eye, he smiled and raised his glass and nodded towards Johnny, who was trying to explain an English joke to the bemused Pawel via its translation into French by a somewhat-inebriated René.

Eamon, too, was storing this mentally, hungrily, knowing all the while that these moments would one day be all he'd have to remember of his son. Then perhaps he would come back here and, with Maurice's talent, he could watch an illusion of such times as these.

♬ ♩ ♫ ♪ ♬ ♪ ♫

The following morning, as Johnny was showering after another gruelling session with Pawel, Eamon put his head round the shower door. "Johnny, Father Jerome has asked to see you after breakfast. He is very frail, so it won't be a long visit, but he was insistent. Abbot Gregor and I will go with you. There is no need to wear a robe; as you know, here we only wear them when and if necessary. Nor do we stand on ceremony. Jerome is beyond all that, but to see you and talk with you for a short while will give him great pleasure."

Johnny towelled off and began to dress. "Dad, just why is this work I'm going to do so special? I mean…OK, I'm supposed to go out and talk to people about the next Teacher, but let's face it, any one of the people I've been with in the last few years could do that."

"No, Johnny, the Forerunner is special. You have yet to come into your full power. That's why you are going from abbey to abbey—because in one of them, the Descent will occur, and from then on everything will change. You will no longer be Johnny; you will be the messenger of the Age of Aquarius. Now hurry, let's have breakfast, then go to see Jerome."

As they joined the early morning crowd, Pawel told Johnny, "I have a feeling that when you have seen Jerome, you will need to give time to yourself. He may be old and ill, but the power in him is intense. I think of all the leaders in our abbeys, he is the most powerful, even now, though the abbot of the Dawn would be the closest. I'll see you tomorrow, early."

Johnny looked round but did not see Mara. She spent most of her time with the old man, caring for him, reading to him (he loved Agatha Christie novels), and keeping him company. It occurred to Johnny that he had never asked what her talent was.

Johnny finished his meal and went looking for Eamon. He found him in the garden with Gregor. They were sitting on a bench looking to the snow-covered mountaintops. He stood quietly, waiting for them to speak first.

Abbot Gregor sighed and stood. Eamon followed him. "Let's go. He will be ready for us now." He led the way through the garden, passing Sister Dagmar as she gathered vegetables for Maurice. She stood aside to let them pass, head bowed. That puzzled Johnny; so far he'd seen no sign of deference to either of them.

A sense of import flooded through Johnny. Something lay ahead. Something strange and new. Something close to the time he had helped Lea birth her second child. Something was building in him, gathering strength and purpose; the power at the base of his spine was beginning to unfold. "Johnny" was withdrawing, and the Forerunner was taking over.

The two men with him looked at each other and drew back, walking behind Johnny as he led the way to a part of the abbey he had not seen before. They passed under an ancient archway and approached an oaken door. Johnny raised his hand and it opened to allow them entrance.

On a hospital bed against a pile of pillows, the man who had once been Jerry Muldoon from County Sligo struggled upright. Mara went to help him and turned to Johnny only to see a man she did not know. That shy man was now a Priest of Power.

Johnny's clothing dropped away, leaving him clothed in Light. Eamon and Gregor went to their knees, heads bowed. Johnny's voice held the timbre of muted thunder. The face was that of a man who had walked through centuries and held their memories. Yet when he spoke, it was in the Gaelic tongue of Jerome's childhood.

"*Beannachtaí,* Jerry Muldoon. *Tháinig mé mar a d'iarr tú. Bhí luach is airde ar do chuid oibre agus tugtar luach saothair* the gift of Light. *Tóg é ó mo lámh agus sosa ann, bheith i do dhuine leis. Fanann na daoine sin a raibh grá agat dóibh agus beannacht an Ard-Aoise ort. Fáiltíonn Dia ársa na talún tú isteach ina gcuideachta.*"[13]

Gregor heard a sound and turned. The doors were open, and the room was filled with abbey people drawn together in silent grief.

The face of the old man lit up. He sat up straight and held out his hands. Johnny took them in his, then bent his head and placed a kiss on the old man's brow. A rose-coloured light manifested above, then flowed down and into Jerome, outlining him for those last few moments.

"Bless you, bless you. May your mission bring the new Teacher to the world."

The Forerunner gathered the frail body into his arms, lifting him effortlessly, and held him up to the rose-coloured light. The grey head sank onto his shoulder, and with a sigh, Jerome Muldoon went to his ancestors.

Johnny placed the now-empty body back on the bed and, turning, left the room. The others gathered round, some weeping, some silent, but all

13. "Greetings, Jerry Muldoon. I have come as you asked. Your work has been of the highest value and the reward of the gift of Light is offered. Take it from my hand and rest in it, become one with it. Those you loved await you and the blessing of the Most High rests upon you. The ancient Tuatha de Danaan of your land will welcome you into their company."

wondering at the rose-red mark on Father Jerome's brow left by the kiss of the Forerunner.

The abbey members all made their farewells, then left the women to their age-old task of preparing the dead. Johnny was nowhere to be seen, so they all went about their usual tasks. At midday they fasted, taking only water, and spent the day quietly and mostly alone. When evening came, clad in white robes and each bearing a lighted candle, they went in procession to the Hall of Ceremony. Two by two, man and woman. Desmond Hinault arrived late from Jersey, delayed by flight problems but in time to join them. Eamon came last, alone.

As they entered the hall, the members separated, men to the right, women to the left, and took their places on each side of the catafalque. It was then that Johnny emerged from the shadows in a simple robe of pale gold, overlaid by a black scapular with its hood drawn, shadowing his face. In his hands he held a bell and a striker.

Johnny approached Gregor and asked a question. "What was this man to you?"

"He was my superior and my friend."

The bell was struck once. The quality of its note manifested as a golden shimmer in the air.

The questioner moved on. "What was this man to you?"

"He was my teacher and friend."

The bell sang out.

"What was this man to you?"

"He was an older brother and friend."

The bell sang.

"What was this man to you?"

"He was my sustainer and my friend."

The bell sang.

So it went on, to each one the question, and from each an answer: my priest, my companion, a father, a confidante, a fellow traveller, a light in my life, a guide, an ideal, a leader. To Eamon, he was "a man searching for an answer, and a friend." To each answer, the bell gave voice.

The questioner turned and lights brightened the temple. At intervals round the circular space stood figures of those who had been the Teachers of humanity down the ages. Some known, many unknown, but all had lifted humanity towards the far-future time of their destined culmination. Each age had been overseen by a Teacher and heralded by a Forerunner. The questioner saluted each one with the bell, then took his place before the marble altar in the east.

Behind Johnny a figure slowly began to form, tall and well-formed, copper-skinned and wearing an Egyptian kilt. Round his neck was a twelve-strand necklace of gold studded with turquoise. In one hand he held a golden ankh. His face and head were that of a jackal.

With one voice, those gathered saluted the figure as it solidified. "Hail Anubis."

The figure passed into the physical body of Johnny and approached the catafalque. At the command of He Who Opens the Ways of both birth and death, there rose from it the image of young Jerry Muldoon. He faced the western wall, where a boat filled with those who had come to meet him waited. The apparition of Father Jerome turned to those who had honoured him and smiled silently, sending his thanks and his love, then entered the boat and set sail for the Field of Reeds with Anubis at the prow.

The physical form that had housed Anubis crumbled to the floor. Eamon caught Johnny as he fell, exhausted by his efforts. The others covered Jerome's body with a crimson cloth. It would lie in that state for twenty-four hours and then be put to rest.

Eamon and Pawel got Johnny to the medical room, washed the sweat from his body, and fed him small amounts of food and hot lemon and honey. He remembered nothing and had to be told what had happened.

Abbot Gregor and Eamon then spent hours talking with the other abbeys. Things were moving faster than had been expected, and not just with Johnny. Colby had linked up with Bucky and Florrie. Tango's training was advancing as well. He was now a solo performer ranking high in the charts and thinking about Hollywood. Word went out to all abbeys and the Watchers: "Be on your guard. Strengthen the links between you. The Dark is now aware of Johnny and his progress."

Abbot Gregor had now recognised Johnny's main talent: he was a "carrier," meaning he could "loan" his mind and body in service to an exalted spiritual essence, and for a short span of time his own body and mind could be indwelt and used by a being of high degree. Such a talent was rare, far more so than even Wolf's ability to shift. It took careful handling and training to cope with being a "psychic envelope" holding two minds at one time, even when the human was aware of the sharing. In ancient times it was a talent valued and sought after; in modern times it was seen as possession and considered either evil or dangerous, often both.

The news spread through the abbeys and among the Watchers. For the next few days, every telepath in every abbey worked round the clock relaying information concerning the training of a carrier. Particular attention was given to how to cope with the inevitable strain on the human mind. Desmond spent half his time researching ancient teachings sent from the Abbey of the Throne. He spent the other half helping Johnny cope with the mental strain of living as two different identities and healing the trauma when he came out of it.

Mara revealed her own talent. Previously, it had been simply healing, but now she opened up to the challenge of helping Johnny retain his own identity even when holding the knowledge and memories of minds like Imhotep, Anaximander, Socrates, Solon, Matthew and Mark, Yeshua (briefly), Bruno, da Vinci, Galileo, and Newton. From every age and every race—often just for a few minutes, sometimes longer—they spoke. Some simply shared themselves with Johnny, implanting memories, places, voices, and emotions. All of them held and gently increased the talent to accommodate the different depths, types, and powers of each indweller.

It was like sitting with a madman: Johnny would change voices, languages; the way he sat, walked, gestured; even what he ate or wouldn't. He didn't seem to notice day or night but lived in a continuous moment of awareness. Then he would suddenly fall asleep for several hours only to wake, shuddering, as a new mind would take over. Sometimes he would cry out in his own voice, "No, no, no more. Please, no more! Let me be. Let me be…"

Eamon was beside himself watching his son's mind taken over, taken apart. In the short spaces of peace, Eamon held Johnny in his arms and spoke gently in the ancient Romani tongue his mother had taught him: old folktales, snatches of poetry, memories of fireside times.

Then, during one almost-violent episode, Mara held Johnny's hand and sang to him, sang his own song, "Mountains of Gold." The result was incredible. Johnny stopped shouting and lashing out and turned to her. For the first time in five days, he recognised someone of his own time.

"Mara. Oh God, Mara, hold me. Hold me. Don't let me go. Let me rest, just rest."

She led Johnny to the rumpled bed and laid him down. Then, without a thought for Eamon and Desmond, she stripped and lay down beside him, holding him close to her warmth.

Desmond took Eamon by the arm and they left the room. "She is what he needs to bring him back to normality. He is safe now."

Back in the main hall, Eamon strode back and forth. "How could they do this to him? How dare they! They are supposed to be on our side! They came close to driving him insane."

It was Pawel who told them, "I could see them. The trouble is not with them, nor does it come from them—it is time. Time is always in the present. Only we think of it as past and future. Johnny is existing in the wholeness of time, so it seemed to us that it was all mixed up. But to those who are teaching him, each one is in *their* time. Johnny must learn to select their moment in the wholeness. It is part of his training. We can only stand and watch and be there for him. Soon he will learn how to do it. Then he will be able to reach into time and select a moment and live in it for a while. All this was because he opened himself to assist Jerome to pass over. He didn't know how to close down properly. When he wakes, he will be calmer. It may happen again, but not so violently, and he will learn to control it."

Gregor nodded. "I see now. He needs to speak with and learn from those who have lived through a new age or who, like him, were and are able to join with others like him. We do not have to teach him. The others, some of whom have been Forerunners, will teach him to cope with the ability to live both within and outside of time. We have not seen a new age approach for two and a half thousand years, so of course we, like Johnny, have to learn how to deal with the work of a Forerunner. All we have to go on are legends, folktales, and books written by those who saw but did not understand what they were seeing. I think this is why Mara was sent to us. 'They' foresaw this and prepared for it.

"My friends, we can now sleep and rest. He is safe, and so are we. Tomorrow we must let the other abbeys know what we have seen, and it must be recorded and taught as part of our work. When the next age begins, our descendants will know what to expect. Soon we will have a day of inner peace and introspection.

"Maurice, please place a basket of suitable food and drink outside the door, and include a thermos of coffee plus some of your special apple pie. Johnny is fond of that. Mother Amalia, I think later, after they have rested, young Mara may have need of your counsel."

Abbot Gregor turned to Eamon. "My friend, share my quarters tonight. I have news from Mr. Buckland, and I also have a bottle of Laphroaig Lore single malt, a gift from the emir. Maurice, open the wine cellar. I think we all need to sample the gift of Dionysius tonight."

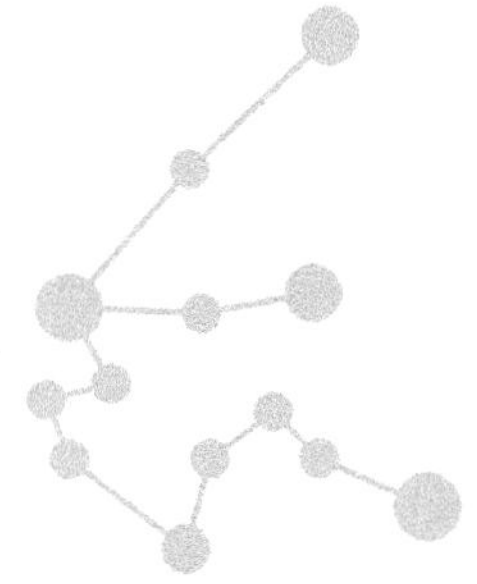

CHAPTER THIRTY-THREE

6 July, 6:00 p.m.
Elstree Studios, London

Tango was in his element. Alone in the soundproofed cubicle, his link to the control board feeding his voice back to him, he had everyone's full attention.

I need a hot-blooded woman on this cold, cold night
And I ain't gonna let her go
But when sun comes up an' the lovin's done
Well then it's time for me to go

The music cut off as Frank pounded on the control panel. "No, no, no! You've done it again, Tango! You must put the full emphasis on the *lovin* or you'll not get the rhythm in the right place. Keep to the bloody beat, you stupid bastard. It's 'But when the sun's come up and the *lov*in is done.' Just once can you do it right? That was the seventh take. I swear to God, if you don't do it right this time, I'm quitting, and I'll take the fucking song with me." He slumped in his seat, head in hands.

Bucky turned to the director and grinned. “Musicians…They're like a load of bloody ballerinas.”

Tango stormed out of the cubical and threatened to punch Frank in the face, but the musician gathered up his score, including the manuscript for a new film's background music, and walked out. All hell broke loose as the producer and director tried to calm their star down and stop their musical director from walking out.

Frank had risen to the occasion. He had not only written what promised to be a number-one hit song but a musical score for the film that was already spoken of as an Oscar winner. A fact that, not surprisingly, really upset Tango, though he already had a platinum disk for his own recordings.

Bucky went after Frank, and they kept up the pretence of an argument. Finally, reluctantly (but hiding an internal grin), Frank had returned to the studio for another try. Equally reluctantly, Tango had finally recorded the song exactly as Frank had written it.

It was gone nine in the evening when Bucky and Frank got back to the penthouse where the rest of them waited, agog with excitement to know what had happened. Florrie had laid on a great dinner. As they ate and talked and laughed together, Bucky sat back, marvelling that despite all that had happened, they had stuck together.

Surprisingly, White Heat was in demand as a backing group, both for singers and advertising, and money was flowing in. Most still lived in the penthouse; only Lyle and Ginny had bought their own apartment, needing extra room for their growing family. Liam and Biff still roomed together. Frank was content with his old room and rented a studio with a piano in which to work without disturbing the others. The new inmate from the Abbey of the Winds had fitted in well. As a trained musician with a formidable illusion talent, Colby got on well with them all. Florrie was in her element, cooking and looking after them all. At last she had a family to look after, but in her heart she often cried over Johnny.

Tonight the main topic was the row between Tango and Frank and the effect it had on Tango's “shadow.” For several weeks De'ath had been showing interest in Colby, sharing a table at coffee break and trying, unsuccessfully, to suss him out. One day at rehearsal, the lights in the studio had driven the temperature up, and the boys shed their shirts. Colby turned to fold away his shirt, displaying a Tlingit soulcatcher tattoo across his shoulders. De'ath went rigid and, turning, ran from the room. He threw up in the corridor and again in the washroom. Finally the studio medic dosed De'ath and sent him home with instructions to stay there until his system had cleared itself. His absence had freed up Tango, and for several days he was almost the man they had once known.

Colby had explained that the soulcatcher was an ancient symbol of protection. He'd received one as a gift from his shamanic grandfather on his fourteenth birthday. De'ath had given Colby a wide berth after that and took no further interest in him, but Colby used his inherited power to extend a protection over the group whenever the Dark one attended a rehearsal. He was also compiling a report for the Aeon and had requested the presence of Wolf if he was available.

As the night drew on, one by one they turned in until it was just Florrie and Bucky sharing a nightcap of Scotch with Colby and his usual hot chocolate. The young musician rose, walked to the window, and stood looking down towards the river. "Florrie, how long is it since Johnny was here?"

Florrie drew in a quick breath. "Oh, it's years now. But I think of 'im every night about this time. We get news from Eamon, and at Christmastime and on birthdays we get cards. And since 'e left Tibet, a couple of times we've had a few minutes on the phone. But it's not the same as being able to put my arms round 'im. I know 'e has important work to do, but it's hard."

Colby was silent for a while. Then he said, "Bucky, how much is there still to do on this film score?"

Bucky downed the last of his Scotch. "If we can keep Frank and Tango from killing each other, maybe two weeks. Why?"

Colby left the window and returned to his chair. "Wolf is coming over. He and I have some undercover work to do. It would be easier if you lot were not around; then we could do what we need to do and not have to keep tabs on any of you at the same time. Would it be possible for the others to be out of London for, say, ten days? I can arrange a cottage in Ireland for Lyle and his family, and I thought Biff and Liam might like to explore the nightlife of Stockholm. I can arrange all of it with no problem."

"Well, the lads could do with a break, and Ireland sounds great for Lyle and Ginny. Frank might like to go with them. What do you think, Florrie? How about a wild ten days in Amsterdam or Buenos Aires?"

Colby smiled. "Oh, I have just the place for you and Florrie and Frank. Florrie knows it well. It's called the Abbey of the Aeon, and Johnny will be there. We can't have all of you there—it would be too dangerous—but the three of you would be OK, and we'll arrange for the others to spend time with him later on."

Florrie's shriek of delight had Biff and Liam rushing out of their bedroom. Liam, who disdained to wear anything in bed but a willing blonde, grabbed the nearest covering, which happened to be a vase of roses complete with thorns.

"What the...Florrie, what is it? Are you OK? Is the place on fire?"

A tearful Florrie raised her head from Bucky's shoulder. "No, dear. No, it's just that...Well, I'm going to see Johnny. Oh, Bucky, my boy. My boy! I'm going to see him!"

Thirty minutes later, when everyone had calmed down and another bottle of Scotch had been opened, Liam looked over at Florrie and said in a quiet voice, "Florrie, there's just one really serious problem ahead, and it may scupper this whole plan."

The laughter stopped immediately. Florrie went pale. "What is it, Liam?"

Liam looked down at his glass and nodded, then looked up at her and said, "Florrie, you do realise you are going to have to get all these bloody thorns out of my dick?"

7 July, 1:30 a.m.
Tango's new apartment in London

Tango stood alone on the balcony of his apartment and looked out over the sprawling, brilliantly lit vista of London below. He looked at the crystal glass in his hand, filled with expensive Veuve Clicquot. Slowly, deliberately, he turned the glass over and let its contents drench the park below. Then, just as deliberately, he flung the handcrafted glass after it and listened to the smash of glass as it hit the ornamental fountain.

He leaned on the balustrade and stared out into the night. What Tango had just destroyed would have been worth more than he had earned in a month as a bartender in a swish hotel with a sideline in "being available" to lonely, elderly (and rich) widows. Now the women in his bed were more likely to be film stars, the daughters of billionaires, and minor royalty.

Tango drove top-of-the-range cars and joined the jet set on their yachts. Everything he wore had been made by hand. On his wrist he wore a Patek Philippe watch. If things went well, next month he'd be in line for a Hollywood contract for a remake of the film *The Student Prince*. So *why*, he asked himself, was he remembering the noisy, untidy, bottle-strewn apartment in old Chinatown, listening to Frank trying to compose a new song with Biff and Liam arguing at the top of their voices, the steady thump of Lyle and Ginny making out in their room, and Johnny quietly reading a book on poetry? And Bucky. Yes, Bucky, who was always willing to hand out an advance or pay a betting bill without letting the others know.

Tango could picture it all in his mind: those first hand-to-mouth days; the early morning train journeys and making sure the instruments were safe and the stage gear was washed (sometimes); the endless meals of pizza, fish and chips, or often just a stale burger; the gradual climb up; and finally, the smash hit with "Mountains of Gold." Damn. Damn. Damn. He missed them, missed the smell of backstage dressing rooms, the banter with the dancing girls as they clattered past, their tap shoes ringing on the metal stairs.

It was all in the past, and this... Tango turned and looked through the glass doors at the luxury of his apartment. This was the present. With all its luxury, was it worth what he had once had? The closeness, the feeling of being part of a wholeness. Even though he had never been as fully accepted as Johnny had been, Tango had been included, had been a living part of it all.

With a moment of absolute clarity, he realised that he had been offered that closeness right at the start and had chosen to reject it, to make himself an outsider. Tango had always been that; his mother had been the only person he had really loved or been loved by. His grandmother had hated him, a bastard brat, the result of a near rape after too much drink.

A rap at the door brought him out of his reverie, and Tango went back into the room and opened it. The woman who stood there was the daughter of a shipping magnate, expensively educated, equally expensively dressed, and as empty-headed as a factory hen. But she was warm, she was alive, she was willing, and for a few hours she would drive away the loneliness, the emptiness. And most of all, she would lessen the darkness that surrounded Tango when De'ath was there. Tango would have turned away from De'ath if he had been strong enough, but somewhere, in some deeply hidden place in his soul, there was a reason why the three of them—Johnny, De'ath, and himself—were in some way linked.

"Well, aren't you going to ask me in?"

Tango stared down at her, and the old shadows enfolded him again. "Of course, darling. I have been waiting for you. All of you, from head to toe. Come on in. The champagne is waiting."

The Darkness relaxed. All was well; Talfryn Garrett was back in their carefully woven trap. But it had been close…He had come close to remembering, regretting, and—even more dangerous—understanding. To every effect, there must be a cause; to every cause, there will be a reason. But those reasons are multiple, and much depends on which one is needed and how it is dealt with.

♬ ♩ ♫ ♪ ♬ ♪ ♫

Miles away, across the wind-driven waters of the Channel and up into the snowy reaches of the Pyrenees, Johnny raised his head. Beside him, Mara stirred but did not wake.

Johnny rose and went to stand by the window and reached deep into the "star chamber" of his mind. In thought and vision, he crossed the distance between them and touched the same mental point in Tango. He surveyed the emotions, the fears, the hopes, and the despair at not belonging anywhere or to anyone, and he replaced them with love, strength, and images of times together.

♬ ♩ ♫ ♪ ♬ ♪ ♫

Tango woke with a shout. The room was empty, his partner gone, but for the first time in years, he could feel Johnny's presence. A warmth spread through him, bringing a sense of belonging, as if in a totally different place they were together. He flung back the duvet and rose to his feet.

"Johnny, is that you? Where are you? What's happening?"

They were joined by something neither had felt before, an Immensity of love so powerful, Johnny quailed before It. Then he reached out.

"I'm wherever you are, Tango. Somehow, what is happening has a meaning for us. We'll meet again, boyo. Not for a while, but it will happen, and it will be hard for us both. But remember what we had once. It's still there, will always be there—you must believe that. Everything has a reason, Tango: birth, life, and death, and everything has two sides. Nothing exists without an opposite because opposition, when it's fully understood, reveals the ultimate unity. Be blessed, brother."

The Immensity expanded and enclosed them both. *All will come about as decreed. You were chosen for this work.*

For a fractional moment, the Immensity and the Darkness faced each other, two halves of what had once been a balanced whole and, in the infinity of time, would be so again. Then all was as it had been before, and both men slept dreamlessly.

7 July, 9:00 a.m.
The penthouse, London

The apartment was bustling. Bucky had been up with the birdsong arranging a break for everyone. It was short notice and there were sulks from the studios, but he maintained the lads needed it, especially after the fracas with Tango.

Colby had dealt with the travel and accommodation for Lyle and his family and for Biff and Liam. When Bucky commended him for all the arrangements, he grinned and tapped his nose. "We don't just learn to do tricks, you know, and there are always people who can help to work miracles. Now you, Florrie, and Frank will take off tomorrow morning from London City Airport at 9:30 a.m. It's a private jet, so you'll be nice and comfortable. Frank, there's a perfectly tuned piano at the abbey, so you don't have to sulk. You can still run off the odd chart-busting song."

Colby turned to Lyle and Ginny and handed them a padded envelope. "Here's the address to where you're going and a list of things you can do while there. A limo will pick you up at 9:30 tomorrow morning and will be there to bring you back."

He then turned to Liam and Biff. "You two fly out from City Airport at 10:00 a.m. It's a private flight and will take about an hour to get to Stockholm. A limo will take you to your hotel. Enjoy!" He handed an envelope to Liam.

"What about you, Col?" asked Biff. "Why aren't you coming with us?"

"I have a date with a Navajo wolf…I'm going to do some hunting. Have fun, all of you. And Bucky, tell Abbot Gregor I want a bottle from his rare whisky hoard for arranging all this. Now I must go and buy some dog biscuits, flea powder, and a strong collar and lead. You can't just walk round with a timber wolf in London and claim he's a guide dog. I'll see you all when you get back." Colby grabbed a small weekend case and left.

Liam turned to Bucky and grinned. "All respects to you, Bucko, but he'd make a bloody good manager. He's wasted living on the edge of nowhere, meditating."

Florrie patted his arm. "You'd be surprised what else he can do, and it's not meditating."

An imperious knock at the door had them all tensing. Everyone scattered, sitting, reading. The TV went on and Bucky went to open the door.

A six-foot, rangy, copper-skinned man stood with a hand resting on the lintel. "You will be Mr. Buckland, I think. I'm here to meet up with Colby."

Bucky held out a hand. "And you will be Wolf. I have heard of you from the brigadier. Please come in. Colby has gone out, I'm afraid. He made a crack about buying dog biscuits and flea powder."

Wolf's face split into a grin, displaying a set of white teeth that justified his name. "One of these days my teeth will meet in a delicate part of his anatomy. I was unavoidably delayed, but I can pick him up. But since I am here, I would appreciate meeting you all and perhaps beg a coffee from Mrs. Buckland, of whom I have heard a great deal." He lifted her hand to his lips.

Florrie glowed. "Well, it is getting on for lunch time. Would you join us, Mr. Wolf?"

"Just Wolf will be fine, and may I have permission to use your name?"

Bucky intervened. “We are all on first names here.” He proceeded to introduce everyone while Florrie and Ginny set about making lunch, having handed Wolf a steaming cup of black coffee.

Just then, Lyle’s daughter came toddling in from Florrie’s bedroom, where she’d been napping. Rubbing her eyes, she looked round and saw Wolf. Her mouth dropped open and she gave a little shriek of delight and ran to him with her arms open. “Doggie, big doggie!” She flung her arms round Wolf’s knees.

He put aside his coffee and lifted her gently into his arms, the others standing stupefied. “What is your name, little girl?” he asked.

“I’m Mary-Clare. Why do you keep your doggie inside you? Doesn’t he like to run?”

“Yes, he loves to run. But in the city there is no room, so I keep him safe inside me.”

“Can I see him, please? I promise I won’t pull his ears ’cos doggies don’t like that.”

“Well, before I let him out, I think we had better ask your mother and father if they mind.”

Wolf looked over at the open-mouthed group round them. Ginny spoke first. “His gift is pure, and so is his heart. I knew she had the Sight, but it has never shown until now. So let ’er see.” Lyle came close and put his arm round her.

Wolf put the child down and took off his leather jacket. He knelt down and began to shake his body, once, twice, and suddenly his human form peeled away and in its place was a large timber wolf. His clothes lay in a heap, and Biff gathered them up. Mary-Clare laughed and cuddled close, and for a while they played together while the meal was set in place. Then Wolf gave her a lick from chin to forehead and went into Florrie’s room to dress again.

When he came back and sat down with them, Wolf said quietly, “When she is of school age, watch her carefully. She will mature quickly and will need help to deal with what will be very strong psychic power. With your permission, I will let the abbeys know, and her normal schooling will be provided for. She is of the new wave of humanity that Johnny will proclaim.”

A few hours later, Wolf left to catch up with Colby, leaving a young family overawed by what had happened. It was the subject of discussion for the rest of the day.

The following morning, they all left for their various destinations. But Colby loaded a large "dog" into his Range Rover, and together he and Wolf went hunting.

8 July, 12:30 p.m.
The Abbey of the Aeon

The limo drew up outside the abbey doors and Maurice got out to get the bags. Bucky woke from his doze with Florrie's elbow in his gut. "Uhh?"

"Wake up, Bucky. We're here. We're here!" Florrie clambered out of her seat as the door burst open and Johnny came rushing out.

"Florrie, Florrie! And Bucky...Oh God, it's so good to see you, to feel you close." Unashamed, Johnny wept over them as they all came together in a tangle of arms and heads. Then Frank joined them, and for few minutes there were no words, just tears and small sounds that meant nothing but conveyed emotions and feelings. After three years, they were together again.

Finally Eamon and Gregor came and urged them inside. Mother Amalia had suggested that only Eamon and Gregor would be with them this first day; after such a long separation, having the whole complement round them would have been too much. She had arranged for just the six of them to share this time and get over the tears, the explanations, the things that needed to be said and shared. In the smaller suite reserved for times such as these, Amalia and Maurice had arranged a light lunch and given strict instructions to the others to let them have this day to themselves.

Having been shown their rooms and settled in, they came together to eat and talk, to share events, happenings, and experiences. They listened to Johnny explain what had happened since he had been taken from them: his introduction to his half-brother, the escapade in Muscat, and the journey over the mountains to the Abbey of the Dawn.

In turn they told Johnny of the struggle to keep the group together, of the rise of Tango and his eventual solo career, of the coming of De'ath, and of the meetings with the brigadier and Margaret. They laughed over Bucky's story of what had happened at the Ducking Stool.

They talked through the afternoon, through dinner, and later over glasses of Scotch until Frank fell fast asleep in his chair and had to be woken up and put to bed. Later still, Florrie wept in Bucky's arms until they both slept deeply and dreamlessly.

Eamon and Johnny stood together in the garden and watched the moon cross the sky and begin to dip into the mountaintops. Then they too, worn out with emotion, went to their beds and slept.

10 July, 8:30 p.m.
The penthouse, London

Colby stood back from the bowl and accepted the glass of water Wolf held out. He rinsed his mouth several times, grimacing as he did so. "Dear God, I've seen depravity in my life, Wolf, but that was beyond belief. All those men—mostly old, but there were young ones there as well—sitting in that rat-hole of a cinema, watching that filth…And the smell as they…Well, as they…" He closed his eyes against the memory and swallowed hard. "And that ghoul De'ath moving from seat to seat behind them, imbibing that tainted energy and relishing it. At least Tango doesn't go to those places. Yes, he takes energy that way, but he takes it from young couples, high-class concubines, and university rave ups. But it's only a matter of time before he falls." Colby shuddered.

Wolf handed him a small shot of whisky. They were, at Bucky's insistence, staying at the apartment. Then Wolf went to the window and looked out at the deepening skyline. "Time for me to hunt," he said quietly. "Rest up, Col. I'll be late."

Wolf opened the door to the small balcony, divested himself of his clothes, and shifted into the form of a sparrowhawk. It was hard to keep hold of and not natural to him, but years of training made it possible for short periods of time. Colby watched him take flight, then made for the kitchen and supper.

Wolf made contact with the nearest Watcher, a Jamaican-born night watchman going on duty. Signals of identity were exchanged, and information was passed. The hawk turned in a wide sweep and headed for Tango's luxury apartment. He found a viewpoint on a tree looking into the main room and exchanged the hawk form for that of a London pigeon. Then Wolf watched.

De'ath strode back and forth, describing his afternoon activity. Tango made no effort to hide his disgust, but his tormentor elaborated. "I feel good. It was a great afternoon; the place was almost full. The football game brought a lot of extra men into town, and they filled the place up. I am at the peak, ablaze with energy! You are a fool, Tango. Too choosy. Energy is energy no matter where it comes from, or from whom."

Tango lifted his head from his film script. "Energy from the ball juice of a drunken, worn-out pensioner is not my style. I get what I need from more salubrious sources as, when, and *if* I need it." His eyes glinted with malice. "After all, I'm not two thousand years old and in desperate need of it."

De'ath spun round and lifted a hand to blast him, but a warning flashed into his mind. *Do not injure him, or you will be replaced.* He snarled and stormed out of the apartment.

Tango set aside the script and rose to his feet. He wandered onto the balcony and looked out over the city. A pigeon on the railing looked directly at him. He considered taking its life energy, but it seemed too much trouble. The pigeon extended it wings and rose, turning as it did so, and let loose a dropping on Tango's handmade silk shirt as it flew off.

De'ath was simmering with rage and, though he would not have seen it as such, jealousy. He stalked unseen through the dark, hidden, vicious underworld of London. It had once been a village on the edge of a great river. But first the Romans, then the lost, hungry, dissolute, and desperate found their way to it. They built a town that reached out and grew and grew, but it always contained a pocket of the vileness that lies at the heart of every big city.

He wandered through streets alive with evil. De'ath drank it in and feasted on its energy. For thousands of years this had kept him alive, kept him going, kept the fear of nonexistence at bay. He opened up to the pain, terror, despair, and hopelessness of it all and relished the power it gave him and those from the far past who had set him on this path. He stole the last heartbeat of a homeless war veteran who had starved to death. Drank in the sobs of a fifteen-year-old escaping from an orphanage as she was assaulted by drunk tourists. He laughed with delight at the terror of an old woman being beaten for the little she carried in her trolley.

Tracking him, unseen in the form of a filthy street mongrel, Wolf sent out calls for help. The dead man's essence was gently gathered up and comforted by an angelic. A policeman on his way back to the station took a shortcut and found the young girl bleeding in the gutter and called for help. A couple of sailors buying coffee from a street vendor saw the old woman being assaulted and proceeded to beat up her attacker, then bought her tea and a sandwich from the vendor, one of them slipping money into her pocket.

When finally De'ath had drunk his fill, he turned—and saw Wolf. The battle was short and sharp. Wolf could not fight such an ancient and powerful opponent alone, but he could (and did) siphon off the stolen energy and dissipated it in the form of a short but violent thunderstorm that flared over London. Bleeding energy, De'ath fled back to his hideout and nursed his remaining energy. He feared the warriors of the abbeys, but he feared his own superiors even more.

In the early light of dawn, Wolf returned to the apartment and, helped by Colby, set about ridding himself of the remnants of evil that clung to him. Then and only then could he sleep and rest with Colby guarding him. As his sleep deepened and became normal, Colby opened up a link with the Aeon and with his own Abbey of the Winds. Quickly and concisely, he relayed what had happened, its results, and the effect on Wolf. Only then did he seek his own rest.

13 July, 9:00 a.m.
The Abbey of the Aeon

During the last few years, Johnny had endured an unremitting round of training, learning new skills and exercising powers he'd never imagined lay within him. Now, for ten blessed days, he would get to revel in the company of those he loved so dearly. They walked in the garden, bathed in the indoor pool, were fed royally by Maurice, and talked endlessly about the "old days." They shared childhood memories, and in the evenings Johnny and Frank played and sang White Heat's greatest hits for everyone.

Abbot Gregor had relaxed disciplines and eased down the usual work (with the exception of Pawel, who insisted on Johnny's fitness regime). Taking Bucky and Florrie into their confidence, Eamon told them it might be the last time Johnny would have what could be called a "real" holiday.

Johnny and Mara had become an accepted pair, and Eamon had told Gregor he would take full care of her in the future and would see that the Forerunner line continued. Eamon set out to enjoy and relish every minute with his son, knowing that this "oasis of time" would have to last him. All the abbeys felt the same way. They were, had been, and would be privileged to see, speak to, laugh with, and get to know the Forerunner in the time before he began his mission. But Gregor had one more surprise for him.

At breakfast one morning, Abbot Gregor announced that Amal had flown in the night before and would be joining them for two days, and he was bringing a guest. They were on their way now and would be arriving momentarily.

"Quicker than that! I am already here," said a voice behind Johnny's chair. A voice he knew, a voice that had kept him sane through those first horrendous weeks. The voice of a man who had willingly endured punishment for his brother's misbehaviour. Johnny's heart leapt. He spun round, sending his chair flying.

"Ring! Oh God, Ring, you're here! Really here. I've missed you so much, *mi prala*. Everyone, this is my brother. Gregor, Mara, all of you, come and meet him." He went off into a mixture of Romani, Sanskrit, and English that had everyone laughing.

Florrie hugged Tze-Ring, but Bucky regarded him cautiously and said, "So you're the—" He paused. "The one who stole Johnny that night in London?"

Tze-Ring held his hand and said, "And you are the man who moved heaven and earth to find him and never gave up." No more was said.

Amal joined them, and a delighted Maurice served up a second breakfast as Johnny and Tze-Ring settled down to fill each other in on all that had happened since they had said goodbye.

♫ ♩ ♫ ♪ ♫ ♩ ♫

A deep sense of purpose settled over the Aeon. Everyone knew, each in their own way, that this was a special time for them all. Those of the abbey drew back a little to allow Johnny to share himself with those he loved so much, but in doing so were themselves rewarded as they watched Johnny change, grow, and settle more deeply into what he would become.

Mara now knew her role and accepted it with all the love her own sweet nature held within. Florrie contented herself by watching Johnny and helping with the daily round of locals who regarded the abbey as a "drop-in" medical centre. Bucky spent some time with Gregor, Eamon, and Tze-Ring, calling them "the three wise men." Under their gentle encouragement, his ability to project astrally strengthened and became more controlled. Bucky also spent time with Sister Genevieve and Mother Amalia, and to his surprise and secret joy, he was invited back to the abbey with Florrie for further training.

But the biggest surprise was Frank. His joy at finding a concert grand at the abbey was like watching a firework display. He spent hours simply playing odds bits of music, modern and ancient. Then on the evening of their fifth day, as everyone relaxed after dinner, Frank sat as usual, letting his hands wander over the keys. Tze-Ring suddenly held up a hand. All conversation stopped and followed his pointing finger.

Frank sat with his hands resting lightly on the keys, eyes closed, his face blank. He was enveloped slowly, as if someone was pouring vapour over him, and suddenly he seemed to be wearing another form: eighteenth-century clothing, a bewigged head, knee breeches. The hands became almost solid; the music changed, became commanding, strong, without hesitation; the face developed into someone else.

Leon came to his feet, drawn to the man now sitting at the instrument, a look of worship on his face. "Handel. It is the master Handel! He is Indwelling him."

For almost an hour, the entranced composer of modern rock and roll music played the music Handel did not live to write. As the last notes died away and the indweller left, Frank shook his head and said, "It's been a long day. I think I'll turn in." He smiled at them all, said goodnight, and went off to his room, leaving a totally stunned group of people behind him.

Gregor broke the silence. "My opinion, for what it is worth, is that the higher levels have deliberately brought together not just the Forerunner and his mate but, for reasons we may not yet understand, they have surrounded him with a group of extra talents. Perhaps as guardians, but I think also as establishers of lines of descent that will be needed in the coming age." He stood and faced the bemused group.

"I think the group you knew and know as White Heat carries within it several different talents that will disperse into the gene pool of the coming age. I sense this is not the only group; there will be others. My friends, we are privileged to be present at a rare event: the gathering of those whose descendants will shape the Age of Aquarius, as well as witnessing the coming of the Teacher of that age.

"The young man who just left us will, I have no doubt, become the Handel of his time. Florrie, you have the ability to cure by sound. Bucky, as a Watcher, your ability to project will be invaluable. I am certain the others will slowly add to the circle of Watchers. And, of course, there is the Betrayer. The stage has been set, the cast has been assembled, and we of the abbeys are the producers and stage hands of the coming drama. We, my friends, are the writers of history."

♬ ♩ ♫ ♪ ♬ ♪ ♫

Two days before they were due to leave the abbey, Bucky got a call from the studio. After a prolonged discussion with Frank and the rest of the group via the phone, he told them they would have to leave at once. Some of the background recordings had been destroyed in a studio fire, and though some had been saved, at least a third would have to be re-recorded.

The rest of the group had been recalled and would be waiting for them at the studio. They were two months away from completion, and the director was going berserk. Tango's recordings had been saved, but there were long days of work ahead to meet the deadline. Gregor was arranging a flight.

Florrie was in tears as she packed. Eamon comforted her. "There'll be times when you can see him, Florrie. I'll let you know where he is and what's going on, but this film means a lot to the group financially and in terms of work."

By midday, the car was waiting and goodbyes were exchanged. Johnny hugged Florrie. "I'll keep in touch with you now, at least a couple of times a month. There won't be as much distance between us as before."

Frank, still bemused by his unexpected link with the past, told him, "I have this idea in my head, Johnny. I want to write an opera based on Shakespeare's *Hamlet*. I'll stick with the group a while longer, then I'll take time off to write it. Take care of yourself. It's been great to see you. This place is great, and Greg told me I can come whenever I need peace and quiet."

The car was packed. Bucky and a tearful Florrie got in, and Frank, clutching a sheaf of hastily written notes, took his place by Eamon, who would drive them to the airport. They had a rousing send-off and then the car disappeared into the mist.

Johnny stood and watched them out of sight, then said quietly to Gregor, "I thought it would be just as it was before, but it was…different. It will never be the same again, will it?"

Gregor rested an arm on his shoulder and sighed. "No, Johnny. Everything changes. It's an immutable law. Everything changes."

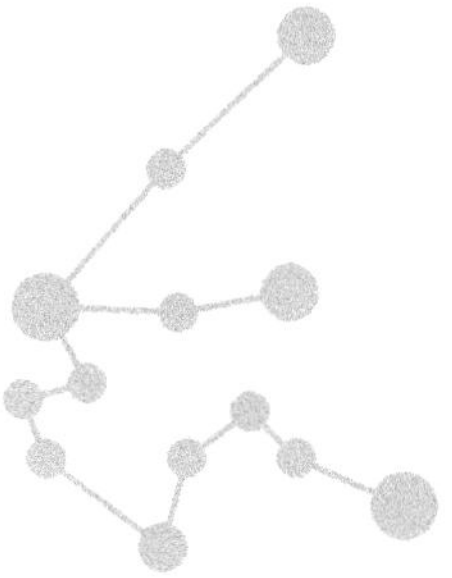

CHAPTER THIRTY-FOUR

31 July, 2:00 p.m.
The Abbey of the Aeon

The brief interlude of retrospection over, the abbey went back into its usual routine—almost. Much of Johnny's time was to be spent with Gregor, sometimes alone, but often with Eamon and Tze-Ring, who had been given extended leave. His initial workload of weeding and garden work would no longer be part of his day.

Johnny was learning to fine-tune his psychic gifts working with the others. His days were long and hard, beginning with his daily workout with Pawel; his nights were spent with Mara. They both knew the destined end but accepted it and lived for each moment as it came.

He often walked with his teachers in the gardens beside the small lake. In his solitary time, Johnny pondered what he was learning, amazed at the strength of purpose and dedication of those who gave their whole lives to the growth of truth. Johnny was especially interested in the founding of the abbeys, the work of the Watchers worldwide, the different talents that appeared in the human race, and the fear they induced in those without them.

"Communication has always been an important key," Gregor told him one day, watching Tze-Ring feed the ducks with biscuits from Maurice's hidden stash. "Everything communicates in its own way." He plucked a flower from a bush and held it gently. "This has no voice, yet it can tell a bee where to find its pollen by exuding a scent. It draws the bee to it by colour. Its petals offer a safe surface for the bee to land and burrow deep into the flower's heart. In effect, the bee mates with the flower to produce the end result of honey. The flower is the male enticing the female bee to come close so it can offer its gift. The bee, heavy with pollen, takes it back and adds it to the store already there. From this comes honey, known for its sweetness and healing qualities. It is the age-old pattern of creation: mating, the passing of a substance to a container, where it is then brought to maturity and becomes different to what it was in the beginning. But always there is communication. This comes in five stages.

"Sight: the ability to see where what is needed can be found. Scent: to track down what is needed. Touch: the softness, the welcome that offers warmth and safety. Taste: the exchange of bodily fluids, like birds feeding their young by passing food from mouth to mouth, strengthening the bond. This equates with a human kiss. The four senses were all there. But humanity needed more. It needed *sound*.

"It saw and desired; it smelt and was invited; it touched and was comforted; it tasted and was satisfied. When humanity developed a voice, the last link needed was made. It spoke, and communication became possible. The brain, hidden in its dark, silent temple of the skull, could make contact with what was outside. What was the first word? We do not know, but we can surmise…

"*I AM. YOD HEH VAV HEH.* I am what I am. I will be what is ordained for me to be. I will make creation as I am. I will create consciousness of self in all life.

"This was followed by another important change: names. We all know the importance of names; they hold the key to the hidden self. One of the least-remembered quotes from the Bible speaks of God giving the task of naming the animals to Adam."

Johnny leaned forward, listening intently, forgetting for a moment the discomfort of a new set of bruises courtesy of Pawel's latest set of exercises.

Gregor paused for a moment, thinking, then resumed. "Names bring about separation and expansion. No two things are identical. Even a duplicate is different because it is not the original." He took a biscuit from its packet and bit into it. "That includes human beings. The more there are, the more differences occur. Variations in the use of the senses can and have happened since the beginning. Mother Amalia's sight in real life is weak, hence her glasses, but the high vibrations of subtle bodies are visible to her. Pawel, Eamon, and René can hear and interpret the incredibly fine vibrations of human thought patterns. Maurice can create a thoughtform and lay it over another object with such precision you see only what he wants you to see. Desmond can see the inner workings of your body and, to a certain extent, alter or manipulate them. All organs of the body have a unique vibration. Florrie can tune in to that and increase or decrease it."

Abbot Gregor paused and stole another biscuit, then went on. "Some, like you, can create a copy of the physical self and extrude it long enough to convince others it is really you. Very rarely someone is born into a body made of particles so loosely integrated they can be changed in shape and form, like Wolf. In the beginning, such people were seen as evil and were slaughtered. Eventually humanity, acting as a whole, mentally created forms that were beautiful, strong, big, and able to do magical things and called them gods. They *gave* powers to them, sacrificed to them, and 'obeyed' them.

"But the outcasts came together and sought refuge in the lonely places of the world: mountains, forests, deserts. They experimented among themselves and learned by trial and error to control their talents and to increase and diversify them—and more importantly, to hide them when they were with those who feared them. Whatever It is that guides the fortunes of this world, It has a purpose, a plan to which we mortals are not privy.

"We know every two thousand years or so, Earth comes under an influence linked to a zodiac point. We realised early on that this brings on a new phase of human growth, an event always heralded by a human being of a special type. We name them the Teachers of the Ages.

"We have traced this back to the Age of Leo, but with little to show for it. It seems to equate with the time when the first real cities were built. That appears to be the first time humans lived in a contained area and abided by what would be the first laws. They kept together under the power of a single human: a king, as a lion rules his pride. Cuneiform writing came into being and records began to be kept.

"The Age of Cancer was one of discovery. Humanity overcame its fear of water and began to venture out of sight of land and learned to steer by the stars. We think the Teacher of this age may have been connected to or might have been Oannes, a being who, it is recorded, emerged from the sea each day to teach new ways of living and working but returned to the sea at night. The image of the 'fish-man' who taught them is still with us. We see it in the fish-head shape of a bishop's mitre. Strangely, the Teacher of the future Age of Pisces would also be connected to water, and the image of a fish is often found in Christian symbology.

"In the Age of Gemini, hieroglyphs began to supersede cuneiform. The duality of rule came into being with the worship of Isis and Osiris, Set and Nephthys. Also in this age, the idea of the Opponent versus the Teacher comes into being. We see this in the slaying of Osiris by his 'brother.' The difference between them is made obvious by the different colour of their skin. It might even be the first time skin colour became a point of dissension. But Divine rulership and the Will of the Gods became a requirement for leadership. In this age, the art of the storyteller was used consciously as a means of training. Humanity was able to consciously build mental images and use them. Extra senses and ways of communication became acceptable.

"The Ages of Taurus and Aries brought the advent of countries rather than just fortified cities. The Bull and later the Ram were sources of wealth and of sacrifice. There were several who could have been seen as Teachers of the Age, and our kind were much sought after. It was a time when divination, prophesy, and speaking in tongues were accepted. The advice of oracles and diviners was sought by rulers, warriors, and those seeking power. In that time, we could walk about and be proud of our skills."

Gregor paused and looked for another biscuit, but Tze-Ring smiled and showed empty hands. He sighed and looked at his watch. "It's time for me to make my contact with the others. Eamon, please take over for me, and Tze-Ring, when you have time, take a car into the village and purchase some more biscuits. We must replenish Maurice's hidden stash so we don't have to resort to stealing." He blessed them and strode away to his office.

Johnny turned to his father. "So when the Age of Pisces arrived, what happened?"

Tze-Ring interrupted. "We had better go inside. I can feel a storm approaching, and it's going to be a heavy one."

Johnny's face lit up. "I love storms! Where is the best place to watch it? We had snowstorms at the Abbey of the Dawn, but a real one with thunder and lightning…I haven't seen one like that since—" He paused, then went on. "I'd love to see a real one again."

31 July, 4:00 p.m.
Elstree Studios, London

The last shot faded out, and in the viewing room, the screen went dark. The small group was silent for a moment, then the director let out a long sigh.

"It's good, bloody good, and the background music is even better than the one that went up in smoke! Congratulations, Frank. That theme song will hit the top ten for sure, and the background stuff really grabs you. Tango, if this doesn't get you the lead in the Prince remake, there's no justice in the film world."

Tango's face lit up. "Thanks, Max. This project will do wonders for me, and I'm due in LA soon for a screen test. The second one, so they must have something in mind."

Frank, sitting in the back, nudged Bucky with an elbow. "He's lapping it up. Thing is, I'm pretty sure he'll get that film. You can't get away from it: He's got the voice, but they'll have to lower the score. He doesn't have the tone or power in the top notes, but he's got the looks and the arrogance."

Bucky chewed on a fingernail. "Damn right. If it wasn't for that walking scarecrow he's attached to, I could almost wish him luck. But let's face it, we've all done pretty well out of this TV special, and we'll make a bomb from the film score thanks to you."

"Right, thanks everyone. It's wrapped and up to the back room, boys." The director bustled out accompanied by his PA and secretary. Bucky and

Frank made their way to the parking area and found Tango leaning against their car. He came forward and held out a hand.

"I just wanted to say thanks, especially to you, Frank. I know I'm not your favourite person, but the song you wrote was incredible, and with luck it will help me get that film role. If there's anything I can do in return, you only need to ask. Bucky, I'm sorry to leave the group, but this is a big chance for me, and you'll be busy with background stuff from now on." He turned away, then after a few steps turned back. "If you ever see Johnny, tell him I do remember. He'll know what I mean."

Tango headed for his own car and drove off without a backward glance, blaming the headwind for the moisture in his eyes.

Bucky drove silently for a while. Then he said, "Do you know what he meant back there? It almost seemed as if he knew we had been with Johnny. But how?"

Frank shook his head. "I don't know any more than you, Bucky. I wish I did, but I do know this is not the end of it. I think when it does end, it will involve both of them. They were always meant to be together for something big."

In his head, Frank could hear the words that had haunted him since that last eventful day in Tibet, the words of the man who had reminded him so much of Johnny: *The Forerunner is always in danger.*

31 July, 4:30 p.m.
The Abbey of the Aeon

Johnny was in his element as he watched the storm from the old bell tower. The three of them stood cramped together in the narrow confines as the wind sent snow flurries down into the valleys. The mountains never lost their topmost layers but wore them like white lace collars. Thunder sent peal after peal of sound leaping from peak to peak until the whole valley below vibrated like a drum. But when the rain began, they made a hasty retreat as the wind blew it directly at them.

Laughing like schoolchildren, they negotiated the winding stairway and headed for dry clothing and cups of hot coffee. In revenge for the inroads made on his biscuit tin, Maurice commandeered Johnny and Tze-Ring to peel the vegetables for the evening meal. Eamon, because of his seniority, escaped kitchen chores but volunteered to feed the livestock and close up the stables against the storm. Then with two or three hours until dinner at eight, they settled by the fire that at this altitude was always needed.

Eamon took up where Gregor had finished. "With the advent of Pisces the world changed, and for such as us, not for the better. Monotheism was slowly breaking down the idea of a pantheon of gods and powers for different aspects of creation. It substituted the idea of 'one god for everything.' The basic idea was sound, but humanity had become more independent and more open to the ways of the Betrayer, the opposer. Opposition is not evil of itself, but when used or manipulated by untrained human minds, it can and did become so. Our kind tried to redirect the over-soul of humanity, but they had tasted a power they were not strong enough to resist. Even the advent of the Teacher of the Age did not manage to get it back on track. So, the only course was to allow it to cause its own downfall.

"The new teaching promised immortality—something humanity desired above all else—but only after physical death. The opposition offered wealth, power, and position here and now. Our kind became the scapegoats of both sides. One accused us of setting ourselves up as Pagan gods and the other tried to use our 'differences' for their own ends. Between the two, we had no choice but to withdraw as we had done before and bide our time.

"Once more we sought out the hidden places and divided our people among them. We took with us our treasured and most sacred pieces and slowly built a haven where we could preserve our skills and powers. But we lost so many to those who feared us. Even those with minor talents were set upon and tortured: men, women, and even children. It was then that we conceived the idea of the Watchers. Volunteers went back into the world and began to search for anyone with talent. We helped them to disguise their powers and gradually spirited them away to what, by now, had become the prototype of the abbeys for deeper training. But it took its toll on some of our best people all through the ages that followed. There was a time when there were ten such places of safety, but many were betrayed and destroyed. One disappeared completely hundreds of years ago...We still do not know what happened to it or even where it was situated.

"The Watchers became experts at hiding their skills and established lines of communication throughout the world. We became the custodians of books, paintings, artefacts, and sacred objects. By the end of the eighteenth century and then onwards, things became easier as humanity learned more and more. They began to ask questions and search out answers. Our influence grew stronger, and we used our skills to build bigger and better abbeys and kept up with everything new as it became available. There are few countries now that do not have a hidden set-up of Watchers and links to powerful people with influence and access to whatever we may need. It was how we managed to spirit you away: yachts, boats, planes were all placed at our disposal.

"Now we face the biggest test of all. For the first time, we can prepare ahead for the coming Age of Aquarius, an age of communication. And not just with humanity, but with those who have been waiting patiently for untold millennia for us to join them. When that happens, we will cease to be a small solar system and become part of a galactic family. But first, we must find the Lost Abbey. We think, if it is still entire, that it holds the key to the future."

Johnny sat silent, stunned by what had been revealed. Eamon and Tze-Ring watched him, waiting for his reaction. Gregor had rejoined them and stood silent and attentive behind Johnny. Johnny stared into the fire and was silent for so long Eamon made as if to touch him, but Gregor shook his head. Finally Johnny raised his head and spoke.

"You said there were six working abbeys. I've seen three of them. Chile is the fourth, and after that I'll be sent on to the fifth, the Abbey of the Waters up near Alaska. Where is the sixth?"

Gregor moved round and took a seat by the fire. "It is the most isolated of all the abbeys and is situated on the island of Rishiri in the Sea of Japan. You will need special clothing. It is difficult to get to, and those who run it are small in number. There are just ten of them, but they are among the most talented of our people. Having said that, we do have many single… shall we call them…adepts who prefer to live alone. Their work is mainly that of observation on all levels. You will meet with them when the need is there."

Johnny continued to stare into the fire, then said, "And the Lost Abbey is still out there?"

"Yes. We last heard from it in the 1800s. The abbot sent word that they had been discovered and had lost two of their people. The members of the abbey were tending people in a remote mountain village that had been devastated by typhoid and saved many of them. However, the local priest denounced them as 'witches' and led a rabble to the abbey to destroy it. The abbot had foreseen this ahead of time and prepared for it. When they arrived, only the abbot remained. They tortured him for three days, but he had cut out his own tongue and severed his fingers so he could not speak or write…Long enough for the others to disappear. We never heard from them again."

"Where was the abbey before that?"

"In the mountains of Thessalonica, but there is no trace or even ruins to show where they had been. It is probable the rabble destroyed everything and razed it to the ground. We have often searched the area since that time but found nothing. Why do you ask?"

"Because last night I dreamt I was walking in the mountains. I thought I was back in the Abbey of the Dawn, but it was not Tibet. I don't know where it was, but it was really vivid. I remember asking someone who was standing behind me where I was."

"Did you get an answer?" asked Gregor, suddenly coming to his feet.

"Yes. He pointed to the peaks and said, 'They are the Accursed Mountains. I will be waiting for you.' Then I woke up. I remembered it when you mentioned the word *mountains*, and it seemed…seemed to fit."

"I've never heard of them."

"I have," said a voice behind them. Sister Dagmar rose from a nearby table where she had been sitting with Mara. "I've been there. I was just out of college and there were five of us: my cousin Gerda and I and three boys, two of them brothers and one a Swedish boy, Zebastian. Zeb's mother was Albanian and came from the north. The whole family was into rock-climbing, and as we talked about getting a group together, Zeb suggested the Accursed Mountains in Albania. They offered spectacular climbs that were relatively unknown at the time, and it seemed ideal. The very name was intriguing.

I have some photos on my computer. I don't know why I kept them...Especially after the tragedy."

"What happened, Dagmar? Is it possible to speak of it without pain?" Gregor motioned her to a seat near the fire.

"After twenty years, it's time to put it to rest." She took the seat offered and all drew close, ready to offer comfort if it was needed.

"There were just eighteen months between Sven and Lars, and even for brothers, they were very close and did everything together. Lars even thought up the idea of Gerda marrying them both: the first triune marriage. We all laughed, but Gerda refused to choose between them.

"Zeb made the travel arrangements. His Range Rover could take the five of us and our equipment, and we had it all worked out. It would take four or five days to get to our destination in Albania, driving in turns and camping at night. We left in early June and drove to our destination: Tirana.

"We rested a few days, but the men wanted to get to the climbing area, so we set off for Shkroda. Gerda and I were new to rock-climbing and kept to the easy climbs, but the men were after the difficult routes. Rock-climbing is not like mountaineering, where you have ropes and pitons and a degree of safety. Rocks are freehold; you climb using only hands, feet, muscles, and sheer strength.

"They took off into the mountains while Gerda and I swam and sunbathed on the beach. The men came back full of enthusiasm and begged us to go back with them. The views were incredible, and Sven had found a route that seemed unclimbed and wanted to try it out. Lars said it was too dangerous, and for once the brothers argued.

"We left the next day. They were right, the mountains were breathtaking, but I was uneasy. There was some influence there that seemed... not threatening, but as if it was waiting for us. I was just eighteen, and my talent was weak and unrecognised.

"On the third day, Sven announced his intention to try the new climb. Lars went spare. He begged him not to try and even offered to try it himself first, but Sven just laughed. He took Gerda's hand and kissed it and said, 'I will name it after you, my love. Consider it a betrothal gift.' We were stunned. This was something new; had Gerda finally chosen?

"Lars got up and left. Gerda tried to make light of it and said she had yet to make up her mind, but I knew. The next day, we left early for the climb. Lars had said no words to his brother, and I felt a tension round us. Sven kept hold of Gerda's hand, and we all noticed it.

"Sven had made a list of the hand- and footholds and had marked them on a photograph he'd taken from below and enlarged. Zeb went first and we walked along the track, keeping him in sight as much as possible. Every now and then he would shout out to let us know he was OK. It took five long hours before he finally reached a safe point from where he could re-join us. He was covered in sweat and there were cuts and bruises all over him, but he was jubilant. 'It's a great climb,' he said. 'I think we should register it. It's demanding and needs careful spacing in some areas, but it's definitely one for the experts.'

"Lars began to strip off. 'Me next,' he said.

"Zeb stopped him. 'It's too late, after two, and by half past three, the rock face will be in shadow and too dark to see where the holds are.'

"Sven added his voice. 'Wait for the morning, Lars. It's too dangerous, and I don't want to lose you, brother mine.'

"Lars hesitated, then shrugged and gathered up his equipment. 'OK, tomorrow it is. And I'll cut those five hours down to four and a half.' We laughed and made our way back to the hotel.

"It was a strange evening: Sven and Gerda stayed together, but Lars drank more than usual and slept in Zeb's room. Zeb was really worried and said it was foolish to climb when stressed, but Lars was determined to try.

"By eight the following morning, we reached the point where he could make the first crossing before beginning the new route. We watched Lars make the first thirty feet safely, then went up ahead to the point where he would make the final climb up and back onto the track. Unlike the day before, we were silent. A foreboding hung round us. Sven kept Lars in sight as he made his way across the sheer rock face.

"It was almost three hours into the climb when Zeb said, 'I can't see him. He's under the overhang.' He shouted down, but there was no reply at first. Then we saw a hand reach out and grasp a hold. Lars came slowly into view almost fifty feet below us, with over one hundred and fifty feet below him. We stretched out, looking down and willing him on. I saw him reach out for the next hold and prepare to swing out…A voice inside my head said, *Now the debt is repaid.*

"Lars forced his sweaty fingers into the crevice, and the stone broke away. He flailed from side to side to reach the next hold, but it was just too far. Sven ran for the ropes and he and Zeb threw them over. Gerda was screaming Lars's name over and over as he hung on just one hand. Sven cinched the extra rope round him, and with Zeb and I bracing ourselves against the expected weight, Sven went over to save his brother.

"Zeb looked at me. 'Even together we can't lift them both.' We tried, we really tried. Sven reach out and grasped his brother's hand and tried to swing him to a new hold, but their hands were too slippery. Much later, Sven told us, 'He smiled at me and said, *Be happy, brother mine*. Then he let go and fell.' It took three days to find his body.

"I photographed the area, and for three years in a row, I went back. You see, I loved Lars, but he had eyes only for Gerda. I never told anyone until now. I know the area well. There are a lot of caves, almost all of them unexplored. The locals think they are haunted. I found one or two that go far back into the mountains but didn't dare go further. But I remember seeing ancient markings on the walls.

"It was years later that my talent to affect plant life began to emerge. I went to agricultural college, and on a conference trip to England, I met with a Watcher. He taught me to accept my talent and helped me to adjust. I thought for a while there may have been a chance…but Lars was the only one for me."

Dagmar sighed and rose to her feet. "I'll find the photographs for you."

Johnny felt the egregore of bonded fellowship enclose Dagmar and strengthen her as she left. He also sensed the pinpoint of light that followed her round—the light he had, until now, thought was a manifestation of her talent. Now Johnny saw it for what it truly was. He turned to Eamon with a smile that lit up the whole room. "Lars is so close to her! She just doesn't see him. She is so wrapped up in her memories."

Gregor placed a hand on his shoulder. "Gently, Johnny. Don't rush into the situation or we could lose her. The shock might be too great. We may be gifted, but we can still be mentally and physically overwhelmed. I think as she looks at the photographs after so long, she may sense his presence.

"It has been a day of wonder and revelation. We need to replenish the physical self with rest and sleep. Tomorrow we may be able to find the Lost Abbey, or at least what they left behind for us to discover."

As they prepared for bed, Johnny watched Mara as she brushed her waist-length hair. Then he rose and went to stand behind her, wrapping her in his arms. He kissed the soft skin just below her ear and said softly, "When the time comes, remember what we saw and heard tonight. I will always be near you. No matter where you are or what you are doing, I will be there."

She turned in his arms and lifted her face to his kiss. "We will do what we were always destined to do, be where we need to be, endure what we were born to experience. Our reward will be an eternity together."

In the still hours of the night, a single point of light manifested in the Hall of Ceremony. It expanded to fill the entire abbey and the hearts and minds of those within. It moved from room to room, changing colour as it went and leaving the scent of spikenard in its wake.

Dagmar slept, and in her dream she walked with her lost love in the mountains of Albania.

Deep within those mountains, the Guardian stirred, and a wave of joy pulsed through her substance. Soon she would be free to join her companions.

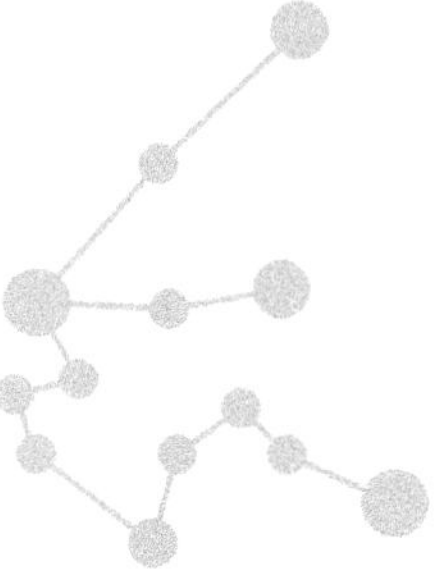

CHAPTER THIRTY-FIVE

3 August, 3:00 p.m.
Caravelle Productions, Los Angeles

The camera tracked slowly up towards the balcony and Tango turned to face it, focusing slightly to the right. The intro began softly as he drew in his breath and began to sing.

The continuity girl held her breath. The sound engineer closed his eyes and, for once, simply listened. Behind the camera, the director and the producer of *The Student Prince* looked at each other and shook hands.

Lost in his own world, Tango sang on, way past the time allotted for the take. He reached for the top note and held it. The music died away, and he stood there savouring the moment of completion. Then the silence was broken as the entire crew burst into applause.

Tango blinked and became aware of people crowding round him, shaking his hand, patting him on the back, expressing their excitement and pleasure. Then the producer asked Tango to come back to his office to sign the contract. The part was his. He had arrived!

The adulation, the praise, the feeling of being the focus of attention—of being *loved* for himself—was overwhelming. Tango dashed the tears from his eyes and smiled, shook hands, and exchanged words with people who admired him. The lonely, unloved, unwanted, deprived child deep within flowered under the praise.

♬ ♩ ♫ ♪ ♬ ♪ ♫

Much later, in the small hours, Tango sat on the edge of his bed and looked at the contract he had signed hours before. He'd made it. He would be—he *was*—a star in the making. Everything he had ever wanted was now in his reach. He hadn't seen De'ath in days and didn't want to, but there was one person he needed, really needed, to speak to. Tango reached for the phone and put a call through to London.

4 August, 11:30 a.m.
The penthouse, London

Bucky put down the phone and breathed a sigh of relief. It was in the bag: White Heat would be backing the headline solo artist in the Royal Variety Performance in November.

He looked at his watch: 11:30. A bit early for lunch, but what the hell? He deserved it. The phone rang as he put on his jacket.

"Yeah, who is it? And be quick. I'm on my way out."

"Bucky, it's me, Tango. I just wanted to let you know I got it. I really got it! I signed the contract this afternoon. I'm starring in the remake of *The Student Prince.* I wanted you to know and to share it with you. I wanted to ask you, Bucky…Please, if you can, let Johnny know. It feels great, Bucky. I feel I'm really worth something." Tango's voice tailed away. "You there, Bucky?"

Bucky suddenly knew, felt, understood what it meant to him. "I'm glad for you, Tango, really glad. I'll let everyone know, and I'll get word to Johnny. I promise."

"Thanks, Buck. And tell him…I remember. Bye." The phone went dead.

Time stretched, altered, changed vibration, and split into three silver threads. Three lives met, merged, and—for an instant—become one. One thread knew itself to be worthy of love, the second understood the true meaning of forgiveness, and the third saw the final moments of its destiny.

5 August, 9:30 a.m.
The Abbey of the Aeon

"Please, Gregor, I *have* to be there. We can delay the flight to Chile for a couple of weeks; it will make little difference to the overall training. I'll work an eighteen-hour day if I have to! I've done it before! But I *need* to be there when the abbey is uncovered."

"We have no idea what we may find. Perhaps just a few books, artefacts...very likely human remains."

"No!" Johnny turned to face him and spoke with a note of authority. "The Guardian saw to their interment. She was the last and has remained as she promised to do. I'll release her."

Gregor came to his feet, ready to reprimand the younger man for his lack of respect, then stopped. What faced him was no longer Johnny, but a figure of power in an aura of violet light. He and those with him went to their knees as the jackal head bent towards them.

"The Guardian has waited long for her release, her passing held in abeyance at my decree." The voice, faintly accented, was deep and musical. "Once the area has been cleansed and made secure and its new leader seated, the rebuilding can begin. Then I will Open the Way for the Guardian. The Forerunner will be needed. Also Sister Dagmar."

"It will be as you wish, son of Light." Gregor rose to his feet and bowed.

Johnny blinked and in his own voice said, "I could do with a cup of tea. Do you think Maurice could rustle up some sandwiches? It's almost lunch time."

♬ ♩ ♫ ♪ ♬ ♪ ♫

It was decided that Tze-Ring would guide the abbey for the short time they would be away. Eamon went to make travel arrangements, and Gregor went to talk to Dagmar. He also spoke with the other abbeys, sharing the news that the Lost Abbey had been discovered and a small party would be going to open it up, cleanse it, and see if it could be reinstated or if a new building would be needed. Within forty-eight hours, offers of both labour and money came pouring in. Dagmar took more persuasion and was reluctant but finally agreed.

♫ ♩ ♫ ♪ ♬ ♪ ♫

In mid-August the ever-obliging Amal flew them to a private landing strip in Northern Greece. A camper van and an off-road vehicle were waiting for them with a note from the emir, offering any help that might be needed. They had decided to drive to Valbona rather than flying in and hiring vehicles; if anything needed to be brought back, there could be trouble with airline customs.

Attempts to make contacts within Albania had failed, but before they left, a message was relayed to the abbey via Florrie. It came from one of her Romani contacts. A man called Yannick Hoxsha would meet them in the region of Krasniqi with information, then stay and drive the camper with Gregor and Dagmar, leaving Eamon and Johnny with the smaller vehicle.

Amal changed the tyres for some more suitable and then they took the road to Valbona. Along the way, Gregor filled Amal in on the new discovery.

It took six hours of tortuous driving to get to the meeting place with Yannick Hoxsha. He met them at a turnoff that looked even more hazardous than the one they were on. Yannick sat at the side of the road, his horse grazing the sparse bushes. He rose to his feet, taking off his battered hat, and Eamon greeted him in the ancient tongue of the Romani. He offered tobacco, tea, and bread in the traditional way.

Yannick and Eamon spoke of weather, of horses, and of life. Then a piece of paper was offered and accepted. They shook hands and Eamon turned away, but under a stone by the roadside he left a brightly coloured scarf wrapped round a generous gift of money. Yannick ignored it until they left.

Johnny smiled, remembering the ancient way. Too proud to ask for payment, Yannick could accept a gift of tobacco, a gift of tea, or a gift of bread. The scarf was for his woman, the money just something he found "lying around."

They resumed their journey and came into Valbona as the evening lights came on. They booked into the small and slightly run-down hotel they had selected, not wanting to call attention to their presence. Over dinner they looked at the paper Yannick had given them. It was a plan of the hidden abbey and the way into the cave system that had kept it hidden for almost two hundred years.

They woke to a day of mist and intermittent showers and dressed accordingly. Their cover was that of a group of botanists and their tutor studying the area prior to their master's degrees, and they would be camping out for a few days. Amal stayed in the hotel, in touch by phone in case help was needed.

All was quiet as they set out for their destination. One of the small local buses took them to a sheltered area of Lake Ohrid, and from there they went on foot.

After hours of walking, they stopped to rest and check the map. A steep climb would take them over one of the lower peaks, from the top of which fell an eighty-foot waterfall into a small valley. Behind the base of the falls was the entrance to a cave system, avoided because of frequent rock falls.

After a short discussion, they began the climb with Eamon leading and Gregor bringing up the rear, Johnny and Dagmar in front of him. Though all were fit, it was hard going and slower than they had hoped, with Johnny and Dagmar slowing them down. When almost at the top of the climb, Gregor called a halt.

"We must make it to the entrance before dark," Abbot Gregor said, drinking from his canteen. "We can't camp on this slope; it's too dangerous. We have to make it to the cave mouth below, or as near as we can before dark. Let's go." Wearily, they gathered their gear and began to climb again.

Some thirty minutes later, Dagmar called out, "Gregor, look! Look!" She pointed to what looked like a narrow path that led straight to the edge of the climb. For a second there seemed to be a misty form hovering over the edge. Dagmar went scrabbling over to where she had seen it, ignoring Gregor's warning shout.

"Lars, I'm coming!"

She reached the edge and, to their horror, seemed to jump. Then Dagmar's head reappeared. "It's an old path, very narrow, but it joins another lower path. We don't need to get to the top; we can go this way and save time. It's dangerous, but it's doable."

Eamon looked across at Johnny, knowing his fear of heights. Gregor studied the narrow ledge, then raised his head. "She's right. It is doable, but it's as scary as hell."

Dagmar took off her hiking boots and socks. "Lars said to go without boots; it's easier to feel the ledge," she said confidently.

Eamon and Gregor looked at each other, then at Johnny. He gritted his teeth and bent down to take off his boots. "Let's get going," he said.

Four gut-wrenching hours later, with sore feet, aching muscles, and in Johnny's case, a determination that one more test like that and "they" could find another Forerunner, they reached a level area alongside the waterfall. Dagmar said nothing, but they knew she was conscious of her lost love close to her. She hummed to herself as they ate a simple meal fortified with hot tea from the thermos.

Eamon called Amal on his phone and relayed their whereabouts as a precaution. Then they settled into their sleeping bags and slept soundly. Around them rose a wall of vibrant power, held in place by two very different forms. What had once been Lars Sorensen greeted the Guardian, and together they kept watch over the sleepers, healing aches and bruises and replacing badly needed energy.

18 August, 11:15 p.m.
Tango's apartment in Los Angeles

Tango punched the password for his apartment into the keypad and kicked the door closed behind him. He was exhausted. Costume fittings all morning, vocal training (like he needed that!) in the afternoon followed by publicity shots, and just when he thought he would be able to grab a meal and an early night, he'd been landed with a TV interview due to go out the following day.

He looked at his watch. 11:15...A shower, a hot drink with a shot of Jamaican rum, and then bed. He groaned at the thought of it: cool sheets, darkness, and oblivion for as many hours as he could get away with.

"At a guess, I would surmise you have found being a star in the making is not as exciting as you imagined it would be."

The figure that rose from the velvet-covered lounge easily matched Tango's nearly six feet. The grey silk and elegant cut of his suit proclaimed its Italian heritage, as did his olive skin, black hair, and dark eyes.

"Who the hell are you and what are you doing here? Get out *now*, or I'll call the police!"

"Oh, you won't do that. We don't want to upset things now that they are going so well, do we? I mean, it wouldn't do your new image as a heart-throb much good to know you have...shall we say...a close companion, now would it?" The man sauntered over to Tango, ran a manicured hand down the side of his face, and leaned in to place a kiss on his lips.

It was the first time Tango had experienced this, and everything in him exploded. He swung at the handsome face only to find his fist stopped in mid-air by the inhuman strength of the stranger's hand.

"Tut-tut. Such a reaction. Well, let's see if this works better." The figure folded in on itself, changing and re-adjusting, and the bemused singer found himself holding a soft feminine form that fitted herself to him with an easy grace. Her face and figure exuded a scent that wrapped round Tango's senses and increased the pressure behind his close-fitting slacks.

But his time with De'ath had not been spent in vain. Whatever Tango was, he was not stupid, and he had studied the Dark arts in the years since his split with the group. In many ways, his inner life had run parallel with that of Johnny's. Tango's association with De'ath—though he had hated every minute of it—had resulted in a working knowledge of the inner powers, powers that now stood him in good stead.

"I wondered where De'ath had gone so suddenly. I gather you have taken his place. So, what is the price? I know there will be one, so you might as well come clean and I'll let you know if I am willing to play along."

Tango walked across to the drinks cabinet and poured himself a neat whisky.

"Let's talk. Do you have a name? And by the way, let's get something straight right away: I'm not gay. So quit with the façade and let's put our cards on the table. It appears that who and what I am is of interest and use to your 'kind.' It's time I got to know what and why. Also—and this is important—what do I get out of it, and what do I have to do to get it?"

Tango's unwelcome guest returned to his original form, poured himself a drink, and went and stood by the open window. He looked out over the City of Angels and thought briefly of how damned unsuitable that name was, then turned to Tango.

"Since I am in no sense of the word human, my name would be meaningless to you, but for now we can use Desiderio, Desi for short. I am what you already suspect: the opposite of what this city is named for. You would say *demon*; I prefer *daemon*. The first is wholly on the side of the Dark. The second is...shall we say...prone to work for ourselves and for whoever offers the most attractive price. We...recruit—I think that is the word—those who can swell our numbers. Humanity thinks in pairs. Two of everything: black and white, good and bad. In actual fact, everything goes in threes. Black, white, and grey. Good, bad, and indifferent."

Tango sat and listened.

"We got rid of De'ath—he would have left you soulless. He had to go and will not be back. But you have something we look for: the desire to have, to take, and to enjoy whatever can be had purely for the self. When we reach a point where we can become a wholeness, we will absorb everything and become a Oneness to rival the opposite One. Then the Great Battle will take place. There can be only One. We look for life forms like you who desire all for themselves. We absorb them and grow strong."

"What do I get out of this?" Tango asked.

Desi turned and smiled. It was not really a smile—more of a hunger. "You get everything you have ever wanted...for a while."

19 August, 7:00 a.m.
The Accursed Mountains, Albania

Yesterday's climb and the descent into the valley below should have left them exhausted. Instead, they woke rested and alert. Dagmar was the first to wake and, to Johnny's embarrassment, stripped off to bathe in the icy waters of the lake. The men, to her amusement, made do with a quick hands-and-face sluice. The tea in the thermos was cold, and though energy bars did not equate with eggs and bacon, they sufficed. Within the hour they had re-packed their gear and set off for the cave entrance behind the waterfall.

The first surprise was the power of the waterfall. Gregor studied it, then said, "Going through that will soak us to the skin. Then we'll freeze inside the cave. There has to be another way in."

Eamon studied the map he'd been given. A roughly drawn set of marks drew his attention. "Johnny, my Romani is a bit rusty. What does *rosu chavi* mean?"

Johnny looked over Eamon's shoulder. "It's a drawing. *Rosu chavi* means 'red stone.' Mama always wore a necklace of red stones, but when we had to put Granddad into a home, she sold it. She cried a lot over that."

"She would. I gave it to her, and those red stones were Persian rubies. The drawing shows three stones close together. Like those just to the side of the falls, and they are near enough to a red colour. I wonder..." Eamon splashed across the shallows and studied the stones closely, then put his shoulder to one and pushed. Johnny and Gregor joined him.

With the three working together, the stones slowly slid to one side, revealing a narrow entrance close beside the falls. Gregor drew in a breath. "This is it! This leads to the Lost Abbey. I can feel its power. The Light be praised." He paused to take a powerful torch from his pack and looked back at the others, his face almost exalted, then stepped forward into the darkness.

Gregor moved slowly, mindful of the uneven surface. His torch played over the walls, revealing images and records of the indomitable will to survive by a small group of people. For two hundred and fifty years they had kept their ways, powers, and purpose alive. He tried to communicate to the others via his mobile but with no success.

The way twisted and turned, and many tunnels led off the main path, but the symbol of the abbey (three interlaced triangles) carved over the lintels showed the way. Abbot Gregor added his own mark to each one to guide himself back. Finally he came to an open space from which four tunnels led off. He looked at his watch. Thirty minutes had passed, and he judged he was half a mile into the interior. It was time to turn back.

Gregor played the light over each entrance and paused at the third. Cut into the stone under the three triangles was a star pattern with one star circled. It was a pattern Gregor knew well: Sirius. He paused. Every instinct urged him to go on, but there were those with him who deserved to share the moment. Abbot Gregor turned and made his way back.

The others came to their feet as Gregor emerged, shaking dust from his clothing and hair. "Well, is it what we were hoping for?" Eamon demanded. "For love of heaven, man, is it? Is it?"

"Yes. I got to what I think is the entrance to the main area, but I want us to be together when we enter it. I need others to verify what we may find. I think it will affect us in different ways. There's an incredible power there, but it's been unused for hundreds of years. We have no idea how it will respond when awakened. It may reach out to us as a group or as individuals. We must be prepared.

"Eamon, contact Amal and tell him to send word to all the abbeys. Ask them to set up a circle of their strongest people and build a protective barrier around this area. That will give us time to cope with whatever we find. Also, we need a working group of fully trained people to go through whatever is found in there, then close it down. I don't think it's possible to use the abbey in its original form. A new abbey will have to be built, preferably close by.

"Dagmar, we need your powers to thicken the forest around here to make it even more difficult to find a way through, but also to implant the way in into our collective memory. Can you do that?"

"Yes, Gregor, but it will take time. Maybe several days. And we need extra supplies."

Eamon was already talking with Amal and reported, "He's in touch with Tze-Ring, and the word is already going out. They are checking with the other abbeys to see who can be spared. Getting supplies to us is more difficult. They don't know exactly where we are."

Johnny interrupted him. "I can help there. Yannick Hoxsha's people haves a *dukker*[14] among them; Florrie said so. I can reach him or her through either crystal or water. We may have to go hungry for a day or so, but I can guide Yannick to us with supplies."

"Is that safe?" asked Gregor.

"Yes. They are familiar with Florrie, and like all Romani, they are used to keeping secrets. They are a small group and poor, and I think they would

14. Fortune-teller

be in need of shelter for the winter. Maybe we could offer them the camper van as a gift for their help. For such a payment, they will repay us with utter silence, complete loyalty, and help with supplies. But we need to ask the emir's permission to make the offer. Dad, call Amal back and ask him."

After a meagre lunch, Dagmar went foraging in the forest. Eamon spoke with Amal and got permission to offer the camper van as a payment; they could hire an extra vehicle on their return.

Dusk fell early in the mountains and gradually, one by one, they fell silent. Gregor suddenly felt very tired and sat down, his head in his hands. Johnny went to him, placed a hand over his heart, and matched its beat with his. After a few minutes the older man looked up.

"Thank you—it's easier now. Let's all get some sleep, and early tomorrow we will enter the Lost Abbey together."

Johnny found a quiet place by a clear pool and mentally reached out to the *rawnie*, the grandmother of the Hoxsha family: "A holy place has been found, kept secret. We need supplies. In return, we offer our modern vardo for you and your family to shelter you through the winter and aid your travel. I can arrange for it to be brought to where we met with Yannick. This is where we have made camp tonight. Do you know this place?"

He repeated the message several times, waited, then repeated it again. The Romani power was strong in this country, and Johnny was confident his message would be received.

Just before dawn Johnny woke and went to sit by the pool. The water rippled, then cleared to show a wrinkled, elderly face. The old woman held up a loaf of bread, then made a walking motion with her fingers, then held up her forefinger. Johnny nodded, placed his hands together, and bowed his head.

He woke Gregor quietly. "Supplies are on their way. It will take Yannick a full day to reach us. We can wait for him to get here or leave one person behind."

Gregor shook his head. "We all need to be there. The power level will be high after so long. Spread over the group, it will not be as dangerous. If the power is too strong, it may be tainted by its long incarceration. We'll wait. We have waited for several hundred years. One more day will not be too hard to bear."

Dagmar, as always the first to rise, emerged from the trees with an armful of forest herbs and roots, some wild mushrooms, and, amazingly, three pigeon eggs. She set the herbs and roots to simmer and made a sparse but edible breakfast with the last two rashers of bacon and the bird's eggs. Then Gregor drew a sketch in the dust of the layout he had memorised from the day before.

"I'm certain they would have set up protection around anything of value, so we need to be on the watch for booby traps. When in doubt, don't touch, don't make a sudden move, and be ready to duck. Think in terms of Indiana Jones. Johnny, what time do you expect Yannick?"

"I would think just before sunset, which means he will have to spend the night here. There is something about him that makes me think he knows more than seems possible. The *pivley rawnie* I spoke with seemed to be aware we were looking for something special."

Eamon stood up and looked towards the mountain. "Whatever is in there, it's waiting for us. I feel its weariness and its longing to rejoin those who went before. I feel them also; the expectation is palpable. But we can't risk starting until Yannick leaves. All we can do is rest and prepare."

The sun was setting when Johnny came to his feet, looking towards the trees. Then Yannick appeared, by his side a dog showing more than a touch of wolf. Both carried packs of supplies.

Johnny went forward. "*Cushti bok, miro phral.*"[15] He greeted Yannick with the traditional Romani handclasp. The others joined in.

Yannick had brought supplies for three days, providing they rationed themselves. He also brought two bottles of local wine, which they shared along with the evening meal.

As they ate, Yannick spoke of his small family. They travelled a set journey in the spring, summer, and early autumn. The fairs and festivals so beloved by the Slavic countries provided a market for their wares: wooden carvings, hand-spun wool, woven rugs, and of course, fortune-telling. Yannick and his sons were metalworkers mending pots and pans, sharpening knives and axes, and doing farrier work, but they always returned to the "family holding."

15. "Good luck, my brother."

Yannick expressed his gratitude for the gift of the camper. The present vardo was older than Yannick himself and offered little winter shelter for the five of them; he and his sons slept in the stable of a friendly farmer a few miles down the road. Also, their goods and services sold at the fairs were not as lucrative as they had once been, so he and his sons hired themselves out during the winter, but being Romani made it hard to find work. This year, the family would be warm and dry thanks to their gift.

To find Johnny was of true Romani stock through his mother and to speak his own tongue with him warmed Yannick's heart. He sat for a while, listening to them talk and thinking deeply. Then he turned to Abbot Gregor as the leader of the group and, with Johnny as an interpreter, offered information that stunned them.

"My family has lived here for generations, and we hold many secrets. Long, long ago, there came over the mountains a group of holy ones, five men and three women. They were skilled in the healing arts, and though exhausted and homeless, they saved the lives of many of our people who were stricken with a strange illness. They spoke of persecution, torture, and the hatred of their way of life by those with no understanding. The Romani have always suffered such things, and we welcomed them. They needed a place of safety where they might live in peace and where their treasures could be hidden.

"We told them of the ancient caves deep in the mountains and for months helped them to build a place of quiet, peace, and safety. There are two areas there: one was used for living, the other to hold the treasures they had brought with them. That second place is guarded by a door with a special lock. Both the door and the lock were made by one of my ancestors who was skilled in the art."

Yannick spoke of the arrival of the abbey refugees as if it was yesterday, and those listening held their breath.

"Our tribe was bigger then, and the brethren offered help for those who were sick and taught the children. We in return helped them to make the caves habitable and kept them supplied with basic foods. And all the while, we kept their secret. They said that one day their own kind would seek them out, and when that happened, we were to offer our help. Slowly, they began to pass, but always there was one who stayed and did not pass but kept guard. When we had great need, we would come here and ask for help. Sometimes it was in coin or small gifts that could be sold; sometimes it was instruction. When war came close, we hid there, often for months, venturing out only for food. Always, the Guardian kept watch."

Yannick paused and was silent, then spoke again. "The door to their sacred place was made to their instructions, and its lock was designed by my ancestor. Two keys were made: one for the Guardian and one for my ancestor, to be passed down until it was time for the door to be opened."

Yannick paused in his story and took a leather thong from round his neck. On the end was an intricate key, in form and shape unlike any they had ever seen: some five inches long and with three sets of prongs.

"This has been passed down in my family since that time. We knew one day you would come. Now I give it to you." Yannick placed the key in Abbot Gregor's hand.

The silence round the small fire was deep. The abbey personnel crowded close to look at the legendary object in Gregor's hand. In the silence that followed, Gregor stood and held up his arms, invoking the abbeys to join together in the moment of renewal and re-integration. A soundless shout of joy, halfway between a greeting and an amen, sounded over the mountains in a clap of thunder that broke windows for miles around.

In the abbeys, everything stopped. Those sleeping came awake, and all headed for their Halls of Ceremony to offer thanks and welcome home the lost ones.

♫ ♩ ♫ ♪ ♫ ♪ ♫

Early the next morning, Yannick made ready to leave. Gregor asked him to be with them when they opened the door, but he shook his head.

"That is for you and those with you, *miro phral*—I just kept the promise made by my people. I will send word that between the Romani and the People of the Key, there is an understanding."

Johnny translated, then spoke with Gregor and turned back to Yannick.

"For this gift, we give thanks. It is no small thing that you offer. I offer you a name, address, and phone number. If you are in need, no matter what, call or send word and help will be there for you. This man has much influence, and long ago a woman of the Romani saved his life. He has never forgotten his debt."

Johnny handed Yannick a paper with the emir's details and watched him leave.

21 August, 7:00 a.m.
The Abbey of the Dawn

High in the snowy peaks of the Himalayas, the frail figure of the abbot sat supported by the strong arms of Chambha. His voice was faint, but it held its customary note of authority.

"Soon we will experience the reunion of the seven abbeys. We must celebrate, Chambha. Our unwilling protégé has proved his worth. I think perhaps a special meal after the ritual of reunification would be appropriate. Then, if I may ask for the use of your energy, dear friend, I would like to 'see' the opening and make contact with Brother Johnny. I confess I miss the sound of his laughter."

♬ ♩ ♫ ♪ ♬ ♪ ♫

In the Abbey of the Throne, members gathered together and, while waiting, listened again to Frank's tone poem. In the Aeon, the Abbey of the Waters, and that of the Winds, they too awaited the moment of reunion. In the north, on the island of Rishiri, the Abbey of the Snows bathed in the aura of the borealis as they joined their combined power with that of their fellow abbeys.

21 August, 8:30 a.m.
The Accursed Mountains, Albania

In the little valley, they checked and re-checked: water, torches, extra batteries, knives, rope, energy bars, a small first-aid kit, matches, and face masks in case a long-closed door loosed something unbreathable. Abbot Gregor carried a powerful lamp with a long-life battery to save their smaller torches; he also had red markers in his pocket. They all wore lightweight helmets to guard against falling rock.

Eamon went first, then Johnny, with Gregor and Dagmar bringing up the rear. As they approached the entrance, they were all aware of the combined strengths of the abbeys surrounding them.

Dagmar secured the guide rope to a stone and handed the roll to Eamon. Between the rope, the rough pencilled plan, and the markers, they would be able to find their way back in an emergency.

Moving slowly, they entered singly, feeling the sudden drop in temperature as they left the sunlight. All of them followed the beam of Eamon's torch, saving their own as a precaution.

The paintings on the walls were mixed, some ancient and badly faded, others drawn at a much later date and detailing the occupants' struggle to survive. Here and there, there was the odd word in Romani or a rough drawing of a vardo, but such efforts to record events petered out as they made their way slowly inward.

Dagmar voiced her thoughts. "They tried so hard…At times it seems they came close to giving up. I can feel their despair; it clings to the walls."

The way ahead turned and twisted and at times almost doubled back on itself. Here and there, Eamon's torch picked out other tunnels, some wide, some narrow, and others almost sinister. Hour after hour, they made their way forward. Then Eamon stopped and shone his torch round, revealing an open, circular space.

Gregor caught up with him and set down the larger lamp. He busied himself with the stand for a moment, then hit the switch.

They looked round, dumbfounded, speechless, and unable to take in what they saw.

Years of study and discipline failed Eamon. "Bloody hell!"

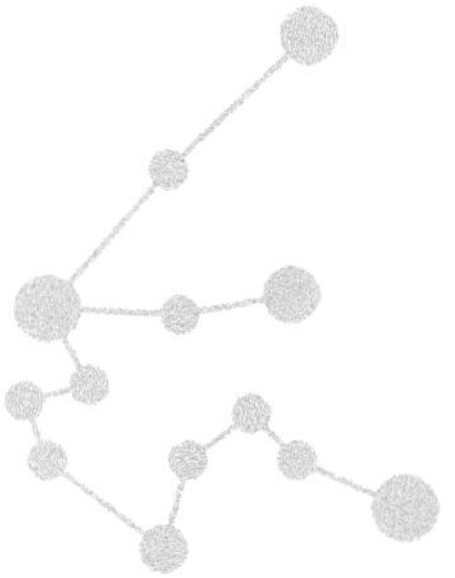

CHAPTER THIRTY-SIX

21 August, 11:30 a.m.
The Lost Abbey

The almost-painful brilliance of the powerful lamp flooded the circular space in which they found themselves. Tunnels led off in different directions, each one covered by a hanging that had once glowed with colour but now hung limp, faded, and in tatters. A niche had been excavated between them, each one filled with the dehydrated body of an original member of the Abbey of the Crown.

One opening was closed by a carved wooden door. The depth of the carvings showed its strength, and the intricate metalwork of the lock showed the skill of its maker. Three roughly made wooden benches, one overturned, and a single chair filled the space and surrounded a small altar. The top of the altar was covered by a paper-thin square of gold and a silver candlestick holding the last piece of a long-burnt-out candle, yet the air had retained the faint scent of that last flame.

Training and instinct took them to their knees, and the opening chant of the Abbeys of the Sevenfold Powers sounded in the makeshift temple for the first time in centuries:

Seven are the doors that lead to the Temple of Creation.
The first is the Door to Life, opened by the Key of the First Breath.
The second is the Door to Growth, opened by the Key of the First Word.
The third is the Door to Knowledge, opened by the Key of Realisation.
The fourth is the Door to Self-Recognition, opened by the Key of Acceptance.
The fifth is the Door of Transformation, opened by the Key of Surrender.
The sixth is the Door of Sacrifice, opened by the Key of Willingness.
The seventh is the Door of Rebirth, opened by the Key of Joy.

The four voices swelled as they were joined by their spiritual kin of the abbeys, and above the mountains the sun rose to its zenith and cleansed old pain, hurts, and loneliness from that which had been accursed.

The sound of a human heartbeat began to be heard, faint at first and then stronger. A feminine voice stole into their minds like a small bird to a nest. A pinpoint of light rested over each head and drew just enough energy to sustain an ephemeral, almost indistinct, feminine form in a grey robe.

"It has been so long—so long—but I held to my trust that you would come as was promised. Then one came, having made a willing sacrifice out of love; he strengthened me and chose to wait with me. Now, when the power is passed, I can gain release. He will remain with she who will take my place. When the time is right, they will be granted their joining.

"Gregor Theodorakis, tomorrow you may open the door. You will be told what is needful to do, how to handle the treasure of the abbey, and where the new Abbey of the Crown can be raised. A blessing rests upon you all, and upon those who have kept their promise."

Silently, the group made their way back, and the one who walked unseen with Dagmar surrounded her with his light.

A surprise waited for them at their camp: a warm fire, hot vegetable soup, coffee strong enough to hold a spoon upright and sweetened with honey, plus bottles of Raki, a fruit-based brandy similar to a Yugoslavian slivovitz and with much the same effect. Amal and the entire Hoxsha family greeted the group with hot towels, good food, and an understanding of their need for rest and quiet. The women saw to their comfort. The sons gathered wood and kept the fire going. Yannick sat and smoked his pipe, his young daughter close to him playing with a stuffed toy, the first she had ever had.

Johnny suddenly broke—the pressure, the power, missing Mara, and something he couldn't name overcame him. He bowed his head and wept. The old woman drew Johnny's head to her lap and stroked his hair. In a surprisingly strong voice, she sang a lullaby to a tune he remembered from his childhood. Eamon took Johnny's hand in his and, for the first time in many years, felt the presence of his lost love surround him.

One of the sons produced a flute and played for them, and one by one the group members crawled into their sleeping bags and slept. The Romani family banked the fire and settled down; the dog snuggled close to the girl. Only Dagmar remained awake a bit longer, sensing the presence of Lars close to her until she slept.

♬ ♩ ♫ ♪ ♬ ♪ ♫

Deep inside the mountain, the Guardian attended to her duties for the last time. Before each of her former comrades, she bowed her head three times and manifested the scent of frankincense and myrrh.

"Brother Marek, blessed be thy rest and thy dreams. Soon I will join you in the Light.

"Brother Amos, blessed be thy rest and thy dreams. Soon we will sing together as of old.

"Sister Janika, blessed be thy rest and thy dreams. Those who come will tend thy garden.

"Sister Hestia, blessed be thy rest and thy dreams. The son you bore lives in his descendants.

"Brother Leon, blessed be thy rest and thy dreams. Your music still lives on.

"Brother Phillipos, blessed be thy rest and thy dreams. My heart lies with you, my dear love.

"Abbot Nikos, blessed be thy rest and thy dreams. I have fulfilled my task. Tomorrow I will pass the treasure of the Abbey of the Crown into safe keeping. Grant me then permission to pass into the Light."

The shadowed form approached the locked door and passed within.

♬ ♩ ♫ ♪ ♬ ♪ ♫

Dawn broke over the mountains as Yannick rebuilt the fire. His wife set water to boil. The old lady slowly got to her feet and woke the others. Dagmar, used to early rising, helped to prepare breakfast for the Romani; she and the others would fast this day.

With everyone awake, they prepared for what the day would bring. Abbot Gregor sought a secluded spot to meditate on what might be demanded of him. Eamon and Johnny sat together, strengthening their talents with measured breathing and mental adjustment. Dagmar bathed in the icy water and smiled quietly, remembering her dream and already adjusting to the task before her. As the sun sent its first rays into the valley, Gregor called everyone together.

"Yannick, to you and your family I offer the blessing of the Seven Abbeys of Light. You have kept the secret of those we thought lost to us and in doing so preserved knowledge the world will need in the future. Between the people of the Romani and the abbeys there is a bond, and you may call on us when there is a need. I don't know what lies before us, but I ask you to wait for our return. We may have need of your strength."

Yannick took off his hat and placed a hand on his heart. "We will wait and be ready to offer what help we can, *miro phral.* If you find you have need of me within the mountain, I will come; I have permission from She Who Guards the Door. *Vay Duvvel*—go with God."

He watched the four of them approach the entrance and pause briefly. Then, without looking back, they disappeared into the mountain.

In single file, the group followed the now openly marked trail, carrying with them what would be needed. With each step the psychic pressure grew, pressing down on them and heightening their talents. Dagmar became aware of the forest roots digging deep and drawing sustenance from the soil. She sensed the awakening of the life force in the forest and a sense of expectation. *The earth is holding its breath*, she thought and felt the warmth of Lars's presence wrap round her. Eamon felt the presence of his lost love, smelled the scent of her hair and the pressure of her lips on his. Gregor sensed the presence of his former abbot and heard the Irish lilt of his voice. But Johnny felt the pain of Tango's anguish. "Why Johnny? Why me? Why, why, why?"

Johnny heard his own reply. "There are always two sides to the sacred sacrifice, Tango. The slain and the slayer are always part of each other. It takes love and courage to slay what you love, and love and courage to accept the blow and understand the pain of the slayer. The two cannot be separated: Set and Osiris, Yeshua and Judas. What happens on the higher levels is mirrored in the lower levels."

Then Johnny heard, "Welcome." The voice of the Guardian was low and weak. "I must have energy to complete my task. My companions, in turn, offered me the life expectancy they held in order for me to continue my guardianship. I ask of you enough that I may pass on the instructions I was given. I need but one day's energy from each of you, with the exception of the Forerunner. His energy must remain complete. Are you willing? I can accept, but I cannot demand or take."

Gregor stepped forward. "I willingly offer what you need."

The diaphanous form of the Guardian enveloped him momentarily, then stepped back, visibly stronger. Eamon came forward and made his offer and was enveloped. Dagmar came last and, with a smile, held out her arms to her sister in Light. Then the Guardian stood manifest as she had once been: of middle height and sturdily built, her dark brown hair touched with grey lying close to her head and tightly braided.

The Guardian turned to Johnny. "I know you are willing, but your days are needed for the task before you. This is enough for me."

She gestured to the wooden seats, and they all sat together.

"I am Esther. I was given to the abbey by my parents as a child. My gift of the inner sight was difficult for them to accept. To keep me safe from the church, I was sent to another country and finally to the Abbey of the Crown. My life there was good until the blue illness came and the abbey healers moved among the people, curing those they could save. The church deemed it evil to save those 'God had called.' The abbot told us to take the treasures we guarded and seek another place. He stayed behind to delay them and suffered greatly in doing so. He had named Nikos as our new abbot, and twelve of us fled the abbey.

"Over the next year, moving constantly, starving, cold, and homeless, we lost many of our little band. We finally came over these mountains and were found by those named the Romani. With them we found shelter and acceptance. They hid us here, and we made it our place of Light. We brought with us much that could be sold and were able to fit this place to our simple needs. We hoped our fellow abbeys would find us, but years went by and no word came. We hoped and kept our way of life. The treasure and its power gave us strength and advice. But Nikos feared it would be lost forever if no one was left to guard it, so we sought advice from the treasure itself.

"We were told to select one to be the Guardian. That one would receive whatever life force was left from those remaining and, in doing so, might live long enough to see a re-joining with the other abbeys. The Romani began to spread the word of a 'lost place of power guarding a great treasure.'

"I was the youngest, so I was the one who would live longest. The years went by, and as each companion grew older, one by one they gave their life force within to me. I grew no older, but it was a heavy burden to bear as each one made their sacrifice, even Phillipos, to whom I gave my heart and my love. Sister Hestia was the last. Then just me.

"The people of the Romani offered, but the treasure forbade it. They raised energy through dance and song to enable me to keep my vigil, but my ability to maintain form is no more. I ask you to take the treasure and the panoply of the Abbey of the Crown and rebuild what was lost. Choose one to keep the vigil and be the Guardian of the Crown so I may rejoin my companions. But first, come, follow me, and bring the key."

The now almost-solid Guardian rose and went to stand before the door to what was obviously their Hall of Ceremony. Gregor produced the key and Esther instructed him, "Insert the key to the first tine, turn it, and wait until you hear the click. Now push the key in to the second tine, turn it, and wait. When the lock clicks, push the key right in to the last tine and turn it in the opposite direction to the other two. Then and only then can you turn the handle and open the door."

Gregor followed her instructions. Taking a breath, he turned the handle and opened the door.

Around the globe, the abbey telepaths and psychics reached out to each other and combined their talents to relay what they were seeing to those around them. Roughly oblong in shape, the stone walls had been painted to resemble the valley around them. Mountain peaks and trees, the waterfall, and the small lake had been copied with loving care. The outside had been brought inside. Stationed at intervals stood twelve carved candleholders, in which stood cathedral-sized candles. These were lit, and the whole area presented as an outdoor place of worship. One might imagine you were in a garden lit for a nighttime celebration. Wooden chairs covered with sheep fleece dyed deep purple, each with a kneeling pad in the same colour before them, were placed in a semicircle on a floor made of handmade tiles that depicted the zodiac. An altar carved with the same skill was covered with a cloth of handmade lace. The chalice and paten were of pure gold, as were the ampulla and spoon. Everything showed the work of loving hands over long periods of time. Behind the altar hung a curtain, a cloth of gold.

Esther's voice was quiet and full of pride, mixed with tears. "The days were long, and we needed to keep ourselves busy and not thinking too much about the trials behind us and the long years before us. Our Romani friends brought wood, tools, paint, clay—things we could not acquire for ourselves. They also joined us as we worked. Some of the things we made we gave to them to sell. We taught their children to read and write, and those of us with healing powers treated them when it was needed. We also had articles of gold and silver and other things of value that we used to purchase what we could not make. But our greatest treasure we kept hidden." She hung her head. "I have not had the strength or the power of physical form for so long. The cloth has not been moved for over a hundred years. I was hoping to see our treasures once more before…" Her voice tailed off.

Gregor held his breath; some inkling of what lay behind the cloth touched his mind. He turned to Johnny. "Forerunner, will you open the curtain, please?"

Johnny looked at him, startled, then moved behind the altar and drew the curtain aside.

Held against the bare rock of the mountain were two pieces of aged wood, broken from their original shape. Barely recognisable at first, but then their eyes grew used to the dimness, for the candlelight did not reach so far. The broken shape formed what was left of a shaft topped by a cross piece. A broken shard of clay held what was left of letters *N. R. I.* Below it was a circlet of thorns that bore traces of a dark stain.

Esther's voice was whisper-soft. "The Teacher of each age always leaves behind something to remind humanity of their presence. The new Teacher has not yet been recognised…but to have welcomed the one who will prepare the way for Her has made the years of waiting worthwhile."

Esther offered Johnny a square of white linen. He took it and, with shaking hands, lifted the crown of thorns from the wall and brought it into the light. The small group encircled it. Linking their trained powers, they sent a picture of the relic into the unified thoughtform of the abbeys and held it for as long as they could. Then the light died away and they were released from their task.

Esther turned to Dagmar. "I am instructed to offer you the leadership of the rebuilt Abbey of the Crown. If you accept, there is one here who offers to remain with you until your time is completed. He will then accompany you to the Field of Reeds."

Dagmar bowed her head in acceptance, and there shimmered into place beside her a tall blonde man with a brilliant smile. "*Från och med nu kommer vi att vara kära.*"[16] A plume of energy flowed between them and added to the strength of Dagmar's aura.

Esther led Dagmar to the chair before the altar. Instructions flowed from her to Johnny. He took his place behind the chair and lifted the crown

16. "From now on, we will be together, my dear."

over Dagmar's head. Those with her knelt, and he lowered the crown until it rested there lightly, then lifted his hands away. The crown, of its own accord, pressed down until a trickle of blood ran down each temple.

Esther spoke quietly. "Her duties will be given to her. It is best to leave her alone now."

The three men left quietly, returning to the main hall. Obeying unvoiced instructions, they sat around the centre table in a triad formation and waited. It seemed to them that from another time and place soft music began to be heard. There came a stirring, a sensation of something preparing to happen.

From the sepulchres surrounding them, the long-lost fraternity of the Abbey of the Crown emerged, whole and garbed in their ceremonial robes. They stood still, waiting, then bowed low as another form appeared: a man of middle years wearing the insignia of an abbot. His mouth ran with blood and his hands were without fingers, but Gregor, Eamon, and Johnny rose to their feet and bowed. Abbot Nikos acknowledged their salute and, with his followers, formed a double line and walked into the Hall of Ceremony. The door closed behind them, and in the wall niches the forms collapsed into dust.

Time stopped and reached back into its own past. In the Hall of Ceremony, the Ritual of the Assumption of Rule was enacted. Those who waited were joined by Yannick and his sons, bearing small, carved boxes of yew. They reverently approached the burial niches and filled the boxes with the dust, then waited with the others. The door opened and Dagmar stood there, wearing the collar and nemyss of an abbess. In her hands she also held a box: It contained the tongue and the fingers of their former abbot. She laid the box on a small altar, and the others were placed round its base.

"It is time for you to leave," she said quietly. "I will remain, and those who have served through the years will take care of me until the new abbey is built. My thanks for your loving support."

Gregor, Eamon, and Johnny bowed and left, quietly followed by Yannick and his sons. Outside it was almost dawn, and the day rose on the newly restored abbey.

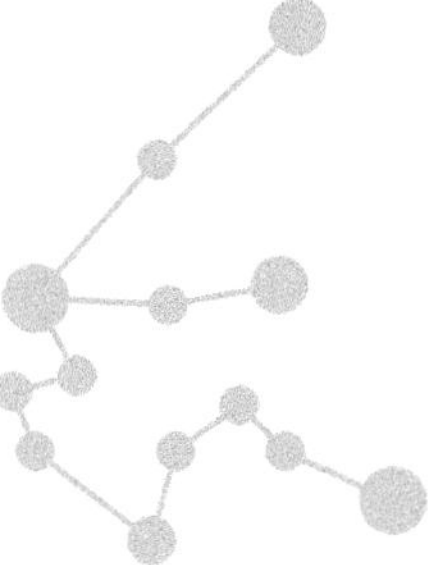

CHAPTER THIRTY-SEVEN

25 August, 1:00 a.m.
The Abbey of the Aeon

Abbot Gregor sighed and sat back in his chair. He took off his glasses and rubbed his eyes. Around the world, the abbeys were interacting and speaking with each other. Most were excited and full of questions and suppositions regarding the lost abbey.

The clock whirred and emitted a soft chime. Gregor stood up, stretched, and reached for the coffee pot. It was empty. He expressed his feelings in his mother tongue. At the same time, the door to his office opened to admit Maurice, armed with a mug of hot tea and an apple pie.

"Maurice, you are a miracle worker! How did you know I needed this?"

"What is the use of being telepathic if you don't make it work for you? You've had enough coffee, and the tea has a measure of Scotch in it. If you want my advice—you seldom take it anyway—you'll go to bed, and I'll have breakfast sent in to you around ten in the morning. Now go!"

Dutifully, Gregor went.

25 August, 10:00 p.m.
The Abbey of the Dawn

In the quietness of the Hall of a Thousand Candles, the frail abbot sat and communed with his spiritual masters.

"The next move will be hard for Johnny. I was against the idea of bringing Mara in so soon. I fear things are moving faster than we anticipated. Events in the world seem to have accelerated. Time grows short, and the Forerunner has much to learn. How goes the training of the new abbess?"

Abbot Nyang Darsip listened for his masters' reply.

"It goes well. She will be ready to receive the Indwelling of the Master at the time chosen. The planetary alignments are now moving into place. We await the Sirius ray of enlightenment at the specified time; the Abbey of the Snows keeps close watch."

The abbot said, "My physical form grows weaker. I would like to see Johnny one more time, if that is possible. I have grown very fond of him and his gift of laughter. He keeps in touch mentally with both his half-brother and with me. I humbly request permission to keep the connection after… after…my departure."

"That has already been arranged. Also, you will be with him at the final moment. He will need help to adjust after the usual trauma. It is anticipated he will adjust quickly. There are those among us who remember his somewhat spectacular entry into the upper realms with a lightness of heart."

The abbot smiled. "Ah, yes. The entry of the Fool into the archangelic realm was quite unexpected…I am grateful for your presence. May the Light surround us all." He sighed and slumped in his chair.

Chambha came with a shawl and covered the abbot, carried him to his quarters, then settled to sleep as he always did: at the foot of the master he loved. From the higher levels, a benediction of Light covered them both.

15 September, 8:00 p.m.
The penthouse, London

Things were different at the apartment. Colby had returned to the Abbey of the Winds, and Liam and Biff had moved to the apartment next to Florrie and Bucky so they could indulge their lifestyle without bothering the others. But Bucky and Florrie were happy as things were. Frank stayed with them but spent most of the time (often the nights) in his studio, composing. Old habits died hard, and somehow they were all drawn to the penthouse to sit, talk, and remember the times of struggle and hardship. Only Johnny was missing.

One night, after one of Florrie's homemade steak and kidney pie suppers, they all lay around finishing what was left of an apple pie and watching a *Tom and Jerry* cartoon. Florrie had been quiet all evening, just keeping the food and drink handy, when the sound of a key in the lock brought them fully alert. They were all there. Who else had a key?

The door opened, and a figure they knew walked in. "Hi, guys! It's good to see you again."

For a heart-stopping moment, they were silent. Then came the rush.

"Johnny!"

"What the hell are you doing here?"

"Johnny, where have you been all this time?"

"Johnny, are you going to stay now?"

"Johnny, have a beer to celebrate!"

"We've missed you so much!"

"Any chance of doing a gig? We can put one together, or a recording! Frank can throw some songs together."

They swarmed over him like ants over honey. Laughing, Johnny fended them off, slapping them on the back, hugging Florrie, and refusing the beer but accepting a mug of tea. He sat down on the old sofa.

"Good God, Bucky. It's time you bought new furniture. This thing still has the same lumps in it." He grabbed the apple pie Liam had been eating and wolfed it down. "Florrie, have you got anything left from dinner? I haven't eaten since this morning."

Florrie headed for the kitchen.

"It's so good to see you guys. Have you missed me?"

Liam laid a hand on Johnny's shoulder and told himself the wetness on his face was just sweat. "Missed you? Well, now you come to mention it, we thought you'd been taken off by the dose of clap you were sporting last time we were together." He paused and looked at him. "You're different now. Looks like you've been taking more care of yourself since you...er...left."

Lyle sat beside Johnny. "You *have* changed. It's as if there's a new Johnny inside you. How long can you stay?"

There was a pause in the gabble of voices. Then Biff said, "You're leaving, Johnny? We thought you were back for good."

Johnny shook his head. "No, Biff. I'm on my way to Chile. I leave the day after tomorrow. I took the opportunity to see you all again, but I can't stay."

Florrie put a tray with the last of the steak and kidney pie, garden peas, and roast potatoes on the side table and watched Johnny fall on it like a young wolf. Speaking over a mouthful of food, Johnny shook his head. "I have a different sort of job now, more like Lyle."

Biff stared at him in horror. "You got religion?" His voice rose almost to a soprano. "You're not going into a monastery, are you?" His words brought all conversation to a halt.

Florrie held her breath. Bucky closed his eyes and prayed silently. The others crowded round Johnny, looking at the dark suit, white shirt, the neat haircut.

"Not the kind you mean. Just a place where you can be quiet and learn about things you thought couldn't happen. The kind of place Colby is in."

Biff looked horrified. "You mean no booze? No sex?"

Johnny laughed and shook his head. "We can drink if we want to. And sex…Well, her name is Mara, and when the time is right, we will marry."

The questions came thick and fast until Florrie put her foot down. "You can talk tomorrow. But now, sleep!"

♬ ♩ ♫ ♪ ♬ ♪ ♫

Bucky held Florrie close as she sobbed uncontrollably. "Hush now, honey girl, or you'll wake him up. You don't want that. We'll not see him for a while after this visit, so let's enjoy every minute we are with him."

"I know, I know, but there'll be so few times now before it all ends. Why does it have to be him? Let someone else do it."

"You know what Gregor and Eamon told us: Everything has a reason and a purpose. And he accepted this life, this work, and its ending. Let's take the time offered to us and enjoy it."

He held Florrie close until, finally, she slept. Bucky remained awake, thinking and remembering, then made a decision. He closed his eyes and reached out to the one person he knew would tell him the truth.

"Sir, I promised I would only call you if it was important, and it is. We know what lies before Johnny and that it has to happen, but can you tell us how long we have with him?" Bucky pictured the message as a bird and set it free. Then and only then did he sleep.

The bird rose up through the levels of space and time and selected the level needed. Below it, the high peaks of the Land of Snows came into being. It reached out and called, and Chambha answered. He rose and gently woke the abbot. "Rinpoche, there is a message for you from Mr. Buckman. Shall I take it, or do you wish to speak with him?"

The abbot thought, then said, "For him to call directly, it will be important. I will take it, but you must enable him to transport."

With Chambha's help, the abbot rose and settled into a receptive mode. "Mr. Buckman, please relax and place yourself in the hands of my companion. He will bring you to me."

Silence filled the small room as it was lifted into a higher level. A ball of light emerged from the solar plexus of Chambha and hovered before the abbot. It took form, and Colin Buckman stood before him and bowed.

Colin Buckman's request was already in the abbot's mind as he raised his hand and blessed the visitor. "You have kept your word, Mr. Buckman, and I will keep mine. Five years was the allotted time given to the Forerunner, but he will leave behind a son, for the bloodline of the Forerunner will never fail. The child will carry the genetic makeup of the Forerunner, which will be passed on as it has been for the last twelve thousand years."

He paused, thought, then spoke again. "You have a good mind, Mr. Buckman, and a good heart to go with it. Circumstances will be arranged so that you and your wife will eventually become the child's guardians. My own passing is imminent, but after an interval of rest, I will be able to establish contact with you. Also, to my surprise, you have begun to understand the importance of the one called Tango as well as the closeness and meaning of their relationship. I will speak with you again, Mr. Buckman... before I pass. Be ready. Now return to your rest."

In London, Bucky murmured, "Bless you, Rinpoche," and slept.

But Johnny lay awake, pulling together his memories of this place, this room, this bed. He remembered leaving the party that night and walking in the drizzle of a London fog. He remembered Tze-Ring suddenly appearing out of the shadows, the motor yacht, the abbot, and the gut-wrenching fear when he realised he was being abducted. The memories came thick and fast: Murad holding him as he hung over the chasm; the peace of the Abbey of the Dawn; the endless lessons; the patience of Chambha; the wonder and the acceptance of knowing why he was there and what was to come. Eventually, Johnny closed his eyes, and he too slept.

The day dawned and brought with it the first gentle hint of autumn. It was still warm and sunny, but there was a scent in the air and a faint hint of colour in the trees. Unusually, everyone was up early and clamouring for Florrie's cheese and tomato omelettes. The coffee pot had been emptied and re-filled so many times that it blew a fuse and they had to borrow Ginny's.

Eight of them sat crammed round the table, all talking at once. Bucky and Johnny exchanged looks and smiled. It was so like the old days: the smell of burnt toast; Liam talking with his mouth full and waving his fork around; Biff taking the opportunity to pinch the rest of Liam's omelette; Lyle feeding his youngest; and Florrie in her element with her family round her. Bucky reached out quietly and laid a hand on Johnny's shoulder. They both knew this moment, this day, was a gift to be remembered and treasured.

The rest of the day was spent talking, sharing. Johnny showed them pictures of the Abbeys of the Dawn and the Aeon and a photo of Mara and himself together. He talked a little of his own "studies." Frank played some of the songs he had written for Tango and one he was currently writing. But they all avoided talk of the future.

Florrie kept close to Johnny. He was leaving early the next day, and everyone was going to the airport. Frank went to the piano and began to play "Mountains of Gold," and Johnny sang, just for them.

The next morning they all gathered at 5:30 a.m. for an early breakfast. Bucky had hired a minibus to take all of them to the airport. Johnny just had hand luggage; everything else had gone ahead. Florrie shooed them all downstairs but kept Johnny back for a few minutes. He stood looking round at the apartment, memorising it all. He held Florrie close. No words were said—none were needed. Then he handed her his key, and they went to join the others.

Heathrow was a madhouse as usual, but as Johnny was flying first class, things were easier. Once he was booked in, they went to have a last drink together. He had two hours to kill, but being without hold luggage made it a lot easier. His first flight would take him to Buenos Aires and an overnight stay. The next flight was to Santiago and another stay over, then a final flight to Ushuaia, where he would be met and taken to the Abbey of the Winds. He was not fond of flying, and the thought of almost four-and-a-half days of being airborne most of the time was not Johnny's idea of fun.

They spent two hours talking over old times and listening to the group's plans. They were in demand for background scores, thanks to Frank's compositions, and provided backing for singers. That and the fact that White Heat was still selling well had given all of them a sizeable income, and Bucky saw to it that they did not fritter it away. Johnny thanked him for that, and Bucky shrugged and blew his nose to cover the odd tear. "You're all my boys," he said. Florrie simply held his hand.

At 9:30 a.m. Johnny's flight was called and the last goodbyes were said. Then he made his way down the ramp and boarded. Once in his seat, he allowed his tears to fall quietly.

The group watched the plane take off. Then, in silence, they went home.

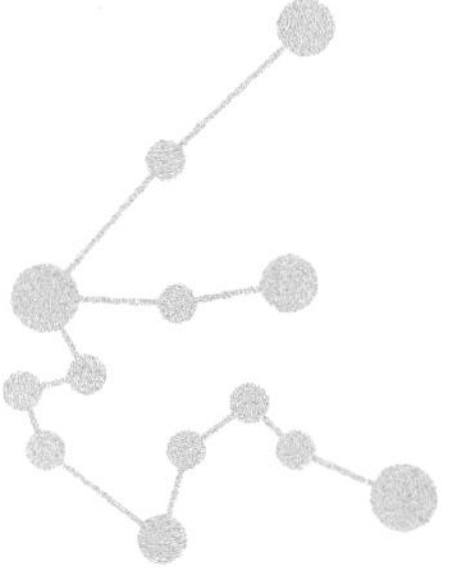

CHAPTER THIRTY-EIGHT

18 September, 2:00 a.m.
Buenos Aires

Even at two in the morning, Buenos Aires was as manic as it had been when White Heat had held a concert there years before. The crowds, the babble of voices at the packed airport, even the hotels were just as busy with people coming and going. The last time Johnny was here, fans had all but stripped the group of clothing. He smiled, remembering Tango and Liam taking off what was left of their shirts and throwing them into the crowd. Tango had added his shoes and socks as well. They had arrived at the hotel in just denims and their underwear.

This time, Johnny was alone and unnoticed. He booked into his hotel at 3:30 a.m., and having slept and eaten on the plane, he tried to adjust to the time difference while standing on the balcony. Then he felt a familiar mind touch.

"Johnny, my brother, is all well with you? Was the journey comfortable?"

"Ring, it's good to hear you! The flight was OK, and I booked in an hour ago. Are you alone?"

"No, Dad is here, and Mara."

The contact changed and Johnny felt the touch of his father, strong and loving.

"Hello, son. It's good to feel you. I won't keep you long; Mara is waiting. But I wanted you to know that Nyang Darsip of the Dawn is close to passing. Chambha will make a link between you when it happens. The abbot was insistent he spoke with you before going into the Light. He has a few weeks, a month at most. Word has gone out to all the abbeys. Mara wants to talk to you now. As she is not a telepath, Sister Amalia will act as her link. Tze-Ring and I will leave so you can talk together without us around. Goodbye, son. I'll be in touch when possible."

A new voice touched his senses, gentle in tone. "Greetings, Johnny. Mara will use my link with you, but I will close down my hearing, so it will be as if you were alone. This is unusual, and I can only hold the link in this way for a short while. Here is Mara."

There was silence, then a voice he knew.

"Mara, my love, it's good to hear you. I miss you so much."

"Johnny, oh Johnny, I miss you also! It's hard not to have you beside me. Gregor told me it will be months before we can be together, but he is hoping to send me to the Abbey of the Waters to meet you there."

For a few precious minutes, they shared feelings, thoughts, and desires. Then, all too soon, Sister Amalia sent a quiet message that the link was breaking up and they made their goodbyes. For a while Johnny sat, his head aching from the effort to keep the double link open and missing Mara's presence. Finally he went to bed, his mind full of things he had wanted to say, and fell asleep saying them in his heart.

Johnny slept deeply and woke late. His flight to Santiago was in the afternoon, so after lunch he did some shopping for Florrie, Mara, and Ginny. He'd post them from the abbey if it had access to a postal service—but from the pictures he'd seen, that might be a problem.

The flight was nerve-wracking, as the plane flew between peaks that looked far too close for his liking. Santiago itself was a smaller version of Buenos Aires, but the hotel was next to the airport and his room was much quieter.

As instructed, Johnny was up and dressed by 7:00 a.m. when a knock on the door heralded breakfast. It was wheeled in not by a waiter but by a tall, slim, copper-skinned man sporting a waist-length braid of jet-black hair. He wore a braided headband and matching wristlet, and his mental greeting reached out clear and bright. "Greetings! I am Wolf, and I am a shapeshifter."

Johnny responded in kind. "Greetings in Light, Wolf. I've heard a lot about your skills."

Wolf smiled. "The Abbey of the Winds is difficult to get to, so I will be your guide, but I am not a working member. I don't belong to any abbey in particular but travel between them as I am needed. Come, eat—we have a long journey ahead."

Cereal, eggs, ham, toast, along with fruit juice and coffee disappeared rapidly, with Wolf ordering an extra helping. "My talent needs and uses twice as many calories as a human body," he explained, adding Johnny's uneaten portion to his own plate. "Do you have a pilot's license?"

"No, I don't. I can drive most things, but flying is something I never had time to learn. Do I need one?"

"No. Many of us fly, but your power is something we do not have."

Johnny shrugged. "It feels as if I don't really have a power beyond telepathy and moving things."

Wolf buttered the last bit of toast. "My own talent is rare, but yours is even more so. Only once in an age is one born to carry the power of a proclaimer. Come, it's time to leave. There's a long day ahead."

At the airport Wolf drove into the area where private planes were kept and serviced and dealt with the paperwork. Then he led the way to where a fuelled Cirrus SR22 was waiting. The luggage was loaded, and Johnny climbed in while Wolf checked the tyres and talked to the engineer. Satisfied his flight plan was verified, Wolf signed the papers, shook hands with the engineer, and climbed into the pilot's seat. Thirty minutes later, they lifted into a clear blue sky.

"It's good weather most of the way. Might be bumpy later on, and Torres del Paine can get misty. If I need to re-fuel I'll call ahead to Puerto Eden, but I hope to get there without that. Then a short helicopter flight to the abbey."

Johnny sighed. "This is as hard to get to as the Abbey of the Dawn."

Wolf laughed. "No, the hardest is the Abbey of the Snows. It can take a week to get there. Anyway, make sure to look down. There are few sights more breath-taking than flying over the islands of Chile."

Silence prevailed as Johnny took in the scenery below them. The entire country seemed to be made of islands in different sizes, shapes, and types. Some were populated, others almost empty. Farmland, forest, mountains, and lakes passed below them, and Johnny was spellbound by the diversity. Wolf pointed out major cities and wildlife preserves as they flew south, but the weather began to close in and he had his hands full keeping the aircraft aloft and hoping they could make their destination safely.

An hour later than planned, they landed as the fog rolled in. "I gather we won't make it to the abbey tonight," said Johnny, shouldering his bag.

Wolf shrugged. "This is typical weather; it changes from one moment to the next. Tomorrow it may be worse or completely clear. The hotel here is small but OK, so let's get going. I'm hungry."

Dinner for three was ordered, two of them for Wolf. Johnny watched as his companion ate everything but the plates! "No wonder you keep moving from abbey to abbey. Keeping you in food must cost a bomb. Have you always eaten like this?"

Wolf drained his third bottle of water and sat back with a sigh. "Until I reached twelve, I was just a hungry kid. Then, overnight, I was eating everything in sight. My Watcher foster parents knew it would happen and prepared me. I had shifted partially before, but only if I was ill or had an accident, like the time I broke my arm or got a concussion falling out of a tree.

"On my fourteenth birthday, my father allowed me a small glass of wine. I'd never had alcohol before, and it triggered a full shift. Boy, that was *bad*. It was like being torn apart. My mother cried, and my father held her back from touching me. I had to go through it alone. Then Dad opened the door and I ran, and ran, and ran.

"We lived way out of town, but there was a wolf pack some sixty miles north. It took me a week to get there. I had to learn to hunt, to eat the catch raw, to avoid humans. By the time I found the pack, I was almost starving. Then I had to persuade them to accept me. They smelt the human part, so I had to fight to belong. I lived with the pack for two years, learning about that part of myself. But my foster parents had prepared me well. After two years with the pack, I went back home and had to learn to be human again. At eighteen I went to the Abbey of the Waters and from there to college and university, majoring in anthropology. Then I returned to the abbeys, where I am happiest. It is easier to live with those who accept me, where I can be useful, and it's a good life. But come, let's turn in. If the weather is clear, I'd like to get off early. It's only a thirty minute flight by copter, and the helipad is on abbey land."

♬ ♩ ♫ ♪ ♬ ♪ ♫

Johnny woke early to find the other bed was already empty. The sound of the shower and a Beatles song, belted out in a rich baritone, told him Wolf was up and about. He headed for the bathroom and stopped dead, then doubled up with laughter. The sight of a naked guy wearing a women's bath cap was too much.

Totally unconcerned, a grinning Wolf turned off the shower and reached for a towel. "I wear my hair in the way of my tradition, but it takes ages to dry, so when I'm in a hurry I cover it up."

Still mother-naked, Wolf ambled into the bedroom and called for breakfast to be ready in half an hour. Johnny showered and shaved, and together they went down to breakfast. Judging by the amount of food provided, Wolf was a frequent visitor.

As they ate, Wolf read the weather forecast passed to him by the waiter. "Looks like it's clearing. With luck we could take off before lunchtime." He waved his fork in Johnny's direction. "You know, you're the first person in a long time that hasn't asked me personal questions."

Johnny went red. "Well, it's not because I didn't want to, but I felt it would be intrusive. I guessed it would be something you do get asked, so… I didn't."

Wolf sat back and looked at him. "They all want to know how it happens, how it feels, does it hurt. I was once asked if I had trouble with fleas!"

Johnny choked on his coffee, then grinned and asked, "Do you?"

Wolf, with a perfectly straight face, said, "No, I always carry a can of repellent with me!"

They both rocked with laughter, then gathered up their luggage, thanked the staff, and left for the airport.

♬ ♩ ♫ ♪ ♬ ♪ ♫

The copter landed with a gentle bump. Wolf switched off the controls and turned. "Welcome to the Winds, Johnny. This will be home for the next few months."

A tall, blonde-haired figure came running across the strip and hauled Wolf out of his seat.

"About bloody time you got here, mate! What kept you?"

Wolf thumbed over his shoulder. "Blame him. I had to drag him out of the local bawdy house!" He grinned at Johnny's red face. "Johnny, meet Brother Carl. He's from your neck of the woods: London."

The newcomer slapped him on the back and shook his hand. "It'll be great to hear what's going on in the Big Smoke." Carl grabbed the baggage and led the way to a Jeep. "You coming, Wolf?"

"I'll check the engine first. It was sounding a bit rough. See you later, Johnny."

After a twenty-minute drive at breakneck speed along a road bordering a spectacular lake, Johnny got his first look at the abbey. "My God. It's a backdrop of *Gone with the Wind*."

Carl laughed at his reaction. "Actually, it's less than one hundred years old. Some guy from the US bought the land and built this replica of a colonial mansion. Then he went bust and it was put up for sale, but it's too far from civilisation and no one wanted it. Our lot bought it about fifty years ago, and it took five years to make it habitable. Its location is just right for us, and as I work with the elemental powers, mainly earth and water, it's great for me."

He drew up at the imposing front door. "Let's get you in. Abbot Jorje insisted you have time to rest and adjust to the atmosphere here for an hour or so. Then you will meet everyone and dinner will be served. Afterwards, coffee, a little wine and conversation, then sleep."

He led Johnny into a spacious hallway and up a flight of stairs. At the end of the corridor Carl showed him into a room fitted as both a workplace and a sitting room; leading out of it was a bedroom and bathroom. "There's a house phone that connects to the library, kitchen, the abbot, of course, and as you get to know everyone, you can add their room numbers. Your belongings have arrived and been put away. It will take a day or so for you to adjust to the atmosphere here; it can get heavy at times. So, settle in. You'll find tea, coffee, and sandwiches over there. Rest up, and I'll be back in a few hours. Dinner is at eight. Welcome, Johnny. It's good to have you here." Carl laid a warm hand on Johnny's shoulder and then left.

Johnny stood for a few minutes, then went to look out of the large window that opened onto a small balcony. A range of blue-grey mountains loomed over the lake. Their silence was like a physical presence, enveloping everything in a protective embrace. It brought back memories of the Abbey of the Dawn, and Johnny reached out to his first teacher, wanting to share the experience with him.

The link was weak and faint. Then Johnny felt the sustaining strength of Chambha adding his power to that of the abbot's. Johnny heard the abbot say, "It holds great promise for you, my son. It is here that you will receive the sustaining Power of the Forerunner line. I will endeavour to maintain my hold on life to be with you at that moment."

Johnny replied, "Rinpoche, beloved teacher, I offer my own power to assist you."

Chambha's link came back to him. "No, Johnny, you will need all your own strength at that moment. I will see to his needs at that time. He sleeps now. Be blessed, Forerunner."

The link faded, and Johnny was alone. He looked round. His clothes had been put away, his books shelved, even his photos and personal belongings had been laid out. So much effort had been made to make him feel welcome. Suddenly, he was desperately tired and lay down on the bed. Within seconds he was asleep.

In the Hall of Ceremony, Abbot Jorje Ortega de Najera gently manoeuvred Johnny's mind into a level of energy replacement and turned to Sister Eugénie. "Keep him at this level for at least two hours. He has travelled far, and his body needs to adjust."

The healer nodded. "I will remain linked to him until he wakes."

Abbot Jorje acknowledged the central altar with a bow of the head and left. The task before him carried great responsibility. It was one thing to prepare oneself for admittance to a high-level spiritual power; it was quite another to teach a stranger to do the same thing. But there was something about this young man that spoke of a readiness to accept the challenge ahead.

The abbot made his way to his own room and prepared to make contact with his spiritual advisors. He needed to find a way to gently unlock Johnny's human persona and allow entrance to the Power of the Forerunner.

♬ ♩ ♫ ♪ ♬ ♪ ♫

Johnny woke to find the bedside lamp lit and the scent of lavender on the air. A woollen robe of silver-grey had been laid on the sofa, together with a matching pair of shoes in soft leather. A deep red cord lay coiled on the table. He rose and stretched, noticing the curtains had been drawn, and looked at his watch. Quarter past seven. Time for a quick shower and shave before dinner.

A knock at the door came as Johnny was tying the cord round his waist, and he called "Come in" as he pulled on the leather shoes and smoothed the hair back from his face.

The tall, strongly built, smiling man who entered greeted him with a jovial "How are you feeling? Are you hungry yet?" His accent spoke of his Trinidad birth. "My name is Roger. Welcome to the Winds, Johnny. Dinner will be on the table in ten minutes, and it's always best to get there first if you want a good choice, so let's go!" He landed a slap on Johnny's back that nearly floored him.

"Oops, sorry! I keep forgetting you lot are so delicate." He grinned down from his imposing six feet four inches, exposing a set of teeth any crocodile would have envied. Like all his countrymen, Roger had the gift of laughter, and he reminded Johnny of Lyle. As they went down to the dining hall, Roger regaled him with the menu about to be put before him. "There's always at least two choices, often three—we're a mixed lot here. Of course, there's always fish; you can't get away from it here. But we only have one vegetarian. Give me a steak any day. Ah, here we are!"

He paused at a pair of double doors and, with a flourish, flung them open with a loud "Ladies and gentlemen, I give you…the one and only Johnny Nova…in person!"

Johnny gasped as a chorus of voices sang out the opening lines of one of the group's old hits.

Roger put an arm the size of a small tree trunk round his shoulders. "Blame Carl. He is a big fan of White Heat, as we all know from hearing your CDs played time after time. Come and meet the members of the Abbey of the Winds.

"Our esteemed and much-loved Abbot Jorje and Mother Simone. This is Emilio, and here's Claudio. Tanaka…Watch him, he's a telepath in at least eight languages. Carl you already know. Sisters Maria Teresa and Eugénie. Last but never least, Dylan from Wales. He can sing every song you have ever recorded. The one already at the table is of course Wolf, already halfway through the menu."

The abbot came forward, laughing. "You must forgive the boisterous introduction. We are happy you are here with us, but we do have a serious side. Come, sit beside me, away from Wolf, who will eat your dinner as well as his unless you are with me."

Wolf grinned and waved a drumstick in his direction.

The menu was the equal of Maurice's best efforts at the Aeon, and Johnny tucked into roast chicken, sautéed potatoes, and an assortment of greens. A robust red wine made locally added to the feeling of a celebration. A selection of cheeses followed, and dinner was completed by a pie of local fruits garnished with fresh cream. Finally even Wolf had had enough.

A communal hall with a large fireplace seemed to be part of all the abbeys, and the Winds was no exception. Everyone settled down on chairs, cushions, stools, and sofas as the group mind of the abbey wrapped gently round Johnny, making him part of them. Like all secluded groups, they were hungry for news, and Johnny shared with them the excitement of finding the Lost Abbey and what had taken place there. As one who had been a part of the discovery, his account was listened to with rapt attention. Finally the fire burned low and the abbot sent everyone to bed, the exception being the watcher who was changed every night and silently patrolled the abbey until dawn. Wolf had volunteered, knowing the others would be worn out with excitement.

Roger escorted Johnny to his door and told him that for the next few days he was allowed to sleep until eight, and a breakfast tray would be outside his door. The abbot would like to speak with him at half past nine.

Johnny was asleep within minutes of his head hitting the pillow, not even waking when Wolf checked on him during the night.

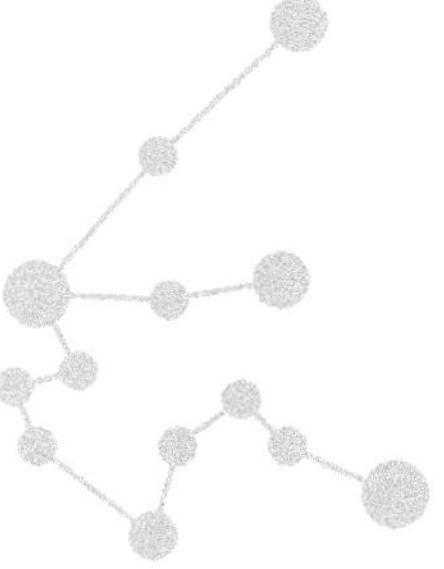

CHAPTER THIRTY-NINE

22 September, 9:28 a.m.
The Abbey of the Winds

At 9:28 a.m., Johnny knocked on the door of the abbot's study and waited.

"*Adelante, por favour.*"[17]

Johnny opened the door and entered a large room furnished as an office but with handmade tapestries decorating the few walls not filled with books. The abbot rose and came to him with hands outstretched.

"*Buenos días.* Did you sleep well, Juanito?" Jorje drew him to a pair of easy chairs with a small table between them. "Have you had breakfast?"

"Yes, thank you. I slept better than I thought I would. After noisy hotels and airports for days on end, the silence was wonderful. But now I am ready to begin whatever I need to do."

"We will take it slowly for a few more days. The atmosphere here has many layers. Some are energetic; others need us to slow down and experience what is being displayed or shown to us. You will find many similarities to the Abbey of the Dawn. I have made contact with Abbot Nyang

17. "Go ahead, please."

already." He paused and drew a deep breath. "He is close to passing, and I will miss his strength and his..." He sought for a word, but could only find the obvious one. "His love. He will always be close to my heart. He will always be a part of those privileged to know him.

"I have spoken with him many times in the past year, and he has advised me on how to deal with this part of your training. It will of course be taken in stages. It will be demanding, so between times you must rest. I know you are aware of your destiny and have accepted it."

Johnny nodded.

The abbot rose, walked to the window, and stood looking out over the lake. He was silent for a few moments, then turned and came back and sat below Johnny, taking Johnny's hands in his.

"You take my breath away. You are so calm, so accepting. In the flower of youth, you have chosen to make an offering few would even contemplate. To face it, to be at peace with it..."

Something stirred deep within Johnny, not yet fully awakened but filled with compassion for the man at his feet. He put a hand on the bent head and a voice that was not his spoke quietly. "Such a sacrifice is not made by one person, but by many. Everyone in every abbey shares the wonder of the event. Everyone needs to allow this to happen, to accept the need for it. This makes it a communal sacrifice. You all share in its power and glory. Also, it is not only the Forerunner who makes the offer. The one who delivers the blow and the one who comes after will make the same sacrifice. Great events need great power to manifest. Nothing is greater than the advent of a new age, and this one is of great significance."

The abbot looked up, startled at the change of voice and the sudden surge of power. What wore Johnny's likeness stood and raised him to his feet.

The voice continued, "We will work together to open the Gates of the Middle Pillar. I also must prepare. It has been long since I used a human form, and it will need effort on my part, as it will need effort on his and on all who share in this undertaking. You will find him easy to work with. I must leave—he is unused to holding my energy for more than a few moments. Be blessed in all you achieve."

The door burst open to admit Roger and Carl, both looking ready to deal with an intruder. Roger grabbed Johnny as he fell, and Carl assisted the abbot to a chair.

Tanaka appeared in the doorway. "I picked up a huge burst of energy. What is going on? It wasn't human."

Roger sat Johnny down in a chair and placed his hands over his heart, adjusting its beat. "His energy levels are low, Carl. How is the abbot?"

"He's OK, just a bit drained. Johnny OK?"

"Yeah…Tan, did you pick up what was going on?"

"Yes, it was a burst of energy from at least level six or seven. It only lasted about four or five minutes. More than that, they would both have been unconscious. If this is going to happen a lot, I'll put in for a leave."

"It was amazing, but keep it to ourselves. We don't want to scare the others."

The abbot cleared his throat and sipped at the brandy Carl handed him. "Is Johnny all right?"

"Yes, sir, I am all right." Johnny stood up and went to him. "My apologies, sir. I had no idea it would happen. I usually can feel it when it's about to come in."

All four of them stared at him.

Jorje wiped the sweat from his forehead. "Does it happen often?"

"No, sir. But lately it's happened several times without warning." Johnny looked at him and said hopefully, "Do you think I might go and lie down for a while? I feel a bit shaky."

The abbot nodded. "Good idea, Johnny. I will see you at lunch."

Carl offered to see him back to his room.

The abbot got to his feet a little shakily. "From what I was told, this will happen a lot more. He is closer to the moment of Indwelling than was thought." He turned to the Brothers. "We have taken on a huge responsibility. The next few months will be interesting! Roger, order some more brandy. We, or I, may need it. I will follow Johnny's example and lie down. Touching that level of power is not something I plan to do often."

Abbot Jorje headed unsteadily to his bedroom, leaving Roger and Carl to explain the sudden surge of power that had filled the abbey. It left the cook planning a cold luncheon while the electrical wiring in his kitchen was checked over and some of it was replaced. The power surge had affected the entire abbey in various ways. They were all used to such power flows, but this had been extreme.

Some miles away, Ulrika stopped her car and looked at her passenger, an unspoken question in her eyes. The young woman beside her nodded. "Drive faster. I am needed."

22 September, 12:00 p.m.
Johnny's room at the Abbey of the Winds

Johnny stood and watched Mara arranging flowers in a crystal vase. As she tucked each one into place, she sang softly to herself. She took the last stem and kissed it. "Take my kiss and give it to Johnny, and tell him I love him."

Mara placed the vase in the window and looked out. The garden below was deep in shadows, and the full moon made her slow and stately way across the sky. Mara looked at the mountains dozing under their blanket of night clouds. "Wherever you are, dear one, feel my love surrounding you. In my heart, I'm holding you close. Feel me, touch me, hear my voice." She ran her hand over her breast and down over her belly and pressed lightly.

Johnny, linked to Mara's thoughts, followed her hand, feeling the warmth, the softness, the roundness...He stopped. Roundness, warmth, growth. A tiny shape that, even as he drew in his breath, he knew, linked with, recognized, and loved. A child. His child. Their child. A living, breathing entity that would carry the line of the Forerunner into the future had entered into life.

With a sudden jerk, Johnny woke from his journey. His physical self was thousands of miles away, but he knew beyond any doubt that back at the Aeon Mara was pregnant with their child. He threw back the coverlet and jumped to his feet, his heart racing, his whole body filled with a new kind of joy, a feeling he'd never felt before, never known before, never dreamed of until this one precious moment. He wanted to run, wanted to find someone to tell, wanted to sing, dance, shout...

"It's always like that. The sheer joy of it, the promise, the hope and the fear, the doubt—the sudden responsibility. But you will cope."

Johnny turned. A woman stood looking out the window. She was tall and slim, with a braid of black hair draped over her shoulder. She turned to face him, her coffee-coloured skin thrown into relief against the pale cream of her robe. The woman held out her hand to Johnny and smiled.

The room seemed to light up around Johnny. He took the woman's hand in his and felt the surge of power rush through him. He sank to his knees and began to shake, then looked up at her, a question forming on his lips, but she forestalled him.

"We meet at last, Johnny Burke. I am Pacia, the Teacher. And you are my Forerunner.

"Johnny, don't kneel to me. Like you, I have not yet come into my full power—that is something we will do together. You have had two big surprises in a short time, so let's just sit together and allow everything to fall into place."

Pacia held on to Johnny's hand, and they sat looking out over the lake towards the mountains. Johnny felt the warm strength of her thoughts flow into him and allowed his own to reciprocate. Twin powers rose from their base chakras, illuminating each sphere in turn as they ascended the spinal channel and emerged from the lotus in a burst of light. Information passed between them at a speed beyond imagining.

Messages flashed from mind to mind throughout the abbey. Everyone stopped what they were doing and made for the Hall of Ceremony. Obeying silent instructions, they donned their robes and prepared the sacred space. Candles were lit and incenses prepared. Throughout all seven abbeys, the news went forth.

In the Abbey of the Dawn, the Hall of a Thousand Candles blazed with light. Chambha carried the abbot in and gently placed him in his chair, then stood behind him and summoned his power of projection. Enclosing the abbot within its sphere, Chambha took a breath and projected the image across time and space to the Abbey of the Winds. Each abbey in turn tuned in to what was happening and used their respective talents to join in the event. Those with the ability helped those who were weaker, and slowly the Hall of the Winds filled with forms of light and shade.

Into the prepared space came the Teacher and the Forerunner. They paced slowly to the altar, took their places on each side of it, and laid their hands on its surface. Above them a sphere of indigo light manifested. Johnny mentally reached for it, and in his hands it turned into a pure-white dove. Slowly, Johnny lowered it to just above Pacia's head. In a language no one had spoken for a thousand years, he asked her a question.

Pacia held her breath for a moment, then answered in a steady voice. The dove folded its wings and burrowed deep into Pacia's prime chakra. She stiffened, and her whole body became incandescent.

Now a sphere of violet light appeared over the head of the Forerunner, and taking the form of a flame it descended, enveloping him completely.

The roof of the Hall became opaque and opened up. A third light of silver manifested. A voice that throbbed with power spoke.

"One to prepare the way. One to give the teaching. One to accept the blame."

The three sources of energy—indigo, violet, and silver—filled the sacred space with an almost unbearable burst of power. It poured itself into the two chakras, and both forms became incandescent. Pacia and Johnny jerked and writhed as if in agony and became forms of pure elemental fire. Those watching cried out and hid their eyes and faces from the unbelievable power filling the Hall. With the light came sound—it could not be called a voice, but held pure sound—a sound heard only once in every age: *Always there must be three.*

In a studio in New York, the electricity failed, and Tango's voice faltered and stopped. He heard from afar a voice asking if he would accept the blame, and he knew without any doubt that this was why he'd been born: to accept the blame.

Tango bowed his head and heard Johnny's voice.

"Now it begins..."

YEAR FOUR

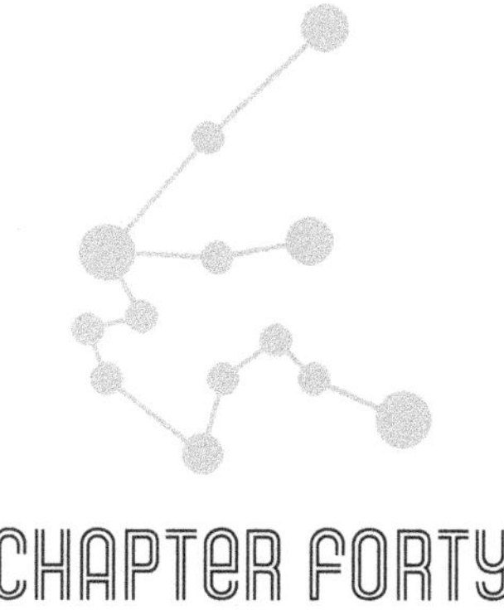

CHAPTER FORTY

9 October, 2:00 p.m.
The London Palladium, stage front

The rehearsal for the Royal Variety Performance was in full swing, though there were still six weeks to go. Celebrities, show girls, dancers, and musicians had spread out over the auditorium in various stages of exhaustion. A constant stream of helpers, costumiers, makeup artists, secretaries, and hangers-on dodged the fast food suppliers trying to keep up with the demands of the weary performers.

At the moment, a group of frustrated engineers were trying to get the mobile stage to actually move. It had come to a grinding halt halfway down, leaving Lyle, White Heat's drummer, using words unbecoming to a practising Christian. The rest of the group helped to remove the extensive drum kit so the engineers could get under the base.

The show's compère was an old hand. He lit his fifth cigarette and sat with Bucky, their legs hanging over the footlights. Screams, shouts, threats, and hysterical stars were all part of their world. Nine hundred and ninety-nine point nine times out of a thousand, it all came right.

Twenty minutes later, a broken roller had been replaced and Lyle was back in his seat. The stage manager had stopped screaming, and White Heat were ready to rehearse.

Bucky looked them over and mentally patted himself on the back. Their new get-up looked good: white and silver with a red flame pattern climbing the outer seam of the trousers and replicated on the sleeves of the skin-tight shirts open to the waist. Shoe and belt buckles flashed and glittered in the stage lights as White Heat swung into their latest hit, "Burning Up the Tracks."

Colby had returned for the Royal Variety Performance, and the Abbey of the Winds resigned themselves to the fact that every now and then they would lose him to the lure of the footlights. They followed the new track with "San Francisco Blues," vocalised by Colby and Liam, and ended with Lyle's superb rendering of "Talking Drums." The timing was good and ended exactly on the time allowed. The next act was beginning to get their things together when there was a yell from the front of house.

"Bucky, hold it!"

All heads turned as a familiar figure came down the centre aisle. Bucky shaded the lights with his hand, and his jaw dropped. "Tango?"

"That's me. Great to see you, Bucko. The boys too." He waved a hand in their direction. "Hi."

Bucky went forward and held out his hand to haul the newcomer over the footlights. "The studio said you couldn't get to rehearsals because of the filming schedule."

Tango grinned. "There was a hitch in the dates and I have a forty-eight-hour window, so I grabbed a plane. I fly out again tomorrow night. So, any chance we could try out the new number here and now?"

The compère came forward, hand outstretched. "Tango Garrett, it's good to meet you. Jesus, this is great! You came all this way just to do one rehearsal?" The ever-ready reporters were already calling their editors.

Tango laughed. "For Bucky and the boys, nothing is too much trouble. Frank wrote this number specially for me, so I'm returning the favour. Shall we get on with it? Unless you need to do something else."

The stage manager was already rearranging the roster. "Hey, you're the star of the show, the top billing. You want it, it's yours."

Tango strolled to centre stage and looked round. Years ago he'd dreamed of singing here—something Johnny had never done. Now *he*, Tango Garrett, was top of the bill, and not just any bill: the Royal Variety Performance.

Frank tapped his shoulder. "We're ready, Tango."

Tango looked round, saw the members of White Heat waiting, and went over and offered his hand to each of them. "It's great to sing with you again. Thank you. I know you'd much rather it was Johnny doing this. All I can say is let's do it for him, OK?"

For a brief moment, something momentous hung in the balance. Then Lyle picked up his sticks. "Let's go, boys! This one's for Johnny." He led them in with a riff that flowed like hot chocolate.

Tango fitted the head mic. He turned to face the expectant crowd and took a breath.

Why did I lose you? Was it something I said?
I've tried to remember, going back in my head
The world seems so grey now that you are not here
I'm lost and alone now, my heart full of fear

I reach out to touch you but no one is there
Your voice fills my dreams. When I wake you're not there
The sound of your laughter will fade with the years
The warmth of your smile and the shine of your tears

Oh, why did I lose you? Did I do something wrong?
Time stretches before me, so lonely and long
Your things still surround me; I can't let them go
Your scent on my pillow, your morning hello

Oh, why did you leave me? Why couldn't you stay?
I'll leave you this rose, love, and I'll walk away
To a life full of dreams that will never come true
And a heart lying broken and alone there with you

Tango held the top note, letting it grow softer and finally die away into silence. A silence that held and held, and then came the roar of applause as the entire theatre exploded. The crews stood, filling the auditorium. Frank bowed his head and gave thanks for the song he had written and the man who had just touched the heart of everyone within hearing. Both the song and the man would be remembered, but for different things and in different ways. Deep inside him, something grew and blossomed.

Far, far away, Johnny paused, listened, and sent back a wave of love, respect, and a closeness that included Tango.

13 October, 4:00 p.m.
The Abbey of the Dawn

The Hall of a Thousand Candles had been dimmed. At the abbot's request, a low couch had been placed at the foot of Tara's statue, where he would spend his last hours. Tze-Ring, Lea, Murad, and the ever-present and faithful Chambha waited and watched as Abbot Nyang slowly and painfully drew each breath. The abbey members came and went, seeing to their daily chores, but sparing what time they could to take their turn in the vigil.

For the last two days, he had only spoken twice, each time the same words: "Is he here?" The answer was, "Not yet, but he will come."

In the early evening of the third day, Chambha raised his head. Tze-Ring woke from his exhausted sleep, and word went through the abbey. "He comes."

They gathered to greet Johnny as his Body of Light crossed the snowy heights and the doors opened to his command. They remembered the sullen, disoriented, frightened young man who had caused so much trouble and the well-balanced, fun-loving, and mischievous individual he had become. Who now entered the Hall was a priest of high rank in full command of his power.

Johnny knelt beside the abbot, and the old man's eyes lit up. Chambha lifted the old man's hand and placed it on the head of the Forerunner.

"Son of my spirit, I give thanks for your existence and for your destiny. Until you entered my life, I confess it had, without my knowing, become… shall we say…dull. Your time with us brought laughter to the Abbey of the Dawn. You were a trial at first, but when you left, you were missed. Now you are close to the summit of your powers. I bless you in the work to come and in its ending, and I will be with you in that time. My own time draws to a close, but it has been a privilege to have been one of your teachers. After a period of rest and reflection, I hope to make contact from the higher levels."

Johnny reached out mentally, and as he did so, he took on the form of the clown with which he had once surprised the angelic world. He wrapped his arms round the old man, letting his love and respect for him manifest as power.

The abbot gave a shaky laugh. "Ah, Johnny, it is good to have known you. Farewell, my son, for now."

Suddenly Johnny and those present were alone. He wept and joined with his own kind throughout the world to bear witness as the brilliantly coloured spirit left its outworn form and became one with the Light.

20 November, 6:30 p.m.
London

London was buzzing. Its streets, hotels, restaurants, and shops were thronged. In just one week, two big events were taking place within days of each other: the Royal Variety Performance and the much-publicised premiere of *The Student Prince* with its star, Tango Garrett. Both events would be attended by royalty and had the whole city in a frenzy. Sales of the film's CD had rocketed and achieved platinum status within days. Predictions of Oscar awards for the film, the score, and its star were already rife.

Tango was torn in two ways. During the day he drank it all in with a hunger for acknowledgement that had been starved since childhood, but at night he was haunted by memories of withholding his grandmother's heart pills, and in dreams often found himself standing by a flower-starred mound of earth in a lonely garden. He'd refused to sell the house, and when he could, he visited the lonely grave and kept it planted with flowers and watered with tears.

Tango's face in lights towered over Piccadilly Circus, smiled out from magazine covers and posters, and teenagers slept on pillows embellished with his portrait. His clothes, aftershave, preferences in food and drink, and his every word were copied and lauded. But in one way, he'd not changed: To the surprise of the group, he insisted on using them as a backing whenever possible and relied on Frank for his "special" songs. So far, three of them had reached the top ten, and he was the first singer to hold all three top places at the same time.

Bucky kept peace in the group by pointing out that it kept them employed and enabled them to report on Tango's movements. Not that he went out of his way to meet them…Only at rehearsals or a one-on-one rehearsal with Frank. Tango had his own manager, an Italian, Desi Agostini, who managed his contracts with the skill of Machiavelli and the temperament of a Rottweiler. Tango only dealt with Bucky as the speaker for the group when they were needed.

Now the Royal Variety Performance was just hours away and performers were making last-minute adjustments to their acts, music, costumes, and—in the case of the Americans—decisions whether to curtsey, bow, or shake hands. A Chinese acrobatic group was practising their English, and a Lithuanian tenor sat in a corner of the wings trying desperately to remember the words of an aria he'd sung hundreds of times and had now forgotten.

The members of White Heat, who were backing Tango as well as doing their own piece, were totally unconcerned. They were playing poker in a dressing room shared with the Chinese acrobats. Colby, whose maternal grandmother hailed from Shanghai, was trying out his Mandarin, to their amusement. A voice over the intercom brought all the heads up.

"One hour and thirty minutes to go. Count down to overture will begin on the hour. Good luck everyone."

At ten minutes to eight, the royal family entered their box and the audience stood for the national anthem. Applause followed and was acknowledged. Then the orchestra swung into the overture, a pastiche of a top-of-the-charts parade that, to the glee of White Heat, included two of their own repertoire. The compère came on, and having softened up the audience and made the royals laugh, he introduced the first act.

In the star's dressing room, Tango walked up and down. This was his big moment, just him and no one else, but he was trapped in his memories. *That dirty little Garrett brat…He don't look as if 'e'd 'ad a wash in weeks. My Amy said she 'ad ter sit next to 'im in school and 'e smelt summfink awful. T'aint right ter let a kid run loose like that. Council should do summat.*

Tango looked in the mirror at his impeccably dressed reflection and made himself a promise: As soon as he had some time free, he'd take a trip down to Cardiff and look up some of his old school "pals." He pondered for a moment. Should he take the Lamborghini or go down in a chauffeured Rolls?

Lounging in an armchair, Desi smiled. He could use those old hurts to great effect. To open old wounds and fuel the desire to hurt back would be amusing and could draw his prize deeper into the trap. Meanwhile, he could watch these pathetic humans amuse themselves.

♬ ♩ ♫ ♪ ♬ ♪ ♫

The evening wore on as act after act offered their skills and were applauded. White Heat closed the first half having received tumultuous applause, and to their delight and astonishment, they received a request for a repeat of "Burning Up the Tracks" from the Royal Box. The equerry who delivered the request also asked if they would consider a private engagement for a party at the Royal Lodge next year, leaving the group stunned and elated.

The second half began with a dance routine followed by the usual array of comedy acts interspersed with singers of varying quality and talent. Finally the compère called for silence and began to introduce the top of the bill.

"Your Majesty, Your Royal Highness, ladies and gentlemen. In a few days we will see the premiere of the long-awaited remake of *The Student Prince*. Tonight we are proud and pleased to welcome the star of the film, the one and only Tango Garrett."

Applause broke out and continued as Tango walked onto the stage and bowed to the Royal Box. The compère shook his hand and turned to the audience with a grin. "Girls, he's even better looking close up than on-screen." There were cheers from the audience, and he turned back to the singer. "Tell me, Tango, how does it feel to be the number one pin-up? Maybe you could give me some tips."

Having been primed as to the answers needed, Tango looked the compère up and down and shook his head, saying, "Maybe with plastic surgery?" Then added off the cuff, "But then, you don't have the voice."

The compère gave him a dirty look and turned to the audience. "Shall we let him sing?" A resounding *yes* rolled back, and the compère left the stage to Tango, who turned to face the Royal Box and placed a hand on his heart.

"This is my favourite song in the film, and it is close to my heart. Tonight, with the greatest respect, I dedicate it to Your Majesty."

It was a masterly piece of crowd manipulation, and they loved it. All over the theatre, people began to rise and turned to the Royal Box. Tango nodded to the conductor. The music began, and with all the skill he possessed, Tango sang an operetta from *The Student Prince.*

As he sang, a part of him seemed to stand alone. Tango knew no matter what the future held, this night was his. For a brief space of time, he was everything he could have been, always had been, always would be. In this moment he lived the lifetime of love and acceptance he'd never known.

As the last note died away, there was a moment of silence. Then the theatre went mad. People stood and cheered both the song and the singer. In the Royal Box, a gracious head was inclined and a hand raised in acceptance.

It took a while for the tumult to die down. Then Tango stepped forward. "Thank you! Tonight I have a new song, written by my good friend Frank Saunders." He turned to the wings and gestured and an uncomfortable Frank walked on, bowed to the Royal Box, then went to the Concert Grand that had been wheeled into place.

Tango continued, "Frank has written the background score for *The Student Prince* and many of my own songs. Tonight you will hear his latest—and his best—song, 'Why Did You Leave Me?'" He went to stand by the piano and, as Frank led the orchestra in, Tango whispered, "He's here, and he's listening." Then, turning to the audience, he sang with everything he had in him and the knowledge of what lay ahead.

Why did I lose you? Was it something I said?
I've tried to remember, going back in my head
The world seems so grey now that you are not here
I'm lost and alone now, my heart full of fear

The entire theatre was silent, listening, entranced by the music, the purity of the voice, and the emotional impact of the words. The last note died away into silence, a silence maintained by a mesmerised audience. Then came the tumultuous applause as the audience rose to their feet.

Tango stood for a moment, dazed by the reception. Then he turned to Frank and took him by the hand and they walked to the footlights, sharing the plaudits together. In the wings, Bucky and the others stood open-mouthed at Tango's gesture and hugged each other. The applause went on and on.

25 November, 7:00 p.m.
Leicester Square, London

Leicester Square Cinema was ablaze with light. The red carpet was filled with celebrities and titles, and the crowds screamed and shouted every time a limo drew up. Inside was just as crowded as TV cameras had a ball, interviewing each famous name as they appeared. Reporters yelled into their mobiles, and cameras flashed every few seconds. White Heat had already arrived and Frank, with Bucky in tow, was talking to studio people about writing the score for a new musical. Florrie, surprisingly calm, was in a designer dress and pearls, and she prevented a nervous Ginny from bolting.

A roar from the crowd heralded another limo, and this one disgorged the female star of the film and, looking every inch the leading man, Tango. Reporters and cameramen left the crowd and headed for him, to the fury of his leading lady. For the next twenty minutes, they posed, talked, and thrilled the crowd. Tango posed for cameras, took selfies with his fans, and charmed elderly ladies with smiles and a kiss on the hand.

Slowly the organisers began to get everyone into the theatre as the cameras waited for the royal car. When it arrived the same enthusiasm was enacted, and it was another twenty minutes before the main stars and guests had greeted the royals and had taken their seats. The lights were dimmed, the credits began to roll, and the opening bars of Frank's score filled the theatre with the promise of love, laughter, and heartbreak.

A few seats away from the main party, at the back of the cinema, Tango's new manager sent out a wave of enthusiasm that permeated the whole building. By tomorrow morning Tango would be a worldwide star. Desi smiled to himself and wondered how his new employer would feel when it all came crashing down.

17 December, 7:30 a.m.
Beverly Hills

Tango emerged from the bathroom, towelling his hair, and walked across to the huge bed. He surveyed the two girls still sleeping there, then leaned down and slapped the rump of the nearest one. "Get up, get dressed, and get out…and you don't need to come back. There's an envelope on the table; share it between you." He turned away and walked out onto the balcony, oblivious of the fact that he was stark naked.

He lit a joint and drew the smoke deep onto his lungs and leaned on the balustrade. Tango looked out over the mountains, then turned to the glint of the sun-kissed sea beyond. Life was good. More than good—it was what he had dreamed of all his life. Wealth, high-quality clothes, luxurious surroundings, and, most of all, fame: the attention, admiration, and envy of those around him. So why did he feel as if he was missing something?

Unbidden, a memory surfaced of a day years ago: his birthday and the group surrounding him with presents, cards, booze, a cheap sponge cake with candles. Aftershave from Liam and Biff; a pair of shorts patterned with musical notes from Frank; a woollen scarf and gloves from Lyle and Ginny; a twenty-pound note from Bucky. Then Johnny had offered a watch to replace Tango's broken one. He'd apologised that it wasn't new; he'd bought it from a local pawnbroker, but it was a brand name, the first Tango had ever owned. Johnny must have gone without lunches and beers to save for it. Johnny, the star. Johnny, who he'd envied so much. Johnny, who always, at Christmas and birthdays, had given Tango something he wanted but couldn't afford. For one wild moment, Tango searched in his mind for something he could now afford to give rather than receive: a gold Rolex, a sports car, a holiday in Barbados…but he didn't even know where Johnny was or what he was doing. *Johnny, where are you? What are you doing?*

"You don't need to think about that deadbeat. You have the world at your feet." Desi appeared at Tango's side. "Get inside and get some clothes on. If you go down with a cold or sore throat, the whole bloody tour will be a write-off. We need to go over the programmes and the extra appearances."

Tango stopped pulling on his shirt. "What extra appearances?"

Desi sighed. "The odd appearance at a hospital. Perhaps a song for the nursing staff, a photoshoot with kids at their school...All that can boost your profile by 200 percent. It may seem like a chore, but it builds your bank account."

Now dressed, Tango shrugged into a sports coat and picked up his keys and wallet. "OK, whatever you say. Arrange it and I'll go along." He hesitated, then asked, "Was there an answer to my call to Bucky?"

Desi turned away. He'd never sent the call. "No, nothing came back. They obviously don't want to know you. Not surprising—you're far above that lot now that they're has-beens." Desi hesitated, then added, "Of course, you should keep in touch with Frank. He's worth his weight in gold with his talent for songwriting." He picked up a sheaf of papers. "Now, here's a list of songs for each appearance. It's a fair mixture of old and new stuff along with encores. You'll need to go through them. I'll arrange a run-through tomorrow."

Tango headed for the door.

"Hey, where do you think you're going? We have to go over these programmes." Desi caught his arm, but Tango shook it off.

"To hell with the programmes. I've been singing longer than you've been around. I'll do it off the cuff. Don't push me, or it'll be you that gets the push. I need fresh air and time alone. Stop pestering me." He headed for the door. "And don't wait up!"

The door slammed behind him, leaving Desi disconcerted at Tango's sudden change of mood. Something was causing a change in the singer, something he couldn't quite put his finger on, but it meant doubling his efforts to bring about the plans his superiors were planning. Desi headed for the balcony, becoming less human as he did so. He reached for a new form, and a carrion crow flew from the balcony and headed out to sea.

♬ ♩ ♫ ♪ ♬ ♪ ♫

Tango didn't return until the small hours. Desi found him on the bed, half-dressed, an empty syringe on the floor beside him and vomit covering the pillows. He let his rage boil over and dragged Tango bodily into the shower and cleaned him up. In a few hours they had to be at the studio to sign contracts. Desi had three hours, four at the most, and he intended to have Tango there, cleaned up, sober, and in his right mind. The only way was to use...darker methods. So be it. It would not be pretty, but Desi's bosses had been more than explicit—he still bore the proof of their anger.

18 December, 11:00 a.m.
Producer's Office, Los Angeles

Dwight L. Hanrahan leaned back in his chair and regarded his newest star with some suspicion. "What the hell is wrong with him? He looks like he's ready to pass out. Is he gonna be OK for this tour? Jesus H. Christ, he looks like shit."

Desi shrugged. "It's this new stomach bug. He's on medication. Give the guy a break. He's here, isn't he? Doesn't that show his commitment?" He eased into the man's mind and poured sympathy and fellow feeling into his thoughts. "You know how it is with these new bugs; you can pick the bloody things up even in a swank hotel. He'll be back on form in another twenty-four. We don't have to be in New York until the day after tomorrow. Where's the contract? He'll sign it, and I'll get him back to the apartment and dose him up again."

Hanrahan waved his hand at the hovering lawyer, who produced a sheaf of papers. Desi poured more strength into Tango and got him to look more in control.

Another twenty minutes and they were back in the car park. Desi slid into the driver's seat. Tango just sat, his system still dealing with the mixture of drugs he'd taken earlier.

Back at the apartment, Desi undressed Tango and got him to bed. He blocked all calls and made it known that Tango would not be available for a full twenty-four hours due to a stomach bug. Then he let go of his human form to become a mist of dark grey and poured himself into Tango's unconscious mind. He cleansed out the drugs still lingering there and began to re-align the mental patterns into their former state.

Many hours later, Tango was sleeping normally and his memories had been rearranged so all he remembered was being taken ill and under medication for twelve hours. Desi, even being non-human, was exhausted. He began packing for the trip and making sure all the papers and tickets were in order. Hotels and transport had been arranged by the organisers. Musicians, compères, valets, secretaries, and the usual entourage needed for such a tour were in place. Desi didn't need sleep normally, but using a human form for long periods was debilitating. He took on his own form and returned to the Dark levels.

♬ ♩ ♫ ♪ ♬ ♪ ♫

Tango slowly opened his eyes, then closed them as his head threatened to split open like a ripe tomato. Cautiously, he tried again. Desi held a steaming cup of coffee under his nose. Gratefully, Tango began to sip it. "Who—What happened?" he asked.

Desi took hold of Tango's T-shirt and lifted him up face to face. He let rip with a selective vituperation any stevedore would have been proud of. He cursed for a full ten minutes before calming down. Then, having given the stupefied Tango another coffee, Desi gave him a blow-by-blow account of the last forty-eight hours. He went on, "You have eight hours to get your fucking head into gear, then we're due at the airport to fly to New York in a private plane supplied by the organisers. We are due to arrive at 7:00 a.m. A limo will take us to your hotel. At 11:00 a.m. you have a meeting with said organisers to talk about your programme. You—that is, we—are invited to dinner at 8:00 p.m. at the mayor's home. Your hostess will ask you, as a favour, to sing for the guests. There will be twenty people there. You *will* oblige with a rendering of 'Be My Love.' You will *not* drink *any* alcohol at dinner, pleading the medication you are taking for your recent 'stomach upset.' We will leave as soon as we can do so politely. You will rest up the following day to be fresh for your first concert at the Lincoln Center. Do I make myself clear?"

Tango nodded.

28 January, 4:00 p.m.
The Abbey of the Winds

For months, Johnny worked to the point of exhaustion. Most of his time was spent with Pacia, learning her thinking patterns, trying to understand her personal view of the teaching she carried within. To prepare the world for her mission, he had to know its purpose, its long-term plan, her interpretation of it, and he had to adapt his own idea of it to his way of presentation. Johnny had been given a sense of joy and laughter at birth, and this was his way into the hearts of humanity. But he also had to prepare them for *her* way of teaching, one that was more serious, more direct, more intensive. The world was changing fast and increasing its ability to understand the universe around it. Johnny learned to move into those times, to foresee what was ahead. He was both amazed and fearful at the prospect: inventions, ideas, philosophies, and the decriers and unbelievers that would stand against him…and her.

When not with Pacia, Johnny's time was spent with the abbot, learning to work with the Forerunner power. The hardest task was adapting his own thought patterns and understanding of how the average human being thought to those of the spiritual power now existing within him. But he also had to cope with his mental and emotional link with Mara. She was entering her third trimester and feeling the pressure of separation more acutely. Arrangements had been made for her to be with Johnny in the Abbey of the Waters, but this meant travelling in winter, always a dangerous time at that latitude. If medical help was needed, the abbey was difficult to get to and get from. Johnny was at a difficult point in his training, and the mental and physical pressure were making it almost impossible to relax.

The abbot stood at the window and watched his charge walking by the lake; Johnny paced to and fro, trying to ease the inner turmoil. The abbot felt a gentle mind touch on the wavelength used by the abbeys. A deep growl filled his thoughts. "I think you have need of me, Holiness. I may be able to ease the turmoil in Johnny's mind. A way I learned as I grew and had to deal with being part of two different species. May I have permission to come to the Winds?"

"You are always welcome here, Wolf. I would be grateful for anything that will help him cope with this burden. The separation from Mara and the coming child conflicts with the task before him and keeps him from concentrating fully on either of them. He needs freedom from both in order to regain his sense of direction. It is a pity Mara became pregnant at this time, but when a soul decides it is time to be born, nothing will stop it. When can you get here?"

"I have felt Johnny's confusion for several days now and have been making my way south in case I was needed. I can be with you tomorrow evening. May I assume my usual quarters and needs are available?"

Abbot Jorje smiled inwardly. "As always, my friend and brother, and I can promise steak for dinner. Will you need Dylan to get word to the local pack?"

"That would be a courtesy, Holiness. I will have need of their group mind, so they need time to prepare the cubs for human intrusion. Farewell."

The abbot sent out a summons, and a few minutes later Brother Dylan knocked on his door. "Enter, Brother Dylan. Wolf is on his way to us. Please see that his quarters are ready. You will need to alert the local pack that he is coming and has need of their group mind. He is hoping to ease Johnny's present confusion by working with them. Is this agreeable to you and to the pack?"

"Of course, Holiness. We will do what we can to help. I will make all the arrangements. I will prepare the den in case it is needed." He bowed and left.

The abbot returned to the window, but Johnny had gone. The evening approached softly, and beyond the mountains a gleam of light heralded moonrise. He watched the first sliver of light appear over the summit and, with a sigh, returned to his desk. There was time to finish his letter before dinner.

♬ ♩ ♫ ♪ ♬ ♪ ♫

Johnny tossed restlessly on the edge of sleep, unable to let go of consciousness. Then he felt a weight on the other side of the bed, something alive. He smelt something familiar coming from the warm fur under his hand as an expensive aftershave teased his nostrils. He tried to stay awake but heard a voice he knew: "Let go, Johnny. I'm with you. Let go. Just rest." Johnny felt the weight of a paw on his shoulder. *Odd*, he thought. *A wolf wearing an expensive aftershave*. He slept deeply and dreamlessly, and the form beside him melted away.

He woke to find Pacia preparing to leave. She had been called to the Abbey of the Throne to prepare the temporary removal of its treasure. The time was coming for all of them to be gathered together, and she would oversee the preparations. She planned to stay briefly at the Aeon, so Johnny hastily wrote a letter to Mara and enclosed a necklace of lapis lazuli he had bought locally for her. The copter taking Pacia to the airport had brought Wolf, to Johnny's delight. He got the usual Wolf hug, and they picked up their deepening friendship on the way back to the abbey.

The shifter looked at Johnny critically. "You've had a rough time lately. The circles under your eyes look like you had a round with Pawel back at the Aeon." He slapped him on the back. "Well, I've got just the remedy for that. I arranged with the abbot for us to have some time together, just you and me. Thought I'd teach you a few tricks of the shifter trade."

"What kind of tricks?" asked Johnny suspiciously. Wolf held out a hand that shimmered and dissolved into a paw.

"This kind. Hey, we're here. Hi there, Dylan, Carl. How's it going with you guys?" With laughter and jokes, Wolf swept into the abbey and produced a bottle of aged brandy for the abbot, and Jorje smiled to hear Johnny laugh for the first time in weeks.

As usual, Wolf had brought with him the little luxuries hard to get in their secluded life. "Just because it's an abbey doesn't mean hair shirts and carbolic soap," he announced. "By the way, what time is dinner? I'm hungry."

Wolf went to unpack, and Johnny turned to the abbot. "He was with me astrally last night, Holiness. I see your hand in this visit. Thank you. I know I have made things difficult for everyone in these last weeks. My apologies, sir."

"The task before you will demand all you have to give. Time spent with a friend for a few days is little enough to ask of those who guide us. They will not begrudge you this time. Let it be a memory to help you bear what is to come."

Dinner was a party, with Wolf telling some of his stories and keeping them laughing. Dylan sang some of his Welsh songs, and as a finale they watched one of the films Wolf had brought with him, a Disney fantasy that they all enjoyed. Wolf caught the abbot's eye and nodded to Johnny, who was laughing wholeheartedly. They both knew this would be a memory to cherish in the times to come.

It was close to midnight when Johnny heard a knock on his door. Knowing who it was, he sent out an impulse that opened it wide, and Wolf ambled in. "Thought you might like a bit of company," he said and grinned. "Humans often find sleeping with an animal friend can help them relax. Children have their teddy bears; you have a wolf."

One of the first things Johnny had learned about shapeshifters was that they disliked shifting in front of others. Almost without fail, they would seek out a quiet place to take on their other form, and again when turning back. He knew what was in Wolf's mind and put out a hand.

"Wolf, you don't need to do this—I know you hate it. I'll turn round or go out on the balcony."

"Johnny, we all know what lies before you. We know we will lose you. This is my gift to you. It shows my trust, my love, and respect. It will be something to take with you and something for me to remember. This is a special time for me, a moment when I have you to myself, to talk with, cherish, listen to, and learn from. People see me laughing and joking and think how much I must enjoy being what I am. But Johnny, like you, I am a rarity. You are for real; I am a freak of nature. I have, after many years, come to terms with the fact I am not, never have been, never will be, fully human. But you and Pacia give me hope that you have come for my kind as well as for humanity."

Wolf stood and stripped off and let the change flow over him. Fascinated, Johnny watched as bones dislocated and lengthened, changed, and settled into place. Fur erupted over the entire body and part of the spine extruded and lashed from side to side. Wolf dropped to hands and knees and whimpered as bones and sinews cracked and became something entirely different. He deliberately slowed the change down so Johnny could take it in.

"Dear God, it hurts you! Each time it hurts you. The pain…Oh God!" Johnny knelt and put his arms round the animal his friend had become and wept for him, for the pain he endured every time he changed. He looked into the dark eyes and caressed the noble head. "This is the most wonderful gift I have ever had, will ever have. I will remember and take it with me into wherever it is I must go. I'll tell Mara to speak of this to our son, and when the time is right, your wonderful, magical kind will take your place among humanity."

Wolf's thoughts reached out and touched his. "My friend and brother, I will guard them both while life lasts. Now, let us sleep."

Johnny snuggled down into the crisp sheets, but Wolf leapt lightly onto the bed and circled, then curled at his feet, his tail covering his nose. A thought laced with laughter touched his companion's mind: "I used an extra dusting of flea powder for the occasion."

They slept, and Johnny dreamed of running with Wolf through the forests below the mountains. But Wolf dreamed of what was to come when this man who meant so much to him would no longer be there, and in his dream, he wept.

During the next wonderful, magical week, Johnny learned slowly and painfully to approach, touch, and link with the wildlife around the abbey. First was the wolf pack attached to Dylan, who, though not a shifter, could communicate with most animals. Fenris and his mate Kala were used to touching human minds, but their twin cubs were wary at first. Wolf spent the first few days with them explaining what was needed.

Then Wolf explained to Johnny, "The important thing to remember is it is not just *you* learning to be a wolf—it works both ways. They also experience what it is to be human, and that includes how you, as a human, regard them. You must monitor your thoughts, ideas, and memories of pictures, films, or TV programmes dealing with the animal world, which can be frightening to them."

In the end, it was Kala who opened up to Johnny. In her mind he learned how to approach other wolves, those below her in rank, and the alphas of other packs. He learned to use scent as a recognition and as a greeting. He learned to relax his entire body in different positions and how to remain motionless under cover. His human hearing became keener, his reactions quicker, but he never quite got to the point of chasing, catching, killing, and eating raw the rabbit he fancied for dinner! Best of all was the moment he joined with one of the great eagles as it soared over the highest peaks of the Torres del Paine. The complete freedom, the feeling of the wind under his wings, of being in control of his environment, brought an exhilaration he would always remember.

Each night, Johnny slept held safely within the mind of Wolf.

On the last day, Wolf, Fenris, and Kala took Johnny deep into the forest below the mountains, and he spent the whole day linked to the combined pack mind, something Dylan envied him. At dinner he said his goodbyes to them all, and during the ritual in the Hall of Ceremony he offered his blessing to each one. He did so not in his name, but in the name of the man who had changed his life: Nyang Darsip, Abbot of the Abbey of the Dawn.

The following day, Johnny and Wolf left the Abbey of the Winds on their way to Buenos Aires. In the hotel that night, Wolf told Johnny he would be flying to Madrid the next day and driving to the Aeon the day after to spend time with Mara before leaving for the Abbey of the Waters; it was too risky for her to travel that far while pregnant. She and Tze-Ring would be waiting for him in Madrid.

When he'd gotten over his excitement, Johnny asked if Wolf would be going with him. "No, brother mine. I have work to do elsewhere. It will be some time before we again share a meal, and by that time you will be a father. But I will meet with you again at the Abbey of the Snows. Come, let's eat."

That night they drank their way through a bottle of top-class Spanish wine and finished off with a well-aged brandy. Never one for lengthy goodbyes, Wolf left while Johnny was still sleeping. On the bedside table, he left a chain carrying a wolf's head in gold. There was no message; none was needed. Wolf would be with him when the time came.

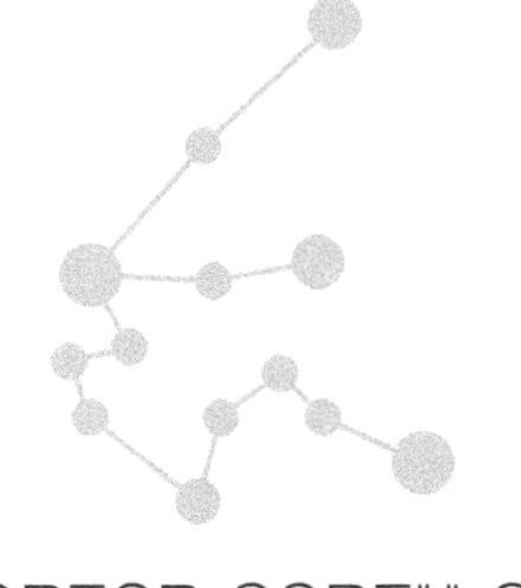

CHAPTER FORTY-ONE

2 February, 3:30 p.m.
Studio set, Los Angeles

"No, no, no!" The frantic director clutched his hair and made a determined effort to pull a handful of his scalp. "Why can't you do the bloody scene as I've told you? For fuck's sake, what is wrong with you? This is the fifth take."

"Because what you want is *not* the way I want to do the scene, and I'm the star. It's my way or nothing!" Tango threw his script on the floor, stamped on it, and stalked off to his dressing camper. The director followed him only to have the door slammed in his face. Don Webster paused and stood for moment, then called a break for the crew and made for the head office.

The studio head, Stan Lowicz, already aware of the situation, was waiting for him. Stan's top director, a three-time Oscar winner and personal friend, was on the verge of a heart attack. Plus, his top star's blatant disregard for the man's expertise was sending the film costs beyond what even he, for all his millions, was prepared to lose. The two men faced each other over the antique desk.

"I quit! There is no way in hell I can work with him, and the crew are with me on this. Hell, everyone from the camera guys to the floor cleaners hates his guts. He wants his own way in every scene, and he's got the whole character wrong. He turns up stoned almost every day. Melissa is scared to death of him. He's tried it on with every female from the makeup woman—and she's in her fifties—to the cleaners! This guy may be the studio's hottest thing in years, but Stan, I'm telling you, he's dangerous. Find some way to break his contract or it's disaster time."

Stan chewed on his cigar. "The bloody agent of his has us so restricted we can't do anything without his approval; he'll sue and enjoy doing it. Shit, he could end up owning *us*."

The two men sat in silence. Then Stan got up and poured two stiff glasses of whisky. He set one down in front of the disgruntled director. "Of course, if anything happened that prevented him from…Well, I mean, if he was ill or had an accident…Not fatal, but, you know, enough to make it impossible to work for a while, say three months, we could legally replace him."

Don raised his head. "I wouldn't want…I mean, we couldn't. That guy he's with, he gives me the creeps, and he's clever; he might suss it out. God forgive me, I'd be willing to try it, but we'd have to replace him. You know, it could work. He's taking a real mixture of stuff, the real expensive kind. We can rig an accident of some kind that will keep him off his feet. Then we'll suggest he dubs the songs. That would keep him in the limelight. But how can we make it happen?"

Stan tapped the side of his nose. "Leave it to me. You go back and let him do the scene as he wants. He won't do it for long."

"How will it happen? I mean, won't it look suspicious?"

"No. The man I'm thinking of was a stunt man for me years ago. One of the best. We just need something to keep him quiet for a month or so. I can pressure someone I know who has a private island where he can recuperate. Throw in a couple of girls to soothe his fevered brow, make it seem as if we really care. I'll put together a couple of suggestions for another film he can think about."

Don tossed the rest of his drink down his throat. "I'll get back and do some grovelling, get him back on the set. When is all this going to happen? It's costing more every day."

"Leave it to me. It'll have to be public to get him a lot of sympathy; he loves attention. I'll let you know the details later, OK? You know, Don, he's good, but there's always someone ready to grab a chance. Stars come and go, and fans are fickle. They have short memories. Tango could have been top of the tree, but he won't last. Yes, he has talent, but no real depth. Get back to the set. I'll be in touch."

TOP STAR IN HOSPITAL WITH CONCUSSION: TANGO GARRETT IN ATTEMPTED MUGGING. THE GOLDEN VOICE DROPPED FROM NEW FILM

Tango Garrett, Hollywood's newest and most admired star, is tonight in a private suite in the Cedars-Sinai Medical Center with a severe concussion. An eyewitness reported, "I saw it happen. He came out of the side door to avoid the fans, and these two guys came at him with baseball bats. One of them was shouting something about leaving his wife alone and that he'd leave him with a scar for life. The second one hit him and knocked him down. Then they got in a car and drove off. No, I didn't get the plate number…It all happened so fast."

Sources say Garrett, whose face was slashed during the attack, has regained consciousness but is disoriented. Work on his new film has halted while a replacement is found. Many speculate the singer's recordings will be dubbed in later.

This is not the first threat to Garrett's safety. He has acquired quite the reputation, with sources claiming there has been recent trouble during filming. The police will continue to investigate the attack.

9 February, 9:45 a.m.
Madrid

Johnny landed in Madrid just before 10:00 a.m. Mara was waiting for him. Her face lit up as he came through the door into the arrival hall. He gathered her up and swung her round. Then, remembering she was pregnant, he set her down gently. Johnny held Mara's face in his hands and drank in the sight of her, the burgeoning shape of the child they had created nestled between them.

Tze-Ring, waiting to greet his half-brother, felt a wave of grief flood through him. The child would never really know his father, would grow up, grow old, and carry on the bloodline as Johnny had done. Maybe he would inherit some of his powers; maybe not. But when the time came for the Age of Capricorn to take the stage, it would be a descendent of that child who would be its herald. There was so little time left to share his brother's life, to laugh and talk and do the things brothers do together.

Then Johnny turned to Tze-Ring and held out his arms, holding him close and sharing with Tze-Ring the thoughts and feelings going through his mind: *I'll never be far from you,* mi prala, *and I'll be waiting to greet you when the time comes.* Aloud, Johnny asked, "Is Dad at the Aeon as well?"

"Yes, and Florrie and Bucky hope to make it over too. Let's get your luggage and get going. It's a fair drive to the Aeon from here."

By 12:15 p.m., Johnny and Mara were cuddled together in the backseat, exchanging news, ideas, and plans for the all-too-brief time they would have together. Tze-Ring settled into the task of remembering and using every shortcut he knew. Reaching ahead, he called on the abbey personnel to join forces and keep the roads clear of traffic, holdups, and potential accidents. In doing so, he cut the four-hour journey down to just under three, and they rolled into the abbey soon after 5:00 p.m. to an enthusiastic welcome from everyone.

Dinner was brought forward an hour to allow for Johnny to adjust to the time difference, but by 9:00 p.m. he was packed off, protesting volubly, by Eamon and Mara, and he fell asleep almost before his head hit the pillow. As he did so Johnny heard, as if far away, the howl of a wolf.

For the next three weeks Johnny made the most of what was virtually a holiday. Bucky and Florrie arrived and filled him in on news about the group and that Frank had written a new symphony, "Hymn to the Sun," that had drawn great praise from the highest quarters of the musical world. Johnny listened to the recording with amazement and spoke to Frank about his transition from modern music to classical. Frank was due to conduct it with the London Symphony Orchestra at a royal music gala the week before Johnny left for Canada, and Johnny was determined to attend. This meant rearrangements. Johnny dug his heels in and refused to leave without attending Frank's time of triumph.

Mara had nearly six weeks to go before the birth, so Johnny's arrival at the Abbey of the Waters would be delayed. Star charts and planetary aspects had to be taken into consideration. All the abbeys went on high alert as they realised the Forerunner had a mind of his own, and come hell or high water, he was not going to miss his friend's big moment or the birth of his son.

11 March, 11:00 p.m.
Las Vegas

Tango had fretted about his enforced semi-retirement while his facial surgery healed. The film was to be released with Tango's dubbed voice, likely to a much reduced reception. Plus, the discovery of Tango's affair with the wife of a highly placed politician became the subject of a nationwide furore, made worse by the fact it involved drugs. After three highly successful films and several top-of-the-charts platinum recordings, Tango's popularity had fallen quickly and dramatically.

Desi had disappeared, recalled by his Dark masters; he had endured an uncomfortable session with his superiors. Without the help of Tango's "alter ego" to boost his presence, his income began to slide, not helped by his continued high life. With his film contract gone and without Desi, Tango had to employ a publicity man. Under the publicist's guidance, Tango had recently began to work the nightclub round, which included a two-month booking in Las Vegas. But Tango's lifestyle of drugs, booze, and women went on, and slowly the glamour began to erode.

Standing by the window, he looked down on the brilliantly lit street below. Light was a strange thing; it made ordinary things look different, and different kinds of light altered the way you saw those things. It occurred to

Tango that it had been days, maybe weeks, since he'd seen real daylight. In Las Vegas, few people saw real light. He thought back. How long was it since he had seen the sun or watched a full moon rise over the sea?

Tango looked back at the girl lying on the bed, her naked body limp and sated, and felt a sickness rise in his throat. Suddenly he needed to get out. Out of the room, out of Las Vegas, out of…where? Where was he? Not just in what state, but in his life, in his mind, in his soul? *What* soul? Did he even have one? Then, out of nowhere, came words, words he remembered that held a meaning for him.

So I went my way from town to town
Just a desperate man with his shoes worn down
I followed the call and the beckoning hand
To a far-off place in an unknown land
I sat beneath an ancient tree
And my heart said, "Be still and listen to me"

Johnny's "Mountains of Gold," the song Tango had always wanted to sing. Suddenly he felt Johnny there, in the room with him.

"Tango, sing it now. Sing it with me."

Tango drew in a breath and began to sing softly. He heard Johnny's voice join with him, adding the harmony.

I looked for love through the cities of despair
I looked for love, but never found it there
Sometimes I thought I had seen her face
In a downtown bar or a dining place

A female voice joined them. Tango felt her, felt them both: the man he envied and a girl whose body lay in an unmarked grave in a deserted garden covered with wildflowers.

Tango broke, flung on a shirt, chinos, and trainers, and ran down the stairs, pushing through the crowded streets. He ran and ran out there, anywhere, desperate for silence, to be alone, to find who he was, where he was, *what* he was. But the words of the song and the voices went with him.

In the darkening sky, the planets moved slowly into their ordained positions, and the world soul held its breath.

12 March, 3:00 p.m.
The Abbey of the Aeon

The relics of the Age of Pisces would soon be gathered together and hidden in a place of power with others of their kind. The Teacher of the Age of Aquarius would provide her own.

In the Abbey of the Crown, Pacia clutched the circle of thorns and watched her blood drip on the tiled floor. The seconds ticked away relentlessly. At the Abbey of the Dawn, the chalice spilt its contents over the feet of Tara's statue. Within its hidden shrine, the Ark of the Covenant gave out a peal of thunder. Three rusted nails in the Abbey of the Winds sank deep into the wooden altar, and in the Abbey of the Waters, a wolf lifted its head and howled as a bloodstained shroud was laid on the altar. In the Abbey of the Snows, a spear that had once pierced the heart of a world Teacher gave off the scent of frankincense. In the Aeon, Mara placed on the altar a silken pouch holding a lock of dark hair.

Power flared and Mara convulsed in pain and collapsed, going into early labour.

Johnny manifested in the Aeon's small dispensary as Eamon carried Mara in. The women were already there.

Eamon hauled Johnny out of the room. "Let them see to her. She won't want you to see her like this. Let them get her ready. She's young and strong, and five weeks early is not as bad as it might have been. Many babies come early."

"I want to ease her pain. I can do it—I did it for Lea. I can do it now."

"This is different, Johnny. The women are trained midwives. Wait until they have done what needs to be done at the moment: wash her, get her into something clean and comfortable…I promise you, when the time is close, you will be with her."

Johnny became aware of a presence—no, two of them. One was Pacia, reaching out to Mara and easing her fear of losing the baby. "He is strong. He is eager to be with you. All will be well." The other presence was faint but held the feel and the scent of Wolf.

At the same moment, Abbot Gregor clasped his hands together and bowed his head. His mind was gently touched by a presence. *It always begins with a birth, physical and spiritual. They reflect each other. Dawn will herald the Age of Aquarius.*

12 March, 5:00 p.m.
Las Vegas

Tango was also facing a birth. He lay curled under a bridge, racked with guilt and facing memories he had tried hard to forget: his grandmother pleading for her pills to ease her pain; the desperation of seeing his mother trying to find work to feed them, standing at an ironing board for hours to earn a pound or two to buy food; her pauper's grave with no flowers or even a stone. Tango had reburied her when he joined the group; it had been the first thing on his mind. Later, he added a headstone, and it was Johnny who had helped him pay for it.

Now Tango faced a new threat: the loss of all he had worked and hoped for. He'd thrown it away because he wanted to show Johnny and the group he could make it alone. He'd done it…and now he was back where he'd begun. Yet again, Johnny had come to him, had shared his song with him. He reached out tentatively. "Johnny? Johnny, are you there?"

But there was just a blackness, a sense of pain, and something happening. Tango got to his feet and began the long trek back to the hotel, dreading the devastating row that awaited him there.

12 March, 5:30 p.m.
The Abbey of the Aeon

The men gathered round Johnny, surrounding him with energy until the women allowed him in.

Mara held out her hand. "He is like you, always trying to be one step ahead of things. Come sit with me. It will help when the pain comes. They told me it will be hours yet, but he's in the right position and doesn't seem to be in any difficulty. Just impatient."

As each pain came, Mara drew in a sharp breath, clutched Johnny's hand, and breathed through it. He sang to her, told her jokes, shared memories of his younger days—anything to keep her mind off the pain. Time passed, and the pains came closer together.

The moon rose slowly into a star-filled sky. Eamon brought messages from Bucky and Florrie and the other abbeys, and Johnny marvelled at the love and strength that surrounded them, unaware he was receiving what he had always offered to others. Despite the turmoil going on in his own life, he was also aware of Tango's downfall and reached out to him as he tossed and turned in a ravaged sleep. Then he felt the presence of Pacia in her Body of Light. With her appearance, everything fell into place. This was the time. This was the moment. This was the beginning of the Age of Aquarius.

All three felt a soul-tearing wrench involving time, space, and power, and...a presence. Johnny sought words to describe It, but there were none. It was so far beyond power It stole his breath. Its purpose was an event nothing could deter, a purpose of which he, Pacia, and Tango were a vital part and always had been. On the astral, a conversation involving Johnny, Pacia, and Tango was about to take place, a Tango that matched them both in power and purpose but was unaware of the conversation on the physical level.

Enclosed in timeless space, the three stood in the presence of a power, purpose, and perfection that towered above them. In a voice of muted thunder, It spoke: "The manifestation of a new age requires the power of three willing sacrifices. The Teacher, the Forerunner, and the Betrayer."

It turned to Pacia. "Knowing what lies ahead, do you still make the offer?"

Pacia bowed her head. "I still make the offer."

The presence turned to Johnny. "Much will be asked of you. Do you still make the offer?"

Johnny, his heart breaking as he thought of his son, bowed his head. "I still make the offer."

The presence turned to Tango. "You came close to withdrawing your offer. You were almost lost to the Dark. Now is the time for truth. You may withdraw if you wish, though it will delay the onset of the age. It will be hard, for I must withdraw these memories from you."

Tango turned to Johnny. “Love and hate are often mistaken for each other. I ask pardon for all that has gone before.” The light of their forms flowed together for a moment, then separated.

Tango bowed to the presence. “I still make the offer.”

The light of the presence grew in intensity and enveloped them all. Before them manifested a great door inscribed with the ancient symbol that held the meaning of time before creation.

In front of them stood an immense figure with the head of a jackal. The voice was deep and throbbed with a power beyond human ears. “I am the Opener of the Ways, and I now open the doors to the Age of Aquarius.”

♬ ♩ ♫ ♪ ♬ ♪ ♫

The cry of a newborn filled the air, and Eamon put Johnny’s son into his mother’s arms.

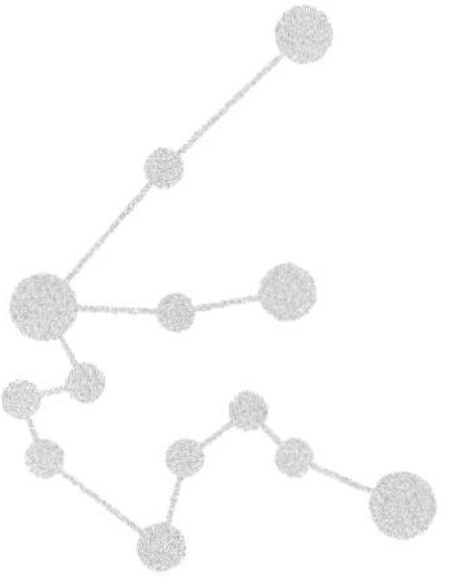

CHAPTER FORTY-TWO

15 June, 9:30 p.m.
The library at the Abbey of the Aeon

Johnny stared down at what he had written. It wasn't all he wanted to say, but some things needed no words, just emotions. He folded the paper and slid it into an envelope. He had one more day before leaving for the Abbey of the Waters, so he would leave it with Eamon with instructions to give it to Mara after he'd gone. He looked at his watch. Coming up to ten…and Jared's feeding time.

He stood up and looked round him, trying to fix it all in his memory. Apart from the Abbey of the Dawn, this was the place he had stayed the longest. Soon he would be on his way north, and after that would come the last of the abbeys, the Abbey of the Snows on Rishiri Island.

Johnny sighed as he left the book-lined room where he had studied for so long and quietly closed the door for the last time. Then he went to spend some precious time with Mara and their son.

♬ ♩ ♫ ♪ ♬ ♩ ♫

At three months Jared was beginning to recognise different faces, smiling and gurgling with laughter. Fed and prepared for the night, he lay between his parents on the big bed, enthusiastically waving his arms and legs around. Mara watched as Johnny tickled him and blew bubbles on his tummy, her thoughts almost choking her as she thought of the empty days and nights ahead. Not for the first time, she battled with her resentment at having to live without the man she loved because of his destiny. His son would grow up with no real memory of him.

Johnny had accepted his future role, but Mara was the one who would have to live with only her memories to cling to. She watched as Johnny, now holding his sleeping son close to him, also fell asleep. Mara tried to remain awake, filing her senses with every second. Reluctant to separate them from each other, she pulled the covers over all three of them and fell into a deep, dreamless sleep.

Johnny woke early, determined to spend every last minute with his family. *His family.* He savoured the feel of the words in his mind. It brought back memories of his own childhood. He too had grown up without a father, but at least he'd found him again, had gotten to know him, laugh and talk and argue with him. Jared would never get to do that. Then Johnny smiled. Jared would have a doting grandfather, and he'd have Bucky and Florrie, Frank, and aunts and uncles who would tell him about his father and share their memories of him. It would never be enough, but it would be something.

He joined Mara as she bathed the baby and fed him. This day would be theirs. As a gift from those who knew and loved them, they gave up this last day of his company so he would have a day to remember just being a partner and a father. He would live every moment of it.

The others gave them space but watched and built their own memories.

28 June, 7:00 p.m.
London

For the last few days, a lecture called "Finding Inner Peace" had been advertised. Free tea and sandwiches were to be provided. Now, in a less-than-salubrious dusty and draughty church in the east end of London, Pacia faced a group of people who matched the condition of the room.

There were eight of them. Two had come in just to get out of the rain. Another, clutching an empty beer can, was asleep. Two were in their early teens, little more than children, hungry and homeless. A man sat in the farthest corner. His eyes were watchful and his clothes bloodstained. A young woman, her clothes neat but shabby, sat clutching a rosary in nervous hands. The last was a man nursing a hand in his coat. His face was tear-stained, bruised and etched with pain both physical and mental. All had sought shelter from the outside world for various reasons. The dingy hall, with its single battered poster, offered what they all needed: shelter.

Pacia's heart ached as she looked at them. She opened it and let a feeling of peace, safety, and warmth flow through the hall. Then she smiled and stepped forward.

"Welcome, my friends. I know it's raining outside, so how about we begin with a hot drink and something to eat? As there are so few of us, there's more to go round, and it will be more of a friendly get together than a lecture. As you know, my name is Pacia, so please use it."

She turned to the two youngest. "My guess is that you are on your own. Is that right?"

The oldest, a boy, nodded. "She's my sister, Angie. I'm William. Billy. Dad was beating Mum again, and I couldn't make him stop. When she didn't move anymore, I grabbed Angie and we ran. That was three days ago. Can we have something to eat, please?"

The young woman with the rosary stood up. "I'll get it," she said. "It will give me something to do." She began to hand round paper mugs of tea and took the cover off a large plate of sandwiches. The young man edged forward and held out an eager hand. The drunk woke up, belched, and lurched back into the rain.

The two women who had been the first to arrive stood up and announced their departure. "We thought this lecture would be about the local church," said the older of the two, "but it seems to be just for the down-and-outs." She took a five-pound note from her purse and put it on the table. "That's to help with the tea and food." They departed into the rain-filled street.

Pacia smiled at the others. "That leaves even more for us," she said, looking round at the five remaining. "Now, let me see. We have Angie and Billy…" She looked at her helper. "And you are?"

"Er, I'm Carol. I was born on Christmas Eve, you see. I came because… Well…" She paused, then blurted out, "I'm strange, you see. I kind of…see things, and it scares me. My mother wants to have me exorcised. She says I'm evil and God has forsaken me. But I can't help it! They just appear and tell me things. Things about people and what is going to happen. And it doesn't *feel* bad; it feels warm and loving, like *you* feel. I know you can help. I saw the poster and knew it was meant for me. I'm not bad. Truly, I'm not."

Pacia put an arm round her. "You are not bad. You are gifted, and all of you who have come here tonight have been brought here for a purpose. Each one of you felt the call and found your way here…to me."

She turned to the man with his hand inside his coat. "You are in great pain. Let me see." Hesitantly, the young man uncovered his hand. The fingers had been broken, and as he looked at it, he burst into tears.

"I'm Steven, and I'm a pianist. I *was* a pianist. Now I'll never play again. I needed money for music school, and I carried drugs for some men. They paid me for it, and I used the money for lessons. But when I saw what it was doing to people and I told them I wouldn't work for them anymore, they beat me up, and one of them stamped on my hand."

Pacia took hold of his good hand and asked, "Have you any family?"

"No. I was brought up in an orphanage, but at eighteen you have to leave. I work when I can get it, and I play the piano in a bar at night. But now…"

Pacia felt a new power fill the room and turned to face the last of the five.

"You," she said, "You can help him."

The man with bloodstained clothing cried out and shook his head. "No, no, no. I can't. They'll burn me again. I can't. I won't!"

Pacia laid her hand on his head. "Peace, Haji. Let my peace become part of you. Let me fill you with grace. You were born to heal, and heal you shall. In my name, you will heal."

A change came over the man after he heard Pacia say his name. She took the broken hand and placed it in his. Haji's form edged with light, and he took each finger and slowly made it straight and supple. The sound of the bones mending echoed in the almost-empty room.

Pacia reached back into the past, and they all saw what had happened to Haji. When his gift became too strong to hide, his community tried to burn him alive as a witch. They saw him flee from village to village and finally stowaway on a boat to England. Three years of struggling to survive had brought him to this moment in time.

An intense silence filled the dingy room. Then it slowly filled with light coming from Pacia's heart centre. A voice that was not a voice but a knowingness and a decree filled the silence with unheard words: *And these five will be the first to follow the Teacher of Aquarius. The Forerunner now spreads the news. Move slowly and choose carefully. Gather these I have brought to you and tend to them. All has been prepared as was promised. Those chosen will leave behind all that they knew.*

The chosen stood quietly as they were slowly filled with inner peace and with grace. Pacia led them into the street. The rain had stopped, and two limos stood at the kerb. As usual, the emir had arranged everything. When all were safely seated, they took off.

Overhead, a meteor flashed across the sky.

31 August, 4:00 p.m.
Las Vegas

It was over. Tango couldn't believe it. In a few short, hellish months, he'd gone from a star to a burned-out shell. From being a millionaire to wondering if he had enough for a flight to New York, or even a rail ticket. Hollywood had torn his throat out, and Vegas lawyers gnawed on the bones that were left.

Tango had watched as they cleared out his penthouse apartment, sold the massive TV and the baby grand. His luxury gold watch was now worn by someone else. Most of his wardrobe had gone; what little he had left was now in two suitcases, one of which he was sitting on. He had kept his guitar by hiding it with the one friend he'd managed to keep: a bit player who, like Tango, had seen better days and knew what he was going through. Tango had been sleeping on the guy's sofa for weeks—when he slept at all.

Tomorrow Tango would shake the dust of the West Coast from his feet and try to scrape a living in New York, but he knew he'd have to let the furore of the last few months die down and lie low. With luck he might be able to get work in the classier nightclubs, but with barely two thousand pounds left to his name, he had to get there, find somewhere to live, feed himself, and go job hunting. That was something he had not done in years, before he'd joined Colin Buckman and White Heat.

Tango picked up his cases and left them by the back door, something else he'd have to get used to. Later that night, he lay sleepless on his friend's lumpy sofa, his stomach protesting at the two-day-old pizza he had eaten. Try as he might, he could not hold back the tears as they streamed down his face and soaked into the thin pillow.

Tango's Body of Light stood with his spiritual mentor and watched. "I cannot even offer consolation by Indwelling it for a few hours," it said, turning to its companion.

The bright being nodded. "It is part of what you offered when you agreed to bring in the new age. The physical selves must endure the lower traumas. But help will be offered when needed to bring about the final Opening of the Way."

When morning finally came, Tango gathered his things together. His friend shuffled his feet self-consciously and held out an envelope. "It's a sort of goodbye and a thanks for the times you got me extra work. It's not much, but it'll get you halfway at least." Tango looked inside the envelope at the bus ticket to Houston. "You can maybe get a couple of days' work there and then make it to the Big Apple. It'll save you digging into what you've got left. I gotta go, buddy—have to be at the studio by 7:30. Stay safe, and keep in touch."

Somewhere deep inside Tango, a small spark of hope flared. After his friend left, he looked down at his cheap watch. Time to leave.

Tango closed the door quietly and left without looking back. He grabbed a passing cab and headed for the bus station. Once there, unnoticed and unrecognized, he loaded his cases and took a seat at the back.

Closing his eyes as they took off, Tango shut out any last glimpse of the gaudy, shiftless, and faithless city on which he had once pinned his hopes of fame. A single tear of self-pity trickled down into the beard he had lately grown as a barrier between himself and the world he had once thought was his.

YEAR FIVE

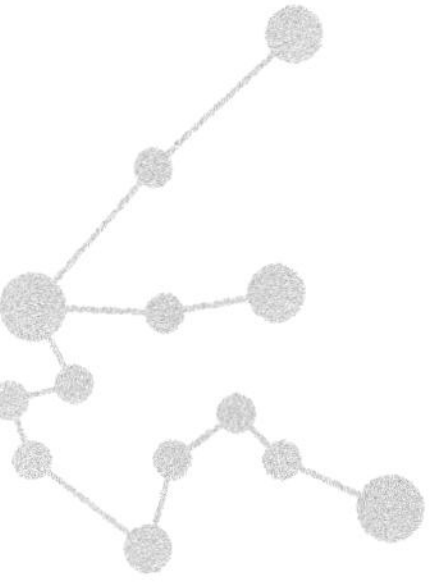

CHAPTER FORTY-THREE

27 November, 5:00 p.m.
The Abbey of the Waters

Johnny sighed and closed his diary, then got up and walked around the room to ease the muscles that had seized up over the long hours of study. Normally he would have gone for a run or walked around the abbey gardens, but a run when the temperature outside was freezing was unthinkable. Since his arrival, Johnny had forgotten what it was like to feel really warm. Now, in late November, Johnny was counting the days to the warmer months. For the first time, he understood why some animals went into hibernation. He'd even thought about doing the same.

The Waters was different than the other abbeys, though the climate reminded him of his time in the Abbey of the Dawn. To his delight, Wolf was a frequent visitor who brought news and videos not only of Mara and Jared but of the others close to him. Frank was working on an opera, and White Heat were still doing background recording work. Johnny also learned that all the abbeys were on alert, waiting for the first signs of the new message.

Here in this lonely and isolated place, all but three of the personnel were of First Nations tribes ranging from Navajo, Zuni, and Hopi to Tlingit, Iñupiat, and Haida. Learning what he could of their language was difficult and caused a lot of good-natured laughter. From the abbey members, Johnny learned to listen to the voices of the earth and its non-human life forms. With Wolf's help, Johnny became aware of the fact that everything that grew had a voice and could be contacted. He listened, fascinated, to the creation legends told him by the brethren and noted their similarity to those of other belief systems. He began to ask permission to join them in their ceremonies. Sometimes it was given, at other times withheld. Johnny never insisted.

Christmas came and went. Johnny spoke to Mara and Jared by phone and sent gifts via Wolf and Bucky. Mostly he lived, studied, and worked alone. The brethren had brought spiritual solitude to a fine art and taught him the finer uses of inner creative work. Slowly, Johnny learned to build within his mind an inner sanctuary. Here he found what the Abbey of the Waters had to give him.

Johnny didn't recognise the Inner Level teacher who guided him back into the past to meet the Forerunners who had served before him. From them, he learned what would be asked of him in those last moments.

♬ ♩ ♫ ♪ ♬ ♪ ♫

One morning Johnny was invited to join everyone at sunrise to welcome the return of light. Everyone gathered together at the circle of stones that, for them, represented a spiritual hogan. Abbot Kanien and Sister Chenoa stood on each side of Johnny, and the others gathered close.

The abbot took a handful of earth and poured it into Johnny's hands, then turned him to face the pinpoint of light as it pierced the horizon. Johnny knew in that moment what was being offered to him and felt a flood of joy and power fill him. He lifted his hands and let the earth trickle through.

"I greet thee, my father sun. Let your light fill thy children with joy and strength."

Brother Zane filled his hands with water to sprinkle the circle.

"I greet thee, my mother earth. I give thee water to enrich the life you give to us."

They all began to circle with small steps, shifting their balance from foot to foot, letting the morning chant call on the twin powers to begin the day.

"The earth is our mother; let us care for Her. Let us honour all life. We open our hearts to the Great Spirit. All life is sacred; we treat all beings with respect. We will take from the earth only what is needed and nothing more. We will do what needs to be done for the good of all. We give thanks to the Great Spirit for each day and follow the rhythms of nature. Let us enjoy life's journey but leave no track behind us, for all must find their way unaided."

With Johnny in the centre, they circled him, laying their hands on him and letting their thoughts, emotions, and blessings flow into him and fill him. Slowly, Johnny felt himself being drawn into their group mind, being filled, accepted, loved, and made a living part of their ancient belief system. He felt filled with the power of the sun and the earth, knew them as part of his own beingness. As they continued to circle, Johnny turned of his own accord to face the empowerment of the sun as it rose from the ocean, and his consciousness left him as he became one with the wholeness of all. He fell into the gentle touch of the Great Spirit, the power of the group souls of Earth's many forms filled him, and he became one with the consciousness of the Great Spirit.

From far away, the spirit body of Wolf joined Johnny and shared with him the brotherhood of earth's life forms. Johnny became part of every root and leaf, flower and fruit, stone and sand, cub and kit, bone and fur, claw and fang. Earth, the Great Mother, gave Herself to him. He knew Her, loved Her, and felt the power of Her kiss. He lived through aeons of time and watched universes come into being and dissolve back into infinity only to begin again.

Johnny knew this was the penultimate point of his training. He understood the symbolism of the door and knew he would be the one to utter the Word that would open the door to the Age of Aquarius.

He came to his senses with the brethren gathered round him. In silence, they returned to the abbey. Soon, Johnny would leave for the Abbey of the

Snows, the last and most powerful of the seven. There he would be prepared for the coming of the Word, the understanding of its meaning, the preparation of the Breath of Empowerment, its correct pronunciation, and its effect.

1 February, 1:00 p.m.
The Abbey of the Snows

Four weeks later Wolf set the copter down on an impossibly small landing field. Johnny opened his eyes and whispered, "Did we make it? Are we down?"

Wolf grinned and shut down the engines. "Sure we did! I know this strip like I know my face in the mirror. I bring their supplies in when it's open. Sometimes it's closed for months."

Johnny peered out of the window. "It's so small. Where's the abbey?"

Wolf pointed to a volcanic mountain dead ahead. "It's one third of the way up there. That's Mount Rishiri. It's almost the same shape as Fuji, and to the Japanese, just as revered. But don't worry, there's a lift—sort of. The abbey is well hidden and few people, bar the islanders, even know it's there because it is actually inside the mountain itself. You'll find it a mixture of laboratory cum observatory cum science set-up cum Shinto shrine. I hope you can use chopsticks!

"All the abbeys have a special purpose. The Dawn is the prep school, and the Throne is the research area. The Aeon is the heart centre, while the Winds are involved with the specialist work. The Waters bring it all together, and the newly found one is the sacred abbey."

As Wolf spoke, several men ran out of a small two-storied building and began to unload the copter. A diminutive and voluble person, obviously the overseer, pumped Johnny's hand until he thought it would fall off and led them into the airport, where a few people who ignored them sat huddled together next to a radiator.

After signing a mound of paperwork, they left with handshakes and respectful bows all round. An ancient off-road vehicle had been provided, and they set out for the Abbey of the Snows. Ahead Johnny could see the looming bulk of the now-dormant volcano wearing a cloak of rain-filled clouds.

"We got in right on time," said Wolf, nodding towards them. "It will be a noisy night. The thunder reverberates through the abbey when it gets rough, but you get used to it."

He drove on, avoiding the stray cattle and farmers heading for their fields as well as the odd hiker. "Do they get many visitors here?" asked Johnny as they skirted a small group loaded with what looked like camping gear.

"Quite a few in the summer. They come to see the mountain, and there are some smaller areas of interest. But summer is short here, so the locals make the most of it by selling locally made items. The women are expert weavers, and the men spend the long winters carving wooden figures, bowls, plates, and stuff like that…We're coming up to the point where we'll have to leave the truck."

"Will it be OK to just leave it?"

Wolf laughed as he drew up and shut off the engine. "You could leave a gold watch here and no one would touch it. The word has already gone round: You are bound for the abbey, and no one would take anything of yours. Abbey personnel are the sacred ones. Grab your bags; this is where we take the lift." He lifted a large duffel bag from the backseat and headed for a wooden gate bearing three hand-painted signs with Japanese words that translated to the Mirror, the Sword, and the Jade Crystal.

"No one would enter unless invited. Come on, let's get inside before the storm arrives. It's close now, and I'm hungry."

Wolf struck the bronze gong hanging beside the gate, and the sound set a vibration going inside Johnny's head that took him to his knees. Wolf helped him up and steadied him. "You'll get used to it. It always hits you the first time."

A robed figure arrived at the gate and bowed, looked at Johnny, and drew in a sharp breath, then dropped to his knees. "*Yōkoso seinaru mono*."

"Welcome, Holy One," Wolf whispered in Johnny's ear.

Johnny hesitantly gave a blessing in return, repeating after Wolf, "*Megumareru.*"[18]

18. "Blessings."

The man rose, bowed, and opened the gate. Beyond lay a tiled pathway leading to a wooden structure, obviously a lift of some kind, albeit not looking very safe. A memory rose in Johnny's mind of another unexpected and equally flimsy lift that operated between the mountains and the Abbey of the Dawn, and he felt a moment of nostalgia. This particular lift seemed to have no means of movement, but he followed Wolf and their silent guide onto the open platform, where the man raised a flimsy-looking wooden barrier. Their guide spoke into a mouthpiece set into the stone wall. There was a short pause. Then came a series of incredibly deep notes in an ascending scale of three, punctuated by a single note deeper than the others. The wooden platform shook, then began to ascend slowly and steadily.

Johnny lost his breath in sheer wonderment, first at the depth of the human vocal notes and then at the result. Beside him, Wolf grinned. "It takes you by surprise, doesn't it? It never fails to hit me in the pit of my stomach, and believe me, this is not all they can do with what they call the God Breath. You'll learn a lot from these people, Johnny, but it may not always be comfortable."

The slow ascent of the platform gave Johnny time to assimilate all that had happened in the last hour or two. In search of comfort, he mentally reached back to his father in the Aeon: "Dad, are you there? Wish I could be with you." But there was no answering mind touch.

The platform came to a halt before an opening in the mountain. Further in Johnny could see what looked like a security door. The place was well guarded judging by the robed figure carrying a gun who stood by the door.

The guard may have been armed, but at the sight of Wolf and Johnny with their guide, he snapped to attention. A whispered conversation took place between the guard and their guide. Then the guard turned to Johnny and knelt before him, laying the gun at his feet. Wolf translated, "He has been told you are the holder of the Word. The powers of the monastery are at your disposal."

Johnny went red, then white. "I really don't want all this bowing and scraping. It has to stop, Wolf. Please tell them."

"You will have to take that up with the abbess when you meet her. I have no power here. You truly don't know how important you are, Johnny, but you will have to admit to it before you leave here. This is where your training ends and your ministry begins."

The security door opened and they went through. Inside, the monastery was sparsely but comfortably furnished. His bedroom was small but adequate, though Johnny was not used to a futon. Next to it was another room fitted with the three symbols of the Shinto: a Mirror, a Sword, and a Jade Crystal shaped like a hook. There was also a bookshelf with several books, a chair, and a table with an impressive computer set-up. Wolf was next door.

Johnny took advantage of the computer to make contact with the Aeon. He opened a message and watched with delight at his son taking his shaky first steps while holding his mother's hands. Then he spoke with Eamon and Gregor for a while.

A sudden knock on the door heralded the appearance of an English-speaking apprentice with a message from the abbess inviting him and Wolf to meet with her in a few hours. Johnny changed into the robe that had been provided and used the futon to snatch a few hours of sleep. Overhead the storm unleashed its fury, but he was too tired and too drained of energy to stay awake.

Wolf woke Johnny just before 7:00 p.m., and they were escorted to the rooms of the abbess. As they traversed what seemed to be a mile of intersecting tunnels, Johnny muttered to Wolf, "You were not kidding when you said it was actually inside the mountain."

"You ain't seen nothin' yet," came the iconic reply.

♬ ♩ ♫ ♪ ♬ ♪ ♫

The quarters of Abbess Iwara Sakura were modest. Her only concession to her age was an electronic wheelchair in the corner. She sat on a plain wooden chair, the legs of which had been shortened so that it was just a few inches off the tatami mat. Her back was as straight as the painted screen behind her. A narrow, oblong window looked out over the slope of the mountain towards the sea. Scented candles lit the room, and a modern radiator kept it at a temperature suitable for the abbess's advanced age, but which the men found overly warm. The abbess sensed their discomfort and told the servant to lower it.

Deep cushions had been provided for their comfort, and on a low table, tea in fine porcelain bowls gave off a delicate aroma. The servant knelt to offer them each a bowl of tea, then retired to another room, leaving them alone. Wolf, experienced in their etiquette, gently turned his bowl several times before drinking in sips. Johnny smiled, remembering his own first meeting with the Abbot of the Dawn, and followed suit.

The abbess watched, smiling, then turned to Johnny and, speaking in excellent English, welcomed him to the abbey. "I spent several years in your country," she added. "I studied physics and astronomy at Cambridge, then went to Harvard in America to gain my PhD. Now I only get to speak English when Wolf comes to visit.

"I have been kept informed of your progress through the abbeys and have my own estimation of your growing abilities. Tomorrow you will be shown around the Abbey of the Snows and introduced to those within its walls. Two of them, plus myself, will be your guides through the last stage of your preparation."

She sipped her tea and breathed in its aroma. "The signs are drawing closer together, and we estimate the time of the conjunction on a daily basis. Such delicate formulae need constant adjustment until the exact moment can be known. By then, you will also be ready, as will all the abbeys and those within them. Your time with us will be exacting, and you will be required to keep to a tight schedule. Nearer to the conjunction we may, for a fleeting moment, find ourselves outside of what you know as time. That can take its toll on all of us. But whatever happens then, you, Forerunner, cannot deviate from your task. Nothing, *nothing*, must fall short of that unknowable space between the two events: the passing of one moment in time and the birth of its successor.

"Before then, you must learn the breathing technique that will allow you to speak the Word. Only that Word will open the door to the new age. Then we will have achieved our purpose.

"Now you will be taken to the dining hall, for you must both be hungry. I advise early sleep—you will need all your strength, Forerunner. You were born for this purpose alone and for its consequences."

The abbess rang a small silver bell and a servant appeared. She gave instructions in her own tongue. He bowed, then turned to bow to Johnny. The man spoke English and informed Johnny that he, Yoshi, was designated to serve him, and should he have need of anything, he should ask and it would be provided. Johnny and Wolf bowed and wished the abbess goodnight, then followed Yoshi to the dining room.

Johnny chose a rice dish, determined to show respect to the abbey, and found it very much to his taste. Wolf, however, worked his way through a steak large enough to feed a small family along with a mound of fries and a salad, then rounded off with two portions of ice cream—his own and Johnny's.

"They have obviously gotten used to your appetite," Johnny teased as they walked to their rooms. "But I must confess, I'm feeling a bit hemmed in. Everywhere is so dark. A lot of lights, yes, but no natural light."

Wolf yawned. He'd been up for a total of sixteen hours and needed some sleep. "Remember, you are inside a mountain. Although they have an incredible air system, you'll still react to the atmosphere of the place, both natural and...extra-natural. It will take a couple of days to acclimate. Now I'll leave you. I can't sleep here; it's too enclosed for my inner wolf. I'll leave my clothes in my room and find a place outside. I'll see you tomorrow, brother mine."

Johnny slapped his shoulder and teased him. "Don't forget to take a poop bag with you. Don't want to upset the locals."

Wolf dug in his pocket and produced a small plastic bag. "I always come prepared!" They parted with laughter.

Later, curled under a snug feather duvet, Johnny thought about the time, not so far away, when his relationships would be out of reach: Mara and Jared, Bucky, Florrie, Frank, the group, Tze-Ring, Gregor, all the people who had touched his life in so many different ways. Where would his consciousness be? Would he be able to see, hear, feel them? Be close to them? Who would tease Wolf about his appetite, run with him through a forest or along a deserted beach?

Johnny reached for the gold wolf's head on its chain round his neck. "I'll miss you all so much. Will you miss me?"

27 March, 6:00 p.m.
Europe

The abbeys kept close watch as Pacia slowly gathered her disciples round her. She was beginning to be known and talked about. Papers, news channels, and radio stations reported stories about her, her speeches, and her meetings with heads of religious, political, and business groups. In her work, Pacia placed emphasis on the future of humanity, its effect on the planet, and the changes there would be in the coming Age of Aquarius.

There were also a lot of people interested in Pacia's apparent ability to heal. The Pope was not among them. The possibility of a female Pope was not something the church wanted to see.

At the moment, Pacia was in talks between two factions in the Middle East. Events were beginning to link up and cause effects that held promise of resolving long-held differences. But the Dark powers bided their time and set in place their own plans. Above, in the vastness of space, two celestial bodies moved inexorably closer together.

30 March, 8:00 p.m.
The Abbey of the Snows

"Well, what do you think of it?" asked Wolf, leaning against an impressive computer set-up. "Not as big or extensive as NASA, maybe. Nevertheless, it will work just as well for our purposes." He turned to Brother Hiro. "Could we see what you have on the meteors?"

Hiro beamed with pride and ran an expert hand over a large console with the ease and panache of a concert pianist. "We have been able to add to our last programme, Brother Wolf. They are much closer. We will be able to predict their final conjunction within days, and by next month within hours and minutes."

Hiro's enthusiasm dimmed as it dawned on him he was happily predicting the demise of the speaker of the Word, who was standing right next to him. He sprang to his feet and crossed his arms over his heart centre. "I beg forgiveness, Holy One. I did not think! I—"

His voice trailed away, and everyone in the observatory held their breath.

Johnny laid his hand on the man's head. "Apologies are not needed when truth is spoken. We all know what is coming, what will happen, and to whom. Hiro, you can show me what few people ever know: the moment when the purpose of their life is achieved. For that, I bless and thank all of you who have worked hard to bring it about."

The entire room stood, turned to Johnny, and bowed.

Hiro turned down the lights and focussed the huge screen. The immensity of the night sky swam into view, a celestial carpet of black velvet embroidered with stars. More wheels turned, buttons were pressed, programmes shifted and changed, and suddenly the screen displayed two brilliant spherical shapes set against a star system.

Brother Hiro went into teaching mode. "There are two main stars contained within this area: Sadalsuud, or Beta Aquarii, and Sadalmelik, or Alpha Aquarii, together with globular clusters and Messier 2. It also holds the star called TRAPPIST-1, which is about forty light years from Earth. The Aquarian system holds about a dozen stars with planets." He adjusted his thick hornrims and went on. "Astrologically, it is ruled by Uranus—not considered the most helpful of the Gods. Aquarius's symbol of water being poured from a container often makes those ignorant of symbology think it is connected with water. In fact, it is an air symbol, as it is the air entering the container that pushes the water *out*." He paused for breath, then realised who he was talking to and blushed. "Forgive me. I am so used to teaching classes."

Johnny laughed and put an arm round his shoulders. "You are a fountain of knowledge, Hiro. I envy your students. Tell me about the meteors."

"They are approaching their...how do you say...rendezvous. And their speed is increasing. Also, the planets of our system are moving slowly towards—" He paused. "Towards their appointed collision point."

The voice of the abbess rang through the hall. "And that, Brother John, is when the Word of Creation must be spoken and the door to Aquarius will open. Continue with your exploration of the abbey. Tomorrow you will begin your studies of the Breath of God, its correct pronunciation, and how to use the power needed to project it. Brother Wolf, I have a message for you from the Aeon. You must return to New York at once. Transport and your instructions are waiting in Tokyo."

Wolf sighed and turned to Johnny. "A short meeting, brother mine, but it was good to spend time with you. I will catch up with you when I can." He gently punched Johnny's shoulder, then turned and left.

Hiro returned to his task of explaining the work of the observatory. A short time later, they heard the sound of a plane taking off for the mainland.

♫ ♩ ♫ ♪ ♬ ♪ ♫

Ten days later, Brother Hiro paused as they walked by the lake at the base of the mountain. He stooped and gently prised a flower from the earth, taking care not to damage its roots. Then he turned to Johnny and held it up for him to see.

"All things conform to the fourfold law," he said with a smile. "This small flower and you both obey that law. It holds true on this planet and on all those graced with the gift of life. The four great powers stand at the corners of life. We know them as earth, water, fire, and air, but more accurately they are substance, fluidity, energy, and space. All four are required before the fifth—power of consciousness, or spirit—can manifest.

"This does not always happen. There are many 'Earths' where only one or two such powers come into being. There are planets where fluidity reigns with just a modicum of substance. The sun above us is pure energy and nothing else. In our own system, there are moons of substance with no fluidity. Space exists in an aura of its own nothingness—at least, a nothingness we cannot see, feel, or experience. But when all four exist together, the possibility of life gifted with consciousness of the self increases in whatever form is most suitable. This flower found in earth a substance, which gives it stability. Water gives it the urge to grow, and the sun's energy draws it upwards so it can manifest in space."

Hiro replanted the flower and held his open palm over it. The plant quivered, straightened, and reached up to receive the blessing offered to it.

Hiro smiled and turned to Johnny. "Each power has a sound: the deep rumble of earth, the rhythmic slap of water against a cliff, the roar of fire, and the soft breath of air. This flower is conscious of the energy I can offer it. It is aware of something greater than itself and strives towards it.

A child grows in the same way, feeding on substance, drinking water, feeling the energy of too hot, too cold, or just right. Humanity adapted its physical shape, grew in strength, learned to cope with heat and cold, and used air to create a voice.

"You will be taught to control all these powers in order to manifest the Word that will open the door to Aquarius. Are you not taught in your belief system 'In the beginning was the Word, and the Word was with God, and the Word was God'? In that one saying, there is more knowledge, wisdom, and strength than your wise men and women have ever realised." He paused and held his head to one side, then smiled. "The abbess asks you to join her in her rooms."

Yoshi, Johnny's shadow, came forward, bowed with a smile, and indicated the way. Johnny followed reluctantly, hating to leave the sunshine and fresh air for the heavy atmosphere in the mountain. Hiro waved and went back to communicating with his plants.

With Yoshi trotting in front of him, Johnny wound his way through the seemingly endless corridors and finally arrived at the door to the rooms of the abbess. Yoshi rang the silver bell and moved aside the exquisitely embroidered curtain that covered it. The door was opened by the abbess's personal servant. It always felt like stepping back in time when in her presence.

Johnny bowed, entered, and approached the abbess with due respect, bowed again and took his seat on the cushioned stool before her. "*Konnichiwa.*"[19] The servants left them.

The abbess leaned forward and tapped his shoulder with her fan. "Your Japanese is improving, though the pronunciation needs to improve. But your efforts are commendable." She smiled, and her wrinkled visage became warm and welcoming.

Another wave of the fan brought tea and the American cookies to which the abbess was addicted. Silence was observed as the tea was sipped, and the required words of appreciation were offered and accepted.

Her sense of tradition satisfied, the abbess got straight to business. "News from the Aeon is good. The work of the Teacher proceeds as planned,

19. "Hello."

and Her gatherings are beginning to be well received. The press are watching with interest. All the abbeys are prepared and primed to withstand the Power of the Opening on the day and the time designated. I am informed that your training proceeds well, but that you will now begin to practice the correct breathing pattern. For though the abbeys will call out the actual sound of each note, you must reproduce it within all four of your bodies—physical, astral, mental, and spiritual—in rapid succession, then bring them all together as the Word is spoken verbally.

"That is the most difficult, as it must be the *last* breath. You will be in pain, but your mind must remain in full control. You must speak with power and intent, but also you must build and hold the image of the Door of Time. When it opens, the symbol of the age will come through into manifestation. The passing age will depart the same way, *but*…it will take you with it. You must take nothing with you! No regrets, no anger, no images or emotions. You depart as you entered: with nothing."

Johnny protested. "But that means my memories…I'll have nothing of *me* left."

"You have no idea of the power this will demand of you. You will pass into a state of unknowingness that will slowly settle into a time of total integration with the All. This will begin to lighten, and with it will come your memories. You will be aware of helpers around you. Also remember that the second of the three who offered will be with you; he will have gone through a similar experience. The third will follow in time. When the Forerunner, the Betrayer, and the Teacher have passed into the All-Time, then your work will be assessed, and you will have access to all you have known and experienced."

Johnny shook his head. "But time will have passed here. I will have missed my son growing, maybe his children…This is not fair!"

The abbess gave a dry chuckle. "Have you forgotten all your teachings, Forerunner? Time does not pass. It *is*. You can pass back and forth as you will. You will miss nothing—not one moment. You and the Teacher are the lucky ones; you know what is before you. Think of the Betrayer, for that one never knows what lies ahead. They live with regret and pain, self-loathing, and the knowledge that for the whole of that age, their name will be reviled and their seeming betrayal will be held up as a warning to others. Each age must have a Teacher to guide it, a Forerunner to announce the coming, and the one who will offer to take the blame. Of them all, the Betrayer's role demands the greatest strength—they never understand until all is achieved. It is always thus. It takes three to bring the age into being, and they all know each other."

Johnny raised his head from his hands. "Tango, he will be the one who…who…"

"Kills you. Yes, Johnny. And your last and greatest task is to persuade him to do it with love and for the Light. If you do not succeed in that, the message of the age will be misunderstood, and it will all be for nothing. It has happened. Not often, but it has happened. *That* is your prime task, Forerunner. The Betrayer must understand why he is doing it, and he must do it with love."

The Abbess paused and regarded the distraught man before her with sympathy. "Would you like some more tea, Johnny?"

"*Why*? Why does it have to be him? He had a rotten start in life. All he ever wanted was to be a part of something worthwhile. I tried and sometimes succeeded, but he was so hurt, so suspicious. I don't even know where he is. He made it to the top, then lost it all. God knows where he is now."

The abbess beckoned him to sit by her side. "He is safe and being looked after for the time being. Giving birth to something new and wonderful is always painful, like all births. This is a time of trial for you all, Johnny. At this moment, Pacia is being imprisoned for trying to bring two warring factions together. Both have turned against her. She will cope, as will you all, Johnny Burke. Deep within himself, the one you call Tango has both loved and envied you. To be the sacrifice is the easiest; it is the slayer who must be the strongest. Dying is soon over and the trauma eased away. To slay what is loved for the ultimate good, and to carry the stigma through the entire age, requires a depth of love beyond all imagining.

"Until now, the emphasis has been on you, Johnny, and it will pass from you to Pacia. Each of you, in turn, will become symbols of the new age. The world will weep for you both, say prayers, light candles, and speak your names with hushed voices in temples built in your honour. But in an unknown place, there will be a patch of earth more sacred than the greatest cathedral. There will always be flowers growing there, and for a time, there will be those who will visit to remember and bless what lies beneath. What the world thinks does not matter, what the world can achieve, will open up the way to the stars."

The tears from his eyes blinked away, Johnny lifted his head. "Is there anything I can say to help him?"

"No. All you can do is make him see that it has been his destiny since the beginning, and now, at the end, it will all rest upon him. If he can understand and do it with love, all will be well." The abbess paused. "You need me to reassure you about Tango. Allow me to do this." She spread her fan wide and reversed it. On the opposite side, a symbol had been painted. "It holds many meanings, among them faith, purity, and knowledge. Focus on the symbol, Johnny, and embed it into your subconscious. When stressed, call it to mind and allow it to take shape in your thoughts. Then project it outwards until you can manifest it at a distance." She waited until the symbol was steady and exact in shape, then snapped the fan shut.

With a start, Johnny came to and thanked her for her help. He quietly left the room and went, as instructed, to the temple where the Breath of God awaited him.

As he crossed one of the small garden areas, Johnny paused. A small plant lay on the path, torn from its place by the cart of a passing garden worker. He bent, picked it up, and gently replaced it, packing the earth around it. Johnny extended his hand over it as Hiro had done and blessed it. The stem strengthened and came upright, and the head lifted and turned towards him. Johnny smiled and said, "Any time, little one," then went on his way.

The abbess smiled and shared the moment with Hiro. "He learns quickly."

Johnny took his time getting to Aoki's music room. Like Hiro's garden, it was outside the main area of the monastery. It also contained a soundproofed room, something the rest of the abbey had learned to appreciate.

At almost six foot, Aoki was tall for a man of his race, and he owed it to his grandsire. He greeted Johnny and led the way into a music room equipped with many different instruments. As Johnny looked round, he recognised items from both Western and Eastern cultures.

He turned to Aoki. "Honoured teacher, I have to tell you I never learned to actually read music, just enough to play a guitar accompaniment to my own voice. However, my friends were the real musicians. They were my supporters. All I had was a voice and the ability to put a tune across to the audience."

Aoki sat at the piano and sent a ripple of notes flowing through the room. Johnny recognised it. "Frank's symphony! You heard it here?"

"No, Nova San, I was there in person. Frank has a great talent that has been opened more fully by your association. I hope one day to meet him and to offer my humble help in opening his talent to the world. But now to you, Nova San, and the task before you. Sound is the only instrument that can open the Door of the Ages. It may seem a small thing, but the vibration of the Word of Creation is done by using the Breath of Kami—you would say God."

Interested, Johnny took a seat closer to the piano. "I have heard much about this phenomenon. Can you explain it in more detail?"

Like all teachers with an interested pupil, Aoki opened up. "It is a moment when one becomes a part of everything that has ever been or is yet to be. It lasts, in one sense, no time at all. In another, it is continuous throughout time. The Breath is threefold: It is desire itself; it is that which is desired; it is the object of desire.

"In simplistic terms, the Breath is pure vibration, and when used with intent, it 'becomes' that which is desired. Understand that the Breath is Creation in and of Itself. It has never 'not been.' It will continue to be without end. To breathe is to be, to be is to know, to know is to sustain what we know as consciousness of self. The Breath is conscious of Itself and desires to share that knowingness with all life. So it pervades the All with Itself, looking for the slightest hint of consciousness. When It finds it, It joins with it and creates more of Itself, then moves on.

"When a life form reaches a certain level, the seed of the Breath takes root in the strongest, and a Teacher is born. When that form is no longer able to sustain it, It leaves and lies dormant until needed once more. All three of those who open the way to a new age hold the essence of the Breath within. As each Teacher passes beyond their allotted time, the remnant of the Breath of God leaves them. Do you remember the last words spoken by the Teacher of this passing age?" Aoki closed his eyes and spoke, his voice deep and resonant. "'My God, my God, why hast thou forsaken me?' Great as those souls are, there is always a moment of fear and doubt. The last shred of human consciousness."

Aoki rose from the piano and stood close to Johnny. He lifted a mobile phone and spoke into it, listened for a moment, then replaced the phone. "Come, let us begin your training. Place your hand on my solar plexus and press firmly."

Johnny did so. With startling suddenness, he felt the muscles tense, then become rigid. Then Aoki's solar plexus pulsed rapidly. Johnny felt a surge of powerful energy that grew in intensity.

Aoki closed his eyes, opened his mouth, and sang out a note deeper than any human voice Johnny had ever heard. The room began to shake. Beneath his feet, the earth trembled. Aoki stood with closed eyes, and as the note died away into silence, he sang out again, and deeper. The sound was almost solid. A thousand claps of thunder would have been a lullaby to this. Beneath them, the entire mountain trembled and shook. Rocks fell from the summit. Birds fell to the earth and trembled where they lay. The room fell quiet. Then, on the third breath, the note was so deep it could only be felt, not heard. Johnny slumped, unconscious, to the ground.

After a few minutes, the phone rang and Aoki picked it up. It was Hiro in the observatory. "We've lost all the light bulbs, and two of the screens have cracked. Three bloody noses, and two of the younger ones fainted. We'll need to buy more cups. It's a pity the abbess insists on china—paper cups would be a lot cheaper. No complaints as yet from the village, but we really must get the alarm working again. But at least you didn't sound the last one; I'm grateful for that…I only have the glasses I'm wearing left. How did our guest take it?"

"He will come round in a minute or two. He stood the first two well. I have high hopes he can stand up to the last one."

Aoki replaced the phone and helped the shaken Johnny to a couch. "Stay still and be quiet for a while. The first time is always a shock. At least you didn't lose your lunch."

Johnny sat with his head in his hands. "Is it always like that?

Aoki held out a glass of water. "No, sometimes it's worse. We only reached the third depth. There are two below that—the last is the one you need to reach. But you do not have to sound it; you couldn't anyway. All you have to do is open a 'space' for it to manifest. The note is conscious of itself and its purpose, but you have to hold the Door of the Ages open for it to come into full manifestation. It is remarkable that you held out to the depth you did."

He went to the cupboard and took out a bag of birdseed. Opening the door to the garden, Aoki spread the seeds liberally. "The sound does not hurt them, but they need to recover, and feeding them helps." Then Aoki helped Johnny to his feet, called Yoshi in, and instructed, "Take him to his room, give him tea, and let him sleep, but see he does not miss dinner."

Still dazed, Johnny followed his guide back to the living quarters and slept. Aoki went to report to the abbess.

♬ ♩ ♫ ♪ ♬ ♪ ♫

"Remarkable. He took it to a depth unheard of for a first time. I do not wonder why he has been chosen. The next age will be one of great change, and some of it will be hard, but my Kami tells me it will open the universe to the human race. I almost wish I could be there when they realise their potential. Almost, but not quite." Aoki rearranged his natural form on the heated support opposite the abbess.

She smiled and picked up her china cup, holding it carefully in her six-fingered hands. "They are a remarkably creative life form, and pleasant to look at, unlike some I have visited. It has been interesting to watch them grow into their power. The coming age will test them severely, but I have high hopes of their eventual acceptance onto the Council." She sighed. "I will miss this liquid. It is very refreshing."

12 April, 2:00 p.m.
Ceuta

Pacia blinked as she staggered out of the prison into the harsh sunlight. After two weeks in near darkness, her eyes burned and watered as she headed for the nearest patch of shade. One of the guards, a young Spaniard, passed her tattered rucksack to her and tucked a piece of paper into her hand. Then he hurried back into the miserable building that passed for a jail in the Spanish outpost on the coast of Africa.

Pacia's rucksack was heavier than it had been. Inside was a bottle of water, a slice of bread, and—glory be—a hat that had seen better days but would provide protection against the blistering sun. She crouched under an overhang and drank some water but kept half against later need. The bread was hard and more than a day old, but it was food.

At last, Pacia unfolded the paper. On it was a rough map and an address. She looked back at the prison building. From an upper window, the young Spaniard looked out and pointed to his right, then held up three fingers and made a walking gesture. She nodded, turned right, and began to walk on feet that had been blistered.

As she walked, Pacia sent a blessing to rest on the head of her unknown saviour. He had held up three fingers. Three streets, three houses, three days? She kept walking. At the third opening, a small boy waited. He smiled, then turned and walked away. She followed him to a door that opened to a courtyard. A woman held up a hand and drew a triangle, and Pacia limped into the cool interior. No word was said, but there were women there. They bathed Pacia, put ointment on her burns and cuts, fed her, and let her sleep with someone beside her. She rested for two days, then was passed from house to house until she reached the harbour.

Amal picked her up at nightfall and took her to a motor yacht in the harbour. Within hours, Pacia was in the Abbey of the Aeon, and two weeks later was once more on television talking to the world about its future. Her scarred face and tortured hands and feet bore witness to her determination to spread her message.

"Allow all to worship as they will. No one faith is above the other. Forget differences—they mean nothing. Heal each other. Look within, honour the gift of life within you, and share it. Look to the stars; they are waiting for you. There are other lives out there. Share what and who you are with them. They have fought the same troubles and won. You also can win. Yes, look to the stars. There is life there, different to you, but waiting to welcome you.

"Humanity is one of many forms of life. There is so much to know, understand, and share. Reach out, and together you can begin the wonderful journey before you. But do it together. There is room for all! The universe is never-ending. You may be black, white, or brown; French, Asian, or African; speak English, Spanish, or Russian; but what you *are* is human. A special life form, one of many throughout the universe. Seek out the others and learn, share, teach, exchange, marry, share beliefs. Make the universe a haven of intelligent life, and in the fullness of time, seek out that which lies beyond…for there is always more to experience.

"This is my message. But who will listen? Ahead is the Age of Aquarius, with many wonders to explore. Together we can achieve so much. Don't throw this away. There are those waiting to welcome you. They are here now. Seek them out. Listen to them. Don't let the power of the coming age slip away. Take it. Use it. Listen to me. Please, listen."

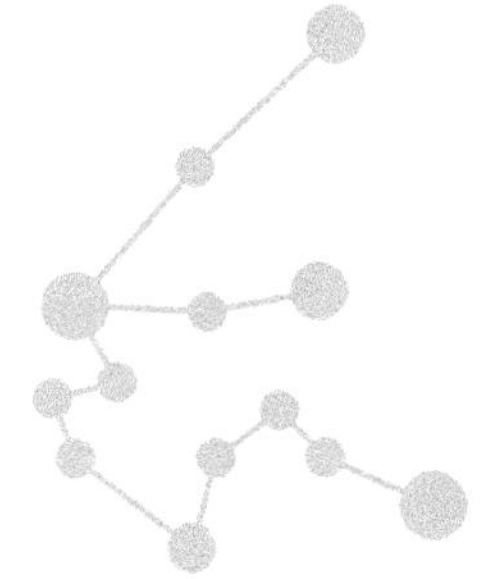

CHAPTER FORTY-FOUR

13 April, 1:00 a.m.
Longwood, New York City

A cutting wind carrying the promise of rain swept along a deserted side street. Discarded newspapers, condoms, plastic cups, cigarette butts, and the rubbish of a city's daily output were scattered everywhere. At 1:00 a.m. the alleyways were filled with cardboard boxes that housed the homeless and the hopeless. The silence held the stench of hunger, loneliness, and misery.

A church clock sounded the hour, and the silence deepened. There came the sound of weary feet, feet that had walked long and hard without any purpose. Into the meagre pool of light of a single streetlamp came a man. His age was difficult to judge. Hunger, fatigue, dehydration, and sheer hopelessness showed in every step. His clothes showed evidence of having been of good quality when new. Now torn, dirty, scuffed, and smelling of long-time use, they were ragged and fit only for the garbage. His shoes were cracked, and one sole was held together with string.

The man carried a plastic bag in one hand, and on his back, the only thing of worth that he owned: a guitar. As he reached the streetlamp, he staggered and clutched at it, then slowly slid down and used it as a support. From the plastic bag he took a piece of bread. It was mouldy, but it was food. He picked out bits and tried to eat, but his mouth was too dry. His head drooped, and a sob shook his shoulders. He cried as only a man at the very edge of exhaustion can cry.

From his pocket, the man took a small knife and opened it. He stretched out his hand and laid the knife to his wrist. He looked up at the new moon as if to keep its image in his mind and applied pressure to the blade.

"I don't think that is a good idea, my friend." A lean, well-muscled form sat down beside Tango. "What you need first is a drink. Here." He held out a small carton of milk. "Sip it slowly or you will be sick."

Tango stretched out a dirty hand with broken nails and brought the milk to his lips. He paused, inhaled the scent of the liquid, then took a sip, and another and another. When he had drunk half of it, the stranger took it away.

"Let it settle in your stomach for a while. Then you can finish it off."

Tango leaned back against the lamp post. "Thanks. It's been a long time since I tasted milk."

The stranger offered him a small bar of chocolate. "Now try this. Take small pieces, and let it melt in your mouth. The sugar in it will give you energy."

For the next half hour, the stranger fed Tango slowly with small pieces of cheese, sips of milk, and finally a piece of bread spread with butter and meat paste. Then he helped Tango to his feet and led him, unresisting, to where a small, battered camper van was parked by the curb. Inside was a single mattress with a real pillow and a blanket. "Rest here. Sleep is a good healer."

Tango turned to him. "Why are you doing this for me? You don't know me."

"We have a mutual friend," said the stranger. "Now sleep."

Too weary and bemused to argue, Tango dropped onto the mattress and within minutes was asleep.

Wolf watched him for a while, then closed the camper door and got into the driving seat.

♫ ♩ ♫ ♪ ♫ ♪ ♫

Wolf parked the camper and walked into the Harbour View Rentals booking office. The clerk reluctantly tore his eyes away from the pornography he was watching and tried to look welcoming.

"I want a double room, twin beds, and a decent-sized shower. Not sure how long for, but at least a week. I'll pay up front. By the way, is there a place to eat close by that does takeaway as well?"

The clerk pushed the register towards him and reached for a set of keys. "Room twelve. Turn left outside and last on your left. That'll be two hundred fifty for the week, and Momma's Place is over the road and round the corner. She does a pretty good dinner, and you can get takeout after 6:00 a.m."

Wolf paid up, grabbed the keys, and left the clerk to his video. He moved the camper to a spot opposite room number twelve and opened the back of the van. Tango was in no shape to be woken up, so Wolf carried him into the room and laid him gently on the bed, then went back for his own luggage and the guitar. After Wolf locked the camper, he stripped his charge and covered him warmly, then stretched out on his own bed and set his inner alarm for 6:00 a.m. and slept.

♫ ♩ ♫ ♪ ♫ ♪ ♫

Wolf gently woke the sleeping man. Tango stirred, sighed, then came wide awake, already reaching out for his guitar—all that was left to him of his former identity. "What? What…Oh God, I'm sorry, officer. I was so tired. I'm going, I'm going—"

"It's all right, Tango. I'm not the police. You're safe. Now get up slowly—no need to hurry. Let's get you into the shower. You'll feel better when you've cleaned up. Then you can shave and we'll have breakfast. Not too much at first; your system won't be used to it. We'll snack later on and get your stomach used to working again."

Wolf helped the bemused man into the shower and kept watch until he was sure Tango could stand without falling.

Tango revelled in the warm water, real soap, and a clean, dry towel, not one used by a dozen before him in a homeless shelter. Wolf shook his head at the amount of dirt a human body can accumulate and put a set of clean clothes on the bed.

Several razor nicks later, Tango pulled on clean underwear, socks, denims, and a warm fleece top. He had forgotten what it was like to feel clean and warm. The trainers were a relief to his sore feet, and when the smell of coffee hit him, the tears began to flow. Tango put his face in his hands and wept. Wolf was quiet. This man had to relearn how to live without fear.

Scrambled eggs on toast, more toast with butter, and honey followed. Finally Tango felt able to ask questions.

"You said we had mutual friends, but I haven't had any friends for a long time. Had some once...Great guys, but I didn't appreciate them and lost them a long time ago. There was one special one. Johnny. He was always good to me, even when I treated him like shit. He gave me the guitar. Never tried to sell that. It was—is—all I have left of those times. That was a long time ago, in London." Tango got up and walked to the window and looked out. "I'd give so much to be back there. I really want to go home, but it's so far away."

Wolf came up behind Tango and laid a hand on his shoulder. "First you need to get your strength back. Then you can think about getting back home."

Tango shook his head. "You don't understand. That needs money, it needs time, and I need to find work. Once I had all the money I wanted, and friends, sort of. They left when the money ran out. All but one. He tried to help. I blew it, but there's still something I have to do. I keep dreaming about it, but it's not clear in my head."

Wolf drew Tango to the table and poured him another coffee. "You don't need to think about it yet. You need to get back to full strength and then, my friend, we'll get you back to London to complete what you have to do."

Tango turned to face him. "Who are you? I don't even know your name. You fed me, gave me clothes, a place to sleep...and now you say you can get me back to London. Why? Why are you doing this? Who are you?"

"My name is Wolf, and as I told you, we have mutual friends. My task is to get you fit enough to complete what you were born to do. First a haircut, then a visit to the gym for a very gentle workout, then lunch, then a sleep before dinner. I'll be looking after you for the time being." Tango protested, but Wolf stopped him. "You don't have to understand—just go with the flow. Now, first the haircut, and on the way we'll buy some new strings for the guitar; two of them are broken. Tonight you can play for me." Wolf handed Tango a denim jacket. "Come on, let's go."

The day passed in a blur, but the extra-gentle workout at the gym exhausted Tango after just thirty minutes. Wolf fed him hot soup and crackers and, as a treat, a cream doughnut. A slow walk in what passed for the local park was followed by an afternoon sleep. While Tango rested, Wolf took the opportunity to report back to the Aeon and the group what was happening. Despite all that Tango had done, Bucky and Florrie were concerned and supportive, though the rest of the group (all but Lyle) were less so.

When he finally woke, Tango spent a happy time re-stringing his guitar and polishing it with loving care. Finally he began to play. At first his fingers were stiff and awkward, but soon he forgot he had a listener, and after a few false starts, the old skill returned. Old memories returned too, and he lapsed into what had once been his mother tongue.

Paham mae dicter, O Myfanwy,
Yn llenwi'th lygaid duon di?
A'th ruddiau tirion, O Myfanwy,
Heb wrido wrth fy ngweled i?[20]

Tango raised his head from the instrument and looked at Wolf with tears running down his face. "The last time I sang that, I caused the death of a young girl." He laid the guitar aside. "When I get back home, I will visit her grave and beg her forgiveness."

Wolf noted the tiny spark of spiritual light that never left Tango's side and smiled.

20. "Why so the anger, Oh Myfanwy, / That fill your dark eyes? / Your gentle cheeks, Oh Myfanwy, / No longer blush beholding me?"

♬ ♩ ♫ ♪ ♬ ♪ ♫

Wolf and Tango stood silently at the foot of the gangplank. Tango's luggage was already on board.

Wolf spoke quietly, still looking out across the water. "I chose a small ship and a second-class ticket, not because it was cheaper—you could have gone first class—but on a bigger vessel and in first class, there was more chance of you being recognised, and that would have been difficult for you. This way you get to the UK with no publicity. But I did tell the purser you were a singer and if he played his cards right, you might consent to doing a bit of entertaining. The people travelling with you are mostly older and not likely to recognise you, especially with the beard. Which, by the way, suits you.

"You'll have five or six days to decide what to do when you get home. Also, you will need this." Wolf passed a padded envelope to him. "There are still choices ahead of you, but Tango, think carefully before you make those choices. Whatever you choose, whatever happens from now on will affect many people. I do not think we will meet again, but I have enjoyed your company and to have been able to help you has been a privilege. Goodbye, my friend. May the powers go with you and help you to make the right decisions."

Wolf laid an arm across Tango's shoulders and held him, for a moment sharing his heartbeat with him. Then he turned away.

Tango called out. "Wolf, wait! Please, who has been helping me through you? I want to be able to thank him, if only in a prayer."

Wolf turned as he opened the camper door. "I'll tell him that even through the bad times, you kept the guitar he gave you and never sold it to buy food."

He drove away, leaving Tango open-mouthed. "Johnny. It was—it is—Johnny!"

Tango dashed away the tears and made his way up the gangplank. He was going home.

17 April, 4:00 p.m.
The Abbey of the Snows

Inside the soundproofed chamber, well below the observatory, Aoki and Johnny sat side by side on their tatami mats. The last rumbles and shock waves of their morning practice had died away. Aoki sighed and turned to his companion. "That was very good, Nova San. You can now withstand the power up to the third level. You have progressed very quickly. The abbess will be most pleased."

Aoki stood and began to stretch his limbs in a series of exercises. It was obvious the sessions were causing him discomfort. Johnny rose and assisted him to a curiously shaped piece of furniture that seemed to offer his teacher a degree of comfort.

"May I offer tea, sir? The work seems to cause you discomfort. Is there anything I can do to help?"

Johnny rang for Yoshi who, on seeing the master's obvious discomfort, called his personal servant, and a tall, heavily built individual arrived. He gently lifted the old man and carried him away.

Yoshi reassured Johnny that Aoki would be all right and tried to explain. "Master Aoki is of a different—" He hesitated. "It is to do with his family. Ah, something they share. Perhaps you would care to walk in the garden or stay here and go over what the master has taught you so far. The breathing exercises are always useful to repeat."

Johnny nodded. "That is a good idea, Yoshi."

The little man beamed with delight. "I will leave hot tea with honey. It will help." He bustled off.

Johnny walked over to the window and looked out over the garden and across the narrow strip of forest to the sea beyond. He felt in need of company and sent a mental probe out over the ocean, touching and seeking. Seeking—

"Johnny?" The image of a sleek wolf filled his mind. It lifted its head and leapt to its paws. "By the grace of the Great Spirit, is it you?"

"Wolf!" Johnny's voice lifted. "It's good to hear you, even if only mentally. I didn't know I could reach this far by myself."

"Johnny, your only limit is belief in your own ability. It is good to feel your energy, my brother."

"Wolf, what of Tango? Is he on his way home? How is he now?"

"He is well, though he needs to exercise and rebuild his confidence. He will be in England in a few days. Pacia is on the same ship and will make contact with him soon. But I have felt the closeness of the Darkness. Do not underestimate them; they have not given up their plan.

"Johnny, I can feel your link fading—your power grows weak. Close down and reserve it. I will send you news of Mara and Jared and also of Tango. Beneath the personality he has built in this incarnation, I have come to know a very different one. Rest now, brother mine."

The link faded as Yoshi entered bearing a tray with tea, small cakes, and a bowl of fruit.

Later Johnny dined quietly with Master Aoki in his rooms, which held comfortable, if somewhat unusual, furnishings. Aoki spoke at length about the power of sound when allied to voice, music, and speech: its variations, levels, and tonal qualities. Johnny learned that each planet and even solar systems came into being on the wings of sound, and that this was true of all things.

Aoki told him, "Your earliest wise ones made this clear: In the beginning was the Word. Each new life does the same, just as every human being is birthed to its own cry. Its true name lies in that first utterance. Sound combined with intent is the basis of what you call a prayer, a spell, and so is the name given to you by your parents. It becomes a sound portrait of the person. The new age must be named, Johnny, or it cannot come into being."

He spoke earnestly, obviously using his own voice to demonstrate the effect of sound. But the effort was telling on him. Aoki sank back in his circular chair and breathed in vapour from an oddly shaped incense burner by his side.

Johnny leaned forward. "Master Aoki, you are not well. Shall I call someone to help you?"

The older man smiled. "Thank you. I apologise for my lack of attention. It is due to a…condition I cannot control, a family trait. I will need to withdraw for a time. But I will arrange for you to have another teacher for a while. He is younger than myself, but very gifted in the use of sound in all its forms. I think you will do well together."

Aoki rang for his helper as Johnny rose and bowed respectfully.

"I bid you goodnight, and I hope to see you again very soon, sir."

The helper entered and bowed to his master, then to Johnny, before lifting the old man into his arms and leaving.

Johnny surveyed the room. Something seemed...What was it? Of all the abbeys, this was the only one where he felt out of place.

He left and returned to his own quarters.

♬ ♩ ♫ ♪ ♬ ♩ ♫

In the unfathomable depths of the Allness to which even time and space owed their existence, Thought stirred. Images came into being and dissolved again and again. In untold millions of worlds, events happened or were prevented from happening. It was virtually untold for anything to disturb the constant flow of change and growth. But once in millions of years...

17 April, 8:00 p.m.
The North Atlantic Ocean

The *Pride of Plymouth* had slid quietly from her berth and made her way through the dark waters to the sea, turning her nose to the open Atlantic and England. Tango stood alone and silent as he watched the land he had dreamed of in his younger years slowly fade from sight. The golden land he had planned to conquer, which instead had brought him to his knees.

"No, Talfryn, it simply taught you lessons you needed to learn."

Tango turned, startled, to face a woman of some thirty years standing beside him. Her eyes held a power that part of him recognised and was in awe of. She held out her hand. "I'm Pacia Adabyo. We have a mutual friend. Johnny Burke, or rather, Johnny Nova."

"I know you! You've been on the news and all over the papers lately. The Pope called you an antichrist and tried to have you banned from Italy. You cured that child who everyone thought was dead."

She laughed. "Don't believe all that you hear, Talfryn. Yes, I lecture and talk to lots of people, but all I do is try to make them see sense about themselves. The Pope has to learn that people have the right to see the Creator as the highest aspect of themselves, and it's a struggle to accept it. I tell the truth—that's all I can do—and hope they understand.

"Your God was fame and fortune. A way out of the guilt of your grandmother's death. Johnny saw it as a way to learn through music about the new Age of Aquarius. We all have a part to play, and yours will be the hardest. This journey is for you. When you reach England, follow what your heart tells you to do. This time will see the end of the Age of Pisces and the dawn of Aquarius."

Tango stared at her. "How does that involve me? I know very little about things like that."

Pacia took his arm and began to walk to the stairs leading to the cabins. "That is why I am here, Talfryn. During the next few days, I will tell you all you need to know. I'll help you to understand how you and I—and Johnny—will open a new and exciting age for humanity."

He scoffed. "That kind of stuff needs special people."

"Exactly, my dear, and it will take all three of us to make it happen. Now let's get some sleep. We have a lot to get through over the next four days."

♫ ♩ ♫ ♪ ♫ ♪ ♫

Tango decided that he did want to provide entertainment for the ship's passengers. Part of his job on board was to mingle with the passengers during the afternoon, but the mornings and pre-dinner times were his own. Once dinner was over and cleared away, the real work began. Talking to people had given him a lead on their favourite songs. The time spent with his mother and his grandmother, both gifted singers, had given him a comprehensive repertoire of songs of the 1940s and '50s as well as modern musicals. His natural charm, when he chose to use it, gave him a very appreciative audience during his performances.

Pacia sought Tango out each morning, and he soon recognised in her the same kind of power both De'ath and Desi had shown. But this power was clean, and it held a purity of purpose he'd never experienced before. When she was with him, he felt different. He slept better than he had done for so long.

While Tango slept, Pacia began to gently ease away some of the traumas of his early life, helping him to understand the lessons they held. Once or twice, Johnny joined her, and Tango would wake with memories of the early days of White Heat. He recalled the feeling of belonging, being valued, the laughter, the warmth, the quarrels and the bickering, and the smell of Bucky's cigars. Between the memories, moments of information were fed to his mind: pressure to remember something important he had to do—something terrible, something he'd done before and had to do again, but for a different reason. Unknowingly, Tango was coaxed into reopening his inner powers, but this time for the right purpose.

♫ ♩ ♫ ♪ ♬ ♪ ♫

Tango's voice flowed over his listeners like honey. Almost all his fellow travellers were pensioners taking advantage of smaller, cut-price cruises. He'd realised from the outset these people were not into the White Heat style, but at an age to look back and remember their youth and songs they knew from earlier days. Without realising it, Tango had sung many of his grandmother's favourites. For the past four days, he had concentrated on the ballad style and recalled for his listeners the music and songs of their past. In the afternoons he had shared some of his past with Pacia, and she had mentioned that the past could hold some answers to his hopes, fears, and doubts. Now, on the last evening, Tango had chosen his mother's favourite song, "Without a Song" by Frank Sinatra.

There was a short silence and then, to his surprise, the audience rose to their feet to applaud. Taken aback, Tango went red and got to his feet and bowed. When it quieted down, he spoke. "Ladies and gentlemen, these have been a very special few days for me. This is our last evening together, and you have made it a very warm and friendly time. Thank you. I have spent too much time in the US, and now at last I'm going home. It has been my honour and my pleasure to sing for you. I will never forget this time we have shared."

The ship purser rose to his feet. "Talfryn, you have brought back many memories for us, songs we loved and sang in our youth. We enjoyed your company as well as the beauty of your voice. We would like to present you with a token of our thanks and our time together. Please accept this with our thanks." He handed over an envelope of money.

The applause was a balm to Tango's bruised soul. He wept unashamedly and shook hands with everyone. The captain brought out champagne to add to the celebration.

Later that night, in the quiet of his small berth, Tango did something he had not done in years: He knelt in thanks and blessed the ship and its company. Tomorrow he would be back home, and hopefully his luck would change.

In her cabin, Pacia shared his thoughts and plans. Her heart bled for Tango. He still had to understand his place in the opening of the new age. She set free her empowered consciousness and connected with Johnny, passing to him the events of the past few days. Johnny, in turn, gently touched the higher consciousness of Tango as he slept.

"Be strong, my brother in Light. When seeming disaster strikes, remember that together we are the three who will bring humanity into the new age. Love, knowledge, and power. Together we made the offer. All will be accomplished at the chosen moment. Rest now."

22 April, 7:00 p.m.
Southampton

Tango stood by the window of the cheap motel room, a bottle of English beer in his hand, and looked over the parking lot. He was back in England, and soon he'd be in Cardiff, where his memories could have free rein to either soothe or destroy him—he'd have to wait and see.

He finished the beer and stretched out on the bed. It had been a hectic day. Customs had been thorough in their search; even his guitar had been X-rayed. Satisfied he had nothing illegal in his luggage, they finally let him go. Then Tango had taken a bus into town and looked for a cheap place to sleep and get his land legs back again.

Tango treated himself to a meal of sausages, mashed potatoes and peas, and another beer. Then he slept, long and heavily, and woke with a sense of purpose. Breakfast was egg, bacon, and beans, with toast and marmalade to follow. The sound of English voices, the blare of traffic, and cheerful music from the café's TV brought home to him that he was back where he belonged. He paid his bill with a sense of pride at being able to do so, thanks to the money Wolf had given him. With the three hundred from the ship's purser and the gift of his travel companions, it meant he had enough—if he was cautious—to keep him until he could find work. But first, Tango had things to do.

After a few inquiries, he found a café used by truckers. There he asked a few questions, bought a few beers, shared jokes, and made inquiries about a possible lift. By 2:00 p.m. he was on his way to Bristol. To pass the time, he played the guitar for his driver, and the two of them sang bawdy songs at the tops of their voices.

Just before 5:00 p.m., his driver dropped him off close to a bed and breakfast used by other drivers. After booking in, Tango again made inquiries. A discreet tenner changed hands, and he had a ride into Cardiff the following day.

Seeing his guitar, the buxom landlady asked him to play, and though tired, he obliged, much to the delight of the drivers and the landlady. It earned Tango a free meal and a reduction on his bill.

He slept fitfully and woke to a day of rain and a drop in temperature. As he paid his bill, the landlady produced a well-worn raincoat and gave it to him. "It was my hubby's," she told him. "He used to sing for the lads some nights, but he's long gone now. It'll keep you dry. You don't want to catch a cold with a voice like that." She saw him to the door, where his lift was waiting, and suddenly gave him a hug. "I love that film you did. You were great, and I'm sorry things went so bad for you after. But here's hoping you can make it big again, lad."

The woman hurried back and closed the door, leaving Tango open-mouthed and a bit tearful. He climbed into the truck and took off for his final destination.

Bristol disappeared behind him. The land levelled out and slowly took on a different look, and within the hour the signs were reading *Creoso y Cymru*. His driver was not as talkative as the others had been. The Welsh tended to keep their distance from those not of their kin, but when Tango began to give the driver directions in his own language, the man's attitude changed. He began to talk, asking where Tango had come from, how long had he been away, and if had he come to stay. Tango showed little sign of wanting to explain, so much of the journey passed in silence.

As they drew near to the docks, Tango gave more directions. "It's Seymour Street, off Moorlands Road. You can drop me here—it's very close. Many thanks for the ride." He handed over a roll of notes.

The driver nodded. He said, "*Diolch. Gobeithio y cewch chi ymweliad da,*"[21] and drove off.

Tango smiled thinly. No, there would be no one to make him welcome.

He walked down a road once so familiar, now totally strange and unknown. Many of the houses were empty, and all needed repairs and a paint job. This was where he had grown up, played football on the street, dodged the stones and names: mongrel, blowfly, Spanish git, popish bastard, and worse. He stood at the gate of number nine and wondered who lived there. There were curtains at the windows, and the front garden looked as if someone had tried to make it neat and tidy. He remembered his mother's coffin being carried out of that door, and much later, that of his grandmother. Tango wondered, and not for the first time, why he had come back. What had drawn him to this place of so many bad memories?

The rain had stopped. The front door opened, and an elderly woman came out to place empty milk bottles by the door. She saw Tango standing by the gate and paused, then came nearer to peer at him through thick glasses. Then she reached out and touched him.

"Talfryn? Good God! Talfryn Garrett! 'Tis himself you are, and you're back. Well, Tal Bach, come in! I'll make a brew and we'll talk."

She hustled the stunned man into the house where he had been born and fussed around him, taking off the raincoat and sitting him by the fire. In her excitement she slid from Welsh to English and back again. As Tango warmed his hands, he listened to her talk while she made tea and opened a Christmas tin of biscuits. She'd been left a small legacy by a former employer and with it had bought the house at low cost. Her grandson had redecorated it and made it habitable.

The past came back with a rush, and Tango fought back his tears. Bronwen Williams had been a midwife in her younger days, and with her own

21. "Thank you. Have a good visit."

hands she had brought young Talfryn into the world. Now she brought him back into the world of his youth with kind words and an outstretched hand.

"There's an old camp bed upstairs if you've nowhere to go tonight," she offered. "I've a cottage pie in the oven, and Maisie next door made an apple pie for me yesterday. There's enough for two! And I'll make some custard. It'll be nice to have someone to talk to. You can tell me all about Ameriky and what it's like there."

Tango was torn between another night in a cheap B&B and an evening of explanations about life in Hollywood. He listened to the wind and rain against the window and opted for a night by a real fire and homemade cottage pie. He accepted another cup of tea and settled down to dazzle the old lady with talk of famous stars he had met. Later, he slept deeply and well in what had been his room so many years ago.

The following day, Tango left after breakfast with a promise to return in a few days. He left his guitar and case on the bed and took just a plastic bag with a few essentials, fully intending to keep his promise. Then he made for the bus station.

Hours later, after a couple of free rides and two bus journeys, Tango stood by the post office of Penwyllt and looked round. The village had not changed since he had last been there, but it hadn't changed for over a hundred years and probably never would. He made his way through the single narrow street. Lights were on and curtains drawn. The inhabitants—those not in the Ceir Coch bar drinking—would be sitting down to dinner.

Tango climbed the steep road leading to the house he had not entered since the death of young Penny. He stood at the gates and looked at the house. He had often thought about selling it, but he couldn't bear the thought of Penny's hidden resting place being disturbed. She needed to be quiet and peaceful, unlike the pain and fear of her death. The path and front lawn were weed-filled, untidy, and neglected, and as the door swung open, the memories long held within flooded out. Tango reeled back and vomited. He took a bottle of water from his bag and rinsed his mouth. Then, summoning his courage, he entered the house.

Thousands of miles away, Wolf came alert. Memories flooded in: gunshots, pain, the smell of his blood, and the need to escape. He sat up, breathing deeply, and sifted through his memories to find what had woken him.

He reached out and touched a mind half mad with fear, horror, and guilt. But before Wolf could grasp it, the memory was shredded with light, love, and forgiveness. Penny had waited a long time for Tango to return, and Wolf settled back down. His help was not needed when something this powerful was already there.

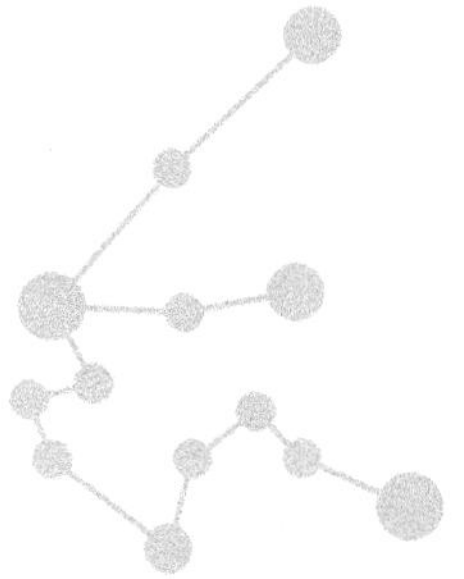

CHAPTER FORTY-FIVE

23 April, 2:30 p.m.
The Abbey of the Snows

"Again, Nova San. Try again. You are almost there. Breathe. Breathe deep. Pull the air down into the belly and feel the note waiting for release. Know it for what it is: pure energy. It contains all that will be, all that is waiting for the new age to begin. Every new invention, every new song, every new experience for your species to explore is held within, waiting for its moment of birth. Feel the breath and feel its strength. Now bring it up slowly and until you can feel it trembling behind the breath…Hold it, hold it. Don't let it loose, just feel what it will be like to release it. But not yet…*Now!*"

The sound of the carrier wave burst out and covered the island. It shattered windows, and here and there a bullock fell dead and birds dropped from the sky. The energy blasted its way across the sea, and several small earthquakes around the Ring of Fire sent panicked inhabitants running into the streets. For a full thirty minutes, the energy raced across the Pacific and encircled the globe, then slowly subsided into quietness. All work halted in the observatory, and in the quietness of her quarters, the abbess smiled as she sipped her tea and sent a mental note to her coworker as Aoki lay resting, coiled in his cocoon. "The Forerunner has achieved control. Soon he will have the Word. Our work draws to a close. Soon we will rejoin our own kind."

The news, verbal and mental, flashed from abbey to abbey. A mixture of joy, wonder, and sadness flooded their hearts. Soon the door to the Age of Aquarius would open and life on Earth would begin a new and demanding level of consciousness. The moment the door opened, a level of humanity would be conceived that could finally reach the stars. There humans would find they were not the first or even the most advanced form of life; it would be a humbling lesson for humanity to accept.

In the observatory, attention was focussed on the narrowing distance between the meteors carrying the Aquarian gifts of enrichment of the mind, body, and soul, gifts that would be released in the moment of the meteors' self-destruction. In every abbey, a voluntary couple would soon conceive a child so their enhanced talents would go on and they would stand ready to train those who came to them, just as Johnny had been trained. At the moment the meteors met, their essence would touch every newly filled womb, every moment of conception, and would enrich each child's mental and physical capacity. It would be up to the individual to use it or lose it. Such moments could produce a genius or a monster—free will was always the deciding factor. The guidance was in the hands of the Teacher of that age. The time was close.

Johnny lay unconscious. Yoshi stayed with him until he opened his eyes once more. Eventually, Johnny rose shakily to his feet and looked round him. His senses had increased far beyond the norm. Colours moved, rippled, and formed patterns. He could distinguish every scent, one from another, and hear voices through the whole of the abbey.

The abbess gently touched Johnny's reeling mind. "All will quieten down in the next few hours, and you will be able to control it. You now hold the power to utter the Word and will know the moment to speak it. Now rest, Nova San. Your training is over. Tomorrow Wolf will come for you—it is time to return to where it all began. It is an honour to have been a part of your existence and your training. My work is done. I and my companion can return to our own world."

Johnny used his new powers to see her, her delicate catlike form covered in tiny iridescent scales, her faceted eyes and multifingered hands. She spoke in her own language, but he understood. Power flowed through him, and he felt regret that all this would be his for such a short time. He reached for the knowledge of her own tongue, offered a blessing, and received one in return.

Johnny went to where his other teacher lay resting and knelt beside Aoki and, having been given permission, touched the gleaming coils. "Now I understand why humanity has revered and feared you. Naga Khan, the Naghareem, the Serpents of Wisdom, who taught Eve the creative power within the body. We have reviled your form down the ages. Master, forgive our temerity. Accept my thanks for your help. May I have your blessing?"

The coils were cool as they wrapped round him, and the tongue touched Johnny's own gently and with love.

The following morning, Wolf's copter touched down gently. The entire complement of the Abbey of the Snows was there to make their goodbyes. The bond of love they had forged in the short time Johnny had been with them became visible.

As the copter rose, Johnny saw a sevenfold coil of light surrounding the abbey and felt a single facet of the light embed itself within him. He realised with a mind-blowing jolt that every abbey had done the same, had left within him something of themselves, something that would be with him in those last few moments. He would leave something of himself in this world. His son would carry part of him and in turn would leave the seed of the Forerunner to await the next age.

Wolf remained silent. The moment was too charged with power for words. He must make the most of what time was left to be with the man who had become the brother he had always longed for.

26 April, 9:00 p.m.
The penthouse, London

"He's coming home! He's coming home! He's arrived at the Aeon!" Screaming her news, Florrie ran from room to room in the old group apartment where Frank still lived. Frank's pen jolted from the slap on his back and drew a line through five bars of his music. "He's picking up Mara and Jared and will be here tomorrow! Bucky? Bucky, where are you? It's Johnny! He's coming home!"

Florrie ran next door and yelled in Biff's ear to wake him up, then flung open the bathroom door to reveal Liam with his boxers round his ankles as he read the racing results. Ignoring his roar of fury and embarrassment, she returned to the penthouse and threw her arms round Bucky as he discussed a deal with a new producer, then headed onto the balcony. There she flung out her arms and yelled to the world, "My laddie's coming home—to stay." Then she covered her face and sobbed.

The group gathered round Florrie, telling themselves they were comforting her but in reality already feeling a sense of being all together again at last. They called Lyle and Ginny and began to make plans for a "welcome home" dinner. Then Bucky, who had been very quiet, came up with an idea that stunned them all.

"I've been thinking. We kept the name of White Heat alive all this time with recordings and as a backing group. What if we put out an announcement that after some years in retirement, Johnny Nova was going to make a comeback? We could do a whole series of two- or three-night specials. You know, TV with some big names as a star host. We'd make DVD recordings, special interviews on TV and radio...We could string it out for a few months, covering all the major cities. And, as a climax, we could wind up with a Wembley sell-out with a worldwide audience. What do you think? Are you up for something like that?"

For a long moment, there was silence. Then came an ear-splitting whoop of joy from the whole group that scattered the pigeons gathered for their evening roosts. Florrie headed for the wine cabinet to fetch champagne. Ginny wept in Lyle's arms, and the whole apartment went wild.

"The good times are back again! God and all his angels be praised," crowed Liam as he grabbed Florrie and danced her round the room. Frank headed for the piano and began to hammer out a souped-up version of "Let the Good Times Roll."

Bucky grinned. "I guess that means a big *yes*! As soon as Johnny gets here, we can sit down and begin to plan the return of White Heat. But remember, he has to say yes as well. Without him, it won't work. While we're celebrating, I'll run the idea by some of our old contacts. But lads, remember, Johnny has to want to do it as well. Now...sod the champagne. Where's the Scotch?"

♫ ♩ ♫ ♪ ♬ ♪ ♫

The following day, Florrie and Ginny staggered from the lift loaded with food and opened the door to see Biff, Frank, and Liam in Florrie's aprons cleaning the apartment under Bucky's directions. Once they'd stopped laughing, they shooed the men out and Ginny finished cleaning while Florrie cooked. An hour later in a clean, tidy, and almost-unrecognisable apartment, they relaxed with tea and Florrie's fruit cake.

There was a knock at the door, and a sheepish Bucky asked if it was OK to come back. He looked round. "Florrie, Ginny, thanks for doing this. I don't know how you did it all so quickly."

Florrie waved a hand. "It would always look like this if you lot put things away after you. I found three pairs of socks and a week's worth of boxers under the sofa cushions! Don't know whose they were, but they need to go out and buy a whole new set because I binned the lot. Now this is how I want it to stay.

"It's just after six, and they'll be here in an hour. We'll all have dinner together. Ginny's sister has taken on the kids for a couple of days, so Liam, pull out the extra leaves on the table. There'll be nine of us. Lyle will be coming direct from choir practice."

"Make that ten, Florrie. We have the big bad Wolf with us!"

Florrie turned, her face lighting up. "Johnny!" She screamed "Oh, Johnny!" and flung herself into his arms. Mara joined in and Wolf, holding one-year-old Jared, became part of the melee that followed.

"We thought we'd surprise you and come early."

Bucky stood silent for a moment, just watching and close to tears. His boys were back together, and though he knew it would be for a short time, it was a moment to remember, cherish, and in the empty years ahead, to recall and relive again and again.

Only one person was missing. Bucky wondered what his reaction would be to the idea he'd been pondering. For it to be as it had been in the old days, they would need Tango, but he needed to tread gently and prepare for the uproar that would greet his suggestion...He'd let them have this evening to enjoy being together. When the moment was right, Bucky would throw in the suggestion and be prepared to duck!

♬ ♩ ♫ ♪ ♬ ♪ ♫

At 2:15 a.m., Johnny and Wolf stood on the balcony and looked out over the sleeping city.

"It's such an ancient city, Wolf, and there is so much going on underneath it. People being born, dying, making love, and planning new inventions and mayhem...And not just here, but all over the world. In twenty years it will look different, but underneath it will be the same."

Wolf said, "Cities change, grow, and die just like people, Johnny."

Johnny laid a hand on Wolf's shoulder and spoke urgently. "Wolf, as the end draws closer, I have become aware of future events. I've made a will, but I want to add a clause if you will agree. I lost my mother when I was a teenager, and I know it will be the same for Jared. You are the one I want to train him, guard him, and share the way of the shapeshifter with him. Will you do this for me? Will you share your blood with him as you once shared it with me?"

Wolf caught his breath. Such a gift, such a responsibility, was overwhelming to one who had never known a family of his own. "Are you sure, Johnny? What of Bucky, Florrie?"

"It needs to be you, Wolf. My first and much cherished teacher has advised me. Let's do it now."

As they stood beside the sleeping child, Wolf extended a paw and drew a single drop of blood from Jared's arm. He took it into his mouth, then placed a drop of his own ancient blood on Jared's lips, and a small pink tongue licked it into his system. Under his breath Wolf chanted an oath in the ancient tongue of his people.

"I swear by my ancestral blood, by my father, the sun, and my mother, the earth, and by the power of the Great Spirit to take this child as my own, to cherish and guide and train him in the ancient ways to be a guardian to those in need."

Jared whimpered and turned in his sleep, thrusting out a tiny hand that, for a brief moment, became a grey-furred paw.

♬ ♩ ♫ ♪ ♬ ♪ ♫

Breakfast was, as Bucky had expected, a riot. Johnny had wholeheartedly backed the idea of a reunion of White Heat and had himself suggested bringing Tango back. Biff and Liam were against it; Lyle, with his forgiving nature, had been ready to forgive and forget; Frank said nothing, just listened. Johnny went to see his lawyers and left them to it.

During the ensuing row, voices and tempers were raised, and every aspect of the whys and the nos, the hows and the whens, were fought out. It still hung in the balance when, after hours of discussion, Florrie, who had been silent so far, turned to Wolf, sensing he might hold the key.

"Wolf, dear. Though you were never part of the group, from what Johnny has told us, you've been with Tango lately. What happened after all the trouble in Hollywood, and do you know where he is now?"

All eyes turned to the tall, bronzed figure leaning silently against the wall. He came forward and took a seat by Bucky. "As you know, I am abbey trained, but I do not belong to any one of them entirely. My 'talent' is extremely rare, so I go where I am needed and serve as a freelancer. In the past weeks, I have spent a lot of time with Tango, and while there are still some dark areas in his psyche, nevertheless he has an important part to play in this time and place. His early life was one of great loneliness, a situation similar to my own. After the early death of his mother there was no love, affection, or attention of any kind.

"I don't know how much of Tango's early life you know. Suffice to say that both he and Johnny were born to fulfil a special purpose. Tango's personal need was for attention and a sense of belonging; Johnny's spiritual task was to be taken from the White Heat group and trained. With regard to Tango, it will be enough to speak of the past seven or eight months. That will give you an idea of what his life has been like and why his inclusion in the return of White Heat is of vital importance."

The group leaned forward and began to listen.

Wolf spared nothing: the early years of beatings; the refusal of Tango's grandmother to acknowledge him other than as "the mistake," "the bastard," or simply "you there"; little food; jumble sale clothes; the jeers and name-calling from other children and even their parents. Tango's only place of refuge was the library. His withholding of his grandmother's heart pills was an escape into the low life of Cardiff, but the key into a decent world was his voice. Bucky found him singing in the street for pennies or the handout of a sandwich. Bucky fed Tango, bought him clothes, and gave him a bed to sleep in until he finally got the beginnings of White Heat together. It took six months and another six of one-night stands, bachelor nights, and weekend singalongs at holiday camps. Nights were spent in waiting rooms so they could catch the cheap early morning train.

As Wolf spoke, he freed the group's memories and rebuilt their feelings of togetherness. He spoke of White Heat's growing success, topping the bill at the Palladium and the international tours that made them world famous and put millions in their off-shore accounts. He also spoke of Tango's link to De'ath and his descent into the Dark.

Having rebuilt their early memories, Wolf then told them of Tango's career developments and how the Darkness had sent a new link to him. His drinking and sexual exploits with married women had caused his final downfall and the departure from Hollywood. But it was the story of finding Tango sick, exhausted, and starving in New York that clinched the group's acceptance, Tango's desire to be back where he belonged. Evening clouds were looming as Wolf finished, though he refrained from speaking of Tango's present whereabouts or the death of Penny.

Ginny turned her face into Lyle's shoulder and wept. Florrie had already cried her way through every handkerchief in the group. For a while there was silence, then Frank went over to the piano and started to put a refrain together. As he played he looked over his shoulder at Bucky. "How about we split the solos between them? Johnny would have the finale—"Mountains of Gold," of course. But I'll put together something operatic in style for Tango. He'd love that."

Lyle agreed. "Yeah, I could come up with a soft underbeat to make it low and sexy."

Ginny began to gather up the cups and glasses. "I'll clear the kids' playroom, and Tango can have that until he can find his own place."

Florrie smiled at Wolf through her tears and patted his hand. "I'll go out and buy some extra bedding tomorrow. He always liked plenty of pillows."

Bucky coughed and discreetly wiped an eye. "I'll draw up a new contract and make a start on announcing that White Heat is back and hotter than ever!"

Wolf felt Johnny's mental touch, warm, enclosing, and full of affection. No words were needed.

♬ ♩ ♫ ♪ ♬ ♪ ♫

The news hit the front pages on the early edition.

"MISSING SINGER RETURNS FROM THE DEAD"
"JOHNNY NOVA'S SECLUSION IN A WITHDRAWN MONASTERY"
"STAR'S FIVE-YEAR BATTLE WTH DRUGS AND ALCOHOL"
"DRUG ADDICTION DROVE SINGER'S DESCENT INTO RELIGION"

Then came the expected demands for interviews, TV appearances, the usual begging letters, along with fans and hippies wanting to renew imaginary acquaintances. But their idol was no longer in London. Bucky had hired extra office staff to cope with the deluge.

Florrie, Mara, and Ginny took the children and two burly Watchers to a secluded retreat away from avid thrill seekers. No one noticed two brightly painted vardos plodding a forgotten highway. They slept under the stars and played rough-and-tumble games with children who went barefooted.

♬ ♩ ♫ ♪ ♬ ♪ ♫

Johnny and Wolf met with Pacia at the rusted double gates of the old house. They passed into the house, filling it with Light, love, and power. The Darkness that had occupied it for so long screamed with fear and tried in vain to escape from its searing fire. The evil that had been done shrivelled and fled into its own dimension. It left behind a human form curled in a fetal position, a form that sobbed and cried and tried to crawl away from the Light that now approached it.

Penny took form and approached the moaning Tango and covered him with her love, sweetened it with her forgiveness, cleansed it with understanding, and offered to take upon herself all he had done and suffered. She took from her heart centre the little cross he had placed there and laid it on his brow. It burned through the human flesh and imprinted itself on his brow.

The three who watched added their power, love, and forgiveness. The shade that had been Penny bowed before them, and Pacia reached out and wrapped the slight figure that once had been so full of life in her own radiance.

"Your wait is over. What you have done, what you have forgiven, what you have endured and offered, has been witnessed and recorded. Now you are free and may follow your heart."

Penny sat with Tango's head in her lap. "I will stay with him. The time approaches, and soon the door of the new age will open. He took on the fate of the Betrayer, the hardest of the three needed to bring in the new age. I will wait with him until that moment comes."

Pacia bowed her head in recognition of the sacrifice being made. "We will complete the cleansing now and prepare for that moment. Now go with those who await you, and rest until you are called. He will have need of you then."

Penny kissed Tango's forehead and stood, her form growing brighter still as she was surrounded by loving arms and sweet voices. The light faded, leaving four exhausted people.

Tango knelt, weeping, at Pacia's feet as she blessed him. Then Wolf came and lifted Tango into his arms. He and Johnny took him to the car. Pacia stayed behind and would be joining them later.

As Wolf drove away, Johnny looked back at the house now burning fiercely. What it had contained had been cleansed completely.

30 April, 6:00 p.m.
London

The laughter could be heard down the hall. It was the boisterous sound of a group of closely bonded people enjoying themselves. Tango stopped short. He was shaking and on the edge of flight. It was a sound he had once, long ago, been a part of, but he had thrown that away because of his desire for self-importance.

Wolf was used to loneliness and to the feeling of belonging nowhere and to no one. He had found the opposite in his friendship with Johnny and knew the loneliness would return when he was no longer there. He placed a hand on Tango's shoulder. "I know what you are feeling. I have been there. And yes, for the first few days it will be difficult, but it will get better...for a time. After that, it will no longer matter. Come, let's get it over with."

Tango squared his shoulders and opened the door on to a bizarre scene: Biff and Liam, draped in bits and pieces taken from Florrie's wardrobe, were attempting to dance a tango to Frank's inebriated version of "La Cumparsita." Florrie and Ginny were in fits of laughter, and the ash from Bucky's cigar (he'd started smoking again) had burned a hole in his waistcoat. On seeing Tango, Frank stopped playing and everything went quiet.

Tango just stood there, head down, preparing to be asked to leave. Then Frank leapt up from the piano and rushed across to him. "Tango!" he yelled. "It's Tango. He came! It's true—we're all going to be together again!" Frank flung his arms round Tango and hugged him close. The others followed.

Bewildered and still afraid he'd be shown the door, Tango just stood there, enveloped by the people he thought he had lost forever. Then the tears came as everyone crowded round and the old tight-knit circle snapped back into being.

Wolf stood and wondered, not for the first time, what it was like to be part of such a thing. He found out a few minutes later when he was drawn into that same group as Lyle came through the door with Mara and the children.

Suddenly the place was full. Wine and food was produced, pizzas were ordered, and the room filled up with voices, laughter, music, and the indescribable feeling of togetherness. For Tango, it was togetherness, a homecoming, that only such a group could build. For Wolf, it was an experience to remember when the loneliness returned, because it would, for a shapeshifter walked alone. But this was a moment Wolf could know and treasure. He sipped one glass of champagne all night and basked in the power of a group mind.

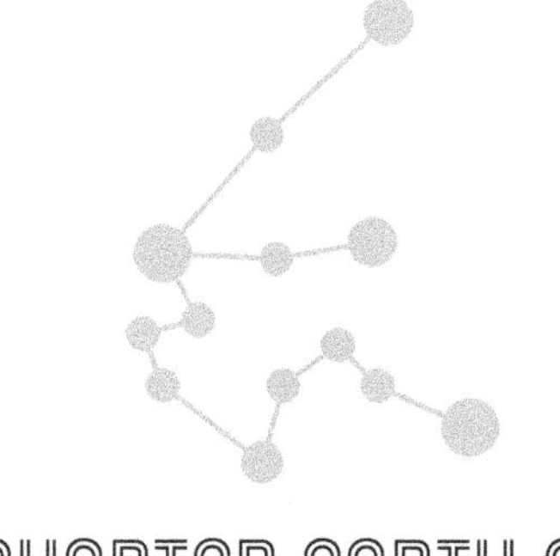

CHAPTER FORTY-SIX

20 August, 12:00 p.m.
London

The next few months were spent in rehearsals, rehearsals, and more rehearsals as White Heat strove to regain the musical closeness they once had. It was hardest for Johnny, as his voice had changed. The breathing techniques of the abbeys had deepened and enriched his natural tenor, giving it a richer tonal quality. Tango's lessons with a top-line teacher during *The Student Prince* had also changed his voice. If anything, it was now better than Johnny's but lacked the power of intent that flooded the emotional content of the words.

Johnny spent as much time as possible with Mara and their son. His father and Tze-Ring kept in touch as much as possible, visiting sometimes for just a day but always in communication. The power links between the abbeys were a constant source of strength, determination, and advice when it was asked for.

Elsewhere, Pacia's efforts to bring the warring factors of the world together were gathering support. Her spiritual presence was beginning to be felt even between faiths. Strangely, it was Biff who sought her out when she visited and spent time asking questions.

Ginny and Florrie spent time designing new costumes. The top depicted their new symbol of five red teardrops, one for each member of the group, making a statement about their closeness. Each teardrop had a name embroidered below it.

Bucky's initial fear that Tango's Hollywood fracas would detract from the tour build-up proved groundless. If anything, it added to it and made him appear to be "dark and dangerous," and he acquired something of a "bad boy" image.

Lyle talked to his Trinidad friends, and between them and Frank, they worked out several electrifying drum solos called "Drums on Fire," "Call of the Wild," and "Haiti Calling."

Frank was in his element, and in the space of three weeks he turned out "Talking Guitars," "Midnight in Madrid," and "El Matador" for Biff and Liam. Then he locked himself away to write for Johnny and Tango.

Ten days before their opening night, Frank reappeared clutching a case full of songs: "You Burn Me Up," "Lullaby for Lovers," "Just Before I Leave You," Laughter in the Wind," "My Last Dance with You," and "I Let You Walk Away." He didn't know it yet, but several would go on to make platinum, and two would become standards worldwide. For Tango, Frank wrote "Come to Me Softly," "You're Too Good for Me, I'm Too Bad for You," and "Let Me Make You Smile." These would be mixed with old favourites and some popular melodies going the rounds. Frank then fell asleep on the couch and went out like a light for almost twenty-four hours, waking only to drink tea and stagger to the bathroom.

♬ ♩ ♫ ♪ ♬ ♪ ♫

Bucky found time to reopen Tango's bank account linked to White Heat and quietly handed him an envelope of money. Despite all that had happened, Bucky had continued to pay in Tango's share every month. Tango sat for several hours going back over the intervening years and hating himself. The following day he went to a lawyer and set up an account for the old midwife in Cardiff. She would have a comfortable old age and never want for anything.

♬ ♩ ♫ ♪ ♬ ♪ ♫

"WHITE HEAT IS REWIRED FOR SOUND"
"BACK ON TRACK AND BETTER THAN EVER: IT'S NOW AND NOVA"
"WHITE HEAT: HOT AND READY TO BLAST OFF"

For months the papers had kept the fans on tiptoes with pictures, gossip, news of rehearsals, dance routines, and interviews. Now with just hours to go before the opening of the tour, everyone was wired to the hilt. Tempers were short; the smallest thing set off screams and shouts. The only calm one was Bucky. He'd seen it all before and knew it was just nerves and tension.

The Royal Albert Hall was packed solid. Tickets had fetched two thousand pounds each. Telegrams, flowers, and bottles of champagne filled the dressing rooms and overflowed into the corridors guarded by hired help. The order was strict: No booze until after the show.

In the hall the noise was deafening, but in the main dressing rooms it was quiet as everyone went about the process of dressing, making up, and preparing for the moment of entry. Frank was already in the wings and making last-minute adjustments. Then the five-minute call went out, and everyone took a deep breath and went to their places.

The house lights dimmed and the audience went silent. There was a mind-blowing roll of drums and the curtain rolled back to reveal White Heat. They stood with their backs to the audience. Then, one by one, they turned to be outlined by a brilliant spotlight. Each was greeted by a thunderous roar of applause. The last light hit Johnny, and the entire hall erupted in screams and shouts. Flowers and gifts were flung onto the stage as Johnny walked forward and bowed. Then he spread his arms to include the whole group in the wave of adulation that went on and on. With a roll of drums, Lyle led them into the first number. Back in the old routine.

It was a night no one would ever forget. Song after song was received with an almost hysterical show of adulation. The new items became instant hits; the old favourites were demanded again and again. The programmed interval never really happened and turned into a shouted conversation between the audience and the stage. Finally Johnny came forward and held up his hand for silence.

"You have been wonderful. You have welcomed us back with such warmth, and all of us are so grateful for your love and support. But we have gone well over an hour of the time allotted and frankly, we need to rest. And so, my friends, do you. Please let us go now before we fall asleep on stage. Lyle tells me he has broken three sets of drumsticks tonight. Frank is almost asleep over his keyboard, and I think Biff and Liam have almost lost the use of their fingers. You have made it a memorable night for us all. But frankly, Tango and I are flat out of energy." Tango came forward to stand beside him and nodded. "We wish you all goodnight and God bless. Until we meet again in Birmingham. See you there! Goodnight to you all." The curtain fell amid screams and shouts and slowly, very slowly, an exhausted audience began to make their reluctant way out and homeward.

Backstage, the emotionally depleted group members were helped to their dressing rooms by dressers and stagehands. Too drained to think about changing, they dropped, sat, or lay on couches, chairs, and in the case of Lyle, on a pile of street clothes on the floor. They slept where they fell. Bucky, Florrie, Mara, and Ginny covered them with whatever lay around and left them to sleep until dawn. They finally woke to a world totally in love with them and their music.

YEAR SIX

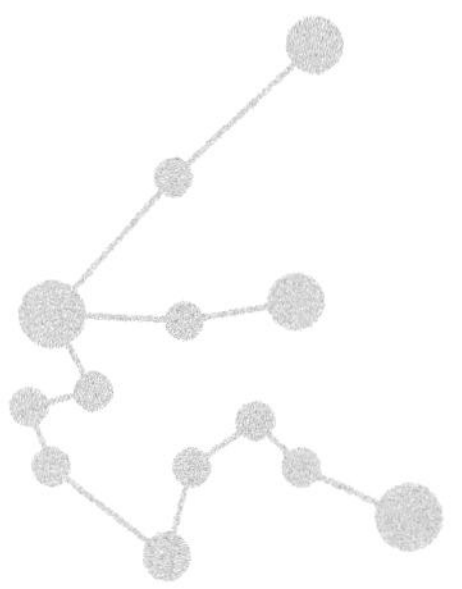

CHAPTER FORTY-SEVEN

13 October, 3:00 p.m.
Birmingham

"Bloody hell."

"Wow!"

"Stupendous!"

"Now that is what is meant by *big*!"

White Heat stood on the stage of Symphony Hall and looked out over the auditorium, specifically at the massive speakers that hung over the seating area. Liam shaded his eyes as he looked up. "I thought those we saw in Sydney were big, but these babies are way out. I think we'll have to look at spacing, maybe even add some back-ups."

"No!" Bucky didn't want any outsiders crowding his boys. "Frank, what do you think?"

Frank called over the head electrician and spoke with him. The man nodded and disappeared. A few minutes later, the speakers began to hum. Frank turned to Tango. "Tango, go down and stand about twenty rows back and in the middle." Tango ambled down and took up the suggested position. Frank stood centre stage, halfway down.

"OK, now let me have a scale, middle C but soft."

The notes rang out and, amplified by the speakers, filled the hall.

"OK, now go up a tone and use a half voice."

Again, the speakers spread the sound evenly over the hall.

"Now let me have full voice, and try some fancy vocals."

Tango took a deep breath and let loose. The hall came alive with sound. Entranced, Tango tried out his full range up to C5, and the speakers matched him with faultless accuracy.

Frank and the sound engineer went into a huddle, and minor adjustments were made. Finally the group came together and went through a vocal sans instruments. Then Frank and the engineer shook hands. "It's all arranged," he said, beaming. "We don't want to deafen everyone, and our type of music going full blast has been known to cause pain and even damage to some people. I'll adjust the personal mikes as well. Let's eat! I'm starving."

Back at the hotel, having eaten their way through three courses, the group divided as usual: Liam and Biff to a club, Bucky on the phone, Lyle to his studies, and Frank working on his oratorio.

Over the last few months Johnny and Tango had reached a tenuous point in their relationship. Tango was conscious of a kinship but could not fully admit to it. Johnny, aware of what the future held, strove to change the feeling of resentment into one of acceptance, hoping it would lessen the blow when the moment arrived. Tango's solo work in the group had helped, but at the back of his mind, there was something he had to do concerning Johnny. Later that day they sat silent, close, but held apart by something with no reason or purpose Tango could name. Johnny lifted his glass and held it out. He smiled at Tango and clinked their glasses together. "Salud," he said.

The tour so far had been a triumph. Birmingham, as always, tried to surpass the London show and did, drawing in crowds from all over the Midlands. Police protection was provided when an overenthusiastic crowd of admirers ambushed White Heat's cars after the show and literally tore their clothes off for souvenirs. The fracas left Lyle with a wrenched back and Biff and Liam with multiple bruises, black eyes, and little in the way of clothing. Tango, who fought back and broke a couple of noses, got a dislocated shoulder in return. Frank missed the whole thing, as he'd stayed behind to re-tune his instrument, but Johnny was left wearing his socks, shorts, and what was left of his shirt. Several clumps of hair were scattered round. That same night, they ran the gamut of the hospital, where the nurses handed out hospital gowns but took advantage to share what was left of the men's clothing among themselves.

It was three in the morning when they got back to their hotel. Bucky's comment was, "Thank God you were not wearing the stage outfits—they cost three thousand apiece." As it had been a Saturday night performance, they had Sunday to recover, as far as was possible. The experience made the Sunday headlines and doubled the advance sales of the venues still to come.

Monday brought offers of videos, one-on-one interviews on TV for each of the group, their own weekly show with guest stars already lining up to offer their services, plus the offer of a full-length film detailing Johnny's disappearance, where and how he'd spent the ensuing time, and his triumphant return. Bucky almost cried at refusing the offer; the financial return would have been in the millions.

Their next show was cancelled based on police advice as they arranged extra protection and everyone recovered from their manhandling, but an extra show was offered in lieu for those who already had tickets. Warnings were issued about legal repercussions, and the days passed in relative peace, though Florrie and Ginny were unhappy about problems recurring. The next three evenings were reasonably well behaved, and as the group packed and made ready for the next stop (still nursing bruises), Bucky made certain they had police protection at the stage door and cars with shatterproof glass.

♬ ♩ ♫ ♪ ♬ ♩ ♫

Liverpool greeted them with a bus-top drive through the city, an event usually reserved for victorious footballers. Biff, Liam, and Tango lapped it up. Lyle gritted his teeth and smiled stoically. Johnny and Frank waved and smiled and wished it was all over. A civic dinner had been arranged, and their womenfolk had been flown up as a surprise. Speeches were made, and Bucky made a gracious reply. Finally the long day ended with everyone falling into bed exhausted. By 8:30 a.m. the next morning, reporters and newsreaders were already waiting in the lobby, but Johnny insisted on the group eating their breakfast in peace. The interviews took two hours, and it was noon before they got to see the venue.

The general opinion of the venue was "It's OK"; the sound equipment was not as good as Birmingham but was sufficient. Dressing rooms got a thumbs down, but as it was just two nights they decided to raise no objections. The venue's capacity was 1,700 against the former 2,300, but because the whole tour had been put together so hastily, Bucky took the objections in stride.

The following two days were given over to rehearsals but were marred by an altercation between Johnny and Tango when the latter's solos were cut to allow for a forty-minute space for fans to ask for favourite pieces. Bucky had been thinking about including the audience in the presentation and wanted to try it out. Tango threw a fit and accused Johnny of asking for more solo time. Bucky finally cut it down to just two requests. Tango, however, was not included on the grounds that the whole tour had been built around Johnny's return to music.

During the event, the presentation itself went without too much trouble, but Tango sulked and took his meals alone in his room. Bucky spent time with him, trying to point out how well the tour was going and how bright the future looked, but the Welshman had tasted fame once and lost it, and he was reluctant to do so again. Tango took to moving round onstage, changing his stance during the solos, and signalling to his fans. He stopped eating with the group, turned up late for rehearsals, and often spent the night away from the hotel.

By the time they hit Leeds and then Dublin, Bucky was furious. Tango's behaviour was beginning to affect the whole group. Although the response was still there and the audiences were, if anything, double what had been forecast, within the group the old troubles were re-appearing.

Johnny was the only one who took no notice and continued to behave as normal. He spent every spare moment with Mara and their son, taking photos and storing up memories. Frank worked frantically and hardly seemed to sleep, turning out new songs for a TV special that would be filmed on Christmas Eve.

♫ ♩ ♫ ♪ ♫ ♪ ♫

When they returned to London, there was a ten-day break, during which time Johnny and his family went to the Aeon to spend time with Tze-Ring, Eamon, and Wolf. A message was waiting for him from the Abbey of the Snows. Short and cryptic, it gave the exact time of the meteoric collision.

Three days later Johnny arrived back in London and began rehearsals for the TV special. Tango had left the apartment, and although he turned up for the meetings, no one knew where he was staying; only Bucky had his number.

Then, just weeks before Christmas, a special newscast broke into all programmes. It was announced that a collision between two large meteors was expected to take place on or about 31 December or 1 January, and the collision would be visible in the night sky over most of Europe. This sent astronomers and astrologers worldwide into meltdown. Warnings and statements of if, when, and where fragments might land battled with prophesies of the unexpected arrival of the Age of Aquarius. These filled the international news, fuelled the idea of a new Christmas star, and rattled churches worldwide, while in the abbeys preparations began to be made.

For the group life went on as usual, and rehearsals for the highly publicised White Heat TV special took on a new intensity. Choreographers worked the dancers to exhaustion. Wardrobes filled dressing rooms and corridors with rails of costumes while weary, harassed, and fraught musicians, stagehands, and production personnel worked endlessly at shifting and re-adjusting props, scenery, and musical instruments. Colliding meteors were the last thing on their minds. The last week before Christmas Eve found most of the staff, including the group, slumped wherever a convenient place could be found.

Florrie, with typical understanding and generosity, had arranged for food and drinks to be available all through that last hectic week and made certain everyone got a sizable bonus. Johnny called a halt on the final rehearsal and a king-sized Christmas cake, mince pies, and champagne was served all round. He thanked everyone for their work and praised their expertise in a speech that many would remember in the years ahead.

The stage was set, cameras in position, costumes ready. Overhead, two meteors entered the final phase.

The dress rehearsal went surprisingly well. Finally it was time to film the TV special. Guest stars included a minor Hollywood actor who kept his mouth shut when he came face-to-face with Tango. All were received with wild applause by the audience. The full two hours went by without a hitch. Then Johnny took the stage for a final goodnight, which turned out to be something no one but those in the group knew about. He came forward and asked everyone to quieten down, as he had something to say.

"These last few weeks have been wonderful, a time to hold in my heart and remember for as long as I live. As you all know, I left the group for many years because there was something I had to do, had to learn, experience, and understand. But you—all of you—welcomed me back, and with me, my long-standing friends and fellow musicians. We regrouped and for a time renewed what we had shared before. This last year has been magical in more ways than you can imagine, but all things have their set time, and for White Heat that time has come. I have another task before me, and one that will take all I have to give.

"My friends, my dear friends, there will be only one more event for White Heat. It will take place at Wembley on the first day of the New Year. You are all invited, and there will be free entry. It is our gift to all of you for your love and loyalty during these past years. It is always best to go out on a high—and I promise it will be a high. It is the right time to say goodbye and God bless. Don't be sad. Listen to our recordings and remember us as we were. We all have things we need to do, see, share, and discover. For ten wonderful years, you have been a part of us, and we will never forget those years or you.

"Come and see us next week and help us make it the biggest and best farewell Wembley has ever seen and ever will see. Goodnight! Drive safely! We will see you then."

Johnny stepped back and joined the group. They faced a stunned, silent, and totally bemused audience. Then came the reaction. The audience surged forward, calling, shouting, crying, and asking questions. Some fought to get onto the stage, but the group had prepared for this. The safety curtain came down, and the group headed for the roof and the waiting copters. Whatever had been expected, it was not this outpouring of grief and dismay.

♬ ♩ ♫ ♪ ♬ ♪ ♫

High above the city, the copters headed for their destination. Every member of the group was silent. Financially, they need never work again. Emotionally, they were already feeling bereft knowing that Johnny had made his decision at last, and in one short week White Heat would cease to be.

Below them a small island came into view, then a large house with room for the copters to land. This was where they would spend Christmas and would be together for the last time as a group. They would share three or four days of celebration, days in which to build memories that would have to last a lifetime. From the copter, Johnny could see Florrie and Mara, with Jared in her arms, as well as Ginny, Mary-Clare, and their youngest, little John. And, standing a little apart from them, alone as always, was Wolf. Tomorrow they would be joined by Eamon and Tze-Ring. This togetherness would be captured and held within a moment of what humanity calls time, but which is, in reality, a constant renewal of what has always been.

There was a gentle bump as the copters landed. Overhead, two intensely bright objects in the night sky drew closer together.

Sleep was the first need, and all six of them stripped, showered, and fell into bed with scarcely a word between them. For twelve solid hours they slept, renewing their mental and physical strength. Both would be needed in the days ahead.

For the first few days, everyone behaved as if nothing had happened. They sat around and snacked, drank, played with the children, talked about the "old days," and shared their thoughts, ideas, and plans. Frank played pieces of his oratorio, Biff and Liam planned a six-week safari trip, and Lyle and Ginny talked about taking the children to Trinidad to meet their relatives. Tango took long, silent walks around the island, sometimes alone, sometimes with Wolf. Florrie and Bucky let everyone do as they wished, just making sure they were there if needed. Tze-Ring and Eamon arrived and spent some time alone with Johnny but left on Christmas Eve.

The tree was decorated, and the children pawed over the gaily wrapped presents, trying to guess what they contained. Everyone had chosen a different coloured wrapping paper: Biff's were in blue and white; Liam's were plain with silver bells; Lyle and Ginny had chosen green with sprays of mistletoe; Frank's were white with Christmas symbols; Tango chose purple and silver. High on the tree was one parcel wrapped in plain gold paper and marked with Johnny's name. Just the one.

Johnny had spent a lot of time choosing a gift for Tango. Tango loved antiques, and anything old, well-used, and treasured delighted him. His own collection had been sold to pay his legal costs. Finally Johnny had found something in a dusty down-at-heel shop in Durham close by the ancient cathedral. He stood looking at it for a long time and wondered about its history, then bought it for the absurdly low price of thirty pounds. Johnny thought about having it restored, but decided against it. It looked right as it was. That, too, now lay under the tree, waiting.

♬ ♩ ♫ ♪ ♬ ♪ ♫

Christmas morning was bedlam. "Breakfast first!" said Florrie. As everyone came down at different times, it ended with the children getting impatient and tearful. Finally, the long-awaited moment arrived, and within minutes the whole room was full of torn paper, string, ribbons, and often very strange gifts. Some Florrie and Ginny hid under cushions or under chairs. Liam and Biff always made Christmas a time for giving the most outrageous gifts, especially to each other. The most hilarious was a personal catheter for Bucky, who was known for having to get up two or three times a night.

For Johnny, there had been just one present: a gift from them all, which he now wore. A twenty-four-carat chain bearing eleven gold medallions, each one inscribed with a name: Bucky, Florrie, Ginny, Lyle, Biff, Liam, Frank, Tango, Mary-Clare, little John, and, in the largest medallion, Mara and Jared. In the centre of each was a small diamond. Bucky had presented the chain, saying that this way they would always be with him. It now lay over Johnny's heart, together with the gold wolf's head that never left him.

Hours later, with the exhausted children napping on the sofas surrounded by their loot, the rest of them sat silent and recovering. Christmas dinner was always an evening meal for them, so for now they sat, drank, and shared memories.

♬ ♩ ♫ ♪ ♬ ♪ ♫

Christmas dinner was almost quiet. For once, Wolf waved away Florrie's offer of a third helping. "There are times," he said regretfully, "when even a wolf has had enough."

Later, while everyone else was watching the TV, Wolf and Johnny walked together by the shore. They didn't talk. All the words had already been spoken, shared, and understood. Both knew it was the last time they would share the closeness that had been there from the very beginning. There was no longer a need for words.

They walked back to where Wolf's copter was waiting. For the last time they embraced, heart to heart. Then Johnny stood back out of the sweep of the rotors. One look, one smile, one wave of the hand, and the craft lifted into the sky.

Alone, Johnny walked back to the house.

26 December, 10:30 a.m.
The penthouse, London

Boxing Day—a bloody good name for it too, as Bucky said later—began with a discussion on the Wembley programme. Right from the start, Tango made it clear that he expected a greater share of the vocals. In particular, he wanted Frank to write something for him that would become as synonymous with his name as "Mountains of Gold" had done for Johnny.

Frank pointed out that with less than a week to go, a new song was impossible to write, let alone write *and* rehearse with an instrumental background. Tango's answer was he could have one of Johnny's songs restructured for his "better" vocal talent. The row this provoked was something that had never happened in the group. Only Frank held back, knowing all too well it would be up to him in the end. Only he could make it happen, and there was no way physically or mentally that he could write and orchestrate a new song from scratch in a week, plus adjust the sound apparatus and rehearse the additional musicians in that time.

Frank's explanation led Tango to play his trump card: Either it happened or he walked away from the whole set-up. Tango sat back with a smile and waited for the capitulation. When it didn't come, his fury was monumental. Florrie and Ginny got the children out of the room, but Mara took her place by Johnny and opened her healing powers, trying to lessen the build-up of fear, anger, hate, and the ever-present sense of loss and lack of attention that had been with Tango since childhood.

Bucky tried to smooth things down. "Look, Tango, the timing is all wrong. We can't change the whole show in the time left to us. Let me talk to some people I know; I might be able to get you a whole show of your own."

Tango turned on him and snarled, "No! I want the group behind me. Not him—*me*! This show would put me in front of a worldwide audience and wipe out all the shit I've gone through in the past few years. I don't want to have to do all the talk shows, one-night appearances, sucking up to people not fit to polish my shoes. I want to rub the faces of those who dumped me in their own vomit. I want the whole thing. I've had it before, and I want it back. White Heat can give it to me without all the arse-licking I did before."

Then Tango turned on Johnny, standing quietly behind him. "I want what is my due. What you've had even when you weren't bloody here. They still called your name and talked about you. Johnny this and Johnny that. Always you, never me. My voice is far better than yours. Another year and you'll be forgotten. God, I hate you, Nova. I really fucking hate you, and I hate that stupid name. I'm finished with you—all of you! I don't need you. In six months you'll be forgotten and it will be *my* name on the billboards. You can all rot in hell! I'm out of here. For good."

Tango turned on his heel and strode out of the room, slamming the door as he went, leaving behind him a silent group. Florrie and Mara heightened their healing powers and gently cleansed the agitated emotions that hung like dirty linen in every corner of the room. Johnny also opened his senses and requested a space of time for peace, balance, and harmony. The abbeys responded, and in an hour all traces of anger, hurt, and desperation had been cleansed. In silence, they all left the room one by one until just Johnny and Mara were left. She turned and smiled, and Johnny took her into his arms and lowered her gently to the floor. Their bodies flowed together, and the last remnants of anger were dissolved in their lovemaking.

In his room and still shaking with rage, Tango was packing. He threw his new, expensive clothes into the cases with little regard for their care and snapped the locks, then paused and looked round to make sure he had everything. He saw the pile of Christmas presents from the group and snorted. They could keep them—he wanted nothing from them.

Then Tango saw Johnny's gift on the bedside table and paused. Of all of them, Johnny knew of Tango's love for old things, and his gift was beautiful. Tango sat on the bed and picked it up. It fitted his hand perfectly. Perhaps in an earlier life, like some people believed in, this had belonged to him. Its blade held the patina of age. The hilt was an intricate design of a coiled serpent that twined about the cross bar. Its open mouth held a gemstone of vibrant green that could be a small emerald or a chrysoprase. He turned it over to look at the Greek phrase engraved on the back of the blade: *Ego eimai fos*. "I am light."

Johnny's gift. Johnny, who had everything that he, Tango, dreamed of having but never would.

Tango stood up, unlocked one of the cases, and buried the dagger under a pile of shirts. Then he picked up both cases and walked out to where the copter waited.

Tango didn't look back as it rose, turned west, and flew towards the setting sun. His lips twisted into a wry grin. *How appropriate*, he thought.

♬ ♩ ♫ ♪ ♬ ♪ ♫

The others put their heads and talent together to adjust for the missing member. Bucky held a hasty Skype session first with the Wembley personnel, then with the relevant publicity people and newspapers. The story being put out was that Tango had been offered a solo career and had decided to leave White Heat. They had all agreed that it was in his best interest and wished him well in the future.

Bucky knew Tango's temperament well enough to guess he would not quibble over that kind of career boost.

♬ ♩ ♫ ♪ ♬ ♪ ♫

For Johnny and Mara, their last day was spent quietly. They knew they were their last few moments together. To the others, the Wembley show was seen as the main group going on, with Johnny dividing his time between them and his spiritual work.

31 December, 9:00 p.m.
London

Pacia's work had taken on a new intensity. She would use the meteor clash as a symbol to open the Age of Aquarius and use its power of communication to unite the warring sections of humanity. She'd already marked out those whose desire for personal power would bring her to her own demise. But, for now, she must wait for the right moment.

Johnny's task was to use the Breath of God to utter the Word of Creation, the Word that would descend and infuse her with the power needed to make her the Teacher of the age. The Forerunner, in turn, could only speak the Word with his last breath—the breath that had to be taken from him by the Betrayer.

As it always had been and would be, each age needed the power of three: the need to become, the need to empower, and the need to sacrifice.

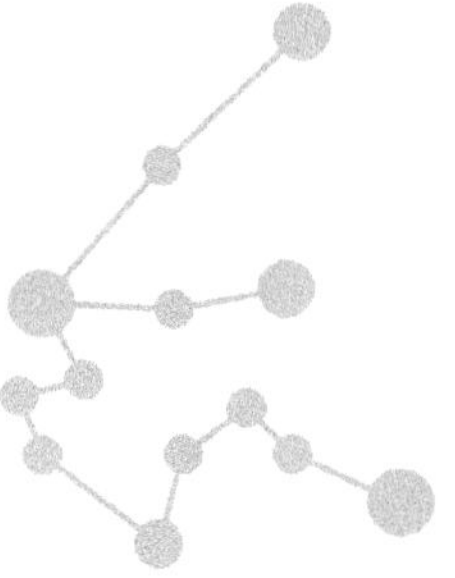

CHAPTER FORTY-EIGHT

1 January, 8:00 p.m.
Wembley Stadium

The papers, reporters, and newsreaders were out in force. Not since the coronation had so many human beings crowded into one space! For the first time, this event was seen as a sign of something far beyond anything that could be imagined. It was attended by politicians, scientists, the priesthood of every world religion, along with those who simply felt the urge to be there. Many didn't even know *why* they were there, just that they had to be. The wise and the crazies mixed and mingled. It concerned all of them. For good or bad, for wisdom or a descent into a new Dark age, they felt called to be there. The noise was a physical entity of itself. In the night sky, two points of light continued to move towards each other.

Pacia stood silent and ready by the water's edge. Johnny stood calm and smiling in the wings, ready to make the entry of White Heat. Bucky and Florrie stood close together, sharing their strength. In a stolen car heading towards the venue, Tango drank deeply from a silver flask as he sped towards his own destiny.

White Heat was well into their third piece, and the crowd was going crazy singing along with them. Every single seat or space they could stand was taken. The musicians themselves had been caught up in the energy of the moment. The open arena was a seething mass of humanity, and centre stage was Johnny. His love for each and every one of them flowed out with every breath.

Those with Johnny were caught up in the outpouring of adulation, but Lyle, his face wet with perspiration, knew something was coming. Something good, something bad, something monstrous. His faith rose up in him, and he felt a presence enter his drums. Biff and Liam were way down, front of stage, playing into the souls of those before them. Frank wept; his hands moved over the keys of their own accord. Beside him, unseen by any but Frank, stood Tze-Ring. His voice was soft but clear. "He has to die…but he won't go alone."

Johnny searched the crowd, looking for the one face that *had* to be there. As they moved into the second half, he saw him way at the back, his clothes soaked with sweat.

Abruptly, Johnny held up his hand and the entire place went silent. He went to the front of stage and called out, "Tango! Tango, come on! Come up! It's where you need to be: with us. With us all together. Come on!"

Tango climbed up onto the stage. Johnny went to him and embraced him. Then they turned to the others. "'Mountains of Gold.' Let's do it."

The silence was absolute as Frank led them into the song that had been written for this moment. They drew together, the two of them, their voices blending with a sweetness Frank would never forget. But over and above the music, messages went back and forth.

Johnny: "Remember, Tango, remember what you—what we—are. This is what we offered to do, but we'll be together, brother mine. There's always three: one to teach, one to open the door, one to offer the sacrifice. Adam, Eve, Lucifer. Osiris, Set, Anubis. Arthur, Lancelot, Galahad. Innana, Ereshgigal, Demuzzi. Yeheshua, John, and Judas. We all have to make the offer, Tango. Do it, boyo. Do it now, but do it with love."

The two men drew together. The knife Johnny had given Tango was in his hand. Tango lifted it and struck.

Tango: "For love, Johnny. Always for love…I didn't know…I love you. I love you."

Johnny drew in his breath and pitched the note with everything in his power, and as the knife went in he sang out the Word of Creation.

The door of the new age opened, and as the meteors exploded, the Age of Aquarius came into being.

Johnny pitched forward. The music died. The crowd fell silent. Liam threw down his guitar and lurched forward. He grabbed Tango, heaved him over his head, and threw him into the crowd. They fell on him, and with hands, feet, and deadly intent, the crowd brought Tango to his own death. Lyle threw down his drumsticks and ran to Johnny, gathering him into his arms and sobbing out the words of benediction for the dead. Above the melee, the pain-filled howl of a wolf rang out.

Florrie looked up and saw the energy burst of meteoric debris as Johnny Nova became one with his name.

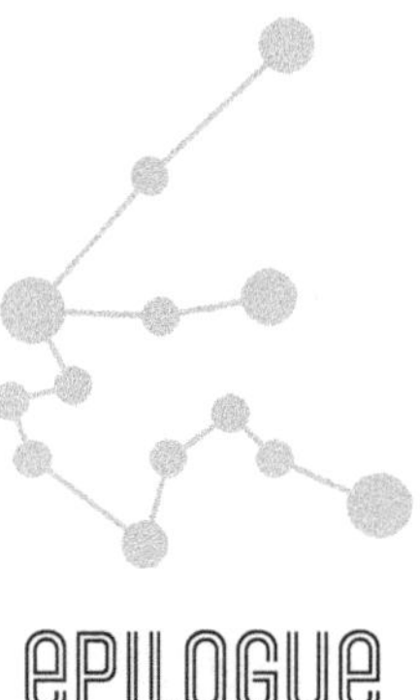

EPILOGUE

Colin Buckman became one of the guardians of the Christos and lived long enough to see Her mission begin to affect the world. Florrie spent her time in the Aeon helping to train others. They claimed Tango's remains and saw to their interment. Bucky and Florrie were honoured by the abbeys for their devotion to Johnny and were buried in the garden of the Abbey of the Aeon.

Frank Saunders left the world of popular music to become an acclaimed composer of sacred music. His best known works include the Johnny Nova requiem "Behold, There Came a Man" and the stunningly beautiful oratorio "John the Beloved." The opening words of its most famous aria—"I stood upon the mountain and beheld the coming of the Light"—echoed Johnny's words to him a few days before his death. It was chosen by William V for his coronation hymn.

Liam never fully recovered from the shock of Johnny's death or his remorse at being the cause of Tango's murder by the mob. He became severely depressed and for a time was a patient in a psychiatric unit. On his release, Lyle and Ginny took him into their family to make sure he was not alone. He died ten years after Johnny, and his last words were, "Tango's here, and he says it's all right."

Biff also had problems for a while, then surprised everyone by applying (through Bucky) to the Abbey of the Aeon for training. He was only a minor member, but his devotion and his willingness to serve in any capacity endeared him to all.

Lyle and Ginny raised their two children, Mary-Clare and John. Lyle eventually became Bishop of Southwark. All were frequent visitors to the abbeys. Mary-Clare followed her father into the church and became the first female Archbishop of Canterbury. She crowned William V of England in Westminster Abbey. John entered the Abbey of the Winds and in due course became its abbot.

Tze-Ring was offered the post of Abbot of the Abbey of the Waters but declined. He took up the task of training the most gifted of the children brought into the abbeys. When the Christos began to establish Her church, it was Tze-Ring who laid its foundation and became Her advisor. He never ceased to mourn his beloved half-brother. At the age of eighty-nine, at the end of a major ritual in the Abbey of the Dawn, the doors of the Hall opened of their own accord and a young man with dark hair and brilliant green eyes stood there. By his side was a full-grown grey wolf. The old man's face lit up and he called out, "Johnny! Johnny!" He struggled to his feet to follow the figure out of the Hall, telling everyone to stay where they were. When they went to look for him, only his cloak lay on the ground. There were footprints from the door to the bottom step, then just unmarked snow. Tze-Ring was never seen again.

Jared, Johnny's son, lived quietly with his family and kept the bloodline and its importance going. Wolf disappeared for almost a year, then reappeared to take up his duties again. He kept a close relationship with Jared and saw to his training until Jared was sixteen. A few years later, the skeleton of a wolf was found lying on the Forerunner's grave.

In the year 2050, Pacia, Creator of the World Faith belief system, was dragged from her car and publicly hanged by a group of fanatics. There were unconfirmed reports of two beams of light appearing on either side of her body.

As Johnny foretold, in the Age of Capricorn humanity must provide its own Christos. But, human or non-human, every aeon must have one who will foretell the coming and one who will take on the task of the Betrayer. Somewhere on this planet, among its myriad of inhabitants, the bloodline of the Forerunner has been kept. It may be in that child in the park, or in the person next to you, or it may be in you!

ACKNOWLEDGMENTS

To Herbie Brennan for his unwavering support and belief in this book for the twenty-odd years it has taken to complete it. And to Carol and Steven Lomax, who not only believed in it but actively bullied, threatened, suggested, and encouraged me to keep at it. Although the storyline scared me witless, Carol and Steven hounded me until I reread it. Maybe I had "come of age" as the world is now approaching the Aquarian Age with all its turmoil. Together, they re-typed (I'm a terrible typist), edited, suggested, pointed out errors and mistakes until finally, after a year of blood, toil, tears, and sweat—and bad language—it was finished. But for three people's efforts and belief, this story would never have made it. So, here you are, the story of Johnny Nova.

Acknowledgments and thanks for your unfailing support and belief to Caitlin and John Matthews and Maria Teresa Harmer.

Other Books by Dolores Ashcroft-Nowicki

An Anthology of Occult Wisdom (twelve volumes)

Building a Temple

Daughters of Eve: The Magical Mysteries of Womanhood

First Steps in Ritual

Highways of the Mind: The Art and History of Pathworking

Illuminations: The Healing of the Soul

Inner Landscapes: A Journey into Awareness by Pathworking

Magical Use of Thought Forms

My First Book of Magic

Return of The Prodigal

Shadows and Light

Silver Sandals

The Atlantean Sacred Cord Meditations

The Body of Light

The Door Unlocked

The Four Kingdoms

The Hill of Dreams (novel)

The Initiate's Book of Pathworking

The New Book of the Dead

The Ritual Magical Training in Western Magic

The Ritual Magic Workbook

The Shining Paths

The Singing Stones (novel)

Tree of Ecstasy

Your Unseen Power